Incredible praise for the world of BLOOD OF TITANS

Smoke and Rain

International bestselling fantasy and winner of NewApple Literary's 2015 Excellence in Independent Publishing Award

"Holmes weaves a tapestry of the forthcoming events with the skill of a thaumaturge…In [the] seductive opening few lines so much of the nidus of this fantasy tale is hinted...Wade deeply into these waters for a fine curtain raiser for REFORGED. V.S. Holmes quite simply demonstrates that she is an artist of significance"

- *The San Francisco Review of Books*

"A well developed and subtly-layered world...filled with compelling characters and dangerous magic"

- *Aurealis Magazine*

"The very first page hooked me with the simple yet elegant narrative…The characters' dilemmas were revealed in perfect timing yet kept me wanting more, and Holmes didn't disappoint with dropping tidbits of emotion, character growth, and internal struggle among all the the action and war-time maneuvers."

- Kathrin Hutson, author of *Gyenona's Children* and The Unclaimed Trilogy

"I couldn't put it down to save my life and I couldn't turn the pages fast enough. The plot line was incredibly unique ... Holmes gave me a lot of the things I look for in a wonderful story and so much more."

- Cassandra Carpio, *The Bookish Crypt*

Lightning and Flames

"The atmosphere surrounding this saga is intoxicatingly real...Very highly recommended… This REFORGED volume elevates the reader even more, adding to the obvious stature of V.S. Holmes' literary presence. Very Highly recommended."

- *The San Francisco Review of Books*

"Holmes' prose perfectly illustrates the incredible, world-shaking horror unleashed when Alea and Arman's magic clashes with that of the gods."

- *Aurealis Magazine*

Madness and Gods

"...This tale focuses on the political struggles of its characters with few traditional trappings of the fantasy genre...it takes fantasy's ability to explore complex issues such as gender, mental health and human rights through allegory, and refocuses back on the issues themselves...while new and secondary characters now take centre stage. The new protagonists are interesting and richly drawn..."

- *Aurealis Magazine*

"Following this fantasy experience is addictive and thoroughly satisfying."

- *The San Francisco Review of Books*

Blood and Mercy

"The series excels in using allegory to mirror contemporary issues and explore them in a unique, thoughtful manner. Frustration, hope and the transformative power of righteous fury ooze from the...The underlying optimism of the series, balanced with unflinching realism regarding the difficulty of change at personal and systemic levels, is a testament to the possibilities of the fantasy genre—and a worthy read for our times."

- *Aurealis Magazine*

Books by V. S. Holmes

BLOOD OF TITANS

REFORGED
Smoke and Rain
Lightning and Flames

RESTORED
Madness and Gods
Blood and Mercy

REBEL
*Treason's Tears**

STARSEDGE: NEL BENTLY
Travelers
Drifters
Strangers
Heretics
Fugitives
*Emissaries**

SHORT FICTION
"Nowhere Fast" (*We Came to Dance)*
"Starfall" *(Vitality Magazine)*
"The Tempest" *(Out of the Darkness)*
"Disciples" *(Beamed Up)*
"Familiar Waters" *(Love and Bubbles)*
"Mere Primordium" (poem, *Mystic Blue Review)*

**forthcoming*

REFORGED

V. S. HOLMES

AMPHIBIAN PRESS

This is a work of fiction. All of the characters, organizations, and events portrayed in this novel are either products of the author's imagination or are used fictitiously.

None of the material within was created, in whole or in part, using AI technology.

REFORGED

SMOKE AND RAIN Originally Published in 2015
LIGHTNING AND FLAMES Originally Published in 2016

Amphibian Press
www.amphibianpress.online
www.vsholmes.com

Cover by Ben R. Donahue
www.bendonahueart.com
Printed in the United States of America

ISBN: 978-1-949693-35-5

REFORGED I

To everyone who has known darkness, and beauty,
and the building of a new life.

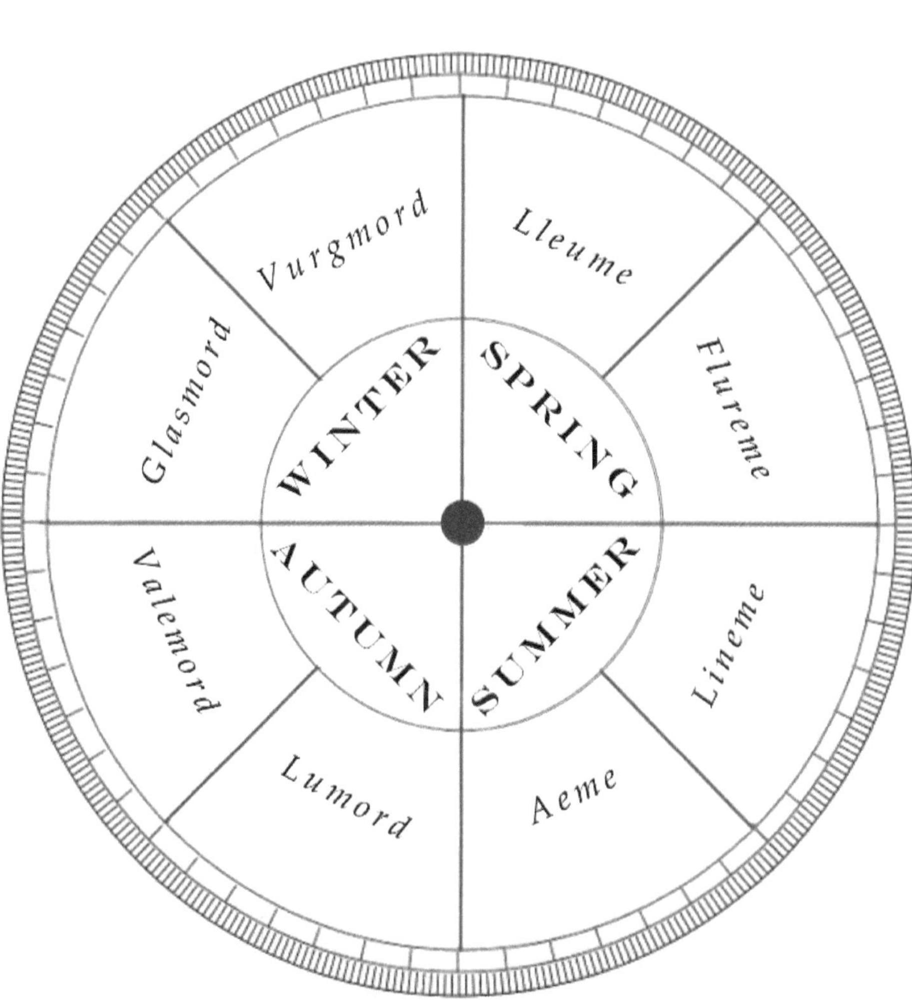
WINTER
SPRING
SUMMER
AUTUMN
Vurgmord
Lleume
Flureme
Lineme
Aeme
Lumord
Valemord
Glasmord

The World Of
BLOOD OF TITANS
N
The Icelock
NORTHLANDS
Neneviir
The
Ilmar
MIRIK
Mirik
Claimiirn
Eastern
Ocean
Ceir
Felden
Iron Sea
Ceir
Athrolan
Fort
Stone
Fort
Shadow
Arc of Zunu
Zunu

RoBal
Ceir
Bodian
BAN
The Hartland
Feld
de
Barran
Ceir
Pardelan
Berme's Eye
Berme's
Teeth
Berrinal
Juniaal
Jade
Forest
Ag
VALE
NAD
ANEN
Vielrona
Oin de Duhtain
Seyn
Cehn
SUNAM
Sashn
Seas
Burning
Waters

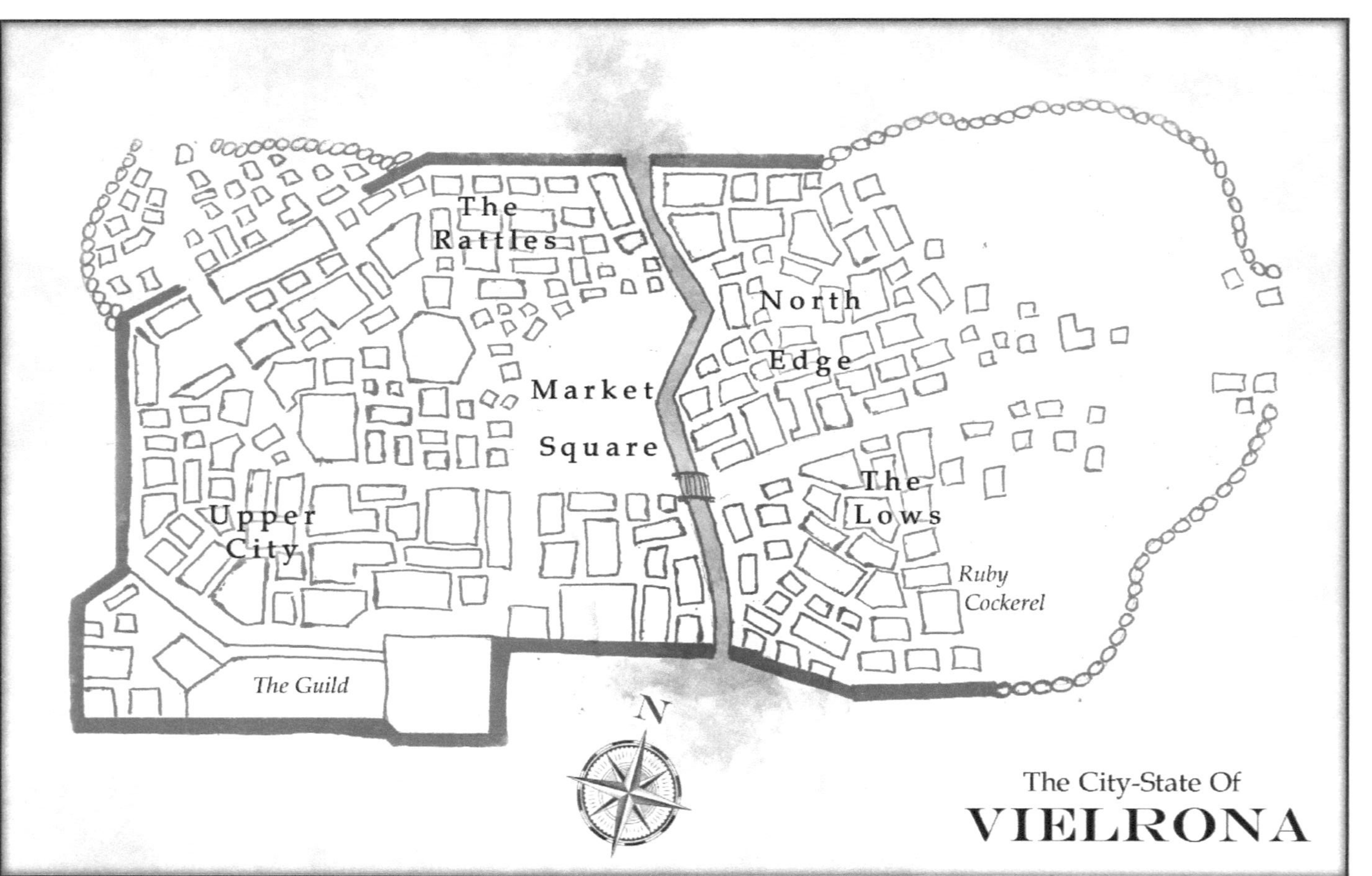
The Rattles
North Edge
Market Square
The Lows
Ruby Cockerel
Upper City
The Guild
N
The City-State Of
VIELRONA

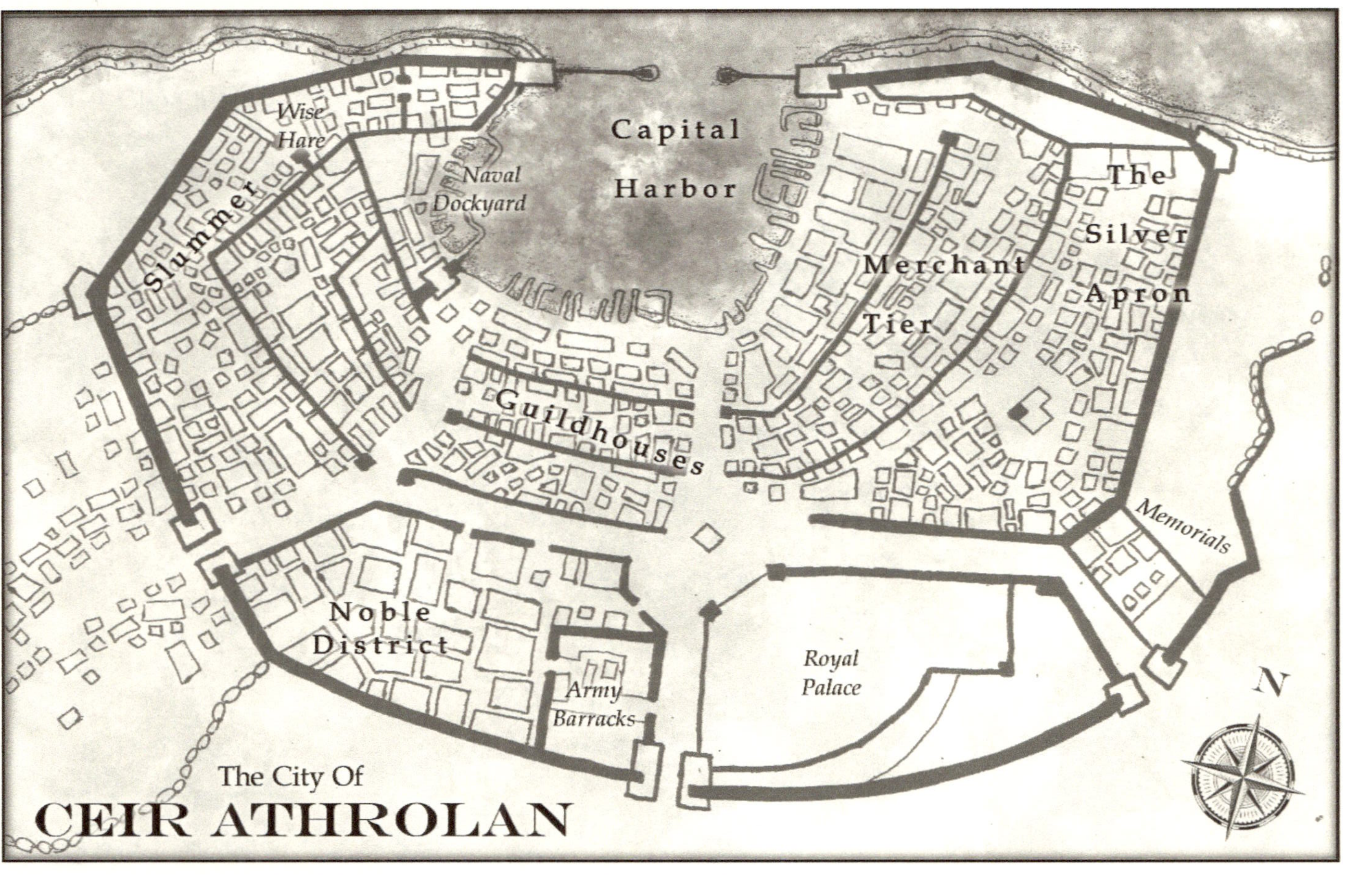

The City Of
CEIR ATHROLAN
Capital
Harbor
Wise
Hare
Naval
Dockyard
Slummer
Merchant
Tier
The
Silver
Apron
Guildhouses
Memorials
Noble
District
Army
Barracks
Royal
Palace
N

New
City
Jug-End
Square
Blessed City
Dockyard
Markets
Royal
Palace
Gods
Walk
Army
Barracks
Gods'
Mouth
Old
City
N
The City Of
MIRIK

The Layers of a Single Life

CHAPTER ONE

The 17th day of Lumord, 1251
The City-State of Vielrona

ARMAN GATHERED BLOODY RAGS from the cots and tried to ignore the five figures by the door. Despite his mother's care, half the refugees who arrived four days before had already passed. He dumped the rags in a basket in the corner, glancing back. Fire chased ice up his spine. It was unpleasant, but alluring, like the burn of alcohol down his throat.

He forced himself to approach the women. *Laen are never simply "women."* In his twenty-three years, he had never seen of the gods' creators. Now half a dozen of them stood in his mother's inn. Arman hastily patted a blood-stained hand over his curls and bowed. "Lady Liane?"

Silver eyes slid over him in absent acknowledgment. "Liane is fine."

"My mother said you're welcome to stay as long as you need. Vielrona promised to guard your people." *Even if centuries have passed and we have nothing to protect you with.* He hoped the Laen could not read minds.

Liane scanned the injured filling the room with moaning, rattling breath. "The gods' army won't be far behind." Liane's hard eyes returned to the youngest Laen, bundled in a cloak. "We thank you, but no place is safe anymore, even one that once worshiped us."

Arman followed her gaze. The girl looked thirteen, though he supposed she could be decades older. *How do Laen even age?* Out of all her companions, she was the only one who looked afraid. And the only one with armor.

Arman shuffled back a step, swallowing bitter dread in his throat. Even rumor of her presence would bring the wrath of armies. "There's a road from the western wall," he explained, not caring that his shaking hand waved north instead. "It's narrow and rocky, so only shepherds use it." He spoke to Liane, but his eyes did not leave the youngest Laen.

Liane's eyes narrowed on him.

Arman back up again, palms up. "I won't tell a soul, I swear."

Liane eyed him a moment longer, then gathered her pack. "We have guards who were supposed to meet us in Cehn, though we were attacked before they arrived. If they come through, tell them our path."

Arman frowned. "How will I know them?"

Liane sighed. A lesser woman may have rolled her eyes. Her hand snaked out and gripped Arman's brow. Cold seeped from her hard fingers and with it flooded an image. Arman jerked away, his jaw clenched against the sudden ache in his skull.

Liane swept past him, the others filing out of the room after her. Arman fell to his knees and emptied his stomach into a washbasin.

Φ

The dim common room of the Ruby Cockerel was deserted. Most patrons sought other alehouses since the Cockerel was transformed into a makeshift infirmary. Arman was grateful for the quiet. He downed a mug of cheap tar-whiskey and poured another before sliding onto a barstool. He was no stranger to death, but the past days weighed on his heart.

A week after smoke appeared on the southern horizon, the Laen arrived in Vielrona. With them came three dozen refugees and the threat of war—all that remained of the desert city, Cehn.

Arman hoped the sting of alcohol would clear his head. When the gods overthrew their creators centuries before, the world fractured. *And the girl who just left is what both sides have sought for decades.*

The oak door of the common room banged open and heavy boots sloshed across the floor. "Fates, this rain is horrid. Picked up out of nowhere."

"Hey, Wes."

A large-boned young man slumped into the seat next to Arman. His tan was several shades darker than Arman's, and heavily weathered by the heat of a smithy. He jerked a blocky head at the ceiling, "They still here?"

Arman shook his head. "Left a few minutes ago."

Wes suppressed a shudder. "Probably them that made the rain. Hide their trail and all."

Arman rolled his eyes and stood to pour Wes a mug of ale. "They can't play with the weather. I'm glad to have them out of the house, though."

Wes accepted his mug with a nod of thanks. "The idea gives me the winders."

"I am all for them winning the war, but that feeling when they look at you—like jumping into the Halen in winter."

Wes eyed his friend. "I never felt that. Granted I didn't live with them. If we're not careful, you'll be chasing after them."

Arman snorted and finished off his tar-whiskey.

"So why are we drinking tonight?"

"You're drinking because you tracked slush all over my mother's floor and you know she won't yell at you if you're tossed."

Wes glanced guiltily at the hardwood. The two had been friends since Wes caught a five-year-old Arman riding his father's sheep around like warhorses. Kepra Wardyn was as much Wes's mother as Arman's. The smith fished a towel from under the bar and began to boot-slide it across the wet floor.

Arman's mouth twitched at the sight. "You're better than a maid. Do away with the smithy and take up a job here."

Wes growled, "What would you do at the forge without me? You've no head for business. You'd be lost." He shuffled carefully back toward the bar to gather the worst of the mess. "You never said why you're drinking?"

Arman glared at the cloudy dregs of his drink. Wes did not strictly count, as he was closer to family, but Arman had promised not to tell anyone. "It's nothing important. Seeing all the suffering upstairs just wears on a man. Most won't ever wake up."

"Azirik's army won't come here, Arman." Wes's muddy eyes were earnest, "We've nothing they want." He took a deep swallow of his ale. "Fates, your mood is enough to make a man drink."

Arman fixed Wes with a pointed stare. "Those women were here, Wes. The god's army followed them to Cehn and they could just as easily follow them here."

"'ll leave you to your brooding then." Wes shrugged. "I should get home, I need to start working on that piece for Reskle in the morning." He buckled his cloak again. "Will you be by?"

Arman nodded, "I have to finish the jewel-work on that hilt."

"You're seeing Veredy tomorrow night though, eh?" Wes waggled his eyebrows suggestively from the doorway.

Arman's laugh scratched in his irritated throat. "Hopefully. There's still a lot to help Ma with, though. Out with you, you're letting the rain in." He winced as Wes's exit rattled the glass in the windows. Fishing a clean towel from the bar, he went over his friend's slush trail again, gaze distant.

It was not a lie that the massacre in Cehn brought battle too close. Arman was barely walking when the rumors reawakened the war against the Laen. This time, the gods—and their human armies—hunted a woman who would bind the world together again.

In the wake of genocide, however, it was hard to hope.

Arman scrubbed his face with a groan. "Azirik's army is looking for her, Wes." His voice was low. He needed to tell someone, even just the empty common room. "The Mirikin are looking for her and she was in my mother's house."

Φ

The 20th Day of Lumord, 1251
The City of Berrinal

Brentemir took a careful sip from his steaming mug of *ucal.* After two months among the Berrin, the fermented seaweed drink was the only thing he would miss when they marched. The rear of the berth house held leather-padded benches and hassocks, across which he sprawled. Despite the few seats left, the building was quiet.

His staff bearer flopped down beside him. Like Bren, he wore the brown uniform of a Mirikin soldier, though Bren's was newer. Ever-increasing height forced him to be outfitted more often than any man had a right.

"Evening, Korir," Bren greeted.

Korir hummed in response. His lidded eyes spoke to time in the massage house.

"You'll miss the attention when we're back on the road." Bren's voice was low. The gray landscape lent itself to silence, and the Mirikin were reluctant to break it.

Korir shrugged. "There are a couple weeks left of negotiations, I'd say."

Bren fiddled with the heavy copper emblem around his neck. The center shone from the number of times he had rubbed a thumb over it during prayer or thought. When they first set sail, he was eager to set foot on anything other than Mirikin soil. The past year hung heavy on his shoulders, however, and he was homesick. He knocked back his drink and raised a hand to order another when a head popped through the door from the front room of the berth house. "Corporal Barrackborn? His Majesty the King asks for you."

Bren sat up with a groan. "Don't bother to save my spot—I might be awhile." He tugged the green wool of his cloak tighter and stepped into the damp air. Haphazard streets and suspension bridges wound between the different rafts. Berrinal was built on natural seaweed-supported islands and constructed rafts, and the constant rocking wore on Bren's nerves. Salt dusted his beard by the time he arrived at the top floor of the embassy.

Mirik may have been an island kingdom, but Berrin seafaring shamed all others. The sea filled every aspect of their world, from patron gods to officers' titles in their army. Bren tidied himself and pulled the leather cap off his short, auburn hair. He rapped on the door softly.

"Your Majesty? Corporal Barrackborn here."

"Come in." The voice was distant.

Bren kept his head down as he shut the door behind himself. "You asked to see me, sire?" He was careful with his words. Azirik was intelligent, but his single-minded drive could be described as insanity. Now the king peered at military maps scattered over his desk. Gray threaded his long red-brown hair for as long as Bren could remember.

"We are leaving Berrinal within a week. Negotiations finalize tomorrow. Save the hideous pomp, we are free to leave anytime afterward. I need a troop to move west. I sent Lieutenant Gransa south several weeks ago to hunt down rumors about Laen in Sunam—their city Cehn was defeated, but they lost the creatures. I want you to lead a second troop west, to cut off their escape in Athrolan."

Anticipation thrummed up his limbs. "I am honored, sire, but would Lieutenant Serik not be more suited?"

Azirik's bright blue eyes flicked up to Bren with an unreadable expression. "Serik has been gone a week."

Bren forgot himself, "What, by Toar, does 'gone' mean?"

Azirik moved to the window, ignoring his soldier's insubordination. "Perhaps you didn't notice, Barrackborn, but Mirik is not what she once was."

Bren noticed. He would have been a fool not to. Fighting for the gods changed Mirik. None dared mention the atrophy of the capital, but even from the barracks across the harbor, everyone could see the toll of Azirik's declared war.

"Many lesser families sought safer cities years ago, when I first honored the gods with our dedication."

Bren did not break the long silence that followed the king's statement.

"Barrackborn, the capital is closing. All the higher born have fled the kingdom. Enough of our soldiers have family in the lower nobility. Serik was one, and he tried to follow his parents. His desertion was punished properly two days ago." He paused. "You are promoted to Lieutenant. You leave in four days at the head of Serik's troop. They're your men now."

Bren bowed his head, "Thank you, milord. I am grateful to do all I can for the gods."

Azirik stared at the maps for another minute. He finally looked up, as if remembering Bren's presence, "You may go."

Bren bowed and showed himself out. He planned to return to the berth house and order more *ucal.* Now he just wanted air. He had always worked hard to overcome his orphaned upbringing, including teaching himself economics. If the higher born fled the city, it did not bode well. The economy would be in waste and the common folk would starve. Commoners were the backbone of any city, and without them, the city would fall.

A particularly large wave made the ground lurch under him. He leaned on the wall at the edge of the ocean, searching for the fogged horizon. A promotion was good, and he hated the apprehension coloring his excitement. *Questioning orders is not my place.* Hunting Laen was an honor, but he wondered, after decades of war, whether the gods would care.

Φ

The 22nd Day of Lumord, 1251
The City of Vielrona

Quiet clicking of Arman's pliers distracted him from the eerie silence. Though preferable to the groaning of the injured refugees, he could not shake the feeling that he was surrounded by the dead. He leaned back to shed more light on his work. The hilt in his hand was intricate, carefully placed garnets and topaz glittering under the single lantern. Though his father had been a true bladesmith, Arman's talents ran closer to artist and jeweler. Wes took over the heaviest smithing. Tending to the refugees cut into Arman's time, but it was peaceful to work while he stayed through the night.

Ragged breathing interrupted his focus.

A woman by the hearth tossed in her sleep. Arman poured a mug of water and crept over to check on her. Dark hair tangled across her furrowed brow. One white-knuckled hand clenched the sheets.

Nightmares. Doubtless, most survivors would have them. He crouched beside the cot and dipped a cloth in the cool water of her washbasin. She muttered incoherently as he wrung it out and draped it over her forehead. Her face was the light brown of the Sunamen, but her pale forearms told him she was not native to the desert. He pressed a finger to the place his mother had shown him, just below her thumb. He was not sure what to feel for, but her heartbeat was strong, if fast. *Dreams, even nightmares, are good. It means she will probably live.*

Once her movements settled, he returned to his seat. The room was quiet again, but he fiddled with the wood handles of his pliers. A few of the survivors had woken, though most were too ill to be truly aware. Between festering wounds, exposure to the cold desert night, and dehydration, it was a wonder any lived to see Vielrona. Familiar sounds from the kitchen below startled him from his musings. Arman glanced outside. It was dawn.

After a minute the door eased open. His mother moved from cot to cot, her fingers feather-light as they checked pulses, fevers, and bandages. Her smile warmed when she glanced up at him. "How are they?"

Arman wrapped his work and tools. "It was a quiet night. That man's fever rose. He barely stirs." He frowned. "That girl, there, she had a nightmare an hour ago. Settled when I put that cloth on her forehead though."

Kepra's face softened when she followed his gesture. "No doubt she has heartbreak. She wears a betrothal ring." She squeezed her son's hand, "Off with you, Wes will wonder why you're late."

Arman changed into a clean shirt before taking the stairs two at a time. A pear waited in the hanging basket at the end of the long bar, and he took a bite as he left. He licked his thumb and pinched the wick of the lantern hanging beside the inn's wooden sign.

Smaller market vendors already tied the wool screens back from their stalls. Shopkeeps hung signs between yawns. Arman tossed a copper guild-mark to a baker. "Morning Fina!"

"Good to see you're back to work. How're the new folks, Arman?" She handed him a small, hot roll from the tray on her counter.

"Most still fighting. Thanks!" He shot her a smile and slipped down a makeshift street. The market spread across the northern end of the Lows and a wide cobbled street cut a swath through the jumble of stands. Arman sidled between a gem vendor and a jeweler before ducking inside his knife stall.

Wes already perched on a stool too small for his bones. "Morning, Wardyn."

Arman nodded back, his thoughts still hazy from lack of sleep. He handed Wes the roll and returned to his pear. "Did you sell the branch hilt?"

Wes sighed, "No, but Megg is eying for her suitor."

Arman made a face at the name. "Which one?"

Wes cackled and laid his whetstone aside. "The richest, you are to be sure." He examined the edge of the blade he held. "Speaking of gossip, did you hear the street-talk yesterday?"

"What now?" Arman tossed the core of his pear into the ditch along the edge of the street and unloaded more wares.

"Mistress Jehan said you took up with the Laen. Said they asked a favor."

"Where would she have gotten that?"

Wes looked at him as if he had been dropped on his head as a babe. "Her boy cleans the privies on your street."

"I know. All the Jehans lie, Wes. They made up that tale that you were marrying the widow of Burrow-heel."

Wes rolled his eyes, "She's about as fetching as my cousin's bull—"

"Not to mention, dead," Arman interjected.

Wes flashed a wicked grin. "Her son, though—he's the proper combination of tall and narrow."

Arman let out a short laugh. "If you ever finish the jasper pommel perhaps you could give it to him."

"Handsome sons aside, Arman, I worry when people talk. Speaking to them is one thing—what's this about a favor? Jehans might lie, but the whole Lows do not."

It was a relief to return to stall-work after days away, but the banter was a too pointed for his tastes. *City gossip is as wicked a mistress as Megg.* He elbowed Wes sharply. "Now you sound like the Jehans."

Φ

The 23rd of Lumord, 1251

Screaming rent the air, followed by the sickly-sweet tang of blood. Hard hands yanked Alea to the sand. Beside her Ahren thrashed on the ground, his body opened by a sword. The strange women her foster-father hosted clustered near the center of the oasis. They're Laen, they must help. *Desperation, not certainty, cemented the thought. Focusing on their silver-tinged forms, she staggered toward them.*

Thrashing flipped her out of bed. Memories of smoke and fear choked her. Gooseflesh followed the drip of sweat down her limbs.

"Settle, miss. You're safe. Settle." The woman's voice was low, the language different.

Careful hands pressed on her arms. Alea blinked into wakefulness. Her head pounded. She drew a steadying breath and took stock of her surroundings. Nothing hung on the sturdy walls, but embroidery decorated the pillowcases and curtains. Several other beds and cots crowded against the wall. *A makeshift infirmary, then.* Everything, from the rough wood to her nightmare seemed incredibly distant and unimportant. Even the pain in her skull throbbed from leagues away.

"Hello." The woman spoke Trade, which told Alea she was near Athrolan. She ducked her head to catch Alea's gaze with her kind brown eyes. Gray striped her brown hair at the temples.

Alea jerked a nod to show she understood. "Where--" her parched throat cracked and burnt.

"In Vielrona, your ally-city. I'm Kepra and this is my inn. Those women brought you and the others here." She helped Alea climb shakily under the coverlet again before handing her a mug from the nightstand. "Drink this, but slowly. Too fast will make you sick."

Bitterness and an earthy aftertaste rolled from her tongue and hit her stomach like a blow. Once she forced herself to finish, Kepra offered water. "You've been very ill, but your fever is breaking." Her eyes flicked to the ring on her smallest finger. "I am terribly sorry for your losses."

Despair was a flooding ache and Alea turned from the proffered mug. She did not want to eat. *If only they hadn't found me, hadn't saved me. If only I never woke from my fever.*

"You need to drink, to eat." When Alea still ignored her, the woman put the mug on the bedside. "I'll check on you again, soon. One of us is always here." She rose, but paused before going back to the seat by the window. "When my husband passed I thought I couldn't go on. It took years, but sometimes the happiness you find after pain is all the sweeter for it."

After a moment the terribly familiar sound of needlepoint broke the silence. Alea buried her face in the covers and wished she could weep. The Mirikin may have taken her home when they destroyed Cehn, but with Ahren, they took her future. *There's nothing left.* Tears would not come.

Φ

The 27th Day of Lumord, 1251

Watching three ill people was far easier than a roomful. Arman fiddled with a loose fitting on a stiletto's handle between cursory glances at the sleeping forms. The blade was satisfactory, but he had made better.

Cold inched up his spine again. His reaction to the Laen was slow to fade. Wes's words the night the Laen left still made him scowl. *I'm not about to run into the woods after them.* Curiosity nagged at him, however.

He glanced out the window, measuring the moon's height with mental thumb-thickness. Any moment now the young woman's nightmare would start. His hands stilled. The Laen said she was part of the governor's household. *Maybe she knows more about where the Laen are headed. And whether the gods' armies could follow them here.*

Right on time, the girl began to toss. Muttered foreign words sharpened with fear. *And anger.* He laid aside his work and crouched beside her bed. His mother said dreams—even bad ones—were the soul's way of facing conflict, helping to understand a deeper part of yourself. Arman was inclined to believe it, but this girl dreamt horrors enough. He shook her foot gently.

She came to screaming. Strings of sweat-damp hair and rolling eyes made her wild. He held his hands out, trying to appear gentle. *At least my hair is yellow, and not brown like the Mirikin who attacked her.* Her gaze flitted between the open window, the beds, the door, calculating. *Finding her bearings.* After a moment, her eyes finally rested on him. They were gray.

He offered a smile with a cup of water. "You're safe. This is Vielrona. I'm Arman." He stopped himself from telling her it was just a dream. *It was real to her, once.*

Her shaking hands spilled water across the coverlet, but her eyes narrowed when he reached to help.

"How long?" Rasping accented her words as much as Sunamen.

"How long have you been here?" He kept his voice low and calm.

Her head jerked in a nod.

"Ten days. Your fever broke the night before last."

"Who else?"

His calm expression faltered. "I don't know who you knew. The Laen brought survivors here and tended you. This is my mother's inn. She said you woke to her, but you mightn't recall."

"Brown hair, kind eyes."

Arman smiled. "Yes. Do you need more water?"

She looked around, the strength on her face crumbling. "I want to sleep."

"I'll make you tea. It'll help."

When he returned she had straightened her covers and was wearing a shawl wrapped around her head. *Right, all Sunamen wear head cloths.* She appeared calm, save for her eyes. Fear and despair brewed there, a distant, approaching storm. He hoped he would not see it break.

CHAPTER TWO

The 29th Day of Lumord, 1251
The Boden Province of Athrolan

"CEHN HAS FALLEN!" The shout rose with the sun. The rider stumbled from his mount and into a bow, breath heaving.

Azirik glanced at the boy. He did not care about the city, or its people, or whether the victory was hard-won. "And? The girl?"

The boy wiped horse's foam from his uniform and did not meet the king's eyes. "No, sir. They escaped, riding north. Tracker says they made for a town called Vielrona."

Azirik scratched the raw skin of his brow. Hot copper was far different from the familiar bronze of Mirik's circlet. The gods' Crown gnawed at him, more than a physical irritation, it itched in his thoughts. "Did you inform Lieutenant Barrackborn?"

"Kellim did, Your Majesty." The boy shifted awkwardly, watching the dismantling tents, the milling soldiers and horses. "Do we make for Vielrona?"

"No. If Barrackborn fails, there will be greater battles to fight than forgotten city-states." Azirik trotted to the head of the forming line. It was sentimental, promoting Brentemir, and trusting that, of anyone in the army, his own bastard would succeed. *We're fighting a divine battle. If ever there was a time for symbolism and fates, it'd be now.*

He may not have wanted Mirik's throne, but four words had cemented his hatred for the gods' creators. *"Azirik, I* am *Laen."* He was damned if he would not see the war through. Most kings gave encouraging speeches at the beginning of a march. Azirik remained silent. The gods' voices trickled through the Crown they gifted him—a gift meant to control as much as to honor. The Crown of the human world was lost, and the Laen surely had theirs. *But I have the gods'.*

"Orders, Your Majesty?" His captain paused as the king rode past.

"We ride north-west, across the Feld. The Berrin will join us and together we face Athrolan." It would take faith and distraction to get an entire army across the barren expanse ahead. Azirik burst into a lope. If all went well, the

Laen would be eradicated in a year. The thought terrified as much as soothed him. The war lasted the entirety of his reign. War was all he was.

Φ

The 30th Day of Lumord, 1251
The City-state of Vielrona

Violence stripped the world naked. Even the gray sky seemed to hang closer than the parched zenith of the desert. Alea watched ponderous, rain-heavy clouds through her narrow window. She was the room's only occupant, now, the remaining survivors well enough to be afforded privacy. *Or dead.* She could not bring herself to wonder at her future. Raw, hollowness gaped between her rips, tenderness scoured from her heart by the bones of everyone she ever loved. A slamming door downstairs heralded Arman's return from work.

"fates', it's biting out there!" He let out a dramatic shiver. Boot falls pounded up the stairs and paused outside her door, but he did not knock until he returned from his room.

"Yes?"

He nudged open the door. "Evening." He grinned when he saw her by the window. "Good that you're getting some air. You want supper? It's chowder. I could bring you some up."

She frowned at his boots, as if they had asked her the puzzling question, "I'm not certain what chowder is." *And no amount of food could fill this void.*

"Ma's chowder is better than any you've ever had!" Arman's smile faltered. "Though if you've never had any, that's not much of a boast." He disappeared, leaving the door ajar.

Alea looked back out the window. It did not seem to matter how she answered. People were as distant as her surroundings were close. A wooden tray clattered onto her bedside table. It held a bowl of creamy soup.

When it was clear Arman would not leave until he saw her eat, Alea tested the food warily. Bitter greens joined sweet vegetables and thin slices of fish. Her stomach's rumbled response startled her. *I don't even recognize hunger anymore.*

"I don't know your name." Arman pulled a chair up beside her bed.

Alea blinked at him, then returned her attention to the soup. "Lyne'alea ir Suna."

He frowned. "Suna—that's the surname of the lord?"

"Cehn's ihal was Ahme'reahn ira Suna." Rolling, guttural sounds of the Sunamen tongue were sweetly familiar.

"You're Sunamen?"

The only people who considered me such are dead. Only when she caught Arman's wince did she realize she spoke the thought aloud. "I did not mean to share that."

"I wasn't certain, with your coloring. You look Athrolani."

"The ihal took me into his household as a favor to an old friend." She finished the soup in silence and set the bowl back onto the tray.

"You've been sleeping better?"

Alea wrapped her arms around her middle. The question was intimate and uncomfortable. "I'm afraid I need more rest. Thank you for the meal."

He seemed to want to ask more, but finally nodded and left, taking her dishes with him.

The stripped mattresses around her looked macabre, an echo of the bodies sprawled across them. Blood soaked into the beds' stuffing. Staring eyes clouded. Voiceless mouths cracked, dried under the sun. Her fingers ached from trying to claw her way to the Laen.

She blinked.

Crescents marked where she bit her knuckles to keep from crying out. *I'm safe. Some people lived.* Sleep was a poor choice with memories so close, but anything was better than being awake.

Φ

The mattress creaked under him as Arman rolled onto his stomach. Evening eased over the land, lengthening the mountains shadows until the sun's warmth was only a memory from summer. He could almost taste the frost in the air, though it was still weeks away from winter. The view from the window was different from that of his bedroom and he caught sight of the faint winding trail through the hills. *I wonder how far they've made it by now.* It was a perverse preoccupation, his curiosity about the Laen. Still, something nagged at his thoughts. Even when they were far from his mind echoes of their power crackled in his bones. It made him itch.

"Where'd you go?"

His attention returned to the woman beside him, tucked into the warmth of their shared sheets. "Nowhere, just thinking."

Veredy turned on her side and propped her blonde head on a crooked arm. "You've been doing a lot of that lately." Her hand traced the line of his brow, as if checking for wrinkles. "I feel like you're lost."

"Not lost. The refugees brought a lot of worries, is all." He snorted and nudged her nose with his. "I don't want to lose this life we're building."

Her small mouth curled into a smile at his use of "we," and she laced her fingers with his. "There's no rush. I'll be here. You have time aplenty to work on your business. Maybe in a year or two, we'll find a place of our own, a place with room enough for children."

Arman smiled too, but he knew it did not reach his eyes. All they had worked for seemed removed now, one step more distant than before. Instead, his focus continued to return to the Laen.

The ice in his bones. The burning curiosity, almost obsession, just shy of dread.

"If it's not the threat of mortality, what has you so concerned?" Veredy asked, clearly realizing Arman was far from letting the dark thoughts go.

Arman's gaze roved over the wood grain of her bedroom walls. "I feel like Vielrona failed them. There was a citadel in these mountains, one we guarded. Did we forget our roots?"

Veredy tossed on her back, frowning. "Arman, we're not their guards. When Vielrona protected them, we had the strength of the Rakos, their fire and fury." She glanced at him. "Did the Laen say something?"

No, they placed memories that aren't mine in my head, images and feelings I can't erase. He hoped the sensation faded once he passed the Laen's message on to their guards. Part of him, though, the piece still entranced by traveling storytellers, would miss the feeling. Perhaps growing up in Vielrona made him view Laen differently. In the distance, the taller building of the Guildhouse dimmed its lights. "They just asked me to look out for their guards—human ones, not Rakos."

Veredy hummed in response, eyes already lidding again. They were unable to meet as often lately, and Arman tried to have the quality of their lovemaking make up for its infrequency. He kissed her brow and dragged himself from her bed. As much as he wanted their relationship to be more formal, too much stood in the way to marry just yet. *"There's no rush. I'll be here."* His thoughts returned to the ring on Alea's finger, the pain in her eyes when she spoke of Cehn. *We don't know that, Ver.* They could have decades left together. They could have hours.

Φ

The 30th Day of Lumord, 1251
The Feld de Barran, Athrolan

"There are campfires in the hills." Liane's eyes did not move from the flickering on the otherwise dark horizon.

Hela settled onto the cold rock outcropping beside her. "Shepherds?"

Liane shook her head. "Unless our luck has suddenly changed, it's the Mirikin." She rose with a groan, pressing a hand to the small of her back. "You going to be alright till dawn?"

Hela smiled and held up a battered lute. "I'll be fine. Besides, this ground isn't comfortable enough to let me sleep. Get some rest."

"Play quietly, alright?" Liane shot a narrowed glare at the horizon.

"I promise."

Liane picked her way down the slope to the nook between wind-worn rocks where they made camp. Dark lumps curled around the screened coals. Liane suspected it was as much for comfort as warmth. A month ago, they numbered twenty-seven, their ranks filled with writhing power of warriors and healers. Liane's gaze lingered on the girl tucked against the belly of a borrowed Sunamen charger. Now only three citadel guards, a historian, and a cook were left to escort the girl to Le'yne. If their guards still lived leagues of bitter mountains and barren grasslands separated them. *And an army of Mirikin soldiers.*

Liane settled in beside the girl's sleeping form. Gentle notes of *Mirrel in Winter's Chill* curled from the hill behind. Head pillowed on the horse's flank, Moera's young face relaxed into a smile. Perhaps a night free of nightmares was worth the risk of Hela's music.

Their journey from the citadel of Emala began as an exodus. Now it was a divine mission. *She might not be able to control it, but I know what I saw.* When the Mirikin attached in Cehn, black fog exploded around them. No Laen ever wielded black power. It had to mean something.

Now, Liane's own silver magic curled over her companions, easing aches, filling muscles with strength. The scent of salt and mountain springs drifted, alien, in the air. It was the only echo of home that still felt real.

"I miss home." Moera's silver eyes blinked open, following the invisible path south, as if she could still see the ruined citadel leagues away.

"I didn't mean to wake you." Liane did not meet her gaze. "Home's Le'yne now, and we have leagues to go. You ought to rest." Her thin lips clamped down on the rest of her words. She missed home, too.

Wind chattered through the dry leaves overhead. On the hill, Hela's music stuttered into silence. Liane raised her nose to the eddying air. It brought the stench of fresh blood and hot metal. *The gods.*

Nerves sang up her limbs, turning aches into exhausted willpower. War did not make time for grief or compassion. She surged to her feet and shook the others awake.

"Wind's changed, it'll bring our smoke right to them." She glanced at Moera, not thinking, "Put out the fire, would you?"

The girl waved her hand over the sullen coals, brow curled in concentration, then frustration. Finally, she kicked the bucket of drinking water into the fire with an exasperated sigh. "How can I bind the world if I can't even extinguish a campfire?"

"You'll learn in Le'yne, I promise. There are teachers there, better ones than I." Liane's voice cut through the soft sounds of the other Laen packing camp. "Move!" The cover of night would only last so long, and the stark landscape of the Feld de Barran offered little concealment. *We must make Namus by dawn*

Hela jogged down the hill, lute traded for her crossbow. "You smell that?"

Liane glanced at the historian sharply, slicing her hand through the air. Moera was already terrified. Panic would only make their ride more difficult. *We'd be dead.*

She coiled her braid under her cowl and buckled her swordbreaker onto her hip. In the citadel, it never saw use. In the wake of the war reigniting, the weapon bore dents and scratches. Muffled hooves thumped against hard ground as the others flanked the charger. The creature flicked its ears, unaware he carried the weight of the world in the form of a girl.

"Go. I'll catch up." Liane watched the Laen disappear into the darkness, pressing against the rising wind. She raised her hands, silver pooling in her palms, twisting tendrils erasing their footprints, wiping the stagnant stink of wet coals from the air. It was a sorry attempt, but she had to try. She did not know how the gods' magic reached across the barriers splitting the world, but she would know the sickening smell, the heavy, itching feeling anywhere. She nudged her stolen horse into a lope.

She missed the desert air, the humid, ocean air whipping over the walls of Emala, and the cry of lemurs in the oasis. Le'yne was as much a home as the hard, cold ground where they made camp. *I miss peace.*

Behind them, a lieutenant pressed his palm into a fresh hoofprint.

Φ

The 34th of Lumord, 1251
The City-state of Vielrona

As foreign as Vielrona's people and streets were to Alea, the sounds were the same. Migrating birds looked like tattered black lace over the overcast sky. *Right, Arman said it was autumn soon.* She was not certain what that meant outside of the most abstract sense. Desert seasons were just the two, though this close to the mountains they occasionally saw frost on winter nights.

Rough wood walls and the single slice of sky were comforting, but she was restless. She rose shakily, finding a sun-warmed basin and pitcher by the wardrobe. Sickness and sweat washed from her body with the water. Weakness dragged on her arms when she braided her hair, but she was cleansed from sweating illness and terror from her body. Both echoed still, but softly.

In a chest at the foot of her bed was a dress in an alarming shade of saffron and a plain black scarf. Breeches were an added layer under the shapeless dress, almost echoing her yelek and tsalvar. Though shorter than the jahi she usually wore, the scarf was enough to protect from the sun.

Not that there's much in the way of sunburning here.

Clinking dishes and low conversation emanated from downstairs. One narrow hand gripped the banister as she descended, steps shaky. Sunamen architecture was delicate, designed to take advantage of any breeze. This inn was sturdy and plain. Arman sat at the bar in the rear of the common room. One foot tapped against the foot-rail, the other hooked around the leg of his stool. He hummed absently as he peeled potatoes.

Words clogged in her throat and, without the swathing layers of clothes, she felt exposed. "Good morning." Nerves pinched her voice into shrillness.

Arman glanced up and waved with one of the potatoes. Distraction shadowed his eyes. "Afternoon, actually."

Kepra emerged from the kitchen, a smile blooming. "My dear, I am glad to see you about."

"Walking's easier than I thought. Will things be busy tonight?" She dreaded a crowd.

"Not for another two hours probably. Farmers' and guards come most often, and they aren't free until evening-fall. Want to sit?"

I want to go home. Alea edged over and took a seat two stools away from Arman.

Kepra slid a steaming mug over to her. "This ought to steady you."

Alea watched the swirling tea for a moment. It smelled of earth and rain. "Thank you—" her voice rasped. She remembered another voice, another mug of tea, the soft hand of her foster father on her brow. Grief was a sandstorm abrading her mind. She tried again, "Thank you for the tea. And your care."

"Ma's the best midwife in the Lows. Even if her draughts taste like cow's piss and pond muck."

The memory of a smile tugged at Alea's mouth. The description was accurate, and it sounded like something one of her foster-brothers would say.

"Arman!" Kepra flicked her dishtowel at her son. "Neither of you've died, and you'd do well to remember your manners." She removed the forgotten potato from his hands. "Get our guest some food, why don't you. I doubt she came down for the company."

While Arman did his mother's bidding, Alea surveyed the common room, noting the mixture of local wood and Sunamen sandstone. "Your people traded with us often. I remember the markets had your wood, your wool."

"Vielrona would be much poorer without trade," Kepra answered. "She's a convenient place to stop between Berr, Athrolan and Sunam. Speaking of, the Guild announced refugees are welcome to stay if they take up work. Something for you to think about."

Alea caught the underlying meaning. *If I stay in Vielrona I'll earn my keep.* Allies or not, the city-state risked herself by harboring the survivors. "I'll think on it." She had nowhere else to go, but the idea of making a life anywhere was distant and uncomfortable.

Arman added a plate of chicken and greens to the bar top before her, but waited until she was finished before breaking the silence. "If you wish for fresh air I'd be happy to show you the city. Or, there's a porch upstairs. I could show you landmarks from there."

Alea fiddled with her fork. She did not care about the city, though surely it was interesting. "I think I'll keep to myself if it's all the same to you." When his expression flickered from curiosity to frustration, a tinge of guilt colored her apathy. "I'm just adjusting. Thank you for the food, both of you, I'll not keep you from work." She beat as quick a retreat as her trembling legs allowed.

"Milady ir Suna," Arman caught up to her at the top of the stairs. "I know you suffered—I can't imagine how, but you have nightmares. Distract yourself, come see the sights. You ought to put the attack behind you."

Honestly, "milady?" The smile on his face did not quell the bitterness in her throat. "Suffered? Nightmares?" Anger sharpened her words, but she managed to keep her voice low. "You think I'm glad I survived? I have no history, no family. My only hope at a future is reduced to memories and sand-weathered bones!" Fatigue and fury darkened her vision. *I'm exhausted.* "Until you understand that, Master Wardyn, keep words like 'ought' and 'should' to yourself!" She slammed her door shut behind her.

Emotions she had ignored raged, released by her angry words. Her weakened legs failed, and she caught herself on the edge of her bed. She crawled to the chamber pot, heaving until nothing remained in her writhing stomach. *Please don't let him hear this.* In Sunam discussing one's emotions was common, but showing them was not. It was something only young children did, who knew no better. *What does it matter? Ihal or Ahren aren't here to see. I'm not Sunamen, not truly.* Fear welled, and she choked on the sobs exploding from her gut. Memories tumbled through her mind, each ending in blood-soaked sand and clouded eyes. She did not know how long she stayed curled on the floor, trembling and weeping.

Isolation was familiar. Not in the usual sense—she had friends in Cehn. Few were close, but Alea never minded. Life was an engaging play she watched, separated from her by an invisible wall.

Now the bubble surrounding her burst and she was raw from the strange wind buffeting her mind. It did not matter others had no such barriers. That wall protected her, and she would rebuild it. Perhaps it protected the world from her.

Muscles cramped when she finally pushed herself upright. She could not bring herself to get back into bed. For better or worse, she had survived. There was little sense or probability in spending the rest of her life in bed. *I need air.* She hated closed spaces. Remembering Arman's offer, she stepped quietly into the hall. It was deserted, but voices drifted from the common room below. *The aforementioned patrons.* At the opposite end of the hall from the main staircase was a narrow door. Finding it unlocked, Alea opened it to see narrow stairs winding up to the smaller third floor.

A door to her left bore a child's scratched letters. *Arman's room.* Another door opened onto a porch. It was barely more than a ledge but looked out over the front of the inn. Alea folded her arms on the open rail and tilted her face up to the sun. Warmth eased across her skin, heated the black scarf on her head and crept up her arms. Cradled in the northern foothills of the mountains, Vielrona was smaller than Cehn. Most of the surrounding buildings were two-storied, the lower half built from thick beams or stone and the upper with plaster. Rooftops sported moss and most houses had kitchen gardens. Plowed fields lay beyond, bordered with a low stone wall. A river wound through the city. Across a bridge sat larger houses built of stone and official looking buildings. Alea supposed she was in what Arman called the Lows.

Awareness bloomed on the back of her neck and she turned.

Arman leaned on the porch's doorway. "It's a nice place to think."

"I like to be someplace high when I have too many thoughts. It makes them seem smaller." She picked at the weathered wood of the rail. "I'm sorry I yelled at you."

"No need. I spoke thoughtlessly. I've seen my share of violence, but it was long ago." He gestured to a wooden chair, the cushion of which he hastily beat clean. "We've lived here since I can remember. I can't imagine what you see, looking at it with new eyes."

Alea sat and looked out at the city again. "It's greener than I'm used to. And cold." She frowned. "You're not part of Athrolan, though, correct?" The vast kingdom was something of an enigma to Alea. Sunam occasionally received news, fashion, and metals from its northern neighbor, but nothing as formal as an alliance.

"No. We are not a part of Athrolan, Berr, or Sunam. Vielrona started as a guard city for a nearby Laen citadel. Most just consider us outlaws now. We've a lot of fine craftsmen here, though, and make decent trade."

"What is your work? Do you inn-keep with your mother?"

"I design and sell blades. My father was a bladesmith and when he passed, my friend Wes took the clients. He does the actual forging, but has little skill for business or art." He faltered as if choosing his next question carefully from a jumble of words. "Did you study in Sunam?"

She frowned. "Ihal was very strict about our studies. He wanted each of us to learn as much about the world as we could. I enjoyed economics and learning about plants and trees—we had so few in the desert."

"What of history? That was always my favorite."

"Not mine. Ihal said we must learn the past, however, so we would not make the same mistakes."

"Is that why he sheltered the Laen?"

Alea's breath hitched. *How could he know about the Laen?* Her foster-father did everything in his power to hide the truth about the strange guests who arrived three days before the attack. She knew from the beginning that the attempt was pointless. *And we were repaid our kindness with death.* "Maybe. He had news for them, something about their first visit years ago. I was too young to remember their first visit. I don't know how anyone could keep that kind of power secret for long." She glanced over. "Sunam's divided in its opinions of the Laen. But Vielrona a sympathizer, since you used to guard them?"

It was Arman's turned to frown. "I would like to think so."

Grief and awe both tinged Alea's view of the Laen. On the grand scale, she wanted them to succeed, but they were also the reason her family was dead.

Mirikin blades opened Ahren, not Laen smoke. "How did you know about the Laen in Cehn?"

Arman glanced at her, his brows raised. "They brought you here. They loaded the survivors onto horses and wagons—the one with the instrument carried you on her back for half the trek."

Nerves thundered through her and she glanced up the street, half expecting silver footprints to lead down the cobblestones. "They aren't still here?"

"They stayed long enough to rest a few hours and restock, before continuing north." Arman's expression was pinched as if something clawed at his stomach.

"It does not matter if they only stayed long enough to use your privy." Alea rubbed the strong bridge of her nose. "The Mirikin will know. They knew which wing the Laen used. It was the oldest part of the building, designed to be a stronghold. We used it for the children."

Arman winced. "They attacked there first."

"And yet the Laen survived." Alea tried to keep the frustration out of her voice, but fell far short. She looked away. "I'm sorry. I'm not opposed to the Laen, Ihal saw to that. But they protected themselves, as my family was cut down around them." She squeezed her eyes shut for a moment. "I can't speak about—" Her voice tripped into a shaking breath and she rose. "Perhaps when I'm ready you could show me the city?"

"Of course. Can I do anything to help?"

"Just...." She squeezed her eyes closed and turned away. "I wish they left me for the vultures."

Φ

The 36th of Lumord, 1251
The Oasis of Cehn, Sunam

Sand hissed under the horse's hooves as An'thor trotted north. He was silent, but alert. His eyes fixed to the ground. His clothes were made for bitter cold and glaciers, but the hardy leather and top few layers were suitable for Sunam's dry heat and cold desert nights. The swath of sand abutting the mountains was hard-packed, closer to his native tundra than desert. *Far easier to track when the sand doesn't move with each breath of wind.* He tugged the silk wrap normally insulating his jacket tighter around his face. An'thor was not lucky enough to be protected by the rich Sunamen tan. His skin was a clear white, the blood vessels a visible purple network just under the surface. Being born in a country where true summer lasted only one of the forty-nine-day months made him less accustomed to sunlight.

Like the Laen, the Nenev were an ancient, dying race. A people of ice and progress, their minds turned like gears. Isolation made them legends, but they were rarely the heroes. A tattoo curled from his bicep, up his throat and across the left side of his face like an eddy of wind. Black ink had long ago faded to an ashy gray from age and weathering.

He noted where hooves kicked aside rocks or scuffed the parched earth. *Seven horses. A wagon. Fewer than when we were separated.* He found one body three hours before, the simple arrow notably Mirikin. He wondered how many Laen would be left when he finally caught up with them in Cehn. His horse's head hung low, gray coat shining with sweat. He looked as tired as An'thor felt. "Almost there, Theriim. We'll rest when we reach the city." He rubbed the weary animal's neck. He felt more guilt from the failed promises to his horse than those to himself.

When he first joined the Laen's escort, there were dozens of the women. Forced to separate during a skirmish to buy the women time, he and the others were days—if not weeks—behind their charges. *Did that cost them even more?* His long life bore witness to too many cities and lives rising and falling to disbelieve that life came in great cycles, but the Laen were the epitome of balance. And he feared they would soon break.

His gaze followed each irregularity of the ground, and it was several moments before he saw the smoke. Even in early autumn, heat haze hung on the horizon. Despite the distorting ripples in the air, An'thor's gut twisted. *This is wrong.* He urged his gray mount into a lope, heart sinking in certainty. Wind moaned as it whipped through the still smoldering city at the edge of the oasis. Loose sand and ash rasped across the sandstone and burnt wood. Even the lower levels of the manor were razed. "This was a massacre." Theriim's ears twitched in response to the low words.

Bodies littered the main street. Those who survived the initial attack and the following flames were methodically killed as the army moved out. An'thor's gaze slid over the light clothes of the residents searching for a gray dress, a cloak. Grappling marks on the sandstone told him the manor was attacked first, and he nudged his mount into the private courtyard. The fountain was mercifully clean, save for a layer of sand. An'thor refilled his waterskin and wiped his face clean, leaving Theriim to drink his fill.

Sticky blood dragged at his boot soles. Desert heat raised the stench of rot, even as the sun desiccated flesh beyond recognition. The household staff had made a stand, and just inside the building's ruins lay the *ihal* and his sons. *Still no Laen. Could they escape this?* Darker thoughts of capture followed on the first's tail. Children's bodies clustered in the garden behind the manor and a pregnant woman sprawled several paces farther. The blood covering her belly told him it was fruitless, but An'thor's pale hands fumbled with her clothes, hoping someone, even a squalling infant might have survived. Instead, his blood-stained fingers closed her dark eyes. A chill unrelated to his sunburn crept through his body. He was accustomed to violence, but he did not enjoy it, and massacres were a different breed from battle. *Azirik, what are you doing?*

Only after searching each building did he admit the Laen were gone. He led Theriim from the manor and through the eastern gate. The Mirikin would be well across the mountains, and he knew Azirik planned to cut across the Feld de Barran of Athrolan. Muscles ached when he crouched to touch the tracks marring the sand. *I'll rest when I know where they've gone.* Hundreds of hoof prints and Mirikin boots disturbed the ground. He noted ridges from wagon wheels and winced. "They easily could be captured." He examined them for a few more paces then turned to call for his horse. If the Laen were captured, he would follow.

Theriim nosed a pile of horse dung on the smaller road north. He frowned. The desert sun made quick work of any moisture. Most of the bodies in the city were already desiccated. The metal toe of his boot broke open the dung. "This can't be more than a week old." His gaze inched over the road's bricks. It was less obvious than the open ground, but he could see where sand was scuffed away. His careful paces turned into a jog as he followed the trail farther north. No more than a dozen riders, many bearing stretchers, if he gauged the depth of the prints correctly.

A toppled league marker heaped by the roadside. Brushing sand away, he tilted his head to read. He could decipher little of the language, but he recognized one name. *Vielrona.* His cracked fingers paused in their exploration. A square of gray linen was wadded into a crevice. Leaving a note was too great a risk, but a tattered piece of clothing was enough. He swung himself onto Theriim's back and turned north.

An'thor knew better than to pray, but the familiar weight of despair in his stomach told him they sorely needed hope.

Φ

The 37th Day of Lumord, 1251
The City-state of Vielrona

Sunlight flooded across Alea's upturned face. With her eyes closed, it was almost like home. The wind brought the scent of damp stone, however, and the low sounds of sheep and cattle from beyond the houses. A breeze tugged at her black scarf, nipping with the promise of winter. The gate clattered shut and Alea's eyes snapped open. "Mistress Wardyn."

Kepra's smile was bright, almost as impish as her son's. "Morning, Miss ir Suna. I'm glad to see you've ventured into our garden."

"Morning," Alea added belatedly. "Might you know where your son is? I wanted to accept his offer to show me about." Whatever Arman's opinion was of his mother's teas, Alea's strength returned over the last few nights.

Her spirit had not.

"I just saw him at the market, but he often comes home for lunch. If he's not busy I'm sure he'll show you about." Kepra lifted the basket resting on her arm. "Let me put this on to roast and I'll find you a cloak." She paused in the doorway, frowning at Alea's feet. "You ought to wear shoes, miss."

Alea glanced down at her feet, covered in the battered sandals she wore all the way from Cehn. "These are comfortable." *These are a piece of home.*

"Suit yourself. Before winter comes, though, we ought to get you fitted for a set of boots though."

Guilt slid into Alea's heart and she tucked her feet under the cover of the chair. She had no money. Borrowed dresses were one thing, but shoes cobbled for her alone were another.

A tuneless whistle heralded the younger Wardyn, followed by his appearance around the corner. One hand sketched in a cheaply bound journal, but despite not looking at the cobbles he did not trip.

He slipped through the garden and was halfway down the path when he paused at looked up. "Milady."

Alea offered what she hoped looked more smile than grimace. "Morning. Are you busy this afternoon?"

Arman frowned, then grinned. "You want to see the city. It was a slow day, I'm sure Wes can handle the stall. I'll grab lunch." He ducked inside then poked his head back through the door. "Have you eaten?"

Alea nodded. She had not, in fact, eaten, but the idea of leaving the sanctuary of the inn churned in her stomach, and she thought it poor form to vomit all over her host's boots.

Arman reappeared, mouth full and humming tunelessly. He tossed Alea a thick length of fabric. "You'll want a cloak."

She arranged the cloth around her shoulders and fastened the worn hook before following him to the gate. Nerves tingled up her arms and her fierce grip on the gate's latch was slow to relax.

Arman either did not notice her anxiety or was pretending not to. "This road is East Twist," he explained around the bite of roll. "If you are ever lost, just ask for it, or for the Ruby Cockerel."

Bright red paint decorated the battered wood sign he indicated. *I never had to worry about getting lost before.* Houses and walls that stood below the tiny porch upstairs in the inn now towered above her head.

"You all right?"

"Cities look larger from their streets."

Arman tilted his head. "Did you never explore Cehn?"

"Not on foot. None of us did. The ihal and his eldest son occasionally went on diplomatic errands, but that was rare. We kept to ourselves. He was always worried about safety, especially when Mirik began to skirmish on our borders."

"I can't imagine that. The lack of exploring, I mean." Arman pointed at her borrowed cloak. "Tie that about you and don't mind the stares. People're curious about the refugees."

Alea did as he suggested, then lifted her chin and drew a deep breath. "Lead on." She tried a smile, which Arman returned before turning back up the road. His longer legs took one step for every two of hers, but he chose an easy pace. East Twist curved sharply and spilled onto a wider street. Clustered, narrow houses overhung the passerby, but that was not what made Alea stare.

"Everything's green. Plants on the roofs. Vines are everywhere." Low laughter startled its way from her throat. She barely recognized the sound.

"Wait a few more weeks—the hills turn red and orange before winter." Arman nodded up the street with barely hidden impatience, "Shall we walk past the markets?"

Winding narrow paths navigated the booths, and Alea was glad for the slower pace forced by their turns. Seemingly little sense dictated the market's layout, but a pattern arose as Arman navigated the chaos. Closest to the fields were stalls offering fruit, livestock, and farming tools. Household wares were the next circuit in. Deeper still, one found cloth and finer wares. Arman mentioned his own blade stall was within the last.

"Do you craft at the stall or just sell your work?"

"Just sell. There's not enough room in the market and we make enough smoke to be a bother. Most workshops are across the river in the Rattles. Wes—my friend who does the heavier forging—lives above our forge." He glanced over as she steadied herself on the stall's wall. "Want to see the river and take a rest?"

"Please." Lively people and colors drained Alea's newfound energy. *It is as if Cehn was a wonderful dream and now I've woken to this disorienting world.* A low wall ran along the edge of the market, the hewn stone forming one bank of the river below. Muttering water and the distant music of a performer several streets down underscored the cluttered noise of the market. Arman perched on the stone, legs dangling over the steady current.

Alea took a spot beside him, peering down at the dark river. Sunken stones loomed in the depth, stained brown with rust. "In Cehn we had a spring—It made the oasis—but no rivers. You're lucky."

"Farther upriver, where it's deeper, we swim."

Alea glanced over, brows arching. "I can't imagine swimming when it's so cold."

Arman lifted a shoulder in a shrug. "It's a bit cold now, but in the summer most at least wade to cool down." He grinned. "Though I don't suppose we know what true heat is."

"I wouldn't think so, no." She even missed the layers of heat, the rippling air so dense it was a final layer of clothing over her skin.

"Besides, if we don't jump in ourselves, our friends give us a push—" Shouted greetings cut his comment short.

Two young men approached from the center of the market. The first called his greeting again. "Arman!"

Arman stood, clapping the shorter man on the back. "I was wondering how long I could avoid you." He turned to Alea, "Milady ir Suna, this is Kam—" he gestured to the man who had first spoken, "and Wes." He nodded to the broad bladesmith. "Lyne'alea ir Suna is from Cehn."

Kam's brown face split into a cheerful smile. "Milady Lyne'alea!" He bowed lavishly over her hand and grinned at her surprise. "It is our pleasure."

Wes nodded his white-blond head. His gaze was respectfully curious. "Welcome."

Heat spread across her face. Attention was uncomfortable, and being singled out as someone new was worse. "Thank you."

"Kam's a locksmith, and I've told you about Wes." He glanced at the latter man curiously. "I thought you were packing in early to finish that blade by tomorrow."

"Patch in the bellows gave again—I had to send it to Heggins this time. It'll be at least tomorrow afternoon before we can have it back." His gaze flicked to Alea again. "Have you had lunch?"

Arman nodded. "Just finished before we left. I was going to show her the rest of the city."

"We're headed to an Upper bar. See you later?"

"Tonight," he promised.

Kam and Wes were lost to the swirling crowd.

Alea glanced over, wondering at the look that passed between Arman and Wes. "They seem entertaining."

Arman scoffed. "Wes is decent, though he has a filthy tongue. Kam loves women too much." He jerked his head in the direction of the finer houses across the river. "Shall we continue? Do you need to rest more?"

"As long as we walk slowly." Truthfully, her legs ached and her back was stiff after so many days in bed. *I can't go back to that room just yet.* She fell into step beside him again, this time walking farther into the nicer part of the market, edging tall townhouses and a public garden.

"Here, try this." Arman stepped into the shade of a bar's awning. "It's not alcohol, at least, not this one." He slid a copper coin across the bar and held up two fingers and made a swirling gesture with his hand by his chin.

Alea watched the bartender combine several fruit juices and a splash of something bright blue. The result was a thick green drink she poured into two large, waxed leaves bound into a conical shape. She signed something to Arman and turned back to the interior portion of the bar.

"Ma Ha-jal makes the best drinks in the entire city. A bit expensive, but worth it. She imports her fruits from home, in Ban."

Alea's tentative sip flooded her tongue with the taste of cut palm fronds, grasses, and something spicy that lingered for a minute. Arman finished his in a few gulps, but Alea nursed hers as they crossed a narrow bridge. The streets were quieter, lined with stone houses. Despite her initial judgment, the city was small. The whole of it could fit twice into Cehn proper. *If it still stood.* Even the cluster of stone buildings Arman explained made up the official halls of the Guild were compact. They crowned the simple city well. Like Cehn's golden sandstone fit in the desert, Vielrona's gray stone and dark wood blended into the surrounding foothills.

"There's a garden in the Guild's walls that's a nice place to walk."

Alea paused to lean against a wall. Her body dragged, and fatigue muddled her thoughts. "I think I might need to turn back." She glanced at the sky. "Will it be dark soon?"

"Not for another two bells, but if you're tired we can go another day."

"I'd like that." She loved the greenery, and her garden at home was a sanctuary.

"Let me see if I can get a ride back." Arman flagged down a small empty cart headed toward the Lows. "Tomas!" When the driver slowed his donkey and raised his hand Arman placed his hand on the seat's edge to haul himself up. "Mind driving us home?"

Tomas' hand stopped him. "Begging your pardon, Wardyn, but I won't have her on my cart." The man's steely eyes pinned Alea in place. "Allies or no, they shouldn't have been brought back. Your girl here was with them. I'll not bring the Berrin or Mirikin down on my family." He paused, shaking his head at Arman, "They'll be the death of you. That is how their kind are."

Arman fell back, frowning. "Good day, then, Tomas." His dazed tone told Alea he was as surprised as she. He was silent a moment then turned to her. "I am sure he just doesn't like strangers."

"He doesn't like the Laen, Arman." She looked down, allowing a loose hank of hair to hide her eyes. She expected cultural misunderstandings, but in a city sympathetic to the Laen, Tomas' fear worried her. *If he fears armies will come here, am I still not safe?* She straightened, pulling a faint smile onto her face. "I would prefer to walk anyways."

Φ

The sun's warmth disappeared with its light, and Arman shrugged deeper into his cloak. The bar Wes frequented in the Upper district was a fair walk away, but the distance usually sobered them up before they reached home. Arman heaved a sigh. Tomas' words irked him. *That is how their kind are.* He assumed most in Vielrona were neutral on the Laen, if not wholly supportive. Now he wondered if he was wrong.

He glanced to the north where the rolling hills of Athrolan stretched into blackness. Somewhere the Dhoah' Laen camped in the wilderness. Young. Hunted. He could not imagine the weight that rested on her shoulders. *Vielrona should have welcomed her, raised our walls, and armed ourselves to the teeth to protect her.* He kicked at a loose cobble with an angry growl. The world needed her, and she needed guards.

CHAPTER THREE

The 38th Day of Lumord, 1251
The City-state of Vielrona

ALEA'S EYES WERE CAVERNS in her face. While the mirror was copper, unlike the silver she was used to, she knew the differences were not due to the material. Her tan paled until she almost looked Athrolani. Grief and illness sharpened her features.

"Alea your eyes, they're darker." Ahren's last words were already faint in her memory. She might never recall the event fully. She wondered if she even wanted to. What she remembered was horrible enough. With an irritated glance at the mirror, she adjusted her makeshift jahi. It was pointless to still wear the garment—sun and wind here were an echo of the desert's ferocity. Still, it was one more layer between the new world and her tattered mind. Her wall was almost complete. She straightened herself and followed the clattering of pans downstairs.

The inn's common room was deserted and Alea paused to admire the space anew. She briefly wondered at the wealth required for Kepra to own such a space, but each furnishing seemed simple and well cared for. She peered at a stylized metal sun hanging above the door.

"Arman's father gifted me that when I told him I was bearing his child." Kepra's soft voice was warm, as was the hand that touched Alea's shoulder briefly. "I thought it made the place homey."

"My ihal had a tiny statue on his desk. It was his wife's favorite. Whenever he held it there was such light in his eyes." She looked down.

"He must have loved her dearly." Kepra bustled back into the kitchen. "Breakfast? How did you find the city?"

Alea sat quietly, fingers brushing the wood of the bar. She felt vulnerable, open, but it was as refreshing as it was uncomfortable. "The market was interesting. Vielronan food smells so different. I like the spices you use." Her throat was tight. "I feel a bit lost. I'm used to whirlwind days."

Kepra paused, her dark eyes resting on Alea for a moment as if gauging her strength. "I'd welcome the help if you wish to keep busy. I have more vegetables that need peeling and cutting."

Alea's smile probably looked desperate, but she could not keep the happiness from her face. She hastily tied on an apron and followed Kepra into the heat of the kitchen. Some of the vegetables were strange, but peeling and chopping were the same in any kitchen. Noontime was accompanied by loud men, sweaty and dusty from the fields, and Arman with a small canvas-bound book. He smiled at his mother and, noting the crowd, chose a stool at one of the kitchen counters. He sat, book open, with a cheap quill in one hand and a mug of stew in the other. He was mostly finished when Alea coughed softly from the farthest corner.

"What are you working on?"

Arman choked on his potato, breath wheezing for a moment before he turned to peer behind him.

Alea waved from her stool beside the stove. She was sure her face was smattered with flour from dumplings, but her hands were too covered to try and wipe it away.

"A design for a client." He raised his voice, "Ma?" When Kepra glanced around the doorframe he continued, "Why'd you enlist Miss ir Suna to cook?"

"Perhaps you could ask her yourself, Arman. Don't be rude."

Arman turned back. "You don't have to earn your keep yet, you're still recovering. And you could eat in the common room."

Alea looked down, smiling. "Business keeps thoughts away. There are too many loud men out there and the kitchen is warm."

Arman still looked surprised when he cleared his dishes. At the doorway he paused. "If you want something else to keep the darkness at bay, there's a library I'd gladly show you."

He was gone before Alea responded, but she turned the thought over in her mind. Her foster-father had a library of his own and gifted her with books. *What titles await me in this city?*

Kepra's voice cut through her thoughts. "I just have to clean. You seem lost in thought—do you need to rest?"

"Arman mentioned a library."

"I'm afraid we only have two books of our own, but the Guild's library is extensive. Were you thinking of visiting tomorrow?"

"I was." Alea swept the countertop clean and began to scrub the wood. "My foster father gave me a poetry book. The collection here might have new ones."

Kepra stared at her a moment, brown eyes thoughtful. "May I ask you something?"

A note in her soft tone made Alea pause. Fingers picking at a stubborn piece of dough stilled. "Of course."

"You were wearing gold and a ring on your finger. Arman said you were in the garden of the manor. You speak of your foster-family and your ihal with the same love. May I ask who you are?"

Alea stared. Many told her she was an intelligent girl without valuable history who would make a good wife for a wealthy commoner. She was lucky her foster-brother agreed to marry her. None of those things mattered now. Alea opened her mouth, closed it, and then opened it again, with the tang of stubbornness in her throat.

Kepra leaned forward and touched her hand. "You don't have to answer. It may deserve some thought. It's hard when we lose the people and places that defined us." She took the dishtowel from the younger woman's hands. "I can finish up here."

Alea thanked her then rose. She stopped just outside the bubble of noise from the other patrons. Her wall was strong and thick. Normally she disguised bitterness as wry wit.

Every wall has chinks.

Kepra's words wormed through her defense, and anger lanced out, cold and crystalline. "I am Lyne'alea ir Suna." Her steady voice belied her shaking hands. "I am the foster-daughter of Ahme'reahn ira Suna, ihal of Cehn. I was to be the wife of his second eldest son, Ahren. Our city was attacked a week before my wedding. Everything I ever knew, ever could have been, is gone. So, I am gone. I'm only certain of my name, which is borrowed, and that nothing will ever be as beautiful as it was before." She kept her composure on her path through the common room, gripped tightly until she closed her bedroom door.

Deep, gasping sobs took her, and she wondered if she could ever stop. She slid to the floor, leaning back against the door. It was solid, only making the familiar things in her memories less substantial. Measured footfalls on the stairs forced her to bite back hitching breath. She bit down on her sleeved wrist to muffle her noise.

She heard a calloused hand press on the door. "Milady?" Arman's voice was gentle.

She did not respond. It was almost dark, but she had not lit the candle by her bed. *I could be out.*

"Ma told me you seemed shaken." He paused. "Are you there?"

She cleared her throat. "I was just resting." It was obvious, but she was grateful he afforded her the lie.

"I'm sorry I made these first few days hectic. I'm not good with grief. Do you want me to let you alone?"

"I don't want to be alone." She wondered if the words were too soft for him to hear. She rubbed the marks her teeth left on her arm.

Rough fabric rasped as he eased onto the hall floor. "I've had a share of grief, but nothing like yours. If I lost Vielrona I'd lose which way was north." He sighed. "I've heard what allowing the Laen to come here could do. Even bringing you here could endanger us. But I see you sitting at my hearth and I wonder how people could be so cruel." He paused as if to check she was still listening. "Would it make it better if you learned the reason the Laen didn't protect your family? If you learned your loss was not in vain?"

"No." Her voice cracked. "If I learned we saved the world, it would hurt just as much. My family was my world."

"I'm sorry, then. I don't know how to make it hurt less."

"Thank you for talking to me. I think I can sleep now."

He rose with a groan. "Very well." He was partway down the hall when she peered into the dark corridor. "Arman, would you show me the library tomorrow?"

His smile was careful. "Of course. I can bring you on my way to the forge."

She ducked back into her room with quick thanks and lit the candle by her bed. Walking the city made her muscles ache and she undressed slowly before sliding under the coverlet. Arman's words helped.

Closing her eyes, she thought of the spicy scent of the wood and curtains of ihal's manor. Merahn's laughter as she held her firstborn. Alea smiled at the memory of Ahren's quick wit. They took a walk in the garden without escort a month before the attack.

His dark eyes had glinted when he saw her, presenting her with a hair comb wrought of silver and studded with onyx and lapis. He had just returned from negotiations in Vielrona and had found the gift in their market. "It matched your gray eyes," he explained with a smile. "I am sorry our wedding continues to be postponed. I would imagine you're anxious."

Alea laughed as she often did, then. "I waited years, Ahren. What is another month?" His hand sliding over hers surprised her, as had the kiss on her brow. "It is only until the rains come."

She had not understood the sorrow in his eyes when he pulled away, thinking it was only from desire. "Alea, you know there's a war on?"

"Ihal mentions it every day."

Ahren's face grew serious. "Do you remember anything from before?"

"I was half a month old. How could I? This family is all I am."

Ahren looked up at the fading light in the desert sky. "I'll protect you. I know how precious you are."

"Precious to you?"

He had answered only by squeezing her hand. Now, half asleep, Alea's mind paused on that. The image of Ahren's face dissolved into his expression when the attack began. He had the same sorrow in his eyes, haunting with the knowledge behind them.

Φ

The 39th Day of Lumord, 1251

"The tomes await, milady!" Arman knocked on her door before trotting downstairs. Alea finished braiding her hair and hurriedly tied her sandals before rushing after him. Arman turned, half a biscuit in his mouth while he pulled on a cloak.

She smiled briefly before looking away, but she knew he saw the shadows under her eyes. Half a pace allowed her to walk in his wake through the morning crowd, but her toes still found their way under more than a few boots. She picked out local Vielronan by their honey-colored hair and tan skin, but the city clearly had a history of opening their gates to those who needed shelter or business. Even still, gazes the slid over Aman paused on her. She wished her borrowed cloak had a deeper hood.

Arman swung open the Guild's wooden gate and showed her up a paved walk to a small building. "I'll come by when Wes and I take our midday meal. If you're tired I can show you home, then."

She nodded, hand on the door-latch. "Enjoy your work." It was rare that she was alone in Cehn, with such a large household. Now that she had little to occupy her time she found herself unsure how to simply exist in her own thoughts. *Especially when they are so dark.* The low room was filled with scattered shelves and boards holding maps and charts. The hearth was lit, but low, and she hung her cloak beside one of the chairs before perusing the tomes. There seemed to be little order to the books' placement. Several books were piled haphazardly atop the shelves. She frowned at the titles: *A History of the Gods, The Way of the Earth,* and *In the Name of Balance: The Teachings of the Laen.* Chills rolled down her arms. *Arman's not the only one to think there was much more to the attack.* The thought made her uneasy.

Turning she saw a new account, one she knew. *Between Desert and Mountain* was a dry retelling of Vielrona's political sparring with Athrolan to the north and Sunam, to the south. One illustration made her pause. It was the Minister of Vielrona meeting with the ihal of Cehn. She traced the artist's rendering of her foster father's face. *His eyes were calmer than that, and his hair was always bound back under his jahi.* She almost smiled, though, at the familiar face.

She shut the cover gently. History was never a subject she appreciated, preferring modern poetry and music. Finding a few volumes of nature-centered verses, she retired to the chair. After a minute she lost herself to golden grain and bitter ice in winter. By the time Arman arrived, she could almost recognize the taste of winter.

Φ

The 46th Day of Lumord, 1251

Alea was absorbed in a book on Vielronan plants when the door opened abruptly. After close to a week visiting the library, Alea knew most of the collection. It was close to supper and she expected Arman. Instead, a tall, unfamiliar man blocked the door.

He paused when he saw her, then doffed his cloak. "Forgive me, miss. I didn't know the room was being used." He stepped closer, allowing the torch at the door to illuminate him. Like most Vielronan his skin was gold. Gray threaded his long pale locks. Lines of a life filled with sorrow and joy etched his broad mouth and fierce eyes.

"I was just passing time," Alea answered. "You're welcome to your business." She turned back to her book, only to be interrupted again.

"I know everyone in this city, by face if not by name." His broad hands rested on the back of the chair opposite hers. "I don't think I'm familiar with either of yours."

Alea closed her book carefully and straightened. "I'm Lyne'alea ir Suna. I'm staying with the Wardyn family."

The man regarded her searchingly before nodding. "I know where you came from and how you arrived. I'm glad you find our city hospitable. Perhaps soon we can have a better conversation." He lifted a roll of maps from a shelf flanking the hearth, and with a smile, headed back toward the door.

"May I ask your name, sir?" Alea stopped him as he was fastening his cloak.

He bowed his head. "Gluan Herdingman. Have a good night, miss."

Φ

"And on top of that, I received two new commissions for hilt repair. It's the fine tooling that I like the most." Arman glanced at Alea. She barely responded to his excited retelling of his day. Her dark gaze trailed along the road as if her body dragged its unwilling mind after it. "Are you alright?"

"What?" Her eyes flew wide and she almost tripped over a raised cobble.

"You seem lost in thought."

She shook her head. "I'm just distracted. I met someone in the library today—Gluan Herdingman. He said he wanted to speak with me."

Arman's laugh was closer to a snort. *Of course, he did.* "That was our Minister. His curiosity got the best of him, I think. He's a good man, if abrupt."

Alea paused on the bridge, frowning. Arman leaned his forearms on the cool stone. Chills curled up his arms, but he welcomed the cold after a day in the forge. Bells from behind drowned out most other noise. For a moment, Vielrona drew a breath, preparing for night.

Arman eyed Alea sidelong. Her profile was lit by the sun setting as she raised her face to the fresh wind gusting down the mountains. She leaned over the side of the bridge, peering at the dark water. Thick blocks of dark gray stone reinforced the banks, dotted with small, scraggly shrubs that found hold between older blocks. "This is beautiful."

She must not see the sewage from the Upper culverts. He smiled. Still, it was nice for someone to call his home beautiful. "You said the desert had no rivers?"

"Except for Sunam's capital. Flood waters from the other side of these mountains meet the sea there. I've never been." Her eyes traced the narrow sandy path along the river and she glanced over. "What lies up there?"

Gooseflesh rippled up Arman's arms at her words. "The ruins of Elanal—the city Vielrona used to guard."

"The Laen city?"

He nodded. "Few visit it. It feels like a grave."

She gathered her skirts and headed down the road. "Arman, you know the biggest difference between home and Vielrona?"

He looked back at the mountains, half expecting to see the Laen standing in the churning waters. "The sand?" he hazarded.

She laughed. "Besides that. It's the layers."

"Layers?" He shoved his hands in the pockets of his cloak.

"In Cehn, everything was layered. We wore layers of fabric; our doors and windows were layers of wooden lattice and drapes. Our hair was done up in curtains of braids and charms under our *jahi*. Even the sandstone of our buildings had layers of gold and red and brown. In Vielrona you have more colors, perhaps—green and blue—but it's simple. Straightforward. It is a different kind of beauty." Her hands animated the descriptions.

Arman wondered if she knew her words described the difference between the Vielronan people and her own. They stepped through the gate to the Cockerel when a sharp voice came from the doorway. "Wardyn!"

Arman tried not to wince and raised his hand in greeting. "Farrow, I've not seen you since last winter. How has the clerk's life treated you?"

"Well, so far." The man was older than Arman by a few years, his orange-gold hair closely cropped. His cream tunic bore the city's insignia on the right breast. Despite his tidy grooming, scars peppered his hands and a long mark over his left brow designated him a former common lad. "When the Minister had me draw this up, I offered to run yours myself."

"Glad I could see you." Arman turned and motioned Alea forward. "This is Lyne'alea ir Suna. Miss, this is Maren Farrow, an old friend."

Farrow's pale gaze was reserved as he handed her a folded letter. "This is for you, miss." He glanced at Arman. "Might I speak with you?" Arman stepped aside to allow Alea past. When the door shut behind her Farrow looked down. "Watch yourself."

"Excuse me?" Sickening dread unfolded in Arman's gut. Despite his introduction, Farrow was not a friend, and had not been for years. But neither was he an enemy.

"The world's not safe and you're only making it worse."

"What are you talking about?"

"First the Laen in your inn, now you're keeping her about? Her family sheltered them, Arman. There's already talk." He rested a hand on Arman's shoulder. "Think of Veredy, if nothing else."

Arman shook the hand off. *Veredy?* She was even less concerned about the Mirikin than he. "It's good to see you," he lied. He watched Farrow retreat up the street before stepping into the inn. Alea perched on a stool, the letter open before her.

"I'm sorry about that. Just reminiscing." Arman jerked his head at the parchment. "What is it?"

"A summons to appear before the Guild with the other survivors tomorrow morning."

Tomorrow? "May I?"

Shaking narrow fingers handed him the letter. The words were neutral and made no mention of any rumors, but it still made Arman's skin crawl with unease. Farrow's words cast a sinister shadow over Gluan's careful words. "It's probably a formal welcome, maybe they'll help everyone get settled with work." It was the third time he lied in the last few minutes, and he did not like the ease with which falsehoods slipped from his tongue. "I'm going to go wash off this forge-filth." If she said goodnight, he did not hear.

Later, with the worst of the grime off his hands and drifting in the bottom of his washbasin, Arman opened the chest at the foot of his bed. His family was not wealthy, but his father had often read to him from one of the few books they owned. It was Arman's favorite as a child, and he suspected they were his father's favorites too. At the bottom of the chest was a slim book wrapped in several layers of cloth and stuffed in a pair of boots he outgrew years ago. Callouses caught on the soft material of the cover as he unwrapped it.

Gold and white detailed the plain green. Inlaid on the cover, was a small portrait, protected by a thin sheet of clear mica. The man in the picture glowered at Arman with eerie yellow-green eyes.

Arman thumbed through the pages as quickly as he could without damaging the delicate parchment. "Page eighteen," he reminded himself. Finding the place, he sank onto his bed and reread the words. He almost had it memorized, once.

> *"Laen are powerful, creators of gods, made of sea and storm, ice and lightning. Beside them stands another race, as fierce as the Laen are calm. Guards made of fire and earth, filled with the rage of earthquakes. They are the Rakos. The Laen claimed their souls, and in return, offered their hearts."*

Under the passage was a note by the scribe. It mentioned the Rakos were all but extinct. Wholehearted defense of their Laen came with a cost. Most died in battle. Others disappeared into the wilderness. Some bred with humans, but their children were unremarkable. As the Laen dwindled, so did their protectors.

Arman turned back to the image on the cover. The man passed as human if one did not look closely. Something in the set of his mouth, the depth of his eyes revealed his monstrous nature. Arman understood how many folks thought Vielronan people had a bit of Rakos in their ancestry—gold hair and ruddy skin echoed in the deeper tones of the portrait. *Ancestry or not, your blood is all but useless.* He shook his head. *You can't even inspire faith, and when the Laen need you most, you're gone.*

Φ

The 47th Day of Lumord, 1251

The double gates to the largest Guild building hung open and guarded. While the rest of the city bustled, stillness muffled the official complex. Several Sunamen faces were among the gathering crowd, and her nerves relaxed a fraction. She was almost used to her simple routine and the sudden turn of events frustrated her. She did not dare to think on what might happen if they city chose not to shelter the refugees. *How could I find another place to live? How could any of us?* As much as Vielrona was not home, neither was any Athrolani city. Besides, news—and superstition—of the attack would precede them. Rumors flew faster than a horse could run.

Dark, warm air drifted from the open doors, and Alea slipped down the hall reaching off from both sides of the foyer. Servants milled about, but Alea noted few differences between the classes.

Someone poked his head through a door directly opposite, scanning the gathered newcomers. "Are you here for the hearing?"

A broad man with a dense collection of Sunamen braids stepped forward, one hand laced with his wife's. "We are."

Dread landed heavily in Alea's stomach. *Hearing?* Fourteen others waited in the small room. Alea examined the faces. The familiar, light brown of Cehn people was a warm breeze to her weathered spirit, but none of their faces were those of her family or friends. Nervous smiles matched her own, however. Seeing their own borrowed clothes, Alea was glad Kepra lent her a clean dress. Sarafan and kokoshnik were the style in Athrolan, but Vielronan women favored loose dresses gathered with broad canvas or leather belts. The one Alea wore was cream stitched with gray. She suddenly missed the comforting weight of her cloak.

No sooner had she found a seat than the man returned, this time holding up a different door. Alea's brows rose as they entered. Strength and age filled each aspect of the architecture. The expected riches were forgone for rough simplicity. Instead of a massive hall, they ranged about the rear of a narrow stone room. It was beautiful in the way the mountains were beautiful due to their might and ferocity. Warm gray walls were unadorned, save for a single banner at the rear of the room. Smokey waxen torches burnt against the stone. Beneath it a long table stood along the wall.

The dozen people awaiting them were the strangest mix Alea had yet seen. Half were the tanned-and-blonde combination typical of old Vielronan families. The others seemed to hail from several other nations. Alea picked out the dark brown skin and shaved head of a Banis woman, and the white skin and brown hair of an Athrolani man. One woman was even Sunamen.

"Order." Gluan sat at the center of the table. Now he wore a small medallion around his neck but was otherwise unremarkable. He fixed the refugees with a pointed stare. "I am Minister Gluan Herdingman of Vielrona." His tawny eyes were those of a hawk. "I formally offer you asylum in our city, but I would like to hear what each of you will gift us with in return. What skills do you bring to Vielrona?"

A man she recognized as a gardener stepped forward. "I tended the ihal'*s* plants in his personal garden. The plants here are different, but I would gladly work in the fields or in the Guild's personal garden. I studied with Burhen the Green, a great botanist of Sunam, and could bring much to your farms and fields."

Many of the headmen scratched notes as he spoke, but Glaun's gaze did not waver from the speaker. When the man was done, the Minister gestured to the city folk who were gathered to watch. "And do any Vielronan speak for this man?"

After a moment an older woman stepped forward. "Minister, sir, my husband was crippled two months ago during planting, and with only two boys to help us, harvest has been difficult. We would provide room and board to this man if he helped us in our fields. It is not work as glorious as gardening, but it would be a start and we sorely need the help."

As one of the last to fully recover, Alea was toward the rear of the line and watched each person find a place. The proceedings impressed her. Some survivors had little to offer, or none to speak for them, but the Minister found a place for each, even if it was only as a messenger or laborer.

"And you, miss?" Alea stepped forward, clasping her hands before her to hide their trembling. "Minister Herdingman, sir, I am Lyne'alea ir Suna. Firstly, I wish to thank you for your kindness toward us. I am literate, and worked as a governess to the children in the ihal's household since I was fourteen."

Her next words were halted by the Minister's hand. "Miss, I will hear your skills, but I need other information first. Am I right you were in the ihal's manor during the attack?"

"Yes, sir. I'm foster daughter to ihal Ahme'reahn ira Suna."

"How did you survive when the city fell?"

Cold crept through Alea's body. Whispers rose from the watching crowd. "I remember very little. I fled toward the outskirts of the gardens. Perhaps the Mirikin already swept through there. There were certainly enough bodies."

"There are concerning rumors—I assume you heard them—about the reasons behind the attack. Was the ihal sheltering more than the Laen?"

"Forgive me, I don't understand your meaning. He hosted six Laen. That's all. He said they came to him before, but I was too young to remember their first visit." *What would I say if there were more to tell?* Perhaps she would have lied.

Gluan finally sat back. "Very well. Thank you for your candid answers. Do tell us of your skills."

"I can do maid's work, and know a bit about cooking, though perhaps only enough for scullery work." She was confidant Gluan would find a place for her, though she did not look forward to meeting another family.

"Do any speak for this woman?"

"I do."

Alea turned, heart thundering. When she had not seen Arman that morning, she assumed he was already working. Instead, he stood in the hall, dressed in his finest shirt and newly polished boots.

"My mother owns the Ruby Cockerel." Arman did not look over, but his hand fluttered a greeting behind his back. "She does what she can, but would welcome help. Miss ir Suna recovered with us and helped much in the past two weeks. I ask that she stays on to help my mother. We would offer her room and board in exchange for her work."

The cold walls surrounding her fragile mind warmed a fraction. She remembered ihal's patient kindness and Ahren's gentle support. *Perhaps such things did not die with them.*

"You are willing to take responsibility for her in Vielrona until she finds her own way?"

Arman did look at her then, flashing a smile before addressing the Minister, "Vielrona is her home, and I gladly welcome her."

Φ

Alea's steps on the inn's stairs were light. Horror sunk in her chest, however, when she opened the door to her room. The bed was stripped and all the borrowed effects she came to consider her own were gone.

Kepra emerged from a room at the base of the stairs down the hall. "Miss, I've moved your things. If you're to be living and working here, you deserve your own space." Her expression softened at the concern in Alea's eyes. "Arman spoke to me last night after you went to sleep. He wanted it to be a surprise. I know it's not much compared to what you're used to, but this can be home for as long as you need."

Alea could not trust her voice. Instead, she ran to embrace the older woman. With Kepra's soft, strong arms around her, she realized she had not touched another person in weeks. *Not since the attack.* Before her composure could truly break, she pulled away and offered Kepra a smile.

"You don't know how much this means." The usual simmer of bitterness dimmed with momentary excitement. She was grateful, surely, but behind her icy walls, there was only exhausted relief.

Kepra's eyes crinkled with a smile very much like Arman's "I'm glad. There's a purse on your nightstand with your wages for your work and a pair of boots by the door. I'll pay you each week." She made a shooing motion. "Go explore your room, but be in the kitchen before third bell—I'll need your help tonight."

Alea was rolling dough for dumplings again when Arman peered through the kitchen door. "Did you see your room?"

"Luckily I did, elsewise you would've spoiled the surprise." She met his eyes. "Thank you. For the room and for today at the hearing." She turned back to the dough with a frown. "I feel as if more was said in there than I realized."

Arman slumped onto a stool. "You must understand we have survived this long by being direct, shrewd, and firm. I don't think he was antagonizing you, simply wanting the truth."

Alea pursed her lips. "I don't understand why he is fixated on rumors. Surely a few Laen cannot make a large difference."

Arman gaped at her. "You're what, seventeen?"

She drew herself up. His words smacked of condescension. "I turned nineteen on the twentieth of Lumord." She faltered at that. "I was unconscious at the time, I suppose."

Arman bowed his head, just kindly enough that it did not seem mocking. Nevertheless, a grin tugged at his mouth. "Forgive me, milady." He sobered quickly. "What do you know of the war?"

Alea looked down. "I learned a little about the Laen. Mostly it was history. My ihal spoke enough of war beyond our borders and I knew the Laen were—are—hunted. I didn't realize how bad it was, though."

"The Mirikin have all but destroyed the Laen." Arman's voice was very soft, as if he hoped speaking quietly made his words less true. "Those that still live are old and hiding. The youngest pose a threat simply because they could birth the Dhoah' Laen."

Alea's heart pounded. *Is that what Gluan meant when he asked if there was something more that ihal hid?* "She's the one that would bind the world, yes?"

"Yes."

Alea shook her head. "I prayed to the gods, like most Sunamen, but ihal taught his children to respect the Laen as well. I made offerings as frequently as any—mostly to Ikate, a goddess of the desert. I never thought the gods were evil enough to murder their creators."

Arman shook his head. "Many histories discuss the Division of the world. I am sure you could find a few in our library. It might do you well to understand how we see things here." He stood abruptly and left without another word.

Gluan's pointed questions drained her enough. *And now Arman's nearly laughing at my perceived naiveté.* Speaking of her faith, when Arman's and most of the Vielronan clearly differed, made it worse. At home, when the heat soured her mood, she lay on the cool stone slabs by the baths with Merahn.

Here she was always cold. Her hand clenched around the dough as waves of homesickness crashed through her.

Φ

The 8th Day of Valemord, 1251
The City-state of Vielrona

Leaves turned from gold to orange and crimson over the next few days. Their flames dotted the hills with brilliance and lent warmth to the cold air. Alea found much in the historical accounts in the Guild's library, and after Arman's pointed remark, made herself familiar with them, despite her irritation. There was nothing of current tensions, in the books, however. An older tome told of the Laen's nature and the history of the Division. This one she returned to each day. Finally, one morning she found a passage toward the back.

> *Before the world was divided, the gods walked the earth as men do now. Their rulers were the Laen and the Rakos. Fiery Rakos governed change and the gods lived under the teaching of whatever element each represented. The Laen kept the balance of life and death, peace and war, chaos and order.*
>
> *The gods were inquisitive and wanted more than what they were given. They captured Lynel, the Laen's leader and convinced her even the Laen's rule had to pass, forcing her to split the world. With the world divided they did not have to live under the rule of either the Laen or the Rakos. Weakened by the rebellion's effect on the world's balance, the Laen were unable to fight the onslaught.*

Alea stopped. She heard the tale a dozen times. It varied with each telling, as all legends did, but she never heard a telling so sympathetic to the Laen. *What side is even right?* She stared out the window. *The balance of nature is important, but could we have lived this long if it was damaged that badly?* She flipped forward a few pages, ignoring the violence of the war that followed the Division. *The war that has begun anew.* Finally, she found a passage, written toward the end.

> *Now, when the Division is centuries past, tales tell of another Laen. She will be more powerful than all before her, for she will be the embodiment of Creation and Destruction. Called the Dhoah' Laen for her dualistic nature, she will mend the world. Her power will cause wonder and sorrow, her touch relief and pain. Her love will bring life, but also death.*

Chills filled Alea's bones. She knew the Laen were austere, but even in a gods-supporting city, she was not taught the ferocity detailed on the pages before her. The image was haunting. *That is what the Mirikin were hunting when they attacked Cehn. They wanted her.* She shut the book with a snap. She was already late to help in the kitchen, and her thoughts were too dark.

Φ

Heat and the clatter of dishes reminded Arman of the forge. Working in the kitchen was usually a welcome relief, and he enjoyed sneaking tastes without his mother's reprimands. Tonight was different. When Alea arrived that evening, he toiled at the stove alone.

"Do you need help? Where's your mother?" She tied on an apron and checked the bread baking on the hearth.

"Please. She went to help Mistress Connolin deliver her second child. You remember her—she has the brown cow that ate from your hand." Arman glanced over. "Pass me that pot over there?"

Alea handed it to him. "Your mother's a midwife as well as a healer?"

"It was her profession before my father died. Healing was just part of it." He piled plates onto a tray. "I'm going to bring these out, check the soup, will you?"

Arman edged through the tables, balancing trays of stew and ale. "Here, Guntar, but this is your last. I'm not carrying you home again." He scowled at the heavyset farmer. "Your sick ruined my better breeches last time." He gathered empty mugs from their table and turned back to the bar. Most patrons chose the same tables, with the bar occupied by traders passing through. With winter and war closing in, such visitors were fewer.

That was not what made Arman stare at the strange man seated at the end of the counter. A fur-lined cloak was tugged about his ears, despite the warmth of the room and he wore a silk wrap around his head.

Arman navigated back through the tables and delivered dirty dishes to the wash barrel. Noting the man had only a glass of water before him, Arman sidled over. "Could I interest you in food, if you're not drinking tonight?" *People who don't drink at inns are trouble.* It meant they were there to do business, and evening business in taverns was rarely legal.

Narrowed eyes met Arman's, solid black, like those of an animal. "Stew, if you've got it."

Arman could only stare. Winding tattoos decorated the milk-pale skin. *I'd bet my best blade his headscarf hides a set of horns.* "Leek soup alright, sir?" He took the man's request, but could barely concentrate. Each time he left the kitchen he checked to make sure the stranger was still there. *I can't let him leave without speaking to him.* A lull came as the first wave of patrons tottered off to bed.

Arman removed his apron and slid onto the stool beside the pale man. "I know who you're looking for."

The man's closed expression darkened violently. "I am certain you don't."

Arman rolled his eyes and pitched his voice to a murmur. "Six survivors from Cehn. Ones who wield smoke and lightning."

The man's eyes widened. "Only six?"

Arman looked down. "I was told to look for you. What do you need to know?"

"What happened in Cehn, and where they are now."

Arman jerked his head toward the upper floor of the house. "Let's speak somewhere else. There is a porch on our third floor. I'll meet you there in a few minutes."

Arman ducked into the kitchen. Alea was adding onions and carrots to the soup. He knew she remembered very little, and what she did recall she wished she could not. *One woman's peace of mind is not worth the world.* "Miss?"

Fatigue shadowed Alea's eyes when she glanced up.

"I need to speak with you. Upstairs. Now." Nerves sharpened the words no matter how gentle he strove to sound. He was grateful she followed him through the common room without protest. The guard had already disappeared. At the door to the third-floor stairway, Arman stopped. "I need you to do something for me."

Wariness tempered the curiosity in Alea's gaze. "Surely, this can wait."

"I'm certain it can't." He pointed to the floor above them. "There's a man upstairs who needs to hear about what happened in Cehn. I know this is hard, I know you don't want to think about it, let alone speak about it, but he came a very long way and it's incredibly important."

Alea pursed her lips, but he saw dread in her eyes. "If you ask me to do this, you need to tell me why. More than 'incredibly important.'"

He squeezed his eyes shut. *I will not tell a soul.* "Why don't you come upstairs, and I'll tell you both."

After a moment, she nodded.

Upstairs, the door hung open and the man paced the short length of the porch, fiddling with something at his belt. Seeing them approach, he stopped, his glower falling on Alea. "I'd rather not tell the town gossip about this, boy, if it's all the same to you."

Alea froze in the doorway. "I didn't come up here to be mocked." Her sharp gray eyes fixed on An'thor. "If it's all the same to you."

Arman ignored the tossed barbs. "Milady ir Suna is a survivor from Cehn, sir. Her family sheltered your charges."

Alea glanced between the two of them. "He's here about the Laen?" When both men tried to shush her, she sank into the chair. "Where do you want me to start?"

"The beginning." Had the pale man's words not been growled through stained teeth, they would have sounded comical. "When did they arrive? How many were there? What did you speak to them about?"

Alea held up her hand. "I did not speak to them. Seven of them arrived a few nights before the attack and stayed in the children's wing—it was the safest part of the building. My foster-sister Merahn attended them. As I was preparing for my wedding, I did not. One was young, younger than me. Ihal visited them but they didn't leave the wing. We all knew what they were, but none dared speak it. They were following up on a visit many years before, I guess." She rubbed the strong bridge of her nose and cleared her throat.

"The attack came at sundown. I was putting the children to bed. I heard screaming, so I locked the doors and went to see what happened. By the time I was downstairs the entire southern wing—including the nursery—was in flames. The Laen were in the garden and I tried to reach them, tried to beg them to help fight, to protect us. Someone grabbed me, the air filled with power and I remember nothing more." Her shoulders shook, and Arman wondered if it was from the cold or emotions.

He placed a hand on the back of the chair. "Thank you. I know that wasn't easy."

"Their power—what color was it? What color was the girl's power?"

"Gray. Silver maybe. The girl didn't use hers, though. They protected her."

The strange man nodded, a satisfied look on his face. "Thank you, miss. I apologize for my brisk nature." He turned to Arman. "And they came here?"

Arman nodded. "They tended some of the survivors, brought them here. They stayed for only a few hours. Their leader—Liane—gave me an image of you and the others and I told them the best way out of the city. North, via the western gate. It is a bad road, but few travel it." He picked at the skin around his nails. The ice, the fire at the memory of the Laen still coursed through him. "What color power does she have?"

The pale man looked out to the north. "I've never seen it, but it should be black."

"She it, isn't she? She's the Dhoah' Laen."

The man met Arman's gaze for a moment, but did not answer. "Thank you for your time, and your dedication. I won't forget it." He paused in the doorway. He did not look at Alea, but his hand rested on her shoulder for a second. "I am very sorry for your losses. Know they didn't die in vain."

Φ

Arman slumped onto a barrel with a sigh. Alea went to bed and the Laen's guard left shortly afterward. Arman did not think to get his name. *He would have lied anyways.* The rest of the night had been busy, but the last round left some minutes ago. *I don't know how Ma does this by herself so often.* As if called by his thought, Kepra breezed in.

She planted a tired kiss on his head and poured herself a mug of tea. "Thank you for taking over." Her smile was wan. "It was a difficult delivery. All is fine now. They have a daughter."

Arman frowned. Something tugged at his mind, but he could not place the memory. "I'm glad they're well."

"You seem distracted, did anything happen tonight?" The lines on her brow deepened and she brushed curls away from his face.

"No." He shook his head, still mulling over the night's events. "Just the usual." He rose. "I'm feeling a bit ill, Ma. Everything's cleaned for tomorrow though." He squeezed her hand absently and trudged up the stairs. Cold still flickered over his body. He hoped it would pass once he delivered the Laen's message.

Candlelight shone from under Alea's door. He paused, frowning at the flickering glow and a memory thundered into his mind.

He peered through the crack in the door. His mother often told him off for spying, but curiosity bested his will. His mother was cleaning the new baby, eyes warm as she swaddled the child. "There, milady. You have a daughter."

The woman on the bed was not Vielronan. Sweat streaked her black hair and her silver eyes were luminous. She held her child as if the baby were her last tie to life. "Beautiful."

"Will you stay with us long?"

Sorrow or pain tightened the edges of the mother's eyes. "I must travel south."

"You can shelter here, there's no need to run."

"Don't pretend ignorance." Her silver eyes flashed. "You know what I am. I can't get far enough away from Mirik and your city is the first place they'll look." Her gaze softened as she smoothed the black tuft of hair on her daughter's head. "She'll have the best chance without me."

Arman leaned too far forward and stumbled. His mother whirled, brows snapping together. "Arman, sweetling, I told you to go to bed."

Arman staggered against the wall, one hand over his mouth to muffle his short breaths. *It can't be.* Many dark-haired women came to his mother for help. It was denial and he knew it. *She was Laen. South could have been Sunam. Cehn. Lyne'alea doesn't remember the Laen's first visit because she was a baby.* He could only guess why they abandoned her. She did not feel the same as they had, and he wondered if she lacked power. Of one thing he was certain, however:

Lyne'alea ir Suna was not human.

CHAPTER FOUR

The 9th Day of Valemord, 1251
The City-state of Vielrona

ARMAN WAS PRONE TO imaginative ideas. A large part of him wondered if this was one. He leaned against his mother's doorframe, steeling himself.

"Just come in, Arman. I can hear you."

He chuckled and stepped inside, shutting the door behind him. Kepra sat at her vanity brushing her hair. A thick wool robe wrapped her thin shoulders, but Arman could see how unkind the years had been. "I didn't mean to bother you."

"What's on your mind, love?" She finished twisting her hair and sat on her coverlet.

He frowned. "Maybe I just want to say goodnight."

"And do you want to be tucked into your blankets too? Arman, you haven't come to say goodnight in a fair few minutes." She drew her legs up under herself, and Arman was abruptly reminded of Alea. "What is it?"

"I need to ask you something, and I need you to understand I've thought about it, even if it seems mad." He perched himself at the foot of her bed. "Something you said last night made me think. Do you remember a foreign woman you were midwife to? I was about four or five at the time. She came from the north and didn't stay long."

Kepra frowned. "I remember all the women I help." Understanding glinted in her eyes, though she looked away.

"Ma, I need to know where she went."

"'South,' is all she said. Arman, you're implying something incredibly dangerous. She seems like a normal woman to me."

The fact that his mother already knew his train of thought said as much about her motherhood as it did the truth to his suspicion. "South could be Cehn. Ma, her birthday was the twentieth." He rested a hand on his mother's clenched fist. "I just want to know if it's possible."

Kepra ran her knuckles down Arman's cheek. "Her coloring, her features, they are familiar. More so now that her tan is fading."

"But she's not one of them, so what is she?"

Kepra shook her head. "I don't know what she is, Arman. This conversation doesn't leave this room. Am I understood?"

Feeling like a scolded boy again, he rose. "Yes, Ma." He stopped. "She's strange and probably dangerous, but for whatever reason, we can't give her up to fate."

Kepra's face softened finally. "I would have raised you wrong if you could." She flicked her fingers at him. "Now let me rest. Next time you come knocking late at night you best be asking to give my ring to Veredy."

The fleeting thought warmed him, but even with the dream of Veredy as his wife, he could not sleep. Strange, violent thoughts filled his head. Instead, he grabbed his cloak from the hook by the door. Flipping his hood up, he strode off toward the tavern lane. Alcohol would help.

A wave of warmth broke over him as he stepped into the Crook and Candle. Kam's boasts already resonated from the corner of the dim alehouse. Arman flopped onto the bench beside Wes, characteristic grin creeping onto his face. "Which story is it: the four trained assassins or the broken-hearted young widow." Arman's voice was low.

"I think it's seven assassins now, but he's detailing the fight on Box Corner." Wes ignored the sour look Kam shot at him. "How goes your strange noble woman?" The words were not unkind, but neither were they respectful.

"It's strange to have someone else in the inn. It's been just Ma and me for so long." He jerked his head at the bar. "I finished that hilt you asked for today—buy me a mug. I need a drink." While Wes gestured for another round, Arman scanned the crowd. He disliked the tone of Wes's words, but he knew they were well founded. Alea was nothing like the city-folk. Even picturing her at their ale-sticky table was laughable.

Guilt bloomed in his chest at Veredy's familiar hazel eyes when she slid into the seat beside him. "Master Wardyn, I don't believe we've met before," she joked.

He only saw her once since the refugees arrived. Playing on her false dramatics, he placed a hand over his heart. "It wounds, that you cannot remember my face."

Despite the jesting, Veredy's expression was guarded. "You've been busy, I hear. How does the lady fare?"

"Well, I suppose. You should meet her."

Veredy fingered the jeweled pin holding up her locks. "Perhaps you should bring her out one evening."

Arman recognized the pin as one he made for her and his guilt intensified. "Do you want to walk?" He offered her his hand.

They ducked out under the cover of Kam's ruckus, and if Wes saw them go, he said nothing. Veredy tucked herself under Arman's arm with practiced familiarity. "I missed you."

"And I you." He squeezed her. "How's business?"

"Good, though I prefer selling in the stalls." She steered them down a quieter street, walking toward the Rattles. "Do you think she'll stay?"

Arman asked, even though he knew. "Who?"

"Your strange noble woman."

"She's not mine," he retorted. "And I have no idea. Ma enjoys her help, but Alea doesn't seem in love with Vielrona." Cold air flooded his lungs as he sighed, enjoying Veredy's warmth against his side and the muted city sounds drifting from the market. Everything was perfect, peaceful. Perhaps it was the threat of winter, or the muted city sounds drifting on the night breeze, but his chest ached with melancholy. "I've missed seeing you lately."

Veredy nudged him with her elbow, but smiled. "I wasn't certain how to deal with your new lady guest."

Arman snorted. "You've never been uncertain in your life." He kissed the top of her head. "Anyways, I don't think anyone knows how to deal with her." *Or the Laen. Or whatever she is.*

"Would you like some tea?"

Arman realized they stood before the door leading up to her room. "Tea would be perfect."

Like many, her rooms sat above the store she worked. Though larger, it was almost as much home as his own room. He peered out the window, taking a deep sip of the liquor-laced tea she poured. "You've lived here a long time, now."

"Several years." She leaned against the tabletop. "When will you find your own place?"

"When I have a woman to share it with." He smiled at her and sat at the table. Strange urgency hardened the playful words. "Do you think you'll take over the shop?"

Veredy made a face. "I hope I can have my own. Mistress Hughen drives me mad. I can only imagine what it would take to buy the place from her."

Arman took her hand, rubbing his rough thumb over her work-worn fingers thoughtfully. "A lot's changed since we were young, you know."

She snorted and wrapped her long tan hands around her own mug. "We're still young by most counts. And you still dance around subjects like a prairie hen." She leaned over and kissed him.

He smiled against her mouth. "You are not mad I've been too busy to see you?"

She moved to sit on the edge of her bed. "You're here, now aren't you?"

Their tension lasted only until he toed off his boots and dropped his belt with a metallic thump. Smiling, he tugged off his shirt and crawled under the coverlet with her. He scraped the bristles of his cheek on hers. Laughter filled the space between them, but Arman swore sadness shadowed her eyes.

Φ

The 10th of Valemord, 1251

Quiet filled with kitchen in the absence of Arman's usual morning boisterous monologue. Alea peered into the kitchen curiously. "Where's Arman?"

Kepra shrugged as she measured out cornmeal. "He went out late and did not come home."

Alea tied on her apron, alarmed. "Is he well?"

Kepra laughed. "Neither Wes nor Kam blazed in here in the small hours of the morning. They always do when Arman finds trouble. I trust he's safe." She gestured at a package sitting on the bar top. "He sent that over this morning for you."

Alea brushed her hands off and unfolded the bundle of cloth. Thick wool cascaded over her hands. New linen lined the cloak, matching the dark green wool. Folded parchment was tucked under the wrought silver clasp.

> *I know you are used to the desert and it is getting colder. My friend cut down my best one for you, and I made the clasp myself. I'm sorry for keeping you out in the cold the other night.*
>
> *I have something to ask you over lunch today.*
> *-A*

His abrupt writing echoed his frank speech. She pressed the cloak to her chest. Woodsmoke and stone were not the same scents as home, but they still comforted her. After hanging the cloak carefully by the door, she set about the morning's tasks.

Arman stumbled in at noon as Alea pulled rolls from the oven. She tossed him one from the previous batch with a smile. "Careful, they're still hot. Thank you for the cloak."

Circles hung from his eyes, but he grinned. "I'm glad you like it." He dug around in the pantry. "Ma? Where do you keep your tea? The stuff from Ban."

Kepra breezed into the kitchen with a frown. "It's ginger, Arman. You ought to bring some with you if you're going to continue to drink to excess." She handed him the packet of herbs.

"I'm not hung-over, I just got very little sleep." He poured himself a mug and slid onto one of the bar stools. "How has your morning been, miss?"

"Good. I think I'm settling in more." Curiosity sparked in her chest, and she perched on the stool beside him. "You wanted to ask something?"

"I did?" Arman frowned, and he took a long sip of his tea. His expression brightened. "Ah, yes. You're safe here, but you've seen violence, and I thought I could help you feel safer."

"What do you mean?"

"Have you thought about learning to protect yourself? Archery, hand-blocks and the like?"

Alea stared. *It's wrong to bear weapons.* Her heart balked at the thought. "If I carried a weapon it'd be a challenge and I'd be attacked. My ihal taught us that. None of his family ever learned combat."

"What?" Arman looked incredulous. He drew a breath. "Milady, with all respect, they didn't carry weapons and Cehn was still attacked. Perhaps if they had they'd be here now."

Stubbornness set Alea's chin. She picked at a splinter on the bar top. "It is childish, but I think part of me thought a hero would rush in and save us. If I can't hold onto that hope, what's left?" She did not realize disappointment crouched in her chest until the words left her mouth.

"You're thinking of the wrong part of the story. In the beginning, innocents aren't saved, the hero's not the hero. He's a child, ignorant of the world. He loses something dear to him and that sets grief into his heart. Depending on the story, that grief turns to vengeance or justice or hardened resolve."

"What do you mean?" His words echoed in her, cracking open something she kept closed for as long as she could remember. *Vengeance or resolve?*

"This story just shattered you. Gather the pieces and kindle the flames. Then you'll be reforged."

Reforged into what? Curiosity warred with culture and made her heart race.

Arman rested a hand beside hers on the bar, like he had when she told her story to the Laen's guard. "There are training halls in the Outer Edge where many of us practice defense and weapons when we may. You could meet me at our stall tomorrow afternoon."

"I just think it is better to use our minds and our words to fight, not our hands," she argued. Deep in her mind, however, darkness unfurled, something hounding to act.

"You're right, but it takes a long time to train our minds to fight that way. Protect yourself with your hands until you can fight with only words."

"I'll let you teach me," her words were little more than a whisper, "but I don't think any weapon could have saved them."

Φ

The 12th Day of Lumord, 1251

Polished steel glinted through the market, and Alea followed it through the crowd. She recognized Wes in the rear of the stall, watching, amused as Arman juggled three daggers in a silver blur. After a few turns, he laid them aside with a flushed grin. His eyes caught Alea's and he waved. "I am glad you didn't change your mind."

"You expected me to?"

He grinned at her barb and nodded in the direction of the Outer Edge. "Shall we?"

Keeping up with Arman stretched her muscles, and by the time they arrived, she was almost warm. The barns that served as training halls lay behind the market, bordered by the stone-walled fields to the north and east. She followed him through the door, nervous.

Sawdust piled on the floor and a shed in the back held worn weapons. Targets hung in a row on one wall, opposite a line of straw dummies. Arman beckoned her to a bench where he handed her a bow and wrist guard. "I thought we could start with the bow. You don't need to be close to do damage." He showed her how to fasten the wrist guard. "This protects your skin from the string." He handed her the bow and sat beside her to explain how to string the weapon. "Loop it over in a fluid motion. Slowly, though."

After several attempts, she succeeded, and she grinned back at him. The motion was awkward and far from fluid, but it was a start.

"Now again." Arman instructed her several more times before finally pointing to a target. "Are you ready?"

Alea's heart pounded in her throat. She took a steadying breath and rose. Arman stood next to her, another bow at his belt. "Which is your strong hand?" When she held up her right, he gestured to her legs. "Stand with your left leg forward, right back. They should be the same distance as your shoulders. Toes farther forward."

She felt foolish. "Arman, my body's not made for this." Her face flushed at his amused look.

"Having a slight build is better for archery." He paused, concern and uncertainty filling his gaze. "Do you wish to stop?"

Alea looked at her hand. Warm wood weighed in her palm. *The world you adhere to is gone,* she reminded herself, *This is your new one.* Facing the target, she resumed her stance.

"Good. Hold the bow in your left hand—it's more precise and your right has the strength to draw the string."

She pulled back the string a few times, letting Arman adjust her grip to her first two fingers. Her shoulder and back ached. After an hour her arm shook, but she drew the bow smoothly.

Arman stopped her as she raised the weapon again. "You're shaking. Starting slow is best, and you're doing well. Do you want to try again tomorrow?"

A tiny smile flitted across her face. "I think I would. Are you coming back to the inn?"

Arman helped her unstring the bow and put it away properly. "I'm meeting Kam and Wes. I can meet you here at the same time tomorrow, though."

Sureness strengthened her steps back to the inn. Burning muscles lit inspiration in her mind and neglected pride uncurled in her chest.

She smiled, lifting her face to smell winter on the wind.

Φ

The 26th Day of Valemord, 1251

Black, naked branches replaced gold and crimson leaves in the two weeks since Alea began training. Even the sunlight lacked warmth, and Alea arrived at the training hall early to warm up after the cold walk. Doffing her cloak, she noticed a circle of men at the opposite end of the hall. Two in the center grappled with bare hands. She watched from just inside the door, curious. After a moment she recognized one fighter's blonde curls. Hand-to-hand combat was something she never saw, though she heard brawls from her rooms.

Arman's forearm swept up into his opponent's neck. *How don't they kill each other?* The heavier, older man ducked under the swing and drove a fist between Arman's shoulder blades. Arman rolled with the blow and came up spinning, hands already guarding. He allowed the next strike to pass then swung an arm across to unbalance the man, a punch going to the lower ribs. When they stepped apart, Arman saw her watching. He shook arms with the man and stepped from the circle, another taking his place.

Arman grabbed a rag from a bench, wiping sweat from his face and neck before going to her. "Afternoon."

She greeted him, looking pointedly at the floor. Sunamen were never seen out of day clothes by any but their spouses.

"Are you all right?"

She nodded, her gaze not moving from the sawdust. "I dislike so much..." she waved her hand in his direction, "skin."

He choked back a laugh and pulled on his shirt, rolling the sleeves up. "Forgive me. Our women often see us in various stages of undress. Most swim nude." He nodded in the direction of the men still wrestling. "There are a few holds and hold-breaks you could learn, you know." He grinned wickedly. "Clothed, of course."

She glared. "I'm sorry if my people's choice to protect themselves from the desert sun offends you."

He held up his hands in surrender. "Of course, milady. Jesting aside, though, not all attackers are considerate enough to stay in bow range. Every woman I know uses hold-breaks to dissuade persistent advances."

Memories of many of the household women's last minutes flashed through her mind and she winced. "Teach me, please." She followed him to a cleared section of floor.

"They'll likely grip you by the arms or hair." He moved slowly, showing her where an assailant might grab. He made her act as the attacker first, show how he could loosen her grip long enough to pull free.

When she mimicked him, her movements were indecisive, and she winced each time she twisted his arms.

"Be firm." He showed her how to form a good fist. "Use their weight and balance to your advantage. Move forward, as if your block was a blow itself."

She felt foolish when he moved her fingers into a better position, but her blow sent him back a pace. She laughed and returned to a ready stance.

"Confidence is everything in a fight. Now try again." Arman's hands flashed forward, grabbing both her wrists and tugging slightly.

Sickly sweet blood soured the desert air. The oasis was dark, and the screams pierced the night. A soldier yanked her arms. Merahn lay a few paces away, eyes wide and blank, pregnant belly drenched in blood. Alea's head spun and a voice shouted at her, though the words were incoherent.

She was aware of gentle arms around her shoulders and a low voice. "You're safe. You're here with me. It's Arman. You're in Vielrona." His murmured litany wormed through her frenzied thoughts.

She opened her eyes. She crumpled to the training hall floor and Arman crouched before her. After a moment she pulled away. Panic still hitched her breath and spurred her pulse. "I was in Cehn. There was a soldier, and Merahn—" Her voice broke and Arman shushed her gently.

"Can you stand?" When she nodded, he helped her up.

"Wardyn, you set?" one of the men called.

"Set. Just a rough move," he called back.

She heard mutters about noble women, but Arman's excuse helped her ignore the worst. She let him keep his arm over her shoulder until they were out of the hall, then stepped away. Contact made her skin crawl in the wake of violent memories. Silence reigned as they returned to the inn. The crowd in the common room was growing, but Arman settled her at a table in the corner.

"If you can't eat that's fine, but I think Ma's tea would settle you a bit."

"Tea would be good. And maybe one of those meat, bread things I helped her bake this morning. A small one though. My stomach is flipping." She closed her eyes and willed a calm mask onto her features. Her walls were not as sturdy as she hoped.

Arman returned a minute later with a tray of meat pastries and two mugs of tea. He sat across from her and set the tray between them. After she took several deep sips of her tea he peered at her. "I've fought since I could run, practically. Kam's damn near the only man in the city smaller than me. So, I picked fights with any lad—the bigger and wider the better."

A small smile curled Alea's mouth and she began to pick at her pastry. Conjuring an image of a young Arman scrapping in the street was easy.

Arman grinned. "At any rate, I picked the wrong man one night. Kam was working, so I was alone, and this man had friends. I thought they'd never stop. My ribs cracked, my nose broke so badly I couldn't breathe through it. One forearm bent the wrong way and my leg was fractured. I don't remember most of the blows. Lying in a gutter, with the rain and scummer from the Upper privies, though? I remember that. I knew I'd die there."

Alea forgot her food. The irregular line of Arman's nose showed where it healed crooked. Surprise arched her brows. Men usually told of their bravery, not being beaten into sewer run-off.

"My Pa found me, finally, and brought me home. It took a long time before I stopped having dreams of dying in the streets. I still dislike the dark." He pushed his hand across the table to rest beside hers. "What you experienced was a thousand-fold worse. It'll haunt you, even when you're awake." He looked down. "I just wanted you to know you're not the only one."

She looked down. "Thank you." Nervous determination creased her brow. "I want to learn, Arman. I need to. I can't stay weak."

"Cehn's attack doesn't make you weak." He interjected. "But I'd like to continue teaching you. Tomorrow we'll go slower." After a moment he smiled. "I'll never speak to you again if you tell anyone that story."

She laughed. "You have my word. I am sure you've never been bested since then."

He stuck out his chest dramatically. "Not even by giants!" The conversation lifted. Arman asked careful questions about her life in Cehn. Familiar words rolled from her tongue, bringing pain, but also peace.

In the following days, Arman added half an hour of hand defense to her lessons. Instead of grabbing her, he showed her how to align the bones and muscles of her body to move him farther. He explained how most defenses could become attacks. Even gruff advice from the other patrons helped.

Exhilaration joined strength and clarity. Deep within, an unnamed shadow grew stronger too.

Φ

The 28th Day of Valemord, 1251

Alea glanced around at the myriad lanterns. "What exactly is this a festival for?"

Arman frowned. "You know, I honestly can't remember." Wes already waited at their stall, Kam and a young woman perched beside him. Arman grinned and ushered her over to the others. "You know Kam and Wes. This is Veredy Cordyn."

Alea's smile was nervous and wide as she hurried over. She offered her hand to the blond. "Well met, Miss Cordyn."

The other woman laughed. "Please, Veredy is fine. Now that we're all here shall we find some supper?"

They stepped into the street, leaving Wes to mind the stall. Veredy fell into step beside Alea. Wood smoke and cooking meat thickened the air and spilled ale and sauces made the cobbles sticky. Alea pointed out a vendor selling roasted shell peas, but Arman made a face.

"You dislike peas?"

Arman waved her comment away. "It's a bad tale."

Kam pounced on the opportunity. "Who are we to deny a lady entertainment?" He grinned and sidled up to Alea. "We were celebrating my twelfth birthday—"

"Fourteenth, you could barely hold a pint when you were twelve," Arman interrupted. "If you must tell her, make it the truth."

"Like you could hold any more." Kam sighed. "We were celebrating a birthday and decided to visit as many taverns as was possible and still be able to walk home."

"They carried Kam," Veredy pointed out.

Alea hid her smile. "I'm sure he made a valiant effort."

"Anyways, the roads were wobbly, and we chose to nap in the root cellar of Master Megurdy's tavern."

"Since Kam was enamored with Megurdy's eldest daughter," Arman pointed out, steering them past the offending pea stand and toward alternate supper options.

"Wes bet Arman, here, that he couldn't eat a whole basket of shell peas sitting on the cellar shelves. He did just that and won the two silver."

Arman tried to interject, but Kam swatted him with his hat. "We were too tossed to notice the peas sported great lengths of this marvelously pink fuzz-mold. Needless to say, Arman was ill for three days and has been unable to eat the things since."

Alea's stomach ached from laughing. "Truly?"

Arman shook his head at his own foolery. "Sadly, while Kam may exaggerate, it's true." They turned the corner onto the broad market street lined with food vendors. Alea gestured to a stall selling desert hare and cacti—one of her favorites from Cehn. "What of this?"

Kam shrugged. "I've never tried it, but I'm willing." He shouldered Alea playfully and she realized he was shorter than she. "You promise not to poison me?"

"Ver and I'll get Wes's and our supper from Ferrin's smoke pit," Arman called over his shoulder. "Meet you at the stall!"

Alea helped Kam pick what to try. Wooden trays piled with dripping food balanced in their hands as they made their way back to the corner. She glanced back to the stall where the others stopped. Arman watched their food cook. Veredy leaned against his shoulder.

"You must have a thousand stories from when you were younger," Alea said wistfully as they made their way back to Wes.

Kam laughed. "I often wonder how we've not had our thumbs taken for stealing."

Alea stabbed a bit of hare with her wooden pick. "You seem to be less rowdy now. Perhaps not you." She trailed off.

Kam glanced at her and realized she was jesting. He grinned. "It was Arman's doing. He was careless and rough—never held to one girl, always wanting to be free of the city. When his father died something changed. Overnight he became devoted to the work left behind and to making a future with Veredy. He's rarely even drunk now."

Alea looked over at Arman. He was engrossed in whatever Veredy described, a bite of food poised, forgotten, on his knife. *So, she's promised to him.* Memories ached in her chest. "They're lucky."

CHAPTER FIVE

The 30th Day of Valemord, 1251
The Village of Marl Kess, Athrolan

"DAMNED WEATHER." AN'THOR TRADED the comfort of the inn's finer rooms for proximity to the back door. With snow drifting through the crack on the side of the window, however, he mentally kicked himself. Being born in a snow-blasted country made him all but immune to cold. He still hated it. *I could do without seeing another flake.* Stuffing a crumpled shirt into the crack, he dragged his chair closer to the window. The dense, white fur of his bearskin hood hid the chipped ivory horns curling upward from just behind his temples. It was only a single evening, and that time would be spent with his black eyes fixed out the window.

A Mirikin troop approached from the east, though the storm hid their campfires. The few scattered Laen citadels were destroyed or abandoned. Those few kingdoms still supportive of the Laen had all but barred their gates in fear of the same fate. Rocky grassland stretched from Athrolan's mountainous southern border to the dense forest at its center.

If the Mirikin caught them, it would be there.

The moon rose. Marl Kess quieted and the village's lanterns were dimmed. An'thor shifted, returning feeling to his legs. Candles flickered in rooms across the way and harness metal glinted on the rider under the stable eaves. The Laen's other protectors rarely met for longer than a few hours, ranging a league or two around their charges. Other than he and Albi'giran, the mounted man below, they were all human. Albi'giran was asai and knew An'thor before the others were born.

A door shut softly down the hall, and he straightened. He pinched the candle out and stepped quietly out the door. Liane paused at the end of the hall, briefly silhouetted by lantern light. Their eyes met. They spoke all of thrice before now, but he would recognize her in a heartbeat. Her gaze was a frozen mountain stream or mist rising from a lake. She hurried silently down the stairs after the others.

An'thor shouldered his sword, buckled on his revolver, left payment on the table, and descended to the stable. The storm muttered around the sharp corners of the buildings, not serious enough for proper winter.

"North?" He swung his saddle onto Theriim's back, glancing over to the other stall.

Hela, the historian, tacked up her own mount, eyes heavy with exhaustion. "North. I think she means to make it to the next town by tomorrow night. At this pace, we're as like to drop dead from fatigue as we are to be shot." She flashed a wan smile at An'thor. "You're joining us?"

"We can't be separated again, not when they're this close. Albi'giran and the man from Ban will flank us by a league or so. Ju-elta, I think is his name."

Hela sighed in response and looped her reins over her mare's head. "I'll see you in the courtyard."

Even dark clothes and layers of scarves and hats could not hide what their true nature. An'thor and another man would ride with the party, the others surrounding them just within shouting distance. An'thor and his gray horse were once known on sight and they relied on that reputation for the first years of the war. Nothing short of a divine miracle or luck could save the Laen now.

"You're the Wanderer, eh?"

An'thor glanced over at the use of one of his old epithets. The Vielronan man who drew abreast joined them just a week ago. "As much now as ever. You come from the mountains, am I right?"

"I am called Henly. What do you think of this Laen-child they've with them?"

An'thor winced. He did even trust the wind to keep their secret. "I think she must stay hidden."

Henly seemed to hear the hint. "I didn't know you folk were for the Laen."

An'thor snorted. "The Nenev are too engrossed in themselves to care about what happens elsewhere. Why did you choose to protect the Laen?"

Burbling coughs answered him. An'thor turned to see a second arrow bloom from the man's chest. An'thor whirled around, whistling through two fingers. One hand whipped his blade from its sheath, the other fell to the firearm at his hip. For once An'thor was glad his race thought in metal and fire. Hoofbeats already pounded behind them.

He thundered up the line of Laen. Vermillion of the Mirikin uniforms appeared over the hill, but the Laen's other guards did not arrive. *Already cut down, then.*

Liane yanked her spooked horse in a circle, eyes meeting An'thor's.

"Ambush! West, go west!"

One citadel guard raised her glaive, then choked on the black shaft of the arrow that burst through her throat.

An'thor winced and dragged his horse's head about. "What are you waiting for? Ride!"

The second Laen fell as they made for the shadow of trees. Tiny curls of gray power wound about the horses' hooves or over their shoulders to block arrows. An'thor lived too long to weep at the sight. With so many dead, the Laen's power was little more than a suggestion.

Your horse is faster. The voice was ice crystalizing in his mind.

He glanced over at the Laen pacing him. It was Liane.

She pointed at the young woman dashing madly in front of them. Her eyes glittered silver. *Go. We're already dead.*

He swerved into the girl's horse, grabbing her wrist. "On my horse, now!"

She gripped his cowl and arm and she hauled herself up behind him. Icy hands locked at his belt and he leaned forward. Theriim surged ahead. Within moments they outpaced the others. Clamoring pursuit faded. An'thor's hands cramped on the reins by the time trees rose before them and he finally allowed Theriim to slow.

"We made it, my lady." He patted the girl's hands, still clenching his belt. "You're safe now." She did not move. An'thor drew Theriim up in the shadow of the forest and reached behind. His fingers came away covered in blood. *Fates, not this.* Dismounting, he pulled her down after him.

Her eyes were glazed with the effort of keeping herself alive. Bloodless lips stuttered, "I'm scared."

"I've got you, my lady." Perhaps this would be one promise he kept.

Albi'giran's red charger skittered up, covered in foam. There was blood on the asai's blade and burgundy hair, but he appeared unharmed. He tumbled from his horse when he saw the girl. "Dammit, no!"

An'thor tore the back of her dress open. "Healers kit, now!" The girl's eyes were beyond consciousness, beyond sanity. Cold radiated from her body. *It's just her power.* She was too cold. He was afraid to break the arrow's shaft, afraid to even field dress. *What if I ruin her concentration?*

He caught her gaze. *"I'm scared."* Fear forced him into action. He snapped the shaft and worked his fingers into the wound. The bronze arrowhead was narrow, hammered with a triangular base. It was designed to bleed. He yanked. Metal came free with a torn flesh and welling black blood. His fingers were slick but managed to grip the faintly-pulsing arteries. He fumbled with the sinew and needle for a second, catching her gaze again. Silver irises faded to dull gray. He wiped his fingers and began to sew.

Albi'giran watched helplessly. There were words for An'thor's actions. *Hopeless. Denial.* She was dead the moment An'thor pulled the arrow from her chest. She was dead the moment they realized her power.

An'thor's frantic attempts at surgery ceased. "You're safe." His voice cracked. "You're safe now." His spirit crumpled with his last shred of hope.

Above, the moon set.

Φ

The 31st day of Valemord, 1251

Despite spending most of the past thirty-two hours on horseback, Bren's whole body hummed. His horse's muscles trembled from the effort to bring them this far. His broadsword was drawn, stained with Laen blood. Early dawn light shone on the soldiers dismounted at the forest's edge. The Mirikin stood in a wide circle around the base of a tree. They looked shaken, but no weapons were raised. Bren halted at the sight of the body lying amongst the roots.

He dismounted, armor clanking softly in the stillness. "Her guards?"

One soldier shook his head. "Gone, sir. They were here, working on her, but when they saw us closing, they took off."

"Cowards."

Bren frowned at the man who interrupted. He edged closer to the body, noting the surroundings. She lay still. Blood and the bruised cast of death covered her skin, but he took no chances. Finally, within arm's reach, he crouched. He tugged off a glove and felt for a pulse. "She's dead. Good shot, Doric." He sat back on his heels thoughtfully. "Sorier, you and Gorden start digging. She'll be burned, broken, and buried. Everyone else, make camp nearby. We're done."

His soldiers lurched into motion. They were as tired as he, and deserved sleep. *Besides, this is it.* He could not look away from the girl's face. Wide colorless eyes stared from beneath a furrowed brow. He knew that expression. Evidence of surgery scattered around the depressions where her guards knelt. He found his knife and turned his attention to her fingers. Cold ligaments and stiff muscle yielded reluctantly to steel, and after a minute he wrapped the token in his kerchief.

Strength left Bren's limbs. He slumped to the dirt with some dignity but rested his head between his armored knees. The sweet tang of blood was so familiar it went unnoticed among the other battlefield scents. It weighed on him. Stifled by the stink of his own sweat, he tugged off his helm. After several deep breaths, he raised his head.

"Fullsen!" Even his battle-shout sounded weary. He managed to haul himself upright and be standing when the boy halted before him.

"Lieutenant, sir?" He swayed where he stood, and no longer had an arm on his right side. He seemed not to notice either.

"You wounded?" Bren peered at the dirty bandages. "You ought to be resting."

"Happened in yesterday before we caught up to you. Healer fixed me up proper. Got a good story for the women!"

Bren shook his head. Fullsen's age was closer to a toddler than a man. "Can you pen a missive?"

"Surely, I scribe with my left anyways."

Bren could not say his own hands shook, or he feared he would be sick all over the parchment if he tried to write the letter himself. He tossed over his writing kit and gestured to the campstool someone erected for him. "Address it to Milord King Azirik. He's on the coast now, I think." He shook his head to clear the fog from his thoughts. "We found the women. Just north of Marl Kess, as expected. There were only six. They had guards, but we separated them. They were cut down. One among them was the girl. She wore armor, and the others protected her above all else, above their own lives. We chased her to the Hartland, but she was already dead, shot down during pursuit." He paused, as much to draw breath as to fight back nausea. *Is it normal to feel this way when war is over?* "I am confident she was the Dhoah' Laen. I will await your orders. Signed Lieutenant Barrackborn." He handed over the fingers folded in the kerchief. "Send this with it."

Fullsen carefully scribed each word, tongue clamped between his teeth in concentration. When Bren finished he glanced up. "Lieutenant, permission to ask a question?"

"Yes?"

"Sir, is this true? What you just had me write. Did we really destroy the Dhoah' Laen?"

Bren frowned. "I suppose we did." They won. He won the war his king began two decades ago.

"You killed her?"

Bren almost nodded, then shook his head. "Doric killed her. Arrow in the back."

The boy leaned forward, eyes hungry for more of the story. This was the event every Mirikin boy trained to work toward. "Did you see them? Did you see her? What did they look like?"

"I did. They were tall, I suppose. Hair blacker than night and skin that glittered, like dusted with glass." He knew it sounded stupid, too poetic, but Fullsen was a boy, and a boy would not care. "Their eyes were silver. You could feel their power, cold, like walking the beach in winter. It was strange. Everything around them, even battle, seemed muffled." He sighed. "I've fought them many times, but this was surely different."

"What about the Dhoah' Laen?" Fullsen asked, rocking forward on his toes. "Was her skin made of metal? Did she have the black claws? Blue blood?"

Bren glanced up, staring at the boy, but not seeing him. He saw a face frozen in panic. Clouded eyes. "No. She looked like just a girl."

Φ

The 33rd Day of Valemord, 1251

An'thor stared at the thick brown of his drink. He drank rarely. It dulled his senses and made for carelessness. He took a slow sip, rolling the acrid liquid around his mouth. It did not matter anymore. *I could drink until I'm tossed, and it wouldn't matter.* Around them the tavern bustled, barmaids weaving around busy tables as patrons shouted as many lewd remarks as drink orders. An'thor and Albi'giran were a fragile bubble of despair in an oblivious, turning world.

Albi'giran knocked back another thumb of tar-whiskey. The grimace was violent on his ashen features. "We can't possibly be getting tossed in an Athrolani bar."

An'thor's black eyes fixed on the other man's. "She's dead." He flung an arm out. "This place will be gone in a year, two years, damn, I don't know, but it'll be gone. Everything will be gone. The world is crumbling and the only chance at healing it is cold and dead on the edge of the Felds." Venom laced his quiet voice.

Albi'giran looked away. It did not seem real. "Perhaps I'm grasping here, but are you certain she was...what you thought?"

An'thor looked down. "The Laen were certain. That's enough for me. I never saw her power and neither did that girl in Vielrona. That they kept her from using it says a lot." He frowned. "You think she was a regular Laen?"

The asai sighed. "I don't know what I think. I'm too cold to think. Too numb."

An'thor looked away. Tears stung his eyes, but the ache in his chest was too deep for weeping. "I almost wish her death caused chaos at once—if the moment her heart stopped the world tore asunder. It'd make it easier."

Albi'giran splashed more alcohol into the Nenev's glass. "Waiting's worse."

"Watching the world devour itself, knowing she died in my arms." An'thor shuddered. "This is worse than anything I could dream."

Albi'giran grinned humorlessly and raised his glass. "To the end of the world."

CHAPTER SIX

The 36th Day of Valemord, 1251
The City-state of Vielrona

ALEA WAS NOT CERTAIN Arman's idea was a good one, but curiosity nudged her into the Vielronan streets. There seemed to be an alehouse on every corner. *How will I ever find it in this?* The walk was cold but along the better lit of Vielrona's streets. She wrapped the cloak tighter around her shoulders and rounded a bend. The kerchief over her hair was less obvious that her jahi, but strange. Her two braids were pinned up around her head.

Cat's Run took up an entire block of buildings. The windows were large, casting gold firelight onto the rough cobbles of the street. The bubbling din of conversation swelled each time the door banged open.

She made out Kam's lively antics through the waving glass and smiled.

"Evening, Miss." A broad man stood, one foot braced on the stairs as he held the door open.

She realized she stood just off the stoop in a daze and stepped in ahead of him with a quick thank you. Shivers erupted at the sudden warmth of the room. Arman's friends monopolized the rear corner of the largest room.

"Fates! The women-folk are outnumbering us!" Kam sat on the back of a bench, boots propped on the table.

Alea giggled and hung her cloak by their table. "This is quite the place."

"Quite," Wes answered. "I'm impressed Arman convinced you to come." He nodded to her kerchief. "You could pass for a local girl." The top two buttons of his shirt were undone, and he wore his hair slicked back.

"Care for a drink? We have strict instructions to make sure you enjoy yourself," Kam explained.

She laughed. "I think I'll start with something light. We don't normally drink unless it's a ceremony. Not to mention your tales warn against the effects of Vielronan alcohol." She slid onto the bench beside him. "Where's Arman?"

"He's collecting our next round," Veredy replied, sitting beside her with a bright smile. "You look lovely! I've always admired dark hair." Her deep brown eyes crinkled at the corners. "Do you dance?"

Alea's brow rose. "We had many household dances—ring dances and the like. Do you do those here?"

Veredy's laugh was kind. "Gracious, no. We jig and have many a skipper. All are paired though. Did you ever learn them?"

Alea shook her head. Nerves were a knot in her stomach, despite the friendliness. Dancing had not crossed her mind. "I'm afraid I don't know a single step."

"Kam doesn't know the steps either, but that doesn't stop him. It's more important to enjoy yourself and move quickly so your toes aren't trampled than get the steps right." She broke off and greeted Arman with a kiss.

He handed her a heavy glass and passed Kam and Wes their mugs. "You two better not thank me the same way."

Wes grinned wickedly. "How else do you expect me to pay you back?" He took a deep sip of his drink. "Our dear Alea fears her dancing skills are not good enough for the noble patrons of Cat's Run."

Arman snorted. "I'm certain her actual dancing skills surpass all of ours." He fixed Alea with an impish look. "However, what we do here cannot fairly be called dancing." As if called by his mention, a flurry of music cut through the conversation. Two musicians stood in the opposite corner. One held a brass pipe, the other a set of lap drums. A second series of notes began what Alea assumed was a song. Though charming, it was closer to a lilting scale, a series of skips. *This is hardly dancing music.*

Wes's offered drink arrived, and she tentatively tried a sip. It was heady and sweet, but warmed her stomach.

"It's mead," Wes explained. "Honey wine."

Chairs were pushed back, and dancing sprung up in the center of the room. Veredy was right—there was little skill involved, but much enthusiasm. Kam was up in moments, putting the other dancers to shame with his cavorting. Alea laughed aloud and began clapping in time. Her drink was finished, and her body was tingling pleasantly. Arman and Veredy seemed lost in a conversation.

Wes nudged Alea gently with his elbow. "What say you? I'm not a very good dancer, but apparently, we'll be well matched."

Alea felt her cheeks flush and she looked down. Panic warred with flattery. *I had no idea he was interested!* "Oh, Wes, I didn't know. I'm afraid I hardly know you."

His laugh boomed. "Alea, my dear, I'm afraid you've deeply misunderstood." He leaned closer. "Though your company is charming, I'd be far more likely to proposition Arman than you."

Understanding dawned on her. She giggled in surprise and allowed him to pull her to her feet.

Φ

Arman was not a dancing man, but lively music had a habit of making his feet tap. He leaned back against the wall, one arm slung over Veredy's shoulders. He worried inviting Alea to a tavern would be a mistake. Instead of withdrawing nervously, however, she laughed. It was her second dance with Wes and her face was flushed. *Granted that might be the mead.*

Winter was normally a dark time, but during war it was often the only season that guaranteed peace. The relief was tangible across the city and he felt his own heart grow lighter. Dark ice and deep heat still echoed the Laen, but he forced it from his mind. Alea was learning how to be Vielronan and Kepra needed his help less, now that Alea was working.

Veredy's brown eyes were alight, and one hand clapped in time on her leg. *She's as strong as I am, but far steadier.* Kam did not exaggerate Arman's antics as a younger man. Driven, and curious, he always wished to leave the city behind. Now, that determination focused on building the best life he could. Laen and Alea and war aside, he belonged in Vielrona. He twirled a lock of Veredy's hair around a blunt finger. *The best life would have her in it.*

He leaned down and nudged her cheek with his nose. "Thank you, Ver."

She pulled away to peer at him curiously. "Whatever for?"

"For being here. Even when I've not been."

"You're drunk if you're speaking that way." She grinned, jostling him with her shoulder. "I suppose I still can't convince you to dance."

He made a face. "Go take a turn."

She rolled her eyes and rose, skirts held away from the dirty floor. It was a two-pair dance, she and Alea trading partners several times as the music continued. She was a good dancer, as Vielronan dancing went and her long legs were as quick as they were strong.

"You are ogling, my man." Kam's chest was heaving, but his smile was broad. "This is Celly." Kam flopped down in Veredy's vacated seat and patted the bench beside him.

A woman stood a pace behind him. Her face was pink, but her expression reserved. She sat and held her arm out to Arman. "Celly Orean." She was several years older than Kam, and confidence lent beauty to her simple features.

"Well met, Miss." Arman grinned, recognizing her as one of the Guild's headmen. "I'm impressed Kam was able to interest someone as intelligent as you."

"Perhaps I find his difference intriguing." She flashed a witty smile. "May I buy your table a drink as thanks for letting me steal your most entertaining friend?"

"If I expect to make it home I should start drinking water, but I'm certain Wes will gladly accept." He rolled his shoulders. Comfort flowed in the wake of warm alcohol, but he wanted to be sober when he spoke to Veredy.

Kam leaned closer to Celly and began another elaborate tale. Arman scarcely listened. The music tittered to a halt while the musicians accepted their own drinks and took a minute's rest. When Alea bid him a breathless farewell he only smiled and wished her a good night. Veredy returned to perch on Arman's knee and introduce herself to Kam's admirer. Arman rubbed a hand down her back. *I've thought about this enough, I made every excuse I could and Ver was patient through everything.*

"Do you want to stay later?" Veredy smiled down at him.

"I'd like to walk. I want to talk to you about something."

One brow rose. "The air would be nice, I suppose." She slid off his legs and he grabbed their cloaks.

Compared to the din of the tavern, the streets were still. Arman slid an arm around her easily. "It seems Kam found his latest lover. I'd worry about a dalliance with someone in the Guild."

Veredy laughed. "Well, she seems as much a handful as he, albeit in a different way. Perhaps she'll settle him a bit. Fates know he could use it." She leaned her head against Arman's shoulder with a sigh. "It's such a journey, to see all of us change. Kam gained confidence—perhaps too much—and Wes is becoming a renowned smith. Even Alea changed in the month she's been here."

Arman realized almost a month passed since the Laen arrived and shook his head. Those weeks seemed to change everything. "What about me?"

"Conceited, are you?" Her grin warmed the gentle barb. "You went from violent boy to brooding man within a few days. Lately, you've realized you can't fix everything."

"That's partly why I wanted to talk to you." He let the statement hang in the air for several moments while he gathered his thoughts. Walking in the cold certainly cleared any alcohol from his mind, but his nerves helped little. "You're strong, and have a clear head when I get lost in my thoughts. You keep me centered. Fates know you're familiar enough with my moods. Ma no longer needs me about the inn as much, and Wes said the rooms beside his are empty now."

Veredy stopped and pulled away. She took his hands and peered into his face. Her expression was puzzled, but a smile curled one corner of her mouth. "What are you saying, Arman?"

He squeezed her hands. "Ver, I—"

Cold slammed into him. It shook his bones and clenched his gut. Breath stuttered in his chest and his knees hit the cobbles with a crack. Cold fled, followed by burning heat. Blood filled his mouth, hot and sweet. His jaw ached. His own groans were faint to his ears like they were another's. Veredy shook his shoulders, but her words were unintelligible.

The screaming in his ears was not his. It was Alea's. He staggered to his feet. "I'm sorry, Veredy. I have to go." Words tore from his throat. He stumbled into a jog then an outright run, leaving her staring, incredulous, behind him.

Φ

Crisp air burnt in Alea's lungs as she made her way along the quiet street. It was close to midnight, but many lanterns still glowed in the surrounding houses. Dancing was more fun than she ever expected, and with Wes felt safe. Even if she and Ahren only loved each other as friends, the wound from his loss was too raw for her to consider romance. Despite the cold, she enjoyed her new freedom. The city was peaceful, open for exploration.

She trailed her fingers along the cool stone of a cobbler's shop, humming the last dancing tune absently. *I'll have Arman show me the gardens soon. Though perhaps they're all brown in the winter.*

Boot falls as she passed an alley made her turn. The street was as deserted as before. "Hello?" Metal hissed against leather raising the small hairs on the back of her neck. "Who's there?"

Two men emerged across the narrow street. They were dressed in dark clothes. Alea was certain the scarves covering their faces were not for warmth. She stepped back until she felt the wall behind her. Whirling, she dashed toward a larger street several buildings down. Hard muscle tossed her to a halt as a third man emerged from behind a workshop. His hand clamped over her mouth as she tried to pull away.

She bit down hard and skittered away when he let go with a curse.

"Help!" She pitched her voice to carry, something Merahn did when she wanted her way. A fourth man arrived. Their clothes were unmarked. Vielronan green marked their irises. *"I will not have her on my cart.... you endangered the city bringing them back."* Tomas' words echoed in her head. *They're fearful enough to attack me? Drive me out?* She wondered what she would do to save her own city. Indecision froze her limbs. Perhaps they just wanted to frighten her. "Please, I know you're scared. I don't mean to threaten your city. Let me go and I'll leave. I promise." She hated the fear in her voice.

"We can't afford that, girl. You get out, so does word those women were here." The speaker drew his dagger. It was a curved, wicked looking thing, and Alea realized she saw it at Arman's stall.

Strange, what one thinks of when they're about to die. They intended to kill her, and her skills at hand-combat were serviceable, but not against four men armed with blades.

Another man burst frantically onto the street. Behind the twisted snarl, his features were barely recognizable. He threw himself blindly onto the closest man. Surprise seized the others only for a moment. Arman landed a blow to his opponent's temple and slammed the palm of his hand upward into his nose, driving bone and cartilage back. He whirled to face the next man. An arm came up to block, but he was too slow. The attacker's blow landed on Arman's chest. He staggered, but rushed forward, fists raised. His steps faltered, and he stopped, staring in confusion at the deep stain growing on his shirt. "Dammit." His knees gave out and he fell face down in a culvert.

Alea stared. *Run. Fight.* She should have used the surprise of Arman's attack to overpower one of the men. Instead, her feet rooted in place. Arman shuddered once in the gutter, then lay still. Darkness churned in her mind. It was angry and roiling. It was despair. It was the loss of something as familiar as her soul. The world trundled past without knowing, without seeing the force building inside.

Now that darkness grew. She spent weeks wishing to die, but this was different. It was anger. It was hate. And hate gave her something to live for. *They are monsters.*

Φ

The ground hit Arman like a second blow. He gasped, gutter water rushing in instead of air. Cold slime from the butcher's lard tub mixed with manure from the gardens. Burning ripped through his body, save for his left arm and shoulder. Those were numb. Dim awareness told him the water downstream from him was awfully dark. *He stabbed me. That's my blood.* Bile rose. Muscles convulsed, but he did not know if it was from fear or shock.

"Alea." Her name came as a gurgle. He expected to see her dead, to see an empty street. Alea pressed against the wall. "Stop," she whispered. Then her features smoothed, and she forced herself up. When her eyes swiveled to the tall man, they hardened. Delicate hands raised before her. "Stop!"

One man rushed forward, blade raised. Arman's world exploded into darkness. It was not unconsciousness enveloping him, however, but roiling black fog. Fighting broke out and he heard a shout, pounding feet, then silence. *They've taken her.*

A gentle hand brushed dirt from his face. Cold hands rolled him over and cleaned the scummer from his nose and mouth. "I won't let you die in a gutter, Arman." Lead and energy laced Alea's voice, and he blinked his vision clear.

Calm erased any concern on her face. Her gray eyes darkened to silver-black, glowing in the dark, like an animal's. Black veins marbled her skin. Bodies lay in the street, black fog drifting from their open mouths where it had choked them.

Alea turned his face to her again. "You're safe." Her palm pressed against his wound, achingly cold. He groaned stomach rolling at the pain. It felt as if ice crystals spread in his chest. Then it was over. Alea sat back on her heels. Blackness streamed into her, twisting under her skin before disappearing. Her eyes lightened to gray and rolled back. She gasped once, then fell.

He reached out but stopped short of touching her. Quick breaths misted the air over her mouth. *The Laen have the wrong woman.* It was his last thought before shock drove his mind from consciousness.

Φ

The 37th day of Valemord, 1251

Blood and muck dripped across the floor of the Ruby Cockerel. Arman scarcely noticed. Kam caught him as he sagged against the banister, still refusing to meet his friend's eyes. Wes banged in after them, Alea cradled in his arms. Arman glanced over. "Hush or you'll wake my mother."

Wes looked thoroughly chastised. "Where is her room?"

"Last on the right. Below mine." He glanced at Veredy, who stood by the door. "Can you go with him, get her cleaned up?"

She wordlessly followed the smith upstairs, leaving Kam and Arman in the common room.

"Arman." Kam's voice was low.

Arman went to hang his cloak, only to realize it was ruined. He bundled it into the hearth. His movements were emotionless, his face blank.

"Arman." The word was closer to a bark. Kam pushed the taller man down into a chair by the sputtering fire. "Sit."

Arman slumped, watching the damp, brown wool burn. "There's ale if you want."

Kam's words were strangled. "We find you both unconscious, covered in blood, and you offer me a drink? Like it's midwinter and I'm selling chestnuts?" He made a disgusted noise and stomped off into the kitchen. He returned with two thumb-glasses and a bottle of tar-whiskey. He drained his glass twice before finally sitting back. "Tell me what happened."

"I can't."

"You can't, or you won't?"

"I won't because I can't. I don't know what happened, Kam. I don't understand it." Arman frowned. "How did you know to come?"

"Veredy. She said you were talking, then you went a bit mad. You ran off. We knew where you might have gone." Kam handed him a glass.

Arman stared at it, but did not drink. His body should be shaking, he should be frozen halfway to death. Instead, itching crawled over his flesh and fire burned in his chest. Nausea clenched the walls of his stomach. *Do I really not understand it, or am I simply refusing to admit what I saw?*

"Whose blood is that?"

"Mine."

Kam stared at him. "What?"

"I said 'mine.' Kam, I appreciate the concern, but I can't handle your questions." Arman sank his head into his hands. Exhaustion crept in. Perhaps if he slept everything would be clearer.

"What about mine?" Veredy stood at the bottom of the stairs, Wes just behind her.

Arman looked away from the hurt in her eyes. "Ver, I'm sorry, but no." He levered himself out of the chair. Leaving his drink untouched on the table, he made his way to the stairs. He ran a finger down Veredy's cheek. "Thank you for coming." He waited while they filed out, then stumbled up the stairs to his bedroom. He stripped off his ruined clothes and cleaned the blood from his body. The wash water was cold, but soothed his fevered skin. At his shoulder, he paused. The mirror by his door was small, but he angled it down. There was no wound, only smooth, red scar tissue. His breath hitched.

It was a handprint.

CHAPTER SEVEN

The 39th Day of Valemord, 1251
The City-state of Vielrona

ALEA IGNORED THE KNOCKING. Each time Kepra brought food up over the past few days she refused to answer. Instead, she sat on her bed and stared at her hands. Now the pounding persisted.

"Milady, it's Arman. Open the door please." When no response came, his voice grew firm. "I can break in. Open it or I'll pick the lock."

His honorific for her irked more than usual. She dragged herself off the bed and cracked the door.

"May I come in?"

She wrapped her robe tighter and returned to perch on the bed. Arman's brows rose at the sight of her room. Clothes from the attack lay crumpled on the floor. His concern did not wane when he took in her appearance.

"I only just left my room today, too." Soft words slipped between them. Confidence, confession.

Alea stared at him. He cleared his throat then picked up her clothes, examining them. "I doubt the blood will wash from these." He dropped them in the tin barrel used for waste. He dipped a facecloth into the stale water of her basin and held it out to her. "Veredy did her best, but you still have blood on you."

She could not move. Too many layers of her fears, confusion, separated her from his words. He hesitated, then dabbed the blood away, wiping the dirt from her cheeks and brow. When her face was clean, he took the metal comb on her bed-stand and freed her hair of snarls and blood. Her hair tidied, he shifted awkwardly. "I don't know how to braid."

She was silent. The dissociation she felt now, was different from the apathy that followed her grief. *Truth is what scares me now.*

He knelt to peer into her eyes. "Are you in there, somewhere?"

Tenderness brushed her mind. She slid from her bed and wrapped her arms around his neck. Her words came out in a tumble close to nonsense. "I thought I was nothing. I thought I was a foster-child saved by my ihal's kindness. I was the reason the Laen came the first time. I was the reason the Mirikin attacked, even if none of us knew it!"

Arman gingerly patted her shoulders. "I know." He pulled back and took her by the shoulders. "I've suspected for weeks. My mother helped a woman deliver a baby—a baby she took south to abandon. But she was not a human woman. She was Laen, and you are her image." He caught her startled gaze and smiled. "This will take a long time to accept, and you could do with some food. I'm headed to the library, but perhaps afterward we might talk?"

Forcing a nod, she pulled away, embarrassed at her condition. When he had gone, Alea risked a glance in her mirror. She looked the same. *What did I expect?* She quickly finished washing and changed into a clean dress. The ordeal in the alley seemed unreal, but the blood on her clothes was real. Kepra bustled downstairs, but Alea could not bring herself to leave the room. *Here I'm safe.* She lay back on her bed, eyes closed. *Between these walls, I'm only Alea.*

Φ

Arman sighed in relief when we saw the deserted room. *Of all my research attempts, I want an audience for this the least.* Leaving his cloak at the door, he found the older historic tomes and scrolls. Several were recently thumbed through, he noticed, all regarding the Laen. *Someone else is curious.* He shook the sensation of being watched away. *They've a right to know what stayed – stays – in their city.* He did not flip to the lengthy pages about the war or the gods, nor did he seek the histories of men. He looked for the Rakos. His old book of tales rested heavily in his pocket, and he wondered how much of it was true.

With a few promising options, he retreated to one of the plush chairs. He flipped through the pages of the first. Toward the middle was a rough copy of the painting adorning the cover of his book. *A Rakos guard of Vielrona, as illustrated by Druca of Berr.* Arman's brows rose. It was an old image—the last of the Laen guards disappeared centuries ago. He turned to the page opposite the portrait.

> *The Laen did not oversee their world single-handed. Of their creation, they picked the most beautiful and powerful – the titanic fiery monsters known as the Rakos – and gave them the ability to take a form like the Laen, to the gods, to mankind. The Rakos were all male to the Laen's female and were everything they were not: chaotic and progressive and passionate. Each bonded to a Laen, guarding her and upholding her wishes.*

Arman sat back. *Bonded?* A seed of certainty put down roots within him. After the Division, the Rakos offered their piece of the world to shelter mankind. In the absence of the Laen, some took lovers and their powers were bred out. Most simply disappeared.

A small map in another book showed Rakos garrisons, each guarding a Laen city. His finger brushed the grayed dot illustrating Vielrona and her sister, the Laen city of Elanal. *We were once so great.* All he read bogged down his mind and darkened his mood. Returning the books, he shrugged on his cloak. He was not ready to go home, or for the conversation with Alea. It would change everything. She needed his strength, but beyond that, he was lost. *I thought the Dhoah' Laen left weeks ago. I sent the guard after them. When she's been in my home, learned from me, danced with Wes.* He shook his head, hoping his thoughts settled into some sort of order. His feet followed the familiar path to his and Wes's forge. He could do with some work.

Sharp scents of hot metal and charcoal filled the air as Wes hammered a blade. The smell was like home. He shouldered the door open. Heat from forge fires rippled in the cold air. Wes stopped when Arman entered, gaze flicking to the empty doorway behind his friend, as if checking for Alea. "Good to see you."

Arman nodded. Tension hummed in the air as much as smoke. "How's work been?"

"Slow. I need an extra set of hands. I'm thinking of asking Farrow's brother. He's been eying our stall."

Arman frowned. "What do you mean? I'll be back tomorrow."

"For how long?"

"If you have something you need to say, say it. Don't dance about. That's my territory." The joke fell short and Arman's words just sounded childish.

Wes shoved the blade back into the coals before it cooled too much. "We need to talk." He wiped his hands clean and leaned back against his anvil. "Do you have a few minutes?"

Arman shut the door and hung his cloak up before drawing up a chair. "What is it?"

"Be straight with me. What happened that night?"

"It was a blur. We were attacked by those men. I don't remember much else."

"Arman, I dealt with the bodies. I cut them to make it look like they fought each other. You owe me the whole story, not just lies and tidbits. You're no hero and I don't think she's your lover."

Arman looked down. "I can't say, Wes. I told Kam the same. I can't tell you, either of you."

Wes slammed his heavy fists onto his workbench. "Dammit Wardyn! This is no longer just about you! This is not about the women you helped flee the city, this is not about Alea! This is about the city, this is about your damned friends. For fuck's sake this is about your home!"

Arman sat back, speechless. Wes never yelled. The man's anger usually surfaced as quiet disappointment. It was never a rage. Arman met his friend's eyes and his chest tightened. *He's afraid. He's terrified.* Arman sighed. "I'm sorry. You're right. I've gotten blind in all of this, and you deserve the truth. All of you do." He stood. "But I still can't tell you. Not until I know the truth myself." He grabbed his cloak and strode back outside. He expected Wes to barrel after him, expected the door to slam. The following silence hurt far worse.

Φ

Alea resorted to mentally reciting poems—even her least favorites—and listing her favorite flowers. Thoughts encroached on her peace. It was childish, and she knew it.

A twisting tendril of Red Tearing
Sticky sweet on the lips then searing
Bunch of Bitter Knot bright and baleful
Can't find Cat Thumb, must be careful
Little pinch of Jani's Lute...

She searched for the rest of the line, her brow creased. A quiet knock scattered what was left of the midwives' recipe. "Who is it?"

"Arman. Had you any plans for the rest of the day?" He smiled when she opened the door and held up a tray of tea and food. He teetered on the threshold, as if uncertain whether he was welcome. "May I?"

She ushered him in. "How was your day?"

"Interesting." He slid the tray onto her bedside table and took one of the mugs for himself. "Ma said you'd not been down, so I thought I'd bring you something." He peered into his tea as he hoped it could answer his questions. "We need to have a talk, milady."

"I know." It was the last thing she wanted, really. Speaking anything aloud made it real. *Inescapable.*

"What happened?"

"They attacked me, said I wouldn't leave the city alive." She still heard their voices, the last few words—threats—they uttered. "They couldn't risk word getting out about the Laen. I thought one might be Tomas, the cart driver. I wanted to fight them, like you showed me, but I froze. When did you arrive?" She waved away his answer. "He stabbed you and I realized something."

"You wanted to fight."

"I wanted to live." She looked down. Her hands were remarkably still. The past months she spent uncertain of who she was. Ice pooled in her heart again, and her stomach lurched. Now she knew. It was unexpected, unwelcome, even, but it was a start. A darker part of her whispered now she had power to avenge her family's death. "My body was cold, and black fog erupted. It filled their lungs." She shook herself. "The thought should sicken me, but it doesn't."

"By the time I was home, I healed. Can you explain that?"

"You don't remember?" Her own memory was blurry, but perhaps more from horror than actual trauma.

"I remember fine, doesn't mean I understand it any better."

"I don't either, really. I just put my hand on you, to stop the bleeding. Something rushed from me, mended your wound. I don't know anything else."

"You fainted. I must have too, because the next thing I remember is Wes dragging me from the water and Veredy shrieking we were dead. They brought us here and Ver helped clean you up a bit." He fixed her with a pointed stare. "The power was black."

"Yes." She refused to meet his gaze. She knew what he was meant. "That man mentioned black power."

"Do you think perhaps you were the reason for the Laen's first visit to your ihal?" He leaned forward, but did not touch her. "You know what you are, and you know you need protection. Appeal to the Guild. Demand they shelter you."

Alea finally looked at him, certainty coursing through her. There was one option left for her and she hated it. As much as she disliked Vielrona at first, it was the only thing she had left. "They'd throw me out on my ear. Any city that shelters me will be in danger. They might protect me if I begged, but I will not."

Arman sat back, realization dawning. "You're leaving?"

She had to. *If I stay here, you'll die. All of you will. I can't cause that again.* "I've thought a lot today. I tried not to, but many things became clear." Confusion and fear roiled in her mind, but outwardly she was nothing but calm.

"Where will you go?"

"I have no idea. The guard mentioned a town—Marl Kess? Perhaps I will go there and try to find him. I may be the Dhoah' Laen, but I need help." Tumbling from her lips was the terrifying truth. She held out her hand, black power marbling her skin for a second before it disappeared. "I am the Dhoah' Laen."

Arman ran his tongue over his teeth thoughtfully. "I know." He offered her a faint smile. "Or some part of me did."

"I am sorry for what I've done to change Vielrona. I'm certain I'll do far worse." She smoothed her coverlet. "Have you told your mother what happened?"

"No. She heard us return, but she assumed we were drunk. I suppose my antics when I was younger have bought us some time."

"Are you going to tell her?"

"I don't know how. There's something else, something beyond what you are, I can't explain." When she made no move to interrupt he rubbed a calloused thumb over his teeth. "I think you are like a river over rocks—one eventually changes the shape of the other. I think you are changing me." He paused awkwardly for a minute. "I don't know what to tell Wes or Kam. Damn, I left Veredy at a poor time."

"Tell them the truth. I'll be gone before long. Then things will return to normal. I'd hate to disrupt your world any more than I already have." Her smile was real, but even she could hear the sorrow in her voice. "I think I need some time."

Arman looked down. "I can't imagine... Let me know if I can help in any way." He rose and offered her a nod, almost low enough to be a bow.

Please don't add bowing to the "milady's" and "miss's." She shut the door behind him without another word. There was nothing to say, nothing she pulled from her throat sounded genuine.

Shadows crouching between her thoughts had origins, histories centuries older than she. *"I know how precious you are."* Ahren's words rumbled into meaning. In her childish romance, she thought he was flirting. Now the idea of Ahren flirting with the daughter of the Laen was laughable.

Certainty, sadness, even the dedication in his eyes and in her foster-father's voice made sense. *They knew. I was never a charity, a babe taken in as a favor.* Guilt and horror eased then. They had known, they had always known, what lay in her veins. *I could have saved them.*

Bloodstained sand had scraped her palms, when she crawled toward the Laen, begging them to help, begging them to save her family, the children from the manor. *Then someone grabbed me and...blackness.* Not the blackness of unconsciousness, but of roiling dark power.

Turning her hand, she stared at the palm. No mark showed where power thundered to her rescue. Only the sickness in her heart from killing lingered. The others must have thought her power was the girl's, separated by a few paces. *Dhoah' Laen.* Black curls, ink beneath her skin, marbled over her palm, twisting between fingers for a moment, then disappeared with the thought. The idea was both unfathomable and obvious at once. She was no more precious to Ahren than air, than water in the desert's heat.

She was necessary.

Φ

Arman let his feet trace old paths of his childhood while his mind wandered. Two months ago, he was certain of everything. Two days ago, he was certain of one thing.

Now he was certain of nothing.

He paused on the bridge and leaned on the rail, looking south. The river was sullen and gray, the shrubs along its banks pitiful in the winter cold.

Aching still echoed in his jaw and he tasted traces of blood. *Up there, somewhere, was a city of her people.* His eyes followed the line of the river through the notch in the mountains. He pushed himself upright and strode back over the bridge. Swinging one leg over the river wall, he dropped to the narrow bank below. Moving was better than sitting still and thinking. *I could talk to Ver,* but the voice in the back of his skull nagged. Wes and Kam would bombard him with questions, but Veredy was different. *How can I tell her another woman's voice came into my head? Laen or not, it's strange.* The stone blocks of the riverbank became rocky strand. His boots hissed on the damp, rough sand. One hand trailed alone the rocks piled at the bends, feeling the thrum of rushing water.

Soon he emerged into the steep valley of the notch. Before him lay what had once been Elanal. Toppled buildings were completely submerged or flooded. One was carved into a cliff face at the head of the valley. A spark of hope lit Arman's heart. *Perhaps I could find something here, something that will help her find a guard, find her people.* Maybe then she could leave, safely, and he could return to being simply Arman. He skirted the ruins nervously. They were less grand than he expected. No surging cold or churning heat struck him. He still felt their consciousness. He edged along the cliff's base, finding the doorway nestled beside the cascading water from higher up.

Perhaps the Rakos have simply been hiding, been sleeping until she needed them. He snorted at the thought. The room beyond was dark and smelled of mildew. It was empty, save for a few smashed pieces of what may have once been a chair. Opposite was another doorway. This one led to curling, crumbling stairs. Arman's feet faltered on the steps. *This is ridiculous.* The accounts were all legends, mother's tales to teach children values and history. The stairs crunched beneath his boots. Nerves sang through him, adrenaline and some ancient animal instinct screaming that he was no longer the hunter here. He finally skittered into a large room. The weight of the little book in his breast pocket burned over the handprint scar.

Two statues stood at the end of the hall. They were not fine, made of precious metals or gems, but carved from simple stone. One stood in a water stained basin long since gone dry. Her hand was raised, the other outstretched toward the ground. Beside her, the man stood on a bed of dead coals. A groove ran around the woman's head, though the adornment was gone. Arman stepped closer to the male statue and fell to his knees. Gold gleamed on the man's carved curls.

"Please, she needs you." He did not wonder if he sounded stupid. "She's here, she's alive and knows who she is and fates, if there was ever a time, it's now. Come back." Silence answered.

Thank fates I didn't tell her I was coming here, hoping to find something. He moved closer, crouching on the rim of the brazier. The statue was familiar—the set of his jaw and the curl of a snarl on his mouth. Arman fumbled with the book. Sure enough, the Rakos on the cover was similar. *Do you have a name?* He flipped the book open and, with a silent apology to his father, slit the silk lining. The painting was the original, signed with Berrin symbols.

He froze when he saw the subject's name. *Kierman Wardyn 657 Vil Ronna.* He glanced up at the statue. *Wardyn?*

Heat exploded through his bones. He knew where he saw that expression before. *It's mine.* Gripping the statue's outstretched hand, he hauled himself onto the pedestal. His calloused hand slid the Crown from the stone head. Blood flooded his mouth, new teeth emerging between his dogteeth and incisors. Itching heat pulsed, and his bloody mouth curled into a wolfish smile.

Alea had her guard.

CHAPTER EIGHT

The 39th Day of Valemord, 1251
The City-state of Vielrona

ADRENALINE CARRIED ARMAN UNTIL he re-entered the city. Excitement and certainty left his body in a rush and he steadied himself on a lantern post. Every headstrong promise he made as a boy was dwarfed by this choice. This was different from fighting, different from promising to marry Veredy when he was grown. *I can never go back from this.* It was not a choice. Something called him, and he answered. His blood answered. If Alea left the city, he would follow. *No,* he corrected himself, *When the Dhoah' Laen leaves the city her Rakos guard follows.* Perhaps there was no distinction between the two, but imagining one slowed his racing heart.

He ran his thumb over his teeth again. The new points scraped his rough finger, longer than any human teeth had a right to be.

He had to tell Wes and Kam something, had to explain himself to Veredy. *Fates, I was going to ask her to be my wife – in earnest.* In the darkness of his confusion marriage was as distant as summer. Whatever his relationship was with Veredy, would be different now, and must wait again. It was fully dusk, and Arman was too tired to face his friends. There was one task left, however, before he could retreat to home.

The Farrow house was a small cottage on the edge of the Uppers, but it bore the marks of old wealth. It took two knocks before the door jerked open. Confusion, fear and anger shadowed Thada Farrow's features. "What is it?"

It was an expression Arman was far too familiar with. "Evening, Mistress Farrow."

She blinked at him, recognition flitting across her face. "Arman, gracious I didn't even recognize you." She ushered him inside, her face falling back into darkness. "Can I take your cloak?"

"Thank you, but no. I can't stay long." The clean, lively house he remembered from boyhood was dim and cluttered.

She drifted into her kitchen. "Forgive the state of the house. I can't seem to find the energy, not after Maren...." She shuddered. "He was such a good boy, I can't understand what happened."

Dread rooted itself in Arman's stomach. *Farrow's dead. He didn't want the survivors here and now he's dead.* Even with strong denial, Arman knew the truth. "I was horrified to hear the news."

She glanced over, as if she already forgot he was there. "Certainly. You two were close as boys. Not as much recently, but he always spoke highly of your family." She gave him a weak smile.

"I'm actually here to see his brother. Is he in?"

She nodded. "He's taken it hard, but he's a strong boy." She leaned up the stairs. "Hiram? Arman Wardyn is here to see you."

A long pause followed, then a door opened softly upstairs. Hiram was the image of his older brother. The shadows on his face matched his mother's. His faint smile did not reach his tired eyes. "Hey, Wardyn."

"Hey." Arman held out the note he hastily wrote before knocking. "I'm sorry about your brother. He was a good man."

"What's this?" Hiram peered at the paper but did not open it to read.

"You're interested in the smithy, and we could use some help. Bring this to Wes and he'll find you some work." Arman shifted awkwardly and heaved a sigh. "Very well, I should be going." He paused at the door. "I'm so sorry, Mistress Farrow. Really, I wish there was something .... I'm so sorry."

Φ

The knock on his door startled Arman. He contemplated pretending to sleep. He was not ready to face his friends again, let alone Veredy, and his mother's compassion would break his tentative composure.

"Arman, are you there?" Alea's voice was gentle.

He opened the door, leaning on the frame. She was a stranger, there were a thousand things he would never know about her. And yet she was the only one who understood a fraction of the horror and power rampaging across his mind. The same terrible secret bound them. "Are you feeling any better?"

She frowned. "I don't know. I guess better, a bit. You look like something the vultures' pecked over."

He glared at her with mock anger. "That's a new insult."

"No, it's Sunamen." Her smile was more open than he'd yet seen. "Do you need to rest, or may I come in?"

He opened the door wider and ushered her in before flopping back onto his bed. "I'm sorry I'm not a better host right now." He watched her take a seat. "This is an interesting reversal—you checking on me while I lie, depressed in bed."

"I just lived through a massacre, Arman, what's your excuse?" Her eyes glittered with wry humor. At some point she had changed into breeches and a short dress. The look suited her.

"I went looking for something to help you. What I found was unexpected, but pieces fit where there were only questions before." He held the roughly repaired book of tales out to her. "What do you know of the Rakos?"

She took it, but only looked at the cover. Thoughtful reservation tinged her gaze. "They're dead. That's why the Laen struggled so much lately."

"Well the man painted there is Keirman Wardyn. He lived in Vielrona when it was still a Rakos garrison. I hoped I could wake him, or call him somehow. In a way I did." The scarred handprint on his chest burned, pulsing with his heart. "You need a guard, Lyne'alea, and I'm it."

"Arman, your loyalty is astounding, but this weight isn't yours to bear." Her words stopped when he drew the crown from under his pillow. Hammered gold shone in the lamp light. Green, veined agates and ivory studded the side. Its beauty, like Vielrona's, was simplicity and strength.

"It's our weight, together. I'm not choosing to act as your guard. My blood is bound to yours. This is the Crown of this world, of the Rakos, and it is mine to bear."

Fear and pity flooded her eyes. "Are you all right?"

"I don't know. I feel powerful and whole. And a bit odd. My damned teeth hurt, and I'm fevered." He sighed. "I'd imagine you understand. I still feel lost, though my path is clearer than ever."

"Trust your instincts, Arman. At least hear me—I trust them." She held the book up. "Mind if I borrow this? I'd like to know more about this strange creature protecting me."

"Of course." He winced, and asked, "Can you please keep this between us? For now."

"Of course," she echoed. Her smile was gentle as she left, but her words stayed, ominous, in his mind. *Am I a creature now? Is it possible to be only partly Rakos, or does the chaos consume you?*

Φ

The 40th Day of Valemord, 1251
The Village of Marl Mere, Athrolan

Clouds shadowed the road ahead. An'thor spent so many years traveling, both as hunter and hunted, he did not know how to stop. Albi'giran disappeared a week before to find his own people, leaving An'thor alone with his thoughts. Now there was only one place left he could think of to go. The lights of the town ahead glittered in the dusk, a speck of warmth in the cold landscape. A decade passed since he last rode this way, but the gravel sounded the same under Theriim's hooves.

Marl Mere was twice the size of Marl Kess, but nestled in the mountains south of Athrolan, it was far less exposed. He supposed that was why Elle chose it. Her house lay on the village edge. It was closer to a hovel than a house, he supposed, but home was home. Dismounting, he drew his horse under the overhang serving as stable and woodshed. As he removed Theriim's tack he whistled the opening strains of *King's Wrongdoing.* The silence inside the hut sharpened. "Aye, it's me, girl."

She waited in the doorway when he rounded the front. He offered a tired smile. "It's been a while. Missed me?"

Her hair was more silver than black now and her eyes haunted, but her smile was bright. "An'thoriend Domariigo, I thought only the end of the world would bring you back to my doorstep."

His expression darkened. "Well, you weren't wrong."

Grief flitted across her face, but surprise did not. "I suppose you should come in. Supper's almost ready." She locked the door behind him and helped him out of his cloak. "I assume you won't put the serious topics off until after we've eaten."

He laughed humorlessly. "You know me too well." He went to the fireplace and put the kettle on before rummaging through the cabinets for tea leaves.

"Please, make yourself at home." She smiled wryly and handed him two mugs before sitting back in the chair. "And pour me some while you're at it. You keep catering to me and I'll begin to wonder why I never married."

"Your son's father was a genocidal maniac who declared war on your race," he reminded her mildly. "Really, I'm amazed you keep forgetting."

She threw a narrow glance at him. "Why are you here? What's this about the end of the world?"

An'thor paused in his tea making but did not turn around. He only said it the once and was not prepared to do so again. "Elle, I need you to return to Le'yne. For good."

"I most certainly will not." Old rebellion lit her tone and he almost grinned. "They don't even know I'm alive. This is as much of a home as anywhere else, and I'm happy here." She looked away. "At least, happier than before."

"This is different, Elle." He set the cups out and poured the water before taking the chair opposite her. "I wasn't lying about everything ending. She was a little bit of a thing from Emala. The Mirikin found us in Marl Kess. We made it to the edge of the Hartland, but they shot her. I tried, I swear, but she's dead." He glanced up at her. "Elle, the Dhoah' Laen is dead."

Her expression was carefully neutral when she met his eyes. "With all due respect, An'thor, you're wrong."

"Elle, her lifeblood drenched my hands—I'm fairly certain I'd know!"

"It's a pity that girl is dead, but she wasn't the Dhoah' Laen."

"She had Liane convinced."

"The true Dhoah' Laen wasn't raised among our people, An'thor. No one knows about her."

"How do you know then?" Something horrible akin to hope unfurled between his ribs and he clenched a pale hand on the chair's arm. He was too old to hope, too old to be enchanted with prophecies and legends.

"Because she's my daughter." Elle's silver eyes were luminous in the dark hut. "And I'm the one that hid her. "

An'thor realized he leaned forward, clinging with desperation to Elle's words. "If you're lying, if you're just hoping, I swear my heart won't recover this time." He steadied himself with a slow breath. "When did you bear a daughter?"

"Bren was six when his father was crowned. I was only a few weeks pregnant—in the human way, again, but I knew this child was different. I could feel her. I kept up the ruse of being human well enough, but I was scared for her. I told him what I was." Her voice caught on the ragged edges of past heartbreak. "And so, the war began."

"You told him?" This was a twist An'thor had not expected. "Why?"

"It was just rumors, at first. But people wondered about me. And I was young—younger—and thought our love was strong enough to stop a genocide."

An'thor could have scoffed, but he did not. He remembered youthful hope too, and the thought that romance could conquer every storm.

"I think you know how wrong I was. He was so desperate to get out of his father's mighty shadow. So, I left Bren, traveled south to deliver her, and found my way to Cehn."

An'thor stared at her, incredulous. "Liane stopped there two months ago. She thought it was a sanctuary."

Elle's brow quirked. "And why do you think they thought that?"

"You said they didn't know about the girl."

She shrugged. "They knew Cehn sheltered me. They did not know I left something behind." Power lit her expression. It was easy to forget, in her little house, what she was. It was easy to chalk her dark hair and pale skin up to Athrolani blood. There was no questioning her race now.

"Fates, Elle, when were you going to tell me?" She kept the world's greatest secret for decades. *Any mother would.* He put his head in his hands. "Cehn was razed to the ground two months ago. There were barely a dozen survivors and they're scattered in Vielrona."

Her eyes blazed with cold and a smile twitched on her lips. "Go back. I believe you forgot something."

Φ

The 41st Day of Valemord, 1251
The City-state of Vielrona

Snow decorated the wall along the river. It was a rare dusting, and Arman thought it a pity to brush it away. Still, he was not fond of wet breeches. He sat cross-legged and watched the water curl and burble under the thin ice. After a moment he heard low conversation approaching from the market. Wes and Kam fell silent when drew up to him.

The former held up a folded piece of parchment between two fingers. "Got your note. When did you start sending message boys?"

Arman sighed. *This is already off to a brilliant start.* "You wanted help."

"I didn't need to learn you murdered his brother from him." Rumbling in Wes's voice echoed the forge.

"That's what I wanted to explain. To both of you. You said you wanted the truth."

Kam's eyes narrowed. "Why couldn't you tell us before now?"

"I needed to understand some things, and now I do." He brushed snow off the wall. "Will you sit?"

Wes's face hardened. "You want us to freeze our bollocks off?"

"I want to be sure you're the only two hearing this. Now sit, or leave." When they both settled, he cleared his throat. "I killed one of those men, not sure who. Only one."

"You said that blood was yours."

"It was. Another got me in the chest. I was down, bleeding out in the gutter. She handled the rest."

"Arman, I took care of those bodies. You telling me I protected her?" Wes looked betrayed. "You've taught her, but not that much. Those men looked like they just died, of their own will."

"I could barely stand. She held her hands up and they died. Then she came to me and pressed her hand to my wound. By the time we got home only a scar was left." *And teeth that don't belong.* "Do you know what that means?"

Silence drifted like a final few snowflakes between them. Like the snow, Arman wished he could let it settle, undisturbed.

"I thought the last of them left months ago."

"So did I. So did she. This is as new to her as it is to us." He met Wes's eyes. "She's exactly what they've been searching for."

"This will bring them down upon us!" Kam spat, finally breaking his unusual silence.

"I know. That's why we're leaving."

Wes shook his head angrily. Arman watched the smith steeling himself to speak. "She saved you, fine. I'm glad of it. You cannot repay all you're given or revenge all you've gotten."

"You have a life here, Arman. And a good woman, which is more than any of us could hope for. Why are you suddenly begging after this girl? You didn't know she existed two months ago."

"I made that promise to Veredy when we were fifteen. As much as I want it, it isn't to be right now. Something inside me answers Alea. Heat takes over." He rolled his eyes at Kam's lewd gesture. "It's not lust. I know lust, I understand it well. This is different. Something has always been there, inside me. Something that belongs to her." His skin itched just thinking about it. "I thought it was because the Laen were in the Cockerel. I thought it was because she was near me, but it is more complicated than that. It is a part of me."

"I won't let you throw your life away, I won't let you go after her." Wes's words were bitter.

Arman knew if there was an argument, he won. Wes's words were just the death throes. He rose. "I'll come home. When this is over, I'll come home." Drawing his cloak tighter around himself, he trudged away. It was not a choice, not exactly. *So why do I feel like I just chose Alea over my friends?* Discretion was important, but he knew some conversations simply had to occur over tea. This was one of them.

The glow in Veredy's windows was a relief as much as he dreaded what he was about to tell her.

The door opened before he even knocked. "I recognize your boot falls on my stairs." She stepped aside. "You might as well come in. Kettle's just boiled."

He folded his cloak over the back of a chair, but was too nervous to sit. "How've you been?"

"You sound like we've not spoken in weeks." She caught his gaze and held it. "Kam said you were speaking to them today."

"Just came from there. It didn't go well." He picked a splinter from her table. "I'm sorry with how I left things."

"When you were about to ask to marry me, or afterward when we dragged you bloody from the gutter?" Harsh words were tempered with her quiet voice.

Always steady. "I can't help this, Ver. All my pretty words are used up and the most I can offer is honesty." His shoulders sagged, and exhaustion swept over him. "This is too hard."

"You have work, a good family. I enjoy our nights together. You'd make a fine husband. We were going to wed when the time came. It would've been good, easy." She turned away, but he heard the catch in her voice, the switch to past tense. "What changed. Explain why I'm suddenly not the woman in your future."

"Ver, it's infinitely more complicated than that." *Is it?* He squeezed his eyes shut. "When I was twelve, I saw this girl, a few years older. I don't even remember who she was, now. But my head whirled, my heart pounded, my thoughts were blurred. I was sick and couldn't sleep—when I did I was plagued with dreams of her. And yet, somehow, I was happy. It was bliss and terror. My world was suddenly controlled by someone else and she didn't even know it." He scrubbed his face with his hands. "It isn't what you think. That's what I feel with Alea, but worse."

"I would have loved you." Veredy did not beg, but her voice teetered on the edge of pleading.

"You still can, Ver, when I come back, I swear."

She whirled, confusion and pain stark on her soft features. "You're leaving?"

He met her eyes. "I'm guarding her until she finds her people. It's my duty."

"Your duty? Damn, Arman, what are you, a soldier? And her people are dead, Cehn fell!"

"Most of them are, yes. But the rest are waiting for her in Le'yne."

Veredy's hand flew to her mouth as if her grief and surprise were nausea she could quell.

"I told you it was more complicated. I don't love her, Veredy, but part of me is bound to her." He risked a step closer and reached out.

She eyed his hand for a moment, then took it. She was close enough to embrace him, but made no move to do so. Her gaze inched over his features.

"What do you know of our city's founding."

"The Rakos?" Her hand grazed his cheek, her thumb pausing at his lips. "Your teeth." When he nodded, she closed her eyes. "Don't say that. Please, just once more be Arman. Only Arman. The man I was going to marry."

He cupped her cheek in one rough hand. "I can be that for you." His kiss was careful and more painful a goodbye than anything. "And someday I will be again."

"I've watched you change since she arrived. You fit here perfectly before, but it's no longer true."

"I'm not certain of that yet."

"I am." She pulled away and squeezed his hand. "Luck and love."

He wanted to stay, wanted to spend one more night with her, but the pain was too much. Wordlessly, he gathered his things and began the slow walk home. His eyes fixed on his boots as they scuffed the paving stones.

Φ

The 44th Day of Valemord, 1251

Frozen ground at the city's edge crunched under Alea's boots. Her gloved hands gripped a small pouch. The grass was brown, and frost rimmed each leaf. She knelt and shaped the dirt into a makeshift bowl. Drawing a knobby brown candle and tinderbox from her pocket, she wedged the former into the ground. Lighting the wick took a few tries with her trembling hands.

Throaty Sunamen words were both familiar and strange on her tongue. "This is not a proper burial, or how you deserve to be put to rest. It's all I can do. You were the best family I could ask for. Ihal, how I miss your guidance, and

Ahren, your kindness. Merahn, your strength and happiness were a balm to me." She drew a breath. "Ahme'reahn ira Suna, murdered on the eleventh of Lumord. Ahren ira Suna, murdered on the eleventh of Lumord. Merahn ir Hirah and her unborn child, murdered on the eleventh of Lumord." She named each of her family as the candle melted.

Hot tears caught in the grief at the edge of her mouth. "These I name are innocent and have done no wrong. May their greatness in life live in tales and their actions not be in vain. May the gods rest their souls and those of the ones they loved. With these words I let you pass into peace." She placed the tatters of the jahi she wore during the attack against the candle. The fabric lit. It still held a faint spicy scent. She stared at the candle for a silent moment. "Henceforth I am Dhoah' Lyne'alea of Le'yne. Lyne'alea ir Suna is dead."

Φ

Nails clamped in Arman's teeth and a deep frown creased his face. He crouched on the Cockerel's common room floor repairing a cracked table leg. His eyes found Kepra in the doorway.

"Do you think you could break the ice off the roof?"

He nodded. "Once I'm through."

She leaned against the bar. "Where's Miss ir Suna? I've not seen her today."

"She's having a map copied from the library and waxed. She should be back soon." His words were careful, albeit muffled. His mother was an astute woman. It took her all of a single evening to piece together Arman's pointed questions and Alea's sudden decision to leave. He had yet to explain he was going too.

"I expect I'll have to ask the Jehan boy to do such chores when you've gone." Her gaze did not waver from his.

He rocked back on his heels and took the nails from his mouth. "You knew?"

She went to him. "You never could keep a secret from me. You look heartbroken and determined and excited in turns." She brushed the shaggy locks away from his brow like she had when he was a child. "Have you told Wes and Kam? Veredy?"

He grimaced. "I'd rather swallow a hornet's nest than have those conversations again."

"They love you, Arman. We are loath to see you leave." She smiled sadly. "It would be worse, however, to see you stay here while half your heart rides away."

"I don't know what I feel, Ma."

"It's always complicated at first. Does she know you're going with her?"

"I've said as much, though I don't think she understands. There's too much in her head right now." His voice softened. "I love you, Ma."

She kissed his forehead. "And I, you. Be careful." She returned to the kitchen, but her preparations were quieter than usual. After a moment, the soft sound of weeping replaced the clinking of pots and pans. *How can I do this?* Arman turned back to the table leg and drove the last nails home.

Φ

When Alea returned late that evening, lantern light glimmered down the stairs. Arman's door was half open, but she knocked.

"Aye?"

She slipped inside. Rumpled sheets lay under a mess of breeches and shirts. "Arman, I had a question." She scanned the list in her hand. "I've found a lot of this, but there are things I'm unsure about, and I worry about what I may have forgotten." She glanced around his room. A bedroll and blanket were bound to a saddle frame. "What are you doing?"

His eyes were fierce when he looked up.

"You're really coming with me?"

He sat on the bed. "When they Laen first brought you here, I promised to help them."

Dread and quilt warred in her gut. She had to leave Vielrona, but as much as she did not want to leave alone, she already caused enough death. "This will change you."

"You already have." Arman shuddered at something in her words. "Whatever this city used to stand for, I'll uphold." He fixed her with a pointed look. "If we're to make this journey, you must trust me. Tell me things even—especially—when you are unsure."

She looked away. *The Sunamen don't confide.* "I don't know if I can."

"Learn. Our world's running, hiding, fighting." He ran his tongue over his teeth. "And all due respect, milady, you make impractical decisions."

She glared at him, indignation erasing the might of the moment. "I beg your pardon?"

"You could beg asylum, but you chose not to. I understand—and am grateful on behalf of my city—for your reasoning, but it would have been easier."

"It'd be selfish to risk bringing the Mirikin down on Vielrona for my mere presence."

His mouth quirked. "Milady, when the world falls to ruin if you die, there's no such thing as selfish." He rested his hand on the bedpost nearest her. "I do understand you, a bit. You're terrified and guilt-ridden. Even with your power, you feel helpless. You have incredible expectations to live up to."

She made a face. "You're not helping."

He waved the parchment. "Not to mention, I wish you'd let me help with this list from the start. I'm afraid we might have doubles of a few things." His face grew somber again. "You have me. You arrived a wounded girl, but you leave as the Dhoah' Laen with her Rakos guard at her side."

Ice flooded her veins and she rested her hand on his, hard and impossibly warm. "And you have me."

Φ

Arman's critical eye was better trained for composition and metals than horseflesh. He peered at the dozen animals in the market's auction stalls, but truthfully had little idea what he was looking for. One man ran his hands down the leg and looked satisfied. What was he looking for? Fleas? Weakness? *Wonderful. How can I be a guard if I can't even find suitable mounts?* Given their current terms, he doubted Kam would meet him, despite the polite note Arman sent begging for help. The Banis understood horses like a first language. He tried to get the auctioneer's eye when a shout interrupted him.

Wes wove through the crowd. He did not look any happier, but his anger seemed to have subsided. "You're not an easy man to find. We had to ask your Ma where you'd gone."

"I've been busy." Arman shifted. He half expected the large man to start a row again. "What do you need?"

"Nothing, but Kam and I have something to show you."

Arman glanced back at the horses. "Can it wait?"

Wes sighed. "Just come on. I promise it won't take long." He led Arman through the crowd to their forge. It was cleaner than before. *Hiram must be settling in.* Kam waited in the wide, covered alley. His brow furrowed as he adjusted a saddle on one of the two horses tethered there.

Arman stopped. "What's this? Where did you get these animals?"

Kam glanced over and offered a careful smile. "Wes and I went to the auctions yesterday when I got your note. He drew your half of the profits from the forge and I helped him pick these two. He saw to it their feet are set and the harness is sound." He shifted awkwardly, looking down. "We've been damned bad friends the past few days."

Wes handed Arman a small bag. "There was some left over. And that bandolier you could never part with is in the dun's saddlebag."

Arman's chest was too tight for speech. He worried their friendship would still be bitter when he left. At a loss, he rubbed the dun's neck. The chestnut nosed at the pear hidden in his pocket. *I really couldn't have better friends.* It drove everything he was leaving even further home. Arman's notion of home had been where he slept at night. Now home would be two places. "We leave at sundown. Can they stay here 'til then?"

Wes nodded. "Hiram will keep an eye on them." He fixed Arman with an unreadable stare. "What are you doing now?"

Arman helped Kam unharness the horses and see them settled. Once he returned to the inn it would be to gather his pack. He was not ready for that, not yet. "Would you mind walking with me?" He did not need to say it was the last time he saw home for a long time. They knew. "Fates, enough with the dour faces, you're not going to a funeral."

Wes glared. "Don't give us a reason to, understand? You have work at the forge already waiting."

Kam shrugged. "I'll miss you, but I get all the ladies you leave behind."

A winding road brought them through the Upper and around the market. They stopped at each of their childhood haunts. Kam told several stories, though they differed from how both Arman and Wes remembered. It was dusk when they finally arrived at the Cockerel, but Arman was ready.

Φ

The gate to the northern road was propped open and Arman sat on it while the horses grazed. Rocky hills rolled into the brown grassland beyond. Alea's soft footsteps made him turn. Bright determination in his eyes was soothing, and she offered him a smile. "Is this it?"

"This is it. I said my various good-byes." He gathered the reins of his dun and mounted up.

She eyed the saddle wryly. "I was worried you'd have me riding sidesaddle." She swung up easily and settled herself. Catching Arman's wistful gaze, she glanced back at the city. He seemed unable to look away. "I'd imagine she'll be green and blooming when you next see her."

He turned toward the road and urged his horse into a trot. "Do you think Azirik will overlook her? Do you think she'll be spared this war?"

Her eyes were sad and steady. "I think nothing will be spared."

The Rocks in the Road

CHAPTER NINE

The 23rd Day of Glasmord
Pardelan Province, Athrolan

THE FAINT ROAD GREW steadily more apparent as the two riders moved north. Their path led across the rolling grassland. "When will we enter Athrolan?" Alea tugged her cloak tighter.

Arman laughed. "We crossed the border this morning, at the river. I think we're in Pardelan province, will be until the forest. We should make the first wayhouse by dark."

Alea hummed appreciatively. "I'm looking forward to a real bed." The first weeks of Glasmord they had camped, avoiding any travelers that would have crossed their path. The road was better kept than near Vielrona. Now that they were within the bounds of a kingdom on unfriendly terms with Mirik, Arman deemed it safe to stop at a wayhouse.

"Riding it makes you understand exactly how large it is. Maps don't do it justice," Alea mused.

"Athrolan's the largest of the northern nations if memory serves. Or Ban, perhaps, but their borders are mostly wilderness or contested with the Vales, so maps disagree." Alea scanned the horizon, more out of pleasure from the deep blue and purple of dusk than vigilance. Sprawling structures of the wayhouse were tucked into a dell below. A few houses scattered about it with paddocks fanning out beyond. Even protected by the surrounding hills, the village was vulnerable in the expanse of fields.

"You were so foreign and scared when we first spoke, I forget you know as much about the world as any Vielronan." Arman laughed, "Conceited of me, really. C'mon, I think our horses could do with a run and I bet they have stew on the fire down there."

Icy air cut through Alea's cloak and burnt her lungs, but she could not help her own smile. Racing over the grassland was a freedom of which she only dreamt. Their horses' shod hooves thudded against the frozen ground as they trotted into the village. Much of the large stables were already filled, and Alea met Arman's gaze over her chestnut's back. "Winter's an odd time to travel."

His mouth was a grim line as he shouldered his pack. "It's the only time armies are slow and camped. Winter's safety during a war." Warmth hit them like a blow when they stepped into the tavern. They cut a winding path through the crowded tables to a booth in the back. Arman shoved their packs under the table. "I'm going to see about a room and exchange our coin. When I get back we'll figure out a plan."

Alea watched him cross the room. She liked the warmth, but not the noise. It was like Vielrona, but this village's business was travelers, not regular common folk in from harvesting. The rowdiest table had a dozen men dressed in gray and white. Tower emblems on their chest marked them as Athrolani soldiers, as did their pale skin and dark hair. They were well into their cups and loud.

"Finally, a chance to get out of the fields, eh?" one man called. "It's about time Her Majesty dragged us southern lads into the campaign. There's only so long a man can hunt bandits before he becomes one!"

Another man swatted the first's shoulder. "I, for one, look forward to visiting Rose Lane while we're in Ceir Pardelan!" The men roared appreciatively, several making lewd gestures.

Alea blushed and looked away, realizing they discussed a brothel.

"They've no rooms left," Arman thudded down onto the bench across from her. "We can sleep on the benches here. It'll be warm, though that patrol will be up half the night." He pushed a tin tray holding bowls of soup toward her. "Drinks are coming."

"Those soldiers spoke of a campaign. Is every kingdom already at war?" She blinked at the tray. "Arman, you forgot spoons."

"Athrolan doesn't use them, nor forks. Just fingers really. Soup you drink from the bowl."

Alea pursed her lips in confused displeasure but did as he told. The soup was hot, if thin. "I hope they at least use napkins."

Arman's gaze flicked to the men at the table. "In regard to the far less barbaric practice of war—the Athrolani fight Berrin raiding their borders. And Mirikin crossing their land in pursuit of the Laen." He shoved a small purse across the table. "Here, in case anything happens. It's Athrolani coin. Always offer half price for anything—"

"And don't show how heavy the purse is. I know, Arman." She watched him unfold the map that brought them that far. "Do you think they made it? The Laen you met, the ones from Cehn?"

Arman's expression sobered. "I hope. But I don't know." Pointing to their route, he continued, "In a day's time our road splits. The West Road leads to Ceir Pardelan, then north from there. The Mountain Road goes north through the forest and—obviously—mountains. It passes fewer cities and at a distance, but goes through Forts Hero and Stone. Marl Kess also lies along it."

"You want to know which to take?" Though her knowledge of her power appeared in one night, Alea did not know how to prepare for winters in the mountains, or the tactics that might protect them as they rode north.

"I've never been out of Vielrona for any stretch of time—I know as little about this as you. I've also been thinking we could leave a note for the guard," Arman suggested.

"What if it's intercepted? We can't expose our route. Even I'm not that naive." She put her head in her hands. "Arman, we should have brought an army and people to do these things for us."

Another patrol of soldiers entered, cold wind on their heels, interrupting Arman's startled laughter. Drunken greetings from their compatriots drowned all but the most persistent thoughts.

Alea smiled wryly. "Reminds you a bit of Kam, yes?"

Arman laid back against his packs. "In that case, they should settle soon—he could never hold his ale." His grin faltered when the newcomers' captain pulled the other officer to the back of the room.

"Good to see you, Captain. We were told the entire military was mobilizing to each provinces' city. This isn't simply raiding anymore, is it?"

"A Berrin force is headed northwest, toward Bodian. They have other soldiers with them—a few score."

"Azirik?"

"More than likely. I'd not like to face that alliance. We intercepted a scout and it seems they intend on attacking the larger forts. My guess would be Hero or Shadow."

Humor drained from Arman's face and he Arman glanced at Alea. She pulled her blanket over her, pillowing her head on the packs. "We'll figure it out tomorrow." Her voice rasped with fatigue. Running from Mirikin was one thing. Dodging two armies across a war-torn kingdom would be entirely different.

Φ

Hot breath swept over Alea's face and the hand gripping her knee was hard. Her eyes flew open to see an Athrolani soldier leaning over her.

"Hello there, pretty thing." His murmur slurred around his thick lips.

Alea scrambled farther back into the booth. Arman was nowhere to be seen and most of the other soldiers were sleeping. "Don't try it." Rage or fear shook her voice. Stale alcohol hung on his huffed breath.

"Come now, I'm a better get than that lad you ride with." He reached to stroke her face.

She grabbed his wrist, gouging her nails between the tendons. Yanking him forward, her other hand snaked up to strike his throat.

He jerked back then snatched the front of her dress. Other soldiers stirred at the noise.

Alea's eyes hardened. Ice crystalized in her veins, in her gut. She slammed her hands into the man's chest. He flew across the room, black fog exploding between them.

He crashed into his companions' table and the room fell silent. Alea's power writhed back into her hand. *Fates, what have I done?* She grabbed their packs and fled through the rear door, tugging her cloak on. "Arman!" She burst into the privy.

He whirled, one hand fastening his pants, the other reaching for a dagger. "Damn, milady, what in the—"

"No time, we've got to run!" She tossed over his pack and dashed into the stables. Horses shifted uneasily, and her fingers fumbled with the harness. It would take little effort to retrace their steps if she continued to expose them.

Arman shoved into the stall beside hers and flung the saddle onto his dun. "Shite, my cloak and the bedrolls."

Shouting rose from the inn and panic flooded her body and Alea flung herself toward the saddle. The chestnut shied, and she slipped.

"Alea, it's winter and we can't afford new ones!" Arman snapped. "Besides, running off is not the action of an innocent woman."

"Innocent? He tried—"

Arman slammed his hand into the stall door. "You know what I mean! Maybe they already know what you are. Maybe they'll understand."

What. Not who. Like I'm a monster, a creature. Alea's terror faltered. "What if this keeps happening? Last time people died, Arman."

He scrubbed his hands over his face as if they could erase the exhaustion. "You ought to wear a sign about your neck that says 'Do Not Touch Me.' If not for your own safety, for others."

Alea's laugh was closer to a sob. "I don't know what to do. I planned to ask them for help, but goodness, I can't now."

"You're the Dhoah' Laen. You can do whatever you wish, and they will obey. Please, just think about this."

"You aren't the one who had a drunk man grabbing you," She reminded. She stared at her hands gripping her horse's mane, unable to decide between fear or anger. The chill in her veins suggested anger might win. "What if my power is black because it's tainted?"

"I don't know how it works, Alea, I just know something in you is dangerous, powerful, and out there, there's an entire world that needs you. I know you think this is your fight alone—"

"It is." *It is. Mine alone. No matter who protects me, who fights for me, or against me. This is between me and the gods.* Icy power or cold fear shuddered down her spine. Lately, they felt the same.

Arman sighed in exasperation at her mulish tone. "What did I say about impractical decisions?" He slipped from the stall to lean on the door of hers. "Those soldiers already fight your war. Berrin attack their borders looking for you. Athrolan's queen refused to ally with Mirik. Why not see if she'd consider you? Whatever family you have left expects you in Le'yne, but you'll never make it across Athrolan without help."

She whirled on him. "My family—my true family—is dead, drying on the sand!" Her thoughts broke on that, and her heart cracked open enough to let sense in. Her pulse pounded in her throat. "I don't want people to die for me. Again. If I declare myself I can't go back."

His gaze softened. "You already can't, milady." Regret in his words made her wonder if he felt the same.

"We could march into Fort Hero and declare ourselves then. Would they turn us away?"

Arman shrugged. "I can't say. You might send a letter—there are couriers here."

"That's as risky as leaving a letter for An'thoriend." She put a hand over her eyes. "This is too much, too soon. I thought I'd have months to decide what to do." She glanced at the stable door. Running was already exhausting. *For someone with the power of Creation and Destruction, I feel weak an awful lot.* She unbuckled her saddle and slid it from her confused mount's back. "There's an officer in there with whom I need to speak."

The inn's front door groaned at her entry. Overturned tables were righted, the broken pieces piled out of the way. Her attacker hunched in a chair with another soldier who must have been a medic. Two officers sat at the booth she and Arman used. She paused at the last step, fixing them with her eyes. She hoped it had the desired effect. "Might I have a moment of your time, officers?"

The captain scrambled to his feet, one hand resting on his sword. The older officer rose slower, without threat. "I thought you'd be leagues away by now."

"I only defended myself." As stern as Cehn was about assault, Alea knew many northern cities had other perspectives. "Your man is alive. Others have not been so lucky. I hope you understand I was not acting against Athrolan, merely one of her men."

The officers eyed her with a mixture of fear and confusion. The captain finally nodded. "I know."

The other man's expression was grim. "Deal with your corporal, Captain Uralon. Make it known a soldier represents the nation. As such, attacking a stranger—especially off duty—on the road will not be tolerated. I'll speak to the lady alone."

Uralon pointed to Alea's attacker and to the door to a back room. Venom and fear soured his glare at Alea as he obeyed. She hoped he could not see her skin crawl.

"Care to sit?"

Alea glanced back to the older officer and she slipped onto the bench across from him. Arman joined them a moment later.

"Sir Elian of Ceir Felden. I'm a gallant in Athrolan's army." Brown Athrolani eyes took them in for a moment before the man offered his hand.

Alea took it. Slipping back into polite court finesse was easier than she imagined after months of rough city life. "I'm Lyne'alea and this is my companion and guard Aud'narman Wardyn." Forcing her hands into stillness, she sat back. "I'm sorry we meet under these circumstances."

"That was quite the trick." Elian met her gaze. "There are tales out of the south about a woman the Mirikin hunt." Elian paused, as if expecting Alea to affirm his suspicions. "They say she is Laen, but different—"

"Stronger." She let black power marble her hand on the tabletop. The undertone to her words and the display erased contemplation from the gallant's face. *Good.* Every moment she kept them off balance was another moment she held sway.

"I heard you leveled eight men in Vielrona. Why didn't you do the same to Uralon's corporal?"

Alea glanced sidelong at Arman. *There are eight now?* "It wasn't necessary." Admitting she had poor control would only hurt them.

"You ride north to Le'yne?"

"First to your capital, where I will ask your queen formally for an alliance." She ignored Arman's glance at the admission. "You already fight my war. Le'yne will come, but this battle is here, so I'll stay." As she spoke she realized it was true.

"I'd offer to escort you to the city, but our route takes you directly past Mirikin camps. Unless you wish to join us, regardless."

"Thank you for the offer, sir, but milady and I do not seem a target." Arman leaned forward. "A patrol of soldiers alone does, and if they escort two riders, even more so."

The gallant nodded in agreement. "I could carry a message. We'll make Ceir Athrolan in two weeks—sooner than you will, and can have Her Majesty's response waiting for you at the last wayhouse before Fort Hero, in Cima."

Alea smiled. "That would be appreciated. When do you leave?"

He glanced outside. "As soon as your letter is written. It's almost dawn. May I take my leave?" When Alea nodded graciously, he stood, barking to one of his men to rouse those of his patrol that still slept. He bowed to them both. "I'll return when we're set to ride."

The calm façade slipped from Alea's face as she turned back to Arman. "I thought he was going to kill me for harming that man."

"I wondered too. I suppose a reprimand is as much justice as you can expect." He handed Alea the leather envelope of his writing tools. "What made you change your mind?"

"Impractical decisions." She grinned. "Besides, I was just saying how we should have brought an army. Borrowing Athrolan's will have to do." She turned to the paper. Inspiration drained from her body. How could she speak to a queen? How could she ask for help when she offered power she did not understand and a city boy in return? "Arman, how can I do this?"

Arman snorted. "Honesty and open words rarely fail. Besides, you're her equal, if nothing else." Ignoring her blanched face, he eased from the booth. "I'll collect the rest of our things."

The thought of being equal to a queen was nauseating. *I want to run. I want to disappear into anonymity in Cehn, the way I always thought I would.* She had a mother. And a brother. *Who wants me dead.* It was only when Arman returned that she began to write. The letter was short and as soon as the ink had dried she sealed it with a plain stamp and tucked it into the oilcloth envelope Elian had left for her.

The gallant returned a few moments later, armored and ready for the road. He tucked the envelope deep into his jerkin. "Ride fast and sleep lightly. Love and luck be with you."

"Safe journey home. Thank you for your help."

He grinned as he rose from a bow. "Thank you for the hope."

The shape of his men waned through the window as they rode out, racing the dawn. She took Arman's hand across the table. "And so, it all begins."

Φ

An'thor jerked his cowl over his horns with a wince. It was the third time he crossed paths with an Athrolani army in the last two weeks. He could not afford to be identified by any army, let alone an Athrolani one. Years of playing kings against one another, of gambling on the larger picture rather than aligning with a single nation, had its cost.

"Make way!" The captain at the fore of the patrol shouted, driving An'thor and his distinctive gray charger from the packed dirt and into a ditch.

An'thor tucked his head down, raising a hand in vague greeting. They rumbled past, and the warrior glanced up to count their numbers. *Even the patrols are smaller than usual. Too few spread too thin.*

One man, a pale fellow who looked still drunk from the evening before met An'thor's gaze. His eyes widened. "Captain, sir, it's the Wanderer—"

"Enough, Ronier! Ride!"

An'thor forced himself not to wink at the startled man and nudged Theriim back onto the road when they rounded the bend. After another few minutes, Marl Kess rose before him in the early morning light, unlit windows glimmering pink with the reflected dawn. His eyes traced the handful of early travelers on the Mountain Road, wondering briefly why they chose such a road in winter. A bitter wind kicked up, and he shrugged into his cowl again.

Even the high walls of the inn's courtyard did little to shelter him, and by the time he slipped into the quiet common room, his cheeks were wind-raw.

"Sup or a room?" The innkeep wiped the echoes of sleep from his eyes and leaned on the bar.

"Both, please. I'll take some tea." An'thor slumped onto the bar stool.

"Sharp?" He held a bottle of whiskey.

An'thor glanced at the windows. Vielrona would keep, and he had time enough before returning to the road. "Aye."

"Name? For the room."

An'thor faltered. Most of his aliases were known, especially in a country whose queen asked him politely to never darken her horizon again. "Ian. Ian Domar," he finally ground out. Out of distraction as much as curiosity, he turned to survey the common area. Pieces of a broken table stood propped against the wall by the rear door to the alley, and fresh scrapes marred the ancient floorboards.

"Had a tussle in here past few nights?"

"You could say that. War makes people more finicky than a spring colt. Some soldier attacked a woman, his officer made them leave before the sun rose." He shook his head. "Time was they'd care who wore the tower of Athrolan on his breast."

An'thor sighed. He did not remember such a time. Humans were always monstrous in one way or another. "I hope she's well."

"She did worse than he—broke that table tossing him across the room. Think she was gods-touched or something with the smoke in her hands." He glowered and disappeared into the kitchen.

An'thor surged to his exhausted feet and crossed the room to examine the table. New wood rotted around fresh breaks, spongey as if left in the rain a season. *Laen.* Except, every Laen he knew of was already farther north. Or dead.

When the innkeeper emerged, An'thor's tea was drained and he leaned over the bar. "Before you set about my room, master, tell me something—the smoke, in her hands, was it silver?" Theriim was too weary to press on now, but An'thor already slavered for the road.

"She's no Laen, if that's what you were thinking." The man shrugged. "We were asleep, me wife overheard the soldiers this morning, though, as she tidied up. Said it was black. Figured it must be some god-curse."

An'thor strode to the window, gaze following the memory of the travelers on their way to the Orn de Galen. "Must be," he echoed.

Φ

The 38th Day of Glasmord, 1251
The City of Ceir Athrolan

Rain clung to the white stone of the tiered walls, washing streets clean as it ran down to the harbor. Queen Tzatia watched the rivulets running down the glass of her window. Clear days afforded her a view of the gardens on the east of the city and the ocean beyond the cliffs to the north. A patrol arrived a few minutes before, erasing the day's peace. Missives, rather than poetry, stacked the broad writing desk before her. A lavender kokoshnik pulled back lengths of gray hair. She glanced over at her head retainer. "One of my gallants will arrive in a few minutes, Master Valadai. I would like to receive him with tea." Her quiet voice cut the silence and her ladies in waiting paused in their stitches.

She moved to the window, one long hand brushing the window's stone frame. As much as she called it war, it did not feel like it, not yet. She wondered when the exhaustion and frustration would come. Already it shadowed her soldier's faces.

Valadai stuck his head back in, "Your Majesty, Sir Elian is here already."

Tzatia waved a thin hand. "Go ahead."

Mud and rainwater that smelled of horse followed the gallant in, despite the cloak folded neatly over one arm. He had cleaned his face and slicked back his hair, but that was all. Tzatia's heart sank. *Whatever this news is, it's too important to wait.* Elian took a knee, a fist over his chest. "I pray Your Majesty is well."

She inclined her head. "I hope the same for you. What news do you have from the south?"

"I bring two messages. I wrote to you about the Berrin man we caught. We saw the army he spoke of within the next few days. They move toward Bodian and plan to take our larger forts."

Tzatia resisted the urge to sigh and turned back to her steward. "Master Valadai, send for General Aneral and Commander Dorcal. It's urgent." He let he maid in as he left. The queen waited until the tea was laid out and Sir Elian sat with a cup before nodding for him to continue. "The other news?"

He drew a travel-stained leather envelope from his jerkin but did not hand it over. His gaze turned to the ladies in waiting. "Perhaps this should be delivered privately, Your Majesty?"

Tzatia's eyes narrowed. It was unlike Elian to presume, and she never saw his hands shake around his tea the way they did now. "Ladies, you're dismissed. Countess Fiena, you may stay." When all but her Lady of Honor had gone, she fixed her gallant with a stern look. "Care to tell me why you require such privacy?"

"We met her at a wayhouse in Marl Kess," Elian explained, finally offering the envelope.

"Met whom, Sir Elian? Goodness, could you be more cryptic?" Handwriting she did not recognize addressed the plain paper. Simple beige candle wax and a blank circle snapped easily under her long fingers. She tilted the paper toward the gray light from the window.

Your Majesty, Lady Queen Tzatia of Ceir Athrolan,

I met your gallant on the road north and he was kind enough to deliver this letter to you. I hope it finds you well.

My name is Dhoah' Lyne'alea of Le'yne and it has come to my attention that we share a common enemy: the Berrin and Azirik. It would benefit us both if an alliance was formed between your great nation and myself. I carry a powerful artifact north with me and an ever-greater legacy in my blood."

Tzatia looked up at Elian, her hazel eyes wide. Echoes of thunder bloomed in her chest. "Goodness."

Elian laughed softly at his queen's manners. "My reaction was a bit stronger."

"You are certain she is what she claims?" She wanted peace as much as the next nation, but if built on falsehood, it would not last long.

Elian's skin paled further. "I've never seen anything like it before. One of Captain Uralon's men, drunk, tried to assault her at the wayhouse—he's being disciplined—and when words and blows did not dissuade him, she flung him across the room with black fog. Black, Your Majesty, not silver. I met with her and her guard. He called himself Wardyn and was not right, either."

The queen frowned. *Not right?* War brought legends and monsters scuttling out like wood roaches after a storm. It was only a matter of time before even An'thoriend appeared from hiding. "What do you mean?"

The gallant shrugged. "You know when you face down an animal?" He faltered, then, "Perhaps not, but he made my hair stand on end. It wasn't an evil feeling though."

Tzatia turned back to the letter.

Myself and my guard, the Rakos Aud'narman Wardyn, hope to make your city in five weeks, at which time we could discuss this further, if you indeed accept our alliance. I understand the risk of formally linking your kingdom with my cause, and I would hold no resentment if you choose to decline.

I also know, however, that together this war would not be impossible.
Fates be with you
Lyne'alea

Outside the rain sluiced down the glass, obscuring her view. Elian was content to let silence fall until the general and commander's arrival. When the gallant rose to go, she held up a hand. "Stay, Sir Elian. I have a feeling our commander will need more evidence than this." She waved the letter wryly as her two highest officers entered.

General Nei'pheras Aneral rose from her bow first and waved for Elian to remain seated. "You look exhausted." Her brown eyes flicked to the queen.

Between the plain uniform and the light orange braid wrapped around her head, it was clear she came from the sparring halls.

Tzatia gestured for them to sit. As much as she ruled Athrolan, like any monarch she relied on the sharp minds and dedication of her officers and consulates. *Fates help us if Dorcal is in one of his moods.*

The commander of Athrolan's navy was as tall and broad as Eras was short and wiry. He sank onto the couch, eyeing Elian's appearance with his characteristic sour frown. "Your Majesty, you have news?"

"News, yes, but take some tea," Tzatia answered. "We're not at war. Not yet, at least."

The two sat, the commander's blocky worn hands dwarfing the teapot as he poured.

Perhaps it was nerves, perhaps it was hope, but Tzatia's fingers trembled as she rested the letter in her lap. "Sir Elian brought word from the road and a letter. I trust he can debrief you on the Mirikin and Berrin movement at a later date. But you both must read this." She handed the paper to the general.

A nose like a ship's prow led Eras's blade-sharp ashen face. Now her androgynous features settled into neutral curiosity.

Despite noble backlash when Tzatia promoted the sharp-tongued colonel to general twenty years before, the soldiers obeyed Eras with faith and respect. Like many half-blooded, she was a study in opposites. Her Athrolani heart may have been her human father's, but her calculating mind was her asai mother's. Cousins to the horned Ageless, the asai's gray skin and analytical ways caused skepticism in the nationalistic Athrolani elite.

Eras's pale gaze settled on her hands after she handed the letter to Raven.

The massive, ruddy man took a long slow sip of tea once he finished reading. "Permission to speak my mind, Majesty?"

"Granted," she responded dryly. Frank speech and bull-headed patriotism made the man infamous, but not likable.

"Ignoring the fact that I don't believe her claim in the slightest—I'm well aware what she would gain if she joined us—we have the second-largest army on the continent. What, exactly, do we receive in return?"

The queen peered into the dark tea swirling in the bottom of her delicate lavender cup. Greater good and the balance of the world mattered more to Raven than the greater good or the balance of the world. "She's incredibly powerful. The title of Dhoah' Laen could rally both human allies and otherwise. Her Rakos guard alone is a testament to that."

"This Wardyn fellow?"

The queen turned to the gallant. "Sir Elian, care to explain?"

"At first they seemed human—looked human enough. He's colored like a Vielronan. She could pass for Athrolani if you didn't look too hard." He faltered. Raven was intimidating, even if his opinions were not shared. "But they aren't.

Human that is. Meeting her eyes was like watching a storm approach, one you know you can't ride through. And her guard was barely-checked ferality."

"A Rakos, Commander," Eras interrupted. "The Earth Shakers. He alone has great abilities, or could. Your Majesty, what do you think? What military news is there?"

Elian shook his head. "We've seen evidence of Azirik's army—he cuts north now, while another force moves northwest. Scouts would know more. Skirmishes wear more on our spirits and strength than our numbers."

Eras leaned forward. "We're already mobilizing several companies to the cities. The skirmishes were little threat, but an army of four thousand? Any word on Mirik's numbers beyond this force?" The Military aspects of her brain clearly whirred into motion.

Elian shook his head. "Nothing. There are between fifty and two hundred Mirikin accompanying each group of Berrin, but I have yet to see anything that indicates Azirik himself."

"Lord King Azirik, Sir Elian," the queen reminded gently. "As disturbed as he may be, he is still a king."

"Forgive me, Your Majesty." He looked to the Commander. "There has also been no word on the location of the Berrin navy or their numbers."

Eras sighed. "It makes me uneasy. Our intelligence from the island itself is all but silent. Under King Brenteric their army neared fifty thousand. Whether it has grown or shrunk, I can't say. Your Majesty, I wish to increase patrols surrounding the border forts and vulnerable holdings." She leaned forward, "I was planning to visit Fort Stone to see about joining with some of the Bordermen warriors. Should I stay?"

"Increase where you see fit, general. Sir Elian—where did Dhoah' Lyne'alea plan to go from the wayhouse?" Tzatia asked.

"She's marching north as well, and I pray she doesn't cross paths with King Azirik. I told her we could have a response waiting for her at Cima."

The queen glanced out the window, wavy with downpour. She had not offered asylum to the Laen fleeing through her kingdom, but neither had they asked. *And here she is, rising from the shadowed south.* "The Lady Lyne'alea will be at Fort Hero within two weeks. Commander Dorcal, I would like you to escort her north. General, join the Commander when they pass Fort Stone on their way here."

"We protect her?" The lines on the Commander's face deepened. "We don't even know her abilities."

"She seems to think she and her guard are worth my entire force," Tzatia drew a breath. "The Dhoah' Laen offers us an alliance. The gods have their army. Perhaps it's time we give her ours."

CHAPTER TEN

The 47th Day of Glasmord, 1251
The Province of Rodda, Athrolan

WHISTLES SOUNDED OFF AS An'thor thundered into the Mirikin camp. Campfires were unshielded, and the tents were plain beige rather than camouflaged green. *Azirik is growing brazen.* His chest heaved in the cold and his cheeks flushed purple.

"Wanderer!" Azirik's rasp arched across the camp. He leaned on his larger tent, as if the travel-stained canvas was the only thing keeping his body upright.

An'thor handed his reins to a waiting page and bowed to the haggard man. "Sire, forgive my lateness."

"There's a lot more than that to forgive. You can rest and eat later. Get your ass in here." The king lurched into his tent.

An'thor refrained from rolling his eyes. He knew Azirik and his temper for the entirety of the man's forty-five years. It never scared him, and certainly did not now. Shouldering his pack, he crossed the camp and ducked under the tent flap.

Azirik paced the width of his tent, gray-brown hair like ruffled feathers. "Explain to me why Lieutenant Barrackborn reported you were among the Laen's guards a month ago."

"Lieutenant? That's a steep promotion. Being the king's bastard is lucrative—"

"Shut it."

"So, he still doesn't know?" An'thor shook his head. Azirik's affection for his son was obvious to anyone who stepped back from the picture. That he did not kill Brentemir upon learning Elle was Laen was evidence enough.

"Answer me," Azirik growled. "And if you claim Barrackborn's mistaken I'll execute you on the spot. Your face is as recognizable as a broken nose, even without the horns."

An'thor sighed. *Azirik knows this dance, though not as well as I do.* If the king ever intended on killing him, he would never have entered camp. "Sire, I brought you inside information for years. Same with your father before you. Surely you know what it takes to get that information."

Azirik's erratic strides resumed. The boyhood potential and singular drive were twisted into genocide and mania. It burnt the small part of An'thor that once cared about Azirik. "You agree the girl was what we thought?"

An'thor's heart clenched at the memory. Dhoah' Laen or not, a girl died in his hands. "I never saw her power myself, but they protected her above their own safety, and she was young. I am confident your lieutenant's instincts were not wrong." He stressed the new rank.

Azirik scowled and sank into the folding chair by his camp desk. "I didn't think it'd come to this."

An'thor's snowy brows rose. Paranoia and vitriol he expected. Confessions were new. "What's that, sire?"

"I thought they'd surrender. I thought they'd give over the rule of the world to the gods. Cycles and all that." His ice-blue gaze lingered on a heavy chest on his desk.

An'thor would bet his last breath it contained the Gods' Crown. "What about the bigger picture, Azirik? It is worth destroying the world? Legends say that's what'll come of Moera's death."

"Moera." Azirik paused on the name. "Moera, Liane, Nema. Elle." His gaze returned to An'thor's at the last. "Such unassuming names for women who wield Destruction. Myths and legends are often penned by the people they're about—present company included. If I didn't want my people eradicated, I'd probably threaten apocalypse too. Besides, their world might end, but a new one always comes."

An'thor winced. Though he had not always supported the Laen, fates knew he understood how hopeless humanity was on its own. "I think you ought to examine the truth behind those legends."

Azirik's eyes lingered on An'thor for a moment, then another, before he breached the silence. "What's your game, Domariigo? You don't always play by my rules, or Athrolan's, or the gods', or the Laen's. But I've still not figured out your strategy. You give me fair enough information that I know you're not wholly against us, but neither do you seem to be loyal."

An'thor heaved a sigh. "Not everything's a game, Your Majesty. Not everything's a warren of traps and double-crossing." *Except, this time, it is.* He let the conversation lapse again. He was tired. Tired of chasing titanic creatures across desolate land. Tired of lying so much he lost track of what he truly felt. *Humanity needs a guide, and the gods aren't it.* "Is that all, sire?"

"For now. Where will you go from here?"

"I've a citadel to explore. In the meantime, I hear Athrolani armies are moving north. You'd best steer clear."

Azirik hummed, staring at the chest again. "Athrolani armies don't concern me. Once we're clear of Rodda I'll have to decide whether to head straight north or move west. Eventually, we'll meet the Vales."

An'thor's gut sank. *North? And the Vales?* It was not enough to ally with the largest navy of the known world, apparently. His mind lingered on the two figures riding through the wilderness, alone and unprotected. "I heard Her Majesty Tzatia bolsters Fort Shadow. Striking there would be a greater blow." An'thor did not know the soldiers. It made it easier to damn them, to let them die for a greater good they probably did not care about. "Was there anything else?"

Azirik shook his head and waved at the tent flap. "See me before you leave, but otherwise you're free to rest up."

An'thor left without answering, preferring not to disturb the troubled king's thoughts. *Fates know what would be churned up from the muck of that man's mind.* He turned left toward the stable tent to grab his bedroll only to collide with a lanky soldier.

"Toar, sorry Domariigo, sir." Bren muttered, running a distracted hand through his already disarrayed hair. "Didn't see you there."

An'thor waved the apology away but watched the Lieutenant wander toward the mess. Darkness hung around the man's gray eyes, and in the dim light An'thor picked out the strong nose shared by the young woman in Vielrona. *You have Laen blood, boy.*

The furrowed brow, however, was new on the soldier's usually jovial face. *Killing titans of creation doesn't sit well with you, eh?* Shrill whistles cut short further musings, followed by the bark of new orders to prepare for a march to the north-west.

An'thor winced. The lives of the several hundred men stationed at Fort Shadow may be forfeit, but the Dhoah' Laen's path north was clear.

Φ

The 48th Day of Glasmord, 1251
The Province of Rodda, Athrolan

"The stew's good?" Arman slid into the seat next to Alea and tossed a heavy key across the table. He pulled his bowl closer to his growling stomach. Game proved scarce and lean during their month on the road.

Alea lifted a shoulder. "After the past weeks, I think muck-water would taste good."

Arman choked on his mouthful, laughter sharp. "My manners are influencing you, milady." He caught her scowl at the honorific. Though it seemingly irked her, she had yet to explain why. *Besides, people will be bowing and scraping over her soon enough. I'll be damned if I don't respect the Dhoah' Laen.*

"The inn's busy," she noted, as much fatigue in her voice as curiosity.

"Barkeep said the army's fully mobilized. Most folk are running north, those that can. Soldiers like to get into town when they can to have food and women—prices of the rooms show that well enough. I'd not have paid half the cost a few weeks ago."

"We could have camped again." Hesitancy hung on her voice.

Arman grimaced. "If I have to watch you slice mold from that hunk of cheese one more time I might go home, Rakos blood or not."

Alea rolled her eyes and flicked a stray piece of onion at him. "I'm too polite to tell you what I'd be happy never seeing again." She glanced out the window. "The army moves to the cities?"

Before Arman could speculate, the barkeep paused at their table, tray balanced on his wide shoulders. Pulling a thick envelope from his belt he asked, "Yer name was Wardyn? Aud'narman?"

Arman flushed and nodded. "Arman, yes." His unwieldy given name was not a boon during childhood.

"Came this morning," the innkeeper explained, handing over the letter.

Arman thanked him but waited until they were alone to look at the envelope's face. Gobs of rich, blue wax sealed the heavy, expensive parchment. Flowering vines wrapped Athrolan's tower emblem. Excitement lit in his veins. *The Queen.* "I think this is for you."

"Are you finished?" Alea waved at the food.

Arman drained his bowl and gathered his pack before following her up to the room on the third floor. It was cramped, with two beds against the far wall and a single, narrow window. Hooks by the door held his cloak and the chest across the room hid most of his cluttered traveling gear.

Alea sank onto the nearest bed, dumping her pack at her feet before patting the coverlet beside her. "Read it with me?"

He perched next to her, heart thunder in his ears.

> *Dhoah Lyne'alea,*
>
> *It was with great interest we received your letter and we are deeply honored with your hope to ally yourself with Athrolan. Sir Elian informed us of your route. Our naval commander, Sir Raven Dorcal, awaits you at Fort Hero to escort you to Ceir Athrolan.*
>
> *It is our sincerest wish that together we can end the bloodshed threatening both our borders and your people. In the spirit of such, Athrolan invites you to a formal audience with Her Majesty the Queen.*
>
> *This past week we declared war against the lake nation of Berr and will do the same against, Mirik upon the swearing of our alliance to you and Rakos Wardyn.*
>
> *Until we meet,*
>
> *Her Majesty Queen Tzatia of Athrolan and the House of Xain*

Alea's shoulders sagged and the letter fell from her fingers. Arman picked it up, finishing the final paragraph. "What is it? She said yes."

"I know." Alea's voice was quiet.

"You don't seem happy." The elation, the relief, he expected was not there either. Instead something bright and furious uncurled in his gut. *Rakos Wardyn.*

"I am. I'm proud. I'm relieved." She drew a breath. "At least, I know I'm supposed to feel those things."

"But you don't?" He turned to look at her fully.

Her eyes were dark and unreadable. "It doesn't seem real. Whatever part of me realizes it is real, feels guilty. I caused war across the entire continent."

For years Arman saw soldiers on the horizon, smelled smoke too strong to be simple campfires. *It did get worse since she arrived, though.* "It's not exactly your fault," he equivocated.

Alea's pale face curled into a frown.

"War, I mean. It's Azirik's fault, it's the fault of the men who follow him. It's even the fault of the gods, milady, but it's not yours." The bright fire in him flashed. "You'll save the world from chaos. You just haven't yet."

Alea made a face. "I always liked the tales of people who chose their fate. It's not very heroic to make do with what you've got."

Arman shrugged. "None of us choose our fates, not at first. Out of sheer bad luck, you were born with this power. Now you've got to deal with it. What you do, now that you know, is what will define you. That's why I always liked the stories of An'thoriend, or The Talent and Tempest."

Alea smiled weakly. "We only heard those ones rarely." She glanced at the door. "Mind if I get ready for bed?"

He slipped downstairs and through the door to the stables. Warm scents of horse and hay were a balm to his homesick heart. The two halves of him were exhausting to maintain, but quiet moments away from Alea were enough to remind him who, exactly, Arman was. Their horses were tucked into two stalls at the end of the stable beside a tall gray and a hulking, feathered draft.

Though they were already curried, he found a brush and ran it slowly over his dun's flanks, humming to himself. It was well past dusk. *Wes is getting ready for a night with Kam, who's waiting impatiently, chattering by the door. Veredy would be finishing her tasks at her kitchen table with a mug of sharp tea.* The fire in his chest sputtered and dimmed. Whatever he felt for Alea, it was not the comfort he shared with Veredy.

"What do you say, Hartward?" He asked his horse. "Think we can make it home in time for midnight? Maybe I can channel fire and wind and fly us there, like the Rakos before me."

The animal's coat gleamed gold under the shielded lantern light, but he did not answer.

Hot tears pricked his eyes at the thought of clattering across Vielrona's cobblestones on a fiery steed. Even in his heroic, childish daydreams, he did not recognize himself.

"I'm impressed."

He whirled. A pale face loomed from the darkness of the stall behind him, black eyes glittering. Even with the cloak's hood raised, chipped, ivory horns caught the light.

"Easy there. You can put down that hand." The warrior's dark eyes lingered on Arman's mouth.

Arman stepped back, realizing his fist had coiled at his ribs, ready to strike. Copper tang filled his mouth. "You startled me, is all."

"I'm not one for manners, usually."

That's abundantly clear. Arman dropped the curry comb into its basket and leaned on the stall wall. "So, you've finally found us. I wondered if you'd hear the news."

"I did, but not from town gossips. Those are new." He pointed to Arman's teeth.

Arman shook his head. "I guess the Rakos weren't as dead as folk thought. Milady woke whatever was in my blood."

An'thor's laugh was metal on stone in the quiet stable. "You're as much a Rakos as a Banis hare, boy. You're a boy in a man's boots! If the Rakos lived, they'd have woken long before now."

Arman's pride stung, but enough of him agreed to keep from snarling at the Laen's former guard. "Perhaps we didn't have a good reason before now. Mock me all you like, but I've gotten her this far."

The pale man jerked his horned head at the crowded inn looming above them. "I heard about the mess in Marl Kess. She knows what she is?"

Arman nodded. "We didn't know, when you came through Vielrona. I suppose they thought the power was that girl's."

An'thor looked down. "She's dead. And the rest of them, too."

Arman's gut twisted, and he pressed his brow on the stable's worn, splintered wood. "I'm sorry."

"So am I."

"You came here to protect us, then?" Arman asked. As much as he did not like the Ageless warrior, it would be stupid to refuse the help. "We're meeting Athrolan's commander in Fort Hero before riding on to the capital."

An'thor grimaced. "Raven and I never got along. Racist bastard." He regarded Arman again, foul expression turning thoughtful. "There are a few roads ahead of me, but none lead to Ceir Athrolan. Not yet, at least. I'm exiled there, and besides—I think your girl has enough protection."

"It's a long way to Ceir Athrolan," Arman reminded. "What's your name, should we need to find you again?"

"An'thoriend Domariigo. Ian Domar if I'm in Athrolan."

Arman's heart skipped, and he peered closer at the haggard, tattooed face under the cowl. *Exiled from Athrolan.* The pieces clicked into place. "Either your parents had a cruel sense of humor, or you're as much a legend as Alea."

"Oh, my father was cruel, alright, but not much for humor. I'm afraid the legends that name bears are all my doing."

Arman expected awe, overwhelming power. Instead, standing before his childhood hero, he mostly felt disappointment. "You're not what I expected."

"Well, no, the stories wouldn't be very good if they were entirely accurate. Besides, age catches up with everyone. Just took a bit longer for me. You'll come to understand that, being forever bound to the Laen."

Itching crawled up his skin and the ache in his jaw deepened. *Forever is a long time.* Memories of home, of Veredy, flashed through his mind, juxtaposed with Alea's eyes as she healed him in the gutter. It was as if his very soul burned.

An'thor turned, hoisting a saddle onto his gray charger's back. "I'll see you again, sooner than you'd like, I imagine. I've got armies to re-route and lieutenants to convert."

Arman rolled his eyes at the purposefully cryptic farewell. "You don't want to see her?"

"You'll convey my message, I'm sure." He glanced back and handed Arman a folded parchment. "Oh, speaking of messages—her mother asked me to give her this."

Arman stared at the letter, raising a vague wave at the warrior as he led his horse into the courtyard. *Her mother.* He took the stairs to their room two at a time.

Alea curled under the covers, eyes closed. The candle rested at his bedside. Shucking off his boots and jerkin, he settled on his bed, letter in hand. Faint snoring drifted from the other bed. *Let her sleep.* There would be time enough to read another, arguably more important letter. Before crawling under his covers, he tucked the letter into his pack beside the Crown. He pinched the candlewick. "Good dreams, Alea."

Φ

The 1st Day of Vurgmord, 1251
The Borderway Forest of Athrolan

The Mirikin army tents smelled of refuse and sweat. The few thousand men sprawled over cots and across battered camp tables. Most gambled, some tended weapons. Bren sat in the glow of an oil lamp, reading. His large feet splayed across his messy bed, slush from his heels staining the sheets. A scratched name designated the boots as his, though few other soldiers had feet his size. Calloused fingers held the thin book gently. One broad hand ran through his short auburn hair when he paused at a difficult word.

Laughter drew his attention to the closest table and, for a few minutes, he watched the card game, absently. Mirth died, however, when three figures entered the barrack tent, shaking the night's mist from their shoulders and hair.

Mania in King Azirik's eyes had an exhausted shadow, now. Mirik's crown glinted in the yellow light. He waved for his soldiers to sit again and began without preamble. "We ride out tomorrow. Western patrols report the Vales joined us in the name of their patron god Ren-et. Therefore, I'm splitting our numbers. Five regiments will travel west—Second and Fifth attacking Ceir Felden, not far from here, the Third surrounding Fort Floodbane.

"The First and Fourth will cut north through the Hartland to meet the Vales in the west. Each Regiment will be augmented with Berrin and Vale forces. Berrin will join our remaining four Regiments and move north along the mountains. For now, I will travel with the lattermost. Questions?" He glanced about. When no one spoke, he waved a dismissive hand. "About your will."

Reading held no interest for Bren now. Vague emptiness drifted in his chest. No one asked if he wanted company as he left the tents. Their camp perched on a ridge overlooking the Athrolani city of Ceir Bodian. Crouching on the rocks, he stared at the lights below. *Did Mirik ever look so lively?* He barely remembered Mirik's streets, though he must have lived there before moving into the barracks. The city proper was empty of city-folk for years. Families moved across the island or to the mainland, pushed away by war.

He sat back on his heels, enjoying the mist on his face. Fatigue dragged at his spirit. His forty-three men would ride north with the Seventh Regiment and he was happy for the respite from battle.

In the last few years, Bren saw more of the world than he ever thought possible. Uncertainty clouded the excitement since the Dhoah' Laen's death. Hate of the Laen was his mother's milk. As much as he convinced himself it was the letdown after reaching a long-sought goal, his mind returned continuously to the memory of her clouded eyes and the cold, bloody fingers in his kerchief.

Footsteps crunched across the gravel below him.

His hand dropped to his hunting knife. "Who goes?"

Azirik's Ageless informant appeared a moment later, leading his horse up the rocky ridge. He let his mount drop his head to nose a frosted tuft of grass. "Just me. You're out here in the cold?"

Bren loosened his grip on his knife's hilt. "Tents smell of rot and piss." He shifted, guilt blooming again. "I heard Azirik questioned you. I'm sorry I mistrusted your loyalty. I didn't know what to think, seeing you run with them."

The man shrugged, but his gaze was as calculating as his stance was casual. "You've good eyes. War's complicated, and good information is never easy to come by." Room for another?"

Bren shuffled over, bequeathing his already-dried spot of stone to the informant. Bren offered him a flask. "It's wraith," he apologized.

"I like wraith. Drank it a lot more when I was younger. Didn't like who it made me, though." He took a small pull then handed it back with a wince. "Still tastes as good."

Bren chuckled and took a deep sip. Staring at his boots, he finally asked, "Were you there when that girl died?"

An'thor's face twisted in gnarled grief. "Her name was Moera. She died in my hands and I thought the world would end right there."

Bren's eyes narrowed. Pain echoed in the man's features, reminding Bren of his own uncertainty. "Which side are you on?"

An'thor's face cracked into a grin. "You're a soldier. You should know there's no such thing as sides. I fight for peace. Azirik knows that means I'm sometimes his ally. Other times not."

Bren took a gamble. "How did you deal with it? Her—Moera—dying? I know the world didn't end, so that part was a myth, but how could you stomach it?"

An'thor shifted, staring at him in silence for a moment before returning his gaze to the city below. "I went to visit your mother. We were friends before she fled your father."

Bren's guarded curiosity exploded into interest and distrust. "My father died before I was born. She was escaping war, not him. It's why I was raised a soldier."

"A mother doesn't abandon her child unless she has to. Ever wonder why she left you behind?"

Bren's instincts screamed at him. *He should be speaking with the king.* Though they were acquainted, Bren would not expect the man to drink with him. His hand returned to his knife. "Isn't His Majesty expecting you?" Azirik may easily brush aside questionable loyalty, but Bren did not.

White brows arched, but Bren was fairly certain An'thor's surprise was feigned. "I thought Azirik told you. Best forget I ever said anything if you want the war to be as simple as 'sides.'"

Nerves and nausea warred in his gut. Whatever concerns the Dhoah' Laen's death planted now blossomed, and the flowers were ugly. "An'thor, what did you think His Majesty told me?"

The Ageless man shook his head and hauled himself to his feet with a groan. "Your mother escaped because she was Laen and she carried the fate of the world in her womb. The world didn't end when Moera died because she wasn't what you thought."

Vacant eyes. Cold blood on his kerchief. *She looked like just a girl.* The bottom dropped from his gut. He went years without caring who his parents were. The Mirikin army was his family. "My mother was—"

"I'd not go bragging." An'thor's casual tone was gone, and his black eyes bored into Bren's.

He was abruptly reminded of how inhuman the warrior was. "And his Majesty knew? How could he let her go?"

"Azirik waged war because your mother broke his heart. He refused to claim you as a son because he loved you and it was as close as he could bear to killing you."

Bren scrambled to his feet, now numb from the cold. "Wait, you knew this whole time? Did others? Why did you tell me?"

"Corporal to Lieutenant is a large leap. It's obvious, but I think most assume you're just his bastard." He jerked a thumb in the direction of the tents. "If you're going to cross the world to murder someone, I thought you deserved to know she's your sister."

Bren's stuttered response was cut off by a swell of voices as Azirik exited his tent.

The king glanced over in time to see An'thor swing into the saddle. "Wanderer?"

An'thor shook his head and urged Theriim back down the ridge.

Azirik's face twisted into confusion and he turned to meet Bren's stare.

Bren knew his every thought was apparent on his face. He stepped back to distance himself from where the informant had stood, but it was too late.

"What did he say?" the king rasped. He dismissed his guard with a curt wave and strode toward Bren.

The lieutenant opened his mouth but found no words. His eyes searched Azirik's arched nose, heavy jaw. Older, but identical to his own. *Fuck, he was right.*

"Lieutenant?" Azirik asked again, barely a pace separating them.

"You're my father?" Betrayal made his voice as hoarse as his king's.

Azirik's knuckles were white around his sword hilt. "Does this change your resolve?"

"Toar, I don't know!" Bren rubbed his hands over his face. "All this time you never told me, made me murder my mother's people? Laen-blood or not, kin-slaying is damnable!"

Azirik's fist slammed up into the left side of Bren's jaw, cracking his teeth together.

His vision exploded, and he dropped to the ground, world spinning.

"Get out, Brentemir," Azirik growled. "If you're here by morning you'll be dead." Without another word, he strode into the camp.

It did not matter that Bren did not want to choose. His decision was made for him now. Staggering to the tent took a moment, belated adrenaline roaring to the fore. He could not think about what came next. Choice books tumbled into his pack, along with his heavier boots and a few clothes. He tucked the pack into the shadows behind the tents and went to the armory wagon. A friendly greeting drew a smile from the man on guard.

"Just need to mend some things." His bruise-stiff smile belied the pounding in his chest. The man laughed and motioned him through. Once inside, Bren wasted no time. Sword and knife already hung at his belt. A quiver and bow were next, the oiled string going into his belt pocket. He was a lousy shot, but game wasn't going to fence with him. His metal studded jerkin was folded in the chest for his troop, but he found it easily. He averted his eyes from the vermillion double-diamond on the breast denoting his rank. That and his vambraces, rerebraces, and greaves went into another pack. Mail thigh-guards were too heavy. He dropped the bag out the back of the wagon and folded the armored jerkin over his arm.

"Thanks," he shot over his shoulder before grabbing his pack and the bag from the rear of the wagon. Crossing the camp with measured, slow steps dissuaded any suspicion. His horse was tacked, and he was packing the saddlebags by second watch.

A pointed cough sounded from behind him.

He whirled, wondering how many more surprises it would take to stop his heart for good.

His first-corporal leaned on the post, frowning. "Our orders are to move out at dawn. Not now."

"Sorier, please." He returned to loading his horse. "Leave it."

"I saw you argue with His Majesty. You're not an angry man." The man was a dozen years Bren's senior and had helped raise him in the army way. If anyone knew Bren, it was Sorier. "Lieutenant, you deserting?"

Bren rested his head against the saddle. *Is that the word? Surely there's one milder, concerned with blood ties and sanity.* He caught himself halfway through the rationalization. "There's no word for what I'm doing."

Sorier shrugged. "Then I'm coming with you. You're my officer. Doric'll come too, if you only look at him. You could use us."

Bren winced. Loyalty was a painful reminder of what he would leave behind. *I'm abandoning them.* He reached into his pack and ripped the rank-badge from his jerkin. He pressed it into the older man's hand. "Your orders are to stay with the army, Lieutenant Sorier. Doric too."

The older man frowned at the fabric in his hands, not understanding until he heard the title of his promotion. "I pray we meet again."

"If we do, it will be across the battlefield, so I pray we never do." Bren mounted up. "Fight well and stay alive." He could not bear to look back until the darkness and distance swallowed Sorier's figure.

The Mirikin army rode out four hours later, taking advantage of the fog to cover their passage north. Bren watched them pack up from the surrounding hills. He patted his horse's flank dismally. "Happy Midwinter." The army faded into the trees leaving only lines of hoof prints and cold fires.

And him.

Φ

The 3rd Day of Vurgmord, 1251

"I disapprove of your methods." Alea reached for the spit of bacon only to be driven back by Arman's territorial growl.

"You burnt it three times in a row. I'm not risking the last of it." He poked the meat carefully. Violent sizzling of fat hitting embers widened his grin.

"You'll smell of lard for the next two weeks. Especially if you continue to wear that damned jerkin." She sat back, confident in her barb.

Arman just rolled his eyes. "It's warmest. And my other one has a busted shoulder."

"Perhaps you should have brought your mother along." She watched as he tended their food. The ridge where they camped was more exposed than she preferred, but there was evidence of previous fires. She pulled his pack toward her. "Let me see."

"It's in the left side." Arman pointed with his knife. "I can mend, but can't get the thread to hold on that."

Folded, travel-stained parchment found her hand first. She glanced at the front and frowned.

Lyne'alea ir Suna

"Arman, what's this?"

He glanced up, face paling under its tan at the sight of the letter. "It's for you."

"I can see that." She turned it over, searching for a sender's name, but found none.

"A few days ago, when we were in town, I met the Laen's guard. You were already asleep, and I guess, in the excitement of the queen's letter and the first snowfall, I forgot. He asked me to give you that, though."

Alea's nerves were as travel-worn as the letter looked, and what little patience she usually had was gone. "A man with horns gives you a mysterious letter and you just forgot?"

Arman looked away. "I'm sorry. These days wear on me as much as you. I'm exhausted. And it's not mysterious. It's from your mother."

"My mother—" emotions choked her words and she fumbled the letter open.

My dearest Lyne'alea

There are no words for how much I miss you. I realize I don't, truly, know you at all, and when we do meet, it will be as strangers. It breaks my heart, but I cannot wait to see the woman you've become.

Leaving you and your brother was the safest thing I could do. I couldn't hide what I was, but without me, you both might survive. I hope in my absence you've grown strong, and he's kept his heart through Azirik's rule. I hope you understand.

Hope is what keeps me alive now.

Please know our paths will cross, if not yet, soon. And seeing you again will be the happiest day of my life.

Until then, luck and love daughtermine.

Elle

"She wants to meet me, someday." The frozen ground betrayed her, pitching her into an abyss of confusion and anger, and something dangerously close to the hope her mother mentioned. *Brother?* She scanned the words again for a name, a clue whether he was left in Cehn too. *"Kept his heart through Azirik's rule."* Left in Mirik, then, perhaps.

Arman did not meet her eyes, as if staring at bacon gave her some modicum of privacy. "I'm sorry I forgot," he repeated.

"Did you read this?"

Arman frowned. "Of course not."

She handed it to him, tucking her knees up under her chin and staring into the fire. When he was through, she whispered, "I thought the Laen created only daughters."

Arman glanced back at the paragraph mentioning her brother. "I think life's more complicated than we realize."

"Half-brother, then," she muttered. She was not sure why the "half" mattered. *Mother. Brother.* Not "foster" anything but blooded family. Conjured by memories and fear, the image of her brother was a hulking man, twisted between Laen and human, a monster at his calculating king's right hand. A man never meant to be. *Otherwise, why wouldn't he have fled too?*

Arman sighed. "This is more dramatic than a Berrin play. You might as well complete the final act and claim Azirik is a god and your father."

I've an entire family, alive and aware of me and I've never met them? Never heard a word?" Hurt and anger were easier than facing the new facts bombarding her mind.

"Alea," Arman's use of her name dragged her attention to his fire-bright eyes. "If she'd kept you with her, you'd be dead."

"Did the guard say anything else? Why didn't he join us?"

"He mentioned re-routing an army, mysterious bastard. And besides," his eyes were luminous across the fire, "he said you were protected enough."

Alea barely remembered her time recovering in the Ruby Cockerel, but she would bet their entire purse his face was not the same as the nights he watched over the refugees. *There's fury in his heart, and a light in his eyes.* She tucked the letter into her bag and cleared emotion from her throat. "You just have to braid it before sewing. It makes it stronger." She held the jerking in, clarifying, "The thread."

"I told you I couldn't braid."

Alea almost asked when he told her such a thing. *When I was covered in blood, reeling from discovering I was the Dhoah' Laen.* Her face grew still, and she picked at the tattered threads of his jerkin. Even an attempt to distract herself sent them plummeting back to serious topics. "I don't know how we've made it so far, through so much change."

Arman set the bacon aside to cool. "Just a step at a time, as you've done up until now. You learned you were the Dhoah' Laen just months ago. There are a thousand pieces you'll discover about yourself. And you're not alone."

"Just know whatever bloodshed there is," she warned, "I'll see this battle through."

He settled beside her. "Then until I can no longer lift a blade or bow or fist, so shall I." He gestured to the thread in her hands. "Enough doom-talk. Show me how to braid."

CHAPTER ELEVEN

The 10th Day of Vurgmord, 1251
The Province of Boda, Athrolan

BRUISES STIFFENED BREN'S JAW. He blinked against the bright light. After a moment he realized he stared at an evening sky. Naked branches overhead were black veins in the white marble of the moon. His body ached from the hard, cold ground.

Icy rain stung his face and his jaw cracked as he licked drops from around his mouth. Thirst clawed his throat. He rose with a sigh and bound up his bedroll. Sudden decisions were well and good, but the day afterward was rife with uncertainty. Sleeping through most of it did not help his spirits. *There's nowhere to go.* He hummed softly as he tacked up. The tune faltered into quiet when a soft voice cut through the bare trees. Drawing his knife, he crouched to peer from under his horse's belly.

Two riders moved up the hill, switchbacking along the snow-scattered trail. Bren eased his horse back into a thicket, looping the reins over a branch so he could free them quickly if need be. *I could be a traveler.* A glance at his uniform erased his optimism. Even without the officer's badge, deep green and vermillion trim were blatantly Mirikin. *Toar, I should have planned for this.* Except he had not planned anything. His stomach twisted.

The riders crested the hill. Halfway across the clearing, the woman caught sight of his horse in the thicket. She dragged her horse to a halt and fumbled to draw her bow. "Arman!" The woman was young, Athrolani, though her friend appeared Vielronan.

Probably runaways trying to get married.

Her companion snarled and drew a knife from a bandolier across his chest.

Rumbling filled Bren's head, distant thunder, distant ocean. It did not matter that she was clearly inexperienced with her bow, or that the man could barely keep his seat. Instinct told Bren he could not win this fight.

He narrowed his soldier's eyes on her, catching the echo of silver in her eyes, the ferocity in her face. The rumbling grew louder. Tightening his fingers around his knife, he stepped from behind his horse.

Her hand flew out as if she could grip his throat from a dozen paces away.

Cold flooded his chest, his very blood obeying the mountain's winter.

"What are you waiting for?" The man growled.

The woman tilted her head, examining Bren's features. "He's alone."

"I don't give a damn if he's trussed up as a harvest pig, he's Mirikin."

Bren's brows shot up. "I like her better."

Silver eyes met his gray and air left his lungs. They were a vast scattering of stars and he was dwarfed by their majesty. His knees cracked on the frozen hillside, knife clattering to the ground behind his limp hand. Something akin to joy, to fear, bubbled in his chest. "Toar, I thought we killed you."

"You're Azirik's man?"

He could not look away from her. Pointing to the livid bruise on his face, he replied, "I'm not sure whose man I am now."

"Azirik would punish desertion with death." Arman shifted his weight, causing his horse to shuffle.

Bren shook his head. "I think he made an exception for his bastard son."

The woman's gaze did not flicker with surprise. Instead, she lowered her hand, but only slightly "Let's just leave him. We have a long way to go."

"It's a trap, milady."

"It's really not," Bren argued. "If I returned to their army I'd be dead. Please, just leave me." Loneliness ached, and the next month was a mystery, but he was not ready to die.

"Why'd you leave?" the woman asked.

I was too good for them. I was given a dangerous mission. Azirik was too scared I would overthrow him. A thousand lies would make him sound stronger. "I couldn't do it anymore."

The blond man circled, cutting off the only passible route down the hill. "Bullshite."

Bren fixed his eyes on the Dhoah' Laen. "His Majesty—my father's—informant, An'thor, came to me on Midwinter Eve. Told me the truth about everything, about why Azirik never claimed me."

"An'thor as in, the legendary Wanderer?" Arman interjected.

"Yeah, An'thor, An'thoriend, the Wanderer, the Madman of Ice." Bren made his index fingers into horns. "Whatever you call him. He worked for Azirik as an informant. I suspected he was double-crossing us."

The woman refastened her bow, boots crunching on the ice as she dismounted. She crossed the clearing slowly, ignoring Arman's protests. Bren wondered if she knew the air cooled as she approached.

"He came to us too. Twice." She nudged his knife with her toe, sending it skittering downslope. "I suspect he enjoys playing puppeteer with our lives."

Bren swore frost curled around each of his organs with her every step closer. Whispering, he agreed, "Seems like. He said my mother fled because she was Laen, and she carried the world in her." He forced himself to meet her gaze. "I think he meant you."

Anger then horror hardened her face and she stopped less than a pace from him. Tilting her head, her expression softened into curiosity. Her hand brushed his face, drifting snow on his weathered cheek. "I know your face. I've seen paintings of Azirik." Her hand paused at the pale eyes and tapped the bridge of his arched nose. "Those, though. Those are mine."

He swallowed hard and the stillness broke. She backed up, stumbling over bare rock until she collided with her horse. "Arman, it's him."

"Maybe the entire army knows about your mother's son, milady. He could be parroting a line they've all memorized just to save his own skin."

She shook her head, seemingly unable to look away from Bren's features.

"Do you think I could stand? My knees aren't what they used to be."

Arman did not answer, but dismounted too. "What're you called, anyway?"

"Lieutenant Brentemir Barrackborn. Former lieutenant, now, I suspect."

"You never really explained why it's former."

"I've been thinking too much. Questioning when I shouldn't have been. Killing that girl—the one we thought was you—was the hardest thing I've ever done." He picked at the ragged skin around his nails. "I decided to fight for you."

The Dhoah' Laen pursed her lips. "You're a terrible liar. You had no intention of fighting for me."

Bren's face heated. "Won't you kill me outright if I say otherwise? With your..." he wiggled fingers in a poor illustration of power.

"No." She jerked her head at the man behind her. "My guard might, but I wouldn't." She straightened. "We were going to camp here. You might as well share our fire—I don't trust you not to kill us in our sleep. Ceir Bodian's a day's ride away. Tomorrow I expect you can find the road."

After a halting nod, he pulled himself to his feet. As he moved to untack his horse once again, Arman shouldered him aside.

"I'm taking your blades, and you'll be tied to that tree." The man's yellow-green eyes narrowed on him. "You're still a harvest pig to me, no matter what she says."

Φ

An audience made laying camp awkward, and more than once Alea and Arman bumped into one another. Her hands trembled at every task and her conversation—if it could be called that—with Bren repeated in her head until she could have recited it. *"I think he made an exception for his bastard son."*

"What're your names?"

She jumped, surprised at how loud his voice was after only camp sounds and the thunder of her own heart. "I'm Alea. He's Arman." She flashed him what she hoped was a smile, but might have been a grimace. "You said your name was Brentemir?"

Arman growled from across the camp and dumped his gathered firewood with more violence than strictly necessary. "Did it occur to you that he's a spy?"

Frustration flashed through her at the accusation. *Of course, it did. Of course, he could murder us in our sleep.* It was why he was tied to the tree. She set water to boil, tempted to dump it over both men's heads and be done with it. But when she saw what lay behind his eyes, just a few shades shy of hers, she knew. It was the same fear and dedication and confusion in her own heart. Despite her fair words, she unrolled her bed across the fire from their surprise prisoner. "I just know."

"He's Azirik's blood!"

"So's she."

The words crashed into her mind and she whirled on the man. "I think we can argue fine without your commentary, Barrackborn!"

Arman looked between them, incredulous.

Instead, she stood. "I'd rather dig the latrine than listen to this. Don't kill him while I'm gone, Arman, I'll hear it if you do." The woods beyond the firelight were mercifully quiet, but there was no peace inside her skull. She hated how much she longed to trust the man, how terrified she was of being alone and still longed for solitude. How *did everything become so complicated?*

As much as Arman complained that she made irrational decisions, she knew it was only because he never saw the thousand thoughts crossing her mind before she made a choice. He did not hear the cacophony in her head as she crossed the clearing to touch Bren's face.

"...his bastard son."

Up until he spoke those words she assumed they were half-siblings. But she knew the Laen. Days catering to them in Cehn and a healthy curiosity told her they might have had dark hair and silver eyes, but their noses were aquiline. Their chins sharp enough to break mountains. *But ours are strong, blocky. Human.*

She peered at her hands, ordinary under the dark winter sky. Perhaps that was why Azirik hated the Laen so. His lover, his son, his daughter bore the blood he swore to destroy. *How can I mend a world when my own bloodline is so broken?*

It was fully dark when Alea returned to the awkward silence of the campfire. Arman glowered over his mending. Bren held a book on edible plants in his roped hands.

She poured herself a bowl of stew and settled partway between the two men. "Did you give him something to eat?"

"He had his own in his pack." Arman fussed with the jerkin and thread in his hands, expression mulish. "I'm just glad we ate the last of the bacon yesterday. I'd not want to share it with him."

She sighed and turned her waning interest in conversation to Bren. "Planning on taking up as a healer, Bren?"

Bren jumped at her voice. His large eyes widened further and glanced at Arman before answering, "I'll read anything. I'm slow at it, but I enjoy learning."

"You learned a lot in the army?" Small talk was increasingly hard, but she was willing to try.

"Not the kind you mean. I was raised in the barracks from the time I was six and learned just about everything I know there. But there were few books to share among the other orphans." He lifted the book. "Besides, this might be useful."

"You've been a soldier since you were six?" Horror raised the hairs on her arms. How could Azirik teach children to kill?

"Close. I was an errand boy at ten, and began training at fourteen—two years early 'cause I was tall." He shook his head. "I didn't know my—our—ma was Laen."

Would it change anything had he known? *What agency does a child have, though?* She put her head in her trembling hands. "This is confusing. I don't know whether she expected me to be happy or angry about you—honestly I don't think she ever expected us to meet." *Perhaps after the war.* Shaking the thought away, she explained, "We wake at dawn. Arman, take first watch."

Boots discarded, she retreated to her bedroll. The man across her fire killed people—her people. He thought he killed her a month ago. *Yet here he sits, claiming he doesn't want a soldier's life, saying he's my brother.*

She buried her face in the hard camp pillow and wished she did not feel like weeping.

Φ

The 13th Day of Vurgmord, 1251

The wind changed, drifting across the camp bringing the scent of metal and horse. Arman shoved himself upright, shaking clear the fog of fatigue drifting over his thoughts. A glance told him Bren was still a lump against the tree, huddled in his cloak. Alea curled into her bedroll by the fire.

Something clacked on the hillside below.

Hooves. Arman crept across the clearing to the ridge's edge. Beneath moonlight, the rocky trail was a white ribbon winding between naked, black trees. Even with the good vantage, he could not make out the crests on the riders below. *Layered wooden armor, Berrin maybe?* It was possible they would miss the camp, but it was a stupid risk to take.

He rushed back to the fire, staying low and keeping his feet on the quiet exposed rock, rather than the crunching snow. Donning his bandolier, he crouched beside her and pressed a hand to her shoulder.

"Arman, what—" Her words died at his expression. She slipped from her bedroll and shoved her boots on, shivering in the night air. Belongings were haphazardly shoved into her pack and she buckled her bedroll across the overflowing flap. "How long?"

"Ten minutes, maybe less." Arman dragged their horses behind the thicket as he saddled up. He caught her glance at the still-sleeping Bren. "As far as they know he's their ally."

As he cinched the girth, his horse nosed Bren's and let a low whicker.

An alert sounded on the trail below.

"Shite, shite, shite!" Arman hissed, tossing his saddlebags over his dun's back.

Alea swung up first, yanking her reins free and turning her prancing mount in a circle. "Come on!"

They rushed through the trees, faces whipped by branches, horses' hooves clattering up the rockface. Hoofbeats rumbled close behind and Arman whirled, heart in his throat and blade in his hand.

Bren, bonds hanging loosely at his wrists, reached over and tugged his sword from Arman's saddle.

"How'd you get loose?" Arman growled.

"If you think those were secure, you're lucky you haven't had to capture anyone more dangerous." He urged his charger faster, pacing the lighter dun up the trail and over the crest of the hill.

Alea glanced back, black brows knit in a frown. "What do you think you're doing?"

"There's nothing for me in Ceir Bodian. With you two, however, there could be."

Arman's lip curled, distrust souring his already nervous stomach. There was no time to argue. Cries went up as the Berrin discovered their campsite. Ahead, Alea bent over her horse's neck and they tore through the forest. Arman swore and pressed after her. The time for secrecy was over. He snarled at the soldier beside him, "You gave us up!"

Bren rolled his eyes. "No, ass, you forgot to stamp out the fire!"

Φ

The 14th Day of Vurgmord, 1251

"Where're we going?" Bren rubbed down his charger, noting a tremble in the horse's left hind leg. "I'm not sure how long Knell here can go."

"North." Arman heaved his saddle and packs from his dun. "Who names a war horse 'Nel,' anyway?"

Bren sighed and pressed his sweat-streaked brow to his mount's damp neck. "Her full name is Death Knell."

Instead of responding, Arman stalked over to where Alea crouched by the stream. Thick trees and near breakneck speed helped them outdistance the Berrin an hour before. Twisted trunks crowded the road and trickling water filled the air. Cold dawn light broached the mountains half an hour before.

Alea glanced up from filling their water skins and called over to Bren, "Fort Hero. Just over that rise, I think."

"And when we arrive, harvest pig, you and I are having a talk," Arman added a curled lip to the threat.

"I think you've spoken enough for the both of us," Bren shot back. He still questioned his motives for joining them. Surely, he could have formulated a passible excuse to the Berrin, at least long enough to escape to Ceir Bodian. *Arman's right to be suspicious.*

He did not know what the future held for him, what career he might cobble together with knowledge of maps and murder. All he knew was the woman crouching by the stream needed to survive.

"Need a hand?"

He glanced over, frowning. Exhaustion hampered his usual observation. "What?"

Alea stood by his horse's head. "You're just staring at your tack. Thought you might need help."

Bren let out a hoarse laugh. "Tired, is all. And, Toar, the last week—months even—have been trying. I'm not even thirty and I feel like I've lived eighty."

She hummed in response and set about picking burrs from Knell's mane. "I know. Sometimes I catch myself wishing I died with the rest of them." Her gaze met his. "You said 'so is she,' when speaking of your blood. Azirik's blood."

Looking away, he uncinched his girth and slid the saddle free. "You getting at something, milady?"

Her gray eyes rolled. "Please, don't start calling me that. I can't break Arman of the habit, but I'd rather not hear it from both of you." She began tidying the charger's tail. "I just didn't know, until you said it."

"Who did you think your father was?"

"Laen don't have fathers. They—we—are formed of power and borne in a Laen's womb until birth. That's how it's always been told to me."

Bren frowned. Different legends were told to the Mirikin soldiers, ones he heard echoed in Fullsen's excited questions about blue blood and claws. *They rip life from men's loins and leave them broken, hollow and mad.* It was a small wonder Azirik spun that version. "You think you're not?"

"I don't look fully Laen. Even if I were raised as one I'd never be as tall, or my hair so dark. Or my nose so sharp," she laughed through the last descriptor.

Bren rubbed the bridge of his matching nose. "Maybe that's why."

She frowned. "Why what?"

He shrugged, and let Knell loose to graze on what little grass frost left untouched. "Maybe Azirik's blood is why you're the Dhoah' Laen."

She made a face, clearly unwilling to entertain the thought. "I'm sorry, but that man's a monster."

"Probably," he agreed, twisting his back to stretch, "but he has a singular dedication. Monster or man, he's mighty."

"Do you think you can keep that part of our shared blood between us, at least until I make sense of it?" Her pale eyes were moons through thunderheads.

"Of course."

She nodded and retreated to the river without another word. After another minute, with the sun properly on the horizon, they remounted. The final league was easy, hills cradling them as they wound north. At the crest of the next rise, the slopes were cleared of trees. Tucked in the swale stood Fort Hero.

In its center stood a fort surrounded by double walls. The first looked over ten paces, the next another five more.

Double walls surrounded their sanctuary, each several times Bren's height. Mirik may have had a fast army, and a formidable navy, but little compared to the sheer wealth Athrolan sunk into her military.

With a whoop of excitement, Alea urged her tired horse into an easy lope. A week ago, Bren never imagined he would be following the Dhoah' Laen into an Athrolani fort as an ally. *Is that what I am?* The title joined "deserter" and "bastard" in his heart, drifting, still unrooted. He forced the thought away and raced after them.

Alea reached the guards at the gate first, relaying her message. Wood groaned, squealing against itself before the gates swung outward. The garrison was the size of a small town. Stables stretched the length of the left wall. Barracks stood on the right and ran along the rear in an "L." The fort was rough but clean. Wood smoke hung in the air, joining the scent of cooking meat. A pen of chickens stood by a smokehouse.

The things I could tell Azirik. Noting the bows trained on him, Bren spread his empty hands over his thigh and pulled a smile he did not feel onto his face. He strangled the treacherous thought before it fully formed. *I won't be a deserter twice. Betrayal will not be my name.*

A squire trotted up to take their horses, face lit with curiosity. "What can I do for you?"

Alea dismounted, rolling her shoulders. "We're expected. I'm meeting Commander Dorcal." Glancing at the ramparts, she followed the archers' line of sight back to the former Mirikin soldier. She offered a faint smile to Bren, but turned back when an unremarkable man emerged from the barracks. Three circles and dots around Athrolan's tower emblem designated his rank of naval commander.

"Dhoah' Lyne'alea?" While he was Arman's height, his muscular breadth belonged to a larger man. Chin-length dark hair was clearly cut for function, not style. Blocky features settled into reserved respect. "I'm glad to see you arrived safely."

"As are we," Alea answered, nodding to his bow. "You are Commander Dorcal?"

"Yes, Dhoah' Lyne'alea. Sir Raven Dorcal, Commander of Her Majesty's navy. I have orders to accompany you north to the city."

Bren's brows shot up as he eased himself off his horse. Mirik and Athrolan shared an ocean, and he was raised with stories of Dorcal's ruthless command. It was fitting the commander was a mountain of a man, but Bren expected features as sharp as his orders, not pockmarked cheeks and a lumpy nose.

"We're grateful for your aid. This is my guard, Aud'narman Wardyn of Vielrona and Lieutenant Brentemir Barrackborn," Alea glanced pointedly at the soldiers still sighted on Bren, "who recently joined us."

Despite his clearly Mirikin name Bren noted a few arrows unnocked. He did not relax. Whatever Alea said, wherever his path took him, he was Mirikin in an Athrolani fort during war.

"I'm eager to hear all you've encountered, Dhoah', once you've washed and eaten." The commander stepped back with another, stiff bow. "Welcome to Fort Hero."

In a matter of minutes, Alea disappeared into the officers' quarters for her own bath and meal.

Another squire escorted Arman and Bren to the soldiers' bathhouse. It was little more than a shed off the barracks. Fire-heated bricks surrounded a waist height wooden tub in the center. For a fort, it was a great luxury and further testament to Athrolan's past wealth. It was only a few hours past dawn, so the room was deserted.

Heat rushed up Bren's skin as he dunked into the water faster than his body adjusted and he hissed through his teeth. Arman disarmed himself of the various blades of his bandolier and boots.

Bren's eyebrows rose at the pile of weapons on the bench. *Well, that's an obvious statement.* He sunk deeper into the water as Arman joined him. Silence hung undisturbed for a long time before Bren opened his eyes. "It was a long journey from Vielrona?"

Arman's head rested on the rim of the tub. Tips of unusually long dogteeth poked from his mouth. "Yes." His tone was bland, not rude.

Bren itched to ask about the fangs, but held his tongue. Nosey questions would only complicate their situation. "I'd never left my city until a few years ago. I was more excited about seeing the places in the legends than battles."

"Why did you come with us?"

Bren frowned. If this was their supposed talk, it was easier than he expected. "Since killing Moera, my mind's been odd. I didn't lie about that. When he learned I knew about my blood—both sides of it—he told me to leave." He gestured to the healing bruise on his face. "Under to uncertain terms. Perhaps that was the step I never could take on my own."

"Moera. You knew her name."

"Not at the time," Bren sighed. "His Majesty is a driven man, but lately it borders on insanity. He plans to raze every city that sheltered the Laen."

Arman pinned him with a level stare. "Every city?" When Bren nodded, Arman tilted his head, calculating. The glint in the man's eyes was unnervingly reptilian. Arman said no more. Once he scrubbed the rough, lumpy soap from his skin and hair, he stepped out.

Bren followed a moment later, shaking out his clothes.

"The handprint on my chest is from milady." Arman's words were sudden. "I was bleeding out in a gutter and she healed me. Her skin burnt mine. She has that effect on people, Barrackborn. If you're honest, loving her will be your only pain." He laced his shirt and was gone.

Φ

Alea twisted another strand of hair into her braid, frowning into the shaving mirror over the washbasin. A knock made her rein-worn fingers falter. "Yes?"

"It's Arman. Might I have a word?"

"Of course." She shot him a tired smile as he entered. "Feeling better?"

"Much." He settled into the chair at the desk by the window. "I can't believe we're here. Feels like forever and just moments since we left Vielrona."

Tying off the end of her braid, she perched on the edge of her bed. "Cehn is like another lifetime."

Arman examined his hands as if memorizing the exact blisters and callouses. "You need to be careful."

"Excuse me?" She did not want to be berated, not after finally arriving at safety, and certainly not by Arman.

"Reaching out to Athrolan was a necessary risk. Bren isn't necessary. In fact, he's dangerous. This world is big and dark and unfriendly." His eyes pierced her. "This alliance with Athrolan will take time from your learning. With an enemy lieutenant knowing both our movements and Athrolan's, you could get us all killed. Wanting a family isn't worth that."

She smothered the anger flashing through her and settled for snapping, "I don't blindly rush into things without thinking, Arman. You're not privy to my every thought."

He sighed but seemed to either see her point or lose the will to argue. "I know. I feel so poorly equipped to help you, to protect you. I'm clever and quick, but I can't promise I'd win against a trained soldier."

She looked down. "If I could master my power enough to control when I use it I'd suggest I just protect myself."

He gave her half his usual grin, long teeth flashing in the dim morning light. "Eh, at least you got more than a pretty smile to work with."

Whatever frustration she felt waned at Arman's old humor. "It's been a long few days. I'll be careful if you'll give him a chance."

His frown returned, and he rose without answer. "The commander told me breakfast was in his study."

The room next door held a broad desk, perhaps more suited to holding maps, arrayed with anemic squash and cheese. A few bowls held dipping sauces.

Alea found the nearest chair, stomach protesting at her manners. Luckily, Raven appeared in the doorway with Bren a moment later.

"I trust you've found everything satisfactory thus far?" he asked, sitting across from Alea and serving her a plate.

Alea thanked him and nodded, "It's a relief to have some respite from the road life." She watched, envious, as the commander ate deftly without dirtying his fingers. *That's a skill I'll need if we're dining with the queen.*

"I'm glad we could help. What of your journey so far?"

The simplified version of events was easier, but without the confusion and pain, it was as if she told him someone else's story. "You know much of what happened after Marl Kess—we received Her Majesty's response and continued north, to here. Bren found us just today—yesterday, actually. We barely slept last night, with Berrin on our trail."

Raven's expression remained neutral until she was through. He regarded the now-empty plate before him and sighed. "Quite the tale you've got. Athrolan is another two-weeks' journey." His gaze flicked to Bren. "Pardon my curiosity. You're a lieutenant, but not of Athrolan."

Bren pushed his food aside and cleaned his hands before meeting the commander's eyes. "I was Azirik's man until my perspective changed. I earned my rank, so I use it, but my loyalty is to Alea."

Raven's eyes narrowed, but he let the topic be, and turned his questioning, instead, to Arman. "Dhoah' Lyne'alea didn't include your title, but I assume you're her Rakos guard?"

"Yes, though Rakos is what I am, not a title."

Bren's eyes widened at that admission.

Alea rubbed her temples. The tension was childish and, at least for Arman, out of character. "Commander, forgive me, but I think our energy is better spent discussing the future, rather than displaying who is most loyal and trustworthy." She fixed Raven with a pointed stare, ignoring Bren and Arman's embarrassment. "What are your plans for the upcoming journey?"

"In two days, we depart with a troop that will come through Pardelan. We'll talk the mountain pass—Scree Notch—and when the road cuts west we will move north. Fort Stone lies in the Ru'un Felds, and that is where General Aneral awaits us." He faltered, "If you agree, of course."

Alea tried to mentally trace their journey on her memory of Arman's map. "I look forward to the meeting."

Change of guard echoed from outside and Raven pushed back his chair. "There are the minutiae of traveling to organize. If you've no more questions, would you excuse me?" When Alea gestured to the door, he retreated without another word.

Alea rested her head on her arm. *These will be a long two weeks.* "He seems terse."

Arman shrugged. "I don't mind a man who doesn't mince words."

"I'm more concerned with the ones he did use," Alea interjected, "But I'm sure war puts us all on edge."

Bren glanced over. "Honestly, I understood war better than this. I have no idea what to expect."

"Did you only pay attention to the lessons about killing innocent people?" Arman added a raised brow to his jibe.

Oh, for fates' sake. Alea glared at him. While he and his childhood friends frequently poked sarcastic fun at one another, the acid in his voice was new. "I thought we discussed this?"

"I need something from our packs." Arman's lip curled and he strode from the room.

Bren's jaw tensed, and he glanced at the door. "Does Arman dislike everyone?"

Alea winced. "No. He's usually teasing and quiet, but when he speaks he means it. He fears for us—for me."

"He's loyal, bond or no." His gaze turned to the old altar in the corner. It bore the red and copper of the gods. Dust clung to the cold candles, and the few flowers were shriveled. His hand rose to the copper emblem around his neck.

"We're as lost as you," Alea offered, following his gaze. As much as Cehn respected the gods, her foster-father was not the most devout man. *What would it be like to lose my kingdom and my faith in one night?* "I know why you left the army—why Azirik left you, rather. But why did you come with us?"

He peered at his blocky hands, as if the whorls and lines of his palm print held the truth of his motives. "I don't know, honestly. Ceir Bodian held few options for a man in Mirikin uniform. I think the sense of adventure took over. These last months under His majesty weighed on me. I'm fine following orders, prefer it sometimes, but not when they might break the world." He seemed to search the air for words. "When I looked at you, saw your might, the weight was replaced by relief and awe."

"I understand the orders. Arman, Commander Dorcal, even An'thor, they shunt me about, as if I'm not strong or clever enough to do it myself." Alea glanced up, wistful. "But following their orders is so much easier than making my own sometimes."

Bren chuckled. "No words are truer. Thank you for trusting me, at least a bit."

"Arman thinks it's because I want a family, but I think it's because I recognize your uncertainty."

"Family? What of our mother?"

"She left me in Cehn, protecting me with anonymity. Ihal and his family raised me, with kindness and good education. I was even supposed to marry his oldest son."

"Cehn." Sorrow in Bren's voice turned the question into an apology.

"Were you there?" There was no judgment in her question, but resignation.

"Not for—only later to pick up the Laen's trail."

Alea tilted her head. *He can't say it. And he says "our mother" so easily, like his heart always knew he had a sister.* It was a romantic notion, and not one she entirely believed, but it made her loneliness less.

Arman's return interrupted any response from her. The blond man slumped into a chair and dropped a beg between them. "I begged a bit of bootblack from the soldiers—thought we could use the task to keep our minds light for the day."

Alea smiled at the awkward attempt at friendliness and joined them as they drew their boots off. After convincing Arman that she could, in fact, do her boots herself, Alea carefully set about the task. It was meditative, though unfamiliar. By the time she completed her first shoe, Arman finished his and was partly done with her other.

She wiped her hair away from her face. "I didn't think it would be so messy."

Bren glanced up. "You truly have never blacked a boot before?" Deep brown buff stained his large deft fingers.

"I lived in the desert—we wore sandals, and I suppose serving women polished them," she retorted, feeling heat bloom on her cheeks.

Propping her boot beside its twin, Arman frowned and rubbed boot buff from her cheek with a rough thumb. "To think, one day they'll be stories of the Dhoah' Laen blacking her own boots in a fort. They auction off that rag there, in your hand."

Alea glared at him, hoping such a thing would never come to pass.

"Or create a shrine to it, there's space there," Bren added, jerking a thumb at the gods' shrine behind them.

Arman glanced over, perhaps deciding if Bren's words were in jest or judgment. Despite himself, his lips quirked.

Alea giggled, mirth a flood of relief after running for so long. "Maybe then we'd afford to stay in inns rather than wayhouse benches," she retorted and threw the rag in question at Arman's face.

The 14th Day of Vurgmord, 1251

"She needs rest!" The low argument woke Alea close to midnight. Recognizing Arman's lilting tone, she tugged her clothes on.

"I'm sorry, Master Rakos, sir. Commander Dorcal said it can't wait."

Arman snarled something that sounded like a Banis curse.

That respite was short-lived. Alea tugged her traveling clothes on and was lacing her boots when Arman knocked. "What is it?"

He shrugged. "Commander Dorcal called for us." Grim fatigue on his face set her heart racing. Shouts in the courtyard a moment later made it stop.

Halfway to the commander's study Bren appeared from the stairs outside. He grimaced. "Commander Dorcal's in the courtyard with the body."

Arman took off after the soldier, but Alea stood a moment, staring at her feet. *The body? Not more death.* A darker part of her rose, clamping around her vulnerability. This was war, and the refuse of war was bodies. Clenching her teeth against nerves, she followed her brother and guard.

"Dhoah' Lyne'alea, here!" Raven's shout arced over the torch-lit fort, drawing her eyes to the cluster of soldiers.

Sickly sweet scent of rot hit her before she made out the heap on the packed earth. *And something that reminds me of Merahn's orange pie* – "Don't touch it!"

Raven shot her a stern look. "With all due, respect, milady, it's just a body – "

"Oasis Betrayal. It's a poison that gives off the smell of oranges, sir." She explained, craning her neck to see the condition of the body. A shock of red hair poked from under a dented Athrolani helm. Lividity stained what was once white skin now stretched with bloating. "Rot usually hides the sweetness."

The commander ordered his men to step back, frowning at the body. "Small wonder, then. He arrived strapped to a half-dead horse. Those are Berrin arrows."

"Playing on your sympathy," Bren explained with a shake of his head. "Folk ought to be able to bury their dead."

"Anything else you'd like to warn us of?" Raven asked Alea.

She shook her head. "Just burn him. Those who touched him ought to wash, and dump the water in the latrine. I can't remember anything else. It's a common poison, though, someone else might know more." Already the adrenaline trembled in her hands and she yearned for space to breathe, to run.

Raven gripped the roots of his brown hair. "How far behind you were the Berrin?"

"Hours, though we lost them quickly. I doubt they knew who we were," Arman answered, tossing a glare toward Bren, "Unless they were told."

"I was racing beside you the entire time, you – "

"Doesn't matter if they knew," Alea interrupted, "people talk, and the commander this far inland will cause gossip."

"And Ceir Bodian's guards sent word of campfires in the hills. Three leagues to the north there are signs of an army's passing – Azirik's I assume?"

Bren nodded. "And there's another two crossing Athrolan."

"I can't count on both my hands how many raiding parties have been reported to General Aneral." The commander motioned for men to deal with the body and strode toward the barracks. "Anything more, Lieutenant?"

It was the first time the rank was not spoken with distrust.

"Five regiments ride west along the southern border. They aim for Ceir Felden, the Hartland and a large fort there, along the river." He frowned as he forgot the name.

"Floodbane?"

"Yes. The other four move north. I believe a smaller Berrin force plans on joining them."

"Well, one of those forces turned and marches here." Raven's eyes narrowed on Bren. "When we've more time, I hope I can get those details on a map."

Bren swore. "Even just a single regiment has over a thousand soldiers, most mounted. And there's the Crown, though I believe Azirik rides north of us."

"Crown?" Alea asked, stepping into the study and flopping, exhausted into a seat. Her dark thoughts settled on the gold circlet in their packs.

"Yeah, one of the three world's Crowns. The gods gave Azirik theirs." Bren looked down. "It was gifted just after we discovered what—who—escaped from Cehn."

Alea paled. She suspected the gods would lend Azirik power, but this was different. She was hundreds of leagues and months away from Le'yne and the Laen's Crown. "How does he use it? His plans?" She caught sight of Raven's pale face and wondered what, in her expression, disturbed him so.

"He intends to destroy all allies you've gained. Clouds of acid. Waves of blood. The whole apocalypse." Bren's trite words were low, heavy with horror and shame.

Alea closed her eyes, gathering her thoughts. "Then we leave at dawn. It's not safe to wait for the patrol, Commander, we risk further attack."

"Further?" Arman asked, "That man was poisoned, probably by that arrow."

Bren shook his head. "It's a well-known one, but expensive. You don't use it unless you want it to spread."

Raven glanced at Bren. "You're insinuating that was an act of war?"

Alea pressed her hand between them. "I'm saying it, sir. And even if it was a single attack and his horse just staggered home to die, Commander, it still means there are enemies in these hills and I need to cross them."

"The Berrin forces will arrive in half day at most. Our escort will never make it here in time. We ride at dawn."

Arman's tan hand gripped the back of Alea's chair. "Sir, we've slept less than four hours in the past two days." Heat rolled from his skin and Alea did not have to look to know he bared his fangs.

"I'll take my personal guards," Raven promised. "If we ride hard we'll make it. Hero will give us time."

"We should pack, Commander."

He tugged a map toward him, and a stack of cheap parchment for missives. "I'll see you at dawn."

Arman followed Alea back upstairs, pacing the room as she packed.

"What?" she asked when he sat at the desk a moment, only to rise and pace again.

"You didn't share things with me at first. You should keep that caution with Bren—"

"Enough." She forced her tone to remain level. *I still keep so much from you, Arman.* Saying so would do little to help, however, and only start a bigger argument.

His green eyes widened at her hard words. "Lyne'alea?"

Now you use my name. "His appearance was sudden and raises questions, but I already answered the most concerning ones for myself. He may have mentioned Azirik's plans for Vielrona, but that part of his life is over. We need his information. We need his strength." She stopped his stammered excuse with a raised hand. "My instincts are rarely wrong. You're the only one who won't trust me, and I don't know, for fates' sake, why!"

Arman scoffed and stormed from the room, leaving her shaking with frustration and flooded with ice. Between Arman's anger and the commander's terse nature, she already dreaded the weeks it would take to get to Ceir Athrolan.

Wrapping her braid around her head, she stuffed a shapeless hat over her hair. Already the borrowed men's shirt hid most of her shape. Whatever image of the Dhoah' Laen Azirik had, she did not resemble her. *I just wish I felt like her.*

Orange light spread from the small window as torches lit the body in the courtyard. Even through the sturdy wood, the smell of rancid meat filled the fort.

Alea pressed her brow to the window. Through the wavy glass the blaze could have been a festival bonfire. *Azirik has the Gods' Crown.* She barely knew anything about the Crowns—as much a legend as the gods themselves, and just as unseen. The most she understood, they enabled a person to channel all the race's power without being consumed.

A faint, softer orange glow rose on the horizon and she shook herself from the inertia of too little sleep. Shouldering her pack and sweeping the room a last time, she slipped from the room. Already the fort was a mass of soldiers and guards, orders called between crowing roosters and whickering horses.

Alea was happy to see her chestnut horse in the courtyard, ears pricked and one rear hoof cocked as she waited.

"Pretty girl, Sunaf. You have faith in me, at least," Alea murmured, rubbing a firm hand down the animal's gleaming neck. She missed the lean oasis dogs, happy to play or lounge without judgment.

"Are you ready?" Raven strode from the stable, leading a charger as broad and blocky as he.

Alea nodded and swung into the saddle, hips already protesting at the too-familiar movement. Sizzles and pops emanated from the burning body in the corner and she forced her churning stomach to settle. Bren and Arman appeared a moment later, both armed. Cloaks covered even the commander's rank, and beyond the plain blue and brown of the commander's personal guard, they almost looked like common folk. *The best-armed common folk this road will have seen,* Alea mused, counting the weapons stashed under packs and beside pommels.

Raven handed over a missive to the fort's young gallant before mounting up and motioning toward the north gate. "Ride out!"

Alea fell in behind Bren and Raven, with Arman beside her and the guards taking up the rear. Hooves hammered with her heart, a trot that the horses could hold for hours. *I doubt my nerves will last that long.* Silence reigned as they left the fort's cleared apron and crossed into the forest. Though tense, no one seemed willing to break the quiet with the usual road-banter.

Even as the sun climbed the sky, then retreated in dim afternoon, the day never warmed. Alea flexed her gloved hands, willing the feeling to return. The month on the road put many of her expectations for comfort in perspective, but cold was one thing she refused to get used to. *That and the death.*

Arman's gaze roved from his saddle to Alea, to the road, then back. "Trade you for your thoughts, milady."

"I wish you wouldn't call me that. We're friends."

"Alea, then," he corrected. When she was quiet for another moment, he offered, "I'll go first. I was thinking that the legends never tell of how much riding there is. I'm liable to grow a saddle right from my arse at this rate."

"Maybe we'll stop soon. There's not much light left." She drew a shaking breath and lowered her voice. "I was wishing I could pretend my own death and hide. Run away so I could live in peace."

Arman's voice was low, perhaps from sorrow, perhaps from fear. "I doubt even that'd stop them. Besides, Moera already gave you that chance."

"It's only sometimes."

Ahead, Raven signaled for a halt. Arman and Alea had made their own schedule for much of their ride, but Raven set a firm pace. They moved off the road to where a small river looped about a deep grove. Sunaf pranced, ears flicking at the sound of a distant howl.

"Wolves?" Alea asked.

Bren scanned the surrounding forest. "I never heard wolves until I came here. Azirik drove them out of Mirik with the Laen."

"Hopefully they stay in the hills," Raven muttered, swinging from his horse and handing his squire the reins. "Everyone will have an hour watch, excepting you, Dhoah' Lyne'alea and Lieutenant Barrackborn. If you want to bathe, take turns in the river. It's cold, but a hot spring up in the hills makes it less than bone-chilling."

Alea was unbuckling her saddle when a small hand appeared beside hers.

"May I, Dhoah'?" Raven's squire was barely into adulthood. A squire's skullcap topped her shorn, dark hair and her beige skin spoke of Berrin heritage.

"If you'd like, miss...?"

"I'm Squire Tzemine of Ceir Felden."

Alea offered her hand, "I suppose you already know me."

"I do, Dhoah'," Tzemine answered with a grin and even deeper bow.

Unclipping her pack and bedroll, Alea found a good spot by the campfire Raven's guard laid. She and Arman bathed rarely while on the road, as most of the Felds were too exposed or lacked suitable streams. *It might be winter, but I'll never forgo the luxury of a bath.* Swimming did wonders after hours in the saddle.

Loamy ground dipped steeply to the river's rocky edge, held together by the iron grip of ancient, twisted roots. Piling her clothes on a dry stone, Alea stripped to her underclothes. Within the river's sharp curve the water was deep, and she counted to three before steeling herself to jump. Freezing water forced a yelp from her as she surfaced.

"Milady?" Arman's call was laced with worry.

"I'm fine—the water's frigid!" Her words tripped over her chattering teeth, but her skin grew numb within moments. She quickly scrubbed herself and raked her fingers through her hair. After a last dunk and lap across the river, she scrambled out and dressed.

Bren laughed at her quick reappearance, "It must have been cold—I don't think I've ever seen a woman bathe that quickly!"

Mock distain accented her glare as she wrung water from her hair. "You try washing a braid that reaches your rear in under a minute."

"It's why I cut mine!" Tzemine added from across the clearing.

Alea tugged on her cloak. "Besides, frozen mountain streams are a far cry from desert oases." Having repacked her clothes, she turned her attention to the fire. "May I help with dinner?"

"I think Captain Metters and I have it under control," Raven answered. Even the bathing banter did not bring a smile to his face. "Rest if you can. We'll ride again after midnight."

Icy water woke her exhausted body, and Alea settled herself at the base of a large tree just inside the circle of firelight. Since the attack at the wayhouse she skirted the fathomless black power within her. *I'll need a modicum of control if I expect to ever win this.* She closed her eyes and leaned back, stepping down into herself with her mind.

Φ

Arman watched Alea relax against the tree then turned to Raven. "I'm taking a swim, keep your eyes on her, please?"

The commander's gaze flicked from him to Alea then to Bren, but he nodded.

Arman dumped his pack beside the stream, unbuckling his various blades. Placing his dagger within easy reach, he stripped and dove into the water. *Fates!* Cold drove the air from his lungs. It was gloriously familiar to swimming in meltwater from the hills surrounding Vielrona. He skimmed the stony bottom. *This must be what flight feels like.* Surfacing, he flipped and floated on his back. Above the dim sky tangled in black branches.

A wolf howled closer.

Shouts and Alea's terrified scream ripped through the air.

Arman scrambled up the icy bank. Grabbing his knife, he crashed through the brush to the camp. Rain misted the air. Their belongings were scattered across the camp. Horses panicked, rearing to get away from the chaos, Tzemine struggling to keep their reins.

Beyond, the forest was calm. Arman lurched, slipping on ice forming across the bare ground. Rumbling shook the ground, water pooling as if pulled from the earth itself. *It's shivering.* Arman's gaze flew to Alea.

She was not Alea anymore.

Shadows twisted under her skin. Vicious wind whipped her hair. Black fog roiled across the ground. Salty cold crashed against Arman's mind.

"Barrackborn, get the others back, beyond the circle!" Growling in Arman's voice brokered no argument.

His gaze did not waver from Alea's face. He stepped closer and her power surged, black coils twisting like an injured snake. Mentally, he reached toward her. "Milady." Screaming of wood straining under the pressure of wind and magic was the only response. Arman pushed further, brushing the gold of his own power.

Alea. This time he only spoke with his thoughts. Swelling pressure faltered, but did not ease.

Her eyes flickered open, freezing his chest faster than any icy river. Pure silver shone under the darkness writhing across their surface. *Arman?* Her voice was distant, desperate.

It's me. He risked another step toward her.

You're glowing, all white and gold.

Arman glanced at his outstretched hand. She was right. *So are you – silver and black.* He took another step. *Come back. You're drowning.*

Tremors shook her power and he realized they were sobs. *I don't know how.*

Follow the strand of your soul – the silver – back to the surface.

How do you know what it looks like?

I can see it. Veins of your soul-blood overlay your physical ones. "It's beautiful."

Her skin brightened, silver more than black.

A thunderous crack echoed across the camp as a massive pine gave way. It crashed into the picket line. Splinters exploded through the air and a horse screamed, blood flying. Raven hauled Tzemine away as she crumpled, vomiting.

Alea dove back into the depths of her power. Ice coated everything around them, the smell of the sea rising as power pulsed from her body.

Pressure increased, forcing Arman to his knees in agony. Her skin softened, dissolving with the force of her power. *She'll kill herself.* Thunder echoed the thought.

Heat flooded his muscles and he dragged himself upright. Behind him, the fire roared, towering above their heads. Sharp scents of metal and smoke cut the cold. *Stop, Alea.* His voice softened. *You're safe. You're safe with me. Come back.*

After a breathless pause fog rolled back, sinking into her skin. The silver of her consciousness eased to the surface and then faded too. She blinked, and was Alea again.

He rushed to her, gathering her in his shaking arms. Her body was still colder than the stream and set his heart aching. The campfire stuttered back into its coals. "Never do that again!"

She drew a ragged breath, hard hands clinging to him. Her skin began to warm, and she pulled back. "Arman, your clothes?"

He looked away sheepishly. "I was swimming. You'll be all right?"

She ran a hand over her hair and nodded.

He waited until she met his eyes and nodded again before backing away. Bren met him a few paces away and handed Arman his pack.

"Thank you." Arman peered around the camp while hopping, one-legged, into his breeches. "Where are my damned boots?"

"Wardyn, we need to leave." Raven's voice barked across the camp. "There's not a patrol in Boda that didn't see that mess." Smoke from the raging fire spiraled into the sky. Rent bones of the horse sprawled in a puddle of blood and flesh echoed the broken wood of the trees.

"Give her a minute," Arman began.

"And what about my squire, eh?" Raven snarled.

Arman glanced to where Tzemine huddled beside Raven's guards, shattered arm cradled before her. He blanched. "Right. By the time everything's collected she'll be ready to go."

He gathered Alea's things and brought them to her, crouching to take her hand. "What happened?"

"I'm not sure." She shrugged.

"It's important." He frowned. "Why did you go into your power?"

"I wanted to see if I could control it. I need to understand it better."

"Fates, Alea, this isn't something to play with. It's Creation and Destruction. You could have killed us all, killed yourself!" Seeing the fragile look on her face, he sat back. "We'll talk about it when you're calm."

"Dhoah' will you ride double with your guard or brother?" Raven had the horses ready and one of his men doused the fire. "My corporal's horse...fell."

She glanced at the bloody tangle and winced. She refused to meet Tzemine's gaze. Nodding weakly, she allowed Arman to pull her to her to her feet and climbed up behind him.

"Move out," Raven commanded, nudging his horse into a trot.

Silence reigned again, but inside Arman's mind was a storm of questions.

Φ

Trees thinned as mountains closed around them, rocky outcroppings breaking through the vegetation. Close to midnight, they stopped at one such boulder.

"No campfires," Raven warned, "but everyone should rest."

Bren watched Tzemine stagger to the lee of the boulder and slump to the ground. Her pale face was white, and her jaw clenched. Alea and Arman seemed wrapped in exhausted conversation, so he grabbed his pack and sat beside the squire.

"Is there anything I can do to help?"

Pain sharpened her headshake. "I'll get it set when we're at Fort Stone."

"Would you mind if I looked at it?" he asked. "I've seen a share of injuries—I'm no healer, though."

She shifted and laid her arm in his hands. "I don't know if it's broken or simply out of place."

Swelling and bruises marbled her elbow, but no bones jutted at wrong angles. *What do I know?* He shrugged and carefully returned her limb. "I wish I could tell. I've something that might help, though." He fished his lighter cowl from his pack and looped it gently over her opposite shoulder in a makeshift sling. Next, he found his battered relief bag. At the bottom was a small wax paper packet of gray powder. "Put a pinch of this under your tongue. It'll make you feel a bit tossed, but you won't feel as much pain. Or, at least not care that you're feeling it."

She let out a dark laugh and did as he said. "I'd cut the damn thing off if you told me the pain would stop."

He grinned and leaned back against the stone. "I've been there. Cracked both my knees when I was your age—still don't feel right—but the pain was sickening."

Raven sat heavily beside them. Rare concern crossed his features as he took in his squire's appearance. "I think you should stay in Fort Stone. Rest up. I'll manage on without you," he smiled faintly, "somehow."

She closed her eyes, lines of pain already fading from her face. "We'll see, sir."

Bren glanced over at Alea and Arman again. They had finally fallen asleep. "I'll ride with Alea once we move, give Arman's horse a rest. Not that I'm terribly lighter than the two of them." He glanced at Raven. "Fort Stone is just over those mountains, yes?"

"Yes, but it's not an easy ride. We'll arrive the day after tomorrow." His dark eyes narrowed on Alea's sleeping form. "Assuming there are no more unforeseen events."

"She'll be fine," Bren promised. As sure as his words were, what he witnessed hours before chilled his blood. "She's just young and tired."

Raven glared into the darkness. "She's unpredictable is what. I'm not good with such things."

"I'm better with orders to follow and men that know their duties, too." He sighed. "There were men in Mirik's army who—despite their own devotion—got physically sick whenever the gods spoke through Azirik. Some can't stomach the divine or powerful."

The commander frowned, as if determining whether there was insult in the words. Deciding there was none, he sighed. "I've never been good with the idea of the Laen or gods. Another being, deciding a man's fate? Wielding power we can't? It's not right."

"The way I see it is I can do things you cannot, just as you can do things I cannot. They take that to a different extreme."

Raven shuddered, "The feeling of fog on my skin, and the smell of the sea—I was raised on the waves. That felt like an abomination. And the way she made the fire rage—she's dangerous."

"The fire wasn't her, commander." When the man frowned at him, Bren glanced over to where Arman sat beside Alea. "Alea's not the only one with power. We've a Rakos with us. When they learn their power, you'll be glad they fight for us."

CHAPTER TWELVE

The 15th Day of Vurgmord, 1251
The Mountains of the Orn de Galin

RAVEN'S SPYGLASS TRAINED ON the entrance to the pass ahead. Rising sun forced mist from the hills. Alea pulled up at the rise and slipped off of Bren's horse to stretch. Dawn was a welcome change after their seemingly endless night. Bren and Arman dismounted to scout the road behind while Raven planned the next step of their journey.

Alea watched Tzemine lean on the saddle of her round remount. *Say something.* Guilt made it far easier to pretend the woman did not exist. Alea sidled up and offered the horse a slice of hard apple. "How are you feeling?"

Tzemine's glazed eyes roved to Alea's features. "Been better. Been worse. Your brother gave me something." She blinked rapidly, to focus. "And you?"

Alea found a smile curled in the corner of her mouth. "Been better," she echoed, "been worse."

Tzemine's laugh rasped, dragged over the cobbles of exhaustion. "I somehow made it this far without a serious injury. At least mine has a better story than most squires' do."

"I'm sorry." Alea finally blurted. "I shouldn't have tested my limits with others around. I could have killed you."

Tzemine shrugged, then paled at the pain from the movement. "Damn. And if death scared me, Dhoah' I'd not be in the navy." Her barely focused gaze fluttered again and finally settled on Alea. "Not to speak out of turn, Dhoah' Lyne'alea, but be careful. Commander Dorcal's will not be the only one who's skeptical of your abilities. I'm one of the only girls in the navy—the army has many, but not the navy. You and I, we have to do twice as well as they expect to earn half the respect."

Alea frowned at her hands, knotted in the horse's mane. "I suppose you're right."

"Do you mind if I close my eyes? My mind feels like my uncle's sponge cake."

Alea chuckled and shook her head. "Of course. Please, let me know what I can do?"

Tzemine hummed noncommittally and rested her head on her horse's neck.

Alea settled at the top of the rise beside the other Athrolani guards. Her body hummed with energy and weakness and she wished she could crawl into a cave to avoid her embarrassment. Tzemine had a point. *Who'll ally with a Laen who almost kills everything?*

Sinking into her power was easy. Controlling it once she was there, however, was the difficult part. Perhaps it had been the firelight or the sound of horses. Perhaps it was the faint echo of comradery. *It reminded me of Cehn.*

Seeing Arman through the veil of her power changed something in her. She was not the only monstrous thing in the world. His body was lit from within by white light, brilliance through thunderous gold. Power was within his blood, not the other way about. *Perhaps I need to surround my power, not let it surround me.*

It terrified her. Cold tingled through her veins, the bitter bite of Destruction.

The chestnut she rode from Vielrona bumped her shoulder, knocking her from her reverie. "Hello pretty girl," Alea murmured. She caught the grin of the younger of Raven's guards and smiled back. "Yes?"

He glanced at her sidelong, fidgeted a bit then finally spoke, "I expected the power and the violence and the cold. I didn't expect you."

"Honestly, me neither." She handed the last slice of her apple to the mare. "I can tell Commander Dorcal has no love for me or my power, and yet your queen was eager to join us. The gallant we met, Sir Elian, was kind. I'm rather unsure where we stand, actually."

The man laughed. "The commander is a tough man, but a good one. He knows Her Majesty is making the right choice. Honestly, you and your guard give me the twitches, but I'm quite certain I'd rather be on your side of things."

Alea raised her brows questioningly.

"Mirik's vermillion would look terrible on me."

Her giggle sounded strange and loud in the soft morning air. She hesitantly offered her hand, the way Arman would. "I realize I didn't catch your name before."

"I'm Corporal Narier." He bowed over her hand and nudged the guard on his other side. "Metters."

The older man set aside the map unfolded on his knees and "What?"

Narier jerked his head toward Alea pointedly, "This is Dhoah' Lyne'alea."

Metters offered his hand warily across Narier. "Captain Metters." He turned back and pulled his hood up again. "I think we would be better off going into the pass now. There's light enough, but not too much."

Narier snorted. "I think the ocean would dry before Commander Dorcal went into anything without analyzing it eight ways."

Shouting cut through the quiet. A moment later Arman sprinted up the hill, his face grim. Birds startled from the trees not far behind. "Berrin!"

Bren pounded up after him, spinning to face the road behind them. He leveled his broadsword. "Toar, how does that man run so fast?"

Raven surged to his feet, tugging a sword from his sheath. He grabbed Arman's arm as the man rushed past. "We can't outrun them?"

"They're a minute behind us, if that." Arman raced across the clearing and jerked the mare's reins from a startled Narier. He shoved them into Alea's hands. "Ride."

"I won't leave you all here, and I don't know the road!"

"It's the only road, Dhoah'" Narier interjected.

"We won't outpace them and there aren't enough of us to go with you without dooming the others."

"Tzemine—"

The squire sported a manic grin beneath her glazed eyes. "Still have my strong arm." She swung into her saddle and leveled a rapier.

Arman gripped Alea's hand for a fleeting moment. "Go. We'll catch up when its safe."

Guilt and frustration warred in her gut. "*...when the world falls to ruin if you die, there's no such thing as selfish.*" She gripped the reins. "I'll see you soon." With a quick kick, she thundered into the pass.

Φ

Heat exploded through Arman's body. He unsheathed two knives and moved to where the road dipped down a slope of scree. Lowering his stance, he leaned to put weight on his back leg. Muscles burned, but were ready and loose.

"Any minute now," Bren cautioned. "You need a horse?"

"Better on my own feet," Arman explained.

Metters retreated for better range for his crossbow. The others fanned across the crest of the rise.

Nine Berrin emerged from the trees. Mounted on shaggy mountain ponies, they were far better suited to the pass than even the Athrolani's massive chargers. The man in the lead pulled up for a moment, surprise on his face. Thrusting his arm in the air, he let out a whoop.

Chaos erupted. Arman whipped his arm, snapping his hand forward as he released his blade. He raised the second before the first struck home in the throat of the lead rider.

Bren charged forward with a bear-like rumble. Twisting, his broadsword hamstrung a horse in the upswing and slicing the rider in the reverse. A third blow ended the man. Raven's style was twisting and methodical, long blade whirling in arching loops. For a man closer to the size of a bear, the grace surprised Arman.

Burning pain told him an arrow passed through the flesh of his right thigh. He snarled and hauled himself up the saddle of another rider, succeeding only in pulling the woman halfway from her pony. Slashing across the Berrin's throat, he shoved her into another rider. Bren dragged the second soldier from the saddle and drove his sword through his ribs.

Stillness fell. Blood clung to Arman's clothes and a gash he did not remember getting stung on his cheek. Limping through the bodies, he found several of his blades. He preferred close combat, so his weapons never left his hands, but mounted attackers were another tale.

"Well, at least we have more horses now," Bren remarked. The others were silent as they checked wounds and cleaned weapons. Tzemine was an unconscious lump on her horse, though it appeared to be from pain, rather than further injury. Bren's victims were cloven in parts and Raven's kills were clean as were Metters. Narier had a penchant for beheading.

Rapid, hissing breath rose from the man at Arman's feet—shot with one of Metters' bolts. He tried to hide it, eyes vacant, but trembling in his hands betrayed him.

Arman crouched. "Commander!" Grabbing a fistful of the man's stained uniform, he pulled him up. Frustration flooded him, shaking his hands and lending thunder to his voice. "Honesty, or you'll wish that arrow flew truer." The Berrin's eyes widened, perhaps at the threat, perhaps at the fangs framing the words. "How many are you? Where are you headed? Are there patrols ahead? Traps?"

Raven crouched at Arman's shoulder. "I'll do that." He reached for the man.

"They're the reason she's riding alone!" Arman whirled back to the soldier. It wasn't frustration anymore. It was fury.

"None!" The man sputtered, "The rest joined the army. Nothing lies ahead." Desperate defiance in his eyes doomed him.

Heat roiled from his skin in waves and the rippling air tipped his equilibrium. White fire filled his skin to bursting, pouring through his hands.

The wounded man convulsed, and his eyes rolled back. As quickly as it rose, Arman's power faded. He dropped the man in the dirt and strode toward their horses. He had the truth.

Raven checked the Berrin soldier. "He's dead." He turned to Arman. "We get little from a dead man, Rakos!"

"I already have my answers." Arman cleaned his weapons and clipped his pack onto the saddle.

Raven glanced between guard and dead man. "How?"

Narier fixed Arman with a narrow stare before mounting up. "I think he saw his thoughts, sir."

Arman ignored Raven's shudder and dragged his wounded leg over Hartward. "We've lost enough time. There's something waiting for us, before Athrolan. Something about a storm."

Φ

Thin air carried noise father. Alea's horse clattered between the steeply sloping walls of the notch. Panic subsided to bubble faintly under other thoughts. Mainly, she was tired and sore. She left the trees behind an hour ago. Cold chafed her cheeks and stiffened her hands. Gray mountains echoed the overcast sky, backlit with faint midafternoon light.

Patting her horse's neck, she mused, "I thought if there were fewer trees I'd feel more at home." She watched her mount's ears flick toward her. "The similarities between the desert and a rocky mountainside aren't enough, apparently. In Vielrona I'd have bled to see this – to see anything remotely close to home." Perhaps more than the landscape changed.

It was well past lunch, but her stomach was too tight to eat. *How could I just leave them there?* She fought men in Vielrona, and the soldier in the inn. What was a Berrin patrol? Her laugh pierced the still air. *I'd have killed my friends and allies if I tried.*

The road was barely more than a glorified trail, scree and rocks winding up the mountainside. Sunaf labored over boulders tumbled into the road with last week's rain. Then she heard it.

Low muttering, like an angry chatter of stone. She scanned the horizon. Nothing broke the monotonous gray, no sign of life other than sorry moss clinging, frozen to the rock. Tracks along the roadside could have been prints of a large cat, or whomever last used the road. She was no tracker but it made her hair stand on end

The sound came again closer. Sunaf panicked, head bobbing and ears flicking. Alea whirled, trying to place it. The call echoed from ridge to rock face to cliff.

She scanned the ground for a sign of anything as the trail faded, reappeared, then faded again. *"There's only one road."* She did not know these mountains. She did not know any mountains – the only ones she knew were the shifting landscapes of sand dunes.

Wishing she was a league behind, fighting alongside her friends, she drove Sunaf faster. They took off up the trail, winding along what could have been a riverbed. It ended abruptly. Rugged stone steps climbed up one side and the path of scree led into a narrow chasm between two walls of rock. Stone leaned in, the weathered walls ancient and decrepit. Raven said Fort Stone lay beyond the mountain and a single rider traveled faster than six.

Sunaf's hoof-beats cracked and echoed as they followed the canyon's curve to the east. Alea's nerves sang at the closed space. At one point she was forced to lift a leg from the stirrup to scrape through the narrow passage. Her pulse raced until she ripped herself away from the ragged rock gripping her breeches and cloak.

The walls fell away, and she emerged on the steep northern side of the mountains. She drew her mare to a halt to stare. Vielrona had snow, certainly, but this was something else. Dry air whipped ice and snow into bizarre shapes topping each broken rock. Wind moaned as it sculpted, a mournful artist caught in the emotional act of creating. Everything glittered. Clear ice glowed green against the dark rock, and the gravel before her seemed turned to Banis diamonds.

"No amount of reading could prepare me for this." She stared for another moment, memorizing the view. A bitter wind whipped the hood of her cloak, tugging it from her head with its sharp fingers. As beautiful as the mountainside was, she had little wish to make it her campsite. Leagues separated her from rest. With a sigh, she nudged her horse down the faintly visible path.

Φ

The 16th Day of Vurgmord, 1251

Panicked whickering woke her. Her horse tugged at the tether, kicking up snow as she paced. Alea clawed her way free from her bedroll. She grabbed the rope and pulled Sunaf's head down until she could only snort in fear. "I can't hear when you're making such a racket!" Her warning hissed through chattering teeth.

Thick clouds obscured any sign of a moon in the dark sky. No sound came, no rattle of hoof-falls on rocks, or distant voices. She listened for the snarl of a hunting cat, wondering momentarily what predators made such a bleak landscape home.

Wailing swept the mountainside. It grated in her bones, worse than a knife against glazed earthenware. It reminded her of the rending metal in Arman's angry voice, but horribly different, echoing with all the sickly, sulfurous places of the world. She pressed herself farther under the overhang.

Now she heard claws against stone. Dislodged pebbles tumbled across the ice. The shriek came again, closer. If Alea was a betting woman, she would have sworn it sounded furious.

The scratching of nails on stone faded, and after a moment she heard a last call, far distant. She glanced up at her mount. Sunaf's eyes still rolled, but her breath slowed. Alea shrugged deeper into her bedroll again. She was too nervous to rest, but there was another hour before dawn lit the treacherous slope. She had no idea how far behind her escort was, but she imagined the commander would drive them through the night. Chills crawled up her skin at the thought that they would encounter whatever creature stalked the mountain.

There's no one here I can hurt. She settled against the rock. *I owe it to them to try.* She did not plunge into the black wellspring, sinking, instead, into her consciousness. Her mental eyes fluttered open. Twisting black vines wrapped her silver veins. *Just learn to recognize it.* Blackness lapped at her soul blood. Bitter salt lingered in her mouth. She had never seen the ocean, but recognized the depth. *The ocean creates and destroys. It's like me.*

She extended a hand and tugged a sinuous piece of power free. Juggling it took a minute, but soon she tossed it from one hand to the other, like a child with a lentil ball. *Usher it. Don't force.* It twisted, fibers spinning into thread. If it was a thread, could it be a knot? A net? She grinned and began to weave.

Φ

As unimaginative as the Athrolani forts' names seemed, Alea realized they were apt. Steep mountainside slopes leveled into a craggy maze of rocks. Wind swept away any errant snow. She expected trees to reappear, but only dry, brown scrub brush broke up the monochrome gray. Even the wind smelled like stone. By midday the outline of the fort emerged against the bleak landscape.

Alea's horse stumbled for the hundredth time and she slowed, checking the animal's leg. When she looked up, the fort was before her. Perched atop a butte, the garrison overlooked craggy surroundings. It was carved from the rock itself, with two storeys of weathered wood above the three of the stone walls. Against the flat gray sky, its silhouette was grim. Iron-colored pennants twisted sullenly from the three flat-topped towers. She licked her parched lips and nudged her horse up the winding ramp carved in the butte's face.

"Let him pass!" The voice arching from the gatehouse was as rough as the landscape.

Gates a dozen paces high creaked open, anointing Alea with stone dust as she rode through. The fort was laid out much like Hero, though larger and built of stone. Soldiers lined the thick walls, watching her with a mix of skepticism and curiosity. She tugged the scarf from her face and raised a hand in peace. Boots scuffed the stairs and an officer entered the courtyard.

Alea could not decipher the exact rank marked on the tunic's breast, but its complexity told her it was high. "I'm looking for General Aneral."

The hand shielding the officer's eyes was rough and narrow. "I am she." The general handed Alea a water skin. "From where do you ride?"

Alea's brows rose and she took several gulps before handing the skin back. She offered her hand. "I rode from Fort Hero. Before that Vielrona, and before that, Sunam." Fatigue roughened her voice erasing the gravity she hoped for. "I am Dhoah' Lyne'alea."

"Forgive me, I took you for a boy in those clothes." Eras took Alea's hand and knelt, touching her other knuckles to her brow, lips then chest in salute. "I am General Nei'pheras liu Aneral of Athrolan's Army."

Alea's legs threatened to give way. *Nerves, or the fact that I haven't eaten in a day?* She steadied herself on Sunaf's shoulder and answered, "I'm very glad to meet you."

Eras rose and took her arm. "Let's get you inside." She led the younger woman to the door. "How did you come to be separated from the troop?"

"We were forced to leave Hero with only the commander, his squire and two of his guards. A Berrin patrol caught us just before the pass and my guard sent me on ahead." She staggered as they turned a corner in the corridor.

"We'll talk more when you've eaten." Eras shoved open a wide door and ushered her into the mess hall. Fort Stone was easily twice the size of Hero and furnished to accommodate over two hundred men. The dining area alone was the size of Vielrona's Guild Hall. Seating Alea at a long table, Eras set the soup in front of Alea and sat opposite. "I apologize for our lack of fine dishes. We rarely pay host to nobility and the soldiers would just break it."

It was impossible to determine whether the hard-faced woman was jesting. "I've eaten camp fare for weeks. This is more than enough. I'd be happy if you had spoons and forks." At the general's wry shake of the head, she sighed and tilted the soup to her lips ignoring how it burnt her tongue. Oily, thin broth was better than flavorless dried meat. As she ate, Alea surveyed the general's unusual features.

"A surprise, am I?"

Alea blushed, caught staring. "I'm not used to warriors who aren't…." She searched for a non-offensive word. That the general was of a different race was obvious, but Alea had no idea which one.

"Human?" The general's eyes crinkled in what Alea supposed was a smile. "My mother was asai, what you might call 'Stonefaced.' My father was human. Athrolan is more open than her neighbors—you can count yourself lucky for that." She glanced down at Alea's empty bowl. "Let me show you to your room."

Narrow stairs wound up to officers' quarters above the barracks. Eras twisted over her shoulder to talk to Alea as they ascended. "You're lucky you left Hero when you did. It fell."

Alea's eyed widened and she trotted to keep up with the general's long paces. "Fell?"

"Several of the soldiers were poisoned, most of the rest were killed when the Berrin burnt it to the ground. How far behind were your companions?"

"No more than half a day's ride I'd expect."

Eras unlocked a door partway down the hall and stood aside to let Alea enter. "They'll be lucky to make it here. The mountains are treacherous." She handed Alea the door's key. "If you need anything, just ask. Once we know more we can meet to discuss our journey to the capital."

Alea wanted to ask about the creature she heard on the mountains, but her body ached too much for speech, and enough concerns weighed on her mind. "Thank you for having me, General."

Eras fixed her with a level stare. "I'm grateful to live to see your arrival, Dhoah' Lyne'alea. You're needed more than you know."

Φ

The 6th Day of Vurgmord, 1251

Arman peered up at the walls of Fort Stone's courtyard, looming against the moonlit sky. A uniformed figure watched from the stairs as they dismounted. Raven raised a hand in greeting as he unloaded his pack. "Hope we didn't wake you, General." He glanced at Narier and Metters. "Get Tzem to a healer then you're dismissed. Thank you, men."

The two officers helped the pale squire from her horse and ushered her toward the barracks.

Arman followed the commander and Bren up the stairs to the landing where the general waited. He grasped the general's arm as Raven introduced him. "Well met, General Ma'am. Is Lyne'alea safe?"

Eras nodded. "Seventh room above the dining hall. She had a hard ride." She turned to Bren, "Lord Prince Brentemir—"

Bren held his hands up, ruddy face reddening further. "No, I'm not any sort of prince. Lieutenant is fine, if you must."

"Lieutenant then. I've officers' quarters set aside for you and Master Wardyn on either side of Dhoah' Lyne'alea's. Is there anything else you need?"

"No, thank you," Arman offered, shifting his heavy pack to the other shoulder.

"Then we'll speak tomorrow. Rest well." She ducked into the fort, Raven following after.

Arman hurried up the stairs and unpacked his bag in the dark. The hearth was laid, and it took him a minute to find the tinderbox. Whatever Bren gave him to help with the pain of his arrow wound made his body feel hot and humming.

The fire lit, and a knock sounded at his half-open door. "Arman?"

He rocked back on his heels with a smile. Alea stood in the hall, head resting against his doorframe. "Evening," he greeted.

She slipped in, waiting for him to rise before embracing him. Her cold arms were hard around his shoulders. "You're all safe?"

"More or less." He patted his thigh. "Got some scrapes, but we'll all live. Bren's a beast in battle. Your ride was safe?"

"Mostly." Her eyes were colorless in the firelight as she frowned. "Something stalked the mountainside, but I can't say whether it was an animal or not." A jaw-cracking yawn interrupted her words.

He laughed. "I feel the same. I'm glad you made it."

"I'll let you rest, but tomorrow the general said we'd meet."

"Never a moment's peace, eh?"

"I doubt we'll have much in the way of peace until we reach Ceir Athrolan." She rolled her shoulders and nodded to her room next door. "I'll let you settle in. Night."

"Goodnight, Alea." When she had gone, he shut the door and stripped his travel-worn clothes off. There was no bathtub, but the water in the pitcher had warmed enough by the fire to scrub the worst of the dirt and blood away. It was true that he was exhausted, but his mind was too busy to find sleep. Something tailed them through the mountains as well. The fear and nagging familiarity made his skin crawl.

Φ

Raven sank into the chair beside the fire. Eras poured them both a drink and took the other seat. She had plenty of work left to do, but some conversations deserved a drink, and Raven looked like death in boots. "How was the ride?"

"A nightmare. Any news from the cities?"

"Fort Floodbane is besieged. From what they can tell there are roughly two thousand—mixed Berrin and Mirikin. They fight the same cause, but are disorganized. It seems to make it worse for us, though, unable to use one tactic."

"We'll send reinforcements to break the siege?"

Eras shrugged. "We'll discuss it with Her Majesty. These first steps of war will decide the rest." She took a slow sip from her glass. "What of the Dhoah' Laen and her companions?"

"I'm more skeptical of Her Majesty's choice than before. The girl can't control her power."

Eras eyed him. "Is it your observation or superstition speaking?"

"She was testing it, or practicing, or some such when we made camp and lost control. Killed Narier's horse and dislocated Tzemine's arm. I've always trusted my gut and yet the Queen chooses to ally us with her."

"You act as if Dhoah' Lyne'alea is the only one who is other than human. The Rakos certainly bears power, though his limitations are unclear. And then there's me." Her tone was pointed. Like most stubborn, nationalistic folk, Raven's rules had glaring exceptions.

Raven looked up sharply. "That's different."

"It's not."

"Their power's unnatural."

"Unnatural to whom, Raven?" Her voice was gentle, if exasperated. "I have abilities that aren't natural to a human, but are to the Asai—and the other way about. Their gifts are those of the other halves of their bloodlines." She sighed, "Try to see them as people—human or not—as least enough so we can avoid civil dispute. If you become a foul-tempered misanthrope I will not forgive you."

He drained his glass in response. They sat silently for a few minutes as Eras finished her drink.

"I should be in bed." She stretched and rose with a quiet groan.

Raven watched as she put away the glasses and bottle of alcohol. "Are you going alone?"

Eras's back was to him and she ran a hand thoughtfully along her desk. "Tonight I am." She did not move until he retreated to his own chambers. When the hall was quiet, she sat back down in her chair by the low fire.

She had no patience for a touching physical reunion with her intermittent lover. Despite Raven's distaste for anything remotely foreign or inhuman, he was unwaveringly in love with her, and had been for far too long to call it simple infatuation. She scrubbed her hands over her face before pulling a stack of unread letters into her lap.

Most were short missives from her gallants, which she skimmed. Nothing had changed, in that everything was changing. There was a letter from the queen, which she could not answer until meeting with the Dhoah' Laen in the morning. At the bottom of the pile sat a plain envelope without a sender's name and sealed with scummy, colorless wax.

Her heart hammered. A decade had passed since she had seen such a letter. She ripped the paper as she broke the wax. Spikey penmanship was a balm to her brown gaze.

> *Eras,*
>
> *I trust this letter finds you well. I heard Athrolan declared war – about time, if you ask me. I also heard rumor of that woman you escort north. I met her weeks back, before she knew. Interesting, that.*
>
> *I was hoping to be involved in the fun, though Tzatia is probably less than willing to have me. I hope you might persuade her otherwise. When you read this, I'll probably be cresting the de Galin's headed east. Send response to the wayhouse on the Berrin border just past Glas – I'll stay there for now.*
>
> *All my luck and love,*
>
> *-An'thor*

Eras traced the edge of the paper thoughtfully. An'thor was as close to a brother as she had ever come. In their long lives it was not unusual to go years without word, but the past ten were the longest they had gone. *Only a war of divine proportions would bring you from hiding.* As happy as she was to hear from him after so long, her heart ached. If An'thor offered Athrolan his sword, then their situation was dire, indeed.

Φ

The 17th Day of Vurgmord, 1251

Eras leaned back against her desk, crossing her boots at the ankle. Her personal study was cramped, but far preferable to the rather public, albeit larger, tactics room below. "For those of you who do not already know our guests, we are joined by Dhoah' Lyne'alea of Le'yne and her guard, Rakos Aud'narman Wardyn. The tall fellow in the back is her brother, Lieutenant Brentemir Barrackborn, defector from Mirik."

She ignored the irritated look Bren shot across the room. "It's our duty to escort her to the capital. Her Majesty summoned us to court upon our arrival." She glanced at one of the two captains. "Vinden, half your men will accompany us, leaving Captain Hure in command here." Her gaze swiveled to the two tanned warriors by the fireplace. "To those of you who are new," her sharp gaze flicked to Alea and her companions, "these are the warriors Monareka Elang and Iere Ugan of the Bordermen. Warriors, the queen asks you to join us in Ceir Athrolan as representatives of your people."

Monareka, the Border woman, nodded. "I'd be happy to, ma'am, but I can't speak for others. For the most part, we act autonomously. From what I hear, though, if we spread news among our people, dozens will join."

Eras's clear eyes pinned Bren. "Lieutenant, what intelligence do you bring with you? When did you desert Mirik? What are their numbers?" She checked herself a moment. "Forgive me. We haven't been privy to Azirik's movements."

"Might I have a map?"

Vinden unrolled a rough, unwaxed map on the table.

After orienting himself, Bren grabbed a pot of red ink. "The Berrin army's close to forty thousand. Units of around a thousand accompany each of Mirik's regiments, of which there are nine. Each regiment has between one and two thousand men, some mounted." He drew red "X's" along the southwestern border of Athrolan. "He sent two regiments each to attack Floodbane and Ceir Felden, and a fifth to another, which was undetermined when I left. They'll be joined by new allies, the Vales. I know little about their numbers or them as a people."

"And the remaining regiments are those headed here?"

"They're moving northwards along the mountains, though His Majesty—Azirik, sorry—didn't announce their goal. I'd suspect an attack on Ceir Athrolan if they had greater numbers."

Narier snorted. "Can someone explain to me how Azirik funds that many men with a deserted city?"

Bren shrugged. "The island still produces glassware and brick. With no civilians to worry after he's drained most of our--their--treasury. The past few months we lived off the land and Berrin hospitality, to be true."

Raven leaned forward, impatient. "What of the navies? Are either being brought to bear?"

"There is talk of such an attack," Bren continued, "But many of our ships were dismantled for material, metal sold off to the Berrin. Only about a dozen of the original eighty ships are still afloat."

"And the Berrin have a total of four hundred and twenty-eight ships, divided into three navies," Raven groaned. "What I'd give to have that many. As it is we have half. If it comes to a direct battle we will be lost within an hour. Thank fates we only have the single coastline."

"What is the grand plan?" Eras's eyes narrowed.

"Constricting the cities from their resources." He paused. "How many soldiers does Athrolan's army have?"

"That is our advantage. We have three hundred thousand."

Bren whistled. "If there's no naval movement you might have a chance."

Eras pointed at the new marks on the map. "I need to copy that map. Commander, I'd issue missives to your admirals. We leave tomorrow, early. Questions?" When none arose, she patted a hand on the desk. "All but your guests—dismissed." The officers left, followed shortly by the Bordermen.

When they had gone, Eras turned back to Alea. "The way will be dangerous—more than before. The Bordermen know this land better than any, but many aren't keen on allying with us. Not surprising as we've done enough to destroy their heritage and land. It'll be a short ride—less than a week, but I want to be clear that should something happen you two will not look back. It was foolish to send Dhoah' Lyne'alea over the pass alone."

Alea shuddered. "I'd not want to squeeze through that chasm again."

Raven's eyes widened. "Dhoah' that wasn't the road. The road went over top. Narrow and treacherous in winter, but fates, better than the death-trap."

"Well I'd not ridden that way before and what you folk call roads, I'd hesitate to call a goat path," Alea retorted.

"My point, exactly," Eras interjected, driving them back to the topic at hand. "Do not stop until you reach the Iron Sea. A ship is to meet us there, in Marl Mere, but they have orders to sail with just the Dhoah' should it come to that." She straightened. "Enjoy the night. I hear there will be drinking."

Raven cracked a rare smile. "That's every night. I'd best get a head start on the men, as is my duty."

Φ

"Then, An'thoriend slew the last assassin, blades flashing in the sun, his ice-tipped horns stained with blood!" the Athrolani captain recounted loudly. Fort Stone's dining hall was crowded, soldiers ranged around the fire telling tales and tossing dice. The group of Border warriors watched with expressionless faces.

"With the last intruder dead," the soldier continued, "An'thoriend turned to his love, Jessamine, Princess of Clamiirn. He saw, then, that in the battle she was struck down—by an arrow meant for him! On that day, An'thoriend, the mighty hero, swore he would never love any woman but her equal, knowing such a woman did not exist." The man finished by clutching his heart dramatically. The crowd cheered as he bowed.

"An'thoriend?" Alea turned to Arman, "Is that our An'thoriend?"

Arman scoffed. "I doubt he would consider himself 'ours,' milady, but yes."

"He's a hero in tales? Are there many about him?"

"A few. They were very popular with my grandfather's people, so I've heard. He's mostly an old tale now."

Bren glanced over. "I think even Azirik only believes half the tales now. They've been friends—well, acquaintances—for decades, like King Brenterik before him."

"I doubt there is a king or queen An'thoriend hasn't befriended," Arman agreed.

Someone found a wooden flute and began abusing it in the rhythm of a dance called "Sailor's Hip." Several soldiers jumped up and began to make wholehearted fools of their honor, kicking their heels back and lifting their knees high. After several moments the few maids joined in. Narier strolled over to the Dhoah' Laen and offered his rough, square hand. "You look like you could use some fun, though I can't promise much skill."

She laughed shyly and followed him into the dancing. Bren inched closer to the fire pit. This was familiar—loud men and women, laughter that would fade by morning. He glanced over at Arman curiously. The younger man's gaze was impassive as he watched Narier whirl the Dhoah' Laen about.

Is that it, then? Does he love her? Bren had enough experience with the physical aspects of affection, but love was something he pushed from his mind. "If you don't want her to dance with him, best ask her yourself next time instead of glowering."

Arman shot him a glare.

Bren chuckled. "You'll never have a woman that way."

Arman turned the full force of his gaze on Bren, "I've 'had' women, thank you. And I have one such woman back home who'll have me when I return. Milady is different. I don't imagine you'd understand, harvest pig."

Bren heard the dismissal and ambled to one of the tables. Grabbing a chipped mug of foaming ale and took a deep gulp. He eyed the serving girl who ducked from the kitchen for a moment.

"Forget it, she's smitten with Captain Fieren." The female Borderman from the meeting held out a hand. "Reka." Swinging a leg over, she settled backward in the chair beside him. Like her fellows, her skin was a light brown and her hair a warm black. "I congratulate you on your journey thus far—Toar knows it's been nothing but blood for the past weeks."

"I've only been with them for a fraction of it—I can't imagine how just the two of them made it. Some of your people allied with Azirik, but not your tribe?"

"We have tribes, loosely, but our first allegiance is to ourselves. I saw how joining Azirik destroyed my people. I expect you know something of that." She fingered the small tattoo on the bridge of her nose. It was a faded orange and black butterfly.

"What does that mean?" Bren asked, gesturing.

"We're marked on the day we become a warrior. We choose something befitting our character."

Bren smiled. "Our tradition was to become significantly tossed with ale. Yours is much more dignified." He raised his mug, "Care to join me?"

Φ

Arman stumbled up the stairs. Alea retired long before and only Bren stayed up with the Bordermen and soldiers. Ale already caused the Rakos's head to throb. He groaned. It would only get worse with morning. He thudded against his door, searching his pockets for the key. Halfway through his search, he slid to the floor and lay still. "Ouch."

What made me drink so much? It had been years since he was properly drunk, and the road was no place to dull his senses. *Barrackborn said I was unfaithful to Veredy.* He squinted, bringing his thoughts into better focus. "Vielronan ale is sweeter." *The drink or the woman?* "And we did not have this obsession with dancing!"

He addressed the door, "Who even likes to dance? Alea. Of course, she likes to dance. I don't even know a step." A door creaked beside him, but he was too wrapped up in griping to care. "Of course, I barely sleep when we're finally in proper beds. What is a little back cramp to Arman the Rakos, Great Guard of the Dhoah' Laen?" His head banged against the floor as he turned.

Alea sat against her own doorframe, a pace away.

"Hello, milady." He heard the warmth of alcohol in his voice.

"Hello." She smiled. "I think you drank a lot of ale, Great Guard."

He fluttered a hand at her dismissively and made a rude noise. "I used to drink Wes under the table."

"Wes doesn't drink much," she countered.

"He stopped after one night up against me!" He paused his boast, realizing how it had sounded. "Not like that—he's never tried a pass at me."

She laughed. "I'm sure you were a fearsome sight."

He nodded, wincing as the hall spun around his skull. He looked over again, suddenly serious. "I used to think I was. Wes and Kam and I, we were the trouble-tricks of the Lows. You know, when you are so young you feel immortal? I thought I'd never feel more alive than I did then." He continued, pouring his thoughts into the words without thinking. "It's funny, looking at you makes me feel more mortal than anything, and yet invincible. More than when I first felt lust, more than my first brawl. I'm fire. I'm wild." He trailed off and stared at her. *What are you saying?*

Her expression closed, eyes darkening. "You should have stayed."

"You're too interesting. I think that's why Barrackborn's words irked me. I feel guilty for not missing home more, missing her more." He realized she had not actually heard her brother's tease, but he did not bother to explain. Instead, he took her hand impulsively, callouses scraping her palm. "You're worth all the pain of the fire you start, Alea."

Her face flushed, and she drew back. "I think you need to sleep, Arman."

Without answering, he released her hand and watched the door close behind her. Burning raced up his arm from her touch and everything he could see in her face. *Don't go down that road,* he commanded himself. *That is the last thing this journey needs.*

Φ

Alea stared at her door. The warmth in Arman's eyes and the tone of his voice worried her. It was not the ferocity. She saw that look before, on men watching her foster sister. Seeing it directed at her was uncomfortable. Arman was clever and the wear from the road did not hurt his features, but he was a friend first. She did not mind the idea of taking a man, but Arman was another story. *He's too brooding, too dedicated and our friendship is new.*

Flipping over, she stared out the tiny window etched in the wall. She needed to sleep. Her eyes closed, and she imagined she was dancing again. There was no war, just music and someone to dance with. Below the sounds of merriment continued and, for the moment, Fort Stone was the calm in the eye of a storm.

Φ

The 18th Day of Vurgmord, 1251

Condensation beaded on Arman's skin. Clouds rolled like waves of a white sea and his heart thundered at the sight. The chill did not ache in his bones, though it surely should have. It was as if a fire was banked in his chest. A voice cut through the sky. "Brother?" Mountain peaks jutted into the clouds. Perched on the top was a familiar figure. "Arman!"

"Arman, wake up!" Hands ripped his blanket away.

He lunged up, scrambling to get his knife. He blinked and realized Alea stood in his room. Her eyes were horrified and puzzled, "What?"

"You were screaming, and I came in to check, but you were…burning."

"Burning?" He glanced around, which filled his head with pounding. Scorch marks marred the thin wool of his blanket, crumpled on the floorboards.

He dug hastily through the tangle of smoking cloth, finally pulling out the heavy Crown. It looked unremarkable in the dim room, save for the faint smoke curling from the metal.

Alea stepped back. "You're not burnt?"

"All of me hurts, but I suspect that's the ale, not the fire."

"Did you do something to wake it up?" She fumbled over the right words. "How do you feel?"

"Like I deserve. But, no, I wasn't doing anything. I was asleep." *I was dreaming of flying.* "What time is it?"

"Dawn, we ride out soon."

He hauled himself to his feet and gathered his things. "I've got to pack, I'll meet you downstairs."

When he emerged with his pack, the courtyard seethed with soldiers, weapons, and horses. The Bordermen seemed indisposed to riding, but officers already sat ahorse, as anxious as their mounts to be moving. Arman wound through the crowd to where Hartward waited.

He reached for the reins, but the animal squealed and shied from his touch. He tried again, and the horse whirled, teeth snapping closed a breath from Arman's forearm. Arman dragged the mount's head down by the bridle. He forced it to meet his eyes. "fates', I'm not going to eat you." After a moment it finally ceased its panic, though still pranced when Arman swung up. He settled in the saddle and glanced up. Eras watched him, her unfathomable eyes narrowed.

Alea sidled up to him with a nervous smile. "I think my feet will forget how to walk if we keep riding." She glanced at the stormy dawn sky, "That won't make this journey any easier."

He snorted and nudged her with his knee. "Soon you'll be in Athrolan and dressed in silk and pearls and not remember the road's name."

Thunder rolled at his words, a promise of memorable weather. Eras raised a fist and whistled as the first stinging beads of hail began to fall. "Move out!"

Riders spilled from the gates and into the storm.

CHAPTER THIRTEEN

The 19th Day of Vurgmord, 1251
The Ru'un Felds of Athrolan

RIDING THROUGH THE RU'UN FELDS was little better than the gravel pass through the mountains. Conversation was as much about avoiding hazards as impending war or how much everyone drank the evening before. REKA KEPT PACE WITH Alea's horse. "Even I'm growing tired of these rocks, and I was raised here." She pushed her myriad braids from her face with a sigh, "We rarely travel on one path, though."

Reka kept pace with Bren and Alea's horses. "Even I'm growing tired of these rocks, and I was raised here," she commented, tucking one of her myriad braids back under the stone-studded leather band across her brow.

Bren smiled humorlessly. "It's funny how quickly the magic of home fades."

She eyed Alea. "Perhaps it's because I never had a sibling, but I can't imagine deserting my father for my sister. Begging your pardon, Dhoah' Lyne'alea."

Alea's cheeks heated. "I'm not sure it was so simple as that. I didn't even know about him until a few weeks ago."

Bren shrugged, shifting in his saddle. "I didn't know he was my father until the end. He was ashamed of me. That changes things."

Arman trotted up from behind them. "Your turn at rear-guard, Reka and Bren."

The former lieutenant groaned and turned his horse about. "I'm liable to fall asleep if I stare at this ocean of gray any longer."

Reka rolled her eyes, as expressive as the Bordermen got, and followed him down the line.

Arman moved up beside Alea. "He has a point."

"I never thought I'd miss trees. Even the grass is brown." She jerked her head toward the grass waving half-heartedly in the lee of larger boulders.

"Do you need to rest?"

She shook her head mutely. Truthfully, her bones ached with the cold and her body shook. The longer they were in the saddle the closer they were to Athrolan.

Arman placed a hand on her frozen hands, wrapped in mane and reins. He swore softly. "You should have said you were ice."

"This is war, Arman. We're not meant to live in comfort. I'd rather make the best time." His hand was warm, but the heat was eerie.

"I'm sorry for my words last night. Drink makes me a fool."

"I understand." Chewing her chapped lip, she continued, "Merahn and I listened to the servants who drank sometimes. They mostly boasted, but occasionally spoke of women."

"Those are the two things often occupying men—their deeds and women." He chuckled, "Even so, I'm sorry you saw that."

"It makes you human, Arman. When you're always so respectful, it's almost as if you're not real." Her words must have stung, for he pulled away.

His hard eyes narrowed on something far ahead. "Look, milady—forest."

Φ

The 22nd Day of Vurgmord, 1251
The Village of Marl Mere

Arman's heart faltered at the sight of the sea when they emerged from the forest. Dark water stretched to the horizon, large enough to be an ocean. A broad gravel strand swept along the edge of the forest. Down the beach, Marl Mere's few thatched cottages bustled with life, but the pier jutting from the shore was the only thing that had seen recent repair. Still, it swayed with the waves sweeping from outside the harbor. Moored at the docks were three Athrolani naval vessels, garish beside the plain brown fishing vessels.

Arman glanced over as Eras drew abreast. "Those ours?"

"One is. Commander Dorcal arranged for one of his mariners to meet us." She glanced up at the sky. "It seems we'll have clear sailing."

The horses skittered uneasily across the loose boards of the bobbing pier. Alea's face flushed in the sea air, her dark hair whipping about her face. She smiled broadly.

"*M. Xavier* is ours," Raven gestured to the largest ship. Long and narrow, she was made for slicing waves. Her double masts—the taller in the center, the shorter in the aft—were deep red wood, polished from wear, as was much of the dark deck. Thick white rails ran along the side, and symbols for luck were carved in the figurehead's belly. Each of the naval vessels bore the prefix "Magisterial" shortened to "M." The two ships flanking her were of equal decoration and bore the names *M. Vichore and M. Tursio.*

It took many minutes for the horses to be led into the cargo hold and tethered in their small stalls. Alea paused at the bow, staring out to the mouth of the bay as the ships made ready for the voyage.

Bren leaned on the rail beside her as Arman hauled himself into the rigging. "At least he seems pleased."

Wind swallowed Alea's laugh. "And you don't."

Bren made a face. "I hoped I'd grow out of my seasickness, but even the look of the water sets my guts dancing."

"Well," Alea said, lifting her face to the air, "Let us hope our winds are fair."

Φ

The 24th Day of Vurgmord, 1251
The Iron Sea

Arman's legs tightened around the mast. Sailors mostly ignored him, and he was happier in the air. For the first time, the close trees of the forest had made him anxious and he was grateful to have open air. Scuttling clouds caught his eye. The thoughts of the Berrin soldier echoed in his mind, a nervous voice in the back of his skull.

Gray thunderheads built on the horizon before them. Despite his cautionary words to Alea, he spent some time testing the limits of the heat building within him since entering the Laen citadel months before. He closed his eyes and focused. Rising wind buffeted his consciousness as it shot from his body and through the air.

Copper and crimson veined the clouds.

Dread ran down his spine. *The gods' power.* Sucking wind dragged his mind closer and he swore as darkness engulfed him. Stinging rain steamed on his skin. He pushed fistfuls of power into his hands, fumbling with the new sensation. His palms sizzled as he shoved the white fire into his muscles. Heat engulfed him, and he lurched free.

His eyes flew open. Sweat soaked his clothes, but he was still perched on the mast. His hands, gripping the rigging, were as transparent as white smoke. *Fuck!* He shouted and lost his hold, spinning toward the deck.

Φ

Alea leaned against the bow, eyes closed and face tilted to the sunlight straining through the dense clouds. Beside her, Bren retched over the rail. He straightened and wiped his mouth before returning to fidgeting with a frayed bit of rope. It seemed to distract him from the nausea rampaging through his stomach.

Behind them, the general paced the length of the ship, occasionally trading words with their captain. Alea followed the conversation, though she could not hear the words. "I love this."

Bren grimaced. "I envy you."

"Not the pitching ocean," she clarified, "the journey. For the first time since leaving it feels like we're making progress."

"When does the confusion end? My world's replaced with something entirely different." He rested his head on the rail, though perhaps it was from seasickness, not despair.

Alea turned to him. *What can I say? That it gets better?* She was not sure, yet, whether it did. "When my city was destroyed, my only thought was to survive. Then in Vielrona, all I wanted was to die. It was a violent transition but came in stages. Eventually, I helped around the inn. Then Arman taught me to fight. Then I learned I was Dhoah' Laen. Sometimes I wake thinking I'm still in Cehn and I long for desert air and the smell of the bazaar drifting up to my window. Someday the pain will fade, I think, but a piece always remains."

"I feel useless, Alea," he confided, "I'm your brother, but I just met you. I wonder how I can love you, yet I think I might. And you are surrounded by these legends—Stonefaced generals, Rakos guards. What use could I possibly be?"

He winced when she placed her hand on his but did not pull away. "You're Azirik's only son. You're the heir to his throne, technically. That makes you powerful."

He groaned. "He claimed to have an heir but never spoke more of it. I suppose I know why. Perhaps it's not even me."

"Perhaps." Her grin turned wry. "Besides, power's not all it seems. However hard we try to show them we protect them." Heat swept through her, sparked with white and gold, followed by panic. *Arman?* Atop the mast, Arman's body shook. Darkness grew on the horizon.

She must have clenched Bren's hand, because he looked up, following her gaze to the rigging above. "None of the ocean storms in Mirik looked like that."

Orders pierced the air as they sped toward the building clouds. A reply wove down against the wind. Unoccupied sailors climbed to better vantage points, ready to furl the sails. Gathering clouds obscured the northern horizon, wrapping east and west. Above, the wind began to moan.

"Toar, what is that?"

Shouts drew their attention to the sliver of clear sky above them. Arman crashed to the deck. He pushed himself to his shaking knees.

"Arman?" Alea flew to his side, biting back horror at the man's appearance. Metallic gold and white spots formed on his skin where each raindrop landed and evaporated with a hiss.

"Storm's not natural."

Humming climbed body from the storm's power and the heat radiating from Arman made her dizzy. After a moment she dragged meaning from his words. "Not natural?"

He pressed his forehead to hers.

Jumbled images of red-laced clouds unfurled in her mind. It drove the breath from her body. Her blood chilled. *Keep your head!*

The sky growled, and Bren shot a furtive look at the clouds. "We should go around this."

Alea returned to the bowsprit, ignoring the gazes following her. "That's what Azirik wants." Without looking from the storm, she called back, "Hold your course, captain!"

"You're mad, Dhoah' Lyne'alea! I've seen smaller storms destroy ships larger than this."

"None on deck but the crew," she ordered, ignoring his warning. "Hold your course."

Arman managed to stand. "This isn't the time to prove yourself."

"Stay up here if you must, but there is no choice." Her vision already darkened with anger. She had been attacked, her family killed, but she would not let Azirik take Arman or Bren.

The others wasted no time disappearing below. Silence descended on the ship, save for the captain's commands. Alea planted her feet on the wet, bucking deck, bracing herself against the rail. She would need her hands free. *Pull the power up.* Black ropes curled from her palms until she held handfuls of writhing tendrils. Her eyes glowed through the black shadows flitting on their surface. "I'm ready." *I hope.*

She threw her arms downward, fog spreading like liquid across the deck. It hit the rails of the ship and arched into the sky. A shadowy dome bathed the ship in an eerie glow. Rain splattered through, its course altered but not stopped by the strange barrier.

Lightning laced from the seething clouds.

Azirik! For a second, she saw a man standing on the gravelly shore of Marl Mere. Liquid magic coiled from his outstretched hands, matching the red jasper and copper Crown he wore. His brown hair twisted wildly in the wind and his lips peeled back from his teeth.

She screamed at him.

Clouds boiled in response, spouting lightning. An errant tongue of electricity caught Alea. Freezing agony exploded through her muscles. Even without the veil of power over her vision, her skin glowed. Pain tore itself from her throat in a scream. Her grip on her power faltered and she collapsed against the rail.

The dome of power over *M. Tursio* flickered and collapsed into the waves. Even over the howling weather she heard the mast creak and snap. Their captain shouted something, but she gathered her power again. It was a violation, the gods using lightning against her, the greatest form of creation and destruction in one element.

Arman rushed toward her, but she whirled, hand flying out. Black fog pinned him to the mast. She could not erase the fear from her mental voice, *I'm fine. I'll be fine.* Wrapping her power around the electricity still flashing through her body, she swallowed the lighting. Twice, thrice, a dozen times she was stuck, embracing the bolts and sending them into the clouds.

In her mind she saw Azirik drawing his power back, his face pinched and angry. He fell to his knees as the blood-colored magic trickled back up his arms and into the Crown.

With nothing left to fight, Alea shuddered and dropped to the wet deck. Her body felt hollowed, vacant in the wake of so much energy. A single thought sent her from consciousness: *lightning is mine.*

Clouds receded slowly. Traces of lightning flickered over Alea's body, sprawled at the bow. Arman pulled away from the mast only when the last spiral of black fog retreated into her skin. No one moved until one of the sailors began to murmur prayers to himself. The captain's "all clear" allowed the others to reemerge. Bren crouched over Alea. Eerie blue-silver still glowed from her skin. A trembling hand touched his shoulder. Arman swayed behind him.

"I wouldn't touch her," Bren warned.

Arman wrapped his bare arms around her, heedless of the power lapping his skin. He carried her below deck to her bunk. Bren followed, sitting nervously on his own pallet. Arman flopped against the wall at the foot of Alea's bed. His hand rested on her ankle.

"What was that?"

"She knew she could do it. Somehow found control." Arman's eyes lidded with exhaustion. "Fates help those who stand against her."

Φ

The 26th Day of Vurgmord, 1251
The Northern Shore of the Iron Sea

The stale smell of seawater ad tar clung to the close air of the ship's bunks. Bren's shift watching Alea had just begun. He tucked himself in the bank across from hers, book perched in his lap. Nausea prevented him from concentrating on the words, but with calmer weather, he managed a few lines at a time.

Alea burst upright, choking and wheezing. Her wide eyes were their usual gray-blue.

Bren steadied her. "You're safe."

"I can still feel it. The lightning."

Bren winced. "I'm glad I didn't see you struck. I thought you wouldn't make it."

"Where's that faith you gods-fearing folk have?" she shot back. Her face sobered. "So did I, for a moment. My muscles feel as if I've run miles."

"It hurt?"

She shrugged. "I couldn't get away from it. When you hurt a foot, you can distract yourself. This was everywhere. In my power even. It hurt, surely, but I almost liked it. It felt old, natural." She fiddled with her blanket. "What happened to the other ships?"

"The *Tursio* went down. Her mast snapped, ripped the hull right in two. Some of her men were able to climb aboard the *Vichore.* They're a few days behind, but she'll come into port for repairs. She's limping, but she'll live."

Alea looked away.

"You didn't kill them. The storm did."

"I didn't say I had."

"Your face did. I've killed. I know what it looks like."

"I killed men in Vielrona. I barely remember it, but it's always there, in the back of my thoughts. Arman tells me it couldn't be helped, that it was my power, not me."

"No amount of denial helps the guilt. I've tried, and it doesn't work." Bren sat back. "He's wrong. It was you. You are your power."

She glanced at him, gaze blade sharp.

His eyes were gentle, and he took her hand. "You killed them, and it's all right."

Φ

The 29th Day of Vurgmord, 1251
The East of the Hartland Forest

Dense trees sheltered the army from the incessant wind off the Felds. Numbering just over two thousand three hundred, the combined Mirikin and Berrin moved slowly. Only the officers and vanguard were mounted. Captain Orrin glanced again at the hint of sun through the canopy. A mile ahead the lieutenant of the vanguard signaled they closed in on their destination. Azirik's missives dictated they meet at the fork of the river. The knight leading the Mirikin regiment took up the rear, though their men had not remained completely segregated.

The vanguard began to lay camp within sight of the forest, at the joining of two rivers. By the time the last ranks arrived, shielded cook fires burnt and the sun was low. Orrin was studying the maps when an alert for an approaching ally went up. He hurried from his tent to see Azirik ride in. The king brought only a patrol with him, as well as a few others Orrin did not recognize. Azirik's seat on his white charger was flawless, and Orrin winced. The Berrin were not horsemen by any stretch of legend, so Orrin never minded that he sat his mount like a sack of fish-guts. That is, until he saw Mirik's king, who rode as if born to it. Shaking away the injury to his pride, he raised a hand in greeting.

Azirik's men set up their own camp. The four strange companions followed the king as he went to Orrin. Two, unmounted, dressed in buckskin, the others in flowing robes.

Azirik took Orrin's arm. "The sieges are going as planned, no substantial enemy reinforcements thus far." He spoke without preamble. "How goes the march?"

"Fair. We made good time across the Felds."

"My men are glad to be out of them—the wind is torture."

"Reminds us of home," Orrin said with a hoarse laugh. "You rode from the Iron Sea?"

"Through the nights." Azirik's face twisted. "We caught word the chit still lived. We thought to end her in the sea, but she has a better idea of her power than our informants led us to believe."

"What is your next move?" Orrin sat by his fire and gestured for Azirik to join him. "Return to Mirik?"

Azirik regarded the fire thoughtfully. "Mirik's served her worth. I need an outpost on the mainland. I have one in mind." He gestured to the warriors at the edge of the firelight. "I bring allies. The ones in skins are Bordermen. They prove invaluable to our journey and I hope these two will accompany you on your next assignment."

Orrin peered closer. Their tanned skin was tattooed, one bearing lark's wings on his cheeks, the other fox-tracks across his brow. Bone and wood fastened their myriad braids. The fox-marked man offered his arm, "I am Vuli and this is Kire."

Orrin greeted them before turning to the others. They were tall, with layers of cloth wrapped over their breeches. Tight leather caps topped their heads "You are the Vales?"

The brighter-clad man nodded. "Ju-al Rones the Junior. I'm an interpreter and this is my guard, Baj-ik. His Majesty King Azirik requested I help with discussions when my fellows arrive."

Orrin turned to Azirik once again. "Are we still to attack Fort Shadow?"

"It receives reinforcements in a week—response to the sieges no doubt. Make certain you've claimed it before then." He handed the general a thick envelope. "This is the intelligence the Bordermen found. The Athrolani may retaliate, as Shadow's close to their capital. Let them fight you, but do not let them win. I want you to occupy them for as long as possible."

"You're moving your home-post and need them to be distracted?"

"I'll expect regular reports," Azirik continued without answering the question. "You'll remain well informed of the enemy—Vuli has a companion traveling with the Dhoah' Laen." He glanced over at his emblazoned tent beside Orrin's own. "We'll be gone before sunup. Come pray with me."

Orrin followed him into the dark green tent. One wall held a wooden altar, flanked by two soldiers. Priests' robes belted over armor were an eerie sight. Azirik knelt before the altar, pushing back his hood. Orrin did likewise, nervous. He knew the rites, but no Berrin was as devout as Azirik. The Mirikin crown glinted as Azirik placed it on his lap. The king produced a hollow bull's horn from his belt and poured fine ash into a copper disk. Priests poured a few drops of dark oil over the ash while Azirik cut a shallow slit in his forearm. Blood dripped into the disk.

He took Orrin's arm and cleanly made a similar wound. As his blood joined the strange mixture, Orrin noticed the hundreds of healing slices on Azirik's arms. *He has done this countless times.* He regretted his own poor observance of rites and holidays.

Metal hooks in the ridgepole held the disk. Ash, blood, and oil slid slowly down the copper. "From the ashes of your enemies, from the blood of your servants, from the oil of your temples, I beg you hear your devoted soldier." Azirik bowed his head. "I beg you speak, Desmondu, lord of all gods, son of Numon Laenslayer. I beg you: tell me your orders, so you may rise again."

Nothing happened for a moment, then the mixture on the disk writhed into the shape of a face. Orrin was struck by how decidedly human it was. Perfect in its proportions and symmetry, perhaps, but quite human. Bright auburn hair crowned the god's head, and his russet skin shone. Pure copper eyes glowed from deep-set sockets.

"Azirik." Perhaps it was the distance and the medium, but his voice was emotionless. "Orrin too, lovely."

"Lord Desmondu." Azirik bowed lower, not even glancing through his lashes. "My thanks for our luck and victories thus far."

"Not as many as I would have liked. What happened on the Iron Sea, Azirik?"

"She reflected the power back, I think. It was a mistake to use lightning. If we capture her, we need a way to bind her."

"When you capture her, you will kill her without delay." The rebuke was cold.

"Of course, my lord." While not contemptuous, Azirik's reply was not humble either, and Orrin found himself admiring the way the king held his own against the Lord of the Gods. "And in what way do you suggest we kill her?"

"She can die, like any Laen."

"Do you not wish me to destroy her power as well?"

The god paused, a frown appearing. "As my father did with their leader?

"Numon destroyed her completely, did he not? How was it done?"

"Capture and bind her. We will end her together," Desmondu decided.

"The metal-woven ropes were useless against the others of her kind. Do you suggest chain?"

"Make them with the Crown. Make them of steel. She is untrained, I don't see why you can't craft one that will hold her." Desmondu sounded impatient. "Speaking of, don the Crown, will you?"

Azirik unlocked a drawer in the altar. Resting on red velvet was the Gods' Crown.

Orrin's gut lurched at the sight. He heard Azirik possessed the Crown, but seeing it was different. Irregular blood-color jasper studded the hammered copper. The king placed it carefully on his head, arranging the braided lock from his crown to hang over the metal in the back.

"I'm tired of not always seeing what transpires." Desmondu's voice was abruptly casual. "I thought you might wear it more often." Seeing the tightness on Azirik's face, he laughed lightly. "Oh, come now. I know it's uncomfortable for mortal men, but do realize it could be worse." Ferocity hardened the final word.

The Crown buzzed, biting into flesh.

Azirik gasped. Metal squeezed through the thin layer of flesh and fused to the skull. His eyes screwed shut and he let out a low moan. Blood oozed down his face. Acrid smoke from burned bone lingered in the air. Azirik no longer had a choice to wear the Crown. He met Desmondu's gaze, "Am I mistaken, or do you no longer trust me?" His voice was clipped with pain.

"One of your men deserted you and still lives. You lost on the Iron Sea. To a girl-child. I trust you'll do your utmost to bring us victory from this point forth." The god's face disappeared from the disk, leaving a strange silence. Orrin looked over at the king. Unease writhed in his gut at the sight of metal melded to bone and skin. He saw gory deeds in battle, but this was worse. *"Gods help us," has a new meaning after this.* He helped Azirik to his feet. Unsure of what to say, he glanced over. "There was a deserter?"

"A lieutenant. He joined them. If I knew before he was gone, the problem would have been rectified." He gestured to the tent flap, "We've a long ride ahead and little sleep behind us. Send word when you sack Fort Shadow."

Orrin heard the dismissal and bowed. "Of course. May the gods guide your sword." The saying tasted stale on his tongue.

His faith was unwavering, but invoking the Lord of the Gods did not change him the way he expected. After seeing the strength with which Azirik faced his deity and punishment, Orrin respected the man far more. The king would cut the right path. Kneeling at his own, smaller altar to the Berrin's patron gods of the sea, Burme, he began to pray anew.

"God of Sea, of rhythm, of change, grant us victory in this battle. Grant us freedom from the dictatorship of the Laen. Grant us sight to see our paths and heart to choose them. Shield our presence like fog over waves and speed us home on your winds. Save us from error and corruption and the wrongness that runs in the blood of the Dhoah' Laen and her fellows." The image of the Crown searing Azirik's flesh flashed through his mind. "Lastly, grant us peace."

CHAPTER FOURTEEN

The 30th Day of Vurgmord, 1251
The City of Ceir Athrolan

WHISPERS WERE HARD TO IGNORE, but the storm was still fresh in everyone's minds. Alea emerged from her bunk to see they had passed from the sea into a broad river. Grassy hills rolled way on either side of the steep banks, dotted with copses. Tall deer with white banners for tails bounded away as they passed and Alea found she was smiling. By mid-afternoon, the river widened, and the scent of salt drifted in the wind.

"Will we see the ocean?" Alea peered forward, eyes trained for the sight of waves.

Eras smiled at the young woman's eagerness. "We'll enter the harbor from it. I regret to tell you it looks much the same as the Iron Sea. The waves are bigger perhaps."

Alea shrugged. "It smells different enough."

When they emerged, it was into the open expanse of the ocean. Beside Alea, Arman's mouth fell agape. Green black depths surrounded them, and a deep chill filled the air. Waves taller than a man crashed against the boat. Stark white cliffs rose to the left, carved by centuries of constant wind and water.

"It's amazing," Alea whispered. In all the poems she read, none did the view justice. Wind caught their sails and the ship picked up speed. The *M. Xavier* scuttled around a bend where the cliffs dipped inward. Nestled at the center of the inlet sat Ceir Athrolan. Ceir Athrolan was carved in broad tiers in the cliff down to the harbor. Towers flanked the harbor, dwarfed only by those along the city walls. Bright turquoise banners flew from their jagged tops. White roads, shining like silver, ran along the harbor warehouses. Homes and businesses were built above and, several levels higher, sat the palace.

Spanning the port's entrance was a bridge, supported by stone pylons thousands of paces tall. They glided underneath and into the harbor. Arman's hand brushed Alea's Doubt had rooted firmly in their minds since Fort Hero. Now, for a moment, it lifted in her mind.

Fishing vessels and merchant ships clustered across most of the docks, but walls cut off a deeper section to the right, crowded with massive Athrolani battleships. It was there they made berth. Unloading took far less time with an entire naval yard's worth of dockhands to help. The horses were thinner from the voyage but eagerly pranced as their hooves met firm cobblestones.

"One last ride, milady," Arman groused.

Alea settled herself in the saddle with a resigned sigh. Knowing her destination was visible at the top of the city helped little. "What of our things?"

Eras appeared beside her on her bright red remount. "They'll be laid out in our rooms by the time we arrive."

Raven and his guards took up the rear while Eras led them up the white cobbled street. Aqueducts arched along the largest of the roads. The first tier from the docks housed lower class businesses and taverns, the quality growing higher as they ascended. The widest road ran east-to-west, curving around the northern wall of the palace and bordering the royal gardens before entering the distant woods. Rising above the city like a second sun, was the palace's whitewashed dome.

At Eras's raised hand, they entered the courtyard, the gates rolling closed behind them. Falling water from the fountain replaced the sounds of the city. Stables stretched the length of the palace's western wall.

Eras handed her reins to a squire and turned to the steward who appeared from the dark double doors to the palace. "Afternoon, Master Valadai. Is Her Majesty receiving us already?"

The steward chuckled. "Guests this important? Her Majesty has been ready for the past two days. She understands the value of a bath and fine clothes for such things, however."

Eras sighed in relief. "I've grown soft in my cushioned palace life. These days on the road wore on me worse than usual. She turned to Alea, who dismounted shakily. "We'll see you again soon. Relax while you can."

"If you are your companions would all follow me?"

Alea's balance still rolled from the ship, but she managed to accept the steward's bow with a nod.

Despite the might of the city, delicate architecture decorated its palace's foyer. Glass made up the north wall, behind which was a small aviary and indoor garden. Alea's wonder at Vielrona's castle paled in comparison to the awe at Ceir Athrolan's splendor. Between the hall's series of marble arches hung mirrors and mosaics.

Eras and Raven retired to their permanent residences on the other side of the palace, while Valadai showed the others to their guest chambers. Alea's were in the corner near the southeast tower, Arman's beside it and Bren's next to his.

The steward handed them the keys. "Maids will bring whatever you ask, and water is being drawn now for your baths. Midday meal can be taken in your rooms, though the gardens are beautiful in such weather." He smiled. "Might you need anything else?"

"No thank you, sir," Alea answered, hoping her exhausted expression resembled a smile.

"If you think of anything, I'm Master Valadai."

When he had gone, Alea threw open her door and dissolved into nervous giggles. "Our own staterooms! Can you believe it?"

Arman grinned. "At times like this, it is hard to imagine you being the embodiment of Creation and Destruction."

She waved a dismissive hand at him. "I suppose it'd be terribly embarrassing for either of you to be excited over finery." She stepped into her chambers. "I'll see you at supper, then." Her door blocked their rueful laughter.

A large, curtained bed took up one wall, and a sitting area and desk sat opposite. The private privy entrance was hidden by a silk dressing screen imported from Ban. Excitement bubbled through her.

Dhoah' Laen or not, this is the fanciest room I've seen in my entire life. Dove gray and light blue were suspiciously akin to the colors of the Laen and she wondered if the room was decorated specifically for her. Turning in a circle, she admired the finery once more before rushing to answer the knock at her door.

"Dhoah Lyne'alea, your bath," a maid called through the thick wood. A girl a few years older bobbed a deep curtsy when Alea let her in. "I'm Girre, my lady. Welcome to Ceir Athrolan."

Alea smiled. "Thank you, Girre. The city is beautiful!"

The corners of Girre's eyes crinkled as she bustled into the privy. Plain gray tiles surrounded a large copper tub set into the floor. The water in it steamed and Alea let out a preemptive sigh of pleasure. Girre laid out a box of different scented soaps and scrub brushes, tucking up the skirt of her palace uniform. She dipped a hand into the water and nodded. "That should do, my lady."

Alea undressed and slipped gratefully into the hot water, submerging herself completely for a few seconds. She leaned back against the heated sides of the bath and let Girre comb out and wash her hair, stiff with salt and travel.

"Have you lived in the city your whole life?"

"I have, Dhoah'. I was raised just above the warehouse district. My Pa owns a lending house for the smaller shipping companies."

She remembered the prestige of working in the manor and assumed it would be the same. "Your family must be proud that you work here."

"Indeed." Girre's cheeks glowed. "Begging your pardon, but I'm amazed to hear how far you traveled—and almost alone."

"No need, Girre. Sometimes it surprises me too. I had much help." She dipped her head back in to rinse the soap from it. "Would you mind if I simply sat here for a spell? My body feels the traveling."

Girre excused herself, taking the traveling clothes to be cleaned. *Or burned.* Alea closed her eyes, letting the heat work knots from her muscles. Through the stone she heard Arman's voice, speaking with excitement as he wondered at his own heated bath. She laughed. *He's just as much a country-lad as ever, despite what he'd have us think.*

When she finally emerged, a tray of food awaited her along with an envelope. She pulled on one of the dresses Girre must have brought and knocked on Arman's door. There was no answer and she was about to knock again when Bren poked his head out from one door down.

"He went into the city with Raven, said he needed something. I've not eaten yet, want to join me?"

His chamber was much like hers but decorated in brown. It seemed even Athrolan drew the line at decorating with Mirikin vermillion. They sat at the small table and began to eat, enjoying silence and company. Chilled soup and rolls were simple and flavored with rosemary. When she finished, Alea leaned back with a contented sigh. "I wondered if we'd ever make it here."

"I know. I was growing rather used to the Berrin chasing us. I'm almost sad to see them go."

Alea threw her napkin at him. "Careful what you wish for there, brothermine."

He smiled roguishly, "Are you looking forward to Arman and myself making asses of ourselves tomorrow?"

She frowned. "Tomorrow?"

He reached over to his desk and waved an envelope identical to the one she had forgotten on her desk. "We're invited to a ball. It will be our informal introduction to the court, after meeting the queen."

Alea blanched. "I have nothing to wear!

Bren snorted. "I should write Azirik and tell him I've found the Dhoah' Laen's weakness—she's completely lost in the face of no fashionable dresses."

Alea glared at him, then shrugged. "It can't be that bad. I learned some etiquette. Customs differ but respect does not."

"It's a bit easier when everyone's bowing to you and not you to them." Bren rose abruptly. "I heard the palace library is the best on the continent, care to find out?"

Alea smiled. "I'll let you explore on your own. I could use some rest." She waved him off and returned to her chamber and undressed. The coverlet was smooth and the sheets soft. *In the excitement of travel, I've forgotten the bliss of luxury.* She rolled over, looking up at the canopy on the bed. "What happens after war? The tales never tell you that."

Φ

Arman dangled one leg outside. The wide stone sill of his window provided a perfect seat. Winter in Ceir Athrolan was cold, but he enjoyed watching the city lights grow as dusk approached. Raven's brief tour only included the main streets and was conducted on the way to the navy barracks beside the harbor.

As much as he was a country boy, it was a relief to once again be surrounded by tall buildings. The expansive storefronts along the main streets impressed him, but nostalgia caused him to dally among the markets.

He glanced at his hand. Each time he looked down part of him wondered whether he would be made of smoke again. The Rakos were dangerous and temperamental by all accounts, so most rumors about them were just that—rumors. *I was away from my body, using my power.* He closed his eyes and let himself drift. His power rose, and he wrapped it around himself, like a cowl. After a moment he opened one eye. Resting on the windowsill, his hands were paler, tan skin all but invisible. Lines of veins, ligature, and knots of muscle were like white smoke. Only his bones still appeared solid. A grin blossomed at the macabre sight. *This will be useful.*

A knock startled him, and he quickly shook himself free of the power before answering the door.

Alea smiled up at him. "I'm headed to look at the gardens—care to join?"

"Of course." Grabbing his cloak, he followed her down the hall. Narrow doors in the base of the southeast tower led out into a quiet orchard. Palace Way ran overhead, ivy climbing the supporting pillars and arches. The garden was cold, but sheltered enough to still boast some greenery. Somewhere water trickled. Arman sighed appreciatively.

"It's beautiful," Alea agreed. Gravel crunched underfoot, and Alea stopped to admire the white, parchment-like bark of the spindly trees. "Even the trees match the marble." Winding paths led to the arched entrance of the memorials and cemetery. Instead, Arman found a stairway up to the top of the city wall. It ran to the edge of the cliffs, looking out over the ocean. Brilliant orange washed the sky as the sun set.

"In all my dreaming I never thought I would look on the sea. If I'd known it looked like this…." His gaze caught her cloak's familiar silver clasp. "Milady, you should find a new cloak. That one's near to tatters."

"It's no such thing. I like it. It feels like home." She peered down at the waves catching the light and rested her hand on his. "I'm glad you came to see the ocean with me."

Her words were simple, but his chest tightened. He squeezed her hand. "I am too."

Φ

The 31st Day of Vurgmord, 1251

"By Toar." Bren whispered his curse, but Alea glanced over. "This place is huge compared to Mirik!"

Alea elbowed him as they followed Eras down the shorter, central hall to broad double doors. Raven was otherwise engaged, but the general offered to escort the group to their audience with the queen.

"Galvanaeu of Ceir Pardelan." Eras greeted the boy standing just outside the doors. "Certainly the most enthusiastic of our squires."

The squire jumped to attention when he saw the general and bowed before stepping inside. After a moment he returned to beckon them in.

Upon being announced, the general knelt. The others followed suit.

Alea stared. Only about ten paces across, the room was beautiful. Banners from each of Athrolan's cities hung from the walls. Mirroring the massive one over the rooms behind, a small glass dome shed bright winter sunlight across the flagging.

Lacy silver wire edging the queen's purple kokoshnik accentuated her height. The lavender silk dress was square necked and the latest fashion. Brown eyes appraised them. "Dhoah' Lyne'alea. Amazing to have you grace our halls. I trust your journey has been fair?"

Alea rose from her curtsy and clasped her hands to hide their shaking. She knew how to address nobility, but standing before the Queen of Athrolan was intimidating in the least. "I am honored to be your guest and thankful for our lasting alliance."

"As am I. Your letter stated you brought your guard with you?"

Alea stepped back, gesturing to Arman who stood. "This is Aud'narman Wardyn of Vielrona. He is Rakos." She heard Arman's gulped breath and hid a smile. *At least he's as nervous as I am.* "I also bring a valuable ally in my brother, Lieutenant Brentemir Barrackborn."

The queen's eyes narrowed. "That's a Mirikin name."

Alea nodded once. "He defected to our cause." It was not strictly true, but the more powerful they looked, the better. Three young travelers in a throne room were scarcely impressive.

"I hope you're enjoying your stay thus far. Forgive me for such a short visit, but I must meet with the Banis ambassadors." A gentle smile flitted across the queen's features. "We will present you to the city and nobles tonight, and formally ally tomorrow, but I wished to catch a glimpse before then. We'll talk more tonight, I am sure."

"I look forward to it." Alea curtseyed again before allowing Eras to show them out. When the doors closed behind them, Alea let out her breath. "Fates."

"You handled that better than I did the first time I met Her Majesty." Eras glanced over. "I tripped and mispronounced my own name."

Alea could hardly picture the general as anything less than controlled. "I met a fair share of nobility while living at the ihal's manor. Queens are a different breed, though."

"Her Majesty Tzatia and I don't always see on level, but she's a force to reckon with." The general paused at the front entry chamber where their paths parted. "We'll meet three hours after sunset to be announced to the ball."

Arman winced at the reminder. "Will it be as nerve-wracking as that was?"

Eras's brows twitched. "You'll have the entire court watching you, as opposed to a dozen guards and clerks."

Bren groaned as she left. "I think I'd prefer to take my chances with Azirik."

Alea rolled her eyes at his dramatics and returned to her room. *My first days in a legendary city and all I want to do is sleep!* Still, she had little time before Girre arrived with her dress, and time alone was increasingly rare. She fished a book from the small shelf above her desk and settled on her window ledge.

She was still there when Arman arrived two hours later.

"Milady?" He knocked on the doorframe.

She glanced from the view of the city and smiled in greeting.

He took a seat beside her and nodded to the rich skirts tucked under her knees. "Athrolan becomes you."

She shrugged. "I suppose. Are you looking forward to the ball?"

He made a face. "I'm excited to see the finery and the food, not to be paraded about like a stuffed peacock."

She snorted. "It'll be something to tell your grandchildren—your night as a prince."

"I think this journey has provided far more interesting stories." He glanced down at his hand, flexing the fingers. "So much has changed, I expect to wake up from a bizarre dream."

She watched him a moment, mirth fading from her heart. He grew into his role without protest. Youthful energy leftover from boyhood was becoming the diligence of a man. *And the fire of a Rakos.* "I rather miss the quiet of the forest and the tales you told to pass the time."

"I do too. My tales seem stale and colorless when we sleep under the dome of Ceir Athrolan's palace."

She ran a hand along the spine of her book. "They never seem stale to me." Her voice softened. "Whenever I was scared or lost, I'd tell them over to myself. It wasn't the same, but it was comforting. You spoke the words so factually it was no small stretch to think them true."

"I just became the guard to the Dhoah' Laen. What could be myth after that?" He held up his hand. "I discovered something, right before the storm. My hands turned to smoke."

Remembering the heat radiating from him when he crashed to the ship, she shuddered. "I've never heard of such a thing."

"Me neither. Another thing to study while we're here." He pointed to the book, forgotten, in her lap. "Speaking of studying, what's that?"

"A history of the Xain house and how they changed the architecture of the city. Quite dull, really."

Girre's knock interrupted Arman's laugh.

Alea called for her to enter and rose to put her book away. The maid stepped in, a large box under one arm. Seeing Arman, she flushed and looked away. "Apologies, I didn't know you had a guest." She curtsied. "Good evening, my lord."

Arman made for the door. "And to you, miss." He glanced at Alea, "I'll see you shortly."

When he was gone, Girre let out the breath she had held. "Forgive me, but he makes me nervous."

Alea frowned as she stepped behind the dressing screen. "Truly? He's a kind man."

"That may be, but the look in his eyes—he'd kill if someone stepped the wrong way about you. You're lucky to have him." Girre dropped the box onto the stand beside Alea's wardrobe. "Have a look at your gowns, my lady. The top one is for this evening, and the one beneath is for the Ceremony of Alliance tomorrow."

Masses of silver dupioni banished any lingering fatigue. "I can't wear this!"

Girre looked up from making the bed, stricken. "Does it displease you? We used the finest!"

Alea laughed. "Oh, it pleases me plenty. I've never seen anything so fine. I meant that I don't feel worthy to wear it." Steeling herself, she ran a hand down the rich silver silk.

Girre gave her an odd look. "Begging your pardon, but I heard you grew up a noblewoman."

"I was the foster-daughter of a Sunamen ihal, like a duke or governor. We had fine things and a beautiful home, but nothing like this." She fingered the black ribbons gathering the loose sleeves of the underdress before laying it carefully over the stand by her bureau.

Beneath was a more somber gown. The black-on-black brocade gleamed subtly. She drew it out and held it to her body. The shorter overskirt showed silver cloth beneath, which matched the jahi folded around the shoulders of the sheer sleeves. While the first gown dripped with embellishments, this exuded simplicity. "This is wonderful."

Girre drew several petticoats from the wardrobe.

"I take back everything wonderful I said about your city," Alea grumbled at all the layers. "I'll be unable to draw breath with all of that under my…." She stumbled over the strange word.

"Sarafan," Girre laughed, helping her into the layers before slipping the underdress over Alea's head. "Now, turn about." She tugged the overdress into place and fastened the buttons. "Now sit, I'll do your hair and face paint."

"Do you think I'll look the part?" Nerves made her insecure, and the fancy fabric did little to make her feel like herself.

Girre smiled. "My lady, this is court armor. In this, you could be a princess yourself."

Alea caught sight of the black gown, waiting on the wardrobe for the ceremony the next day.

In this, I might be a princess, but in that, I could conquer gods.

Φ

Sundown arrived with a herald of every palace bell. Arman straightened his white tunic for the hundredth time and fussed with his curls again, before stepping into the hall to meet Bren.

The former lieutenant glanced at him wryly. "Toar, we wash-off well!"

Arman mock-scowled. "I did all right, but that orange makes you look like a right prat." He indicated the deep vermillion of Bren's tunic. They were dressed similarly in breeches—Bren's a deep burgundy, Arman's white—with embroidered tolstovka under their tunics. Arman fiddled with the wrist of his green shirt nervously. "Has she come out yet?"

Bren shook his head. "Women take forever with their face-paint and baubles. We should get to the foyer before they announce us."

"They won't without her." Arman cast a last glance at Alea's door, then followed her brother down the hall. They met Raven and Eras just outside the throne-room door. Raven wore his sword and was dressed as they were but in pale grays and turquoise. The latter did not become him.

Eras's calf-length sarafan was made of teal silk and split in the back and front, as if for riding. Underneath she wore a bloused white shirt and breeches. She grinned, and Arman was surprised to note she was attractive under the hard exterior. "Once Her Majesty arrives, we'll be announced. Arman will have Dhoah' Lyne'alea's arm, and Brentemir, you will have mine." She glanced at Raven, "Monareka will join us shortly, you may escort her."

Bren leaned back against the wall to wait. Reka arrived a moment later, dressed like Eras, but in saffron and brown, accompanied by a striking woman.

Arman glanced at them, then froze. His gaze inched over Reka's companion. Alea was dressed in brilliant silver. Every inch of the silver silk, from the thin straps to the lace hems of the skirt was embroidered. Ribbons gathered the bloused sleeves of her black underdress. The upper half of her dark hair was braided back and held under a blue and black net. Her kohl-rimmed eyes met his and her nervous smile broke the spell.

"You look nice." He smiled. "I hardly recognize my road-partner."

She wrinkled her nose, "I'd rather be able to breathe!" He frowned, but she waved the comment away. "Never mind, I'm just nervous."

Doors swung open and a path cleared as the heralds called for order. Brilliant colors and lights glinted just beyond.

"Give me your arm!" Alea hissed. Gripping his elbow, she whispered, "We almost fit in here, with all the nobles."

He jostled her with his arm and stepped into the throne room. Wooden panels folded back, and musicians now sat where the throne had been earlier that day. Now it rested on a larger one at the back of the ballroom. Networks of gold-washed chains held chandeliers across the bottom of the dome. A cleared circle surrounded the area where the queen awaited them. She wore lavender as before, but now it was deeper and trimmed in the same blue that decked the walls.

Alea's curtsey tugged Arman into a bow. "We're honored to be here, Your Majesty."

Tzatia beckoned them over, "Dhoah' Laen, let me introduce you to my court." The silent nobles around her craned to catch a glimpse of the legendary guest.

Alea moved to stand beside the queen, Arman a step behind. Music began, and chatter renewed. Arman's gaze followed Bren enviously as the lieutenant disappeared with the military members of their group.

"Only four of Athrolan's seven provinces are represented officially tonight," Tzatia explained. A tall, elderly man approached at her gesture. "This is lord Tevon, Duke of Pardelan. His son, Geladai, is one of our naval commodores."

Alea bowed her head. "Well met, my lord."

"I saw your sister, Lord Tevon," Tzatia noted. "If you would, tell her I wish to introduce her to Dhoah' Lyne'alea."

Tevon smiled. "Of course." He bowed. "If you excuse me, I'll sample the newest fare of your kitchens."

Tzatia laughed and waved him away. "We grew up together," she confided. Over the next few minutes, she quietly introduced Alea and Arman to the Earl of Ceir Felden and the Duke of Ceir Tetran. As the latter moved off, Eras called the queen away.

Alea put a hand to her brow. "This is confusing. All these foreign names and white faces blend together."

"I just hope there won't be an examination where we must remember each one." Arman glanced over at the small clusters of dancing. "Even a waltz would be better than sitting through this procession of nobles."

"Dhoah' Lyne'alea." A well-dressed man in blue filled Tzatia's place. "I'm Sir Daymir of Ceir Athrolan, Her Majesty's nephew." Even without the mention, his dark hair and brown eyes spoke to the relation. Daymir glanced at Arman. "You must get weary of this. I certainly did when I was new to court." He ignored Arman's narrowed eyes and turned back to Alea. "My aunt suggested I give you a dance."

Alea glanced at the extended hand. "I'd be delighted."

Φ

Daymir's brows rose at Alea's steps. "You know many Athrolani dances?"

She smiled. The dress and press of people made her dizzy. "A very few. We learned traditional ones from surrounding lands. Lately, I've been practicing the less formal steps, however." Steady notes became the quick pace of a four pair dance and Alea enjoyed the brief introductions as they exchanged partners. By the time the second dance ended she was breathless and her cheeks hot.

"Shall we find a quieter corner?" Daymir pressed a glass of lemon water into her hand and found a small alcove across the room.

She tried not to collapse onto the cushioned bench across from the nobleman. She observed him over the rim of her glass. He was over ten years her senior, but his eyes and energy were youthful.

"What do you think of our city?"

"She's beautiful," Alea answered, wondering what, exactly he meant. As friendly as he seemed, she knew his type.

"If you have the chance, you should see the surrounding hills. I'd be happy to ride with you, if you'd like."

Alea smiled, but she felt her guard rise. "Perhaps. I know Arman expressed an interest."

"Your guard?" Daymir glanced across the room. "Is he truly Rakos?"

"Yes. He is learning himself, though, like I am. He will be incredibly powerful." She took another sip of water. "You bear the title 'sir.' Are you a gallant?"

"I am, but my duties differ." His gaze traced the dome above them. "Athrolan is not as beautiful as she once was. I hope you might brighten her a bit."

She followed his gaze, thinking of An'thoriend. "She's faded with grace, if you insist she has at all."

"The legend of you didn't fade." His thin face was intent.

Her gaze flicked to him, but she did not answer. There was interest in his eyes. Not lust, something more calculating and curious. He was powerful and intelligent. Moreover, he knew it.

Φ

Arman took a deep sip from his goblet of mead. "Uncomfortable clothes aside—a man could get used to this." He enjoyed the swirling colors and music, but only from a distance.

Reka's lips thinned. "I need the quiet—this many people in one room makes my skin crawl."

He laughed. "Fair enough."

Reka nodded to where Bren sat close to a pretty young woman whose name Arman could not remember from their introductions. "I think he wants to get used to this life!"

"These people aren't like those he's accustomed to. The nobles play to keep, especially with the power he could have."

Reka shrugged, "You people are too preoccupied with power. Besides, he says he doesn't want it."

"He may get it, either way. I think Her Majesty wants him to take up Mirik and be an ally." Catching Alea's brother's eye, Arman waved him over.

The former lieutenant maneuvered his way through the crowd, leaning against the wall beside them. "How is your evening?" He grabbed two pastries from a passing page.

"Not as entertaining as yours, apparently." The Bordermen had the unnerving habit of never smiling, which made it hard to tell a joke from the truth.

Seeing the crinkles at the corner of her eyes, Bren laughed and waved her words away. "It's harmless flirting."

Arman snorted. "Careful. Nobles are a different breed."

Bren ignored him, scanning the crowd for Alea. She danced with Daymir again. "Lady Fariel mentioned the queen's nephew—with Alea—is next in line for the throne." He offered Reka his hand. "Dance?" When Reka glanced up in surprise, he grabbed her hand.

"I suppose you're the only one who might tread on my feet as often as I do yours. I might actually look good by comparison." She followed him out, and they pranced around. Bren laughed at their clumsiness and wrong moves and at the good-natured or haughty looks they received.

Φ

Breathless, Alea appeared beside Arman at the refreshment table. "I forgot how many muscles dancing involves! You think hand-to-hand fighting takes strength? Try a three-step! I'm glad that woman pulled Daymir into conversation or I'd never have gotten free. "

Arman laughed. "You looked like you were enjoying it."

"You're not much for dancing?" She found a hand-plate and piled it high with candied fruit. "Have you tried anything? Is it good?"

Arman hid a grin at her barrage of questions. "Try the brown things. They're filled with cream. You'll enjoy it—it's too sweet for my tastes." He gestured to a free bench along the wall. "As for dancing—I never was very good. I hate making a fool of myself, especially in front of people I don't know. Wes says I'm too proud."

"Hence why you ended up fighting through half your boyhood?"

He shot her a glance, one brow raised. "I thought you weren't going to mention that story."

"I wasn't going to tell anyone else that you were acting like a paving cobble for several hours. I said nothing about reminding you you're human." She lost herself for a moment as she tried the small pastry Arman indicated.

"Only part of me." He grinned broadly, displaying his teeth.

She wiggled her fingers, marbling her skin black in response. "Look at us, dueling powers for fun in the corner of a ball because we lack the socializing needed to mingle."

"I thought you liked dancing with the heir to the throne."

Alea's brows rose. "He failed to mention that." She picked Daymir out in the crowd. "The dancing was fine, but he looks at me oddly."

"I think he's trying to gauge you. You're new, but unlike the other young, pretty women he has paraded before him, you're Laen, you're powerful, and you're intelligent."

"I'm certain other noble women are just as intelligent, Arman, but I see your point. I guess I'm not used to being scrutinized."

"If you're finished, may I?"

Alea stared at his half-smile and offered hand. "Are you taking my plate or asking me to dance?"

"If you can't tell, perhaps I should rethink the offer." He glanced over at the musicians. "I might as well make a fool of myself where rumors can't get back home to Veredy."

Alea giggled and took his hand. "Depending on how poorly you dance, they just might."

Stiff steps lacked his usual grace, but his fingers on her back were gentle. He caught sight of Bren and Reka and snorted. "No one can argue he was raised in the barracks!"

Alea followed his gaze to where the two cut a wide swath through the other dancers. "Just think of the steps like combat motions."

He watched the surrounding partners and tried to follow suit. "Strike, kick, step aside." He responded. His eyes softened. "I suppose this isn't terrible."

"I promise I won't tell Veredy. She might think I bespelled you if you're dancing at a palace ball."

Arman's smile faded, and he stepped away as the music ended. A strange series of expressions crossed his face, but he finally settled on a faint smile. "You should enjoy a better partner, thank you for tolerating my lack of skill."

Alea watched him go for a moment before being swept up in another dance, this time opposite her brother. She did not dance with Arman or Daymir again, but by midnight her yawns were jaw-cracking.

She retreated to a corner to gulp down another glass of lemon water. The ball was beautiful and the dancing lively, but something nagged her. *I don't feel like the Dhoah' Laen. I feel like an imposter. This city's grandeur is not meant for me, but some powerful inhuman creature.* That thought stalled what remained of her excitement. *Is that really what the Dhoah' Laen is? Is that what I must become?*

Her stomach churned, and she ducked out of the room, racing to her chambers. She was tired, and the journey taxed more than just her body. Tearing out of her fine gown, she scattered tiny pearls across the floor. Without the trappings she felt more herself, but that was little comfort. She curled on the floor, naked in the dark. The tiles of the privy floor bit into her bare knees. How soon until she gave up being human?

CHAPTER FIFTEEN

The 31st Day of Vurgmord, 1251
The City of Ceir Athrolan

PURPOSEFUL KNOCKING WOKE ALEA. She felt as if she had just closed her eyes, but the sky was light.

"Dhoah' it is Valadai. Her Majesty wishes to pay you a visit in a quarter of an hour."

Alea scrambled from the bed. "Of course, thank you!" She pulled on the dress from her audience, running a brush through her hair and re-braiding it.

As she tied the ribbons gathering her sleeves, Girre knocked and entered. She placed a tray of tea and bread on the table of the sitting area before straightening the bed sheets.

"I trust you find the bed comfortable?"

"I was reluctant to leave." Alea smiled. She had forgotten what it was like to talk with other women and a sudden wave of sadness took her breath away. She pressed her fingers to the bridge of her nose.

"My lady?"

"Forgive me. You remind me of my foster sister. I miss her dearly."

Girre bobbed a curtsy. "Thank you, my lady."

Valadai's introduction of the queen cut short Alea's response. She rushed to stand by the sitting area.

Tzatia swept in, the picture of calm and benevolent charm. "Thank you for receiving me, Dhoah' Laen."

"It is a pleasure to see you again, Your Majesty. Will you join me?" She motioned to the chairs, sitting across from the queen. She waited until Girre poured them both a cup of tea and left before speaking again. "To what do I owe the honor?"

Tzatia savored the tea for a moment before fixing Alea with her dark eyes. "You speak noble language well, but let's drop the pretenses. I won't judge you for frank speech." Wry wit in her eyes held the sharpness of a younger life. "I came to discuss our business today and your stay here."

Alea leaned back, relieved, but wary. The queen bore her sixty-odd years with grace. Something about her iron-colored hair and fierce features reminded Alea of the Laen. *And I see the calculating mind she bequeathed to Daymir.*

"It's tradition to accept an alliance as a favor, to which you would respond with gifts during the ceremony." Her cheeks rounded with a smile. "I think you see the folly in such a thought when it comes to you and your guard. It may be that you need more defense, but..." she paused, as if finding the proper words.

"One does not request gifts from titans or gods." Alea shoved her fear away and gripped the chill in her chest. Her love for economics paired with Daymir's claim that Athrolan faded told her enough. "You need us. You need the inspiration of a cause."

"Did your wisdom come when you discovered your power or were you always so astute?"

Alea laughed softly. "Perhaps a bit of both. I was ignorant of many things I see clearer now. I don't know whether my new insight is due to age, experience or something entirely different. My foster-father claimed intuition and insight were observations when our conscious minds were not ready to see the reasons. Perhaps I am simply listening now."

Tzatia's clear gaze took the younger woman in without judgment. "You spoke of staying in among us for some time."

"Most assume I'll run to Le'yne. What I can learn from my people can wait. I can't expect any to fight for me if I do not first pay my dues. Besides, I can learn things here that I can't in isolation."

"Athrolan will fight for you. Judging by my visit with the Banis ambassador, they will as well, despite their views toward women."

"I am not a human woman." Alea's words were soft, as much out of fear for the truth as manners. She put down her cup. "I need you to understand that while my safety is important—"

"That is a gross understatement."

Alea flushed. "I'm not given to conceit."

"You have a right to it. Forgive me, please continue."

"While my safety is imperative," she amended, "I need to be in the battles. I need to see the bloodshed. I must learn all I can about our enemies and my allies, so I might better train. For myself as well." Her last words were whispered, and the queen did not press the matter. "Arman would argue I should be shut away, lest I stove my smallest toe. That can't be."

Tzatia hid a smile. "I understand. I'm afraid I must get ready for the ceremony, but thank you for seeing me." She paused at the door, fixing Alea with her pointed stare again. "If you need anything, do let me know. I am no longer young, but I understand the sharp edges of power and how deeply they can cut."

Φ

Conversation buzzed behind the doors to the throne room. Alea could hear the patter of pages' shoes against the stone as they hurried about last minute errands. Eras paused on her way by. "Dhoah' Lyne'alea, Commander Dorcal agreed to escort you into the ceremony today, as a show of support."

Alea winced. "Who thought of that one? The man detests me."

Eras's pinched expression could have been displeasure or a hidden laugh. "Very well, would you prefer Arman?"

"Milady can be on my arm." Arman offered.

Alea drew a breath and closed her eyes. *Who thought deciding how I enter a room would be my greatest decision.* "Thank you, general, and Arman, but I think I can walk up to a dais on my own. If I can't, the world has greater problems."

The general held her hands up in surrender. This time her expression was certainly a disguised smile. Eras ducked into the throne room and pulled aside the herald. Silence fell as the queen's entrance was announced. After a moment Valadai opened the doors for them.

"Dhoah' Laen Lyne'alea of Le'yne." Alea schooled her features into calmness. *This is the moment you win over an entire kingdom.* Still a single large room from the ball, it was bright and filled with many more noble families than she met the night before. Tzatia stood at the larger dais in the rear. She dazzled in pure white and turquoise. Stitched white rays on her elaborate headdress drew gazes to the rough-cut aquamarine set in the official crown.

Alea's steps down the aisle were measured. Pens scratched against parchment as scribes detailed the scene. *We're making history.* Arman was announced as she ascended the dais, hobnails in his boots clacking against the stone. *Even his boots sound cocky.* Humor brought a smile to her face as she turned to face the queen.

"On behalf of the kingdom of Athrolan, I welcome you to our city."

"We are honored." Alea hesitated, unsure of how to proceed. Arman's hand was feather-light on her back. "Honored by your agreement to an alliance, Your Majesty."

Tzatia gestured to the podium, where a long sheaf of parchment sat, weighted at the corners. Heralds brought it forward. Burnt into the wood above the declaration was the symbol for honesty and honor, encircled with script.

The queen placed her hand over it and read the vows of the alliance, though she surely could have recited them. "I, Tzatia of the North, Queen of Athrolan, Lady of Ceir Athrolan, swear to defend you as I defend my people. I swear to respect you as I respect my family. Your enemies shall be mine, and your allies will be counted among my own. Your losses will be felt as ours and your victories will be our victories." The herald dripped wax over a loop of turquoise and white ribbon at the bottom. The queen imprinted it with the ring on her middle finger. "In the name of Athrolan, I swear an alliance to you and your cause, Dhoah' Lyne'alea."

Valadai brought forward a chest inlaid with gold. "May I present to you this gift to show our gratitude?" She held onto it a moment as she turned to Arman. "It has been safe-kept in our treasury, but it belongs to you."

Arman bowed and took it in one arm. Nestled within was a long, brown leather whip. The handle was curved slightly and gold-washed. He lifted it out carefully. He flexed his fingers, feeling the weight. Vicious spines jutted from the tip. Handing the chest back to Valadai, he hung the whip on his belt by the ring on the hilt. "Your Majesty, I thank you for this noblest gift." The sincerity in his voice kept the words from sounding trite.

Alea stepped up to the podium then, placing her hand over the symbol and repeated the queen's words. Her voice faltered at "losses." Her chin trembled.

Arman placed his hand over hers, low voice helping her finish. "Your losses will be felt as ours and your victories will be our victories. In the name of the Laen, I swear our alliance to Your Majesty Tzatia of the North and your kingdom of Athrolan."

The wax was melted again, and a black ribbon looped through it. Alea reached out and pressed a fingertip to the hot wax. Her heart thundered. She should reciprocate the queen's gift, but was scared of losing control. She closed her eyes and brought her power up the way she practiced. *Just a layer,* she thought, *just a shell, for protection.* She held her free hand out, toward the queen, beckoning.

Tzatia stepped closer until the Dhoah' Laen's palm was inches away. Black power curled from her hand. "Your Majesty, I offer a gift to your people. Of my power, Destruction is the best known, but there is also the gentler side. With the might of my power, I promise none shall ever wear Athrolan's crown whom does not hold her highest in his heart." The black fog curled around the crown jewel above Tzatia's brow, weaving into the heart of the stone and around the metal binding it. "I swear as long as I draw breath, I will keep your people, our allies from harm." The power sunk into the crown and disappeared. Silver and black faded from her eyes and she stepped back.

Tzatia took her hand and spoke the words that bound pacts for as long as they had been made. "So, it is said."

Φ

The hills behind Athrolan rolled away into the distance. Standing atop the southeast tower, Arman could not see where they became the barren expanse of the Felds. The new weight of the whip at his belt was warm, but far less than the pointed consciousness of the Crown in his room below. Daylight faded over the ocean behind him, and he pretended the lights of the town on the southern horizon were those of Vielrona.

The journey north was exciting, bizarre, and horrible in turns, but he was ready to go home. Crops would be planted soon, and Wes would pick up additional work fixing plow-blades. Veredy would mend winter dresses. Her tan legs would be bare as she waded into the river on warm days.

"Enjoying the view?" Narier leaned against the parapet beside him.

Arman glanced over at the corporal. "Wishing it was a different one, more like."

The soldier's expression softened with understanding. "As beautiful as the city is, it sure isn't home, I'll agree with you there. You didn't strike me as the homesick type, though. I thought the Rakos lived and breathed the Laen."

"I wasn't always Rakos." He looked down at his hands on the worn stone. Veredy claimed there was no longer a place for him in Vielrona. She was wrong. Even if the world's bones shook and he forgot his own name, Vielrona would be home. "I have someone waiting for me."

Narier's brows rose, "Now that's unexpected. Does she know?"

"Know what?" *I miss her? I'm practically soul-sworn to another woman? I'm a monster?*

"That you might not come home."

Arman stared at the man. "Milady's allied. She'll stay here and learn what she can before traveling to Le'yne. When she is ready to battle the gods, I'll be there. Until then, I'm going home."

Narier looked away, his expression guarded. "There are words for what you're feeling right now. Fear is one. Denial is another." He pushed himself upright and turned to continue his watch. "Tell yourself what you must to sleep at night, Rakos," he shot over his shoulder, "but once war gets her teeth in you, she doesn't let go."

THE RAINS OF SPRING

CHAPTER SIXTEEN

The 32nd Day of Vurgmord, 1251
The City of Ceir Athrolan

EACH TREMOR OF PAIN drove air from Alea's lungs. It built, fear filling her mind. Lunging upright, she gasped for air that would not come. Her stomach was in knots and shudders of pain and anger wracked her body. She scrambled to the privy and brought up everything she had eaten the night before. Finished, she sat shakily on the couch, blinking at the faint light streaming in her window. Fluttering still filled her chest. It was not physical, but still very real. Sadness echoed. *What is this?* Waking from dreams was disorienting, but the feeling usually vanished when she awoke.

She washed her face and changed before knocking on Arman's door. He did not answer, and she was about to leave when he rounded the corner. He had clearly been up for far longer than she.

"Milady?"

"Something woke me—a terrible feeling in my chest." She felt foolish.

His expression was grim. "Fort Shadow—it lies on the edge of the Hartland, across a river. A message came a quarter of an hour ago. The Berrin massacred them." He frowned. "Do you think that's what you felt?"

Alea shrugged. She was too tired to deal with massacres and strange sensations. "Perhaps. I'll wake Bren. I suspect Her Majesty will call a formal counsel."

"She has. An hour before noon." He gave her a sympathetic look before ducking into his room. "I'll see you there."

Alea's steps to Bren's door were slow and thoughtful. *How could I feel that?* Where was the pain and fear and sadness from? She knocked loudly on her brother's door. When there was no answer she tried the latch. Finding it unlocked, she pushed it open. "Bren, of all times to sleep like the dead—" She stopped in the doorway, jaw dropping. Her brother was curled around Reka's tanned and bare body. The woman sat up at Alea's voice.

"Oh, good morning, Dhoah' Lyne'alea." Her eyes smiled, and she rose to collect her clothes. "Bren." When he grunted in response, she continued, "Your sister's here."

Bren yelped and sat up, pulling the blankets far higher than necessary. "Toar, Alea! Don't you knock?"

"She did."

Alea just stared at the floor, stammering an apology. "I'm so sorry, Bren! I just found out about the attack and wasn't thinking you might spend the night with someone. I thought you were asleep. I'll be in my room." Turning to go she realized Reka was leaving too and the prospect of meeting her at the doorway was incredibly awkward. She stayed where she was, eyes glued to the floor.

Reka's eyes crinkled again. "Stay. I heard 'attack.' I suspect I'll see you both when counsel is called."

"An hour before noon." Alea echoed Arman's words faintly.

"Thank you, Bren."

Alea blushed again as the door shut behind the warrior.

"Wait a moment. I'm going to dress. Then we can talk." Bren grabbed clean clothes far more hastily than Reka had and dashed into the privy. He was silent, then called through the half-open door. "I didn't mean for you to see us."

"Clearly." Her embarrassment was fading into entertainment. "I wasn't expecting to see her—any woman—bare in your bed."

He stuck his head through the door. "What do you mean by that?"

She sighed, exasperated. "I forget some people are more liberal with their affection and the display of it." She paused. "May I sit?"

"Of course." Bren finally emerged from the privy. "I'm going to order tea—the shock of you appearing has worn off and my head hurts."

She smiled. "You do seem to enjoy the punch here a bit much."

He sat on the edge of the couch and ran his fingers through his hair. "I think I'll stick to ale from now on." The gaiety of the days before flew from his face at Alea's expression. "What is it?"

"The Berrin and Mirikin took Fort Shadow."

"I swear the Athrolani have the least imaginative names."

Alea smiled faintly. "There will be a counsel." She frowned. "Bren, I knew about it before Arman told me."

"What do you mean?"

"I woke up with this terrible ache and a fluttering in my stomach. It was like silk being pulled through me." She shuddered. "It made me sick."

"Did you drink the punch?" When the jest fell flat, Bren took her hand.

"It was as if I felt their anguish."

"You're the embodiment of Creation and Destruction. It's no wonder you feel such things when they happen on a great scale."

"Why did it happen now?"

"You never felt anything you couldn't explain?"

She looked away. "Sometimes in Cehn, I'd wake up feeling queasy, not knowing why. My ihal said some people had nerves. It often came when there were assassination attempts on our house." The tea arrived, and she sat back, taking a few sips to calm herself. She took a deep sip and looked up, "Bren, you and Reka—"

Bren groaned. "Truly, Alea?"

"I never guessed love between you two."

He laughed. "Alea, she and I are soldiers—warriors—not nobles. Our bodies are ours to do what we wish. If we both want company and warmth for a night or two, then so be it." He glanced at her, having the decency to blush. "In Cehn things were different?"

"I was betrothed before I was a woman." It was as if that part of her life belonged to someone else, and she was no longer worthy to speak of Ahren. She ran a thumb over where her betrothal ring used to rest on her smallest finger. "Our emotions were guarded, including love. It was a privilege to see someone express their feelings. Now I just feel as if things were left unsaid. It must be wonderful to have such control and freedom over your body."

Bren frowned. "You were betrothed? When Cehn was razed.... I am so sorry, Alea." He sat back. "You should feel the same freedom. If not with your, ah, love, then with your body. If you don't control your body, how can you control your power?"

Alea wondered the same thing. "I have a battle to wage, I can't be preoccupied with sex."

Bren laughed. "I'm glad you trust me, but I think this discussion would be less awkward had we been raised together."

Φ

Mutters and frowns filled the council hall. Seated between Bren and Arman, Alea was stunned by the gathering. One of the men at the far end of the table rose and went to her.

"Dhoah' Laen, it's an honor to meet you. I arrived too late to meet you at the ball." His dark eyes were friendly. Like most of the high-ranking officers, he was of middling age, raw bulk having given way to padded muscle. "I am Colonel Hamacad of Ceir Felden. I command the North Regiment."

She grasped his arm, pleased by his surprise at the gesture. "Well met, Colonel. This is my friend and guard, Aud'narman Wardyn, and my brother, Lieutenant Brentemir Barrackborn." After both had greeted the man, Alea gestured to the men and women gathered at the end of the table. Are they all gallants?"

Hamacad shook his head. "The woman with the curls and the green insignia is Colonel of the Mountain Regiment, Curiel of Ceir Mere, and the bald man beside her is Admiral Sedden of the Navy. The rest are commanding gallants, right enough, but there are seven more who are unable to leave their posts, along with the Colonel of the South and Admiral Fess."

Thumping boots announced the arrival of the general and commander. Officers rose and slapped their fists to their chests. Reka slid into place beside Bren. The crowd settled only to stand again as the queen entered with a bevy of scribes.

Silence fell when she leaned forward. "Greetings. Athrolan suffered a great loss at Fort Shadow. The attack came early this morning from the forest. We must act immediately. Shadow is far too close to Ceir Athrolan to let this wait. She was supposed to receive reinforcements in two days. This they must have known." She looked to Eras. "General Aneral, what do you suggest?"

Eras looked down at the table. "Sir Indred, would your men be ready in two days?"

"They would, ma'am."

She turned back to the queen. "Indred's outguard has long been our fastest and is among the greatest decorated. Speed and force, Your Majesty, are paramount. With your permission, I'll muster the army in the city, excepting those men previously engaged."

"Permission granted, general. Sir Indred, what do you plan when you arrive?"

Indred pulled a map toward him. "Though it might give us an advantage, we can't move north and swing about. It's how they attacked, and the woods will be rife with scouts." He glanced at Eras, "Ma'am, how many did they number?"

"Over two thousand."

He winced. "We'll be hard pressed if we attack outright."

"Permission to speak?" Bren's interjection was confident, if rude. At the queen's nod, he leaned forward. "The Berrin are used to fighting in isolated groups, like they do on their ships. They're unused to organized combat on a large scale."

"So, if we attack wholly we could have an advantage?"

Bren turned to Eras. "General, I request to ride with the outguard. I could be of use, having fought alongside the enemy."

"And I have my dozen—more if I send word today." Reka crossed her arms. "If rumor serves, Azirik and the Berrin have Bordermen allies of their own."

"Granted, both of you." Eras made a note in a canvas field book before her. "Indred, ride out as soon as your men are able. Attack in the early hours if possible. We know this land better than they and that river may prove an ally in itself. Prepare, sir." Indred and his men filed out.

Alea turned her gaze to Tzatia. "This isn't my vengeance," she said softly, "but it is my war. I ride with them."

Raven's hand clenched into a fist on the table. "Your Majesty, do not allow this. Her power—however well intended—is uncontrolled and unpredictable. I cannot let her wield it beside our men." Refusing to meet Alea's eyes spoke to how cowardly he knew the words were.

Tzatia thought for a moment. "I understand your worries, Commander, but Dhoah' Lyne'alea is not mine to command."

Alea swallowed hard. *I saved you on the Iron Sea.* Keeping score, however, would do little good. "The commander is right. I am untrained. I hope to go, not to use my power, but to learn more about those we fight against and beside. That knowledge may aid me once my power is fully controlled. I studied healing as a girl, perhaps I can be of use."

Now it was Arman's turn to look at her incredulously. "You can't be serious, milady. This isn't a necessary journey across the countryside, this is war."

"I'm aware," Alea snapped.

Tzatia's eyes flicked from Raven's glare to Arman's worried frown, to Eras's thoughtful gaze. "It is your choice to make. You would be safest here, but I can't hold you."

"Then I ride out with Sir Indred."

Eras rose. "Your Majesty, I ask that we discuss the battles in the southern campaign. If Indred needs more men in a week or two, he should have them, but neither should Fort Floodbane or Ceir Felden lack manpower."

"What reports have you received?"

Eras's lips thinned. "The intelligence does not add the way I feel it should. Floodbane was attacked first and while there has been constant fighting, no headway has been made. The forces are almost equally Mirikin and Berrin. They seem only interested in picking at our men, not overtaking. It could be due to close numbers. They've not exhibited weapons we can't counter.

"Felden was attacked within a week by twice as many. It worries me most. They're poor and small, and it's a city, not a fort. It could turn ugly if we're not careful. I sent word to Ceir Pardelan and Ceir Meron asking them to send men to Floodbane and Felden respectively, but with Shadow I fear the attacks are too close. Can we spare men? I called the non-commanding gallants and they'll bring personal troops to aid us, but I think all are concerned about where the next attack will fall. Lieutenant Barrackborn tells us Mirik's numbers are higher than we would have liked and the Berrin navy is unstoppable."

Raven muttered something about testing that, but said no more when Eras's gaze flicked to him.

She looked back to the queen, "I worry many of our enemies' numbers are unaccounted for. We were told they moved north along the Orn de Galin, but nothing has been seen."

Tzatia checked that the scribes penned everything. "General, that may have been the most you've said in your entire service to me. Send word to the gallants to the south and east. Indred will have reinforcements. When we learn more about Shadow's situation we can decide on Felden and Floodbane. To move rashly will risk much. Commander, I want you to increase our navy as much as able. Bring your ships home. I want a blockade around Mirik and along our coast against the Berrin should they come."

Her officers bowed their assent and she stood. The others did likewise, Eras and Raven echoing her next words.

"For country, for kinsman, for honor—may love and luck be with you." The signet ring of Athrolan clacked as she placed her palm on the table's worn wood.

Φ

The 34th Day of Vurgmord, 1251

Bren finished loading another few tent rolls onto a wagon before stopping to take a long draw from a water pail along the barracks' wall. Helping the outguard's three captains pack the wagons and ready weapons made the past three days rush by. Activity roiled between the palace and barracks as food and supplies were gathered.

This was familiar to him—gruff men and mud had raised him from boy to man. Athrolani soldiers were no different from Azirik's, but for the grudging respect they afforded him. One of Athrolan's fifteen cavalry battalions, the outguard numbered nine hundred men. Instead of riding with the usual wagon for every two patrols, each man of the outguard carried everything he would need besides a tent and larger weaponry.

Bren watched the bustle before him with a contented smile.

"Comparing us to your own?" The gravelly voice belonged to a broad, heavy man. His thick hair and short beard were gray. Bren recognized him from the counsel and squinted at the white-ringed insignia on the man's breast, trying to remember the symbols for Athrolan's officers. "Indred, right?"

"Yes. Two marks in white means a gallant." The man offered with a wry smile, indicating the dots beneath the encircled white tower.

Smiling back, Bren offered his arm. "Gallants are like our knights."

The gallant took the arm. "Sir Indred of Ceir Bodian. You've met my middle son, Vinden, Captain of the company at Fort Stone."

"I look forward to riding with you.

"And I will appreciate your input on the enemy."

Bren glanced over, "Your comment, about comparing your men to Azirik's—"

"It was not out of distrust," Indred assured. "I fought in several troops and commanded others before this guard. One cannot help but compare."

"For one, I've never seen this many soldiers for a single city."

"Our cities to the south have their own battalions as well, though smaller than Ceir Athrolan's three." Seeing two men carrying a bundle of arrows, he shouted across the courtyard. "Those are made of wood, not lead, Yarren. For fates' sake, lift them!" He turned back to Bren. "You were a lieutenant?"

Bren nodded. "I commanded a score of men."

Indred straightened. "I look forward to riding with you. I should make sure the wagoneers are squared away. I'll see you at dawn." After a few paces he turned with a grin, "Lieutenant to king is a mighty leap."

Bren trudged over to help cover the wagons, trying to ignore the weight in his stomach at the gallant's words.

Φ

Arman dropped his head to the table with a groan. The surface was littered with supper, strategy, and maps. "I'll go mad if I stare at another piece of parchment. Fancy a walk in the gardens?"

Alea sighed and raised her head from its own pillow of maps. "Arman, we're going to war. Real war. The gardens can wait."

"Milady, you need to have a few moments peace or you'll never survive this."

"I did, at the ball."

"If you enjoyed being paraded around and jostled by a hundred strangers then I don't know you as well as I thought."

She laughed. "It was enjoyable." Finally relenting, she started collecting their papers. "Very well, I'll clean up here if you get my cloak."

His smile proved much of his fuss was an act. As he left his room, he collided with Bren.

"The men are almost ready." Alea's brother said by way of greeting. "Where are you off to?"

"Milady and I are taking in the gardens. We've been staring at tomes for too long."

Bren's face lit up. "I was hoping to see the memorials before we left."

A pained expression crossed Arman's face. "As entertaining as your company is, perhaps you could visit another time?"

Understanding dawned on Bren's face. "You're trying to court her!"

Arman glared at him. "Don't be ridiculous. I'm trying to convince her not to go to war. It'd be mighty hard to do with your warmongering arse following us about and negating my every word!" He ducked Bren's playful punch. "I'll see you tomorrow." He met Alea in her doorway as he exited with her cloak in hand.

"What was the shouting about?"

"Bren and I had a friendly disagreement." He gestured to the hall, "Shall we?"

She took his arm as they walked slowly up the stairway to the monuments. The sun was almost gone, but the glow lit the white stone of the tombs. Alea ran a finger along the writing of a headstone. "It's odd—all they put on these are surnames and dates."

"Some have phrases."

"Epitaphs. In Cehn we called them 'hralji.' They were written by loved ones. No one is entombed without one. There are dates of birth and how long they lived, but none of death." She looked down. "I wish I was able to give my family that."

Arman put a hand on her shoulder. "When this is all over, you can."

Alea paused at the newly turned earth of a soldier's grave to murmur a prayer before following Arman to the cliffs. There was no wall between the monument-dotted hills and the cliffs, so Arman plopped down on the grass at the edge. "Why do you say prayers, even if you never knew them? Even when the gods don't listen?"

Alea frowned. "In Vielrona, I read a philosophical book. It said that people are made of two things—a spirit, made of their experiences—and a soul. The soul is the purest form. The spirit is locked in mortality and fades when they die. The soul passes through the Laen's power into the wellspring of energy in Le'yne."

Arman looked over. "Milady, they say Rakos are soul-sworn to Laen. Is that truly my soul or is it just a pretty name?"

"Your soul." She looked down. "Arman, I wish you weren't forced into this life. It'd be difficult without you, but I'm still sorry."

Arman gazed at her in silence for a long time. He picked up a small rock from the cliff and threw it far into the ocean. The splash was too soft and distant to be heard. "I brought you out here to ask you not to go to Shadow."

She looked over. "Arman, you know that's not possible."

"It is, though. The world's been without you for decades. It can survive another few months while you learn in safety."

"It's been without me too long already! I must make up for that time. You know how important this alliance is. You stood beside me in that throne room and swore their battles would be ours. How can you tell me to stay home and mind my knitting? You told me to use weapons. You told me to fight."

"I also told you to be practical." He sighed, tearing at the grass beside him. After a moment he tugged a tattered piece of parchment from his pocket. "I've been trying to write home, trying to explain everything that's happened. I want to tell them I'm safe, you're safe. I want to share all we've seen. I can't seem to find the words."

"And how does that relate to the cost of Banis silk?"

"Because if you go to this damned battlefield I have to follow you!"

She stared at him. "You want to go home. You want me to stay safe, so you can run back and tell your tales? Boast to your friends? Impress Veredy?" She rose, careful of the cliff's edge. "Then go, dammit. Be gone, whatever it takes to release you from your bond." Her voice shook through forced calm. "I need to sleep before tomorrow. I'm sorry if taking promises seriously is inconvenient to you, but I'm going to Shadow, with or without you."

"Lyne'alea!" Arman watched her stalk into the darkness without answering him. Heat erupted over his skin and he watched his flesh twist and dissolve into smoke. A snarl brimmed on his fangs and he glared out at the ocean. As much as Alea thought the duty was forced upon him, he knew it was not true. *I chose this.*

He just wished he knew why.

CHAPTER SEVENTEEN

The 34th Day of Vurgmord, 1251
The Northern Coast of Athrolan

BREN TURNED HIS BAY cob in a lazy circle. "Welcome to campaign life!" He grinned, gesturing to four horses tethered by his remount. "Yours and Arman's."

Alea secured her personal pack to the frame on one of her liver chestnuts. Her eyes were somber as they took in the light buckboards filled with fletchers and smiths.

"Never seen an army before, eh, sistermine?" Bren was in his element.

"Not like this. Aren't the soldiers nervous?"

"We're raised on army-life. This is like going home. Grief for fallen comrades will fuel rage against the enemy and deepen the bond among survivors." He widened the loose circle his mount paced around her.

"You miss it."

"It was simpler." He watched a wagon loaded with all manner of peddler's goods trundle up the road to the south.

Alea jutted her chin toward it as she checked a buckle on her main mount. "What's that?"

"An army can't survive without its trail dogs. Better food than we can cook, with alcohol and women or men to forget the days. They're not conscripts, with enough right to ride where they may, but they gain protection from us."

Alea watched as more wagons joined the trail-army. *Marches aren't the glorious shining endeavors they are in tales.*

Soon, Sir Indred called for order and the line of buckboards moved out, flanked by soldiers. Marching wound up the narrow trail through the hills. Warmth crept in now, tinged with the scent of approaching spring. Alea fell in alongside what she learned was the tenth patrol. The pace was brisk but not urgent.

"I thought you were the commander's guard," Alea noted when Narier drew up beside them.

"Perhaps I took an interest in your safety." He smiled good-naturedly and jerked his head at the front of the column. "I'm Indred's officially. He just loaned me to Commander Dorcal for the journey to get you."

"Speaking of your safety, where's Arman?" Bren glanced across at her curiously.

Alea's face darkened. "I've not seen him this morning. He could be halfway to Vielrona by now and I'd not know."

Bren's brow shot up. It was obviously a tender subject, but curiosity won. "He said he wanted to convince you to stay in the safety of the city."

"Safety was certainly not foremost among his reasons." Sadness replaced the anger in her tone. She thought he might be one constant she could rely upon. Bren shot her a worried look, but turned to Narier to swap tales of the road.

Though only two days from the city, the ride to Fort Shadow was long, and what comfort Alea gained in the saddle was vigorously tested. The outguard moved quickly for such a large group, and while the first hours were filled with jokes and laughter, the afternoon wore on in quiet. Only the occasional captain riding back or forward cut the monotony of thudding hooves and other horse noises.

Mid-afternoon brought a dusty looking Indred into their midst, calling for the men to change mounts. "How goes the road, milady? Lieutenant?" With no specific title by which to call him, the Athrolani soldiers chose his Mirikin rank and gave him the respect due a captain.

Bren grinned, road dust darkening his teeth. "I missed the marching, sir. Your outguard is an ingenious adaptation."

Indred nodded his thanks. "Dhoah' Lyne'alea, I'm sure you could take a turn on the seat of a buckboard." It was clear by their wary looks that the tenth patrol's two squires would rather she did no such thing.

"I've grown used to the saddle, but thank you."

"We'll camp at dusk and ride out early, but easy. We must save our strength if the Berrin choose to surprise us." He continued down the line, passing the word along.

Reka jogged up beside Alea as the gallant rode off. She lasted only an hour in the saddle before joining the other Bordermen on foot. "You should take his advice. Even I'd rather brave the seat of a wagon than ride on meat."

Φ

It was closer to night than dusk when they finally pulled up at a copse of trees. A patrol had been sent ahead with the tent wagon and the camp waited for them. Quiet clusters tents surrounded small fires as they cooked amongst themselves. Tomorrow they would pass within sight of the large town of Marl Orna, but would not stop. True supper would not happen until they made final camp at Fort Shadow.

Bren stayed awake long after Alea retreated to her bedroll. Twirling the amulet around his neck, he stared at the firelight, singing under his breath.

"I am a soldier and bled have I
For country and king, I will fight.
At last we stand 'neath
the gods' light
I am a soldier now, bleed will I."

"What is that?" Arman crouched at the edge of the firelight. He looked as travel worn as the others, though Bren had not seen him at all that day.

"Kind of you to join us, Wardyn." Fatigue stole any sting from the barb. "It's the symbol of Toar." He waited for the younger man to attack him for wearing a gods' amulet, or laugh at his devotion. Neither came. "Many Mirikin soldiers wear something of the like. It means peace, in case we die without our blessings said."

"You really believed in them." Curiosity, not scorn, deepened Arman's tone.

"I saw the power they gave Azirik and the sway they had over him." He shook his head. "But it was always indirect. I never saw them. Only heard their voices. Not like seeing Alea."

Arman cleared his throat. "I told her I wanted to go home."

"Toar, why?"

Arman shrugged and unrolled his bedroll beside the fire. "Because it's the truth. I don't want to guard her any less, I simply thought her staying would let me go back for a time."

"I doubt any real respite will come." Bren crawled under his own coverlet and stared at the firelight on the tree trunks. "If it does, we'll be too wrapped in war to realize it until it's over."

Φ

Dawn sunlight pierced through the bare branches moments after the call to rise. Alea groaned softly, but crawled out of her bedroll and began to pack. Her movements stilled when Arman appeared from the center of camp. Their eyes met for a second, but she said nothing. She buckled her belt and clipped on a dagger and quiver. The movements were practiced.

"You're getting used to the road."

"It's the only familiarity I have left." She gestured to her saddle-frame with her elbow as she tied up her hair. "Mind handing me that?"

Arman did as she asked before lifting his own pack, already tied up. "We ride out in a quarter of an hour. The boys will be by soon to wrap up camp." He left without another word.

Disappointment and anger churned inside her, and she closed her eyes against the ache. The outguard left the cover of the sparsely wooded hills and entered the northern Felds within an hour. Grasses waved, tall and brown, unlike the scrubby gray of their southern counterparts by Vielrona. At noon they passed within shouting distance of Marl Orna, but continued toward the ominous smudge of smoke on the western horizon.

"At least the road makes it feel like progress is being made." Arman nudged his mount over to hers. "I wrote them, you know. Before we left. You could send a letter too."

"I wouldn't know what to say, Arman. They aren't my family. You seem to have forgotten I can't go home." Regret followed her bitter words, but she was saddle-sore, her shoulder ached, and her head pounded.

Indred called for a halt close to evening. The ground sloped gently down to a vast plain. The broad ribbon of a river tucked close to the expanse of the Hartland reaching north and south. Fort Shadow stood between the forest and the water. The enemy camped around the fort, guarding themselves with rushing water. Smoke hung over the scene. Pyres still burnt, though it was unclear if they were sending the Berrin's dead to peace or the Athrolani to damnation.

"We camp on this side of the river. Squires will set up sleeping tents, men you erect guard posts and barricades." He thrust his hand in the air, signaling to continue.

Alea stared at the remains of battle. Spears pierced the ground at intervals along the near side of the river. Each bore something on its tip. "Are those wards against us?" She peered closer before Arman could stop her. They were the heads of Athrolani soldiers, disfigured and holding parts of their own bodies in their mouths. "Fates." Fighting the urge to vomit she bit down and squeezed her eyes shut.

Arman put himself between her and the sight. "Let's find where we'll be sleeping."

For once she was inclined to agree. The camp came together quickly, soldiers' tents arranged in a loose horseshoe facing the enemy camp, well out of bow range. At the center were officers' tents and makeshift strategy halls, with the infirmary tents forming the arch of the horseshoe. The entire camp was subdued and Alea crawled into bed before supper, too tired and shaken to eat.

Φ

The 36th Day of Vurgmord, 1251

Shrieking Athrolani horns pierced the damp air. Alea's eyes flew open and she flattened herself farther to the ground. She peered under her tent flap. Bren's bedroll was empty and cold when she pressed her palm to it.

A moment later Arman crouched beside her. "Berrin, trying to take the banks." He tugged her to her feet. "Come on." He led her along the east side of camp, farthest from the enemy. Bordering the southeast edge were scores of picket lines.

"They were unloading wagons when I went to sleep last night and now it's a small city."

"They know their work." Arman pointed to the northeast. "The trail-army set up along there and the mess fires too."

Alea glanced up as a long roll of thunder followed his words. "What about the attack?"

Arman shrugged. "They're skirmishes, not more than a dozen men to each side. It's been happening all morning. We erected barricades, but the work is slow. The first two times I woke, panicking like you did. Now it's routine, I guess." He kicked at a rut with his boot. "Care for breakfast?"

Hunger roared to life in her stomach at his words. "I could eat three." The soldiers moved in practiced chaos. Some attended their kit, groups of others rushed past to follow orders. The change was drastic. Men who seemed somber the day before were boyish, even in the face of bloodshed. Mess fires were low, most soldiers having eaten close to dawn. Arman found a mostly-edible meat-and-pepper mixture layered on toasted bread.

Alea crouched beside him at the cook fire. The silence was still awkward. *At least we're speaking now.*

"Arman!" Bren hurried up, barely waving at Alea. "We're banking the river. Wagons, anything that can be spared is going into the barricades. We need hands."

Alea looked up at him. "We're making new banks?"

"The river's too open. If any cross, we need to be close enough to shoot them down without putting ourselves in range."

Arman rose and shoved the rest of his second breakfast into his mouth.

"What of me?" She could not sit on her hands until someone relieved her boredom. "What can I do?"

Arman waved his hand at the infirmary as he followed Bren. "The healers could use help. It's safe there. Help the wounded and dying."

She stared as he and Bren jogged out of sight along the makeshift road between the tents. *Dying? Already?* Loneliness returned, and she wrapped the rest of her meal for later. She smelled the infirmary tents before she saw them and was glad she had not finished breakfast. Cloying scents of blood and sick hovered about the place like a wet cloak. Breathing through her mouth, she pushed through the tent flap.

Camp chairs were padded with cloaks, shirts and whatever else could be found. Cots filled the rear. She learned rudimentary healing in Cehn, but never practiced. Nor had she ever seen the aftermath of battle. It was a loud mess. There were enough wounded to make her heart falter. A man's sudden groan as he shifted his seat caught her attention. His stance was awkward due to the arrow through his thigh. It stuck fast at the fletching. The more seriously wounded men meant he had to wait. He offered her a smile that was closer to a grimace.

Nerves disappeared. "May I help?"

"You think I'd say 'no'?" He turned and winced as his muscle tightened around the wood.

"Stay still." She pushed up her sleeves and looked closer. Her fingers were gentle as she probed the skin around the wound. "Might you have a knife?"

He handed it to her wordlessly. She cut his already ruined breeches away from the wound. "You're lucky it missed the vessels." She gripped the arrow just below the fletching. "This will hurt." Her words were apologetic.

"Obviously. Just do it."

She snapped the fletching off then gripped the arrow at its head and tugged. The soldier gasped, and she faltered. Large steady hands covered hers and helped guide the bolt free.

Crouching behind her was one of the largest men she had ever encountered. Fuzzy brown hair and bright hazel eyes made him more comical than intimidating, as did the healers' apron stretched across his girth. "You did well, but a smooth pull hurts less. Stitch him up, then keep going." His smile was gentle as he handed her an apron and a packet of thread and needles. Old joints groaned as he rose. "Your help is welcome, Dhoah'."

As she threaded the needle she realized her patient was silent. She glanced up and found him staring.

"Dhoah' Laen?"

She did not answer. Arman's anonymity when he was alone was enviable. *No wonder he and Bren avoid titles where they can. With titles come expectations and I only know half the legends I'm supposed to become.* "Hold still."

"You're younger than I thought you'd be."

She sewed his wounds quickly, pressing an icy fingertip to them when she was done, willing them to heal. She wiped her hands clean as she rose. "It won't have an infection."

"In this rain, how can anything not?" He fell silent at her pointed gaze. He grabbed a makeshift crutch and bowed his head to her. "Thank you, then."

Alea worked her way through the tent, attending lesser wounds and stitching the men who bled for her. Rain arrived after noon, slow fat drops that drenched everything in moments. She sank gratefully into a chair in the supply tent. The cold remains of her breakfast were slimy.

The large healer joined her a few minutes later and offered his hand with a smile. "Captain Guffe. You do good work. Fates know we need help." He handed her his water skin. "You're welcome as often as you like."

She took a few gulps and handed it back. "I'd like that. I feel useless elsewhere. I'm surprised how well they receive me."

"Some are in enough pain not to care, but I think they respect you for holding your weight in camp duties—especially one so inglorious. You were raised noble and perhaps they expect you to act as such."

She leaned back with a shrug, eyes lidding.

"Most are patched enough—you should rest. These days are longer than many are used to."

"There are a few more I'd like to visit. I'll rest when my brother and guard return."

He eyed her. "Why did you follow us out here?"

"I need to learn more about battle before I know how I can help." When she looked up, she realized how weak her words made her sound.

He laughed kindly at her expression. "We're all still learning."

Φ

The 37th Day of Vurgmord, 1251
The City of Ceir Athrolan

Elle paused at the gates. One cracked hand shaded her eyes as she peered up at the jagged towers. It had been years since she dared enter a city, longer since she saw Ceir Athrolan proper. "Do you think she's here?"

An'thor's dirt-darkened face was somber. His head-wrap was carefully tucked around his shoulders. The southern clothing was clearly uncomfortable for him, but the last thing they needed was recognition. "It should be easy to find out." When they stopped at a market stall for food, An'thor leaned forward. "I heard tell the Dhoah' Laen is here, in this city."

The shopkeeper nodded as he folded oilcloth around their bread. "Was until three days past. She marched to Shadow with the outguard. Tell you though, my cousin Leni said she didn't look much like Laen to her—just a girl-child."

Elle ignored An'thor's speculative response to the man and turned to look up at the palace's dome. *She was here.* In three days, hundreds of leagues separated them once again. She glared at An'thor as they headed farther into the city.

"Don't turn those eyes on me like that. We made the best time we could. You'd be useless to her dead, and then you'd never see her."

Elle frowned. "Forgive a mother's desperation."

"You could have seen her in Marl Mere."

"I doubt either of us are ready for that conversation. Besides, a dirty fishing dock was not safe for such things."

"I still can't believe we're going to Mirik. This is the worst of all your idiotic plans—including bedding a Laen-killer. Twice. At least."

"You've had as many poor plans as I." She hoisted her pack higher. "And you agreed to go with me." Stepping aside, she allowed a wagon laden with weapons to clatter past. Leaving her daughter was agony. It hurt worse than leaving Bren, almost, because it had been a choice. Bren had a father—even if he was a madman. The prospect of seeing Alea—holding her—was surreal.

"Do you think she'll hate me?"

"I'm not the man to ask about familial relations, my dear." He pointed to a small building high above the eastern edge of the harbor, dodging the question deftly. "We'll find our beds there."

Elle followed him, not really listening to the practical litany the warrior kept up. "Why would she go to Fort Shadow? It's the worst place she could be."

"You stayed in Azirik's court for years, knowing he planned the genocide of your people. She comes by stubbornness justly."

Φ

The 39th Day of Vurgmord, 1251
The Athrolani Camp at Fort Shadow

Two hours before dawn, Bren shook Alea awake. "Messenger just arrived from the capital. Calls went out a few moments ago for the officers." He handed her a jerkin "Get dressed and bring your cloak."

"It's still raining?" She tugged an extra shirt on under the jerkin and followed him out.

"The way the soldiers tell, it'll last days." His words grumbled. "Mirik had fog during this season, but outright rains were rare. This is asinine." Most campfires they passed barely smoked.

"Arman?" Alea shrugged into her cloak until just her eyes were exposed.

"He relieved some men building the blockades. The man has the energy of a god."

"More like a Rakos." Alea ducked under the tent flap Bren held open for her. Quiet fell over the gathered officers at her entrance. A few others trickled in, bringing cold and wet with each opening of the tent flap. Arman settled beside Alea a few minutes later.

When all were assembled, Indred leaned forward, "I received a message from General Aneral. Her scouts sent word that reinforcements are arriving for the Berrin in two days. She planned on sending another battalion to get this business done quickly, but she can't. Two raiding parties were sighted near the capital and larger forces too. They seem to mass toward the northern coast. The rest of the men stay in the city in case of attack."

Soldiers groaned. One gallant leaned forward. Her face looked as tired as Alea felt. "What's our course?"

"We stay."

"Excuse me, Sir Indred, I don't understand." Alea stood to better see the man. "Why can't we attack before the reinforcements come? Or retreat until we gather a proper force?"

Muttered retorts followed her words, but Arman's glare silenced them.

Patience was tempered with condescension in Indred's eyes. "They attack in small forces, biting our flanks while we erect barricades. In the time it would take to rally an attack now, they would overrun the camp. If we retreat, they would attack as we fled. We are the barrier between them and Ceir Athrolan. There is no retreat. We're taking the only course left to us—laying siege to Fort Shadow."

Alea's stomach dropped. She barely heard the details. Noting her expression, Bren excused himself and led her from the tent. He found a miraculously dry spot under an awning several paces away and pulled her aside, "Alea, they don't expect you to know tactics."

"But I made a fool out of myself. My people were right, we have no place here." Her gesture took in the entire camp.

"The Laen warned you away from this?"

Alea shook her head wearily. "The Sunamen. My foster-father taught that we don't use weapons. We don't kill. These things are disgraceful and cowardly." She rested her head in her hands with a groan. "I have done all."

"Alea those rules are not upheld in Athrolan, for one, possibly anywhere else. They were certainly not meant for the Dhoah' Laen." He put an arm around her. "You're not a disgrace or coward."

"But surely I'm useless. Arman enjoys being a soldier. Without me, he's simply a man. He likes that. I can't even blame him. Everything happens so quickly, and I feel as if I can do nothing. I've not learned enough. I should be training myself or studying."

Bren arranged mud into little ridges with his toe. His fidgeting betrayed his confusion as to how to comfort her. "Alea, sometimes the only way to learn is by doing. You're valuable in the infirmary and I know more men would be dead without your hands." He looked down at his boots, huge in comparison to hers. "Before I mastered the sword—before I was even allowed to pick it up—I had to clean the armor of every soldier in the army." He ignored her frown. "And I cursed it, swore up and down, and thought I'd never be a fighter. When I finally picked up a weapon I understood why I had to clean armor. I had learned how every style fit. I know where straps held pieces together and where gaps appeared when the wearer moved. With a sword in my hand, I was deadly because of the knowledge I gained cleaning that armor."

She tilted her head back to look at him. "You're saying this is my armor cleaning?"

"I guess. Often, we learn the most when we're uncomfortable. We just don't see it until later."

Talk spilled from the tent as the officers filed out. Arman followed them, pausing as he caught sight of Alea and her brother. Bren beckoned him over, but the man shook his head.

Alea looked up to see him disappear into the rows of tents. "I wish he understood I want to be his friend. I want to laugh with him."

"Let him see you as a person, under your titles and power. Stop trying to be perfect." He sighed. "I need to see to the barricades, but we can talk more tonight if you want."

"Stay safe." Soon the infirmary would need her, but she could wait a minute. She rose, leaning on the awning's pole and watched the rain.

Φ

The 45th Day of Vurgmord, 1251

Berrin sacrifices stained the river red. Each morning something met its demise—usually a goat, chickens when supplies dwindled, and Athrolani soldiers when they were lucky. Arman would never have recognized the gentle river and rolling fields from their arrival. Rain turned fields to mud and foot rot was as much a danger as battle wounds. Heavy sandbags reinforced the eroding bank, but were already half-submerged in muck. Stacked four high, all but the topmost protected the camp from the rising water.

Pallets made from wagons and branches leaned outwards, guarding against enemy archers. Incessant dampness rotted them in places and with the constant barrage of arrows and water, they needed continuous repair. Arman headed to where two men worked at such repairs. They were covered in water as much as tar and greeted him wearily.

"Thank fates," one groaned as he tugged off his oilcloth suit. "I thought duty-change would never come." He handed Arman the protective gear.

The Rakos pulled it on and tied it closed before clambering over the sandbags. Another man relieved the other worker and handed Arman what was once the top of a barrel. Arman painted one side with tar before slapping it over a large leak in the slats. Nailing it in place, he coated the edges, then shoved a support beam in place to hold the new repair. The work went on for much of the afternoon. What was once good, strong wood brought for such a duty, was now dismantled carts. Arman paused to peer through the gaps in the boards. The Berrin watch was changing, barely visible through the sheets of rain. He shook water from his hair and turned back to his work.

Horns sounded deafeningly close.

Arman flung himself behind the sandbags and fumbled with the laces of his oilskin suit. He flattened himself in the mud, knives palmed.

A soldier pressed to the ground several paces away. "Skirmish, just over the wall!"

Arman counted silently. At five, he rushed toward the sound of fighting. A mass of Athrolani, Berrin and Mirikin seethed at a hole punched through the pallets. *Damn!* If the walls were breeched, they were doomed. He jumped into the fray. Mud and blood and water slicked every surface.

A Berrin woman lunged at him, teeth bared like his. Her blade rose, and he ducked under her reach, knife flashing up between her ribs. She collapsed, plunging him under the churning water.

Boots came down on his hand, sending his knife into the depths. Remembering street brawls in Vielrona, he rolled, grabbed someone by the legs and hauled himself up, ducking as they swung and missed. It was an Athrolani squire. The boy backed up, apologizing. An axe thudded into his collarbone. Arman whirled and leapt on the attacker, pummeling him into the muck.

The skirmish lasted only minutes, though it felt like eight times that. Arman groaned as he crawled back up the sandbags and through the barricade. They won, barely, and could repair the new hole. He cleaned, dried and sheathed his knives—excepting the one that was now ground into the riverbed. Adrenaline and giddy confusion were still thick as soldiers milled about.

Arman pitched his voice over the drum of rain. "Get the wounded to the infirmary! Bring more wood and tar!" He bent over his work, ignoring comments about his speed, his ceaseless energy. After a breath, others joined him and the gap in their defenses began to close.

Hot light filled Arman's heart. It was small, but familiar. He had known its warmth in Vielrona, but it was only now, after its absence, that he recognized it. It was the glow of a hearthfire, the light on the first day of spring. He smiled wolfishly as he slammed nails home. *Belonging.*

Φ

Alea hunkered under the rain sheet stretched over the infirmary tent entrance. Moments free from the smell of blood-drenched dirt were rare. The week following the decision to lay siege felt like a month. She pulled her cowl tighter.

"How are they?" Arman ducked under the cover and crouched beside her.

"We lost the three brought back yesterday and the man whose leg we took won't make it through the night." Her eyes were distant, the gray more a glaze than glimmer. "I expected blood. I expected it to come from a battle under the sun and then over. Men would die, but I wouldn't see it. Half the time I only get tremors in my chest that mean something terrible is happening. The other half I'm too tired to notice the feeling. I'm afraid to grow accustomed to it, and guilty because I'm relieved that I am."

Arman picked at the tar coating the back of his hand. "After I killed my first man, in Vielrona, I lost my lunch. I don't know what's worse—that I was sick then, or that I no longer am." Scouting with the others ended in skirmishes more than once. Twice the army had tried to mobilize at night and both times the Berrin had known long before much progress had been made. "You should have stayed in the city." The familiar litany held more sorrow than frustration now.

Φ

That night the campfires were low and the soldiers quiet. Despite the calm of the evening, Bren could not sleep. Though each had their own tents, Bren layered them into one large rain screen surrounding the campfire. It warded off the worst of the damp and cold. Unable to lie still, he tossed onto his side and glanced over. Alea's bright eyes fixed on him. They were surrounded by tear-smudged dirt and ash.

"Alea?"

"Go back to sleep."

"I couldn't sleep anyways." He propped himself on an elbow and inched closer to her. "What is it?"

"I'm the reason all these people die." Tears leaked from the corner of her eye and trickled into her ear.

Bren reached out a blunt finger and swiped it away. "I wish I knew how to comfort you."

"How could anyone love me, fight for me, when all I leave is death in my wake?"

Bren wrapped his arms around her. "Alea, in wars people die. Soldiers will die for you even if they've never met you. They fight because they know you fight for them too. If they protect you, even with their deaths, their families will survive. You gave up the home you could have had in Vielrona and will give up a life in Athrolan to protect this world. That's something worth loving."

Her tears soaked into his shoulder and he held her tighter. "That's why I love you. That is why Arman loves you."

"Arman tolerates me. He's friendly enough, but I'm just a duty he'd rather not have."

Bren frowned. He was fairly certain Arman's feelings were far more complicated—and stronger—than she thought. "I think you're more than that. He warned me at Fort Hero that loving you was dangerous, but he'd be much more so if I crossed you. How would he know it was dangerous if he didn't love you?"

"He might have started as a friend, but his Rakos blood forced him into this, it soul-bound him to me."

Bren's eyes widened. *No wonder his mood wavered between loyalty and frustration.* "Perhaps this war will let you understand one another better. Death doesn't care about titles, and when faced with it we often learn to feel the same."

"Perhaps afterward we can be friends."

Bren shrugged. Whatever relationship she had with Arman, it would be far more complex than friendship. *Besides, I know what comes of "afterward" and "maybe later," and it's never happiness.* Waiting bred regret.

Φ

The 1st Day of Lleume, 1252

Days bled into weeks more literally than any cared to admit. Makeshift bars and brothels provided by the trail-army were welcome diversions. For the most part, Alea steered clear. Her work in the infirmary left little energy for much else other than sleep. Bren, however, spent much of his time among the trail-army tents, learning about his new allies.

He sat in one of the low chairs scattered around an ale tent when Reka slumped down beside him. Stains marred her leather armor and her braids had matted into thicker locks.

"Skirmish?"

She took a deep sip of his ale, then another smaller one before motioning for her own mug. "Third damned one I've seen in the past two days. Your way of fighting is stupid."

Bren was used to her blunt speech, but the Bordermen still baffled him. "What other way of fighting is there?"

"A single fighter against another. None of this army deershit. Strength against strength, skill against skill."

Bren stared at her, incredulous. "Your people have no armies? No united force?"

"There's no honor in it." She scoffed. "A warrior must stand alone."

"You're a very different people. Mirik only allowed female soldiers two decades ago. Athrolan has for a long while though, clearly."

Reka shrugged. "Always making it about gender. Our people are just people. If a man or woman chooses to change roles there is a ceremony called the ruak. It changes our position in society, but not our value or sex—unless they wish it to, of course."

Bren nodded. "I suppose that makes sense."

"Can you explain your obsession with massive forces?" Wooden beads at the end of her braids clacked as she tipped her mug back.

"What one man cannot accomplish, many can. If you think of it simply as an invasion, yes it seems unfair. But to protect your people? Doesn't it seem worthwhile?" He waved for a second mug for both of them.

Reka leaned back and rested an ankle on her knee. "Our children are born with knives in their hands." The corner of her mouth quirked. She was adopting the smile of the Athrolani, but only just. "It's the warrior's duty to care after children and whoever nurtures them. If she or he cannot, then they wouldn't be granted their mark of strength. Sometimes that means running or hiding."

"The butterfly?" Bren pointed to her nose. "That hardly seems the symbol of strength." His tone was teasing, and he pointed to one of the other Bordermen in the bar tent. "Even the crow's wings on Iere there seem more intimidating."

"Not all strength is brawn." She gestured to her muscled frame. "If it were, many would not be warriors. Iere's wings are not those of the crow, but the stork—notice the gray. The stork remains in place, waiting for the frog. It's a wonderful hunter, for he can stalk anything for hours. My butterfly is for the strength of spirit through change."

"Apropos considering your choice to join us while others did not."

She waved a hand. "Enough of my people. Tell me of your time with Azirik. What's he like?"

Bren shrugged. "You mean other than a madman? Serving under him was unpredictable. He was volatile and impulsive and tireless. He was more general than king. I think he saw himself that way as well, maybe it saddened him."

It was late and cold when they returned to their tents. Alea was already tucked into her bedroll and Arman dozed by the campfire. Bren stared at the quiet tableau. Sleep seemed the only peace any of them had now. He wished he had half of Reka's strength.

Φ

The 4th Day of Lleume, 1252

Horns sounded since dawn, cutting through the hiss of rain with aching regularity. Alea crouched beside a man on a cloak spread across the ground. They had long run out of cots. His eyes were vacant and his breath uneven.

Guffe stopped in passing. "How is he?"

"Mind is gone. Breath rattles." She pushed her hair back, not caring that she left a smear of fate-knew-what across her brow. "How much leaf do we have?"

"Little. One more unopened package and a third leftover from yesterday." The leaves came from a mountain bush, and she wondered if they were the same that Bren gave to Tzemine weeks before. Powdered and ingested they helped with pain in small doses.

"Save it then. We'll hope he's beyond pain." She pressed a hand to the dying man's. Rising before dawn and working past dusk dragged her energy, and putting her heart into the work weighed on her spirit. There were hours of work left, but this man had been under her care for three days. In his few lucid moments they had spoken about his family. She waited, hand over his, until his chest no longer rose. Under her fingers, his heartbeat faltered, then ceased. Her grip on his hand tightened. A faint copper-red glow crept to the surface of his chest, spreading down his arm. It melted into her hand. Sadness fluttered in her chest.

Their souls.

She backed away, heart hammering. *Souls cross to Le'yne through me.* She shuddered. *All this time I have been feeling deaths.* Turning to the apprentices at the door, she swiped at her damp cheeks. "We'll need a burial team."

Φ

Arman rested against the pole of tent, just out of the weather. Frequent messengers between the capital and the camp brought orders, news, and mail. The last bundle held three letters for him. Two were from Wes and Kam, the former mostly discussing business and city news. Arman slit open Kam's curiously. It was the locksmith's first letter, though Arman had written twice. The first line made him laugh.

> *Arman,*
>
> *Wes convinced me to write you, since your Ma and he were both sending things. So, hello. How has the journey been? Wes reads aloud what you write to him. I can't believe you saw the Orn de Galin. Lucky arse. Things here are much the same as ever. Remember Celly Orean? Gluan's headwoman? We'll be wed at the beginning of the month, the 1st of Lleume. It would be grand if you could be here, but I doubt you're able.*
>
> *We heard about the attack on an Athrolani post – Fort Shade or something. Keep your lady safe. Come home soon, will you?*
>
> *Kam-Rit*

Homesickness bled through his chest at the familiar, distracted tone. *They've been wed for a few days now.* The realization that weeks passed while the letter found him made him wonder how long news of something serious would take. Kam's ignorance of names and locations that were now familiar made the distance seen greater. Shaking his head, he turned to his mother's letter.

> *Arman,*
>
> *It grows warm here. Kam and Celly are to be wed. They let a house on the corner now. He has a better head on his shoulders and runs the business out of a building by Wes's.*
>
> *We miss you. We get news from the travelers. Most move south, away from the war. There's a siege to the northeast, though it's far from us. I hope you're well away from that mess. You weren't born for battle. What news of your return?*
>
> *All my love,*
>
> *Ma*

Arman hung his head. His last letter was lighthearted and sent from Athrolan. *How can I write anything without being dishonest? Each time they beg me to go back.* He tugged his writing kit over and wrote a short response to Kam and Wes. He paused on the first line to his mother. Bren glanced over from across the fire when the quill-scratching paused.

"Writing home?"

"Damned if I know what to say."

"Not the truth. The few of Azirik's men who kept families never told the truth until they were safe in their wives' arms again."

Arman laughed. "I was thinking of including every detail. 'Mother dear, nice to hear from you! Not dead yet, though I've been close six times now. Alea is the Dhoah' Laen, I forgot to mention, and I grow scales when ticked. How goes the inn?'"

Bren laughed, running a hand through his hair. "I suppose that would go over poorly." He frowned suddenly. "Scales? You grow scales when you're angry?"

Arman sighed, eyes rolling. "Of course not, but the Rakos did. Those are probably the only tales she knows of them." He scratched a few more lines. "It's odd. My friend back home married two days ago." He could not explain the heaviness in his chest.

"The world goes on without you, even if it seems to have stopped here."

Arman finished the letter wordlessly, sealing it before tucking his kit away and moving closer to the fire.

"Arman, when was the last time you spoke to Alea?"

The blond man shrugged, "This morning. Or perhaps it was last night. Who can tell in this weather? She asked if we'd run out of tea."

Bren sighed. "I meant actually talked with her."

"I talk to her all the time." Catching Bren's stern look, he amended his words, "Honestly, it was over a week ago. We talked about growing used to bloodshed. Why?"

"I don't rightly care that you were forced into a soul-bond. It's shit, I'll give you that, but she's your duty. If she doesn't trust you or confide in you, your task will be much harder. Stop thinking of her as the Dhoah' Laen. Stop thinking of her as the naive Cehn refuge. Look at her. All of her. She's a woman and at least a little bit human—glowing eyes and black-snaked skin aside. Treat her thusly."

He wanted to retort, wanted to tell Bren to take his Toar-blasted advice and shove it somewhere dark and painful. Except Alea's brother was right.

Arman looked away. Alea brought out the worst in him, often because she brought out his fear. She also brought out the best. Their entire friendship was built on his assumption that he gave her everything she needed him to. He never paused to ask what she actually needed—or realize what she gave him.

She was laughter on dark roads. She was playful curiosity and unexpected crass humor. She was power, she was grace, she was immeasurable determination. Arman slumped back against the tent pole as the truth hit him. "Damn."

"Realized you've been an ass?"

Something much worse. "You could say that." Whatever other earth-cracking revelations he may have had stopped as Alea arrived. "Milady, you look like death."

She swayed with exhaustion. The shadows under her eyes were darker than ever and her hands were chapped badly enough to bleed. Thumping down between the two men, she rolled her eyes. "Not a way to win a woman over, Arman."

He tried again. "How long did you work? You were gone when I rose this morning."

"Guffe's assistant came to me two hours before dawn. I thought the point of a siege was to weaken them. Instead, I think they're like hornets—odd, water hornets. We just keep making them angry."

Arman snorted and took her hands in his. "Bren do you have any of the grease you use on your scars?"

Bren tossed over a small pouch filled with herb-smelling balm he bought from the trail-army. "Works wonders when old wounds stiffen in the cold and wet."

Alea smiled tiredly as Arman smoothed a small amount over her knuckles, working it carefully into her abused skin. "Thank you."

Bren poured a bowl of stew from their fire and offered it to his sister. "It's a bit spicy but better than tasting the mud."

She glanced at it and sprang to her feet, hand pressed to her mouth. Wide-eyed, she shook her head violently before disappearing into the maze of tents.

"Toar, what did I do?" Bren stared incredulously after her.

Arman shook his head, dumbfounded. "Damned if I know. Even I don't think your cooking's that awful." He pulled on his cloak and rushed after her.

Φ

Alea fought nausea high in her stomach. After so much blood, the sight of food—even stew as good as that had smelled—made her chest tight. *How can they deal with this?* She stared at the faces of the soldiers. It did not matter where she went, but suddenly she was in the center of the trail-army tents. Wood smoke and alcohol almost hid the pervasive scent of mildew. She ducked inside the first ale-tent she saw and sat at the row of camp chairs designating the bar. A heavy woman frowned at her, taking in Alea's worn appearance.

"What can I get ye?"

Alea stared at her, unsure, not even caring that she was finally anonymous. "Something. Anything." Her head dropped to her hands. *What am I doing?* She always took things in stride. It was the Sunamen way—wear a brave face as the river sweeps you along. After meeting Eras, Alea tried to emulate the calm leadership the general displayed. *Why do I break when everything finally stops for a few minutes?*

A small glass of dark green liquid clunked onto the bar before her. It smelled bitter and sweet at the same time. There were barely more than two gulps in the glass. She took a tentative sip. Burning choked her at first, but she forced down the rest, resisting the urge to gag. Realizing the barmaid still stood in front of her with raised brows, Alea slid the glass over with a nod. She did not trust herself to open her mouth. Alea tipped the contents of the second glass down her throat as well. Her stomach warmed.

"Need a third?"

"I think she's had enough already, thank you." A calloused hand planted itself on the bar from behind her.

Alea turned to find herself face-to-face with Arman's stern expression. The world continued to swirl, and she steadied herself on his arm. "Arman."

He helped her straighten and tossed a coin on the bar before leading her out. Once free of the confines of the tent he turned her to face him. "Fuck's sake, what were you thinking?" His grip on her shoulders was almost strong enough to hurt and his teeth bared.

Her stomach roiled as the world spun again. "Arman?" She held his forearms.

"People are fools when they drink. I would know. But you? You're blundering into a tent of lonely drunk soldiers, none of whom recognize you covered in blood and dirt! Who knows what happens to your power when it mixes with alcohol—you could be unable to defend yourself or destroy the entire camp!" He drew a rattling breath.

"I wasn't blundering, and while you may not recognize me covered in blood, most of the men here would—I don't wear ball gowns to sew their wounds! And if I get hurt, fault the lonely soldiers, not my drinking." She wished she could storm off again, but the ground was less steady than before. Instead, she closed her eyes and sighed. "Are you angry with me?"

"Yes!" His voice cracked on the word and he crushed her in an embrace. He took another breath. "No. Not truly. You scared me is all." He pulled away. "Why did you run?"

"Bren's stew looked like what I held in men's stomachs today."

Arman winced. "No stew then. You need to eat, though, and soon, before whatever you drank hits harder."

"It was green," Alea noted as he steered her back to their camp.

Bren looked up as they stepped inside the ring of firelight. Relief washed his face. Alea waved excitedly. Warmth, like she had not felt in days, filled her body. Her chapped lips were pleasantly numb.

"Milady, sit down." Arman kept his exasperation in check. He pulled a cushion up for her. "And for fates' sakes, stay put." He unwrapped the strip of meat he bought on their way back, spitting it over the fire.

Alea sat, then flopped onto her back and stared at the sliver of sky through their smoke hole.

Bren watched incredulously. "Arman, unless I'm very much mistaken my sister—the Dhoah' Laen—is tossed."

"Wish you were." Arman watched her eyes roam over the stars. A smile twitched his mouth. "She had a hard day. I think she thought the numbness of alcohol is learned in one night."

Bren leaned forward with a wicked grin, "Sistermine, I've never seen a traditional Sunamen dance."

Alea sat up excitedly, but Arman put a firm hand on her leg. He glared at Bren. "Be nice."

Bren shrugged good-naturedly. "So, how do you feel?"

"It tasted like fire and...ugh." She shuddered.

Arman laughed and after a minute handed her the meat. "Careful." He watched her eat. "You're lucky, milady. The first time I drank was with Kam and Wes. I think I drank my purse empty."

"You think?"

"Well, I don't remember and couldn't find it the next day."

She offered him her half-finished dinner. "I think I'm done with this."

Arman handed it to Bren. "I'll get you into bed. Dawn will come too early."

When she stood her vision tunneled and blood roared in her ears. She stumbled with a yelp and caught herself on Arman's outstretched hand.

Bren laughed. "Hurry, Toar knows which of her powers comes out with alcohol. Three coppers it's not Creation."

"Five it is!" Alea shot over her shoulder as Arman half-ushered, half-carried her through the makeshift flap that separated her bedroll from theirs. She tugged off her boots before dropping her bloodstained jerkin and overskirt on the chest beside them.

He handed her a dry cloth for her rain-soaked hair and wrapped a blanket over her shoulders. "I'm sorry I yelled at you." He helped her slide into the bedroll on her cot. He pressed a hand to her shoulder and turned to go.

"Arman?"

He glanced back.

"Can you stay until I fall asleep?"

He sat at the foot of her cot and leaned back against the wall. She curled onto her side and rested her head in his lap.

"Why were you scared?"

"What you did tonight is unlike the Lyne'alea in my head. You're stronger and wiser and I never expected you to drink to forget." He sighed. "I forget that you're human, sometimes. If you're just a title, just a figure in a legend, you can't drift out of my reach, somewhere where I can't protect you. Why did you need to forget?"

"Guffe has me do more to help, asks me to tend the worse wounds. I've not seen violence like this since Cehn. I held a man's hand as he passed today. I hadn't tended a stomach wound before. It brought the horror back." She glanced up at him, "I never told you, but I was about to marry my foster-father's second eldest son, Ahren."

Arman looked down. "What was he like?"

"Kind. He would have made a good husband. We were friends." She paused. "I saw him gutted. His last act was to cut down the man attacking me while holding—" her breath caught on the sharp edges of memories "—holding everything from spilling out through his stomach."

Arman rubbed his thumb over her shoulder. "I'm sorry."

"I forgot the details until today. I loved him. Not romantically, perhaps, but it was love." She took Arman's hand, pressing it to her brow. "Promise me something?"

"Of course."

"Promise me you'll be my friend—not just my guard. My mind won't make it through this without a friend."

"Promise." He was silent for a moment. "I don't think I would have gone."

She hummed questioningly at him.

"Home, I mean. Even if you stayed in Ceir Athrolan."

Her eyes fluttered open to look at him. "You were so sure you wanted to go."

"Wanted to, sure. It was desperation, though. Veredy said there was no place for me there, and I fear that. But I wouldn't have chosen this path if I wasn't certain I could see it through."

"You only chose to shelter me in Vielrona. Not the rest of this."

"Actually, that's not true."

She turned to look at him, willing her eyes to focus. This was important. "But your blood—"

"Forced me to do nothing. It asked. I agreed. It was a choice. You're wonderful and powerful and precious and I chose to protect that."

No answer came. That he chose this was more terrible in her mind than being forced. The trust and faith choosing her took was terrifying. She buried her face against his hand and closed her eyes. If nothing else, she would make his choice worthwhile.

Φ

The 9th Day of Lleume, 1252

Bren slumped against one of the reinforced banks, not caring he was as damp as if he had swum in the river. He relieved Arman an hour before, more out of force than need. The Vielronan man's stamina and devotion bordered on eerie. Had it not been so useful, Bren would have been nervous. He pulled the amulet from under his tunic, staring.

"Ey! Barrackborn!" The shout drifted along the barricade. "Guard change on the edge of the Vale camp."

Bren pressed the charm to his lips before rushing after the others. They took full advantage of the confusion of guard-change. Bren crouched at the foot of the ladder that led up and over the barriers. A volley flew overhead, allowing the Athrolani to surge over the embankment with less danger.

Bren skidded down the rough wood and onto the partially submerged rocks and sandbags in this shallow stretch of river. He lifted his sword with a growl as they smashed into the Vale guards. The enemy camp responded, soldiers rushing to defend. Within minutes, bodies were underfoot and blood covered weapons and armor. The fighting pushed into the river, half the wounded drowning before injuries claimed their lives. Bren shoved a man down and thrust his blade into another when the call for retreat sounded. He stumbled back when a hand gripped his booted ankle in a vise grip.

"Lieutenant?"

He glanced down to see a pale face and bright red hair under the helm. "Doric?" Bren lifted the man's shoulders from the water. He hoped to never see the men he led under Azirik. Now one of his best lay at his feet. Bren could very well have put him there.

"You could have let us come with you." Blood leaked from the young man's mouth, smearing on his freckled cheek.

Bren ignored the shout for him to get behind the embankment. "You would have been killed, Doric."

"I have been anyways." He shoved himself away from his former officer, dragging himself up on a rock.

Bren stumbled to safety, but watched from behind the shield of the barricade, cursing his luck. Doric had followed Bren as if he was a hero. Though irritating, the earnest boy's quick humor grew on Bren. He deserved better than death at the hand of a treacherous former officer. He could have told himself the boy's wound was not from his sword, but it would be a lie.

Cowardice crouched in his chest as he waited for the Mirikin to retrieve their wounded and dead. It was stupid to wish he could bring the boy back. All he would face in the Athrolani camp was torture or imprisonment. *He deserves to die a battle-death.*

When Doric was finally hauled out of the water his brown eyes were empty, and Bren turned away. He knew how soldiers were buried during war, with their brothers-in-arms. There would be a short ceremony, maybe a call for silence, or a salute.

At the campfire, Bren avoided Alea's questioning look. His personal pack rested at the head of his bedroll and he drew it over. Tucked in the front pouch was a battered and tarnished brass disk along with a small jar. He laid the disk on his bedroll and poured a dollop of the dark, oily contents of the jar onto the brass. He made a small slice on his forearm; as blood dripped into the oil, Bren began to whisper.

"From the earth of your land, from the oil of your temples, from my blood, I beg you to listen, Toar. I may not be a gods' man any longer, but I don't pray for myself." His words were soft, but he did not hear Arman's boot falls. "One of your soldiers passed today. Many did. This man, Wellir Doric, was young. He was a good man and tried to live a blessed life, as well as he was able. He does not deserve to roam without purpose, with only memories to haunt. Let him find peace in your halls." He pressed his fist to his brow, then wiped the liquid from the disk with a cheap cloth before burning the fabric in his lantern.

"Do you pray for all of us?" Arman leaned against the tent pole, his face unreadable. His arms were crossed.

"There's no harm in asking for another to be put to rest."

"When you pray to those who wish your sister dead, I think there might. And you didn't answer me." Arman's voice was low, but not angry.

"I don't pray like this every night. I pray in my head. I ask for peace when our allies pass and touch the symbol around my neck. You've seen me."

"You just invoked the god of death. I think this is a bit different."

"Arman, today I killed someone I used to lead. A boy."

The fight left the Rakos's body. "I find it difficult to imagine how you can support milady and still pray to the gods. But I understand your need for solace."

Bren looked down. "It's a habit. They only answered Azirik. You never prayed?"

Arman shrugged. "Not truly. Vielrona had all sorts, but we've always been a Laen city. My mother would often appeal to the fates, or our ancestors, but it was usually to make me mind."

"Now what do you worship?" Bren could not imagine a life without faith.

Arman's mouth quirked, "Isn't it obvious?" He jerked his head at the tent flap. "Alea is making supper. Join us."

CHAPTER EIGHTEEN

The 23rd Day of Lleume, 1252
The Athrolani Camp at Fort Shadow

A SOLDIER THUMPED DOWN onto the stool beside Alea with a sigh. "You're the last person I expected to find here."

She glanced over and smiled. "Narier." She gestured to the dirty bottles behind the counter. "Might I buy you something?"

"Allow the Dhoah' Laen to buy my drinks? There must be a law about that."

"If there is such a law, I could probably change it. And I only offered the one."

He snorted. "Blood-ale then, if you wish."

She ordered two then made a face. "Blood-ale? I'm trusting you, but it sounds atrocious. Please tell me it's from the color."

"Probably. We use juice, I think. It comes from the Northlands, though, so all bets are off about what made it red originally." In the lantern light, she saw pockmarks dotted his delicate features.

She eyed the deep red liquid curiously. "Does one sip this, or throw it down their throat?"

"I'm of the school that no alcohol should be 'thrown.' If it tastes like Toar's asshole, then it's your duty to appreciate every horrid burn."

Alea's brows rose. "So, if one were of the other schools, would they throw this?"

He laughed. "No, I don't suppose so." He clinked his glass against hers, "To your health."

"And to yours." The drink was served warm and burnt like too-sweet honey as it slid down her throat. Nutty and bitter aftertastes rolled on her tongue. She smiled, eyes still narrowed. "I think I like your school better."

"You didn't drink much before this?"

"No. In Cehn we only used it for ceremonies, and it wasn't strong or good enough for any casual purposes. I did try some Vielronan mead. And several nights ago, I found myself tossing back something that smelled like a swamp. That neither began nor ended well."

Narier shook his head. "More accomplished than I expected, milady, I'll be honest. I forget you weren't raised, you know." His eyes flicked back to her and warmed. They were the rich brown of worn wood. "Scum-runner. The green drink you had."

She pretended to retch. "Fates, that's one I don't think I could 'appreciate' regardless."

"Shall I buy you another? Blood-ale, that is." His grin was wicked.

"I wouldn't mind a hot cup of tea. Our camp ran out four days ago."

He laughed. "I doubt you'll find any here, but we've got some at the officers' mess."

"Then might I walk you back? Or was your night just beginning?" She was lonesome, and Narier was easy to talk with.

"Just beginning, but I had few plans." He rose and handed her cloak over. "Besides, finding tea for the Dhoah' Laen is a worthy task."

The officers' mess proved less grand than implied, but they had a heavy chest full of dry goods. He rummaged through it for several moments. "We've the traditional Athrolani bergamot, and some spicy thing that only Metters likes." He held up a green tin triumphantly. "Ha! I can't pronounce the name, which means it must be a fine blend."

Alea laughed. "Athrolani is fine." She watched him put the kettle on the fire and ready two mugs. "Where are you from?"

"Ceir Felden originally. My parents own a little sheepfold just outside the walls. I was never one for the flocks, though. Luckily, they had four boys before me, so my joining the army wasn't much of a loss. It's beautiful in a gray way. Much of the coast is. I don't think I'd mind settling there, though. Maybe when I'm too bent to walk straight." The kettle squealed, and he shook his head ruefully. "Look at me, prattling on like a hen." He poured her mug and handed it over. "We ran out of honey a week ago, I'm afraid."

"I prefer it this way. What was it you said—it should be appreciated, even when bitter." She stared into the tea with a smile. She missed conversations that did not involve death or gods.

"Are you still with me?"

She nodded. "I was thinking how much I've missed talking to people. Arman and Bren worry about me too much to let their guard down."

"I'm far from tired. Would you like to talk?" Narier grimaced, "I suppose your guard will be worried for you."

"Arman's got shift and Bren is wrapped around Reka." Though the words sounded harsh, she was not sure why. "I'd be happy to talk."

He smiled and raised his tent flap. "I promise to not mention sheep for the rest of the night."

Peering around, she saw that the tent was roughly the size of hers, but he knew how to use every corner of the space efficiently. A stack of rain-wilted missives lay forgotten in a pile on his desk. Some had begun to grow mildew.

"So, was Cehn very different?"

"In many ways. It is odd how it's not the obvious things, but the little things. How people fix their hair or express love. Those are the things I miss the most. It's lonely, despite—or perhaps because of—what I am."

"You don't seem like the Dhoah' Laen right now. You seem like a woman."

Alea's chest ached at his words. In his eyes, she was human, allowed to be afraid and happy and drunk. She glanced at his camp cot and at the tent flaps to the empty officer's mess. "Would you mind if I stayed the night?"

His eyes widened, following the path hers had taken. "With me, you mean? Here?"

She looked away. *This was a bad idea.* "I'd like to be just a woman for a little while longer."

His expression softened, and he set down his tea. "Of course, you can stay." He stepped closer and reached out to brush her face. The touch was careful, but not fearful. Moving past her, he rolled down the thick tent liner over the inside of his door. When he returned, he was smiling, "May I call you Alea?"

She smiled back, "I'd like that." She doffed her cloak and hung it beside his before turning back. Her hand paused his as he unlaced his jerkin. "Could I?" Her fingers hummed as she untied the leather. Goosebumps followed his movements as he unbuttoned the back of her dress. Cool fingers brushed against her bare shoulder and she jumped.

He paused. "Is this all right?"

"Yes, just cold. I'm not used to this. But I like it." Her words were a jumble, so she glanced back with a smile.

Realization dawned on his face, "Oh, Alea, I didn't know." He continued unfastening the buttons with new focus. "We'll take our time then."

It was not exactly as she imagined. The tent was cold and the air damp, but they burrowed under his blankets. She expected the pain, but not the smiles and certainly not sharing laughs. Afterward, she lay on her side, blanket pulled over their heads for warmth. "This is much better than drowning my thoughts in drinks."

He laughed. "Agreed." He cocked his head at her, "Though I could argue the drinks brought us here." His tawny skin was peppered with dark hair.

She gestured to her own pale skin. "Do I look like the Dhoah' Laen now?"

He pretended to examine her critically. "I've never seen one naked."

She flicked him. "Silly, you still never have."

He frowned. "What do you mean?"

"You've seen me unclothed, but naked is different. Few people are ever seen naked."

"Ah, you mean the soul-bared honesty part."

She nodded. "In Cehn one was never seen naked by anyone, save for their spouse. I always thought they meant the clothes. Now, I think it was more likely the other way. It was rare anyone was seen without masks in place."

"Do you think anyone will see you naked?"

She shrugged. "I hope so, in my distant future."

"Well," he pulled her closer, "In the meantime, I'm happy to see you unclothed."

Φ

The 25th day of Lleume, 1252

Arman groaned and changed course as an alert went up. He wanted to speak to Alea, but she would be busy tending the wounded from the new attack. Horns sounded again, and Arman slid to a halt. *Those aren't attack alarms.* A narrow alley between the mess tents and brought him to the center of camp. A throng gathered by Indred's tent. Bren already stood among the officers, holding a serious conversation with Narier. Alea appeared moments later, still wearing her blood-drenched apron. She flashed him a smile and craned over others' shoulders to see.

"What is it?"

He shrugged, "I only just realized it wasn't signaling an attack."

The crowd parted for approaching riders. Clean Athrolani uniforms of the new soldiers looked almost foreign next to the weathered tabards of the camp's soldiers. General Aneral raised a hand in greeting and drew her horse up. Though her mouth softened in a brief smile at the relief in the tired soldier's eyes, her gaze was hard. Her lips thinned when her boots splashed into the muck.

Indred shouldered his way through the crowd and saluted her quickly, "General, you are a welcome sight."

"What the fates happened here?" She tugged her gloves and helm off. "The last missive you sent was written two weeks ago. I arrive only to find starvation and blood. I ordered you to lay siege on the Berrin, not yourselves!"

"The siege—if you can really call it such—does as much harm as good. The enemy is weak, but their resolve isn't."

Eras waved his words away. "Call a council, save the reports for then." She shot her squire several orders before striding over to where her tent was being erected. Moments later the call for officers went out, though few had left the circle around the new troop.

As the council tent filled, Eras edged around the table to Alea. She grasped Arman and Bren's arms in greeting and bowed her head to Alea. "I'm glad to see you whole." Her eyes lingered on the shadows under the young woman's eyes and the hollows of her cheeks. "You've learned some of war, it seems."

"I have."

Indred dropped into his chair with a weary sigh. At Eras's gesture, he leaned forward, "We estimate their numbers are a thousand four hundred or so, but ours are half that. They've yet to take the advantage, which makes my skin crawl. It's like waiting for a man to bleed out. We've tried to mobilize but they counter before any ground is gained."

"What of the scouting missions in the forest."

Indred pointed to the map, "The Berrin erected ditches and walls, makeshift, but manned and armed. The rear door is repaired. They have three lines of men camped back there, with guards and such, as much as a hundred paces into the tree line. We're unable to discover much else about their camp—visibility is horrid in this weather and the river's too high now for crossing."

"Where's Kerin? He should have no problem scouting."

"Dead, ma'am."

She sighed. "Send another scouting party before dawn, river be damned. If the Bordermen agree, I'd like them to go." She rubbed the bridge of her nose. "Five minutes here and I'm frustrated. I admire that you've lasted weeks. This would be so much easier if we could just torch them."

"Why can't we?"

Her copper eyes flicked to Bren. "In this rain? Oil just washes away, and we'd need a fortune of it to light anything so wet. Otherwise, they'd all be burnt in their boots. This damned campaign already threatened to drain the military coffers."

Arman leaned forward, a thought making furrows in his brow. "What about potash?"

"You want to grow a garden to feed ourselves?" Vinden's comment drew chuckles. Even poor jokes were appreciated after the bleak weeks.

Arman ignored him. "Hass Orean's barn exploded after being struck by lightning."

"A barn exploding? That's the most you can give us?" Indred sighed and turned to Eras.

Narier cut off whatever comment the gallant planned. "He's right, sir. Barns get struck all the time, but the most they do is burn usually. When potash gets wet it turns to stone, so we have to keep it dry, usually with metal bins. My Da used my old armor usually."

Eras's brows rose, "Lieutenant, you realize armor is the property of the kingdom."

"Not the point, ma'am. The only barns that exploded were those with potash in them. Not sure why, but every few years it would happen. If the stuff wasn't so good for growing, we'd have done away with it years ago."

Arman nodded his thanks at the man. "We've been burning grasses and trees for weeks now. Raid every campfire here and we'll get enough."

"And how do you propose we cover the Berrin camp in ashes without being seen? Last I knew, none here can fly."

Bren grinned. "General ma'am, permission to go visit my old comrades?"

Φ

The 26th Day of Lleume, 1252

Wood smoke and fates knew what else tangled Alea's hair. She raked her fingers through it, exasperated. "I swear if we're here for much longer I'll cut this mess right off!"

Narier glanced over with a smile. He was perched on his camp chair, scanning recent missives. "I like it down. I mean, your braid is nice too, but with it down you look more...."

"Mad?" She lay back on his cot with a sigh.

"I was going to say wild." He scratched a few notes in his officer's log. "I think the Dhoah' Laen should be wild. Untamed."

"If I get much more dirt on me I might be mistaken for a monkey. I think that's as close to 'untamed' as I'll be." She began her braid, staring thoughtfully at the floor. "I want to go on the scouting mission tomorrow."

He finished his sentence before turning to look at her fully, "You make it sound like something is preventing you from doing so." He crossed his arms and leaned back. "It wouldn't be Arman, now would it?"

Her fingers halted in their work. "Your intuition is uncanny."

"No, I just listen when people talk. Barrackborn mentioned Arman was less than trusting in your ability. I admit I was surprised he was the one to be overprotective, as opposed to your brother. Thank fates I was wrong. I worried Barrackborn'd beat me senseless for taking you to bed."

Alea blanched. "You told him that?" She was not ashamed by taking a lover, but she certainly did not need Bren knowing.

"Fates, no! I do have some respect, Alea, even if I'm crass. He was at your camp when I returned the purse you left here the other night. I think he figured it out."

Alea flushed. "Regardless, no, he's certainly not the one stopping me from scouting. He'd probably worry if I asked, but he lets me make my choices." She frowned, "What do you mean, Arman doesn't trust me?"

"If he trusted you, he'd realize you have a good head and are stronger and more able than you might have once been." He fixed her with a pointed stare. "If you're asking me for permission to go, to make yourself feel better about not telling Arman and sneaking off, forget it. You don't need anyone's permission, least of all mine, but take your guilt up with Arman himself." His smile returned.

"I wouldn't mind if you waited to talk to him though. I hoped to have your company tonight."

She laughed and grabbed his hand, pulling him down onto the cot with her. "I suppose I'll consider it."

Φ

Alea woke sometime after midnight, arm numb and tingling from where Narier's head lay across her elbow. His dark lashes fluttered in sleep and the shadows of expressions flitted over his face. *What are you dreaming about? Is it war? When you dream is it glorious or terrible?* Her arm began to burn from loss of feeling, but she was reluctant to move. Her relationship with Narier was mostly friendship, but their time was precious. Humor and easy acceptance of whatever she chose to be was a balm against the pain and confusion that came with both war and duty.

She sighed and carefully extracted herself before kissing his cheek. "Stay safe." Anxiety, not cold, drove her to dress quickly. The familiar path between Narier's tent and her own seemed longer than usual and she broke into a jog. Bren was the only one in uniform, the rest of the scouts dressed to blend into the monochrome landscape. Her clothes were mottled, and she smudged additional dirt over her cheeks and nose before buckling on the leather breastplate Bren had found for her. Dawn was still an hour away when she arrived at the river's edge.

Reka glanced up at her from where she crouched by the barricades. "Glad to see you made it." The four Bordermen wore broad leather belts equipped with weights and straps. Wicked looking hooks curved down from guards on their forearms. Two other scouts and Bren arrived a moment later, their banter light, but quiet. Alea looked down, hoping to keep her presence undiscovered for as long as possible.

Reka scratched a hasty map in the mud. "We'll cross upriver, keeping to the hollows until we're well past both our banks and theirs. The river will pull us back toward the camps, so each of my men will have one of you strapped to their belts. We use the hooks to drag ourselves along the bottom and we'll breathe through bladders of air." She smudged the map out and began unbuckling the straps on her belt. "We have an hour to get under the trees, understood?"

Through her lashes, Alea saw the green cast to her brother's face. They moved quickly, darting from hollow to hollow. Campfires seemed terribly bright, and Alea felt far too close to the glow of the Berrin camp when Reka motioned for them to approach the river. They knelt in the sand of the bank. Softened ice from the river's edge bobbed away, green in the floodwaters. Reka tugged Alea over. "You're with me." The warrior crisscrossed belts over Alea's shoulders, strapping the Dhoah' Laen to her back. She handed back a bladder of air and Alea tied it around her wrist.

Walking the few steps to the river while pressed together was awkward. They moved steadily to avoid dangerous splashing. Water that was waist-height weeks before was over twice that after the rains. Even through Alea's several layers, the river sent a dull chill to her bones. and she found herself hoping she would just wake up, warm on Narier's cot.

Reka glanced back as the water lapped around their shoulders. "Save your air as long as possible. Hold your breath and don't worry about me. The belt will keep us together. Do not lose the bladder." She drew a long, slow breath and slipped under the churning surface.

The weights in the warrior's belt helped drag them to the bottom. Water pressed down on them and Alea wished the belt was tighter. Her eyes squeezed shut. *Are we moving at all?* Her lungs ached, and she let the air stream out slowly. The trail of bubbles tickled. She touched the mouth of the bladder to her lips and sipped a breath.

A steady *tug-pause-tug* on the belts around her shoulders told her they did indeed creep forward. She squinted, daring to open her eyes. The water stung. The river was black, but she made out the lumps that were their comrades. Rocks dotted the sandy bottom and caught debris from upstream. She could feel the power in the water, the lifeblood of the fields and hills for leagues. She drew a third breath as the ground sloped up. Soon they emerged on the far side. Water sluiced off them noisily and Reka winced, motioning for them to move slower.

Alea stumbled as Reka released the belts. She felt incredibly heavy after the buoyancy of the river. Iere pulled parchment from a waterproof pouch. A corner had dissolved, but it was otherwise intact. They edged through the trees

Φ

Bren trained a spyglass on the fort. He whispered details to Reka as she scratched notes on Iere's parchment. He had doffed the oilskin suit, Mirik's vermillion and green bright against the gray of the forest. "I'll wait until an hour after dawn to light it, unless I'm discovered. When we take the fort Alea can use the vantage for whatever she needs." He lowered the glass, "That's all I can see from here. I'll head in now if you're set. I'd rather get this over with."

"I'll go with you." Iere rose from his crouch. When Bren glanced over questioningly, the warrior shrugged. "The bastards can't tell us apart."

Bren edged forward, Iere a silent presence at his back. When he was just outside the firelight he threw his shoulders back and strode into camp. *A man with a goal is never questioned.* He paused at the base of the fort, dumping a large handful of potash behind the general's tent. They made their way purposefully through the camp, placing mounds wherever it was driest. Bren emptied the last of the potash along the rear of the Berrin mess tent.

"What are you doing?"

Bren straightened, schooling his face into angry imperiousness before turning. "I dropped my purse, idiot. I can't see anything in this dark." His eyes met the bright brown of a Mirikin soldier's.

"Barrackborn? I heard you deserted."

Blood rushed in Bren's ears. *Toar I didn't think of this.* He did not recognize the man, but that meant little. "Deserted? Toar, the shit you people believe. Milord king gave me a task and I carried it out."

The soldier eyed him skeptically. "It was King Azirik himself who told us." His eyes flicked to the warrior behind Bren. "Iere, he's one of the Athrolani now, isn't he?"

Bren's heart plummeted at the words. If the Mirikin knew Iere's name, he was doomed. He looked over his shoulder at the Borderman. "You're the informant we've been trying to pin the past two weeks?"

He heard the scrape as the soldier pulled his sword free, but did not bother to look. Instead, he grabbed the lantern hanging from the mess tent and smashed it over the potash. The explosion was bright and hot and gave him the moment he needed. Grabbing a torch as he passed the center of camp, he retraced their steps, lighting the potash as he went. It was an hour too early, but it was all he could give them. Alarms sounded on his heels and he skittered through narrow tent alleys. Hoofbeats gained on him as he reached the trees. "Retreat!"

Arrows peppered the ground. He slid behind a tree. Reka's eyes were panicked as she shoved the map into her shirt. "What happened?"

"Iere is a fucking traitor is what!"

"If the attack is happening now, I need to be in that tower. I can lay shields on our men."

The words hit Bren like a bucket of river water. His gaze swiveled to the young woman pressed against the tree beside him. "Alea?" He shook his head. "This is nothing like we planned, you need to get out of here, power be damned."

Reka popped up from her crouch, shooting an answering arrow at their pursuers. "Get to the river." A bolt struck her just below the ribs. She faltered but stayed upright. Her draws were weakened, but a gurgled cry said they were no less deadly.

Bren thrust Alea before him and ran for the water. Hoofbeats grew louder. The sullen glint of the river appeared ahead. A horse burst from the trees beside them, spraying wet loam into Bren's face. The rider grabbed Bren's bright tabard, sword sweeping down and across the lieutenant.

Warmth rushed over Bren's collarbone, followed by distant, stinging pain. His sight blurred, and he found himself suddenly face down in the muck. The ground smelled of copper and mildew.

Φ

The 26th Day of Lleume, 1252

The energy of suspense hummed up Arman's limbs. He was as eager as any to see the stalemate end, but battle made him nervous. He had yet to see Alea all day, and he hoped to convince her to stay back from the actual battle. *She'll have plenty wounded to contend with.* Arman ducked under the tent flap of the infirmary, shaking rain from his shoulders. He raised a hand to greet Guffe. "Have you seen milady?"

The healer tied off a stitch and sat back on his heels, puzzled. "She left with the Bordermen to scout." He frowned, "You didn't know?"

Arman's gut clenched. Without bothering to thank the man, he rushed from the tent, searching for any form that could remotely be Alea's.

Attack horns peeled. Fire exploded behind the enemy lines. *This is too soon.* The camp burst into action. Armor was tugged on and weapons gathered even as boots were tied. Eras's battle-shout ordered formations. Another horn shrieked at the southern edge of camp, announcing an ally.

Arman crossed the camp at a dead run. Blood drenched Reka's jerkin. One arm wrapped over Bren's shoulder. Alea's brother had a wadded shirt wrapped around his throat. It, too, was black with blood. Arman could not discern who held up whom.

Indred called for a stretcher for Reka and Arman dogged them back to the healers. The gallant pressed Bren onto a stool.

"What happened?" He waved a surgeon over. "Can you speak?"

"Ambushed." Bren's voice rasped. "Iere betrayed us. He's been with them from the beginning. Everyone but us is dead or captured. I would be too, but the bastard doesn't know a sword from his ass." Bren hissed as the surgeon unwrapped the makeshift bandage. The gash was deep, but missed the largest artery. Blood pulsed slowly.

"What about Dhoah' Lyne'alea?"

Bren fell silent as the healer drew thick threads through the flesh of his throat. Shame in his eyes said enough.

Indred paled and fled the infirmary, shouting for his captains.

A shadow fell over Bren. Arman's entire body burnt. He pulled the taller man up by the bloodstained collar. "Where is she?" Something beyond fury shone in the Rakos's eyes.

"I kept her with me as long as possible. I went down. I'm sorry."

Arman's fist collided with Bren's jaw, spraying blood and spit. He struck the lieutenant's eye next, splitting the brow before Bren retaliated. He drew blood from Arman's lip and felt a shift of bone as the heel of his palm met the bridge of Arman's already crooked nose.

Rough hands pulled Arman back and Guffe shouldered between them. "Fools!" He pushed Arman back another step, "Don't we have enough enemies?"

Bren held up his hands in surrender and returned to his seat.

"I have work aplenty without my charges killing one another." He regarded Arman's face for a moment, then shoved his nose into place with a fluid motion. Shaking his head, he left them in silence.

"Fuck! Damn!" Arman's newly opened nose bled again. He glared at Bren before storming out of the tent. Rage erased most of his pain, leaving only an ache. Heat rippled over his skin.

He did not care that Eras had a careful plan for the attack. He did not care that he was injured or that anger made him reckless. His hands should have shaken as he buckled on armor. Instead, they writhed with smoke.

"Arman, there's half a battalion out there." Bren leaned on the ridgepole of their tent. He was pale from blood loss.

"I thought you needed to rest." The venom in Arman's quip burnt.

Bren paused, as if weighing the chance Arman would attack him with the blades he strapped on. "You should wait until the attack subsides. Adding more to the confusion will only get people killed. Besides, in this mess I doubt you'll be able to get through the Berrin to wherever they're keeping her."

"They'll panic and kill her before that." He held out his hand, "Give me the map you made out there or let me go in unaware. Either way, I leave now."

"Give me time to eat, get some water. I'll go with you."

Arman fingered the hilt of one of his throwing knives. "I'll meet you south of the barricades. I leave in a quarter of an hour, with or without you."

Minutes passed like hours as Arman waited for Alea's brother. He glared up at the paling sky. They needed the cover of night. The river roiled before them, the water a mess of rocks and debris washed from upstream. When Bren finally arrived, he gave him no greeting. "How did you cross before?"

"You don't want to know." Bren shuddered. "And I don't intend to repeat it."

Arman pointed to where a tangle of logs and cattle carcasses snagged on a submerged rock. "We can stand until there, or close to it." He glanced back. "How's your neck?"

"I'll be fine." Bren followed the smaller man into the river. Water lapped halfway up the barricade. It was icy and drove the breath from their lungs. "Toar!"

Arman kicked Bren after the second volley of curses. The attack provided a diversion, but Arman would not push their luck. *If only we had time to do this properly. I'll regret it when I can never get warm and dry again!* Behind him, Bren lost his footing. He grabbed the lieutenant by the armor and thrust him forward. "Go, dammit!"

After too many bitterly cold minutes, they dragged their silt- and water-logged bodies onto the far bank.

"You could have told me you were planning to just walk across the damned river. Then I'd have known better than to come." Bren's breath was ragged, and his hands shook.

Arman was too adrenalized for sympathy. He hauled himself upright and made for the undergrowth. "And you could have told me you were afraid of water!"

Φ

Dried blood stiffened Alea's brow. Fabric scratched her face as she blinked. More rough cloth was stuffed in her mouth. It tasted like dirt and old wine. She shifted carefully. Dull clanking told her the weight on her ankles was chains. Closing her mouth around the gag, she sniffed, hoping for anything that could tell her more about her surroundings. *Burning cloth. Blood. Mud.* She could have been anywhere in either camp.

Timid voices rose in her head. It had been months since she felt this weak. She hated feeling enclosed. *Last time I felt so weak I wished I could die in Vielrona.* She was tired of being cold and wet. She was tired of being shuffled about. She was tired of being weak.

Ice filled her mind.

She rolled her head on her neck and found the hood was loose and untied. Grimacing, she worked the burlap from her face. If she could see, she could fight. With a last violent headshake, the fabric fell away. She spat the gag from her mouth. The dim room was circular and made of stone. *The fort, then.* There were others along the wall, bound as she was. Some had shoved their hoods off too. She recognized only one of the men who had accompanied the scouts. She caught his eye.

He frowned, eyes narrowed on her hair, her face. Realization dawned, and he blanched. "You should have stayed!"

She smiled. "Getting captured was not my plan, but I can attack just as well from here."

Boots on stone heralded the Berrin officer who burst in a moment later. The sound of battle spilled through the door after him. His gaze traced the line of prisoners. He looked as tired as the Athrolani. His eyes barely paused on Alea.

For once she was glad people expected her to be taller, older, or more beautiful. She dared not close her eyes, but she tugged at the chill wrapping her veins. She pulled rope after rope into her hands.

The Berrin drew a knife and crouched beside the furthest prisoner. "I'm sorry. I have orders." His slash was swift and deep. He moved to the next without watching the man's death. Even soldiers had their limits.

Alea's heart hammered and her hold on the power faltered. This was a test she was not prepared for. Shouts from below grew louder, heralding a new attack.

"Do something!" The Athrolani man next to her nudged his boot into hers.

Her focus plummeted when the Berrin man looked over. Cold gripped her skin and she knew black marbled her face. His eyes widened, and he opened his mouth to shout. The time for faltering was past. Power flowed along her limbs and filled the chains. The metal binding her tarnished, rust blooming across the iron. Her power ate away at the stone, pitting it until her chains fell free of the masonry.

She staggered to her feet, eyes never leaving the officer's. "I know you have your duty, but so do I." Swelling power broke from her body. Black fog exploded from her open mouth and filled the room with churning darkness.

The power roiling from the fort was not obvious at first. It crept across the ground like rising floodwater. Cold soaked into hands and boots, halting adrenaline and rage. Despite the rain, thirst crept up the throats of the soldiers, faint but persistent. Those closer to the blast watched droplets of water burst from their skin to skitter across the ground. Soon it was not just water ripped from their bodies, but lymph and bile and blood. Water trickled, moving ever faster as it wound between the stones and swirled up Alea's legs. And each death burnt through Alea's mind.

Φ

Arman sidled through the hastily-repaired wall. He did not bother to see if Bren followed, or if the Mirikin's broader shoulders fit through the gaps. Like the Athrolani camp, this one was more chaos than battlefield. Arman paused in the shadow of the concentric walls leading to the tower. Bren thumped down next to him.

"Have any ideas for that?" He gestured to the expanse of bare ground between them and the tower.

Arman ignored the question, hoping for something to come to him. *We need a diversion.*

Muffled moaning shook the tower stones. Darkness writhed from the windows, slipping down the battered walls like a plague. Arman grabbed Bren's forearm and jerked his head at the power bubbling from the battlements.

"I think we've got a diversion."

Arman lunged toward the tower, but Bren jerked him back. "Wait," the man rasped.

Something in his eyes told Arman it was fear, not exhaustion that tore his voice. The air dampened. Behind them the river roared, bursting her banks. Screams and the clash of battle faded, drowned by the howl of a rising storm. Mud sucked at his boots and Arman glanced down. Rivulets trickled between his feet, flood water and rain drawn toward the roaring darkness within the tower.

Screaming came again, but it was closer. A Berrin captain dashed toward the tower, sword at the ready. several paces from the door she faltered. Her knees cracked as she fell. Arman peered closer. *Was she shot?* Pearls of water bloomed on her skin, growing, joined a moment later by beads of blood. They trickled down her skin and into the mud. The woman screamed, her voice cracking as if parched. More fluid drained from her flesh, body convulsing as she was mummified alive. Her desiccated body cracked, delicate bones loosened from their joints.

When she fell, it was in a puff of dust.

A Mirikin soldier tumbled from the tower window. His uniform was stained in blood, flesh twisted and stiff, as if tanned.

"Is the world ending?" Bren's voice shook. "Did they kill her?"

Arman shoved himself off the wall and stumbled forward. Each step was a stagger against the dragging power. "It is her."

Sounds of fighting rose from the building, and the writhing darkness turned inward, roiling back through the windows to defend itself.

"Cover me!" Arman shouted over the moaning wind. He shouldered into the room, shivering with the ice growing in his hair as he crossed the threshold. Power curled up the stones, rattling the floors above. Arman eyed the ceiling nervously. Berrin soldiers rushed down the stairs, shouting orders. "Milady, come on. We ought to go!"

If Alea heard him, she showed no sign. Her eyes swiveled to the new attackers. One hand reached to Arman. Blackness twisted around him. It dragged his knives from their sheaths and flung them toward the approaching Berrin.

Arman stumbled, distracted. It was only a moment, but the foremost soldier crashed into him. Arman shoving the man down the stairs behind him. He stood, panting in pain, before rushing over to Alea.

Power writhed back into her body, water dripping from her limbs. The other prisoners were lifeless and still. Their parched bodies looked like they had lain in the desert for weeks. Arman staggered as he reached her, catching himself on her still-outstretched arm. Nausea danced in his gut. His face paled and he crumpled to the floor. A dark stain spread across the front of his jerkin.

"Arman?" The daze lifted from her eyes and she fell to her knees beside him, hand fumbling against the wound.

"Bastard got me."

She took his face in her hands. "You'll be fine, you just need a surgeon." She balled her discarded hood and pressed it against the welling blood.

Numbness crept through him, death chasing the fire from his fingers. He thought of his last letters home and what his mother would think when she got the news. *I should have been more honest.* He moaned low in his throat as his body descended into shock.

Alea pressed her hand to his chest, like she had in Vielrona. His skin dried and decayed at her touch. Shuddering gripped his limbs.

"I chose this. It's all right." He had minutes maybe, but time enough. "Remember when I said you were in the wrong part of the story? I said you had to gather the pieces?"

She nodded. Her jaw clenched, hiding the tremble of fear.

Wrapping his fingers around the back of her neck, he willed himself to focus on her eyes. "This is when you're reforged." He knew what was in his heart, what he wanted to say. Instead, he found three words that would give her courage, ease the guilt rooting in her chest.

"It doesn't hurt." It was not the time for declarations. Honesty would only bring regret and confusion. Last words were not for the dying, but for those left behind.

CHAPTER NINETEEN

The 26th Day of Lleume, 1252
The Battlefield at Fort Shadow

BREN HATED WATER. SICKLY squelching under his boots as he crossed the battlefield did not help. The battle lasted no more than an hour. As a soldier, he knew it was often the strangest things that turned the tides of war. This outshone them all. The corpses surrounding the fort were something out of nightmares. Skin tanned into leather wrinkled around shrunken flesh. Eyes were hard marbles sunk into papered skulls. His sister did this. Somehow, she ripped the water, the very lifeblood, from these people. Tripping over an outstretched arm, Bren glanced down. The uniform was Athrolani. Her power seemed indiscriminate.

Azirik's a damn fool, the gods are fools. They can't fight this. Nothing can. He shoved past the destroyed front gate of the fort. The bodies here were worse. Stairs creaked under his boots sending rot tumbling after his steps. He paused in the doorway to the mess hall. It was dark inside, but he heard weeping.

"Alea?"

Surprise replaced grief for a moment when she looked up, "I thought you were dead."

He shook his head and sat back on his heels beside her. Seeing Arman lifeless was strange. A man so full of fire and ideas snuffed out in one move. "Alea, we need to get back. I'm not certain the building is sound." She barely resisted when he pulled her into his arms.

Bren glanced up at the two Athrolani they passed on their way down the stairs. "Bring her guard back, will you?" He watched Alea as they wound through the destroyed camp. The aftermath of battle was often grim. The silence that followed their passage, however, was different. Alea's eyes rested on the bodies she desiccated. Her expression was knowing, but without remorse.

It made his skin crawl.

Φ

Alea stood in the infirmary tent, arms wrapped around herself. She did not move, but energy raced through her. It was beyond anger, beyond grief. Surgeons and apprentices bustled behind the hastily erected curtain. Bren shifted for the third time. It was obvious he had no idea what to say.

"Will you give me a minute?" Her voice sounded strange in her ears. "I'm sure they need help out there."

"Alea—"

Her eyes flicked to him. They still swirled with darkness. "Now."

Finally alone, she turned back to Arman's body. The healers were careful when they cleaned him. Death was not a pretty thing or a dignified moment. She pushed aside his shirt breast. The new wound was a purple blossom in the center of the handprint scar. A discarded surgeon's kit sat on the ground beside him. Her icy fingers managed to thread the needle and tiny, practiced stitches mended the torn muscles and flesh.

It doesn't hurt.

The lie rang in her ears. Even with his dying breath, he tried to protect her. She had listened to Arman talk about forging often enough. The steel was heated, hammered, tempered, heated again, hammered again. Their entire journey hammered her, burnt her, the pain quenched only briefly. She was ready for it to be over. *This is where you're reforged.*

Smooth silver on his chest was marred by purple flesh. She caused this. Arman would have disagreed, but Bren knew. *Your actions are yours alone.* If she claimed the credit for the men without foot rot and the wounds that did not fester, she must also claim the fault for the punctured lungs, the torn ventricles, and the stilled muscles.

Healing a dying man was not easy. It was impossible when Destruction iced her veins. *I have another side.* The cold was different now. It was a cool drink in the desert heat. It slid through her body like dew. She crawled onto the bed beside him and tucked herself under his arm. Her brow pressed to his. Her mind crept through his body. Relief filled still muscles and chased the sickly smell of death away. She traced the glowing white that overlaid the gold veins of his soulblood. She sunk into herself. A tiny thread still led from his body through her, the footprints of his soul. That was the path she followed.

Outside the rain began anew.

Φ

Blackness surrounded her. Occasionally silver flashed, lightning far above clouds. Before, she stood on the shore of this ocean of power and drawn from it. Now she waded in. Trails of red wove through the fog, like game trails in the snow. This was the unseen aftermath of battle—lines of souls winding their way to death. She found Arman's straight path, the gold glimmering up at her through the darkness. She did not think about what she was doing. She did not glance back to see the blue-black prints her bare feet left behind. She did not think about the pain creeping into her physical chest so far away.

It seemed like hours before the pillowy fog under her feet became coarse, black sand. Gray cliffs rose before her. She did not need her eyes to recognize the place. Her power knew. *I crossed into Le'yne.* Her eyes lingered on the spires topping the cliffs. Someday soon that would be her home. She shook the feeling of dread away and stepped into the crevice. Light reflected from the damp walls, lighting her path. The floor was damp and cold. It did not smell of earth and mildew the way she thought a cave should. It smelled of rock and salt. It smelled of eternity.

The tunnel ended in a vast cavern. If her physical body had been there she was certain frostbite would have set in. The ceiling was too distant to see, as were the far walls. A great sphere floated in the center. Pulsing red swirls moved beneath its silver surface. The air in the room crackled with energy, like the sky just before a storm arrived. Alea reached out and pressed her hand to the surface. The icy light seared her palm and she stepped back with a hiss of pain, cradling her injured hand.

You cannot do this. The voice thundered from all around her, mighty and ancient.

Alea peered up at the sphere, "Who are you?"

I am all the Laen that have passed. Our souls hold those of every being that once lived. We are the shell that keeps them safe. The light pulsed faster. *What you ask is too great. A piece of you will be left behind until you are an empty husk. You will cripple yourself and thus the world.*

Alea stared at the swirling surface. A month ago, she would have hung her head in shame and fear. She would have fled at her ancestor's words. Instead, her voice was thunder, "The world is already crippled! You are bound to the minute, controlled laws of balance. I am the greatest balance."

This is a dangerous path you walk.

Alea ignored the warning and pressed her hands again to the surface. The pain ripped through her hands, knifing up her arms. Her vision burst into lights like shattered glass. She drew more power and forced her eyes open. The surface writhed now as if in violence. Or pain. It thinned under her hands. Wetness trickled from her palms, trickled between her fingers and down the backs of her hands. Screaming filled her ears, but she did not know if it came from the sphere. Perhaps it was hers.

Stop!

Alea forced herself past the pain in her head, the distant pain in her heart. She roared and ripped a hole in the veins of her soulblood, bleeding herself to add to her power. The agony made her mind go blank.

Sharp stone bit into her shoulder. She blinked, her mind clearing. An ugly gash marred the silver surface of souls. Sickly black liquid bled from the raw edges. Later, it would haunt her sleep, make her sick, but not yet.

"Arman?" She dragged herself up and thrust a hand through the sphere's wound. She called again.

A glint of gold approached through the swirling crimson. It emerged, standing on the brink of the opening. It was a man made of white-gold fire. His head tilted.

"Arman?"

The figure reached out, hand brushing hers. His light mingled with her soul-blood, sealing the bond he never spoke aloud.

"You gave me your life. I am giving it back. I don't know if I'll live through this war, if I'm even meant to. I want you to go home, to live, to have children. Tell them these stories."

He took her hand and climbed free. Neither looked back at the bleeding sphere. She led him back through the tunnel, steps stumbling as her power weakened. She tripped, and Arman's gold hand caught her. She did not pause at the ocean of her power. There was no time. She plunged through, unable to keep them above the surface. She swam through the twisting fog, Arman's burning hand clutched in hers. Her hold on her power guttered. The thunder of her heartbeat was now a faltering patter. She thrust Arman's soul through. The murmur of his mended heart echoed as waves closed over her head.

Φ

Bren wandered aimlessly through the tents. There was plenty to do, surely, but many hands complicated most tasks. At the edge of camp Eras perched on a barricade. The general's hard eyes watched the Berrin and Mirikin prisoners being processed across the river. Bren leaned on the wood beside her. "They'll be questioned?"

Eras nodded. "Her Majesty has the Royal Inquest. They'll do the unpleasantries." Her eyes flicked to him, though her head did not turn. "The Rakos?"

"Dead."

Her lips thinned, "I was hoping he would be a boon in the war to come. Perhaps I've read too many tales, but I had the image of fire and crumbling mountains."

"I read the same tale, ma'am."

"Saw the bodies out there, the ones near the fort. That's something I didn't expect. I thought she couldn't control her power."

"She can't. Not well, at least. If she could, I think none of those bodies would be wearing Athrolani tabards."

"Did she kill him?"

Bren shook his head. "Berrin dagger, from what I saw." He ran a hand through his hair, wincing as his fingers caught on a matt of blood. "She'll need time after this. She needs peace, safety. I'll take her back to Athrolan myself. When the time comes she'll be ready, I promise."

Eras glanced over, "She was lucky in her guard, but she's just as lucky in her brother. Whatever either of you need, name it."

Bren pushed himself upright. "Thank you, General." He made one more circuit of the camp before winding his way back to the infirmary. Alea needed her space, but he was afraid to leave her alone with her thoughts for too long. Silence bred darkness.

He ducked inside, edging through the cots and between surgeons. After pausing nervously outside the privacy screen, he rapped on the tent pole. When there was no answer he peered inside.

Alea curled into her guard's arms. Her eyes were closed, and her arched nose rested against his brow. One hand gripped his, the other rested on his chest. Its palm was burnt red and oozed blood and clear fluid.

Bren winced and knelt by the cot. "Toar, Alea, what have you done?" Dread crept into him when she did not even stir. A thousand terrible possibilities flew through his mind. He reached out and placed a hand on her back. She was cold, her pulse faint and slow.

"She'll be all right." The low voice was tired and familiar.

Bren glanced back, confused. Movement returned his gaze to the cot.

Arman's eyes opened slowly, blinking. He wrapped his free arm carefully around Alea and held her gently.

Bren stepped back, mouth moving silently. A sick feeling filled his chest. This was too much. This was too far. "What the fuck is this?"

Arman glanced up. "She's exhausted."

"Not that. You—" Bren could not finish.

"I was dead. I know." Arman's gaze moved back to Alea. His eyes burnt with something that made Bren's heart twist. "She brought me home."

Φ

The 30th Day of Lleume, 1252
The Northern Coast of Ceir Athrolan

The wagon under Bren lurched. He sat up with a groan, rolling his stiff neck. "Toar, I didn't think I'd sleep." He glanced over at the makeshift bed over the axels. Alea was still unconscious.

Arman trailed one hand absently through Alea's hair, fanning it on the pillow around her head. His eyes flicked to Bren's.

The soldier's stomach lurched. He was as superstitious as any Mirikin soldier, but something told him this was different. *He's wrong. You don't come back from death. Not sane, not human.* It could have been his mind running wild with the fear, but he swore Arman's gaze was luminous in the dark wagon. He shook away the queasiness and peered out at the road. "How long until we're there?"

"Another day, maybe two. Depends on how many roads we've got to rebuild from the rains. It's close to noon now. You slept through the night."

Bren pushed aside his question of when Arman slept last. Instead, he nodded to Alea. "Are you sure she's alright?"

"She is. It's a long journey to make, back to her body. And she's making it. Time is different in there, in our heads. Slow and fast at once. When she wakes, you'll see, she'll be the same Alea you remember. I promise."

Bren looked away. *That's a lie. Just like you.* "You don't live through what she did and remain unchanged."

Arman shook his head. "She's Laen. I think both of us could stand to remember that more."

"You might be right about that part, but even if it's just in the way people look at her, she'll be different. I remember the feeling when I first killed a Laen. I couldn't forget it. Even if I lost my mind like the old king of Athrolan decades ago, I'd remember that awful feeling until the day I die." He lurched to his feet and navigated his way to the rear of the wagon. "I think I need to stretch my legs."

"I'll stay," Arman offered, though he had yet to leave Alea's side for more than an hour. "And Bren, she's strong. Strong enough to handle it."

"It doesn't matter how strong you are," Bren countered, swinging himself over the wagon's side. "Some actions change you forever."

Φ

The 32nd Day of Lleume, 1252
The City of Ceir Athrolan

Alea sat on the edge of her bed for a moment, taking stock of her surroundings. Slate flagging was decorated with a familiar blue rug. Gray velvet curtains were drawn, but a bright sliver of sunlight told her it was day. She rose with a groan. It felt as if she had run for leagues. *Or swum.* Her steps were slow as she padded across the room to the wardrobe. Familiar lengths of silver and black silk met her eyes. *Ceir Athrolan then.* She thought about calling for Girre, but was afraid to burst the comfortable solitude.

Instead, she drew her own bath, watching the swirling water tumble into the tin washtub from the boilers below. The lump of lavender soap seemed a silly luxury after living through weeks of siege. Hot water was blissful, and she slid in and closed her eyes. She must have slept for days, and she did not remember waking. Marveling at the rough callouses on her hands, she scrubbed her skin and hair. What few curves she had were gone, her hips and elbows obvious and hard. Only when her fingertips were ridged and pink did she climb out. She dried and donned a simple dress tucked behind the fine gowns. A small stack of letters waited on her desk, but they all looked handwritten. *I can't quite face personal questions.*

She drew the curtains back. Sunlight was golden and warm, she tilted her face up to it and smiled. Her body ached, but a walk would do her some good. She pulled on a new cloak that hung by the door and stepped out into the hall. The palace was quiet, and she passed only a few household staff on her way to the gardens' entrance. All but the mildest of winter's bites melted with the rains. Alea remembered an arbor tucked under the arching road and made her way down a narrow path. She rounded a bend and stopped. A familiar blond figure was already sprawled across the bench. Arman held a small book over his face and his boots were kicked off.

He lowered his book, finger tucked between the pages. "Good afternoon." His expression was open and warm, but honest.

She knotted her cloak in her bandaged hands. She was not ready for this. "Hello."

His pale brows arched, "Come sit?"

She jerked a nod and stepped carefully up to the bench. She perched on the edge, her muscles as tight as if still at war. "What day is it?"

"The thirty-second of Lleume. Bren's here too, though many of the others stayed behind."

"When will you go back?"

"Back?" His face softened. "You mean to Vielrona." He sat up, fixing her with a stare. "When this is all over, perhaps. Until then, I'm wherever you need me to be. I can only imagine what feelings are going through your heart, but guilt should not be among them. If you think I want my duty to you to end because—" He swallowed hard "—because I swore until death and that was achieved, you're wrong. I'll protect you and your people as long as there is breath in my body, no matter how long I may have gone without it." He nudged her with his shoulder. "That's what a soul-bond is to me."

She smiled, still afraid to break the fragile shell around her mind. "Budge over?" She sat beside his feet and propped her own up next to him. "How many people do you think we could fit on this bench?"

He laughed and picked up his book again.

She tilted her face up to the sun. "What are you reading?"

"Me? A lowly common lad? I just look at the pictures."

Alea noted that the book had no images on those pages.

"It's a history of Claimiirn."

She smiled. "If I remembered your sense of humor, I would have considered making you wait longer before waking you up."

A shadow crossed his eyes. "It felt like eternity, you know."

Alea shivered a chill away. "Where's Claimiirn?" The time would come for questions and curiosity, but she was not strong enough for them yet.

"It's Athrolan's mother city. It was the capital, but fell to an Ageless invasion." Arman laid his book open on his chest to keep the page and rested a hand on her ankle. "The queen asked if I wanted an honorary title in the army."

"What did you say?"

"I respectfully declined. I'm taking the surname of Arrowlash, though. He's the Rakos from whom my ancestors are descended. I thought it fitting and I'm not who I was months ago."

"If not for me you would have been."

"You've not done me any disservice. I'd have missed the adventures, the excitement. I'd have missed the people and even the finery here." He squeezed her ankle. "I would have missed you."

"I think I'll go to Le'yne soon."

"You won't take me with you." The words were too certain for a question.

It was more than the momentum of war driving her. Even now Athrolan's walls closed in around her. The whispers were fearful after what she had done. *Is it that I killed a thousand men, or that I brought one back?* Rumors did not scare her, nor the people who whispered them.

She was scared they were right.

"I'll return." She stared out at the gardens as he returned to his book. The trees were leafed in brilliant green and blossoms peeked from vines. She did not see them. Instead, she saw a shadow creep into her thoughts. It hovered on the edge, but she felt it grow.

Φ

The 35th Day of Lleume, 1252

The letter had been specific if brief. Alea turned down the alley, brow furrowing as she stepped over a dead animal. This was not the meeting she imagined. The inn indicated on the crumpled parchment was in the worst district Alea had yet seen. Perched above the naval yards, the narrow houses were poorly lit. Great arching aqueducts cut through them, shadowing the streets.

The road turned sharply and spilled into a dim square. Alea glanced up at the sign creaking in the spring breeze—*The Wise Hare.* Music and laughter within seemed honest enough and Alea pushed through the door. It was a small, dark tavern, but warm. The rich smell of bread and meat covered stale alcohol. She scanned the room for a quiet table, finally finding one nestled in the opposite corner. Her clothes were fine enough to make a statement, but so was the sharp dagger at her belt.

It was several minutes before the door opened again. Alea glanced up from dipping a piece of beef into the small bowl of sauce. Her hand froze, and she stared at the woman in the doorway. She had never known her mother, and it was ridiculous to think she recognized the woman. Still, the dark hair and the violence of her features were unmistakable.

A month ago, I'd have run to her, yelled at her perhaps. Maybe even wept. Alea stayed seated, waiting for the silver eyes to finally rest on her. When they did, Alea nodded once.

Elle approached, eyes lit with excitement and fear, nested in tired lines. "I worried you wouldn't come."

"I almost didn't." Alea pushed the tray of grilled meat into the center of the table. "Help yourself, there's enough for two."

"You know who I am, then?"

"I know what you are. Who you are was plain in your letters." Alea wanted to be excited to finally meet the woman who had birthed her. A fragile shell still protected her mind, however, and mostly she just felt numb. "How long have you been here?"

"We arrived just after you left for Fort Shadow. An'thoriend went east to gain more intelligence. I hoped you would bring your brother."

"He left for Mirik with the Athrolani navy two days ago." Alea examined Elle's blade-sharp nose and large eyes.

"Did they find Azirik?"

"The city was deserted, everything torn apart. The Mirikin had no intention of returning. Athrolan will raid the city for anything to give us the advantage. Bren thinks he can help with that."

"And you? Will you stay here?" Elle dipped her meat deftly, clearly familiar with Athrolan's disuse of utensils.

Alea shook her head. She found herself suddenly unable to meet the woman's eyes. "I can't stay here." Her voice caught on the words. "Neither Athrolan nor I could deal with that."

"Where will you go, then?"

Le'yne had been her destination since discovering what she was. *So why does it feel like I'm running?* She finally looked up. Her eyes were more gray than blue. "I think it's time I go with you. I'm ready to learn control. I'm ready to learn what I am."

"Le'yne it is." Elle's smile did not quite reach her eyes. Decisions that broke the soul were not meant to be accompanied by mirth. She slid her hand across the table. It did not touch Alea's, but simply rested beside it. They were both worn and cracked from a life turned difficult too quickly.

In her lap, Alea's other hand clenched into a fist. She did not want to face the souls she left scarred and bleeding. There was very little she still held dear, and none of it could go with her. "Can you leave tomorrow?"

"Whenever you're ready."

"Then meet me at dawn. Waiting won't help anything." Alea left without another word, shrugging into her cloak despite the balmy night air. Tattered threads of her mind were barely beginning to weave themselves back into something that resembled sanity. Whatever she had yet to learn would push those threads farther. She wondered if they would hold. The shadow encroaching her thoughts darkened and the image of the bleeding souls flashed through her mind.

Alea decided there were two darknesses that filled a person's mind. The first came when her family died. Watching them scream and beg broke her. It filled her with despair and bitterness. It made her angry. That anger fueled her resolve. It bled determination into her limbs and gave her the will to live. It gave her something to hate.

There were laws in the world that were unbreakable. They were mountains' peaks, the sweeping wind off the desert. They were mighty things. The second darkness rooted when one broke those laws. It was slow and creeping, like thunderheads on the horizon of a summer day. She wondered if Azirik's mind was shadowed like hers was now. She could ignore it. Still, it rattled around her mind like dead leaves heralding the bleak chill of winter.

I'm a monster.

END OF BOOK ONE

REFORGED II

A Darkness in the Mind

CHAPTER ONE

The 36th Day of Lleume, 1252
The City of Ceir Athrolan

THE WIND OFF THE OCEAN bit at Alea's cheeks with salty teeth. She smiled, not minding the cold. It was a lover's bite, nothing more. She preferred the hour just before dawn. The city below barely stirred. It was as if she were the only woman in the world. It should not have been a comforting thought. She leaned on the palace parapet. Below, a runner was bringing her letter to the queen and to Arman. She hated goodbye, hated explaining herself. *The Dhoah' Laen shouldn't have to explain herself so often.*

"You thought you could sneak away without me knowing?" Arman's voice was low, the hint of a smile blunting the accusation.

"Not really. I thought I might try, though." She brushed a strand of black hair away from her face. "I leave today. In an hour."

"So you said." The blond man leaned on the wall beside her. "Are you nervous?"

Nervous was such a simple word. Emotions were not simple things. Yes, she was nervous. She was terrified. The shadow crouching in the back of her mind was excited. "A bit. I'm not certain how to feel. Elle's my mother, but I have no memory of her. I'm excited, too. Learning to control this thing will be good. Hopefully I'll learn more about myself as well."

"And what then? Will you be full Laen? Cold? Austere? Proud?"

She looked over incredulously. It did not matter that she knew he was afraid, that she could see the tremble in his hands. "You're scared I'll be different? What if I want to be?"

"You act as if you're alone in this battle. All the Laen do. You never share your plans. You're not alone. You never will be." He dug his fingers into the rough, weathered stone. "Fates forbid you actually tell me anything."

"You've been a part of this journey since the beginning."

"But have I known any detail until I absolutely had to? Did I know you were going to battle before you announced it to the queen? Did I know you were hurting before you got drunk?" He shook his head. "Damn, I didn't know you would draw my daggers in Fort Shadow until it was too late."

She closed her eyes. She was tired. Sleep could not banish the deep, aching fatigue that weighed on her mind. She was too exhausted to deal with one of Arman's tempers. "Perhaps if you assumed I was a person, those decisions wouldn't have surprised you."

"How can I protect you when I'm ignorant? Your refusal to explain anything cost me my life!"

She drew back as if he'd slapped her. This was why she hated good-byes. Everything left unsaid bubbled to the surface, jumbled and painful. "What?"

"You disarmed me in the middle of battle."

"And you have no idea what I paid to bring you back. You may have been there, you may remember it, but you will never understand the cost." Her words were low, almost a curse, almost a sob. She shoved away from the parapet. "I don't know how long I'll be gone—a week, a month, a year. However long it is, I hope to fate I do change. And I hope when I come back I'm everything they need me to be." She hunched her shoulders as she trotted down the staircase. The wind howled through the series of open windows. It was still a lover's touch, but this time it stung with anger.

Φ

The 39th Day of Lleume, 1252
The City of Mirik

Bren tilted his chair back on two legs. His feet ached. He had worked the entirety of the day and was glad for the rest. *I'm getting old if a day's work tires me.* Athrolan's navy had set up a makeshift headquarters in Mirik's old army barracks. Though the flags were now Athrolani turquoise and white, it still felt as if he was in the wrong room.

A stack of books sat on his desk, mostly ones he had found in a chest tossed on a rubbish heap. A washed spittoon held three rolled maps. He opened a tattered copy of *Raulde's Tales for an Officer.* The pages smelled of dirt and wet soot.

He winced as someone pounded on his door, but called for them to enter. Seeing the thin man leaning on the doorframe, he scrambled to his feet. "Commodore Veren, good evening."

The man waved Bren's formality away. "The patrol exploring the southeast quad of the city sent word back from the slums a few minutes ago. Said they found something unexpected and need extra hands. I'm sending you and Parlin with the reinforcements."

"I'll be down in a moment, sir." When Veren had gone, Bren gathered his scout-pack with a frown. *Parlin's a speak-well. Why would they need negotiations in an abandoned city?* A thrill of foreboding crawled up his spine. The city folk who worked for the army during Azirik's time were rough. He had never known where they lived—they were like animals, appearing and disappearing at will. After a moment he strapped on his sword and joined the group gathering in the courtyard.

"Patrol said they were in the slums. We'll start there. Keep your weapons ready, eyes sharp." The shipman shouldered his own gear and headed off at a steady jog. The men fell into a line behind him. Bren took up the tail. They'd been scouting for days now, and the men knew the city well. After a dozen minutes they arrived at the broad wall that separated what had been upscale residences and inns from the grime of the slums. The broken gates hung at an angle, allowing them to pass through two-abreast.

"Jug-end Square." The shipman glanced about them. "This place is a warren."

"The east wall, down that way." Bren pointed right. "In all the books it's the worst area." He ignored the muttered insult of "Parchment-nose." *If they had been in Mirik's army, where the predominant order usually involved "later" or "wait," they'd understand.* The city was quiet and the spring rains—heavier than usual for Mirik, but far lighter than those in Athrolan—turned many of the streets into marshlands. The gutters were more formality than functional.

Over the squelch of their boots, Bren heard voices, most in Athrolani. Their path rounded a bend and they entered a small square bordered by haphazardly built and repaired houses. The patrol ranged about, hands on their weapons. Their expressions were annoyed. Surprised, perhaps, but not frightened. Most stared at the largest of the houses. It was an old thing, originally built in the over-hung style of old Miriken architecture. Now it was derelict. Torchlight burnt in the windows.

Bren edge around the men to the shipman who led the original scouting group. "Guilie, what happened?"

"Damned urchin-clan jumped us as we crossed the wall. Stole half our packs before we could blink. We chased them here where they holed up. They're like rats, jabbering in a tongue I've never heard."

Parlin stepped forward, the thin man straightening as he prepared to speak with the thieves. "Men of Mirik, I speak to your natures. We come not to roust you from your homes. We come instead to ask your help."

Bren groaned and glanced at Guilie as Parlin continued. "They don't give one Toar's hair for helping us. All he'll do is make them laugh if we're lucky, drive them away if we're not."

"Parlin's good at speaking to stubborn nobles. Common-folk with heads as hard as cobbles are another thing entirely. Appeasing to their morals will be hard when to a one they look as starved as a man can be and still walk." He glanced at Bren. "You deal with these folk at all?"

Bren's mouth was a grim line. "They've been here since before the city closed. We hired them, traded with them sometimes. They speak Common, but with a Miriken accent so thick it sounds foreign." He absently fingered the amulet around his neck. "There were several dozen then, I think, but those were the only ones we saw."

"Close to a score were the ones that jumped us."

"Azirik said for every one you see there are four more in the woodworking." Bren turned his attention back to Parlin's futile efforts. After another exasperating minute, Bren nudged the speak-well's shoulder. "I dealt with these folk before. Might I try?"

Bren saw the relief in the man's eyes and moved towards the house. The boards creaked as men shifted inside. *Sighting their bows, no doubt.* He grimaced and edged a few paces closer before looking up to the higher windows. "Kit of Jug-end?" He used their word for people. "We mean no harm to you or the city. In that, Parlin spoke true. We come to repair and strengthen her for the war. We thought you'd all have left."

The square was quiet, save for the guttering of torches and the patter of feet behind the walls. Finally a shutter in the door cracked open. Eyes glinted in the darkness beyond. "That ye, King Azirik?" The dialect of the gruff voice left half the consonants from the words. "Kit dealt with ye. Afore ye left the city."

Bren raised a hand against the torch glare to see the speaker. *Perhaps the resemblance is greater than we knew. Who else suspected my blood?*

The door opened and a man stepped out. A stubby, scavenged arrow was nocked to his recurved bow. The weapon was drawn, but lowered. He stared a second longer, then the bow came up quickly, sighted on Bren's chest. "Yer not Azirik."

The Athrolani shifted, raising their own weapons. Bren raised an empty hand. "No, but I'm his blood. I served as a lieutenant in Azirik's army."

"No longer?"

"Mirik was a great city and could be again. My allies, the Athrolani, promise to help make it so. Time was we traded with them." Bren offered what he hoped was a friendly smile. "What are you called?"

"Arik Oland of Mirik." The man did not lower his bow, but his gaze appraised the men before him. "And ye?"

"Former Lieutenant Brentemir Barrackborn of Mirik."

"Yer his son."

Bren had never considered himself Azirik's son in the way most men were sons. *Owning your blood is the first step to surpassing it.* "I was raised by the army, truly, but yes. I'm his."

Arik approached then, curiosity replacing wariness in his gaze. Deep shadows hung under his eyes and hollowed his cheeks. His clothes bagged around thin limbs.

"The years have not been kind to you, have they?" Bren asked.

Arik shrugged. "The city's dead. The army was our only livelihood."

"You're welcome to come across the harbor with us." When the man made no move, Bren prodded. "We've food and we could talk. And it's simply conversation, nothing sworn, nothing promised. Just talk."

Arik shifted his meager weight once, twice, then raised his voice. "'Ken that? King's son wishes us to dine with his ally-men." Dust and mold filtered down as the houses' occupants moved towards the street. Bren could have sworn the men and women suddenly vastly outnumbering the Athrolani had appeared magically in the street. His brows raised, but he extended a hand to Arik. "Thank you, Master Oland."

Arik shook the hand, a grudging respect growing on his features. "Where this sup you offer?"

Bren laughed and did a rough count of the three-score Kit. "I hope we have enough!" The trip back through the city was shorter and the mood lighter. The Athrolani laughed ruefully as they tried to decipher the bright, quick talk of the Miriken. Bewilderment and incredulous stares welcomed the crowd back into the barracks.

The rafters of the dining hall rang with Miriken chatter. Bren wedged himself next to Arik with a smile, sliding a second plate over to the man. "Try these. I'm not much one for gravy, but they're good." He watched Arik shovel the food into his mouth for a minute. "Are you their leader?"

Arik shrugged. "Someone had to take them up. We stayed in the back alleys of the city. There was nowhere to go, no money to buy passage on a boat south. The army was our lifeline."

Bren looked away. "No one should have to eat garbage to live."

"We damn near starved o'er the winter." Arik's thick lips curled. "But now ye come in to take Mirik's crown and shine 'er up bright."

Bren choked on his ale. When he finished sputtering, he waved away the pounding on his back. "I beg pardon?"

"Ye've come to be the new king, yes?"

"I was bred a fighting man. Queen Tzatia will take over Mirik's ruling. Perhaps Mirik might rise on her own again, but it would be years from now. She'll be fostered under Athrolan's guidance." He tried to keep the guilt from his voice, but the expression on the Miriken faces made him turn away.

Φ

The 40th Day of Lleume, 1252

Alea eyed the woman at the bow. Elle was unremarkable for a Laen woman. Her black hair was laced with silver, her bright eyes nested in crows' feet. Years among humans had not treated her well. "How old are you?"

Elle glanced over, brows raised. "Fifty-seven."

"Laen age differently?"

"Slower, usually. It appears you grew like a human girl, though."

"Not entirely." Alea looked out at Mirik's harbor, her gaze distant. She still was uncertain how to treat her mother. "What are we looking for?"

Elle leaned beside her daughter with a sigh. "Simply a place in the woods. Mirik was once a larger island. It broke into three during the Division. One piece belongs to the gods, another to the Laen. The Rakos left their third to the humans as shelter. Because they were here, long ago, this is the place where the barriers are thinnest." She glanced sidelong at Alea. "I don't suppose you wish to spend the night in the capital."

"You want to see Bren." Alea ran a hand through the tangled hair the wind pulled from her braid. She was not sure whether Bren wanted to see their mother yet. He had seemed indifferent. The ship creaked as the sails were furled and she glided up to the dock. "You think he wants to see you?"

Elle's eyes sharpened on her daughter. "You think he doesn't?"

"I think we're at war and every moment counts." Her surrender came as a sigh. "I've letters I want to send before we go, however, and I didn't manage a proper good-bye." She shouldered her pack, not waiting to see if her mother followed. The dock seemed to sway under her feet and she stumbled. *No sooner have I learned my sea legs then I'm back on land.* She laughed softly at herself and took the stairs from the dock two at a time. Mirik may have once been beautiful. The stone was a rich brown and the steep hills beyond thickly forested. Alea made for the barracks, her steps unconsciously quickening as she approached. She heard Elle's murmured apologies as the older woman wove through the sailors mooring the ship.

The barracks themselves were clean and tidy, though Alea suspected it might not have been so two weeks before. Alea waved over a young deck-boy by the flagpole in the courtyard's center. "Might you tell me if Lieutenant Barrackborn is here?"

The boy's eyes were huge as he stared up at her. When Elle appeared behind her, he swallowed once, then nodded quickly. "Right this way, ma'am."

The officer's rooms were more spacious than those of Athrolan's forts, and lined against the outside wall. Bren's door was propped open with one large boot and the sound of turning pages drifted from within. Alea hesitated at the door, glancing back to where Elle waited at the top of the stairs. Finally, she knocked. "Bren, it's Alea."

The sound of scrambling preceded her brother jerking the door open with a broad grin. "Alea! I was starting to wonder if you'd changed your mind. Want to come in?"

"We're only staying for a few hours."

"We? Did Arman come with you?"

Alea glanced over her shoulder. "No. It's someone you've not seen in a long time." She stepped aside and gestured Elle forward. Bren's face sobered. He blinked, then stepped back and slammed his door.

Φ

Bren leaned his forehead against the door. It was rude and pathetic, but he did not care. He had expected to never see her again. Even after hearing Alea and Arman's story, he had convinced himself she was not real. *At least to me.* He wished Alea had warned him, wished that their mother had written beforehand. *I can't hide forever.* He drew a breath and straightened. He finger-combed his hair, certain that he only made it worse. Finally, he opened the door.

Alea leaned against the far wall. Elle's face was downcast. When the door opened, slower this time, they both glanced up.

He could not look away now. "I'm sorry. I was surprised." He shifted then stepped back. "Would you like to come in?" Alea sat on his bed, their mother taking the seat at his desk. He could not sit. His nerves hummed from a dozen unnamed emotions. "I thought I didn't remember you. I thought I'd never recognize your face."

"But you do?" Her voice was low and warm and more familiar than anything he'd ever known.

"I know you." He blinked hard a few times then fell to his knees. His arms wrapped around her waist and his head buried in her lap. "Ma, I'd know you anywhere."

Φ

Alea looked away from the exchange. She was not jealous, exactly. She had just as much claim to Elle as Bren. Her chest was tight and she felt displaced. It was a strange sensation akin to nostalgia, but more hopeless than homesickness. She wondered what it would have been like to mother a child. She had acted nursemaid to many children in the ihal's household, but that was worlds away from motherhood.

When Bren finally drew back, his eyes were bright and his smile delicate. "I hadn't thought you'd come here together." He looked at Alea and the warmth in his eyes dulled her unease. "You have to leave?"

She nodded. "I know you want to talk, but we've little time. None of us are sure how long this quiet period will last. Is it strange to be in Mirik again?"

His expression slid back into that of the soldier. "Real talk can wait. It's a bit uncomfortable being here. This is Selmar's room. He was one of our.... He was one of Azirik's knights. This is home. I learned to fight downstairs and seeing it dismantled is painful. How was the sail?"

"Good enough," Elle answered. "I enjoy ships and sailing—I lived in Marl Mere for a time."

Bren grimaced. "The farther from water I am, the happier I'll be." He glanced over at Elle. "Is Le'yne far? Is it different?"

It was odd that he spoke questions that should have occurred to Alea. She was focused on other things; greater, darker thoughts plagued her mind. They did not allow for trivial concerns. Elle explained the island as she had to Alea, the younger woman only half-listening. Their speech continued to be punctuated by comments echoing greater, pending conversation. Alea thought it was decidedly awkward.

It was during a short period of silence, Bren staring at his boots, Alea at her hands, that the watch called for noon time. Alea's eyes flicked up to Elle.

Bren followed the gaze. "You're leaving?"

Alea nodded. "Can I ask a favor?"

Bren sat forward. "Of course."

She handed him a thin envelope. "Send this to Arman for me, once I've gone." When Bren frowned, she sighed. "We argued."

He laid it on his desk, looked at Elle, then back to his sister. "Very well." He rose. "Will you go alone? Do you want me to ride with you?"

Alea interrupted Elle's impending invitation. "Alone is fine. We'll not take you from your reading." She rose with a brief smile and waited by the door.

Elle touched Bren's face gently. "I know we said talk would come later. Seeing you stand before me, tall and strong and intelligent, fighting for what you love—it makes all the difference. I have made dozens of poor choices. In many ways I wronged you both, but you're flourishing in spite of that." Her smile pulled taut from everything unsaid and she squeezed his hand. "Stay safe."

They stepped from the room, but Bren grabbed Alea's hand as she made to leave. "You may not have been the mother I yearned for, but I'd still like a goodbye."

Alea laughed at that and embraced him. "I suppose when I next see you, it will be war." Her throat was tight. She had wept enough in the past months to not be ashamed, but tears would not come. She glanced down the hall, seeing that Elle stood at the top of the stairs. She waited a pointed moment until their mother descended out of earshot. "I'm scared. What if I can't learn enough? Or in time?"

"You will. Arman will learn his power. I'll build a fort here. We'll all be ready. When the gods come for us, we'll be ready."

"The siege was horrible, Bren. I kept thinking it wouldn't get worse, but it did. I know it still will. I fear I'll lose you both." There was a darker fear that flexed its claws into the edges of her mind, but she would not, could not speak it. "I fear I'll get you killed."

"Alea, you can refuse to give a soldier orders, but when battle comes he still goes to war. You owe that soldier orders and arms and armor to win."

"Arman's not a soldier."

"Horse-shite. He became a soldier the moment he swore his oath."

"I meant he's more than just a soldier." The words sounded petulant.

"Then what of the general and the men of Athrolan? What of Narier?" Alea shot him a scowl and he heaved an exasperated sigh. "Arman might have his head up his arse, but I don't. I know where you spent your nights. It certainly wasn't in the infirmary tents with that orange-haired giant." His tone softened and he took her shoulders. "What of me? We will fight whether you order us or not. The least you could do is accept that and give us what we need for victory."

"This was rather what I argued about with Arman. A bit more heated and personal, but this was certainly a piece." She sighed. She was tired and had no idea what to expect from the next part of her journey. "I hope in Le'yne I learn about myself, not just my power."

Bren hugged her again. "I hope you learn there is no difference between the two."

Φ

The 40th Day of Lleume, 1252
The Island of Mirik

The heavy scent of wet loam drifted between the trunks. It was not yet the wooly green coat that Mirik would boast through summer, but the forest was edged in the glow of spring. Alea followed the narrow path, her strides out distancing her mother's. If it was a conscious gesture, Alea did not indicate. The wood was etched in game and walking trails, the only road well overgrown. Alea was not sure which of those their path was, but it was well worn and deserted. They did not speak other than to remark on wildlife or warn of low-hanging branches.

After two hours of walking, the path curled left, following the base of a steep hill. Elle ignored the turn, pushing on up the slope. The loose leaves from past autumns pattered from under their boots as the two women climbed. The sky above was the clear, bright gray of an overcast day.

Elle paused as they crested the hill. Her head was up, her silver hair whipping back in the wind that swept through the clearing ahead. "There are not many of us left." Her eyes fixed on the center of the glade. A granite slab rested there.

Alea could not tell if Elle's abrupt words were a warning or a plea. Perhaps it was a confession. "Are they all in Le'yne?"

"All I know of. We're the last to join them." Elle entered the clearing, her steps reluctant. "There are just over a score of us now. We were all born from Laen alone. Our power is faint. We have little left."

Alea stopped beside her, looking down at the slab. It was unremarkable save for the lack of leaves dusting its surface. It was dark, reflecting no light, though its surface was smooth. Alea realized her mother's comment had been an excuse. A year ago Alea would have looked around, memorizing the world around her. Now darkness writhed in her mind, pushing her forward, shoving her from the precipice of fate. Her eyes hardened and she stepped onto the stone. "You're wrong. You have me."

CHAPTER TWO

The 47th Day of Lleume, 1252
The City of Ceir Athrolan

ARMAN GLARED AT THE SHEETS of rain sliding down his window. The year's first month lived up to its name's meaning of "Time of Rain." Arman was tired of the weather. He and Alea had ridden for so long that the indoors held no interest anymore. His body itched to be in the open air. *Vielronan farmers planted weeks ago. Wes and I would use the time away from the markets to catch up on work.*

The rain made the wavy glass functionally opaque. He traced designs across it, smiling as the condensation evaporated with a hiss at his fingertip's heat. A knock interrupted his momentary entertainment.

The page in the hall bowed clumsily when the door jerked open. "Master Arrowlash. For you from Mirik." He held out a thick envelope.

Arman thanked him absently as he closed the door and turned the letter over. The handwriting designating the sender was rough, though the writer had clearly strived for neatness: *Brentemir Barrackborn.*

Arman scowled. He dreaded the letter's contents. *He'll tell me she's gone to Le'yne. She's gone to the one place I can't follow.* He broke the seal and unfolded the first piece of parchment.

> *Arman,*
>
> *Alea left tonight. Our mother was with her. It's strange to think the entrance to their world was right here in Mirik. Before she left she asked if I'd send the enclosed to you.*

I hope she returns soon, even if it heralds approaching battle. What of Athrolan? Are you learning about the Rakos or is it all battle-talk? Being in Mirik is strange. We'll be called back in a month's time for a progress report to Her Majesty and I hope to go along.

Bren

Arman read the note quickly, his hand tightening on the envelope as he read the word "enclosed." He and Bren were far from comrades, but they had made strides. In Alea's absence there seemed to be nothing left but to correspond. He made himself write a response detailing the events in Athrolan and any other small talk he could summon. He rang for the page and sent the letter out before turning to Alea's. He almost did not want to read it. *If I don't read her goodbye, perhaps she'll not have actually left.*

He stared at the seal for several moments. It was one of the plain designs of the wax-stamps in the Athrolani guest chambers. She had written it before leaving. The silence in his room was somehow not solitary enough, and so he climbed the southeast tower, where they had last spoken. The rain had slowed to misting.

Arman,

I hope this finds you well. I'm sorry for our argument. I was angry. I've been angry a long time now. I can't even remember why, most of the time. Bringing you back changed me. I suppose it changed you too. Difference is, I did not change for the better.

Seeing you and Bren on the battlefield and on our ride north, I realized how little I knew of the world. My refusal to share with you and the consequences of that are evidence enough of my naiveté. That is changing. I am afraid of what will come. War, certainly, but deeper. I'm afraid what I will become and if I've deceived you all.

It's time I learn to be without your protection. Perhaps when I return I will be able to stand alone. Perhaps I'll be the leader I'm assumed to be. Perhaps I'll be what you need. Perhaps I'll finally be strong.

Luck, Rakos.

Lyne'alea

Arman re-read the letter before tucking it away. He was not certain what to make of it. Her tone was distant, but naked. It was almost an invitation, a prelude to something new. He leaned on the wall, watching the fog writhe around his arms. She was already stronger, wiser. *What will become of her guard when she no longer needs him? What does she think I need from her?* He shook the thoughts away and mentally reached out, feeling the heavy clouds part before his mind. The moisture was a stinging distraction, an icy counterpoint to the burning of his skin.

Φ

The 49th Day of Lleume, 1252
The City of Ceir Athrolan

Eras had felt truly humble twice in her many years. She remembered the inertia that filled her upon reading Alea's words. Eras was reserved, though perhaps not as obviously as Raven, and withheld her opinion until the woman claiming to be the Dhoah' Laen rode into Fort Stone. She was insignificant in the shadow of Alea's might. The Dhoah' Laen had a long road yet to travel, but the sheer potential that filled the girl's veins astounded Eras.

The general leaned back in her chair, watching the firelight lance through the goblet in her hand. Despite her multifold duties, life had been dull in the spring of last year. Sure, Athrolan had warred with the Berrin and Azirik slid farther down the slope of madness. Those were constant things. *Everything changed when Her Majesty received that letter.* Her eyes rested on her own stack of unopened envelopes.

She leaned forward to finger the rough edge of a plain, dirty envelope. Letters from An'thoriend always looked as if they had traveled the world with him.

> *Eras,*
>
> *I would have liked to help during the siege, but I am glad I did not see the end. She is terrifying. Magnificent, surely, but terrifying. I've heard rumors enough about what happened to her guard, about what she did, but nothing from you. It is not like you to avoid such news.*
>
> *Unless it horrifies you.*
>
> *I am moving north, despite my brother still ruling the Northlands. Perhaps I won't be able to avoid him any longer. I intend to visit Azirik one last time, determine where his camp lies, and perhaps see his son before I cross into the tundra. You say he does not want to rule?*
>
> *Have you spoken to Tzatia for me, yet?*
>
> *Love and luck,* fetali,
>
> *An'thor*

Eras traced the Ageless endearment for "sister" with one scarred finger. An'thor had been the only other creature to make her feel as small as Alea had. He took everything with humor, if not with grace. Eras had never had a friend so close. He was right about her reasons for ignoring what Alea had done. She had expected the Dhoah' Laen to be powerful. She had expected her to crumble mountains and flood seas.

She had not expected her to defy the world's greatest laws.

She was glad Alea had left the city. Perhaps when she returned, the horror left in the wake of her actions would be lessened. Now Eras could focus on the Rakos pacing through the palace. *He needs a mentor. He needs what An'thor was to me.* She turned to the small shelf of tomes and journals behind her desk. Many were old, though most were younger than she. Her rough hand brushed the spine of a thin, tattered book.

Her eyes flicked to the letter in her hand. Alea barely had control and she had turned the world on its head. The Rakos were known for their violence. What would Arman do if given the power? Before she changed her mind, she penned a reply, her quill scratching across the paper in swift, fluid script.

The letter was pointed and sent out before the last bell of the night. If anyone knew what to expect from a Rakos brimming with power, it would be An'thor. This war would force them to call on alliances long since turned to enemies. Apprehension grew in her chest. She knew where they would ask her to ride. She was comfortable being Athrolan's rather exotic general. Going home would mean facing a past she would rather ignore.

A frown creased Eras's brow. Arman's unflagging devotion woke a wistfulness that she had long since forgotten. *Raven and I would never have such legend-worthy romance.* They were both too practical for frivolity and too dedicated to the crown for marriage, children or even regular trysts. Her mouth twitched. *But company never hurt.* She made her way across the castle quietly. Raven answered after one knock.

"What is it?" His face was tired, but the lamps said he had not gone to bed. "Another attack?"

"No, nothing so serious. I'm just thinking too much."

He took in her relaxed clothes and the steadiness in her eyes. "Then we'll talk until your mind is eased." He stepped aside to let her in, and closed the door softly behind.

Φ

The 1st Day of Fluerme, 1252
The Isle of Le'yne

Dizziness swept through Alea's body, churning in her throat. The shapeless blur surrounding her cleared, the world solidifying abruptly. Her stomach heaved. She stumbled off the slate slab, blinking in the suddenly bright light. Steep, dark mountains formed the horizon behind her. Cliffs dropped away below her, topped with a cluster of buildings. Blue-green grasses blanketed the fields rolling from the village to the mountains' foothills. She shuddered, shaking tendrils of black and gray fogs from her shoulders. She stepped from the slab, stumbling when her boots met soft earth.

She had expected a mighty city. "This is Le'yne?" Her voice rasped, as if from disuse. Alea was perversely happy to see that Elle looked as ill as Alea felt.

Her mother nodded. "Like us, it has diminished." She pressed a thin hand to her brow. "Shall we get you settled?"

Alea frowned as they descended the hill. "Do they know we're coming? Do they know what I am?" If Elle had not spoken to her own daughter, could she have reached across worlds to communicate with her sisters?

Elle's prolonged silence was far from comforting. "Lyne'alea, your existence is a complicated thing. We thought we knew who was the Dhoah' Laen. When I bore you, I realized we had been wrong. I also realized that living as Laen, fleeing Azirik, would only get us killed. I had almost lost faith in what you were. I never got the chance to tell them about you."

Alea sighed. *Another battle. Another struggle against people who need me, disbelieve me, and don't understand.* Her fatigue and dark mindedness was turning her usual worries into angst. "What did you tell them?"

"I told them I found another of our kind, hidden like I was."

"Are they so far removed from the world that they don't see what happens?" Alea frowned, navigating the steep hill with stumbling steps. She pictured Le'yne like a floating island, omniscient over all the world, watching, directing.

"We feel the world's energy, feel the rising and falling in the balance. Mostly falling now. That is interpreted. When there were more of us we would communicate with our sisters between the worlds. There is not enough power for that now." She stopped at a low wall.

It and the houses were made of stucco, but of a kind that Alea had never seen. It was rough and dark, dotted with glittering black mica. It matched the sand below the cliffs. *Perhaps now is not the time to mention that.* The houses were all of a single level, the roofs tiled in gray slate. Nothing was grand or austere, save for the open hall perched on the highest point of the cliff top. Silent lightning flitted across the dark clouds bruising the sky.

"So will I meet the others now, or will you explain the situation first?" Alea fiddled with her skirts. The houses were lit, and the small sounds of people preparing for supper drifted through the village. Somehow even that managed to sound unwelcoming.

"I'll explain. I'm sure you want to rest and gather your thoughts beforehand anyways." Elle led her through a narrow opening in the wall and onto a gravel path.

The stones crunching under their boots grated on Alea's raw nerves. It felt like being introduced to the Athrolani court again. *Except this time they can't be fooled.* Her lips tightened as Elle paused at a dark cottage nestled against the rise of the hill. Her mother fumbled with the latch then swung the door open. The smell of dampness hung in the still air. Alea followed Elle up the stairs and into the small kitchen. It was cold, and dust lay thick across the countertop.

"Is this where you lived?"

"A long time ago when I was very young." Elle looked about, breathing softly, as if disturbing the dust would break some tentative composure. She shook herself and briskly pulled a flint from a drawer and lit the lamp on the table. She dug a cloth from a stack on a shelf and began to dust. "There are two rooms down the hall. The second one is yours. Make yourself at home."

Alea retrieved the flint from the kitchen and lit the lamp that hung from the hall's ceiling. The light was dim and only served to make the white walls look bleaker. She pushed open the door at the end of the hall, half expecting a barren room with a cot.

Though the kitchen had been left to the mercy of dust, thin sheets covered the furniture here. Another lamp hung from the ceiling and she had to clamber on top of a chair to light it. She dropped her pack by the door and began to pull the sheets away. Her brows rose. The bed was large, the heavy frame carved from the same dark wood as the door. Blocks of slate decorated each of the four posts.

She revealed a desk next, and a large chest at the end of the bed. The pieces were all blocky and simple, lacking elegance or any beauty without function. The sound of cleaning in the kitchen was replaced with low voices. Alea winced. She was not ready to face that challenge. Instead, she unpacked her things, tucking her few clothes into the chest beside a stack of folded blankets. She turned down the bed, but her nerves sang too loudly for sleep.

She leaned her brow against the cool wood of the bedpost and stared out the window. It had neither muntins nor glass, the air eddying through the hole in the wall. *Even the breeze smells strange.* It was balmy, just cold enough to warrant long sleeves. The undulating voices in the other room grew louder. She had spent nights wishing she was not the Dhoah' Laen. Now her anger at potentially being denied surprised her. *What if they refuse to train me?*

She undid her tangled braid and raked her fingers through her hair. She was tired of the debate—she was all powerful, she was coddled, she was terrifying, but an abomination. *And now I'm shut in my room, again waiting for others to decide my fate.* She sighed angrily and threw the leather tie across the room. Sloughing off her cloak and shawl, she strode down the hall and into the kitchen.

Though the village was not what Alea expected, the Laen themselves were. There were only six crowded into the kitchen. Their sharp words stuttered out when she entered. She had stored a smile for this first encounter, but at the stern frowns, she realized it should wait for another day. "There is some dispute?"

"We appreciate your hope and duty to us, miss, but you must realize you cannot be the Dhoah' Laen. Elle is sorely mistaken. It is understandable, given the hopeless times and war. We all grasp at straws sometimes."

Alea frowned, letting the expression line her brow more deeply than usual. She would use everything she had. "Why haven't you told them?" Her eyes scanned the faces of the women before her, but her words pierced straight to Elle. "They wouldn't argue if you had, so don't lie to me. I'm tired of lies." Her tone was quiet, but not calm. Under its surface trembled cold, bitter anger. She had lost so much, given so much for this—her family, her home, her peace. *My humanity.* They would not make it in vain.

"Tell us what, Elle?" It was not the eldest woman who spoke, but she was the tallest. "There is something we've missed?"

"I thought you read the energy. Surely you felt something." Alea's gaze flicked to the woman who appeared to be their leader.

"She refers to the battle at the Athrolani fort." Elle looked over at a woman seated at the table. "Mera, you mentioned a small surge of power. I believe to that is what she refers. She did a noble thing and destroyed a small piece of our enemies."

Mera frowned. "I did see such a thing, but it was shadowed by something else. Something stranger. I fear the gods are attacking us here. I can't say how they would, but our dead were wounded."

The words sunk into Alea's mind, churning, dredging darkness from the corners like footsteps in the silt of a stream. "Actually, that is to what I refer." Anger made her mimic sound mocking, but she did not care. "Your dead, you say. You mean their souls? The great silver shell that holds the souls of all the beings that have ever died?"

The tall woman turned, her silver eyes narrowing to blade-thin slits. "How can you know that?"

"Because I am the one that tore them open. I am the one that made them bleed. You think I have tainted, pathetic, unnatural power. I tell you, you are wrong! I can kill with Destruction and so, too, can I give life with Creation. You say you've not seen the like of my power—it's because you've not seen the Dhoah' Laen. Elle knew from the start what I would become, so she hid me, far better than you ever hid or protected the poor women you thought would save you."

The tall woman stared at her, lips thinned to a hard line. Her silver hair was so thin and light it was almost transparent, and drifted in the wind skirting the edges of the room. "You are a foolish child." She spat the words, but the brightness in her eyes betrayed her fear.

Alea felt darkness roil through her, but she could not be certain if it was her mind's shadow or the blackness of power. It was a heady feeling, cold and electric. She fixed the Laen with a pointed stare. "Then don't you think you ought to teach me?"

CHAPTER THREE

The 3rd Day of Fluerme, 1252
The Isle of Le'yne

DAWN LOOKED MUCH LIKE dusk, which looked much like a dark, overcast day. Alea rose early. She told herself her body was still used to the early mornings on the road and during the siege, but the humming in her limbs told her otherwise. *It's this place. The air, the earth here, it's different.* She was supposed to be learning, filling her days with study and exciting new tasks. She felt useless already. The dress she pulled on felt odd after months wearing breeches underneath and she laughed at how much her life had changed.

Elle sat at the table in the kitchen, staring out the window.

Alea felt as if she had interrupted a private moment and paused, one hand on the door frame.

Elle blinked, as if dragging herself back from a distant, unseen shore. "How did you sleep?"

Alea lifted one shoulder in a shrug she had learned from Bren. "Well enough. It was quiet, and I am used to business surrounding tents or the sounds of the forest." She edged over to the cast iron stove and felt the side of the kettle resting on its surface. It was hot, and she glanced sidelong at her mother. The woman had been up for far longer than a single cup of tea, it seemed. She poured herself a mug, leaning against the counter as she drank. It tasted of earth and stone, but cleared her head. "I would like to meet the others this morning."

"I think you made enough of an impression for a few days, don't you?"

"I meant those that weren't there last night. Your people aren't so few as to number just a dozen."

"They're your people too, you know."

Alea's gaze flicked to Elle. "Then perhaps they should make an effort to treat me as such. I'm beginning to wonder if you're the only one who wants me here."

"You're not making it easy to like you." Elle leaned back. "I wanted to spend the day showing you about the village, making introductions as we go."

"And my teaching?"

"Are you in such a hurry to return?"

"I'm eager to end this war." It was poorly spoken diplomacy. She finished her tea in one deep sip, forcing the liquid down with a wince before turning to rinse her mug in the wash basin. She had schooled her features into neutrality by the time she turned to leave. Alea shielded her eyes against the sky as they stepped into the yard. Lightning glinted still, ceaseless and silent above the clouds that bruised the sky. The house's kitchen garden had overgrown its bounds and the smell of herbs underfoot was welcoming.

Elle held open the gate for Alea. Under the strange, uniform brightness of an overcast day, Alea was afforded a clear view of the village around her. The hill behind them was crisscrossed with decorative gardens and stone sculptures, each section walled in stone. The houses radiated from the hill like a threadbare petticoat. Elle's steps were too calculated to be casual, and Alea's nerves hummed louder. *This is another battle, another hurdle for me to test my power against.* She thought of the other hurdles she had faced and the destruction that seemed to result. *Are they ready for me?*

"There is Ielya, one of our herbalists." Elle nodded to the woman crouched in an elaborate tangled garden. "Much of our time is spent trying to preserve whatever is left of our people—our knowledge and our crafts."

They wove towards the hall and despite the promise of introductions, Alea found the conversation closer to a lecture that included no one but themselves. The walk through the walled areas along the hillside proved more interesting. Most of the sculptures were either abstract feats of balance, the deeper meaning of which was lost on Alea, or memorials. Single Laen sat in meditation or quiet thought before some of the figures.

Alea paused to watch one of the women, brow furrowed. "You said you don't have the power to create another Laen. How is that? Can't you just pull up more?"

Elle fixed Alea with a wary gaze. "What we have in our bodies is finite. It is all each may ever have. When we die, the power passes into another place. If we are killed in certain fashions, then that power is gone forever. Either way, the others cannot access it."

Alea only hummed in response. Her own power was bounded only by the limits of her mind and body. Something told her it was unwise to explain that now. Though the grass had been maintained, the space just under the hall was disused. A line of stones stretched along one wall. They were all roughly the shape of a duck's egg, but varied in size from twice Alea's height on the right to smaller than her spread hand on the left. Alea frowned at the smallest stone nestled in the grass. It was no larger than her smallest finger. "This is a training court."

"From many years ago, yes. New Laen learned to control their power here." She looked at Alea pointedly. "And so will you."

"I understand learning control, but we should focus on a larger scale. My power moves oceans, not puddles and playing with pebbles will not help me win the war."

"Your training is non-existent and I cannot build without a good foundation, which is something you seriously lack. Worse, I must knock down the shoddy one you've haphazardly built without guidance." Elle moved towards the gate to the rest of the village. "There is more for you to see."

The discussion was clearly over, but Alea's mind whirled. She disliked the layered metaphors and the assumption that they knew her power better than she. *They've admitted to never seeing the like. How can they know what will work?*

The other side of the village was much the same. Alea wanted to scream at the monotony. She shook the thought away and tried to quicken her pace. There was only one building large enough for Alea to consider it sprawling. The single door was wide enough to be two, and stood propped open with a smooth stone. Alea realized she had stopped listening to Elle and, instead, stood on the steps. The depths of the room were dim, but the air was fresh. Shelves of books and scrolls lined the walls and stacks of wax tablets stood in one corner.

An older woman paused in wiping down the spines with a dry rag. She pushed her mass of silver hair away from her brow when Alea entered.

"I wondered when you would come. Where would you like to start?" She was not one of the women who had visited the night before.

"The beginning would be best." Elle stepped in beside Alea, her thin lips pursed. "It's a shame she was not raised with knowledge of us."

"If she had been she'd be dead. Now go on." She made a shooing motion with a blocky hand. "I'm sure your house needs attention after all this time."

Elle wavered in the doorway, eyes flicking between Alea and the older woman. When she left, it was wordlessly.

"I'm honored to meet you, my lady." The woman offered Alea a gnarled hand and a bright smile. "I'm Mera. I tend the books here."

Alea glanced around at the books rather than meet the woman's clear gaze. "You're a librarian?"

"Historian, actually."

"This is the history of the Laen?" Alea brushed a finger down the spine of a thin book. "There's so little."

Mera's bright eyes inched over Alea. "Much was lost. This is what was saved and what I've been able to remember. Soon I'll write about you."

"I'm to read all this? Before the battle?" Years of reading surrounded her.

"We have had our entire lives to study and the deepest truths are ingrained in our blood. But you? You're half Laen, truly, yet more powerful than any of us." She drew a breath. "I can't say what you need to know." She pointed to the stack of tablets and returned to her dusting. "Begin there."

Φ

The 15th Day of Fluerme, 1252
The City of Ceir Athrolan

Melt water thundered through the aqueducts, echoing across the city. Spring had set in with a will. It was not the water, nor the wind that woke Arman, but the clanging bells above the barracks. He shoved aside his blankets and peered out the window. The torches on the towers glowed warmly, but were not the massive blazes heralding an attack. He shoved his boots on and made for the door.

He crossed the main entrance hall of the palace and caught a glimpse of lightning through the thick glass of the aviary. The drum of rain grew louder as he crossed from the palace to the stables. Inside the barracks beyond, the buzz of purposeful conversation warred with the sounds of the storm. The men rushed about, many of whom Arman recognized from the outguard. He grabbed the arm of a passing captain. "What is it?"

"Aqueduct burst. We're to help the masons before the warehouses flood." He waved Arman away. "Back to bed with you."

"I can help." The man was gone and other soldiers jostled past, more than a few shooting foul glances towards him. Arman stared after them, incredulous. These were the men he fought alongside just a month before. They had eaten and bled beside one another.

"Rakos, you'll not make enough of a difference to warrant being up." Indred clapped Arman on the back. "Thank you, but we'll do just fine." He turned back to the men, barking orders and ushering them out towards the streets. "Up and out lads! The water will not wait for your boots to be laced!"

Arman watched the men leave. He had attempted to spar with the soldiers a few times since the siege, but to no avail. As soon as he approached, the men disappeared, spitting retorts or ignoring him completely. He sighed angrily. He wanted to say it was the Rakos blood, that it was his proximity to Alea. He knew it was neither. *They look at me and see a man who should be dead. Who was dead.* Looking in the mirror unnerved him too, but he could not walk away from his own skin. *Time was, I might have shunned a man brought back from death.*

He peered down at the warehouse district, half swallowed by mist. He was angry at the men, surely, but more angry at himself. When had he started letting others get the best of his spirit?

Φ

Indred's men milled about the mess of the warehouse district. They hesitated at the water churning between the buildings and the massive arches of the aqueduct. Frost wore at the stone each year, and the cracks finally burst at the pressure of snowmelt behind them. The masons had already arrived, their laden carts parked a tier above.

"Thank fates our kings carved the city in steps, eh?" The officer clambered onto one of the great struts. The broken stone was cleared away to allow metal troughs to reroute the flow. The work was tedious and the icy water sent several soldiers into racking coughs. It was past midnight before masons' mud could be laid. A file of soldiers formed to pass stone along to the jagged gap. One of the men fumbled the slab in his hands as he brushed the eerily hot palm of the next man in line.

Arman glared back at him, his curls dark and plastered to his brow. "No one needs to like me for me to help." He spat the words before tugging the stone from the soldier's grip and passing it alone. He worked tirelessly, ignoring the looks. The stones were held in place by great buckled leather straps until the cement set. The gap was nearly closed when the entire structure shuddered. A deep groan became a scream as stone and metal bowed. Arman watched the straps stretch a second before they snapped. *They'll never make it in time.* He dragged himself hand-over-hand up the iron ladder in the stone support, wincing as shards of stone rained onto his head. He locked his legs around the upper rungs of the ladder and pushed. Heat rushed through him. The stone groaned again, a strap whipping past and biting a deep line over his cheek. The stone held for a breath, then another. His arms screamed at the effort and he closed his eyes, letting the heat fill him. His legs hardened, his arms stiffened and he pressed his full weight against the incredible pull of water.

"I cannot hold this forever!" He pitched his voice over the roar of the water.

Shock only lasted a moment before the soldiers exploded back into action. Another layer of stones was added, more metal bands hammered into place. Arman was dimly aware of the sky growing lighter. Half an hour from dawn, they gingerly released the troughs and knocked away what was left of the broken dam. Arman's body was stiff and he had long grown numb to the icy water still spraying lightly from the cracks. His mind had sunk so deep that it took a moment to realize someone was shaking his shoulder

"Arrowlash!"

His own breath chuffed hotly against his bare shoulder as he peered down at the man. Pain began to creep through his concentration.

"You can let go."

Arman turned slowly back to the stone before him, tugging his hands free. They refused to move for a moment, then wrenched away. He slid down several rungs of the ladder before he remembered how his legs were supposed to move.

At the bottom there were tired grins and a cloak. His back was clapped and hands were offered in greeting and introduction. He found it all very distant and strange.

"Leave him be until he gets food and ale! Man needs to warm up!" The man who had helped him down waved a hand to disperse the men. He glanced at Arman and offered his own hand, despite his words. "I'm Witt, lieutenant under Indred."

Arman flexed his hand into feeling before taking the man's arm. The vague sensation of skin brought his mind crashing back into his body. "Arman." He followed the mass of men moving towards the barracks. Their steps grew lighter at the smell of food wafting from the mess hall. Arman turned towards the door to the palace, but Witt's voice broke through his damp thoughts.

"Rakos!" Witt's shout arched from the door to the baths. "We're headed into the city for drinks after we get dry—care to join?"

Arman blinked. *Melt water must wash all transgressions clean.* "It's morning."

The man shrugged. "We were up all night. We can sleep in the afternoon."

For a moment Witt was another friend, another dark-haired, drinking man. Arman found a grin creeping onto his face and he threw his hands up in mock surrender. "Very well, I'll change and meet you back here." He waited until out of sight of the men before breaking into a run. He may have been an inhuman creature, but he sorely missed having friends. It took him only a moment to change. The numbness that stiffened his skin was replaced by burning, and he absently checked his hands and feet for frostbite before tugging on a cloak and boots.

The inn was a tall, broad building that took up an entire block of houses between two small streets. It was in the residential area two tiers above where the aqueduct burst. Arman followed the soldiers to one of the four common areas and sat down on a stool with a grateful sigh. The group numbered close to a dozen, and more trickled in as the morning wore on.

"Drink up, you earned it right enough." A large man pushed a mug of ale to Arman. "I'm Sousa."

Arman grinned and took a long sip of the drink, watching a few others gather around.

"I never thought that stone would set proper! Every winter this happens!" A dark-haired man made a rude noise two seats down.

The Rakos leaned forward. "Every winter?"

"Not so badly," the man amended, "but often enough." He offered his hand across Sousa. "Kal Smytheson."

Arman took it. "Arman Arrowlash."

Kal laughed at that. "I know." He gestured to the mug in front of Arman. "Be careful with Ma Hexion's fire ale. It'll get you tossed before you taste the second sip!"

Arman grinned. "It burns like the tar-whiskey we brewed in winter back home, though it tastes far better."

Kal made a face and Sousa frowned. "Tar-whiskey?"

"Made from whatever was too rotted to be saved from harvest." The men groaned and Arman grinned.

"Did it at least get you laughing before it killed you?"

Arman took another deep draw. The alcohol must have burnt, he supposed, but it felt only distantly warm. "My friend, Kam-Rit—a true bantam when it comes to women—wanted to bed up with this butcher's daughter two lanes down. We were all out one evening, drinking tar-whiskey, and we told him that we'd brought a love-luck potion from the market. We convinced him that in order for it to work, he had to dance under her window pretending to be a tom-turkey, chortling like the birds do. Poor fool was so tossed he did it. Never heard from the lass, you can believe, but surely got the attention of her father!"

Sousa laughed. "Where's home, Arman?"

"Vielrona's Lows. My Ma owns an inn there."

The Athrolani frowned. "I thought you came with the Dhoah' Laen?"

"We met there this autumn." Arman finished off his drink and gestured for another. "I've guarded her since." He glanced at Kal. "What about you two? Do you hail from Ceir Athrolan or one of her other cities?"

Sousa thumped his chest. "Born and bred in this very district!"

Kal waved the other man's pride away. "I'm from Marl Orna, just over the hills to the south. It's a small town, but nice. I've settled here, though. My wife's family owns an old inn in the slums. Her grandfather built it and I hope to tend it to pass on to our children."

Heat flashed through Arman's mind at the thought. He wondered if he would ever have that kind of peace. "You have many?"

"Only the one, a girl of two, but we expect our second within three months."

Arman raised his mug in congratulations. "May they be strong and wise."

Sousa shook his head. "I cannot imagine a one-woman life, myself." He proved the words by looking over their barmaid as she delivered more ale.

A man across the table interrupted. "That's simple because no woman can stand you long enough, Sousa." He turned to Arman, his grin broadening. "What of you, Rakos, do you take women besides the Dhoah' Laen?"

Burning filled Arman's skin. "Excuse me?"

"Is she more powerful in bed than in battle?"

Arman's nerves bristled and he turned his gaze fully on the man, raising his lip enough that his fangs were obvious. He wondered at the shadow crossing the man's features. "Walk away. Now."

The man fell silent, wary, but still contemptuous. He grabbed his drink angrily, swearing as it sloshed.

Arman looked down at his mug. The sounds of the common room were distant, and his ears buzzed. A hand on his shoulder jolted him back into the room.

"Hasian makes almost anyone angry," Kal promised. "He only joined up for the coin and when battle arose it proved him a coward. He hates us for it, and your lady who sparked the war." He sat back. "So the tales of you and she are true, then?"

Arman frowned. "What tales?"

"That you love her, not just guard her. Love only her."

Arman looked at the swirling brown of his ale. "I'm her guard." He pulled a grin onto his face as he changed the subject. "So tell me of the wonders of Ceir Athrolan."

Φ

The 17th Day of Fluerme, 1252
The City of Mirik

The overcast skies gave way to the pale, cloudless blue of proper spring weather. Winter's chill was all but gone and in the sunshine it was almost hot. Bren leaned back against the Great Wall surrounding the city, legs dangling off the scaffolding as he unlaced his shirt. "We're close to halfway, Lanav."

The soldier laying stone above him patted the sun-warmed rock. "Aye, we should have the entire west wall finished by the time we report to the queen."

The view had improved with the weather. The still, green harbor water lapped over the crumbled breakwater jutting from the tongue of land at the city's southwest corner. The land rose from there in tall, natural bluffs along which ran the wall they now repaired. The dark, blue-gray of the open ocean far below sparkled at the wave's crests. This was not the Mirik Bren remembered.

Lanav followed Bren's gaze. "Looks near warm enough for a swim, eh?"

"I'd give you two gold pieces if you didn't come out singing like a eunuch. The water may look like spring, but it'll not feel like it until well into Aeme."

Lanav climbed down the ladder to stand beside Bren. He peered up at the sun. Their timing was informal as none of the city's bells were re-hung. "What say we take our midday now, Barrackborn? Bring back that frayed rope."

Bren heaved himself up. "I'll be glad when this work is done." He was a man of movement. Construction was not his interest or his talent. Several other teams from stations along the wall joined their path back to the barracks. Seeing the single ship bobbing in the harbor, Bren wondered absently if any books he had requested from Athrolan's library would be among the supplies. Mirik's library had suffered under Azirik's rule. Most of the valuable texts were sold to fund the war. *There is something wise to be noted about giving up knowledge in trade for violence.*

A squire appeared at Bren's elbow when they entered the courtyard.

"Lieutenant, Mariner Helonin wants to see you, sir."

Bren excused himself and crossed to the officer's quarters. The planning room door was ajar, and he knocked at the jamb.

"Come in, Barrackborn." The mariner and several of his officers sat around the small table. A map of the city stretched before them.

Bren took the seat Helonin indicated. "You asked for me?"

"We breached the palace a week ago, as you know. We're opening the treasury tomorrow. Her Majesty the Queen noted you might wish to be there."

"I've no more claim to be present than another." Bren shrugged, but his body hummed. *This is my country!* "Did she mention why?"

"If you take the throne, the treasury, and all that it contains, is technically yours." Helonin fixed him with an intent stare. "Have you thought on that at all?"

Bren ran a hand through his hair. He felt chastised, as if he'd forgotten to practice his stance before training. "Not enough to make a decision." He had made a decision, but it was not one he was prepared to announce to a room of men who expected him to choose differently.

"If you still wish to come with us tomorrow, we leave at dawn." Helonin turned back to the map and began discussing the entrance to the warren of underground tunnels that held the treasury. Bren excused himself and went to find food. It was the same meal he had loved the day before, but now it was soot on his tongue.

"I heard from Dettan they're opening the treasury tomorrow." Lanav thumped down beside Bren. "That why Helonin wanted to see you?"

"He said I could go. Thought I'd want to see what could be mine, I guess."

"They're hoping you'll take her off their hands. Mirik's expensive to maintain. I don't blame you a bit for not wanting it—give up a life like ours for pomp and papers?" He made an exaggerated pantomime of spitting.

Bren laughed and cleaned his bowl with a slice of bread. "Come on, that wall will not build itself."

Φ

The 18th Day of Fluerme, 1252

Bren was certain the Kit flanked them, an unseen shadow among the broken buildings of his childhood. He wondered if they were as hopeful as Helonin. *Do they think I'll have a change of heart when I see the inheritance?* His heart was heavy. His tattered tunic and dented armor said enough about how drained the coffers had been. He had barely looked at the palace since arriving, though he did not admit to avoiding the place.

Now, with boots thumping the faded tiles, he did not recognize it. The halls were dusty and most of the valuables were long since stripped. The main hall was broad and bore a curved double staircase. His eyes lingered there, knowing that in the warren of corridors beyond his father had grown up. Somewhere, up there, something had made Azirik a madman. He tore his gaze away and instead examined the stones under his feet. He ignored the eyes of the other men as they gauged his reactions.

The palace sat on a twisting network of tunnels dug into the cliff-rock. The higher caverns held servants' quarters and the kitchen storerooms. The lower ones stored anything from old arms and armor to forgotten documents. Those to the east were used as crypts. A large, well-lit tunnel led down beneath the throne room to a metal door. It had once been closed with several padlocks and bolts, all but one having been cut through by Athrolan's smiths.

The last took only a few minutes to break through. The doors were pushed open and a collective breath was drawn. In all, Bren thought it rather anticlimactic. He grabbed a torch with the others and stepped through the doorway. Before him, glimmering in the light of the patrol's lanterns and torches, was what could have been his. It was more gold, silver and jewels than he had ever seen in his life. Each alcove of the circular, pillared room held decorative armor, crowns, jewelry and actual coin. Chests, upended, open or locked, were stacked around the pillars and a large cabinet in the back held thick, ornate tomes. Bren drew a shuddering breath. It may have been a greater worth than any lieutenant had a right to see, but it was a poor fortune for a kingdom. He slid his torch into a bracket on the wall and lowered himself onto an intricately carved chair.

Helonin handed each man a tablet. "Pair up and take an alcove. Write all you find and if you can estimate a worth, do so. Captain Quarier and I are watching, so pocketing anything will be unwise." There was scattered laughter as the men began to work. After a moment Helonin went to Bren. "Are you going to help?"

Bren nodded, not looking up.

"Regretting your decision, lieutenant?"

Bren shot the man a glare, though he knew there was no cruelty in the mariner's words. "You and I both know this is a sorry sum to run a land." He took the tablet from the man. "I'm just ashamed to see how far Azirik drained his kingdom trying to kill his daughter."

Φ

The 20th Day of Fluerme, 1252
The Isle of Le'yne

Alea drew the anoher bundle of tablets from the shelf, laying them out on one of the small tables. Her days were spent reading, punctuated by awkward silences over tea and meals. Though history was one of her least favorites, reading was her only respite from guarded stares and blatent gossip. These tablets began a few weeks before the gods overthrew the Laen and were written by one of the gods themselves. He was a god of the ocean, and called himself Berm. *The same Burme that the Berrin worship?* She filed that away for later consideration. The first few tablets described the god's family, the palace and his love for the sea. Alea skimmed the words, though they were beautiful. Before the war she would have enjoyed the man's descriptions. Now she had darker interests. Now she had a war to fight.

She paused when the tone of the writing changed abruptly.

> *This morning the sea was in turmoil and the waves gray. I went to private counsel with King Numon. I expected him to ease my unrest about his speech yesterday. He did the opposite. He told me many of the godlords were tired of paying homage to the Laen. They were tired of them allowing us an understanding of only facets of the world.*
>
> *He told me he intended to overthrow them. I left, unsure if it was possible. Numon called a counsel this afternoon. There, in the center of our hall was Milady Queen Lynelle. She had arrived out of good will, to settle a dispute. Those who follow Numon forced her to think this was the way of balance, the overthrowing of the Laen. And then they attacked.*
>
> *I cannot – I will not – recount the horror or the betrayal that followed. She split the world in three and Numon's guards drove those of us who protested from the palace. The Rakos attacked, but they were too late. The*

palace burnt as we fled before the walls between the worlds solidified. My son was with me, but his mother and my daughter fell.

Now it is evening. We stand on the shores of the Rakos's land. The Isle of the Gods is gone from the horizon, and Le'yne, too. I do not know what we will do, for our brothers and sisters are either dead or traitors. This morning the sea was in turmoil and the waves gray. I should have listened.

Gooseflesh marched along Alea's arms. She glanced up from the tablet. "Mera?"

The older woman looked over, brows raised. "Yes?"

"The gods, the ones who upheld the Laen laws, the ones loyal to the Laen, what happened to them?"

"I cannot say. They disappeared into the piece set aside for the Rakos, hidden among humans. Eventually I imagine their blood faded, as did the Rakos themselves."

Alea ran a hand down the engraved wax, thinking of Arman. *But the Rakos did not die out. Not completely.* She glanced out the window at the ocean, brows furrowed. Below, the waves were gray.

CHAPTER FOUR

The 21st Day of Fluerme, 1252
The City of Ceir Athrolan

THE EMPTY TABLE BEFORE the library's bank of windows served as a pointed rebuke, as opposed to inspiration. Arman glared at it before nosing about the shelves. There were plenty of books that mentioned the Rakos, if he cared to read children's tales. He opened older histories at random, flipping through the pages as gently as his impatience allowed. "'Greatest bond known to man,' 'Powers of heat and fire,'" he quipped, scanning for anything useful.

His broad fingers paused on a history of Vielrona. Though it was dry and held little new information, the card tucked in the back detailed other comparable books. Most tomes had similar cards, and it spoke to the organization of the Athrolani historians and scribes. He backed up a pace, peering down the shelf for the war log the card suggested. It was a slim tome, and battered enough to have been the original, though the penmanship suggested it was a copy. He navigated his way back to the table and opened the cover. He was greeted by an ink rendition of the portrait from his own book of tales.

The man must have only sat for the one. Arman grinned and began to read.

> *The Rakos garrisons scattered across the continent guard the largest Laen cities. It has been suggested that they are forts, like our own, but from what I have seen, that is not strictly correct. Garrison is simply the only word I have. Anyone who wishes to enter the Laen city must pass the gates, and if the sight alone does not scare one off, then the inhabitants of the gatehouse well might.*

It's been said that the Rakos keep monsters, or make them the way the Laen made the gods. If that is true, then I question the Rakos's sanity. These creatures are not made of flesh and soul. They are earth and fire and burning anger.

Arman ran his fingers over the sketch on the opposite page. It was a monster, by human standards. The flesh looked like stone. Some sort of fluid oozed free where the skin cracked at the joints. Great plates curled up at the edges. Any echo of a human shape was overshadowed by the horns branching from the head and shoulders. Lumps on the back could have been wings or armor. It hunched, as if uncomfortable standing on only two legs.

Arman imagined it was a fearsome sight in person, but all he felt was pity. Still, a grin grew on his face. He reached over and tugged the bell pull. *My power may be an enigma and fairly useless thus far, but intimidating armor can never go wrong.*

Arman turned to the serving man who appeared at the bell's ring. "Could you bring me the sketching materials from my room, and deliver this to General Aneral?" He scribbled a few lines on a scrap of parchment and handed it over. When the man had gone, Arman turned back to the book, flipping through to the sections that described actual battle. His ability to transform his arms into smoke was fascinating, but he had yet to read that any Rakos had such an ability. Full-blooded Rakos controlled fire, from what he read, and the explosion of the campfire on the road hinted he might as well.

He spent the rest of the morning designing armor that echoed the monster. He was not a man who leaned towards armor, nor had he ever designed any. *General, please don't tear all of this apart.* In the back of his thoughts was another, the idea that the Rakos had created these monsters. What if he could do the same?

He was almost through the third sketch when he heard the general clear her throat from a few chairs away.

"That serving man told me a dead man wanted to see me. Took a moment to realize what he meant. You look well, for a dead man."

Arman grinned. "Death becomes me, what can I say?"

"Quite. What did you need?"

He handed her the papers, watching for any reaction as she perused them.

After a moment she sat, looking closer. "This is armor."

"Yes. I found a drawing of one of the creatures the Rakos created—Earth Shakers they were called it seems. Though I'm still uncertain what my actual purpose is, I thought looking like a gods' nightmare would be a good start."

"Have you been finding any information on your actual powers? Armor is a good start, and this is a fine design, but it's only armor. Armor protects you, and you are a weapon."

Arman sighed. "There are few mentions of the Rakos in this library—foolish humans too afraid to even mention us in books." Contempt burnt in his words, though it was unconscious.

Eras glanced up from the design, her hazel eyes narrowing on him. "Watch that pride. It can lead to bigotry." The warning was softened by her smile, but only just.

He rose and went to the window, looking out on the overcast day as she continued to examine his drawings. "My temper is getting worse. I have slight abilities, but they are more parlor tricks than anything else. That was the first light in days." He shrugged. "I don't rightly feel Rakos most of the time. I feel things I know are because of the power, but nothing that feels different from myself. Just new."

"I imagine you were always a Rakos in some fashion."

Arman snorted. "For someone who wields fire and earth I did a terrible job in the forge."

"You were a smith?"

"Not really. My father was, as was my grandfather. My friend, Wes, took over the clients when my father died. I did the jewel work and the designs."

"Breaking the earth's natural form would have been hard for someone whose soul was made of earth and metal. I'd bet your designs leaned towards natural shapes and rough surfaces. Organic things."

Arman stared at her. He wanted to make a rude comment about her having knowledge beyond what was rightly appropriate. It irked him that she was right. It irked him that the blood had controlled him for so long. *Have I ever been my own person?* Had he ever been simply Arman? "It doesn't make sense, general. I'm a diluted mess of old, forgotten power."

"That is no excuse for procrastination. We both know you could try harder."

Arman snarled. "I do what I can! Unlike milady I have no race of mentors eager to help me learn, to answer my questions! They're dead! Whatever is in my blood is an echo, nothing more!" Every sentence grew in volume, his words grinding on the stony rumble of his power.

"You have me, but I'll be damned if I feed you knowledge. I don't know what will resonate with your abilities."

"I'm human! I'm no Rakos guard, able to call forth monsters to shake the ground." He stormed down the stairs. He knew the anger simmering under his skin would prevent any more studying. He rubbed his temples as he walked. His words to Eras about his temper had been an understatement, and a large one at that. As a boy he had been quiet, slow to anger. Now the smallest things made him fume. He was not even certain why he was so angry with the general. *Is it because she thinks I'm a Rakos, or because I'm not one?* He had read that the Rakos had fearful tempers, but there was little else about what he could expect as he delved deeper into that side of his ancestry. With a snarl he shoved his hands into the pockets of his light jerkin and made for the barracks.

Φ

Arman tripped over the package on his floor when he returned from the bars. It was closer to dawn than dusk and he bet that his veins contained more alcohol than blood. *And more of either than any Rakos power.* His blurring vision swung back to the package he had kicked under his bed upon entering. He fished it out and tore open the plain wrapping. It was a thin book, bound like a journal, but in leather rather than the usual, cheap canvas. There was no title or embossing. A short letter was tucked into the front.

> *This was written by a dear friend, one whose voice you may recognize. He was one of the last to ever see the Rakos. Among other things, he tells of their powers and what their offspring were capable of.*
>
> *Should you want more advice or clarity, I am here. Though I'd appreciate if you try to leave your bitterness at the door.*
>
> *-General Aneral*

He knew he had been rude, but was grateful the general had enough sense to realize his actions said far more about his thoughts on himself than about her. He undressed and crawled into bed, belatedly lighting a lamp before opening the book. He liked the author immediately.

> *I would like to say this tale began in a time of peace and happiness, but I would be lying. ...*

Φ

The 38th Day of Fluerme, 1252
The City of Mirik

Bren straightened with a groan. "Damned if I'm going to survive this without becoming as twisted as a crone." Crouching for the better part of an hour that day had done little to help his back. He winced with pain and relief as his backbone popped. He trudged up the stairs towards his room with a sigh. His thoughts had darkened in the bowels of the palace and he could not shake the nagging feeling that he had forgotten something.

Helonin waited by the lieutenant's door. "We sail for Athrolan in a week's time."

Bren was used to the characteristic lack of preamble. "The city is coming along well, sir."

Helonin leveled an appraising stare at the younger man. "Will you return here once we are through at the capital?"

Bren frowned at his boots. He understood the respect behind delivering the question in person, rather than by squire, but he wished he were alone to think.

"You've been an asset, at least in dealing with the city-folk and helping the men learn the streets. If you wish to stay in Athrolan, however, you've given us enough."

"One pair of hands can make a difference, and the Kit are still uneasy." Bren glanced at the man. "Thank you, though."

Helonin clapped him on the shoulder. "We'll be glad of the help. There was another reason I came to find you." He drew out a plain iron box the size of his palm. "This is from the treasury. It might mean something to you. If not, then its missing won't matter."

Bren nodded and thanked the mariner again. When he had gone, Bren ducked into his room. He had thought returning to Mirik was the only option. Realizing he could train with the soldiers and Arman in Athrolan made him question his hasty choice. Mirik was home, and he had missed her sorely, but his heart felt every broken stone. He shook the indecision away and sat on his bed. The box was heavy in his hand and he flicked the lid open, curious. A heavy ring was tucked into a bed of forest green velvet. The band was wide and simple, sized for a large hand. The translucent diopside was native to the iron rich rocks of the island. Bronze shaped into a snake wound over the flat face of the olive gem. Bren's mouth fell open. It was the signet ring of Mirik's king.

Helonin had made a bold statement and Bren suddenly made sense of the mariner's words. *If this means nothing to me, it will not matter that it's no longer among Mirik's treasures.* Bren's continued denial of the throne was judged by many. *When the castle is made into an Athrolani fort my choice will have been made.* He tucked the box into the back of his desk's drawer and drew out a blank parchment to write Arman. His letter would be sent on the schooner leaving that night.

Φ

The 48th Day of Fluerme, 1252
The City of Ceir Athrolan

Helonin hid his amusement at Bren's seasickness, but his men were less kind. The lieutenant found himself the butt of most jests during the three-day sail to

Athrolan. The boat docked late in the afternoon and he could not rush down the gangway quick enough. Most of the sailors disembarked to the navy barracks lining the western edge of the harbor. Bren shouldered his pack. The queen was putting him in the palace for the week.

"Barrackborn!" Arman leaned against a piling near the street.

Whatever surprise Bren felt at the man coming to greet him was erased by the man's changed appearance. As he wove through the crowd he noted Arman was now nearly as broad as him. They grasped arms, Bren frowning inwardly at the unnatural dry heat of Arman's skin. "How have you been?"

"Well enough, though rather bored. You?" Arman fell into step beside him as they headed towards the palace.

"Much the same. Rebuilding a city is tedious work." He drew a breath. "It's good to have a change of scene—Athrolan's streets are a bit livelier than Mirik's."

"You mentioned city-people. Are they really as wild as the soldier's paint them?"

Bren shrugged. "They're odd, certainly. Mostly, they are desperate. Hopefully Athrolan will bring enough business to Mirik to give them food and money of their own again. Though who knows if they remember how to live in society." They continued, swapping stories of the days since they had last spoken.

Bren's room was the same as his last visit. Arman leaned against the doorframe while Bren unpacked. "Her Majesty plans on holding the report in the morning tomorrow and the day after. The rest of the week will be to decide what to do from here. Did you have any plans for the evening?"

"Food and drink, in that order. Why?"

Arman grinned. "I have a bar you should see. I can come by your room when we're headed into the city."

"I'll see you then." Bren put away his few belongings, including a thin journal he had used to record the meetings with the Kit. He rang for bath water and spent what was surely an embarrassing length of time soaking. He was dressed when Arman knocked on his door.

"We're meeting the others in the street." Sure enough half a dozen soldiers waited on the corner of Palace Way.

Bren was curious to see the lively greetings they afforded the Rakos, and more so when Arman exchanged laughing barbs with them. He had never seen the man so relaxed and he wondered how much of Arman's grim exterior had been due to Alea.

"This is Lieutenant Brentemir Barrackborn," Arman introduced. "Bren this is Sousa, Kal and Witt. Over there is Joen, Cennen and Hexion. Hex's sister owns the tavern." Bren was warmly welcomed as they started down the street.

"So Barrackborn, did ye hear about the Rakos here saving the Warehouse District?"

Bren glanced at Arman. The sailors in Mirik had brought word of the floods and Arman had mentioned them briefly, but this was news. "No, actually."

Sousa crowed excitedly and began the tale. Somewhere along the line Bren discovered the man's love of story-telling included exaggeration. He repeatedly glanced over at Arman to determine what was fact and fancy. Even without the license Sousa had taken, it was an interesting story.

"And then he put Hasian in his place—nearly beat the man to Toar and back!"

"Enough, Sou," Arman interrupted. "Save some stories for when he's drunk enough to believe them." The excuse was a thin one, but the men accepted it and Sousa quickly picked up another tale.

Bren's interest was piqued. *Exactly how much has changed?* He watched the changed mannerisms of Alea's guard, eyes narrowed. He wondered what she would find when she returned.

Φ

The 1st Day of Lineme, 1252

Buzzing conversation filled the meeting hall when Bren arrived with Arman. The day before had been serious and quiet, but its topics fueled the discussions now. The colonels and general were already there, along with the commander. The noise ceased abruptly when the queen arrived. She smiled as she took her seat, her gaze resting on each of the gathered officers. Bren watched her, curious. *This is what they want me to become—minus the headdress, perhaps.* She looked as benevolent as ever, but there were lines across her brow that had not been there a few months before.

"Welcome, all." She glanced at the scribes perched behind her velvet elbow. "Shall we begin?" The conversation began with new maps of Mirik and reports on the amount of stone used and gained from the city. The treasury reports would take a day unto themselves, but the rough sum put a frown on Queen Tzatia's face. Bren relayed his dealings with the Kit and their way of life. Hearing his home touted like a prize, to be divvied as the spoils of war made him sick. He mentally cursed his involvement in the meetings. He hid a clenching fist under the table.

"Lieutenant?"

Bren glanced up, blood flushing his neck in embarrassment. "Forgive me, your majesty, I was deep in thought."

Tzatia hid frustration well, but her eyes were tired. "Sir Helonin said you had thoughts on the city, the plans?"

Bren leaned forward to orient himself with the maps facing the queen. "I know your majesty intended her for a fort, but I was looking over the plans from King Brenterik's reign and had a thought." He pointed to the swath of cobbles stretching between the city walls and the harbor. Helonin had been unreadable when Bren brought his thoughts forward a week before and the lieutenant was eager to share. "A market here would be perfect for trade—Toar knows the island has enough timber. Trade routes could be re-established. The temple and noble districts, where most of the stone is, could be rebuilt as residences. Fields could replace the old slums and graze royal flocks."

Tzatia's soft cough interrupted him. "Lieutenant, these ideas would certainly raise the city. I think it would be wise to note, however, while there is enough money in Mirik's treasury for such endeavors, we would be fools to spend it thusly. There is a war on, one her king started."

The anger at seeing his home torn apart, bankwasted, and pillaged rose, and determination took the reins of his mouth. "What of afterward, your majesty? I have enough faith in my sister to believe there will be an after. To let Mirik fall when its port could open up the northern ocean, would be madness."

The queen's face hardened. "The northern ocean has nothing but Ageless iron and ice to offer. You speak as if you rule Mirik, when you have expressed distaste for such a title. I remind you that you cannot have the glory and power of a king with the responsibility of a soldier. Choose your course and hold fast to it, otherwise you are simply wasting our time."

Bren's mouth snapped shut and he looked down. He wanted to storm from the room, but it would only serve to drive the queen's point home. "Forgive me, your majesty. Of course you are right." His words were polite, but he spat them from his mouth with venom. He did not hear the remainder of the meeting and was the first to leave when they were dismissed, ignoring Arman's offer to go to the tavern again.

A knock interrupted him as he forgot his rebuked pride in a book. He glowered, tempted to pretend to be out. A second knock came and he jerked the door open. "What, Arman?"

Instead of the expected visitor, Reka leaned against his door frame. "I thought Arman was lying when he said you had holed up here. I heard the queen showed you your station."

Bren made a face. "I'm sure everyone has heard. Did he send you to drag me out to drink?"

"No, but I'm headed for a mug-full, if you wanted to join me." She grinned. "Last I saw you, we were stumbling into the infirmary at Shadow."

Bren tugged on his jerkin and locked his door. "I didn't expect to see you." He tucked his hands into his pockets as they walked. "I thought the Bordermen were scouting with Athrolani patrols."

"We are. My patrol rode in this morning. You'll be going back to Mirik and I thought I'd visit while I could." She turned down another set of side streets, different from those Arman had taken. The road wound along the upper tier of the city, curling around the western edge of the harbor. It was a seedy area above the navy barracks and shipyards. The farther they walked from Palace Way, the darker the alleyways became.

"You don't go to the same tavern as Arman's friends?"

"There are a few I enjoy. Which is theirs?"

"It's called the Lily and Ahonsa, based on some lewd Athrolani myth, if I remember." Bren laughed. "Bars and sex seem to be firm bedfellows."

Reka snorted a soft laugh. She had clearly adjusted to the Athrolani humor. "No, that's not one I visit. I prefer a storytelling to a brawl. Does Mirik have alehouses? Arman mentioned you were eager to be...." She frowned. "You call it tousled?"

He threw a friendly arm around her shoulder. "Tossed. Mirik had only the alcohol that we shipped over, and we drank over the barracks' fires. I'm tired of the company of bone weary men."

Her eyes crinkled in a Border grin. "That the only reason you wished to drink with me?"

"You make me sound like a boor. It could have been for good conversation."

"You are a boor," she joked as they ducked into the loud warmth of the alehouse. "Now, what will our first pints be? Whisky or spice-mead?"

Bren called for the second and they wove through the tables to a set of chairs by the musicians. The tavern was well built for the district. Each of the pillars had been carved into a well-dressed hare standing erect. Some had headdresses and skirts, others tunics and monocles. Bren snorted, despite the obvious quality of the craftsmanship. "Reka, what is this place?"

"The Wise Hare. It might be odd, but they have good music and mead."

As if summoned by her words, the serving woman arrived. A small tray balanced on her pregnant belly. She grinned at them, plunking the drinks down along with a plate of seasoned meat. Reka's feet tapped in time to the quick music after their first two drinks. After the fourth, Bren convinced her to join in the dancing. Her leathers were better suited to the forest, but she moved easily, hands above her head. She twisted in a choppy, yet rhythmic, dance that must have been Border. The firelight highlighted her body and Bren wondered absently how the male warriors could ignore the fact that their companions were female. After a few turns Reka taught him the complex steps to another one.

"What is it?" He pitched his voice so she could hear him over the lively music.

"A dance for luck in battle."

At her words Bren noticed how some motions were parries or strikes. One even looked like the launching of an arrow. He tried the steps again. It was close to midnight when they returned to the palace, their route far more wavering than before. Bren wordlessly opened his door and stepped aside in an invitation. She tugged off his jerkin and shirt, her own already on the floor. As her hands moved to the laces of his breeches he wondered if there was a dance that would make him a good king. Her lips drove the thought from his mind and he fell back onto the bed. Reka landed on top of him with a rare, low, laugh.

Φ

The 3rd Day of Lineme, 1252
The Isle of Le'yne

Gray fog burst on Alea's chest with cold splinters. "Do not close your eyes. You cannot see if someone attacks!" Elle raised her hands to throw another ball of mist.

Alea reached down again, eyes open now, but it was difficult to visualize her power while distracted by the training court around her. She pulled a tendril into her hands and sent it towards the largest stone. It dissipated before it hit. "I don't feel the way I normally do. I don't have those emotions."

She had not had them since the siege. The darkness crouching on the edge of her thoughts kept anything more than the trivial from her heart. She was scared to call it apathy, scared to think she might never *feel* again.

"You have never used your power without fear?" Elle pressed a hand against her brow. "Breathe deeply. Remember the sensation of your power filling you. Follow that." Elle gestured to the smallest stone. "Now, pick it up and turn it over. Gently."

Alea glared at the accidental insult, but turned to the rock. She pushed power through her fingers and shoved. The stone disintegrated into sand. She heaved a sigh. "If the Berrin and Azirik are so powerful, why must I learn the small things? Whatever I must do to them needs to be massive."

"Control, Lyne'alea. Your power is not just a force, not just an extension of your hand, but a weapon. You will need to have control, lest you hurt your allies."

"I am the Destroyer and you have not let me forget the only time I used Creation. Those are not things done at a whim." She turned back to the rocks and focused. By noon, she was no closer to completing the task.

Elle straightened her dress. "Perhaps we ought to start even smaller. As children we would sit for hours, just feeling our power. Unlearning poor habits is harder than learning good ones."

"You act as if we have all the time in the world, Elle." Alea rubbed her face, hoping to scrub frustration from her body. "I understand this is my blood and I have no choice in that, but I've taken up the mantel of a war I had no interest in, even after it robbed me of the only life I knew."

"We are not weak humans like Athrolan's queen. We cannot be dazzled by the first sign of black fog." The voice behind Alea was deep and hoarse. "Learn your ignorance - there were many women we thought might be the Dhoah' Laen."

Alea turned to see the tall, elder Laen from her first evening.

"Lyne'alea, this is Elai." Elle's gaze was fixed on the older Laen's sandals.

Alea met the woman's eyes. "They are dead and I am here. Destruction is not a simple thing to master. It may be easy to forget, hiding in this monotonous world, but war does not wait. I need knowledge now, not in a year."

"You showed incredible stupidity bringing that boy back. You damaged our power irreparably."

"Boy?" Alea turned to Elle, incredulous. "The same boy you asked to bind himself to me? The same boy who is taking up a duty you thought was dead? We took whatever boyhood he still had." She glanced at Elai. This was not a conversation to have when angry, but her only method of communication with the Laen seemed to be argument. "If you wish to teach me, you might bother to understand me first." She stalked out of the yard, realizing she sounded like the child she insisted she was not. "This lesson is done. Perhaps tomorrow one of you will have come to your senses."

She was relieved to find the library deserted. She took up her place at the table and opened a tome. It detailed the spread of the different races and the waning of the Laen's power. *The Rakos died out, the Laen died out, the only gods who were our allies died out.* She disliked the theme.

"We know you deserve respect." Mera's voice was soft and kind.

Alea looked up. The anger was draining from her. "Then why do I feel as if it's the opposite?"

"We're scared of what you can do. You're supposed to save our race. You are mighty and sweeping and terrifying."

"I do not want reverence either. I want to be seen as an equal, a woman, a daughter. I've given up so much for this war. There is very little left inside of me to give." Her voice broke and she looked down, ashamed at her tears. "I know what I did was dangerous and terrible. I know what it made me. Yet, none of you have thought to ask me why."

"I'm sorry, Lyne'alea. Most of us never knew a life other than this. You have. Finish your reading. Perhaps Elle will talk to you tomorrow." She pressed a hand to Alea's arm. "She's never been a master of words, your mother."

"We share that, then, if nothing else." When she had gone, Alea sat back. Bren had told her how frustrating his armor-cleaning had been as a boy. She had thought the siege was her armor-cleaning. Now she was not so certain. *Elle reached me from across a continent. Faint, but Arman saw her.* She touched her power and reached her mind out across the ocean. It was a familiar path. *I swam through this with Arman's soul.* The thought caught in her throat and she shook her head to clear it. She focused her mind and pressed through the electrified barrier between the worlds. Her mind raced over the water. Mirik glowed, a tiny constellation of copper-red stars. She followed the brown-laced ball of light that was her brother's. Curiosity flitted across her thoughts. Though he shared her blood, his soul looked the same as any man's. He sat at a desk, reading.

She nudged his consciousness. *Brothermine?*

He jumped, surprised. "Alea?"

Yes! How are you? I miss you.

"Toar, how are you doing this? Or have I been up too late and am hearing things?"

No, it's really me. How is Mirik?

"We're working through the city, clearing rubble, searching for anything that will help. It's slow. The queen wants to make it into a fort. And you, how are you? Are you learning a lot?" He tilted his chair back on two legs.

I'm learning a lot, though not what I expected. More about myself, which is useful.

"I've been doing heart-searching, too. Everyone seems to want me to be king. We just returned from Athrolan today, actually. During our report the queen told me I needed to choose what role to have. Her exact words were 'you cannot have the glory and power of a king with the responsibility of a soldier.'"

Well then. If you wait too long the decision will be made for you. She laughed at the face he made. *Have you decided?*

"I think a picture is fast forming." He sighed. "Enough of my problems. What have you learned?"

That I am nothing like the Laen want me to be.

His eyes widened. "That sounds unpleasant."

Rather. They argue over how to teach me, what to teach me, and the nature of my power. I read a lot. Some of it is quite interesting. What remains unwritten by the historians is even more interesting.

"I think most history is interesting."

You and Arman both. I prefer fables and poetry, though this is changing my opinion somewhat. I still feel useless. I think we were wrong – this is my armor cleaning. She felt her power shudder and she sighed. *I think I ought to go. I'm tiring. I miss you.*

"I miss you, too. Visit me again, if you can."

I will. Her mind raveled back to her body quickly, leaving her feeling cold and alone. The book would not read itself, however, and talking with Bren had centered her thoughts for the moment. She turned back to the page before her with a frown. She was ashamed of so much, yet none of it was what the Laen told her she should regret.

CHAPTER FIVE

The 8th Day of Lineme, 1252
The City of Ceir Athrolan

ARMAN WANTED ANSWERS. THE last time he wanted information he burnt a man from within to read his thoughts. Arman tipped his head back onto the cool plaster of the dome. Dawn was one of the few times the early summer heat-haze dissipated long enough for the faint shadow of Mirik to appear on the horizon. In the stillness, his heartbeat was thunder. He had yet to sleep, and now it was dawn. The journal Eras had lent him sat on the stone beside him, a silent and patient companion.

He closed his eyes against the blooming light of dawn. *Surely I could ask the other parts of myself.* He sunk into his own thoughts, following the curls of white-gold power that knotted the surface of his mind. The air was a caress on his over-heated skin. There was a history tucked away in his thoughts, a litany of everything the Rakos had ever been. He had not formed a question when he discovered the storm that waited ahead of their ship. It had been a burning, angry concept at the forefront of his thoughts as he punched through the other man's mind.

He gathered the few things he already knew about the Rakos, about his own abilities. He tied them about his thoughts like a cocoon. In his head, it sounded like a riddle. *I am fire. I am smoke. I am thought. I am earth.* The air felt colder as his body began to burn from within. His mind itched. A great tangle of information glowed in the center of his soulblood. It stung his mental touch. He traced the individual lines that snarled together, finally finding a free end. Ignoring the strange sensation, he grabbed at it and tugged. A thousand burning images bombarded him.

A Rakos stood on a mountain's peak, staring down at a statue of a regal woman beside a lake. The city still stood, not yet in ruins. The image flashed to that of a battle at the edge of the lake. Men swarmed the area, and the Rakos attacked. Monsters screamed from above, their tattered wings raining feathers. Flames burst from the Rakos's hands and mouths, smoke spiraling into the sky.

Who am I? Arman plunged down, under the surface of the pulsing knot. A blond man stood in a room, dark and windowless, a tomb without the coffin. He had dragged a body into the darkness and crouched over the monster's head. The man drew his knife and cut around the creature's brow, parting the scales and skin. A glimmer of gold and white shone through the layers of muscle. He parted the flesh further until his fingers could gain purchase on the metal ringing the creature's skull. Bone cracked as he finally wrenched it free. Arman winced.

A pair of yellow eyes blotted out every thought, glaring into his mind and soul with burning fervor. Its voice was manic and keening. It took Arman a moment to decipher the words. Rather, it was a single word, repeated with the ferocity of a madman. "Fear. Fear. Fear"

The 11th Day of Lineme, 1252

Arman began to wonder if the journal's author was quite sane. The humor and the wry biting words were familiar to Arman. He had spoken to men jaded by life. Sometimes he felt his own voice twisting into cynicism. The author certainly knew enough about the world, and it was the type of knowledge not learned in books, but from walking the road. He spoke of the Northlands wistfully, and of Athrolan tenderly. Arman was fairly certain the man that penned the pages before him had also left legends in his wake.

Arman flipped to a passage he had marked with a bit of string. The Rakos were mentioned often, and with curiosity, not fear.

> *I did not understand the true nature of the bond between Rakos and Laen. Nuirene brought back pieces of black rock-metal he called magnetite. They came from a star-fall. The rocks were heavy, and if brought near each other, would fly together. A large piece would collect thousands of tiny particles, but two pieces of the same size would collide with force enough to break a man's finger. Thus it is with power.*

Arman frowned. The man was not sane. Nevertheless, he wandered into the section at the back of the library holding books and maps regarding metals and rocks. It was mostly used by those seeking to build within the city, or to plan where the next mine would be dug. It was deserted and the shelves dusty. He ran a calloused finger through the dust by the tablets labeled "Ma-" and found a small wooden box. Across the top was a blocky stamp titling the contents as star-stone. Arman opened the box to find a small velvet pouch holding two black spheres. At first they looked like polished metal, but the grain and swirls indicated they were, in fact, rocks. With effort he pulled them apart, letting them snap back together with a surprising crack. He repeated the action several times, amused. Finally, he replaced them in the box and returned to the journal.

> *The Laen power acts in one fashion, and the Rakos's in another. Though they are opposite, they are equal and in the equal opposition there is an attraction that cannot be defied and will break all in its path. Sometimes even those who wield it.*

Arman had agreed with everything written, but now, when called an equal to the Laen, he scoffed. At the time he wrote it, the author had never felt the power Alea radiated. Their powers were two pieces of a whole, but not equal ones.

Though better than the isolation before, Arman's life still felt dualistic. He spent the days as Arrowlash, studying, learning about Rakos power. At night he was Arman, drinking and carousing. It was an extension of who he had been in Vielrona. The disconnect allowed him to relax, but he knew eventually there would be no divide. One would bleed into the other and Arman would be lost forever in Rakos flames.

He glared at the ale in his glass, trying to determine whether he minded. The drink was a rich golden brown. Summer gold. It was a comforting color, familiar and warm. *Veredy's hair.*

"Eh, we lost Arman to his thoughts again."

Arman grinned and flicked his gaze to Kal. He let enough of his power into his body to make his voice rumble. It was a fun trick and rarely made them actually remember what he was. "Just deciding how long I should wait before I whip all your arses." He threw down another card, absently wondering which game they were playing. Would a Rakos enjoy drinking and card games? He did not know.

Φ

The 13th Day of Lineme, 1252
The City of Mirik

Bren tossed onto his side, staring out the window. It was dark and the view was poor. He was glad to be out of the tedious meetings, but Mirik did not feel like home. It only gave him more to think about. The queen's pointed words stung more than he admitted. *I am betwixt two roles and I try to act in both with the responsibility of neither.* He briefly wished he could talk to Alea. When he had been Azirik's man and thoughts kept him from sleep, Bren had walked out by the harbor to think, away from the boisterous chaos of the other men.

His boots were on in moments. He crossed the courtyard and slipped through the gates easily, calling a greeting to the guards. His usual course took him around the harbor, but he paused, looking up at the city gates. Changing direction, he chose the abandoned streets of the city. He was certain the Kit tailed him, but that only served to make the night feel more desolate. He turned west at the palace walls, following them to what had once been gardens. They were dense and overgrown now, but made a good ladder up the city walls. He scrambled up quickly, perching at the top to look out over the waves. The walls were complete, ready to encompass the fort and town that would serve as Athrolan's northern-most outpost.

He leaned back against the tree stretching over the stone. "Come out, Oland. I know you're there."

There was silence for a moment, then a rustle as the Miriken climbed up to sit beside him. He was quiet, running his worn hand over the newly-lain stone. "Ye cleaned her up nice."

"Makes me wish I could remember what she was like at her might, before Azirik."

"When yer grandpap ruled."

Bren shrugged.

"What'll her fate be?" Arik fixed Bren with an unreadable gaze.

"Athrolan will make her a fort. She'll be an outpost for the kingdom, for trade and the like."

"And the Kit?"

Bren was quiet for a long minute. "I suspect you can stay here, work for the soldiers."

"And you think that will be different than Azirik? Better somehow? Ye should take her. Ye know her."

Bren put his head in his hands. "I'm not a king, Arik, I'm a soldier."

"Well, we're not a kingdom either. We're a rabble-band of starved thieves and opportunists."

Bren raised his brows. "You have any room open for a new member? If the queen doesn't give up this quest for my future I might run away with you."

"Do you fear the crown?"

"No. I don't deserve it, though."

"That alone would make you a better king than Azirik."

"He thought he deserved the crown?" Bren shifted to get a better look at his companion's features.

"Azirik wept when his pa died. Not in grief, but 'cause he feared the crown." Arik scrubbed his face with a rough hand. "You would really give up a crown for freedom?"

Bren rolled his eyes. "Honestly I'd settle for a hermitage." His face sobered. "What would you do were you in my place?"

Arik's expression grew thoughtful. "I don't know, truly. However I'll tell you this—I could have left the Kit here. I could have run to my cousin on the mainland and never looked back. Many did. I'd not be hungry. I'd not be poor. I'd feel a damn sight younger. But I don't know if I'd be happier." He shrugged. "This is home. She's not a great land, she's not a rich one, but she's pretty and she's mine." He sighed and heaved himself to his feet. "Pity you won't take her. You'd have the Kit's voice."

Bren stared at the dark water below and listened to the man climb down the wall. "How many are you, Oland?"

A long pause prefaced the words that finally drifted up from below. "Three score in the city. Twice that in the green." He used the old Miriken term for the forest. Bren turned back to the ocean. The conversation left him with fewer answers than before. It would be hours before he could sleep and dawn waited for no one. *Did you really expect to escape fate when your sister is the Dhoah' Laen?* He promised himself he would make a decision before be returned to the barracks that night. He sat on the wall for a long time.

Φ

The 17th Day of Lineme, 1252
The Isle of Le'yne

Frustration and embarrassment were familiar to Alea. Learning a new culture in Vielrona had been hard. Acknowledging naiveté while demanding respect had been worse. Neither were comparable to navigating the icy social waters of Le'yne. The day was crisp and the air rejuvenated Alea's wounded spirit as she walked up to the training court. Despite the outburst, Elle continued to teach her, but with little progress. If anything, Alea felt her hold on her power diminishing in the face of stress and distain.

This morning, however, Elle's faint smile was almost vulnerable. The kindness gave Alea pause. She nodded. "Good morning. Are we picking up where we left off yesterday?"

"We both know it's the wrong way to go about things, at least for now." Elle patted the ground beside her. "Instead of starting small with what you do with your power, let us start small with *how* you use it."

Alea sat cross-legged and rested her hands in her lap. "Taking a small piece, you mean?"

"I want you to bring it up, but do not push it out of yourself. Just feel it. Let it simply be around you."

It was difficult. Alea's power bucked like a horse trying to free itself from a tether, seeking any way out.

"Do not force it down. Spread calmness across, like a layer, holding yourself just in check."

Alea floated on a sea of black, icy fog. She glanced down, looking at the roiling ocean beneath her mental self. Lightning rumbled through the churning blackness. It looked like the clouds above Le'yne. Startled excitement broke her will and power flooded into her skin. Her eyes flew open and she gasped, clenching her fists as cold rocketed down her limbs.

"You held it. It was a moment, but you did it." Elle smiled. "Now, try again."

Φ

Alea frowned as she tossed herbs haphazardly into her mug. "I thought we were proceeding with order and precision." She almost succeeded in keeping vitriol from her voice.

"Yes, and in order to do so, I must understand you better." At Alea's accusing glace, Elle sighed. "Yes, Mera spoke with me. It does not change the fact that I'm curious about what you have learned to do on your own. Perhaps I can teach you better if I know what it is you're wielding."

"I don't suppose the other Laen are curious, too."

"If they are, their curiosity will not be satisfied today. It'll just be the two of us."

The pale sunlight lit the training court well and Alea propped her still-steaming mug on the ground beside Elle. She took a few steps away and tried to hide the shaking in her arms as they hung at her sides. She fell into herself, closing her eyes and pulling the swirling black clouds from her center.

Unbidden, thoughts of the past weeks unfurled in the wake of her power. *The Laen are disappointed. I am worthy of their respect.* Her jaw tightened. Another thought bloomed, this time from the darkest shadows in her mind. *I am worthy of their fear.* She stumbled over its bitterness. She gripped her power tighter, pushing the distractions aside and let it pour into her limbs. It filled her fingers then pushed out, towards the mountains, away from the village and Elle. The ground trembled under her physical feet, but her power was too tight for her to hear. She pushed it further, then let it retreat, curling back into her body and mind. The normal sounds of the village and hillside were replaced with terrible silence.

She blinked, eyes opening as blackness faded from them. The walls of the training court had been reduced to rubble. All but the largest stone was a pile of gravel. A ragged handprint had been carved into it, the edges of the fingers and palm coated in curls of hoar frost.

Alea did not have to look to know the Laen below stared from the streets and doorways of the village. Elle had taken several steps back. Alea turned her eyes slowly to her mother. "I rarely tell it what to do. Often I let it behave on its own. I'm lucky I can control it this much."

"You had less control before?" Elle's voice had lost its calm exterior. Fear and remorse rubbed the edges of her words raw.

"I used to sink into my power instead of drawing it through myself. We were on the road between Fort Hero and Fort Stone. I was practicing and my power got away from me. I destroyed the camp, broke trees, and killed one of the horses." She could feel the hard mask on her face cracking.

"How did you stop yourself?"

"I didn't. Arman spoke to me through his own power. When I relaxed, when my fear had lessened, I could control it again. Afterward, he told me to pull the power up instead of surrounding myself with it. Lest I drown, so to speak."

Elle smoothed her skirt with shaking hands. "One of us has studied the way we each use our power. Would you talk to her? She might have insight. I'm afraid I do not."

"It can't hurt." Alea knew she should be ashamed of scaring them, but a small part of her rejoiced. Perhaps they would finally listen.

Φ

Lelil was the oldest woman Alea had ever seen among human or Laen. Her silver eyes were set deeply into nets of folded skin. Her expression was the familiar calm facade. She ushered them wordlessly into her small house and gestured for Alea to sit at the table. Elle, she ignored.

Alea sat, staring at her uncertainly. *Should I explain myself? Surely what I just did was demonstration enough.* When Lelil held out her hand, Alea took it. The loose skin was soft and cool. She kept her eyes open and drew her power up. It was easier each time, as if the path would be broken in like a pair of boots. Lelil followed along the veins of Alea's soulblood. The additional presence was nagging. She withdrew and Alea let her power fade.

Lelil sat back, regarding Alea thoughtfully. After a moment she stood and went to stand at the counter. Her brows furrowed as if something out the kitchen window was distressing. "Are you tired?"

Alea looked up. She had wondered if the woman was mute. "I've been traveling and essentially rootless for months. Of course I'm tired."

"When you use your power, Lyne'alea, are you tired afterward?"

"Yes. Though often there is stress for other reasons as well. War does that."

Lelil ignored the barb. "And when you have used the most, what has happened?"

"It burnt my hands and I bled soulblood through the wounds. I was unconscious for days."

Lelil's expression tightened and she turned to look at her. "Our power is a ball in our wombs. Yours is rooted there, certainly, but it has branches wrapped around every vein of your being. There is little definition where one ends and the other begins. Your emotions trigger your power this way. Each time you pull your power through yourself, some soulblood is burnt away. With time it returns, but if you use too much at once it will kill you."

Elle rubbed her face. "How did you live through bringing that boy back?"

Alea looked down at the veins of power and soulblood still shining through her skin. "I almost didn't. I sank in the ocean, without enough strength to swim. I pushed his soul back to his body, but remember nothing more. Later he said he carried me."

The two women exchanged looks. "He is a strong man, to carry a creature so powerful and not be consumed by it," Lelil noted. She brushed her hands free of invisible dust. "I will discuss with the others what should be done. In the meantime, keep to your reading and mind your emotions."

Alea fell into step beside Elle after their abrupt dismissal. "You are not meeting with them?"

"My opinion is negated by my apparent affection for you. I fear what they will decide."

"Why?"

"I barely understand your power, but I know it cannot be treated the same as ours. Few of them understand that. They think your tiger should behave as our housecats, not realizing the two are different animals."

Φ

The 18th Day of Lineme, 1252

The view of the ocean made Alea think of Athrolan. She had not been there long enough to call it home, but nostalgia tinted every thought of the tiered city. *It is not Athrolan's cliffs I miss, but the person with me.* She shut her bedroom door carefully and sat on her bedspread. She had avoided thinking about Arman or their argument, but now she missed his steadiness. She connected to her power quickly and shot across the waves in minutes. Athrolan was a sea of crimson shimmering with all the souls.

A spot of white-gold pulsed brilliantly through them. She pushed herself closer until she could see him. He sat in the library, several books open before him. A deep frown creased his forehead and tension lined his shoulders. She moved closer to peer at what he read. It was a plain journal, written in simple, spiky writing. She reached out her mind and nudged against him, like she had with Bren.

Arman? The sensation was strange, like sliding off a glass window. He did not seem to notice her. She grabbed at more power. *Arman, can you hear me?*

He looked up, his frown deepening.

Arman!

He rubbed his eyes roughly. "I'm going mad, thinking I can feel her here." He gathered his tunic, folded haphazardly over the back of the chair and headed towards the door. He extinguished the candles and paused. "I miss you, you know. More than anything." He shook his head and left.

Energy drained from Alea and her mind followed her power back to her body. She flopped onto the pillows. *Why couldn't he hear me? Bren could.* She ran a hand through her hair. She felt more isolated than ever. She rolled over and wrapped her arms around her pillow. Elle called for her to come have lunch, but Alea stared unseeing out the window at the rolling waves for several minutes before finally going into the kitchen.

Elle was silent as she prepared their lunch. She set a pot on to simmer and turned to lean against the counter. "Talk to me?"

Alea jumped, surprised at the vulnerability in the words. "About what?"

"Your journey north, your childhood, your first love. There is so much I don't know." Elle's silver eyes were lit with a bittersweet glow. For the first time Alea felt as if she gazed on a mother. The emotion was uncomfortable to see on her normally stoic features and she looked down at her hands. Without eye contact she could be speaking to anyone, or to no one. "You did well, choosing the ihal to raise me. He was a kind man and intelligent. He must have understood more of the truth than I realized. He had many children, the younger of which I helped raise. His second-eldest son, Ahren, agreed to marry me. The attack came a week before we were to be wed. The Laen were there, six of them, and the one they thought was the Dhoah' Laen. I was so angry at them afterward. They abandoned me, abandoned my family after we had sheltered them."

Her voice faltered for a moment and she drew a breath. "You are right that I know little about your people – I was not raised by you, or even in an ally city. I do know about this war and about my power." She paused, forcing her words to be gentle. It was harder than she expected. "After years of inaction, I think action scares you. Last you saw me I was a child, and now you turn about and

I'm grown. Treating me like a child now will not make up for those years." She finally looked up. "But you don't have to. I had a family, one you picked just for me."

"It is not anger behind my reprimands and reserve. It is fear."

"I know what I did was monstrous and dangerous, but did you ever think to ask me why?"

Elle looked down and shook her head. "That is not why I am afraid. I spent two decades pretending you were never born, because if I didn't, they might find you. Two decades of only loving you in my mind and dreams, Lyne'alea. Now you are real and breathing and angry and I'm still terrified to love you." She reached out to touch Alea's hand, but paused. She swallowed hard, her hand falling back into her lap. Neither moved to take the pot from the fire and the silence was broken only by the hiss as it boiled over.

CHAPTER SIX

The 21st Day of Lineme, 1252
The City of Mirik

SALT MADE THE COBBLES sticky under Bren's boots. There was an irony to Mirik being surrounded by ocean and attacking the woman who wielded its power. He followed the path from his first encounter with the Kit. They were odd, he admitted, and questionably sane, but he preferred their company to the Athrolani. Some deep part of him was sickened by the garish turquoise of their uniforms and pennants where vermilion once hung.

He broke into a jog and turned into the slums. The houses were tall, leaning over the street. Jug-end Square was the center of their domain, it seemed, and since the Athrolani's arrival, the place was tidier. If some nicer materials suddenly appeared in the Kit houses, no one seemed to notice. Bren rapped on the central door, eyes scanning the windows around him. Relations with the Kit were certainly civil, but Bren would not go as far to describe them as friendly.

"Ho, Oland." They may have accepted him more readily than they did the Athrolani, but he was still a vague other to the majority. Doors opened and shut and he heard a muttered order for patience. It was better than finding a bolt in his sternum.

The door jerked open. "Barrackborn." Even under the harsh lighting of the lanterns, it was clear Arik's face had fleshed out.

Bren raised a hand in greeting. "I have something to discuss with you." He shot a glance at the hall behind the Miriken. "Might I come in?"

Arik did not move from the doorway. His eyes narrowed on the soldier, head tilting to one side.

Bren did not rush the man, and forced his feet into stillness. The Kit kept to themselves. Often the only visitors allowed were unconscious or dead. He watched thoughts flicker over the older man's features for a moment. "One Miriken visiting another, Oland, that's all."

Arik sighed. The weight of the past decade wiped all fight from his face and he nodded. "Get in, then." He moved down the hall, not waiting to see if Bren followed. The houses shared walls, and the Kit had opened doorways between them. It created a warren of connected dwellings and meeting halls. While the endlessness may have been an illusion, Bren was willing to bet the buildings covered more ground than the actual palace.

Four minutes of walking brought them to a door at the end of a hall. Arik unlocked it and ushered Bren into a small two-room apartment. Dismantled crates formed a table, chairs and the platform for a cot mattress. Without offering tea or ale, he sat at the makeshift table and fixed Bren with an expectant look. "Well?"

Bren sat and drew a book from his jerkin. "Are you familiar with *Rauld's Tales for an Officer*?"

"Somewhat. It was controversial when scribed, if I recall."

"For good reason. Would you do me a favor and read the third piece? 'Treatise for a Common Man's King.'" He slid the book across the table.

Arik regarded Bren, one rough hand on the book's cover. "I'm not in the habit of reading for pleasure."

"Then consider this research." Bren shifted. He needed the man's opinion before he would admit his real reasons for the suggestion.

"Might this have to do with our discussion last week?"

"It might. Humor me though. Mirik is in shambles. She has no government. The only thing that could make her worse could be if Azirik himself returned."

Arik laughed. "You sound more like Brenterik every day." He glanced up, the nests of wrinkles about his eyes deep with mirth. "As kings went, he was a good man." He looked down at the book before them, a heartbreaking mixture of hope and dread on his features. "Is this something you wish to keep between us?"

"For now." Bren rose. "Mind showing me out? I doubt I could find my own way without getting lost. I've only just got my thoughts straightened out and it'd be a pity to starve to death in this maze."

Arik laughed, tucking the book inside his shirt before rising. "I doubt the Kit would let you starve."

Φ

Bren had gambled on having time to plan, to organize the Kit. He had yet to even formulate what he was actually doing. The letter sitting on his desk when he returned from the city crushed those hopes for more time. The parchment probably cost more than the clothes he wore. If the formal hand of a scribe was not enough, the bright ribbons and seals told him it was from the queen and it was no missive. The address stilled his breath.

Addressing His Highness Crown Prince Brentemir, Heir Apparent of Mirik

Bren groaned. Every carefully thought-over piece of his plan fell through with an almost audible clatter.

We wish to express congratulations of Ceir Athrolan and her cities on the reclamation of the harbor capitol of Mirik. Athrolan received word that the city has indeed been abandoned by Lord King Azirik of Mirik and his Gods' Army, and offers her own Naval Commander and a ship of her navy to continue its aide to raise Mirik's capital to its former strength.

Ceir Athrolan and her cities hope that as acting king of Mirik, you will accept our extended hand of alliance against King Azirik and his Berrin allies in this war for Dhoah' Lyne'alea and her people. We look forward to your response within a fortnight.

Respectfully and in peace,

Her Majesty Tzatia, Queen of Athrolan, on behalf of Athrolan and her people

If Bren was unsure of the calculating intelligence behind the queen's benevolent smile before, now he was certain. "Damn, I'm a soldier not a king!" He tossed the letter into his drawer beside the ring and drew a clean sheet of parchment over.

Oland,

Her Majesty called me out. She addressed me as Heir Apparent and all sorts of things and requested an alliance. I hoped we would have more time. Might I meet with you, and all the Kit and our allies? Your earliest convenience would be best.

He sealed it and sent the letter off with a squire. His officer's log lay on the desk. He had not written since leaving Azirik's army. Now he opened it and stared at the blank page before him. *Rauld says that the best way to govern a people is to be that people. Azirik ruined Mirik with her own crown, and wounded the earth with another. Perhaps it is time we ruled without one.* He dipped his pen and began to write.

Φ

The 24th Day of Lineme, 1252

The City of Ceir Athrolan

Arman decided he and Wes should have taken up armor smithing years ago. The sprawling buildings of the royal armory were bustling, yet well kept, giving the illusion of chaos without the actual danger. He had handed over his designs for his armor, albeit with Eras's changes. Now he stared at the rough sketch and estimated price. He could buy his own forge with that sum. Perhaps two. He could retire and not work another day.

The money Wes had given him before they left Vielrona still weighed heavily in his purse, but it was nothing compared to the price of armor. He had not needed money in months and it was a strange feeling to worry about it again. He, Alea and Bren rested in a strange place of indecision. They did not need money, but nor did they work for a wage. Their expenses were covered by Athrolan, but Arman knew it was not an indefinite arrangement. Anxiety raced through Arman's veins. The smoke and metal scent of the forge was a heady concoction. He needed to be outside. He needed air. Armor would have to wait.

He ducked through the smaller south gate between the palace and the barracks and strode down the road. It led up through the wooded hills before forking to the west and south. The air was cool and within a few minutes the sounds of the city had faded. He walked until the trees swallowed him and all but the highest towers disappeared. The forest was full of animal noises and the wind, but nothing menacing. It had been a long time since he had been able to consider the woods safe.

He shook away the thoughts and broke into a lope. A mountain stream gurgled nearby, and he ran upstream, boots tapping as he jumped from rock to rock. His breath was barely gasping. He pushed himself harder, falling into his power, willing his skin and muscle to disappear into smoke. The resistance of air and gravity fell away as his body dissolved. His eyes fluttered open, mind still gripping his power. His limbs were twisting white smoke, nothing more substantial than dust motes in the sunlight lancing through the trees. Only his torso remained, and even that seemed closer to a ghost than a man.

Arman crowed at the success, and his voice was a keening shriek, too guttural to be a bird's, too grating to be human. "What do you think of this?" He had taken to conversing with the golden eyes that floated in the back of his mind. It warped his thought patterns enough to develop new ideas. Sometimes, even, he thought they answered him.

Smoke is only an echo of flame. Where is the fire?

Arman scowled. "I am no Rakos, burning the air with a single thought. I am just an echo of something mighty." He pulled up more power, coating himself with it and urged his legs faster. Except, it was not his legs that propelled him now, but sheer will. His body faded, skin and muscle writhing away to expose transparent organs, insubstantial bones. "If someone struck me with a sword, would it pass through me, leaving me unharmed?"

Fire is stronger than steel. Fire molds the earth as it wishes.

He topped the hill, a broad rocky outcrop with sparse tree cover. He willed his body to move faster, towards the cliff on the hill's southern face. With a final push, he dove over the edge. *Smoke is lighter than most air, floating on the currents like an equal.* Arman did not fall. He drifted, supported by the sun-warmed air that rose from the rock. His grin blossomed into a delighted laugh. The eyes seared through his thoughts, a thousand times more insistent. A wicked scar scored one, turning the edges of the iris a sickly white.

When will you stop playing and come find us?

Who are you? Arman pushed away, peering at the figure. It was a Rakos, all yellow hair and golden skin. *Where are you?*

I'm Eana. I thought I was the last. The grin was wicked and not playful in the least. *You'd find us if you bothered to look.* The familiar litany of a single word began. *Fear. Fear.* The man lunged and Arman gasped, dragging himself out of the tangle of someone else's thoughts. The distraction broke his hold and his body became abruptly solid. With a startled shout nothing like the war cry from a moment ago, he crashed to the ground.

He groaned, rolling over onto his hands and knees. His body was bruised, but nothing felt broken. His skin itched uncontrollably, as it often did after he used his power, but nothing could dampen his excitement. Even his pride was too astounded to be wounded. The Rakos ruled the skies, and now he knew how.

Φ

The 29th Day of Lineme, 1252

"Deal you in?" Sousa's invitation arched across the bar's common room upon Arman's arrival.

Arman snorted. "I'm rubbish at cards, I think we've discovered." He jerked his head toward the bar. "I still owe you." He ordered a round of whatever his friends had already begun to drink and meandered back to their table. Kal shimmied over on the bench to make room as Arman plopped down beside him.

Arman crossed his boots on the table and leaned back with a sigh. His spirits were high and his heart still raced from his earlier discovery.

"Arman, you got dirt and stone all over your boots." Sousa complained, making a shooing motion at the offending attire. "What did you do, wrestle a bear? Witt said you were out in the woods today."

Arman grinned. "I was practicing, testing some things I read about the Rakos." He rarely spoke about the less-than-human side of his blood, and hated the way it made his friends eye him sideways. Still, his mood was too good to be spoiled by a wary look.

Sousa's expression faltered and the grin he hastily pulled onto his face looked forced. The moment was broken by the delivery of their drinks. Arman gulped down most of his first mug, his mind scrambling for a change in subject.

Before Arman could pick a new topic, Kal glanced over with tempered curiosity. "Did you always know what you were?"

"No, I learned it several weeks after meeting milady." He shrugged. "I'll tell you true, though, it explained some things."

Sousa grinned, his change in mood indicating he had imbibed a fair amount already. "Why you had fangs, like?"

Arman whacked the man on the shoulder. "Idiot, I didn't have those my whole childhood."

"So you bound yourself to this all-powerful creature without knowing what you were? Not knowing if you stood a chance in the war?"

Arman stared into the swirling of his drink, absently telling himself that the drink was in fact swirling, not just his head. "I knew my blood when I bound myself to her. I didn't understand all the consequences though. If you saw her like I see her you'd not question it though."

"I think the same about my woman." Kal's eyes were distant and suddenly sage-like. "So the Rakos blood goes back in your family?"

Arman's response was interrupted by a bitter voice.

"Nah, his Ma bedded one damned ugly stranger when his Pa looked the other way. It's how the thieves of his city are – rut with anyone who looks twice."

Arman's gaze narrowed on the broad shape of Hasian standing over them. He straightened himself on the bench and extracted his arm from Sousa's grip before rising.

"Going to shoo me off again? Words do not scare me, little man. Yer just a corpse forgot he was dead." The smell of stale ale rolled off Hasian 's tongue on the tail of his words.

A month ago Arman would have noted it and backed down from a foolish fight. A month ago he would have laughed the stupidity away. Instead, his blood roiled through his veins. Heat raced through his body, rising faster than ever. His retort bubbled into a growl.

"Forget it, Arman. It's like talking to a wall." Kal tugged at Arman's arm. "We'll just leave."

"You can't fight when your lady's away? What's she doing, anyways? Bedding her way across the country? How else would she get any of us to fight for her? Narier said she's not much in the way of looks, but she's a warm place to stick it."

Sousa groaned, hiding his head in his hands. Heat flamed across Arman's face, turning his eyes yellow. He dropped his shoulder and tackled the larger soldier with a roar. A table crashed against the wall, ale slicking the floor. The two men grappled, no one willing to attempt to pull them apart. Arman's head came up for a moment, blood staining his face.

"Damn, he'll kill him!" Sousa shouted, finally reaching for his friend.

Kal shook his head and held Sousa back. "He'll kill you, too."

Arman heard nothing but the pounding of blood in his ears and the screaming of fire in his veins. His vision blurred, everything tinged gold. His hands glowed like white beacons to his eyes. The yield of flesh and bone under his fists was satisfying, and the resulting blood warm between his burning fingers. It tasted salty and sweet. Abruptly he no longer felt any blows. The roar of a landslide in his mind faded as the common room fell silent. He drew back, breath coming in heaving gasps. Blinking rapidly, he cleared his vision.

Hasian lay unconscious at his feet, bruises already coloring his face. A ragged wound marred his shoulder, bone stark against the dark blood and ale staining the floor. Arman shook the remaining haze from his eyes and turned to find Sousa and Kal. Their expressions were horrified. Sousa swallowed hard before pointing to the door.

Arman shouldered his way through the silent bar. No one tried to stop him. His friends followed him out. Once they were all in the street and the door shut behind them, he turned. "Why didn't you pull us apart?"

"You looked like a mad man, Arman."

Arman ordered his thoughts, each one scorching his mind. Adrenaline and rage were a seething ocean threatening to drown him. "Did I draw a knife? Take his? There was a wound on his shoulder."

Kal pointedly wiped his mouth, obviously meaning for Arman to do the same.

Arman reached up to feel his face. It was covered in blood and pieces of flesh. It was not his own. "Toar!" He turned his back, spitting repeatedly into the gutter. "Damned disgusting!"

Sousa looked down, making no argument. "Do you want us to walk you back? Hasian has few friends, but after that, people will come looking."

Arman backed away. "Don't think I can handle myself? Dead man in there says otherwise." His sentences were fragmented, stumbling over the disgust and rage thickening his throat. He would regret the angry dismissal, and the bloody fight, but that would be later. Now his skin itched and company was the last thing he wanted. He hunched his shoulders and strode down a darkened alley. He took a meandering route back to the palace, keeping to deserted streets. Heat radiated from his body, burning the blood from his skin with a sickly sweet smell. He was sane enough to be concerned, sane enough to be terrified. The lantern light in the general's window caught his eye as he approached the palace. He recalled her offer: *Should you want any more advice or clarity, I am here.*

A pregnant pause followed his loud knocking, then a chair scraped along the floor. Eras jerked the door open and peered into the hall. Her gaze inched over the blood-drenched man, but her expression remained unreadable. "What happened?"

"I don't know. May I come in?"

She stepped aside and pointed to a chair in front of her desk. She disappeared into the room beyond, returning with a wash basin and towel. "It's cold, but I suspect you won't mind."

Neither spoke while Arman cleaned the worst of the blood from his face and hands. He sat back when he had finished.

"That's not yours, is it?" Her tone was hard enough for the words to not actually be asking.

"I attacked a man tonight. He was drunk. So was I, until the fight sobered me."

She sat on the edge of the desk before him, arms crossed. "Why?"

"He slandered my mother and milady."

"Then I suspect he deserved it. You've been in brawls before, I assume. But you are not here because you fought your first fight. You were at Shadow, so you're not here because you killed your first man." She paused, her eyes narrowing. "Did you kill him?"

"Yes. I don't know. He wasn't moving." He looked down at his hands. They should have been shaking. "I beat him senseless, tore into him with my hands and teeth."

"Your vision blurred. You neither heard your comrades telling you to lay off, nor felt the blows inflicted upon you."

He was too tired to be embarrassed by the relief on his face. "This is normal?"

"It happens to soldiers to a lesser degree. It's a form of battle shock. What happened to you, though, is not normal. Not for a human man. Not for someone with a little bit of different blood in their veins, like me." She tilted her head at him, as if examining a curiosity. "You're not just a Rakos, are you?"

Arman ran a hand through his hair, wincing as it caught in snarls of matted blood. "I've read about the Rakos, general. There is mention of a change, something that makes regular guards more powerful, able to create the monsters I showed you. I am nothing like either. I'm a shadow of what the Rakos used to be." His elation at turning himself to floating smoke was gone, erased by dread and shame. "That book you gave me, it sounds like it was penned by

An'thoriend. I was raised on his tales, and we met him twice. If he wrote this, he could have seen what I was. That proves that I'm nothing but a freak."

Eras shrugged. "An'thor is a dear friend, but not always present." She fixed Arman with her level stare. "There are some Rakos that were older, stronger, and they had a name. They were called Earth Shakers."

"Those are the monsters, the things the Rakos created."

Eras's expression softened. "No, Arman, they didn't create them. They became them."

Arman stared out the window thoughtfully. "General, could the Earth Shakers fly?"

Her brows twitched upward. "Why, can you?" When he did not answer, she sighed. "Lady Lyne'alea is unlike anything this world has seen. I wouldn't be surprised if she woke far more than the Rakos in your blood." She offered him a faint, sad smile. "One more thing for you to study."

Arman barked a laugh, the sound foreign in a throat raw from snarling. "If I didn't know better, I'd think you enjoyed tormenting me."

"Someone has to. You need guidance, Arman, and tonight only proves that. Everyone is too worried of what Lyne'alea's power would do if unchecked. I worry just as much about yours."

"Well, with a name like Earth Shaker, it's a small wonder." He looked down at his boots. "If I killed him, what will happen? There were enough people in that bar to know it was me. There's no running."

"I think given the circumstances, it will be all right, but be ready. I'll ask around and let you know in the morning."

He nodded and finished his drink. After a moment he looked up. "Do you think I'll ever go back to being simply Arman?"

"I can't say, but I'd imagine it would be difficult." She poured him a glass of water from a pitcher. "The road back home is often long and harder than we remember. Why do you ask?"

"After this, how would I go back to being a smith? An innkeeper's son? To being Veredy's husband? I'm not sure I want to, and that terrifies me."

Eras coughed on her own drink. "You were married? I must have seriously misread your relationship with Lady Lyne'alea."

"Not exactly. I was ready to ask my girl to wed. I was mid-speech when Alea discovered she was the Dhoah' Laen and started screaming in my mind. Awkward, that. I think Veredy misread things, same as you."

Eras leaned back. "Would I be prying to ask if things have changed?"

Arman laughed. "Perhaps, but I know as little as you. I thought we were friends for a long time. Now I'm not sure. Milady is complicated on the best of days." He finished his drink and rose. "Thank you, for talking."

Eras did not look up and her voice was soft. "If you care for my advice, I'll say that war changes people in unexpected ways. Times like these, even the hardest hearts break. Comfort never hurts."

Arman paused in the doorframe. "What about your hardened heart?" It was something he had not considered before. "Do you have comfort?"

"Now Earth Shaker, that is prying."

He answered her grin with one of his own and ducked out of her room. Her words had calmed his racing thoughts somewhat, but his body still stormed with confusion and adrenaline. The heat marched up his skin, leaving annoying prickles in its wake. He locked his bedroom door and rang for water to be pumped into his bath. He stripped down, grateful that a network of pipes averted the need for servants to bring water personally. The solitude suited his thoughts, and it would further damage his reputation to be seen covered in someone else's blood.

He scratched absently as he waited for the tub to fill. The skin of his shoulders flaked away, coating his fingers with metallic gold-white flakes. He frowned and backed up to the privy mirror to get a better look. His skin peeled back from the hard plates emerging from his shoulders. His heart pounded in his ears. *Scales.*

Φ

The 30th Day of Lineme, 1252
The Isle of Le'yne

The music was no tune she recognized. Athrolan's ball room was decorated for a celebration, though the room itself was deserted. It was spring. Her black dress was Athrolani, but the layers were Sunamen. A circlet of leaves held back her hair. Warmth blossomed on her back and she turned. Arman's boots were silent on the stone. He was dressed in white, his tunic stitched with gold. He smiled broadly and he offered her his hand.

"I thought you didn't dance."

"You've heard the tales – everyone dances at the end."

She whirled about with him, the music sounding like laughter in her ears. A breeze lifted her hair. The ballroom was gone and they were surrounding by ancient trees. Their clothes were simple now and their feet bare. What she could see of her hair was laced in silver.

Lines surrounded Arman's eyes – lines from years of laughing. "What do you want?"

The ballroom reformed and he was the youthful man she remembered again. "Is it this?"

She shook her head, heart pounding. "I want peace."

His expression melted into one of sorrow, his cheeks hollowing as his body aged, died, decomposed before her eyes. Still, he spoke, through broken teeth and desiccated lips. "Alea, people like you can't have peace."

She burst awake, the room cloying is its stillness. She needed air. She scrambled from her sheets and across her room, leaning out the window. Deep breaths of the cold air calmed her nerves and her heart steadied. She palmed her eyes against tears. *What was that?*

She pushed herself through her soulblood, using her confusion as an amplifier for her power. She reached out to Athrolan, raging in desperation. She found Arman easily. His soul's colors were brighter, almost blinding. He was in the slums and she moved closer until her mind walked beside him. A few soldiers were with him, joking with one another.

"Come on, Sousa – I doubt that tailor will appreciate you watering his storefront." Arman turned to the straggler standing at the corner of a building.

Alea gasped. His face was inches from hers. Heat rolled from his skin.

He frowned, reaching out. His hand hovered by her cheek and she leaned her head into his touch. His palm passed through her and her heart ached.

I'm here, Arman. I'm right here. Fates, look at me! Hear me!

Arman shook himself and turned back to his friends.

Dammit, Arman! I need you! She fell to her knees as he walked away, a new frown wiping the mirth from his face. She faded back into her body in Le'yne. Her tears returned. It was not practice that she lacked. Something about him was different.

She frowned. She used her power each time she reached out to Bren or Arman. Despite the command to not practice her power, she had, and done so with complete control. She had brought Arman back and it had not destroyed the Athrolani camp. Her eyes were wide in the dark. *When it stays in my body, I am in control.* Her heart hammered with excitement.

She jerked the door open to find Elle in the hall, hand raised to knock.

Elle blinked, startled. "Yes?"

"I realized something. Why were you knocking?"

Elle shook her head at the offered seat. "Elai decided." Her voice tightened. "They plan to bind you."

Alea frowned. She did not know the term, but foreboding crept up her spine. "Tell them not to – I found a way to control my power, just now, that's what I wanted to see you about."

"They won't believe you."

"What's a binding?"

"A mental cauterization. A permanent separation of your power from your soulblood."

Nausea rolled in Alea's stomach. She began to pace. "They want to cripple me. They cripple me and the gods will win." The whirling and planning and panic were familiar. Comfort dissolved into danger, into the drive to fight or flee. This was the road all over again. *Except, now it's not the Miriken who want you destroyed, it's the Laen.* "I may be a monster, but only monsters kill gods, right?" She glanced up at Elle, her eyes burning.

Elle nodded an answer to the unasked question. "Ready yourself. Read as much as you can, center your mind. They will do it at sundown. I'll help you run before then." Her hands trembled and she grabbed Alea's hand, the first contact they had ever made.

Alea looked down at their hands. "How do you know they're wrong?"

"You destroyed our wall and carved your symbol into the largest stone. That is an obvious statement. I think you were wrong that your power does what it wants. It is your will at its purest state. The connection between your will, your mind, and your power is where your greatness lies."

Alea turned and began to pack. "What time is it?"

"Not yet midnight."

"Go, before they figure this out. I'll see you in the morning." When Elle had gone, Alea sat, eyes vacant. An hour passed. When every light in the village was dark, she rose and crept out of the house. Her bare feet burnt with cold as she padded across the gravel and down to the library. The door opened with a soft creak. *Whatever I'm looking for will be old, older than writing, older than thought.* She walked along the shelves until she found the wax and clay tablets. Her eyes scanned the frames fruitlessly.

"You'll not find it, my lady." Mera stood in the rear doorway, her robe loose over her nightdress.

"I don't even know what I'm looking for."

"You want to discover what you are - beyond Creation and Destruction."

"Is there an answer?"

Mera shrugged. "There is always an answer. You are asking whether it lies here or not." She turned and stepped into the small room at the back. "Come here."

Alea followed. The room was tidy. A long desk looked out over the ocean and flashing sky. A stack of blank tomes sat on one side, full ones on the other. "You record?"

"And re-write, if the scrolls are crumbling. There is so much knowledge to be saved." She drew the full tomes towards her. "The first Laen were good about recording. They had a strong connection to the balance that our power stems from. Granted, they all used a single, combined source, as opposed to the finite spring within each of us now. They were like you, in that way. The energy of the world was represented by the three races - the Laen of balance, the gods of knowledge and the Rakos of chaos."

"Where did they all come from?"

"I couldn't say. Many think it was lightning - it is still the only thing that can destroy our power along with our bodies."

Alea winced. "That is how they killed Lynelle."

"They channeled the power of all the gods through the god of lightning, Lord of Storms." She waved the thoughts away. "Enough." She patted the cover of a heavy tome. "The Laen predicted events based on shifts in the world's energy, like a sailor predicting the sea. The world had its own balance, one with greater dips and crests than our power. A huge dip predicted the Division, though they did not know what it would actually be until too late. A swell and an instability predicted you." She handed Alea the tome. "In here there is the war, its outcome and what comes afterward. There are no interpretations, for that is not what we do. That is for you to decide."

Alea regarded the book. "They don't want me to see this?"

"They do not know it exists." Mera rose and stretched. "I leave my study unlocked and goodness knows you must have trouble sleeping."

Alea laughed softly at the fabricated story. She glanced down at the book in her lap, running a hand over its cover.

Mera paused at the door. "Once you know something, you cannot unknow it. I give this to you because you need to know, but I am sorry."

Alea was left alone with her thoughts and a book that grew heavier on her lap. With determined fingers she opened it on the desk before her. At first she did not know what she was looking at. There was a horizontal line across the page with peaks and dips, some more severe than others and some barely a twitch of a scribe's hand. It looked like the charts her ihal's accountant made of profits over years. She peered closer, realizing it was similar, but it mapped power. She had expected something more convoluted, dry paragraphs perhaps. She traced the line with her finger, reading the captions beneath significant changes that had already occurred.

Towards the end she found a ragged dip that continued on for pages. The sight made her heart ache. *The Division of the world.* The corresponding crest on the opposite page made her pause for a moment. It was not as great as the Division, but it was larger than she expected. She had known her power was great, but seeing it stark and obvious was uncomfortable. A rough, ceaselessly changing line followed and Alea's stomach clenched. *Chaos. The war ends in chaos. We lose.* Heart in her throat, she turned the last page. There was another crest, three times the size of her own, larger even than the Division's fall. It trailed off into the binding of the book.

Energy flooded her body and she stared, unseeing at the ocean beyond the window. It was almost dawn. *Whatever happens in the war, there is an after. I might lose to the gods, I might win, but what comes after is more powerful than I could ever hope to be.* Her lips curled in a feral grin and she closed the book.

CHAPTER SEVEN

The 30th Day of Lineme, 1252
The City of Mirik

TWO DOZEN PAIRS OF EYES stared at Bren. It was something he would have to grow accustomed to, he supposed. The older and more influential of the Kit crowded into what looked like a common room. The smell of ale and dead rats confirmed Bren's suspicion that it was once a tavern. The faces before him were ruddy and worn, but fire burnt behind their eyes. He grinned. It was as if he looked into a broken mirror to see a hundred reflections of himself.

"I suppose you're curious. Arik said you were willing to hear me out, and I hope he's right. I gave him a passage to read, from this book." He held up *Rauld.* "It talks of an oligarchy—a government of a few men, rather than one king. They answer to many ministers who represent factions of the people. I imagine it's much how you rule yourselves now."

He had their attention, but he needed more than passing interest. "For a monarchy, it's dangerous stuff. For me, it's the brick for a foundation. For you, I hope it's an answer. Arik tells me I'd have your support should I wish to claim the crown. I'm asking you to join me in governing ourselves. I am a soldier, a military officer. I understand times of war. I would accept the role of acting king as head of the Miriken military. After the war I would step down to rule alongside others. Rauld calls these men Premiers, but that sounds daft to me."

"And why is this better than being ruled by Athrolan?"

Bren peered into the crowd. The lanterns at his feet blinded him to the farthest rows. "Tzatia is not Miriken. She is full of rolling fields and white stone. She does not have the green at her back. She has never stood on the red cliffs and looked out over the open ocean. Call me poetic, but we need someone who knows what we are."

"Why won't you take her up?" This time it was Arik who asked.

Bren met his eyes. Whether the question was curiosity or accusation, he could not say. "Azirik killed this city with the crown on his head. He burnt the soul out of the world with another. Perhaps it's time that we go without one." He glanced from face to face. He did not see smiles, but he saw relief. He had their hearts. "Arik, how many are in Talic, across the island?"

"Three score, ruled by the governor's nephew."

"Send word to them, and to those in the green, call our people home."

A young woman leaned forward. She dressed like a hunter. "Who should we say calls them, then?"

"Say their Military Commissioner is acting king, and he needs them." He knew his hands shook, knew his voice was low, and there were no rafters from which it could ring. A king might need steady hands, a booming speech. He smiled. He was not a king. He was Miriken, and he was home.

Φ

The Isle of Le'yne

Alea stood on the steps of Le'yne's deserted hall. An hour separated her from the dim light that passed for dawn. Alea brushed a hand over the wood of the door. *Elle said we would not enter here until after the war.* Nightly wanderings in places she was not allowed was a childish habit, but persistent. *War is already here, even if they cannot hear the clashing.*

She pushed the door open, surprised when it was not locked. The Laen did not need to hide things from one another, only from her. The air within the hall was still, but not stale. The exterior was plain. *What were you expecting – they dress in gray.* The single elaborate piece was the black wooden door at the opposite end of the hall. Silver and iron spirals inlaid the wood. Some had been treated to look iridescently blue, like a beetle's wings. The design was too regular to be decorative, but too asymmetrical to be artwork. *A language, then.* What it said was lost on Alea, but she recognized the emblem in the center. It was a silver handprint. It was not inlaid metal, rather it had been burnt into the wood. Her fingers shook as she laid her own hand over the mark.

Nothing happened. She let out a wry laugh. She shook away the thought of saying the words around the door. That was too theatrical for the Laen. They focused on directness and a single path. A grin blossomed on her face and her power curled from her hand. It did not sweep across the door's surface. Instead she forced each piece to follow the metal symbols. Sweat beaded across her brow and shoulders.

The click of the lock was soft and the door swung open. The stairwell beyond was dark, but the steps were smooth and broad. Alea's bare soles whispered on the stone as she descended. Something tugged her memory, but she could not place it. Was it the smell of the air? She stumbled when the stairs ended abruptly. It had taken many minutes, long enough that Alea guessed she was at the base of the cliffs. A gust of wind hit her as she stepped through the doorway into blinding light. It smelled of salt and burnt skin.

The pulsing sphere of souls looked different than before. To her physical eyes, without her power, they were blinding, the colors lost in brightness. The black wound across the surface was knit with blue, bruise-colored lines radiating outward like gangrene. She did not regret her choice to bring Arman back. There was guilt there, surely, but it was not for what she had done to the bleeding souls hanging before her now. For them, she only had disdain.

"Why?" Behind her Elle's voice was low, tinged with as much morbid curiosity as fear.

"Why did I do this?" Alea did not look away, merely turned her head to speak over her shoulder.

"Why did you do it for him? Protection?"

"Bren could have protected me. I can protect myself. I thought it was to repay my part in Arman's death. That's true, in part, but not my reason." Her eyes narrowed on the black, oozing wound. Selfishness marred the heroism and further darkened the terror of her actions. "I brought him back because I cannot fight this battle without him." It was not the full truth, but it was as close as she dared.

"But why did you leave them like this?"

"What is this place?"

Elle paused, but seemed to see that Alea was only taking a meandering route to her answer, not avoiding the question. "Before the Division this is where we created the Laen. A birthing chamber, if you will. Lynelle trapped the power of the gods' souls here so they might not access it."

"She trapped your power, too. As long as the gods' souls are bound here, the power of the Laen is trapped. Each of you dies and adds to the cage, but that power is gone, caught here." Alea paused. "I ripped them open because you'll need that power."

"The gods will gain power as well."

Alea shrugged. *Whether I win or lose, there will be an after.* "Then I'll handle them."

Elle shuddered. "You said you found a way to control yourself?"

"Every time I lost control it was because my power left my body. When I was attacked in Vielrona it came on its own, killing those men. In the tower when

I was captured, it destroyed enemy and ally alike. It ripped all of Arman's knives away from him."

"All his knives? He has many?"

"He has a bandolier of them." Alea frowned at the tangent. "But I took them from him and the distraction caused his death. When I work through it, as if it is a glove over my mind, within my body, then I am in control." Her voice grew soft. "I was going to show you, today." She sighed and rose from her kneeling. "It is almost dawn."

Elle followed her back up the stairs in silence, their footsteps comfort enough. The white light of dawn streamed through the hall's open door. It was just warm enough to burn mist from the dew-drenched steps. Alea stopped at the top, looking down at the crowd of Laen who had gathered there. "Good morning." Alea met Elai's eyes. In the back of her mind, the shadow rose. It built, creeping through her thoughts.

"Lyne'alea, what are you doing here?" Elai's face was calm, her eyes almost compassionate. It made it difficult to hate her, and Alea realized she should not, actually, hate the woman.

"I was curious." The road between hate and respect, however, was a long one. "You've come to bind me?"

Behind her, Elle sucked in a sharp breath. "Lyne'alea."

She ignored her mother, eyes narrowing on Elai. *She believes violating my soul is what's best.* "Well?"

"You are dangerous, Lyne'alea. The sooner we mend you, the sooner you can recover and begin to learn properly."

Alea scoffed. "You want to know why I am here, standing on these stairs, unsurprised by this misunderstanding, this betrayal? Beneath our feet is a ball of battered, bleeding souls. Souls Lynelle trapped there in her desperate attempt to save you. She had little time so she panicked. I'm here to remedy what she has done. Beneath our feet there lies an answer, a fact, a task that only I can complete. And yet you wish to cripple me."

"You must not use your emotions as a conduit. They are unpredictable. Your mother only felt the barest emotions for your father, and look at the mess it created."

Alea felt the tense grimace on her face melt into a manic smile. "Exactly! Look at the mess! She bore a powerful son who defied Azirik himself and a daughter that can defeat gods and bind the world together. That's a damn foul mess! I can control my power and I'll die before I let one more person play gods with my life. I am Creation and Destruction." The shadow stalked forward, blotting out every last bit of serenity from the past few hours.

She stepped down from the hall, her grin broadening as the Laen back away. Hands raised, her icy power hit the sky. "I am the Dhoah' Laen. You cannot separate one from the other." She ripped the lightning from the sky, pulling it into herself until she glowed through the black tendrils that writhed across her skin. The energy tingled, sizzled along her nerves. The lightning radiated from her, sparking off stones and buildings and scorching the grass beneath her. "You will not bind me. I am the Dhoah' Laen. *This is not a piece of me*!"

With the final sentence, she let the lightning crackle back through her body and into the clouds. The black curls retreated from her skin and the glow faded from her eyes. Power retreated until she once more looked like herself. She would never be simply Alea again. She read raw terror on the faces before her. Underneath the fear, however, was respect, and utter faith. "If you plan on fighting the gods, ready yourselves, because I am going to war."

Without another word she climbed towards the hills, the Laen parting like waves before the prow of a ship. Elle caught up with her at the slate slab. Alea looked over. "I'm sorry for what I did, but there was no choice."

Elle reached out, tucking a loose strand of hair behind Alea's ear. "They will thank you one day."

Alea laughed humorlessly. "Then you and I have different ideas of how this will end."

"They will need time to prepare."

"They have it. There are a few things I'll need to do before I confront the gods. Thankfully there is only their Crown left." Her battered fingers rubbed one temple absently.

Elle winced. "I'm afraid not. We had ours decades ago—centuries even—but it wound up in Claimiirn. The story of how that happened changes with each telling I'm afraid."

"Claimiirn?" Alea frowned. *Where have I heard that name before?* She remembered a different voice, gravelly with fatigue and lilting over the double "i" like a brook over stones in spring. "That's the old Athrolani capital, correct? I thought it fell before the House of Xain rose to power."

"It did. An'thoriend's brother sacked the place. Said it did no good having men so close to their lands. Not a pleasant man, Edrodene."

"You're telling me no one has bothered to find the damn thing before now?" She shook her head. "When I'm done, I'll find it myself."

Elle's eyes sparkled. "Seems the only way to get anything done with us, eh?"

Alea paused, looking up at her mother a moment. There was a tone there that she had not heard before. There was a fire, a rebellious edge that she recognized from her own rants to the Laen. She grinned abruptly, a real grin that would have fit better on her face a year ago. "Thank you."

"Stay safe—you and Brentemir."

Alea looked down. "Remember this day. Remember the faith you have right now." She stepped back on the stone slab and met Elle's eyes. "Soon it will be sorely tested." The air crackled as it swallowed her whole.

The Cold and Quiet Ache of Duty

CHAPTER EIGHT

The 31st Day of Lineme, 1252
The City of Mirik

ODDLY, MEETING WITH HELONIN seemed less important to Bren. He rapped on the mariner's doorframe, peering into the room. Helonin regarded his tea dispassionately. "Enter."

Bren stepped in and gestured to the chair across the desk. "Good morning, sir. Might I sit?"

"Ah, Barrackborn. Of course." He sat back, fixing Bren with a frown. "I thought you were going with the men to work on the temple district."

"That is why I came to talk to you, actually. No further work is to be done on the palace. I will need access to the treasury documents as well as its funds."

"Excuse me?" The frown turned into anger and impatience.

Bren knew Helonin had little opinion of him. To the mariner, Bren was only a hard worker and occasionally insubordinate. The latter scarcely applied when Bren's true superiors were the enemy.

"What grounds do you have to halt building? This is Her Majesty's outpost. Barring her word—"

"With all due respect, sir, Mirik is my home, not an outpost." He rested a hand on the desk, allowing the signet ring to knock against the wood. "The word of her acting king should suffice." It was barely an admittance, but when he met the mariner's eyes, he saw it was enough.

Helonin's expression softened. Puzzlement furrowed his brow now. "You said 'acting' king. Care to explain?"

"I am Mirik's Military Commissioner. Given this is a time of war, I am acting king until the threat passes, at which time I will rule with equal power as the other Lord Commissioners."

"And they are?"

"When we've determined that, I'll be sure to let you know." Bren grinned wearily.

Helonin laughed, shaking his head. "I do not envy you. What more do you need of me, my lord?"

"I'll take passage on a ship to Athrolan next week. I think Her Majesty will want an explanation in person."

"Wise man. Perhaps this little land is not doomed after all. I'll have the treasury documents sent to your room, and I'll draw up the orders to cease work." He tossed a heavy bag onto the desk from a drawer. "This is what we've been using for the work, and comes from your funds." After a moment he met Bren's eyes and held out his arm. "I wish you luck, my lord. You will need it."

Bren ducked out of the man's office, lightheaded as the knots in his stomach unraveled. He was halfway to the bell tower when the squire burst from the woods. The boy almost tripped in his haste as he dashed into the courtyard. Bren's eyes narrowed. He watched the boy pant out his message to Helonin, who pointed to the tower.

Bren turned back, reaching the open area by the harbor at the same time as the boy and raised a hand. "What is it?"

"She's back, sir."

Bren's eyes widened and he glanced at the woods. He did not need to ask which woman was in question. "When?" His heart pounded.

"She'll be here in an hour. Kit from the green sent word."

By the time the words were out of the boy's mouth, Bren was already running. He called a hasty thanks over his shoulder as he bolted toward the trees. *She's home. She's back.* How much his world had changed in just a year would always amaze him. He reached the hill after half an hour of steady jogging. The old muscles that knew how to march for days were slow to wake, but they remembered their task well.

He finally caught sight of her as he crested the hill. He had thought he would embrace her, laugh his relief for her return, babble about the change of his role and Mirik's future. Instead he stopped. The damp loam was quiet under his heavy boots. She was not the person who left a few months ago. She had been a girl, excited and impatient and angry. He barely recognized that girl's features in this woman's face. "Alea?"

She glanced up, a smile lighting her tired eyes. "Bren."

"You're home." He did not even dare to shift weight from one foot to another.

"I'm home." The ache and darkness in her eyes was fathomless. She swallowed slowly, as if past the lump of everything she had yet to do. "I missed you."

"I missed you too. Somewhere along the path we became siblings, it seems."

She broke into a run and collided with him. Her arms wrapped tightly around his body. "I missed a lot."

He held her for several minutes, chin resting on the top of her head. Cold control radiated from her, drawing gooseflesh from his skin. *She's done it.* "War, then?"

"War."

"Come on. Let's get you settled." He pulled away and moved down the path toward Mirik.

She laughed. "I'm certainly not attacking the gods on an empty stomach." She fell into step beside him. "How fairs Mirik? Last I heard you were upset with the queen's treatment of her."

Bren grinned. "A lot has changed, sistermine. I couldn't face Mirik falling any further, but neither could I really accept the role of king. I'm a fair reader, and one of the more interesting tomes I encountered is called *Rauld's Tales for an Officer.* He had a great mind for strategy, and after retiring from the army, became a philosopher. Do you know of him?"

Alea nodded. "He wrote *To Give the Poor Man a Crown.* It was an essay my foster-father loved."

"I don't know of that one, but I'll have to find a copy. He developed a proposal for a government without a king, ruled by a few men."

"An oligarchy."

He glanced at her curiously. "You are better versed in government than I expected."

She shrugged. "I enjoyed it more than history." She grinned suddenly, and he saw more of Azirik in her than before. "Shall I guess? You've made Mirik's government into one."

"I did." The initial numbness had faded into both terror and excitement. He turned them onto the worn cobbled road that led down to the city and barracks. "For now, I am acting king. This is a time of war, and I am the current Military Commissioner. Perhaps, when things have settled, I will step down."

"No you won't."

He glanced at her sharply. "What do you mean?"

"They love you. You may not be king, but doing away with the crown does not erase the feeling that you are their monarch." She squeezed his hand as they approached the barracks' gate. "But what you have done, I think, will be greater than any harm Azirik caused."

Bren snorted. "Your optimism is frustrating."

"Why, because you think we'll all die?"

"No, because you have faith in people, and I can't see why. Yet, half the time, you're right." He paused at the gate, catching sight of Helonin waiting. "Alea, this is—"

Alea brushed aside the introduction and stepped forward. "I am Dhoah' Lyne'alea."

The mariner bowed over her hand. "Welcome. I am Mariner Helonin. I can prepare a room for you. Will you be staying long?"

"I'm afraid not. A room would be lovely, but please excuse me, there are things I must discuss." She offered him a fleeting nod and moved past. Stunned silence filled her wake.

Bren's incredulous laugh bubbled free when they entered the hall to his room. "You just dismissed a mariner of Athrolan's navy. Without a thought. What, by Toar, did they teach you in Le'yne?" He unlocked his room quickly, letting her in before closing the door.

A smile flickered over her mouth. "Little, other than history, and exactly how impatient I can be. Their choices forced me to learn much, even if it was not the intention." She sank onto his bed with a sigh. "I've rested little, but I'm too full of adrenaline to sleep."

Bren leaned back in his chair, frowning. "Did you argue? I didn't expect you back yet."

"Our opinions differed." She picked at the skin around her fingers, luminous eyes narrowed. "They thought my power should be split from my soulblood."

Bren scoffed. "See, I knew I disliked them for a reason." He adopted a high-pitched voice. "There is a chance we could win. Let's make a mess of it!"

Alea smiled at the mimic. "They're single-visioned, that's all. I had to resort to fear to make them listen, which was unpleasant." She glanced out the window. "Have you gone to Athrolan to talk to Her Majesty about your new government?"

"No. I have yet to even write her."

Alea's brows rose. "You've dismantled her control and reformed Mirik's government without even notifying her? Surely Helonin said something."

"He didn't know until today." He drew the letter Tzatia had sent and tossed it to his sister. "This is what forced my hand. She called me out."

Alea scanned the letter. "Perhaps when I go to Athrolan you could join me, do some of your reforming there."

Bren nodded. "I was thinking of it, but I want to meet her from a point of strength, and I'm not sure I have it yet."

"Will you ever think you do?" Alea smiled at him. "For one so capable, brothermine, you have little confidence." She masked a yawn and rose. "As much as I said I couldn't sleep, I've had quite the few days and ought to at least try. Who knows when our next respite will come?"

He led her further down the hall to the finer rooms. Sure enough, one of the doors was propped open, the bed inside neatly made and a pitcher of fresh water waiting on the nightstand. Alea turned back to him. "I'm glad to be home."

He embraced her again, the tingle of power crawling up his arms from where they touched. "I'm glad you're back. Rest well. I might be working or in the mess when you wake, but the men will know where to find me."

Once she bid him a quick goodnight and closed the door, he returned to his room. A new letter waited on his desk. There was no sender's name on the envelope, only his new title and full name. He unfolded it curiously.

> *Barrackborn,*
>
> *Much has changed since I last spoke with you – for us both, it seems. I heard you speak the other day, in the Kit's hall. Quite the pair you've got, reforming Azirik's government while he still wears the crown. You're a better man than I expected.*
>
> *I hoped that sometime this evening we might speak. Send a response via Oland. He knows where to find me.*
>
> *Until then,*
>
> *An'thoriend Domariigo*

Bren stared at the letter for a moment then burst out laughing. *Alea's home, I'm acting king, Arman is developing power, and now the legend himself crawls from hiding.* He shook his head and rose to find some ale. Writing a response needed drink as much as their cause needed legends. *It's only fitting heroes emerge before battle. Toar knows we'll need them before the end.*

Φ

The 31st Day of Lineme, 1252
The City of Ceir Athrolan

Arman had yet to leave his room during normal hours. Late in the evening he escaped to the library, when he was certain Kal and Sousa were safely in a bar. Hasian had lived, though it was a week before the man could return to his soldier's duties. He could only see shadows through his left eye and his shoulder was too greatly injurred for him to lift his arm higher than his chest. Arman had yet to hear from the queen or the general about any consequences, but he was smart enough to know he was far from safe.

Most assumed it was shame that kept him closeted in his room. He let them assume. His anger had not subsided. For a week it raged, his skin slowly peeling back to expose the marble-like plates. He paced his room now, eyes flicking from the window to his desk, to the door. A small stack of papers sat on the desk, but he was in little mood to read missives. Spotting a stained envelope, he tugged it free. Bren's greeting was as carefree as ever.

Arman,

I miss the taverns already, though my head does not miss the morning ale-sick. I hope your studies are going well. I feel like we've been holding our breath and are about to dive. Maybe I'm just tired of waiting. I'm a soldier, not a mason.

It's good that Alea's learning more, even if she feels it's not what she should be studying.

Arman frowned at that, and peered closer to the letter.

This waiting business is certainly helped by hearing from her every so often, even if her mind connections are faint and the conversations short. I suppose she talks to you more than me. Has she said anything about coming home?

Until then,

Bren

Arman's fist clenched until the paper crumpled. He did not notice the edges smoldering in his hand until the black ashes drifted to the ground. *She goes to him and not me?* It was not that she spoke to Bren. The prejudice toward one another was all but gone. It was the fact that she confided in someone else. *Who protected her?* Anger welled in him. *Who died for her?* His breath shuddered. He had never been this angry. He grabbed his cloak and strode out of the palace before he destroyed something. *You think you can run off and leave me, without a word, and expect me to forget you?*

His steps were certain on the cobbled street leading to the loudest bar the soldiers frequented. Kal and Sousa were among the crowd at the back. He averted his eyes and found a secluded seat. He did not want conversation. He wanted to forget. A distant voice reminded him that it was not really Alea that angered him, but his own cowardice. He hated that he had yet to be honest with her, hated that he had treated her like a child. *And apparently, too little, too late.* He finished his first mug of fire ale.

Kal perched on a stool across from Arman after a few moments. "Wasn't sure it was you, at first. Glad to see you out." He frowned. "You look ticked."

Arman sneered at the man. "Just need a bit of drink."

"I thought the general told you not to drink, said it was part of your warning from the queen." Sousa sat on the edge of the table.

"You're a pecking hen, Smytheson. Everyone needs a drink and a tup."

Kal shot Sousa a look at the unusual vulgarity. "Have you taken lessons from Hasian ?"

Arman voice rumbled. "Leave me be. I'm no company tonight."

Kal shrugged finally, and returned to his table. After a few failed attempts at conversation, Sousa followed.

Arman was nursing his third mug when a hand touched his knee. It was a barmaid who often worked there, but her dark curls were loose and her dress nicer.

"I don't often see ye apart from yer friends."

He gave her a fleeting smile and turned back to his mug.

"Yer lonely."

He shrugged, taking another sip.

"You have been here awhile yet." She gestured to the stool beside him. "May I join you?"

He shoved his own seat down to make room for her, more out of politeness than interest.

She smiled nonetheless. "Ye didn't come around before a month ago. Did ye just join up? They respect you an awful lot."

"I joined the war last year." He wondered absently how she did not know the story.

She leaned back against the bar. "Has anyone told ye that ye look like the Rakos guard?"

He laughed, then realized she was serious. *No wonder she treats me like a man. She knows no better. Nor was she here when I fought Hasian.* "I've heard that a few times. Most say he's taller though." It was not strictly a lie. The thought that he was normal again, even just for a moment, made his heart light. "You're not working tonight?"

"No, it's Mara's night." She grinned. "Care to buy me a honey ale?"

Arman motioned the girl who must have been Mara over and ordered before returning his attention to his companion. "Were you raised here?"

"Just to the west, in the city's villages. I'm one of five daughters, so we each make our own way." Her mug arrived and she took a sip. "Did you come from a large family?"

"No. I helped my Ma run her inn and took over my father's blade-smithy after he passed."

Her eyes widened. "I cannot imagine losing my Ma or Pa." she tilted her head. "Ye crafted blades? Fighting must come naturally."

He shrugged. "I have a hand for knife-throwing and foot combat." He turned toward her a bit more. She was lively and curious, kind if not very bright. "I'm not a killing man, though. I prefer a good celebration—my city loved her festivals."

"Ye had many?"

"One for every forgotten season and some just because we felt like it and others out of habit." His smile was slight, but it felt good. "Does Ceir Athrolan have many?"

"Just the first of the seasons and midwinter and midsummer. We celebrate the first planting and the harvest. Mostly they are for the common folk, thought the palace needs little reason for a ball or feast. Tell me about yers?"

He thought for a moment then leaned closer. His hands waved, as if painting an image of Vielrona with his gestures. "The city is small, tucked into the hills, but every festival the streets are awash with lights. During midwinter we light a lantern for every person we loved and lost. The entire city glows and there is singing and dancing." He explained his favorite details. She bought him his next drink, and he hers until she laughed at each extravagant story. He could almost forget why he had decided to drink.

"Care to catch some fresh air?" Her offer was sudden.

He helped her into her cloak, though the air was warm. They moved further into the city, walking aimlessly. The moon was high in the sky and shed bright light across the quiet streets. It could not have been much past midnight, but the streets were deserted. "You should go south sometime, see the midwinter festival yourself."

She shivered and he absently put an arm around her shoulders, rubbing her arm.

At a street corner she paused, turning to face him. "Ye have a woman to go home to?"

He froze, suddenly realizing where he was and what he was about to do. *You'll never have Alea. This girl is here and willing.* "I've not had a woman in a long while."

"Ye can tonight, if you want."

You're just a man tonight. You have no future with Alea. He tightened his grip on her hand and lowered his mouth to hers. She kissed him once, twice, then lead him up the stairs of the building on the corner. It was a boarding house and her room was small. A single window overlooked the rear alley. Her bed was against the left wall and neatly made.

She stirred the small stove and lit a candle by the bed before stepping into his arms. She was modestly curved and her hands were knowing as they moved up his back and over his shoulders.

He returned her smile and wrapped his arms around her waist, trailing his lips down her neck. She smelled of hazelnuts and her warmth comforted and wounded him all at once. He pulled back and kissed her softly. She backed towards the bed and tugged off his jerkin. The familiar jolt of heat and attraction did not shoot through him. He felt no flush on his cheeks. *It's been too long – almost a year! I need to remember the steps.*

He pulled off his shirt and lay down atop her, propping himself on his elbows to kiss her again. He pulled back to look at her and she smiled. He distantly noticed her eyes were gray green. *Almost silver.* He pushed the thought away and moved to touch her again, but stopped. His body refused to respond. *She's beautiful, and yet my body is as moved as if I'm learning arithmetic.* He nuzzled her neck, willing himself to react, but to no avail. He sighed roughly.

"Are ye all right?"

He closed his eyes, his jaw working. "I don't think I can do this."

"What is it?"

He rolled off her and sat on the edge of her bed.

"Someone is in yer heart?"

He nodded, holding his head in his hands. "I'm sorry. You're a beauty and I would have been glad to be with you." Her hand froze on his shoulder and he glanced back at her.

Her eyes inched over the scars on his chest and the handprint over his heart. She brushed the hair from his eyes. "When we kissed, yer teeth.... Ye don't just look like him, ye are the Rakos." When he nodded she drew back. "The Dhoah' Laen. You thought you could get her out of your blood because we look alike, dark hair and pale eyes."

"Dammit, it's not like that, at least, not on purpose." Arman sighed. *It's not like any human woman could compare.* He knew the words would sound cruel and held his tongue. His eyes flashed yellow and his fist clenched her sheets. Wisps of smoke curled from between his fingers.

Her gaze hardened. "I think you should leave."

He dressed quickly, without looking at her or arguing.

She waited silently until he was at the door. "I'm sorry. Ye seem like ye would make a good lover. I hope she returns your feelings."

He did not answer and let himself out. He bolted to the palace, his mind anywhere but on his steps. He stumbled twice before he forced himself to slow. *This is ridiculous. Who heard of only being able to bed the person you care for?* He shoved his way through his door and fell onto his bed. His eyes stared at the bare ceiling. One hand drew Alea's letter from his desk. It was tattered from myriad readings. Each time the tone seemed different, as if the words conveyed her changing emotions. *Or mine.* He read it again, his fingers clutching the parchment. When the paper singed, he put it away, unwilling to burn it just yet.

He had been happy to spend his life beside her as a friend, a guard. Now he wondered if he could stand that. *Who knows what she wants from this life, if she will be able to get it even. Who knows if I will?*

Heat built. The thought of Alea, both plain and with black fog in her silver eyes made his body ache. He closed his eyes tight and drew a shuddering breath. *Fates help me.*

Φ

The 31st Day of Lineme, 1252
The City of Mirik

Alea found better rest in the rumble of Mirik's barracks than in the peace of Le'yne. Her dreams were meaningless and forgotten when she finally woke. She rolled over, peering out the window beside her bed. It was dark and the moon was high. The air smelled of pine and freshly turned earth. She was still tired, but fatigue and hunger were pushed aside by something more pressing. She settled herself on the coverlet and closed her eyes. Her mind reached out to Athrolan.

The mental journey took moments, not minutes. Burning yellow-green blossomed in the depths of the city when she focused. Arman was in a common district boarding house. She arrived in the hall and stepped into the room, passed through the door as if it was nothing.

The room was dimly lit and it took her eyes a second to adjust. When they did, her breath stopped. Arman was in bed, bare-chested, his legs entangled with those of the young woman beneath him. Her dark curls were loose and her bodice partly unlaced. The floor bucked beneath Alea's feet and her chest clenched.

She did not remember returning to her body, only that she was back in her own room. Ice filled her skin. She was not certain what she felt. It was not as simple as jealousy, but she recognized the acrid taste of it in her mouth. Arman accepted her as the Dhoah' Laen before she even did herself. When she retreated behind the high, cold walls of her mind, he stepped casually inside of them. He did not force his way in, with loud words and narrowed eyes. *He's the only one who can step inside my defenses and not be destroyed.* When the world was a mass of confusing, distant muted tones, Arman was a point of brilliant color as real as her thoughts. Her stomach was too tight to eat, but she could not stand to be alone. Her hands fumbled with the breeches and jerkin left for her.

The mess hall was loud and the smell of food and ale strong. The chatter nearest the doorway died as she entered. Her eyes found Bren's, willing him to recognize the plea on her face.

She was grateful he saved his questions until they were shut once again in his room. She curled her feet under her as he lit the lantern on his desk. He sat beside her, frowning. "Are you all right? Do you want food? There's stew and bread. I think the fish is gone, though."

Her fingers knotted in her lap. The strange space between her mind and the world seemed suddenly greater, and even her own voice was muffled by the distance. "Did Arman speak of me at all?"

Bren frowned. "Not to me, not after our first letters. I sent yours, which I assume he received, since he replied to mine. I heard he bruised up a soldier in a bar for insulting you, but the tale did not come from him." He peered at her. "What is it?"

"Defending me is his duty. He said nothing?"

"Alea, he's a quiet man, and private, at least in regards to you. What is this about? Didn't you talk to him like you did to me?"

"I tried, but it's as if there's a wall between us. I could see him, hear him, goodness I could even feel the heat from his skin. Even when I shouted, it was like he barely sensed me. I was like a ghost. I thought I needed practice, then I thought it was because of the distance."

"Sistermine." He took her shaking hands in his own, but her voice stopped his words.

"I tried again, just now. I wanted to tell him I was home. I thought now that I was back, it might work. It didn't, though I didn't wait long enough to say anything. He was with a woman. In bed."

Bren's eyes widened. "What? No, Alea, you must have been wrong. It must have been someone other than Arman."

Her gaze pinned him, blazing angrily. "Bren, our souls are bonded. I can feel him breathing when he's in the next room. I know him." She turned away, anger bitter on her tongue. "Besides, I could see enough skin to recognize his scars." She pressed a hand to her stomach. "I feel ill, but my body is too tense to be sick. I don't know why this hurts. I can't even say if I'm angry."

Anger was fleeting and hot. They had made no promises, and so she knew his actions did not justify anger. She sighed, placing her head in her hands. Her words were direct and calculated. Behind the wall of eloquence she was safe. *Safe from what? Betrayal?* The Laen had betrayed her, she supposed, but neither had she ever truly trusted them. They had never promised not to hurt her. Had he promised to love her? Love only her? "He promised to keep me safe, keep my heart safe. And here, he's the one breaking it."

Bren's brows rose. "Alea, do you love him?"

She shrugged. "Our bond wasn't marriage vows and I know it. When someone is with you each step, helping you as you help them, facing each hardship and joy together, it's easy to forget."

Bren rested his forehead on her shoulder. "I don't know what to say. I didn't expect this. In my last letter I mentioned that it was a relief to hear from you while you were in Le'yne. Perhaps he thought your silence meant you didn't want to speak with him."

She drew a shuddering breath. She was too empty to weep. If she began, it would drain her until nothing remained, but a husk. "I can't be distracted. I will give all I have to the war. Everything else will come afterward."

Bren opened his mouth as if to speak, but a sharp knock sounded at his door. His eyes lingered worriedly on her for a moment, but he rose and opened the door. A squire stood outside, shifting from foot to foot. "Yes?"

"Lieutenant, I mean, Lord Commissioner, sir. There's a man here for you. Says he traveled a long way and you're expecting him."

"Commissioner is fine, Gecken." Bren glanced back at Alea. "Do you mind?

She shook her head absently. Her grief was deep, but contained behind the mighty walls of her calm and power. A simple visitor would not disturb her. "I can go, if you wish."

He waved her words away. "It's about the war, you should hear it anyways." He jerked a nod at the boy still hovering in the doorway, trying to glimpse the Dhoah' Laen. "Show him up, then, and could you bring tea and mugs?" He sat once the boy was gone and looked back at his sister. "I received a letter from someone claiming to be An'thoriend Domariigo. You said you met him before?"

"Twice. The second time he told me about you, actually. I'm uncertain whether he is obnoxious or impressive."

Bren snorted. "I still don't believe my father's informant is the hero of the stories. The letter asked for a meeting tonight. It's either the legend or a madman."

"There is a statement in there about the lack of difference between the two." Alea offered him a distant smile. Further dark thoughts were interrupted when the squire returned with tea and a cloaked figure in tow. The boy set the tray down on Bren's desk and bowed himself out.

Alea's gaze narrowed on the man in the doorway. The wide cowl of his cloak allowed the lantern to light his pale face, and she noted the wrap around his head was the same as before, albeit further bleached by sun and stained from rain.

Bren rose and introduced himself. "You asked for a meeting?"

"Greetings, Commissioner." The Ageless man's words were rougher than before, as if his voice had walked the road along with his boots. His black eyes flicked to Alea's. Bracing himself against the doorframe with one hand, he slowly took a knee. "Last I saw you, my lady, you were but a promise. Now I look on the realization of every hope we've ever had. How can they think to stand against you?" He hauled himself back up and gestured to the room. "May I, sir?" His words indicated Bren, but his eyes never left Alea's face.

"Certainly." Bren pulled a chair out and began pouring tea.

An'thor unclasped his cloak and folded it and his head wrap over the back of the chair before sitting with a quiet sigh. He took the proffered cup with a nod of thanks and sat back.

Bren's wide gray eyes were fixed on the chipped, stained ivory horns sprouting from the pale man's temples. They were short and curved, like a bull's, barely reaching the crown of his head, but they easily marked him. The open curiosity told Alea her brother had never seen the man without a cowl or wrap before.

His gaze flicked to Bren. "I'm glad to see you were as clever as I hoped. It's not every man I can convince to desert Azirik's army."

Bren pulled a flask from his desk and added a healthy splash of alcohol to their tea. "Azirik did a fair share of convincing me himself, what with the blows and the anger and the threats." Bren waved the memories away and replaced the flask. "We're not here to discuss that, I assume."

An'thor took a deep draught then peered into the cup. "Is this wraith?"

"It is and older than Toar, but good enough for my purposes." Bren fixed the man with a pointed look. "You came here for a purpose, which I assume is better than drinking my liquor. My sister claims you're the An'thoriend of legend, and I know you only as a double-crossing maniac."

An'thor lips quirked. "Both can't be true?"

Bren choked into his drink. "You waltz in here, assuming I'm going to trust my enemy's informant?"

"He's not lying." Alea tilted her head. "This is the man who spoke to us in Vielrona, who told me about you in that wayhouse. He went by An'thor then, too. The Sunamen were not terribly familiar with your tales, but Arman heard a few." His gaze met hers as if over miles, not meters, and she realized his mind was shielded by as many walls as hers. "He bears enough marks of grief for a lifetime as long as An'thoriend's."

An'thor's eyes softened. "As do you, Dhoah" Lyne'alea." He looked to Bren, one brow quirked. "May I continue, or is her word enough."

Though there was no contempt in the man's words, Bren scowled. "Very well, what did you wish to discuss, Sir Domariigo?"

"An'thor is just fine. I am no lover of honorifics. They make lesser men great. I came north to see what Athrolan was doing with Mirik. I arrived in time to hear you address the Kit. I thought I could ally myself with you. It would benefit us both. Will you hear my proposition?" When Bren nodded, An'thor handed him a parchment from his breast pocket.

Bren scanned it quickly before handing it to Alea. It was a letter with a reply written on the reverse side. The front was from An'thor, asking the addressee's opinions on the war. The reply was abrupt.

An'thoriend

I agree it is shrewd for the Ageless to join the war. As king of Neneviir I have already rallied our warriors, though we are fewer than we once were. As always, I weigh the strength of the sides, and the benefits each offers. The choice is clear. You have my approval to approach the new Miriken lord and offer aide.

Until battle,

Edrodene

She looked up. "What do you want from us?"

An'thor ran a scarred finger around the edge of his mug. "I want the Nenev to use their might for something useful, finally." He glanced up. "Honestly, I just want you to win. I'm tired of war."

Alea saw the ache of homesickness in the lines around his eyes. "You want to go back to Athrolan. I remember that tale, how you were banished from the capital."

"Tzatia is a fine queen, but she is scared. The only way I will find my way back into Athrolan is by your side, and I need to return to her. I know that kingdom's voice and she is crying loud and long."

Alea glanced at Bren. "You really aren't certain? Look at him—he protected the Laen for years, chased them across the continent several times at least."

Bren's mouth hardened. "He also informed for Azirik. Forgive me if I can't quite forget that." Bren regarded the Ageless man for a minute. "All right. I'll speak to the Kit."

"They were the first to accept me in Mirik. They brought me to your father." An'thor grinned, the expression making his face a bittersweet mixture of youthful energy and exhausted age.

Alea wondered abruptly how many of them would have the same features before the war was through. "I can entertain him, if you wish to go to the Kit now."

Bren rose. "I hope to leave within the week. Best to iron everything out that we can." He glanced between his two guests. "I won't be gone long."

Alea smiled inwardly. He had not threatened An'thor, or told her it was not safe to sit alone with a man she barely knew. It was a welcome change.

An'thor reached out, placing his hand on the desk beside hers.

It was a gesture so akin to Arman's it made her heart twist. *Will Arman turn into this? A sad shadow of a legend?* She frowned. "What is it?"

"I'm sorry." He looked down. "For my part in where your life has led. Not sorry for my actions, because we need you, but sorry for the pain they caused."

"You did not make me what I am. You may have told me, helped me, but you did not take my family." She leaned forward. "There is something more, An'thor, that you could do for us."

His brows quirked. "Something your brother can't know?"

Alea shrugged. "He has enough to worry after. Besides, it will not be easy, but must be done." She pulled a scrap of parchment from her brother's desk and hastily sketched a ring of metal and stone. She pushed it across the desk's top. "I'm afraid I have no skill at art, that is Arman's expertise."

"Aye, they say those with fire in their minds burn with creativity." His eyes fell to the image.

"It's old, the stones are dark blue sodalite and the metal is iron. It was in Claimiirn. Perhaps it's still there, perhaps it was looted. I need to know if you've seen it."

"I thought the Laen had their Crown."

"Obviously not. It was last seen in Claimiirn before she fell."

"Claimiirn has quite the treasury. It's been ransacked, surely, but if your Crown was found I imagine we'd know. You will search for it?"

"I'll go before the battle. I need to study more, understand the gods."

"When the time comes I will arrange passage for you, if you need it. And I'll keep my words to myself. I passed through the city on my way here. You know Azirik's made it his base camp?"

"It's a risk I must take. Azirik does not scare me."

"I wonder what does."

"I see a sadness in your eyes," Alea's gaze met his, a tenuous connection through the shadow surrounding her thoughts. "A sadness that used to be in mine, before a deeper darkness overtook it. I think you know what scares me."

CHAPTER NINE

The 35th Day of Lineme, 1252
The City of Ceir Athrolan

ARMAN GRINNED AS HE PRESSED back against the wall. His hold on his power was firm. Eras would arrive within a few minutes. She had enquired about his progress and he wanted to show her first-hand his new skills. Sure enough, her knock came. He called for her to enter and glanced down at his body. It was gone. Tucked in the shadow behind his window's curtains, he was invisible.

Eras glanced through the room with a frown. "Arrowlash?"

"Morning, general." He could not keep the impish grin from his voice.

Her eyes narrowed and began to trace each corner and shadow. They barely paused on him. "Are you washing up?" Her hearing was good. His voice had emanated from several paces to the left of his privy door.

"I'm right here, general." He stepped into the shaft of sunlight from the window. He glanced down at his body again. It was nothing more than a dust mote turned golden in the sun's ray. *This power could go to my head.* After a moment he slowly let his power fade from his body. Eras's eyes caught the change and widened as first his bones, then organs materialized. His skin crawled back into view and he met her gaze.

Her years of training and the Asai stoicism held her feet in place, but Arman caught the sudden bittersweet scent of fear. "You become invisible?"

"The eye does not see smoke, not really. I am but smoke drifting on the wind." Fully corporeal again, he spread his arms in a classic player's flourish. "What do you think?"

"I think you're horrifying. I think we can use you." Her eyes flicked to the exposed skin of his forearms. "I think you have something more than smoke up your sleeve."

He followed her gaze to the scales beginning to erupt from his tanned lower arms. "Ah, yes." He rolled his sleeves down.

"You need someone to take a look at that?"

"No. There is nothing a human doctor could do." He looked down. "There is something else I want to show you, but I think it'd be best displayed outside of the city limits."

"I've heard that before, and from men far prettier than you." Her mouth quirked and she jerked a nod at the door. "Shall we?"

Arman's spirits darkened at her jest and he shrugged on his jerkin with more force than strictly necessary. "Apparently my tastes are very narrow, and I regret to inform you that you do not fall within them." He strode down the hall and to the small gate beside the barracks.

Eras shot him a curious glance, but seemed to know better than to prod the testy Rakos. "So what are you showing me? Have you tested the limits of your power?"

Arman shook his head. "Not really, but I did discover something more useful, even than invisibility. You ever watch smoke after you blow out a candle?"

"No wonder you came to Athrolan, if that was your sole entertainment in Vielrona. But I suppose I know what you mean."

"It drifts, it floats. When I'm smoke, I can do the same."

"You can fly?"

He shrugged and ducked under a branch, holding it aside for her as she followed him further up the hill. "I guess." He had been avoiding testing the limits of his power, and was uncertain why. *Milady's power is known – it's beyond true understanding, but it is known to be Creation and Destruction. I, however, am a wild unknown..* He laughed humorlessly to himself. *Fangs and all.* He topped the hill and stepped into the center of the clearing. He noted with sick pride that Eras stayed back along the tree line. The familiar burn and exhilaration of his power filled him with itching and twitching. His body dissolved again, his form rising in white, whirling smoke. He climbed higher and higher, dozens of paces above the hilltop, before calling down. "General!"

She backed up, face tilted to the sky. "Where are you?"

He allowed just his face to reappear, partially fleshed and macabre, but more obvious against the bright blue sky. He grinned. "Up here."

Eras laughed. "You're amazing, truly." Her expression grew stern, the frown a shadow from his high vantage. "But come back down. There is more, more I've read, and more you have not tested."

He sank back to the ground, his anger itching. *Doesn't she know how hard I work?* When he was firmly back on the ground, he crossed his arms. "What do you mean?"

"Arman, you've been avoiding going deeper. Your abilities are phenomenal, surely, but you are Rakos. More than that, you're bonded to the Dhoah Laen. Don't tell me this is all you can do. What are you afraid of?"

"I'm not afraid! I can't do anything more. Not in comparison to her. I know it's nothing, but this is all I am."

She pursed her lips. "No, this is all Arman can do. What about Arrowlash? What about the blood inside you? You think Alea was never afraid of losing control—damn, she did more than once. She still tried."

"I'm not afraid of losing control!" His anger was already roiling. Heat rumbled up his limbs and his nose singed with the smell of forging metal. Coppery fluid filled his mouth as he bit down on the insides of his cheek. *She's trying to help.* The air around his skin rippled with heat and the glade flicked as if under a desert sun. "What's this going to do, general? Make Azirik sweat a bit? Gods won't like a soldier who reeks? Is that it?" The leaves of the closest trees wilted.

"What are you afraid of?"

"I'm afraid of what I'll become. I'm afraid there is no place for what I'll be, in this world, or in hers."

"What have you lost that makes you afraid of that?" Eras backed up further, her eyes wary, but not fearful, not yet. Each word was calculated, and it occurred to him than Eras had trained more soldiers than he could imagine. His powers were different, but the methods were the same.

His eyes squeezed shut. "Her." He felt the sharpness in the air as she tilted her head in a question. "She was able to talk to us, from Le'yne. She spoke to Bren, and never once to me. She left me here with a duty I never once questioned, and didn't even bother to speak to me."

"Arman, she's a complicated creature. She'd be even if she were only human. You know you wouldn't have it any other way. You're afraid of becoming something else—well you have no idea what creature will step off the boat when she returns. You need to be prepared for whatever she has become. You want her to see you as her equal? Become it."

He did not answer. Instead, eyes still closed, he raised his hands. He did what he had warned Alea against and fell into his power. Everything Alea was to him filled his thoughts. *Faith.* He died for her. She had almost done the same to bring him back. *Faith. Complete surrender.* The image of Eana's scarred golden eyes appeared in his thoughts again. *Fear. Find us. Fear.* Arman's power thundered through him, eating through his skin with searing heat. He opened his eyes.

The hilltop was in flames. The trees were black skeletons, his hands white flames. It should have been excruciating, but it was only pleasantly warm. His skin was a network of white-gold scales. He stumbled back. Eras was several paces further into the forest, her forearm raised against the heat and the glow.

His power faded back into his body and the fire around him died to a dull smolder. He crouched and placed his hands on the ground, drawing the blaze into them until it was extinguished. With the threat of forest-wide destruction gone, he glanced down at Eras. "Well?"

She stared at the blackened trees. "What changed?"

"Each step of the way she reminds me what I am, who I always have been, but have forgotten. In Vielrona she was vulnerable. I remembered I was a protector. In her absence, I remembered my anger."

"And now?"

"Faith. I need to surrender myself." He fell back onto the scorched ground, head in his hands.

Φ

The 36th Day of Lineme, 1252

Swelling around Arman's left eye had replaced the stinging of open flesh. The bruises were still obvious, and the green uglier than the initial purple. He was dressing for the training courts when a squire delivered the mail. Atop a letter from Bren was a summons.

> *Regarding your recent behavior, Her Majesty Tzatia requests your presence within the hour.*

Arman's stomach plummeted as he changed haphazardly into a finer set of clothes. Pomp and politics were more Alea's area, but he recognized the importance of this meeting. *The general said I wouldn't be exiled or anything half so dramatic. She said nothing about other consequences.* He raked a hand through his hair and tied it back. It had grown past his shoulders, more an Athrolani style than Vielronan.

The general was leaving when he arrived at the queen's chamber door. Her face was unreadable, but she nodded to him. "It won't take long, I promise."

He watched her go before gesturing for the steward Valadai to announce him. Tzatia was seated on a couch by a bay of windows. Tea sat, half-drunk before her. It was obvious the refreshments had not been brought for his benefit. Her nephew, Daymir, leaned on the broad window-sill, arms and legs crossed. Patience was clearly a familial trait. Arman suddenly wished he had Alea's hand on his elbow, guiding his actions. She'd murmur a soft joke to calm his racing mind and rising temper.

"Arrowlash, thank you for coming." Tzatia leaned forward. "I hope this will go quickly. I already spoke to General Aneral about the events of last week. Quite the advocate you've got yourself there." She sipped her tea, gray eyes flicking to his green ones. "Might I have your own account?"

"Where would you like me to begin, your majesty?"

"The beginning, perhaps?" Daymir's low voice was tinged with humor, but the hard look in his eyes showed it was no joke.

"The soldier crowd was going to the bars, and I accompanied them, as usual. I had a few drinks. It was close to midnight when Hasian spoke out against my Ma and Milady Lyne'alea—"

"Spoke out how?" Daymir asked, "I believe even I have spoken out against Dhoah' Lyne'alea at times."

"Better not have been like this." Arman's voice was steady, but low enough not to be a serious threat. "He said I was a bastard of my mom's paid union and that milady was bedding her way across the kingdom to get allies."

"I don't suppose you could have ignored it?" Daymir heaved a sigh, lips thinned in distaste.

"You ever been drunk, Lord Daymir? Ignoring is not really an option. Besides, I ignored him the last time and he needed a setting-right."

"I don't doubt he needed to be taken down a peg, only your methods for doing so." Tzatia pinched the bridge of her nose with a narrow hand. "You are our ally, and the general explained the situation with your temper. There will still be consequences. Commander Dorcal has a fleet sailing along the Northlands' coastline. There are rumors that the Berrin navy plans to attack us, and that is the way they will come. The general tells me you have some skills that will be helpful in battle, and seems to think you would benefit a sea voyage."

Arman's expression remained aloof, but his mind was scrambling. He felt betrayal at the general's suggestion. *She thinks I can fly alongside the ships? Ignite the enemies' vessels? I've barely discovered these abilities and she wants me to use them in war?* Instead of voicing his anger, he nodded curtly. "Certainly. When do they leave?"

"Less than a month. I will inform Admiral Fess that you will accompany him. He will meet with you separately to discuss details." Tzatia fixed him with a pointed stare. "If you have business here, I suggest you conduct it with discretion from now on."

Arman nodded and bowed himself out. His hands shook as he hurried down the corridor to the general's room.

Φ

Eras rubbed her face wearily. "The trouble is, Raven, I don't think he realizes they're equals. He's too wrapped up in how inadequate he is and he'll hurt anyone who says otherwise."

"I think both of them are insane. No wonder the Rakos died out and the Laen are hunted. They're mad, the lot of them."

Eras rolled her eyes and poured herself two fingers of a dark alcohol. "He won't be happy with me, either, telling the queen and all that."

"Why do you care so much?" His dark eyes narrowed on her. "I'll never understand your softhearted tendencies."

"If you consider me softhearted, Raven, you're the one who is mad. They may not be Athrolani or human or whatever other criteria of yours they don't meet, but they are magnificent. Besides, I needed a mentor when I was lost. Certainly he does, too."

A fist suddenly pounded against the door. "General!"

She shot Raven a pointed look and leaned forward in her chair. "Let him in, will you?"

"If you like ordering people about, get a squire, Eras. I'm a commander not a lackey." Despite his bitter words, he rose and jerked the door open. "What do you want?"

Eras hid a smile at Arman's confusion. The Rakos's face was flushed and she was not in the mood to agitate him further. "Let him in and for fate's sake be civil."

Arman had to step around the commander's bulk to enter, glaring at the man with open distain. His longer hair and beard only punctuated the feral expression.

"Arrowlash, have a seat."

"Have a seat? Do I look like a court dandy, general? You had my confidence." Instead he leaned on her desk, shoulders hunched and head low. It was not a posture of submission, but threat.

It did not work on her. "Arman, this is a monarchy. There is a very long list of people and places I have a duty to and you are certainly in the middle of that list. Her Majesty and Athrolan, however, are much higher." She absently wondered if he would point out that she did not say they were at the top.

He scowled. "Dammit! I've barely mastered my powers and you send me gallivanting out into the north sea."

"I did not send you, Arman, Her Majesty Tzatia did. Would you rather she put you to work elsewhere?"

"I don't take issue with the order, but now?" He shoved himself away from the table with a snarl. His eyes burnt, but it was not anger she saw there. It was fear. "Milady is home, finally, and you send me away?"

Eras's brows rose. *She's back?* The soldier in her sang at the approaching battle, but she had seen enough of this war to face it with dread in her stomach. "She's home? First I've heard of it."

"I can feel that she's here again. She arrived sometime a few nights ago. I was drunk at the time, I didn't realize it until the morning."

"Drunk? Again?" She waved away the excuse perched on his lips. "Never mind." She glanced at Raven. "Do you really think it's wise if you see her in this state? You're ready to dangle me from the window and all I did was inform the queen of a diplomatic solution to your attempt at murder. What will you do when she's not exactly the woman you remember? When she hasn't changed in the way you expect?"

"What the fuck would you know of that?"

She stepped around to the other side of her desk and folded her arms. He was unpredictable and she would rather face him on her feet then seated. *Besides, if Raven draws arms, I'll never hear the end of it.* "It is my job to know the state of affairs in my city, especially in times of war and when there are key players within our walls. You were seen leaving a bar with a young woman. You left her residence a little while later, angry. Well, angrier than usual. I suppose any man would be angry after so quick a dalliance, but regardless, I was under the impression that you had feelings for Dhoah' Lyne'alea."

Arman's breath rumbled in his chest and his eyes darkened. "I never said that."

"You never had to, Arman. This trip to the north might help cool your head. I don't know what Dhoah' Lyne'alea needs for this war, but I'm betting silver it's not a love-drunk school-boy." She had won the argument, if there had ever been one. *All that is left is for him to storm out angrily. I'll get a letter in the next week apologizing.*

He stalked towards the door. "Perhaps the next time you mentor someone, general, draw up a contract." He slammed his way out.

Eras shook her head in the wake of the outburst and poured herself another drink. "This war is making madmen of us all."

"You don't actually think he'd blame her for not being what he wants, do you? That would just be cruel."

She pressed her brow against the cool stone of her window frame. "That never stopped you from blaming me." The sunset was bloody and bruised. The spring storms had passed, but the skies were darker than ever.

Φ

The 37th Day of Lineme, 1252
The City of Mirik

Bren's gray eyes narrowed on the calm harbor. "I'll need two Kit to accompany me. And when I return I'd like whomever stays to organize themselves. We'll appoint other commissioners then."

"Not after the war?" Like Bren, Arik's arms were crossed.

The new commissioner glanced over and grinned. Flanking the main dock with identical stances, they could have been statues. It was not a bad image, two Miriken protecting what was left of their people. "No. If I die, we need organization. I've not come so far on so many sleepless nights to have it fall to shite. Who should I take with me? I'd like one to be you, but I think you would better serve here."

Arik nodded. "Agreed. When proper battle begins I'll come, with the rest of the soldiers." At Bren's surprised glance, he grinned. "You expect the queen to let you prance into battle with three men and a pale freak from the north? I think not. Anyway, take Kemmer A'hane and Aldac Missan. Aldac's a swordsman and knows our common ways. Kemmer's sister to the man governing Talic. She's young, but bright."

Bren nodded. "I'll send them letters this afternoon." He rolled his shoulders, watching as sailors prepared the ship before them for the sea. "I've left instructions for Helonin. He's to work with you as he readies to pull out. Will you see us off this afternoon?"

"Indeed."

"I'll send word from Athrolan about the war. How many you think will come?"

"For you? As many as can be spared. We'll have a few score. Outfitting them will be difficult."

"I'll take care of that. Make them ready before the end of the month."

Arik bowed himself away. "As ye tell, milord." The wry quirk of his mouth lent humor to the formal words.

Bren laughed as he returned to the barracks, the sound fitting for the clear day.

Φ

The 40th Day of Lineme, 1252
The Ilmar Ocean

Bren pressed his brow against the warm wood of the ship's rail. "Fates, not even the journey is easy!" His face was pale, his lips tinged gray.

"Just think, every time you need to come to Athrolan as a diplomat, you'll be at sea." Alea grinned over at him. The same wind that whipped her loose hair kicked the waves higher.

He groaned. With each lurch, her brother leaned over the rail with a hideous wretch. His stomach was long since empty. "Serves me proper, I suppose. Showing up in court and taking over the city they rightly conquered. 'Thanks for doing all the hard work, I'll take it from here!'"

Alea snorted. "Perhaps, though I doubt the hard work is over. Will you return to Mirik before the war?"

"If this is how I have to travel, I'll never go back." His next words were interrupted as Kemmer approached.

"Milord Commissioner, the captain agreed to stay moored for a bit before disembarking. I thought you might like to tidy yourself before entering the city." Her dark eyes flitted from his boots to Alea's and back.

Bren sighed. "You're godsent, Kemmer, thank you. It wouldn't do for our new allies to see me felled by a few days on the ocean." The woman jumped at the informal address and bowed awkwardly. She was closer to Alea's age than his and Bren had tried to break the formal front during the voyage, but Kemmer seemed as stubborn as he. "How long 'til we dock? Did you find that trunk of mine?"

The woman's silence made Bren glance up, despite his roiling gut. The white cliffs of Athrolan rose before them, half an hour's sail away. The noon sun turned the city into a beacon and made burnished gold of the summer-baked grass. Kemmer stared, open-mouthed, at the sight. Bren grinned. "Bit larger than Mirik, eh?"

She nodded stiffly. "Yessir. And your trunk is by your bunk, below. Aldac is dressing as we speak." Her eyes were still wide when she finally turned to look at him, meeting his gaze for the first time. "Thank you, sir, for picking me." She bowed and hurried down to the bunks to prepare for their arrival.

The sound of bells drifted from across the waves. Bren's brows rose. "I guess they've seen the ship's flag. They must know you're with us."

Alea nodded once and went to stand by the bow. She still wore plain clothes, but it did not matter. The chill of the sea flowed from her skin and Bren found even he was wary of meeting her eyes. He paused by her on his way down to the bunks. "You asked if I'd go back to Mirik. How much time are you giving us before battle?"

"I'll know when I determine how far Athrolan is from battle. I don't want to fight a war on my own."

Bren noticed she did not say she could not have done so, if necessary. A shudder went through him that had nothing to do with the pitching waves.

CHAPTER TEN

The 41st Day of Lineme, 1252
The City of Ceir Athrolan

DESPITE TZATIA'S ATTEMPT to see him before his official audience, Bren stayed holed up in his room with Aldac, Kemmer, and An'thor, carefully writing the details of his hastily planned government reform. There were issues that only time and hundreds of discussions would solve, but it was a start. He sighed as he finally he shoved the papers into an envelope and sealed it.

"This is only the beginning, I suppose. She'll have a dozen questions that I'll never be able to answer."

He glanced at An'thor. "When the page came to ask our titles, what did you say?"

"About myself or you?"

Bren shrugged. "Either one might make her scream."

"I politely told him to stick with 'Lieutenant Brentemir Barrackborn and companions.'"

"Toar, you make me sound like a sell-sex."

Kemer tried to disguise her snort as a cough, but dissolved into laughter after a moment. "Mirik's king, a sell-sex?"

He glared at her with mock anger. "I'm not her king."

"You are for now, sir." The hours working together had done wonders for her formal words, though Aldac still seemed to only communicate with single words.

Bren grimaced. "Regardless, we've just over one hundred seventy-six thousand Miriken Crown, which is about a hundred forty-five thousand

Athrolani. It's dismal to run a country on such. I will order my own armor and both of yours. I'm asking for reports on Mirik's armory and requesting half the able-bodied men and women to sail over within the week. They're to train with the Athrolani soldiers until the battle. I'll save money by hiring a seamstress and smithy in Talic to make uniforms and repair what armor we have." He sighed. "I simply do not know how I'm going to do this."

Kemer leaned forward, pushing a loose lock of her hair away. "Begging your pardon. What if you paid the people in titles and land and housing instead of money?" Her voice was quiet, but certain.

Bren frowned and glanced at Aric. "I think the Kit might listen to that." He made a few notes. "Good thought, Kemmer."

An'thor's eyes were fixed out the window. "Will you tax them?"

"That'll be discussed I'm sure. I'll need to build her coffers some how, but our people are already impoverished." Bren gathered his papers, only to dig through them again as a thought struck him. "Kemer, could you send these across to Mirik please? I'll meet with you tomorrow to go over more."

Kemer tidied the pile carefully. "Sir, I was also told to remind you that the war address is in a month."

He frowned. He had forgotten completely about the address. "I have little idea what to expect."

"I'd imagine it's much like the ceremony of alliance, but with more war. It's a gathering of allies. You're to stand beside Her Majesty and your sister."

Bren sighed. "I'm not looking forward to being compared to Daymir." Above, the bells marked midafternoon. He groaned. "The audience with the queen is in half an hour. Go finish tidying yourselves, I'll meet you here when it's time." He glanced at An'thor when they had left. "Why does this feel worse than battle?"

"Because battle only kills you. This will embarrass you, disgrace your name, and ruin your future." His deadpan broke into a wicked smile. "I'll see you in a few minutes."

Bren rested his head in his hands. It was far too late to change his mind. *Would I, if it wasn't?* He heaved a sigh and shoved himself out of his chair. He stepped into the bath, scrubbing himself quickly for the second time that day. *If I'm going to embarrass myself, it damned well won't be because I stink of sea-sick.*

He jerked the wardrobe open with a frown. It held the fine clothes he had worn during his last visit. He was peering into it, still naked, when a light knock sounded on his door. He gathered a towel about his waist before opening it.

Alea was already dressed in the clothes she had worn for their first audience. Something was different, but Bren could not place his finger on it. She glanced at his appearance as she stepped inside. "Having trouble?"

He shut the door behind her and brought his own outfit into the privy. "No, we just had to write an outline of our new government for the queen." He fumbled with the ties of his breeches. "Are you as nervous as I am?"

She shrugged. "Not as nervous as I should be, perhaps. Is Reka in town?"

Bren's face sobered. "I asked after her when we first arrived. Her patrol was among two that never returned last month."

"Fates, Bren, I'm sorry."

"Me too."

He heard her walk over to the window. "Bren, the entire city turned out to watch us ride up from the docks."

"Fame does not sit well with you?"

"I don't care about fame. The entire city was here, and yet no sign of Arman. Do you think he'll be at the address?"

Bren drew a slow breath in silently as he finished combing his hair with his fingers. It was hopeless. "Alea, are you even sure he's in the city?"

"He's here. His room is next to mine. Right now he's somewhere on the roof of the palace. He's pacing and angry."

Bren stepped out. "I don't know what to tell you, sistermine."

She looked over, smiling at his finery. Her eyes threatened to overflow and flood the expression from her features. "Tell me you still love me. Tell me that even though I'm a monster, even though I'm waging war against the gods you worship, you'll still love me."

He wrapped her in his arms, but his words were interrupted by the quarter-hour bells. He pulled away to look at her. Her tears still had not fallen. Her words chilled him and he was even more uncertain than before. He took her hand and stepped into the hall. "Come on, we have a queen to impress." The others waited for him outside the door. Aldac and Kemmer had managed to find vermilion tunics and An'thor had not changed from his usual black leather and fur.

Bren led them to the throne room in silence, his broad fingers still wrapped around Alea's. When the squire stepped in to announce them, he glanced over. "I'll love you until the end of the world, sistermine."

The queen looked as calm as ever, but her bright eyes were wide with curiosity. "Dhoah' Lyne'alea, we are honored to host you again, despite our shared dark future. I trust your journey from Le'yne was uneventful."

All sadness had gone from Alea's face and she smiled graciously. "Indeed. I am honored to be here again. Your city is as beautiful and welcoming as ever." She stepped aside, allowing Bren to come forward.

Tzatia's eyes flicked to him. "Greetings, Lieutenant. Care to explain your cryptic arrival? Last we corresponded you were in Mirik. Not even my own officers will shed light on Mirik's situation."

He approached, giving her the bow of an equal. The rebellious part of him grinned gleefully as her brows furrowed at the apparent lack of respect. "Forgive my lack of communication, your majesty. It has been a tumultuous few weeks. I have come to accept your offer."

Her furrow brows rose. "What are you telling me?"

He clenched his hands around the envelope to hide their shaking. "On behalf of the Commissioners of the Miriken government, I, Lord Commissioner of the Military and acting king during this time of war, accept Athrolan's offer of alliance." He handed the envelope to a squire. "This document details the preliminary plans for Mirik's future. I invite you to peruse it at your leisure."

Tzatia's gaze was unreadable as it flicked to the three figures behind him. "And these are what, your allies? Your fellow Commissioners?"

"These are Aldac Missan and Kemmer A'hane of Mirik. They are my chief officers while I finalize our path to war, your majesty." He turned to An'thor. "And it is my honor to present Warrior An'thoriend Domariigo of the Northlands and Claimiirn. He is my ally in this war, as are his people."

Her lips thinned. "You bring a known exile into my throne room?"

Bren barely hid his relief when An'thor knelt before her, taking up the impending argument. "Your majesty, my return may be unwelcome, but the reasoning is sound. I do not have to be your ally, but I am Lord Commissioner Brentemir's." He looked up and dropped the formal tone. "You think I would let Athrolan go to war alone? As much as you may hate me, I still love this land."

Tzatia's eyes lingered on An'thor for a moment and Bren caught sight of the pale man's gaze. It held a tenderness that was alien to Bren, but he imagined it was that of a father. The queen's face was pale and her eyes fierce, but she drew a breath and rose. Her steps down from the dais were careful. "Well then. We look forward to our future together and the alliance of our joined forces. Lord Commissioner of Mirik, we welcome you, and your people and allies to Athrolan."

Φ

Eras's shifting weight caused her red mare to dance sideways. She assumed the war would require a journey to her former home, but that did not make the duty any easier. Her gaze stopped at Raven. He had come to see her off. "I've commanded the men to follow Hamacad until my return."

Raven had always been the more expressive of the two and she knew he often wondered how much of his affection she returned. She wondered the same.

"I'd rather join you in battle than Hamacad." His voice pitched so only she could hear. His hand covered hers so briefly that she could have imagined it, but for the warmth it left on her glove.

Eras nodded at him and nudged her mare away. "Ride out!" The men broke into a swift trot and streamed onto the road. As she passed through the gate the men were her living cloak, fanned behind.

Φ

The 44th Day of Lineme, 1252

Bren drained the nervous excitement from his body the only way he knew how. The training courts were empty in the evening, the silence punctuated only by his grunts and the shuffling of boots against sawdust. He wondered if Alea wanted to eat supper together, but he could not bring himself to go find her. Darkness wrapped her thoughts and her words since the siege. It was a darkness that even his heart, raised on bloodshed, dared not enter. Even facing it made the bottom drop from his stomach.

It was nearly midnight when he finally lowered his sword and reached for a rag to wipe his face. He froze as he caught sight of the man seated by the door. Bren could only stare.

Arman had changed much since their last visit, and Bren barely recognized him. The Rakos's eyes, fixed on his, glowed yellow. His hair and beard had grown several inches and his skin shone in the torchlight like tarnished gold. "Hello, Lieutenant."

"Actually, it's 'king' now." It wasn't exactly true, but Bren's anger and wariness shoved the boast from his lips without thinking.

"I heard."

"I thought we'd see you sooner." His clipped words were pointed. "You were too busy studying?"

"Somewhat. I leave with a naval fleet for the north soon, and then on to Vielrona."

"More men?" Their tones were equally biting, though the words polite.

"And Rakos." It was the powerful answer to Bren's assertion of king.

It made the latter frown. "And you avoid my sister?"

Arman shrugged. "I saw her arrive." He glanced to the side, but Bren guessed it was as much to hide the confusion on his face as to appear nonchalant.

"The whole city did, you arse!"

Arman's face darkened and his voice lowered into quiet danger. "You never heard what happened to that man in the tavern, did you? I tore his throat out. With my teeth."

It was as blunt a threat as possible. Bren threw his hands up in exasperation. "Whatever this game is that you're playing, stop. Play it with your barmaid whore, your thrice-tupped lass from home. For what I care, play it with your mother, but, Toar, leave my sister be!"

Arman shot to his feet and shoved Bren against the wall. "Bastard!" His voice was a hiss and smoke curled from between his bared teeth. "She spoke to you, but never gave me a word. I guard her. I fight for her. I died for her."

Bren frowned. The smell of burning cloth rose with tendrils of smoke from where Arman's hands gripped his tunic. "For such a perfect guard you were easily swayed into infidelity."

"We never made promises." His face lost its malice and he stalked back to the bench.

"What's going on, Arman?" The argument had clearly run its course. "You're a stranger."

Arman scratched absently at his shoulder. "I don't know. My feelings have changed, but not in the way you might think. I can't make up or down of it. My power changed how I see her. It's as if something crawled inside me and took over. If its nature were the opposite of mine perhaps I could live with it. Instead, it's more like me than anything has ever been. Before all of this I was just a smith who found a strange woman in the desert. I was beneath her. Now I wonder if I'm her equal. I'm so angry all the time. At myself, at Eras, at you. Fates, sometimes I'm angry at her." His face was etched with agony. "Barrackborn, I want her like I've wanted no other woman and I'm so angry she doesn't see me."

Bren just stared. For the second time that day he was lost for words. Finally he scrounged up a piece of history he had read in Mirik. "The Rakos were as old as the Laen."

"Our powers are opposites. Hers are balance, mine are chaos."

"You are everything she is not and she is everything you are not. Arman, you're closer to her equal than anyone. No one, if not you, is worthy to love her." His mouth quirked. "If you stop acting like an arse." He stepped away and turned toward the door. "I'm going to read." He glanced back in the doorway. "You need to talk to her."

"I'm angry."

"You'll regret it if you don't. Besides, so is she."

Φ

The 45th Day of Lineme, 1252

Purposeful knocking drew Alea from the heavy book on her lap. "Yes?"

The steward poked his head in. "Dhoah' Lyne'alea, Lord Daymir wishes to pay you a visit."

Alea laid her book aside with what she hoped was a smile. Her mind was rarely truly present. "Show him in. Thank you, Valadai."

Daymir stepped in on the tail of her words. When she did not rise, he faltered, then bowed. "Good morning, Dhoah' Lyne'alea."

She gestured to the seat across from her. "Good morning. Care to sit?"

He took the place she offered, his pale eyes watching her. "I trust your journey was good?"

"It was uneventful. That is the most we can hope for, during war. To what do I owe the honor?" Despite her agreement to see him, she was impatient and tired of court speech.

He laughed ruefully. "I get your meaning. I was curious about your time in Le'yne." He paused as Giire brought in a tray of tea. When she had gone, he poured Alea a cup. His movements were careful and it was obvious he rarely waited on people himself. "Her Majesty said your return heralded the war."

Alea took the cup wordlessly, stirring in a small lump of sugar. She took a sip and stared at the liquid absently. "I wish Athrolan had *yilj* for the tea. My birth heralded the war, Lord Daymir. The rest is just formality." She sat back, eyes meeting his. "Le'yne was different from what I expected, but served its purpose." She tilted her head at him. "Will you have a part in the campaign?"

He either did not notice, or allowed her easy flip of the conversation. The intelligence in her eyes told him it was the latter. "I studied for Gallantry for a time, but my status as Head of the Royal Treasury prevents me from actually being on the fore lines. I'll have a hand in the planning." His voice was somber. "Shadow showed us we need to prepare for anything."

"Some things we can never anticipate. It's clear that Shadow was just a diversion while Azirik moved from Mirik."

Daymir nodded. "Speaking of Mirik, your brother's declaration came as a surprise. I look forward to reading that document."

Alea's gaze narrowed. "Do you wish Mirik was under Athrolan's flag?"

Daymir flashed her a wry grin. "Athrolan has far too many obligations without dragging a city from the mud. Guiding a new king, commissioner—whatever he calls himself—who has no experience, a bad example, and too good of a heart will be a hard enough task. When I take the throne I do not want to inherit a floundering ally whom we once needed for morale."

Alea allowed the ferocity bubbling in her stomach to sharpen her smile. "It is clear you have not yet read his words. I look forward to your apology when you have."

He stared at her, as if trying to determine how far he had overstepped his welcome. "Perhaps you're right." He sat back, placing his cup on the table. "You said you wished we had something for the tea. Yeel?"

"*Yilj.* It's a spice the Sunamen add to almost everything. I thought it was best with sweet things—tea and fruit and the like. I admit your tea is different, though." The heir's company was too biting to be pleasant, but she decided it was better than sitting alone. "Have you ever had Sunamen food?"

His smile was grateful. "No. I hear the flavors are complex. I enjoy the fruit from Ban. Did you get a chance to meet the Banis ambassador?"

"No, though I got the impression that your alliance with them is tense."

"It's not much of an alliance. They trade in slavery and have become rich in doing so. I know the city-states to their southwest slave-trade with them."

Alea shrugged. "Sunamen did. We only used felons, though. It kept crime incredibly low, actually."

Daymir looked down. "At any rate, we disagree. They are an interesting people and their land is rich. I hope to visit the forest to their west one day—they only have two seasons and the trees grow taller than the mountains, and are so large that other plants grow on their branches and never touch the ground."

Alea laughed. It was a beautiful image, but one out of a child's story. "I think you have been reading fantasies, Lord Daymir." She glanced out the window, at the sun climbing high in the sky. "Would you like to take your midday meal with me? You could tell me more lies about Ban."

He gave her a tiny, joking bow. "Nothing would please me more than to fill your head with nonsense."

Their food arrived shortly and Alea wrinkled her nose as she gathered the meat and bread onto her plate. "Are the Banis as barbaric as you, or do they actually use utensils to eat?"

Daymir shrugged. "I've heard they have so many slaves that they don't even feed themselves."

The dry humor tugged a laugh from her chest finally. "Perhaps I should get a few of my own."

"I was thinking, Dhoah' Lyne'alea, you seemed to enjoy the ball during your first visit. I thought I might suggest Her Majesty hold another one, heralding your return and our future victory against His Majesty King Azirik." He paused, frowning. "What do we call him, now that Bren has reformed the government out from under him?"

"I think Mirik is now two factions—Azirik's military monarchy and Bren's oligarchy." She paused to dip a slice of meat into the heated bowl of gravy and herbs. "I see the sense in holding a ball, but I cannot agree with it. I'll celebrate when I've won."

Daymir frowned. "I thought you would like to have some happiness."

Her eyes flicked up to his. "If I need you to spend hundreds of crown on a single night of excess, I'll let you know." She sat back. "I do like going to a ball, Lord Daymir. I enjoy the music and the food and the conversation. Dancing is wonderful. It's like sparring. Between the steps and conversation I'm too distracted to think about anything more important. This journey, the siege, has been one long, distracting dance." She fixed him with a pointed stare. "Now the ballroom is empty, the music has stopped."

Φ

The 45th Day of Lineme, 1252

Arman crouched on his window ledge, watching the fading light. His lamp remained unlit, and even in the early summer, his room sweltered. The sounds of conversation next door had finally faded an hour ago, but he still seethed. He was past caring that he brooded. He was past caring about most things. Only his anger consumed him. He had been frustrated with Alea before, afraid for her and of her, but never outright angry. Her return only made things worse. Several of the things in his room were broken or burnt from his half-dozen outbursts.

What would she think, seeing you like this?

He snarled at the inner voice. "I don't give a damn what she would think. I know enough of that to fill a lifetime!" His rage rose, like a wave approaching across the ocean. He whirled and began going through his old training exercises. With each block, fire erupted from his forearms and fists, the flesh protected by the scales marching up his skin.

Would she think you pathetic?

He ignored the voice and let fire roar through him. It was not enough to cover himself in flames. It was not enough to singe his rugs with each stamp of his bare feet. The abrupt heat dried the walls of his room, cracking it along invisible faults in the stone. His arms smoldered white-hot. He thought of Alea, the rage and frustration and despair he felt when he saw her. There was another emotion under them all. Something vast and peaceful, but he did not remember its name.

The reddened back of his eyelids flickered with images. It was like reading the Berrin man's mind on the road so many months before, but now the only mind before him was his own. Some pictures he recognized, others made little sense. Memories from Vielrona and the road north scattered among visions of a thin young man ascending the Athrolani throne, the sights of a terrible battle, magma flooding a barricaded city district. Arman drew the power tighter to himself. The cresting wave of power and rage broke over him then. Suddenly he was above a battlefield. Fire covered the ground and chaos crashed in titanic rumbles around him. The ground rushed up to meet him and his body flooded with pain. His chest seized and his consciousness guttered and suddenly there was nothing. His mind was at peace with whatever led him to that end. His body was numb and his vision black.

He dragged himself away from his power, rising back through it until he opened his eyes onto his room, more destroyed than ever. Every textile was burnt, the bed a charred skeleton of former finery.

Do you believe your power now? You believe you are not just Rakos?

He had nothing to say to the voice. The numbness from the vision had been replaced by agonizing tingles. "I've felt that before. I know what that is." He was distantly aware that a dozen emotions stormed through him. His anger was now tinged with poignancy. "I'm still angry, but not enough. I'm her guard and this is my fate. I chose this. And I would choose it again, and I choose it now." He had seen the battle and it was terrible, but his faith was unwavering.

CHAPTER ELEVEN

The 15th Day of Aeme, 1252
The Hartland Forest

ERAS'S SILENCE WAS NOT HER usual stoicism. She pushed the men hard and wondered if it was partly to cover her own nerves. They were well into their third week of riding. The road lay days behind them, abandoned shortly after entering the Hartland. The day before they picked up a dirt track too straight to be a game trail. Occasional stone pillars marked the distance. Whether it was how far they had come or had yet to go, none could tell. The symbols had long been worn away,

Even at midday the sunlight barely filtered through the canopy. The dusky light dappled the twisted trees. The bent rough trunks were terribly tall and so unlike the smooth white trees of Athrolan. Sharp, gray rocks pierced the soil every so often and the track widened and turned to gravel. This area of the forest was familiar. Eras slid her bow into its case and rolled the knots from her shoulders. She drew up her mare when the gravel became paving stones. Two narrow pillars flanked the road. The gray stone was hung with tarnished medallions. The faint breeze clattered the decorations against the moss-covered markers.

"General?" Vinden drew up beside her.

She noted the tension in his back and the narrow line of his mouth. He lacked the skill of a gallant, but not the courage. If he was nervous, the other men would be afraid. "These are Espera's gates. Guards stood here." She nudged her mare forward, but at a walk. "Eyes sharp, man. We'll reach the city just after sundown." The road was overgrown, but had once been wide. The faint rustling of leaves and the crunch of decomposing stone under the iron horseshoes seemed deafening. After an hour, distant grumbling joined the sounds of men and horses. "Vinden, when we reach the river, half the men will make cold camp. You'll bring the others with me into the city."

"Understood, mem."

The grumbling became the roar of falling water. Eras's pace quickened. They emerged onto a riverbank carved from bedrock. Eras raised her hand, but the men had already stopped in awe. Years of water spinning stone against stone carved perfect circles into the bank. Some were the size of a fist, others large enough to swallow man and horse. They stood on the shore of a churning pool. Across the river, water from the mountains cascaded over low cliffs. They were nothing like Athrolan's, but were broad and dark and dotted with hexagonal watch towers. The city itself was small and perched on an island at the foot of the waterfall. A narrow bridge of stairs connected the island to the shore.

She dismounted, allowing the men their gawking for a moment, then barked orders to make camp before jerking her head towards the bridge. The designs carved along the steps were angular and repetitive, as much for decoration as traction. The boots of the half-dozen soldiers following her barely made a sound. Eras did not have to signal for them not to speak. It was evening and any city should have been bustling as it prepared for supper. The buildings were silent. A large tower marked the center of the island and Eras paused before the open doorway.

Vinden placed a foot on one of the stairs, leaning on his knee and Eras surveyed their surroundings. "General, this is wrong. You said there were only a few Asai. I see none."

The lines of Eras's sharp features deepened with concentration. "I've been gone for years. Almost a lifetime. Anything could have happened. The Asai are cloistered enough that we may never had heard of an attack." She nocked an arrow to her bow, fingers curling around the string, ready to draw. "We'll start here." She stepped into the tower, motioning for her men to spread out. The halls were decorated with carvings, but it was austere. Few pieces were solely art. Each blocky design had architectural purpose. Eras knew her men would chalk her expressionless face up to her usual indifferent mask. It was honesty this time. *Espera stopped being home a long time ago.* The young soldier at her back tripped and whispered a curse, then an apology.

She ignored him and eyed the open double doors at the end of the hall. They should have been closed. She crept forward, instinct singing in her ears. *This is wrong. This is all wrong. If they deserted, where is the dust? If they were attacked, where is the struggle?*

She stepped through the doors.

"General, mem." The soldier's hiss was fearful. "You should look at this."

She froze in the doorway, heedless of the young man behind her. The hall took up a whole segment of the six-sided tower. The books that lined the walls were gone, only a few scattered pages left to mold in the moisture. Mist roiled in from the shattered window. The table in the center of the room no longer held maps. Now it held bodies.

Eras did not bother to search for survivors. The chill of the river had kept some rot away, but the mottled cast and sweet smell of the air told her enough.

"General."

She finally turned to the soldier.

He crouched in the hall, peering at an arrow. "This is Berrin."

"It's hard to say when they were attacked. The cold kept them better than usual." She backed out of the hall and shut the doors. *I should bury them.* It would wait until tomorrow. There was little sense in digging graves in the dark. Her two-fingered whistle rebounded off the stone, calling for the others to regroup. She sat on the steps at the tower's entrance to wait for the others.

The soldier shifted nervously from foot to foot, earnest concern lighting his eyes. "I'm sorry, mem. Did you know them?"

She glanced up, wondering briefly if he was as young as he looked. The other men treated her as an expert on the Asai, but distantly, as if she had studied them as a hobby, not been raised in their culture. The boy before her was either too honest or too inexperienced to do the same. "Probably some. Long ago. Not well." She heaved a sigh. "Thank you, though."

The rest of the men arrived from within. Vinden's nodded greeting was grim. "Berrin attack."

She rose. "Agreed. Deserted?"

"Save a few rooms. Looks like someone tidied up—only a few arrows and all the dead stacked." He glanced up at the tower. "This place is eerie enough, the dead only make it worse."

"We'll deal with them in the morning." They were nearing the bridge when footfalls clattered ahead. *Athrolani patrols don't wear hobnails.* They rounded the bend to see crossbows leveled in their direction. Eras raised her hands carefully. "Don't shoot." Her gaze inched over the high-collared coat of the foremost warrior. Other than its gray color, it was identical to the black one Eras herself wore. She reached out, palm up in the Asai gesture for deference. "I'm Nei'phieras liu Aneral, General of Athrolan."

The man in gray frowned. "Daughter of Lenu'phieras?" When Eras nodded, he lowered his bow and placed a hand on hers. "I'm Albi'giran. I know you only by name, but I rode with An'thoriend for a time."

Greetings through, Eras stepped back. "What happened here?"

"It's better told by a fire and after supper. We saw your camp. Might we join you?"

Eras's mouth twitched. "If we can agree to not wave weapons about any more."

Albi'giran's bow was both humorous and genuine. He fell into step with Eras as they returned to the river bank. "You found the tower?"

Her mouth twisted. "Why haven't you buried them yet?"

"We arrived three days ago. We've been scouting, searching for survivors." When Eras looked at him, curious, he shook his head. "None."

The Athrolani guards around the camp sent up whistled warnings, but Eras waved at them. "Hold, they're with me. Lay a fire." She hid a smile at the soldier's grateful sighs. The Asai stayed at the edge of the camp, watching as tents were moved to make room for the fire. Eras's gaze inched over them, curious as to how used to humans she had become. *They are my people, and yet look foreign.* Her features were angular and ashen; those of the Asai were exotic, almost awkward, and gray-brown. Their red hair was long regardless of sex, though it was not immediately clear which were male and female.

As stew was passed about, Albi'giran crouched beside Eras, his bowl balanced on his knee. "This attack—it was due to the war?" His tawny eyes were bright.

Eras glanced over, her surprise mocking. "The Asai are less isolated than I thought."

Albi'giran's smile was humorless. "When we hear stories of the Laen and Rakos, we tend to listen. Our group was a scouting mission to learn more of this war and to protect our secrets."

"What do you mean?" Eras absently watched her men settle into tense conversation with the newcomers.

"We each carry a chest filled with our most precious tomes. Our leaders knew attack would come. They wanted our knowledge to be preserved, if not our people." He scraped his bowl clean then laid it at his feet. "I told you our tale, now tell me yours. You come to ask for help?"

Eras pursed her lips. She was suddenly aware of how expressive she had become while living among the Athrolani. "Her Majesty of Athrolan asked me to see what numbers we could gain."

"And you were sent after half your blood. Do you fight for the gods or the Laen?" Albi'giran's companions glanced over at their captain's words.

"The Laen." Eras forced her hands to stop fidgeting. The Asai read stillness as honesty.

"Ca'nuran, what think you?" Albi'giran's gaze flicked to an Asai woman leaning on a tentpole. Like him, she wore the long coat of command.

"Battle is a cycle. A king too set in his ways, or a land with no one to lead. We rarely involve ourselves and the situation still resolves. Why is this different?"

Eras shifted to see the woman better. "I may have been unclear earlier. You asked if we fight for the Laen. We do. One particular Laen."

Albi'giran's expressionless facade slipped and his brows rose. "I told you, I rode with An'thoriend. I was with him when the Dhoah' Laen was cut down."

"Then you did not ride with him long enough. The true Dhoah' Laen was forgotten in a small city-state. She's trained and returned to us, ready for battle. She has a Rakos guard who has become an Earth Shaker and a brother who is taking over Mirik and allied himself with the Nenev."

The female Asai met Albi'giran's gaze for several moments of silent deliberation. When he nodded, she turned back to Eras. "We'll join you then, when we've laid this city to rest."

Albi'giran frowned. "Will you stay and help us?"

Eras shook her head. "I didn't stay when they were living. I certainly won't for the dead."

Vinden leaned on the tree beside the general, watching as the Asai dispersed into the darkness. "That was it?"

"You expected a conversationalist?" Her mouth twitched. "A great debate? A stirring speech, the inspiration from people united? Really, Vinden, it's like you don't know me at all."

He snorted. "I suppose you are more forthcoming than we realized."

Eras sat back on her heels. "To you I am a stone, to them, a font of expression."

Φ

The 16th Day of Aeme, 1252
The City of Ceir Athrolan

Furtive knocking interrupted Bren as he crouched to bank his fire. He had gotten used to having the evenings to himself at Mirik. He debated pretending he was already asleep.

"I know you're awake—I can hear you messing with the fire." Arman's growl muttered through the door. "Just open up?"

Bren rose with a groan and let the man in. "I suppose I'll have to become accustomed to all-hours-visitors if I'm going to be commissioner." Bren sat on the end of his bed, watching Arman seat himself by the fire. "I was starting to wonder if you were still in the city."

Arman ignored the veiled question. "What do you know of the Rakos?"

Bren shrugged. "Just what I've read, and that's not a lot. Scarce information about you people it seems. They controlled fire, created some sort of monsters." Bren's military training caught the tension around Arman's eyes. "I'm wrong?"

Arman slid from the chair onto the hearth, and rolled up his sleeves. He stirred the fire with his bare hands. The sparks he displaced rolled upwards, across his hands and curled around his forearms. He flicked them away after a moment. He did not meet Bren's eyes.

"You're not burnt." Bren gestured to the yellow, peeling skin on Arman's arms. "Is that what I think?"

Arman stood abruptly and tugged off his shirt. Scales dotted his shoulder blades, wrapping around his biceps and spiraling across his chest. Small ones formed white ridges along his forearms and neck, this skin flaking around them as they grew. The largest, armoring plates were bright gold.

Bren ran a hand through his hair. "When?" He was at a loss. "Toar, what does this mean? You're saying they didn't make the monsters—creatures?" He corrected himself hastily.

"They became them."

"Can Alea do something?"

"She cannot know." The blond man bared his teeth. "This is something out of both our control."

"Then why tell me?" Bren's eyes were taught to see weakness. He picked out the trembling in Arman's hands, the pulse thundering in his throat, but the only weakness in the form before him was in the eyes. "You're going mad." He wished it was only an insult, but the Rakos's eyes were manic.

"I chose this and Alea cannot know." The command held no trace of a question. "I want her to remember me like I was the last time I saw her."

"I won't tell her, not until she asks and I have nothing more to tell her but lies." Arman's first statement caught up to Bren. "What do you mean, you chose this?"

Arman began to pace. "I had to be something greater, so I could help her. I thought of the uncertainty and fear she had when she first learned her power. We are opposite. So I gave myself fearlessly to my Rakos side. I do more than control fire. I create fire. I *am* fire."

"You sound like this is the end. You can't turn back?"

"I saw things in my power—like when I saw that soldier's thoughts on our way from Hero. I saw the future and past. I saw the battle. I felt my death."

Bren suddenly understood. *He needs someone to know. Even if she remembers him whole, he needs someone to know why.* A knock interrupted his next thought.

"Bren?" Alea's voice was soft. "Are you awake?"

Bren's gaze flicked from the door to Arman. The Rakos leapt onto the ledge of the open window. He shook his head, commanding Bren to silence, before jumping into the gardens below. Bren waited a moment then opened the door.

Alea smiled a greeting at him, but her eyes traced the room behind. "I wanted to see you for a moment. I thought I heard talking. Are you alone?"

Bren nodded and shrugged sheepishly. "Just talking to myself. Come in."

She sat in the chair Arman had just vacated and tucked her legs up. "I met Lord Daymir for lunch again. He mentioned a few concerns about your plans for Mirik. I disagree, but many may not."

"What concerns?" Bren knew many took issue with his lack of experience and breeding. Hearing it from a man as powerful as Daymir, however, made his hackles rise.

"How much support you will need from Athrolan. I suggest you meet with him casually. He said he wanted to speak with you and it might ease both your concerns." She shrugged lightly. "Perhaps if you made some plans public, you would gain faith."

He stared at the floor thoughtfully. "Lord Daymir seems intelligent. Perhaps he might have insight for some difficulties." At Alea's pointed look he held up his hands. "Not too much insight, I promise! I can do this without them." He laughed.

She grinned, but he saw it did not reach her eyes. "I just thought I would let you know. I'm headed into the gardens for some air. Care to join me?"

"I should focus on the city. Enjoy the evening, though." Bren took out his captain's log and began turning down his covers.

Alea paused in his doorway. "You haven't heard from Arman, have you?"

"I'm sorry Alea. I wish I had news for you." Bren schooled his features into steadiness before turning. Her eyes were not fixed on his, but on his open window.

Φ

Alea stopped at the room beside her brother's. She had heard voices, conversation, before she knocked at Bren's door. Often she heard someone moving about on the other side of her wall, but there was never any light under the door. When she focused she could feel his location. Sometimes the heat and shimmering power felt only inches away. *And just a moment ago, I felt him in Bren's room. I smelled metal and ash on his chair and heat rolled from his window sill.* Part of her hated Bren for lying, but the rest was still too stunned.

She hurried down the stairs to the garden, not bothering with a cloak. The air was balmy and beautiful, the sky clear. The gentle weather belied the city's dark atmosphere. Clustered in the garden's center were weeping cherry trees, the curtains of their boughs waving in the mild breeze. She found a secluded bench and lay back on it. She kicked off her slippers and let her feet trail in the waving grasses. It took only a mental beckon for her power to rise. Sparks danced across her fingers and palms. She had been practicing with water, but it lacked the excitement of lightning.

She reached out and caught a falling blossom, floating it above her palm as if on the surface of a pool. The silver sparks drifted up from her palm and into the petals. The electricity followed the flower's veins, becoming a miniature lightning storm in the shape of the cherry blossom.

Heat suddenly shuddered through her and she looked up. A figure stood on the path several paces away. Only the silhouette of his shoulder and the golden glow of his eyes were visible.

The lightning in the blossom turned to ice then shattered, littering the ground with jagged crystals that melted after a moment. "Arman?" Her next words stopped him as he turned to go. "You won't talk?"

"There's nothing to say." His low voice lilted familiarly, but there was a new echo of metal.

"You never came to welcome me." Her words were calm, but her heart pounded. She sat up slowly, suddenly afraid she would startle him away. *He's not a wild animal.* She peered closer, wondering at the uncertainty in the thought.

"I didn't realize you were here yet."

She sighed at the feeble excuse. "The fact that my return was heralded from the bell towers aside—I can feel your power across the city, I can feel your pulse. I know you at least sense me, too."

"Is it so hard to think I might not want to see you?" His voice twisted into a snarl. "What did you wish to speak about, anyways?"

Everything. Anything. "What are you doing afterward?"

"After what?"

"The battle. The mending."

The gold orbs of his eyes slivered in a wince and he snorted. "If there is an after."

"I can do this without you, but I'd rather not have to. Why are you bitter? What changed? What made you love another, take her to bed?" She smelled smoke.

He ducked under the bower of the trees. "You could not deign to speak to me while you were in Le'yne, but you snuck about in my thoughts? Can I have nothing to myself?"

Alea jerked back. Her eyes burnt as if he had slapped her. "Perhaps I assumed, Rakos, but I thought friendship meant more than a night's tryst. Fates, we're soul-bound!"

"Our bond was a promise to fight and protect, Alea, not damned marriage vows! I can bed whom I will, without seeking permission!" His sudden use of her name was like a curse.

Alea's hand shook with strange urgency. *Anger.* It had been a long time since she had been this angry. *This is not the Arman I knew.* Her power surged. "You can keep your cheap bar-girl!" A crackling sphere of lightning shot towards him. It collided with a thin wall of flame, handbreadths from his chest. The wall swirled like magma. Alea's power fell, retreating into her arms.

"Think you're the only one who learned tricks?" Arman's dissipated slower, his hair curling as flames licked along the locks. The beds of his nails glowed like coals. Smoke spiraled from between his bared teeth. "You think you really could have stopped that bolt if you wanted? Could you prevent yourself from killing me?" He wheeled and staggered away. "After all, that's what you're good at, Destruction."

CHAPTER TWELVE

The 22nd Day of Aeme, 1252
The Eastern Coast of Athrolan

ARMAN'S STEPS WERE ERRATIC on the dew-dampened grass. He kept his power raging beneath his skin, though it had long since erased the chill of Alea's power. In his mind, he still felt the ice. He paused on the cliff tops, staring down at the dusk-shadowed waves of the ocean. The city was a day behind him. A line of ships dotted the water. *I was supposed to be on one of those. I was supposed to head north.* Instead, he marched east, paralleling their path on the land.

He had left all but his most essential belongings in his room, and the key in the lock. He would not use it again, he was sure. New fire burnt in him, the heat of shame and regret. *She wondered what I'd do afterward.* The cruelty in his words embarrassed him. He could have simply run when she threw power at him, but his anger held the reins to his tongue. It was the only way he knew to drive her away, make it a bit easier to do what he must. *Making amends does nothing, except worsen the hurt when I'm dead. It'd hurt more if we were close.* It might break his heart to drive her away, but he preferred that over causing her deeper grief.

You'll be unrecognizable by the time you regret it enough to change your mind.

He snarled at the voice and quickened his pace. The forest was thick here, and the trees twisted and ugly. His dreams had come more frequently, always the same voice snarling from the monstrous face. It was the voice that taunted him, first with An'thor's words, then with his own. He hated it, but it was a sneering reminder than he was not alone. Each time he sunk into his power the glittering eyes appeared in the back of his mind. The scar over one told him they were Eana's, but he dared not focus on them for too long.

Fear. Fear.

"I'll find you, you bastard. You and the rest of our mad brothers." There were more Rakos in the world. Unrecognizable and forgotten, perhaps, but alive.

Φ

The 23rd Day of Aeme, 1252
The City of Ceir Athrolan

Daymir swirled the berries in the bottom of his liquor glass. The view from his family's manor in the upper tier of the city was one of the best and offered the palace and cemetery beyond. He had been honest to Alea when he said few considered him the queen's heir. The fact remained, however, that he was Tzatia's closest living relative. *And what will I inherit? A bankrupt nation of the dead?* He was rarely given to dour thought, but Bren's recent claim of Mirik's throne had made him think of his own future. He folded himself behind the large desk by the window and pulled over a small collection of parchment.

He was the eldest child of the queen's younger brother. Daymir's sister, Jantia, married young, leaving him in charge of their parents' estate when their father passed. Daymir's head was one of business, and he enjoyed advanced arithmetic and economics while a squire. When he became a gallant, he took a post in the city, governing over the treasury and military coffers, as opposed to commanding men. It was a post that suited him. Now he was glad for the authority and foresight.

The papers before him were the checks and balances of the nation for the last two years. *Since the Berrin began ferreting about on our borders.* Athrolan had benefited from the influx of nobles after Mirik's great exodus—the taxes on wealth increased and the city had padded her pockets, just in time for war. *And war is damned expensive—drains men, resources, money.* The money set aside for such things was long gone and Tzatia had been turning to other savings. Road repairs were two years late and all but the largest unguarded. Daymir helped his aunt pinch and stitch, taxing more and spending less, but it was hard and the cost of protecting their people grew ever higher.

He may have aged, but his interests had not changed since his days as a squire, and his foresight was still clear. "Currow?"

His steward entered with a short bow. "Milord?"

"Can you have thirty-four thousand great-pieces placed aside? Here is the writ authorizing it, and I would like it to be safeguarded in the lower treasury under Authority of the Treasurer. Today, understood?" His words were quick as he wrote the paper for his steward.

"You're the Treasurer, sir." Currow answered with a frown. "Why not have it under your personal authority?"

"Because this is not for me. It's for our future." Daymir sat back. "Now please, time is wasting." When the man was gone, the heir moved back to his window, watching the clouds thoughtfully. *My aunt is a good woman, but too kind. An alliance with a broken nation? The fostering of a soldier-king? These will only quicken our fall.* With Alea on their side they would win, of that he was confident. *The queen looks only as far as victory, and does not see the hole of bankruptcy that yawns beneath us.* After a moment he checked the time and began to tidy his desk. If he hurried, he could see the Dhoah' Laen just before she called for lunch. With a smile, he grabbed his cloak and headed for the door.

Φ

The 23rd Day of Aeme, 1252

An'thor's stern knocking woke Bren midmorning. He groaned a response and dragged himself to let the man in. "What is it?" He tugged on a shirt and hopelessly tried to order his hair.

"I am sending word to my capital. The queen's address is in less than a month. You should be there."

"I was assuming to be." Bren rinsed sleep from his mouth with the stale water beside his bed. "Everyone else is leaving though. Whatever happened to a united front, with allies and all that? Eras is weeks gone and Arman left a night or two ago."

"He saw you?" An'thor eyes brightened with curiosity.

"I'm as close to her as he'll let himself get." Bren sighed. "So why did you wake me to tell me things I already know?"

"Brentemir, this will be your first public appearance as Lord Commissioner. You need something better than the garb of a Miriken lieutenant. Both for the address and for battle."

"I take it all back." Bren flopped onto the bed. "If being a lord means pompous clothing, I renege."

An'thor snorted. "Valadai will get you squared away, and I'd recommend Master Rulhan for your armor."

Bren rose, composing himself. "All right. Why are you writing home? Are you calling them here? I could use a few troops."

An'thor bated. "Yes, and asking them a favor for your sister." He grinned and ducked out of the door.

Bren looked at his bed longingly, but called for Valadai instead. While he waited, he tugged open the chest at the end of his bed. His Miriken armor lay within. It was boiled leather with bronze mail beneath. It bore as many scars as his own skin. *An'thor's right, though, I need to look the part.* He had been taught to mend armor as well as the next soldier, but this was different. He ran his hands over a few of the deeper dents, feeling unexpected nostalgia. *You saved my life enough times.*

Valadai's arrival pulled Bren from his reverie. "Lord Commissioner."

"Master Valadai. An'thoriend informed me that I will be standing state beside Her Majesty for the address. I need to fit my titles."

The man hid a smile well, but his eyes softened. "I can have your measures taken from any clothes you brought with you. What colors were you thinking?"

Bren dug about in his wardrobe for the set that fitted best. His middle had grown thicker since leaving the army. He paused as Valadai's words sunk in. "Colors?"

"Yes, my lord. You may have noticed the court finery here often has a palate."

"Oh. Well. Mirik's colors then. Vermilion and green. More of the former, though. It's a fierce color. Good for a Military Commissioner, don't you think."

"Certainly. And the style?"

Bren groaned. "Something serviceable. I'm not a peacock. I liked the outfit for the ball during our last visit. But with a Miriken half-cloak, please." He stopped Valadai as the man began to bow himself out. "Might you tell me where to find Master Rulhan? He's a smith."

Valadai's smile broke free from its restraints. "Yes, milord. He is the head of the Smithing Guild, and his smithy makes all the armor for Her Majesty's troops. He's behind the barracks and the stables."

Bren flushed and waved his thanks. He collected his armor with a disparaging sigh and headed across the palace. He followed the smell of burning and metal to the rearmost part of the barracks. The rhythmic noise was close to deafening and he had to shout at a young apprentice for directions. Bren dodged through the smithy toward a Sunamen man twice his breadth. "Are you Master Rulhan?"

The man shoved the metal he was working into the coals and turned, motioning Bren into a side room. His dark skin was stained with ash and his black braids were cinched with copper bands. He wiped a hand on his apron and offered it to Bren. "I'm Master Rulhan. What can I do for you?"

Bren took the hand. "I'm Brentemir Barrackborn."

Rulhan's brows rose and he bowed. "Forgive me, my lord." He grinned as he straightened. "Best be adding those titles on there, though, else some might not take you serious."

Bren flushed and held up his armor. "That's partly why I'm here. I'm told soldier's armor is not seeming of my rank."

Rulhan took the pieces, surveying them with a strict frown on his leathery face. "How have you lived this long?" The question was mild, but the smith winced. "The craftsmanship may have been serviceable once, but it looks like a blind man used this for a chamber pot."

"Given the number of times I had to repair it myself, it's a wonder I'm still here."

"Some god must fancy you."

"I think it's more likely my sister scares the wits from any god."

Rulhan glanced up, eyes unreadable. "She does my people honor."

Bren had forgotten, almost, that the Sunamen had raised Alea. "I'll tell her so."

"At any rate, I'll begin from scratch. The lad will take your measures, but first, tell me of your fighting style and your weapons, so I might design the best piece for you."

Bren's eyes widened. He had always worn whatever was large enough. It was often old and ill fitting. To have armor designed solely for him was a novelty. He grinned and began his explanation, looking over Rulhan's notes and making changes where he saw fit. It took the better part of an hour before he was measured and on his way again. He made a mental note to send Arik and Kemmer to get their own armor to be repaired or replaced. He was headed to his room when Alea emerged from her own, dressed in a split skirt dress and breeches. Her mood was reserved.

"Good morning." He smiled broadly.

"How have you spent your morning?"

"Busily. I just came from the arms-smith. An'thor made it known that my armor was not fit for me to wear and I had to order new clothes for the address as well. Will you have new things made?"

"Of course." Her eyes sparkled impishly at his ignorance. "My dress is already ordered though." She paused. "I was thinking about having armor made for myself as well. What do you think?"

"I think if I were Azirik I'd piss myself. Where were you off to?"

"I wanted to find an empty training hall. Being still is giving me nerves."

Bren gestured to the rear of the palace. "Those in the palace are often empty. Care for some company?"

She leaned on his doorframe as he changed into old clothing. "I saw Daymir in passing yesterday. He said you trained together for an afternoon?"

"We did. We spoke little, but he seemed more at ease afterward. I hope we can develop a rapport." Bren made a face. "I hope he doesn't think I'm completely incompetent."

She laughed and fell into step beside him as they headed towards the practice courts. "I think he worries about inheriting as much as you. It would serve you well to become friendly." She pushed open the door to the training hall to find it deserted. She surveyed the room while Bren lit the torches. Racks of wooden or dulled practice weapons stood along one wall. The floor was covered in sawdust. "It smells like Vielrona."

Bren began his forms, broadsword humming through the air. His movements were careful and slow, building strength from the control. Every few steps he glanced over at Alea. Power filled his sister's body, black snakes writhing under the pale surface of her skin. She moved her hands in the strikes and blocks of a hand-fighter, but they were careful and slow. Each strike sent lightning crackling across her fists and up her arms, the block smacking with the force of a wave. The patterns her feet traced in the sawdust were edges in ice. Her hair whipped as she turned, water droplets surrounding her as they spun free from her skin.

When she came to a stop Bren applauded. "Toar, Alea, you're amazing." He began to move faster, adding speed to the force of his blade. They moved in mutual silence, pacing around the room like circling predators. The bell tolled close to noon before Alea spoke again.

"I won't hurt you, but stay in that corner, will you?"

Bren turned to see her in the center of the hall. He frowned, but did as she bade, tightening his steps. After a moment even his movements slowed and he simply watched.

"I have an idea about the battle, but it's rough. I was hoping I might have your input."

"I'm not sure what use I'll be."

"Is Arman still ours?"

"What?" His heart faltered at the ferocity in her eyes. "What do you mean?"

"You saw him the other night. I told you I could feel him breathe. You think I couldn't tell he'd been in your room?"

"Alea, I'm sorry—"

"I'm not angry. I saw him, regardless, and I think I understand your reasons. Thank you for trying to protect me. Is he still ours?"

"You saw him."

"I no longer know the man he has become." Her words were clipped from anger or something else Bren could not name.

"Regardless of his words, or yours, he's yours. He always will be, Alea." He frowned. "What is your plan?"

"Watch." She grabbed his hand briefly, just long enough for icy tingling to wash over him, then she let go. "Trust me." She closed her eyes and spread her fingers. He watched her chest heave with slow, deep breaths. With each inhalation the air grew colder. Moisture dripped down the stone walls, pooling in the sawdust. The puddles grew, the water rising. It crept across the floor towards them and Bren mentally repeated Alea's command to trust her. *I hate water.* He ordered his feet to stay still. The water was a pace away from him when it halted, still rising, but moving no closer. It continued to fill the room, roaring, thundering around them, past waist height. Still it did not touch him. *I'm in a bubble of her power.*

Alea was not, however. The water surrounded her, swirling over her head. It crashed against the ceiling and Bren wondered if he should break her concentration, if she would drown. He was about to call her name when her eyes flew open.

The silver light pierced through the water and her voice echoed in his mind. *Imagine this, across an entire battle field. All our allies protected, all our enemies drowning.* The power in her voice pulled terrified nausea to his stomach. *Imagine the battle field covered in the power of the oceans and the other half burning, ignited with Arman's power.* The water retreated slowly, draining the way it had come. The damp sawdust was the only evidence of her colossal display.

Bren reached a shaking hand to his sister as the glow in her eyes faded. He had seen atrocities as a soldier. They had made his stomach tight, at first, even made him sick. Nothing shook him to his bones like she did. "I'll need a bit of time to process that." He sheathed his sword with shaking hands. Seeing the guarded expression on her face, he felt suddenly guilty. She was alienated enough. "I love you, still."

Her smile was brief, and erased by a frown when he sank on to a bench. "Are you all right?"

"We're going to win." He could only manage a whisper, but there was no doubt in his words.

Φ

Alea tilted her face up to the sun. Though Bren had offered to accompany her to the smithy, she declined. He was dear to her, but his energy sometimes only highlighted her loneliness. A squire guided her quickly to the office in the rear of the forge. The door was open and she knocked quietly. "Master Rulhan?"

The broad man glanced up then stared. "Dhoah' Laen?"

She smiled. The sight of his myriad braids and deep, rich eyes made her heart ache unexpectedly. "You're of Sunam?" She used her native language, throat tight around the familiar sounds.

"As are you, I've heard." He followed her lead and fell into the throaty Sunamen tongue. "What might I do for you today?"

"I'm looking for armor. Something light, simple."

He leaned back, broad hands crossing behind his head. "If you care to have a seat, I'd gladly design you something."

She sat, all nervousness erased by his low voice and the punctuating gestures that he had learned as a child. When he asked about her fighting style, she met his eyes. "I'll need something in metal—no boiled leather, and I'll need to move easily."

He sketched a few more lines on his design and slid it across the desk for her to peruse. "May I ask what town you call home?"

"Cehn. I was raised by Ahme'reahn ira Suna, may he be blessed with peace."

Rulhan's lined face softened into weathered wrinkles. "Oh, I am so sorry. I have not been home in many years, but I am lucky that its streets still bustle and my mother and brothers and sisters are as loud and playful as ever. What do you miss the most, besides your family, may they be blessed with peace?"

"The layers." She looked up, noting the perfect understanding in the man's eyes. "I miss the smell of the sand cooking under the sun and the spices blowing up to my window from the market."

"And the way the palm fronds would hiss in the wind, the sand scuttling across the stones like women on their way to do the washing. I told your brother you did us honor."

"Your words are kind, but untrue. I am a poor example of a Sunamen woman."Alea slid the paper back to him. "This looks lovely, thank you." She rose and made for the door, but his voice stopped her.

"How many sandstorms did you live through?"

She smiled. It was a common phrase, noting the speaker's greater age. "Nineteen years' worth."

"You remember them well, then. You remember the rage with which they beat our walls. All those layers you loved, they tore them away until all that was left were our souls, sometimes." He gestured to her. "Dhoah' Lyne'alea, you are a sandstorm beating against the world. You are more Sunamen than anything."

She pressed her brow against the doorframe. "Do you miss it?"

"Every day. Now, let me get to work on your armor, *ahalni.*"

Her smile broadened at the Sunamen term that meant both "sandstorm" and "terrible blessing." The mirth felt strange on her sorrow-worn features and she maneuvered her way back across the forge. She took a winding route back to the palace, enjoying the sounds of the city and the warmth.

"Dhoah' Lyne'alea, this is a pleasant surprise!"

Alea shielded her eyes to see Daymir crossing the street. She waved a greeting. "How is your day going, Lord Daymir?"

"Well. Would you care to join me for lunch?"

"Where were you thinking?"

"I was just returning to the manor, and planning on having whatever my household prepared. If you have an idea, by all means, direct me."

Alea paused. *What would he say if I asked to find a street vendor? If I wanted to walk the market?* "Yours is a fine suggestion. I have a brief errand to run, then I'll pay you a visit."

Daymir gave her a true smile then. "I'll await you patiently."

Her errand was as much an excuse as anything. She quickly exchanged her training clothes for a light gown. She glanced in the mirror and frowned. She looked like a noblewoman. *How do I want him to see me?* She never cared which side she showed to Arman. She had been weak and strong and distant in turns, and each new change he took in stride. *Until now.* She ignored the nasty voice in the back of her mind and turned back to her dressing table. Daymir was an ally and she would treat him as such. She unbraided her hair and removed all her jewelry. Another glanced in the mirror before she left told her enough. She was unquestionably Laen.

Daymir's manor was one of the largest in the noble quarter. Centuries of water run-off had stained the white stone gray. The high, iron gate was covered with ivy and led into a small courtyard. She pulled the thin chain beside the gate that no doubt rang a bell somewhere deep inside the house. Moments later a serving man swung the door open for her. "Good morning, Dhoah' Lyne'alea, welcome. I am Master Currow, steward of my lord Daymir's house."

Alea followed him through the large front door. The house was beautiful and she ordered her expression into careful appreciation. The finery of the palace was expected, but the beauty here was surprising in a manor for one family, even a royal one. Daymir himself opened the door and his greeting shook her from her admiration.

"Welcome!" He stepped aside to allow her through. "I'm flattered you took the time to visit me. The meal should be ready shortly. Would you like a tour of the house?"

She could not help but grin at his enthusiasm. "Please, it seems lovely." She followed him through the lower storey. The large dining room led into an intimate parlor and a portrait hall. Everything was rich peacock blue, with copper accents. "Does the rest of your family live here as well?" Alea peered at the portraits of his siblings and parents.

Daymir followed her gaze, hands clasped behind him."Only myself and the household. My sister married several years ago, and my parents are long passed. I manage the estate."

"You seem forever busy. Is there much business being heir and treasurer, or is it the estate that concerns you?"

He led her up the sweeping stairs to the smaller upper floor. "All, truthfully. Much of my time is spent with Her Majesty, advising and discussing matters of government. She listens, though I will not truly be considered heir until she grows ill, I think."

"How is it you became heir?" Bren's new duties had sparked her own curiosity.

"Her only daughter passed as a child. There are only distant cousins after me." He paused to let her admire the potted plants on the broad landing at the top of the stairs before opening a door to his private study. It was off the large master chambers and the other familial rooms were down a short hall. Papers and accounts were neatly stacked on the polished wood desk and a tall bookshelf stood behind. A table was set for a meal for two by the large window and two comfortable chairs were pulled out for them.

Alea took one of the seats, happily noting the steaming pot of tea on the table. "Your house is beautiful, Lord Daymir."

"Thank you, though it is my household to which you give the honor. I'm afraid I'm terrible at ordering such things. In the country, where I am unsupervised, things are in hopeless disarray."

She laughed, thanking him as he poured her tea. "Where are your family's estates?"

"The main family land is to the east, by the mountains. We also had a small manor not far from the Hartland with lovely pasture for sheep. I am afraid it has suffered from the latest raids, though."

"I'm sorry to hear that." The arrival of food interrupted Alea's next words and silence reigned as they ate. "You spoke of sheep, Lord Daymir. What does Athrolan trade in?"

Daymir looked at her curiously. "I never knew a woman who cared for politics if it wasn't necessary."

Alea winced at the assumption. "Athrolan is a land very different from where I was raised—in social customs, food and so forth. It interests me." She pointed at the plate before her. "For instance, this meal's flavor is a variation on a theme. Each part of a Sunamen meal has a distinct flavor." She paused, wrinkling her nose. "Forgive me, I met Master Rulhan today. Seeing a Sunamen face brought my thoughts to family and home."

"It must be wonderful to finally have a family." He looked at her with something that she assumed was intended to be sympathy.

"I'm sorry?" She frowned, glancing up from their food.

"Bren and your mother. Perhaps Azirik negates any stability they offer, but still, after not having a family, it must be nice."

She sat back. "Arman made your same mistake. I did have a family. I had a wonderful, loving foster father, and siblings."

"But they did not consider you such. You always refer the them with 'foster.'" His curiosity was gentle, but nonetheless probing.

"To my ihal I was daughter, to the others I was sister. It was I who add the 'foster,' not they. I do it to remind myself of the great gift they gave me, for which I will be forever grateful."

"It seems I place my boot in my mouth each time we speak." He looked down. "Forgive me, I realize I perhaps do not know you as well as I thought."

She allowed herself a smile, though her eyes were sharp. "How could you? We've barely met." She pushed away her empty plate. "But you are interesting enough for me to be curious to know more."

"In that case, if I may return to the safe subject of food, have you tried our maple syrup?"

"Never even heard its name."

"It's made from the sap of a tree we have here—not the paper birches, but another kind. It's sweet and best with breakfast."

"Perhaps with our next meal I'll try some." She rose as the plates were cleared and gazed out the window. She was aware of Daymir watching her, but did not turn to look. *What must I seem to him, this woman who sends his country to war.* Already his words told her enough of his opinions, despite the apology. "I have yet to visit Athrolan's library, but I was hoping to do some research. Is the collection extensive?"

"Quite. Not what it once was, in Claimiirn, but impressive. What were you hoping to find?"

She raised her chin, running a hand over the window's stone sill. "A way to kill the gods." She allowed herself a mental congratulations as he fell silent.

Finally he cleared his throat. "Your light talk and gentle manners make it easy to forget you embody Destruction."

"Creation as well."

"Right. You healed the Rakos." He looked down, making small folds in his napkin. "Do you mind if I ask you about it?"

She did mind, but knew the questions he would ask were not the most uncomfortable. "What did you wish to know?"

"What was it like? Did you fight the gods for him?"

"Souls go through me to Le'yne. It is a deep place, and guarded by the souls of the Laen. I had to tear them apart to find him, but I did."

Daymir shuddered. "Were you scared?"

She frowned. "I think I must have been. I ignored whatever part of me was scared." She watched as he thought over her words. *Please do not ask me why.*

"I heard he left for the south, to raise more allies?"

"I assume so. I want to investigate the library. Would you care to join me?" The invitation was dishonest, but she feared he would realize why she was fleeing the conversation.

Daymir rose, giving her his hand. "I'm afraid I have business this afternoon. Perhaps another time?" He escorted her to the manor's gates. "I hope you find what you are looking for, Dhoah' Lyne'alea."

She pulled a smile onto her face as he showed her out. Pretending at happiness grew harder each time. She wondered absently if it was the fatigue of pretending that caused some to die so young.

CHAPTER THIRTEEN

The 28th Day of Aeme, 1252
The City of Ceir Athrolan

THE SUN WAS JUST RISING when Alea startled awake. She curled into the enveloping library chair, an open book forgotten on her lap. Her shoulder and neck ached from the awkward position she had slept in. She frowned. She had dreamt of Arman and of anger, though she wondered if they were one and the same. She straightened with a groan.

"Dhoah' Lyne'alea?"

Daymir sat at a desk by the windows.

Her face flamed and she sat up hastily. "Good morning, Lord Daymir." She smoothed her hair and skirts. "Forgive me, I must have fallen asleep while reading."

He laughed. "I can't blame you. Some books are so dull. I didn't want to disturb you, but seeing as you're awake, how is your research going? Other than dream-worthy of course."

She smiled. "Well. I've learned a few things that might be useful."

When she did not provide more, he fixed her with a curious stare. "Could I help? I know this library well, and I might be able to answer questions you come across." His smile was easy, and she suddenly noticed how few lines it bore. "I want to be useful to you."

"Your help is welcome." She gestured dramatically to the pile of books before her. "I have yet to start these. I'm going to freshen up, but I'll be back in a moment." When she returned, washed and changed, Daymir had laid out parchment and quills neatly. He was already bent over a newer tome and making notes.

"You've gotten farther in a quarter of an hour than I did in five." She sat across from him in a huff of mock anger.

"I also took the liberty of ordering breakfast, as I assumed you had not yet had any."

She leaned forward, eyes narrowed. "Have you ever been filled with cold? I suspect you might be the real Dhoah' Laen."

He grinned. "Yes, you've found me out."

She matched his smile. The expression was still strange, but it was hard not to smile as their quick wits dueled. "We always seem to eat together."

"I believe conversation is more entertaining when stimulated with food. What have you found thus far?"

"Not a lot. I already know how the gods killed Lynelle. I read something that says their being—soul, I suppose—is linked to their power, but it was vague."

"It's a start." Daymir slid writing materials over to her. "And that is better than nothing."

The rest of the morning passed easily, and in relative quiet, save for the arrival of their meals. Alea enjoyed dipping ham and biscuits in the syrup Daymir had mentioned before. They found small details and vague allusions. Nothing was specific, but an idea began to uncurl in the darkness of Alea's mind.

Suddenly Daymir sat back. "Why aren't you attacking them now? Laying aside the lack of knowledge, of course. Not to judge, but wouldn't it be better to destroy the source of Azirik's power first?"

"Yes, if it were that simple. The God's Crown is a conduit to their magic. They could use it as a well to hold their power, thus preventing me from destroying them. Through the Crown I can follow the connection back to them." She looked down. "So unfortunately, for me to protect this world, we must first wage war across it."

Daymir's clear gaze narrowed with humor. "You're terrifying, you know?"

She flushed, embarrassed and oddly flattered. "So I've been told."

He tilted his head at her. "It's a pity you can't sit on a human throne."

The sudden subject change tripped her thoughts. "There's a law against someone like me ruling? You think the Creator and Destroyer is not enough for me? You wish to not take the throne yourself?"

"None. I think you would make a good queen. There are no laws, for there has never been anyone like you. I guess I assumed the Laen would disallow it."

She ran a hand over a tome's cover to hide her sudden anxiety. "Before the war many Laen worked for high-born families, but none took such positions or married into them."

"Until your mother and father." A wary grin crossed Daymir's face. "Given the power that union birthed, perhaps there were more valid reasons."

She laughed. "Perhaps. After being Dhoah' Laen, a queen's duty would be an easy task."

He snorted and turned back to the books before him. They continued in relative concentration occasionally breaking the silence with a humorous comment or puzzled question. It was relaxing, despite the grim nature of their subject.

When Bren arrived just before noon, Daymir rose. "I'm afraid I must abandon you to your work—there are a few treasurer duties I should see to before tomorrow."

"Thank you for all your help." She smiled as he bowed over her hand and disappeared. Alea returned to her seat, staring at her book thoughtfully, though she did not actually read the words.

Bren took Daymir's vacated seat and fixed her with a serious expression. "Sistermine, what's between you and Lord Daymir?"

She looked up, startled. "What do you mean?"

"You've been spending a lot of time together. It makes me wonder at the intentions on either side."

"On either side? Bren I don't see what you're getting at." Her heart faltered and she looked away. She had been enjoying the attention. It may have only been a shadow of Arman's faith in her, but she would take it. She had purposefully been honest about her nature, hoping to avoid the awkward predicament that Bren now mentioned. "Bren, he called me terrifying. I think I'm safe."

He reached over and touched her hand. "Alea, Daymir seems to have grown an interest in you. He's a good man, I think, despite his opinion of me." His grin was lopsided. "But I want you to understand something. He is a shrewd and intelligent thinker. He's circling you, gauging your worth, though perhaps less analytically than that sounds." He sighed. "Alea, unless you mean business with him, I suggest you pull away."

"I resent you telling me what's best. He's an ally, nothing more. He may be circling, but he would be a fool to think he can gain anything. I am the Dhoah' Laen, for goodness sake, not a noble daughter to be used in a power-bargain, or whatever it is you're suggesting."

"Alea, you were raised a noble's daughter and you are very much able to act the part. You have the bloodline. You're incredibly powerful and not the least bit stupid. You're a perfect match for a king raising his country."

She rolled her eyes. "Why don't you marry me then? Fates, Bren, you sound paranoid."

"I know how he thinks. Alea, you're powerful and terrifying, but right now you are incredibly vulnerable. You have suffered heartbreak. Even if no one knows, it was obvious you saw Arman next to never before he left, and your manner about him has been reserved. Lord Daymir will read into that what he will."

"You never brought this up when I was seeing Narier."

"I didn't think your heart was in any danger then. Also, Narier was obviously just enjoying your company, like you were his. I doubt he ever had any intentions beyond spending nights. I just don't want your hurt over Arman to turn into false affection for Daymir. It'll hurt you both in the end." He closed the book before him with a snap. "He was right in one thing—you should leave the books for the evening. Come get some air with me."

Bren found an open hillock with an ocean view. The garden was quiet, the city's bustle only a distant mutter. Alea leaned her head against her brother's shoulder. "I'm angry at him, Bren, and I wonder if I can forgive him, and whether I should. Yet, I miss him."

"What did he say? Do you mind telling me?"

She was quiet for a minute, sifting through the emotions from her encounter with Arman to untangle just the words. She was grateful Bren knew better than to interject. Her voice was calm and incredibly soft. "I asked why he sought company in another woman. He said I had no claim to him, which is true, and our bond was not that of marriage, nor should I treat it as such. I had no right to dig about in his affairs, for they were his alone. We fought, with our power." Her voice wavered. "Bren, I threw my power at him. He blocked it, but I still tried to hurt him. Before he left he asked if I could have stopped myself from killing him if he hadn't blocked." She looked down, picking at her nails. "He said it's what I'm good at." She felt Bren's jaw tighten in anger.

"Alea." He stopped. "I'm sorry. Those words were not deserved."

"Part of me wants to hate him for it, but I can't. I wish I trusted myself enough to name my feelings." She closed her eyes against the burn of tears, but they did not fall. "It seems wrong to save the world without him beside me. That's why I brought him back." She slumped back. "Bren, my heart hurts." The sorrow and understanding on his face only made it worse. "It hurts so badly that I don't know how to breathe sometimes."

"Alea, did you love him?" It was the second time he asked the question, but the depth behind it was totally different.

She did not need to ask to which "him" her brother referred. "I once told Narier no one had seen my soul bared. It's not true, though I didn't realize it. Arman has seen my fear and my despair. My anger, my determination."

"What about happiness?"

"I guess I hoped we would have time for that, too."

Φ

The 35th Day of Aeme, 1252

The scarf over Alea's hair felt both familiar and strange at once as her past warred with her present. The simple dress and plain breeches were less so. She took back halls to the barracks, her steps purposeful. It had been months since the siege, and she was not keen to make a fool of herself, but she was also lonely. The six-bed bunk rooms were labeled with surnames and she carefully paced down the rows, reading them. The variety of names told her much about Athrolan's trade history.

A young man stopped at the sight of her. "Miss? May I help you?"

She turned and shot him a smile. "I'm looking for Lieutenant Narier."

"You mean Captain? He got promoted last month. He expecting you?" The narrowed eyes were dark and she saw his guard visibly rise.

"No, not really. We're old friends and I'm finally back in the city. I thought I'd say hello."

He shrugged and pointed further down the hall. "Second to last on the left."

She followed his instructions, pausing outside the half-open door. She could hear the muted sounds of conversation and a deck of cards shuffled between calloused hands. Seeing the names on the doorframe she suddenly realized she did not know his given name. Before her nerves failed her, she knocked quickly. The talk paused and a chair scraped back.

An older man whose face she recognized, but name she did not know answered. "What might I do for you, miss?"

"I'm looking for Captain Narier."

"Hold a moment." He ducked his head into the room. "Narier, girl here to see you." He looked back to Alea. "Your name?"

"Alea."

His eyes inched over her and he stepped back a step. "Of course. Forgive me. Narier, it's the Dhoah' Laen."

Narier suddenly appeared in the door, shoving his friend aside. "Thanks, Jall, I'll take it from here." He did not ask her in, shutting the door instead. The hall was dim without the lantern light from the room. "Hello."

Her words faltered at his uncertainty. "Hello. It's good to see you again."

"And you." He ran a hand through his hair. "Dhoah' Lyne'alea, what're you doing here?"

"I thought we might talk, catch up, have a drink or two tonight."

"You're the Dhoah' Laen."

She frowned. Something cold bloomed in her stomach, but she was not sure why. "I always was."

His smile was sad and faint. "Oh. You don't see it, do you?" He drew a breath. "When we were together, during the siege, you were a young woman, bright and nervous with a big, shining title that didn't quite fit. Now she's grown and I can't even see her because you shine so bright, but if I could see through the glow of how brilliant you've become, I think I'd see that girl is gone. I don't recognize what's taken her place."

Alea stepped back, feeling the frown chase her nervous smile away. "Of course."

He had seen her as Alea, when she thought no one else had. Instead she mistook their indifference for fear and respect. Now she only had the latter two. She swallowed hard and shot him a falsely bright smile. "Of course. I'll see you about then. Good afternoon."

She walked slowly back to her room, trembling hands hidden in her skirts. The sound of her retching echoed against the tile of her privy room. She heaved again and again, wondering if she was sick enough everything she had become would fade, all the monstrous things in her mind would disappear. Perhaps Alea would return if she could rid herself of enough. Stomach empty, she lay on the floor, cheek to the cold flagging. It was impossible. There was nothing left of Alea inside her now, only cold and dark.

CHAPTER FOURTEEN

The 42nd Day of Aeme, 1252
The City of Ceir Athrolan

ALEA'S EYES WERE OPEN, but unseeing. Power filled her, but she did not use it. She reached deep into the earth to touch the massive icy pools within the bedrock. It was a way to center herself when insecurity threatened. Consequently, the exercise had become a daily ritual. Knocking cut through her concentration and her power faltered.

After the third knock, she sighed. "Who is it?"

"Daymir, Dhoah' Lyne'alea."

Darkness retreated from her skin and she smoothed her hair. When she pulled the door open it was with a smile.

Daymir's own smile faded when he met your eyes. "Are you all right? Your voice sounded odd."

She gestured for him to sit. "I was practicing my power."

"Hence the glowing eyes?"

She glanced in the mirror. Power still lit her irises. "Forgive me, I know it's unnerving." Sitting across from him, she changed the subject. "I see you have once again timed your visit to coincide with my midday meal. Shall I call for our food and be done with the pretenses?"

Daymir's smile curled ruefully. "That would be appreciated."

When she had ordered their meals she returned to her seat with a quiet sigh. "Our talks are a welcome diversion from dark thoughts."

"I feel the same. I train with the men, but knowing our skills will be needed soon darkens the fun." He tilted his head at her curiously. "You'll ride to battle again?"

It seemed so obvious she almost wondered if he was joking. "Yes."

"We were incredulous that you went to Shadow. I think only respect kept many from calling it foolish, begging your pardon."

"It was foolish." She was surprised by the embarrassment heating her neck. "I knew little about my power and vulnerability."

Daymir smiled. "I'm glad when you lead us next it'll be with the strength of your peoples' teaching behind you."

She looked down, frowning. Whatever her answer would be, it was stopped as their meals arrived.

Daymir apparently had seen, however, and after a few moments he asked gently, "Why did you frown when I spoke of them?"

"We disagree on several points, one being my power and how I should wield it. I can only hope they see my wisdom and aid me in the battle against the gods."

Daymir tilted his head. "Are you worried you can't do it alone?"

She looked down at her food, chewing thoughtfully. "No, but I went into every battle thus far with allies at my back. I would hope the most dangerous of all would be no different."

"Have you made any more headway with your studies?"

"I believe I have. Your notes about the source of their power helped a great deal." She could feel his senses sharpen each time she mentioned how much power she actually had.

"Yes, I thought that would be useful. Their magic can be destroyed along with their souls—though how you could do such a thing, on such a scale, I would rather not think about."

She smiled. "Understandable. I promise you, though, it will be done." She sat back, allowing their plates to be cleared and replaced with tea.

Daymir stared at her a moment, and she stared back, wondering at the dance of allies, nobles and friends. "I have an offer for you." His voice was lower than usual, and his features serious. "The reason I called on you today, actually."

Alea wondered suddenly if the abrupt tone was due to nerves. She had never seen him nervous. She poured them tea then made herself comfortable, waiting.

When they were both settled, he cleared his throat. "Your brother is acting king—an ally, no less. Your father is a crowned king. This makes you Mirik's princess."

She had not thought of herself as such. In the face of her other roles it seemed trivial. "I suppose, yes." His words hurtled toward the territory Bren warned against.

"Once this war is over, what were your plans?" He twirled his cup in his hands, almost splashing tea onto the burgundy brocade of his tunic.

"I hadn't thought on it. My energy is better spent preparing so there is an after."

Daymir took the gentle, yet pointed rebuke in stride with a smile. "And we will all be glad for it, I'm certain. I had a suggestion for you to think over. I stand to inherit Athrolan. With your political power, and obvious wisdom and level head, we would make a good match. It would be a position of wealth, for your comforts and the challenge of ruling for you mind. And," his voice lowered with well-concealed nerves, "I hope the acceptable companionship of myself."

Alea stared at him for several moments, speechless. "Are you proposing marriage to me?"

Daymir shifted. "I am."

She rose abruptly and went to the window, staring out. She felt his eyes bore into her back. She wished she was alone, so she could pace and worry the way she did on nights she couldn't sleep. Instead she stared unseeing down at the gardens. *Marriage.* Two years ago it had been something she needed to survive. She had been ready to start that life. Daymir posed an equally political and pleasant match, but something had changed. Her mind laughed at the idea now. *I'm not a young girl in need of protection. I am the Destroyer of Gods, the Creator of Worlds.* On the tail of those thoughts came another that she pushed aside. She knew who was the best match for her now. She straightened, still looking out the window. "What do you see when you look at me?"

"Excuse me?"

"What do you see?" She turned, letting only a fraction of the darkness inside her show. "When you sit there, on my couch, staring at me, what do you see?"

"I see our ally, I see Dhoah' Lyne'alea." He frowned.

She looked away. "You are so used to getting your way—not because you were spoiled, for I don't believe you were. You work for everything you have, with your mind and your money that you forgot sometimes other people work harder. You are mighty, Daymir, but my mind is darker than yours and my money far less and this makes me mightier than you. You are so used to getting your way that you only see what you want."

"What am I supposed to see?"

"Your aunt made a stupid mistake."

"Her Majesty is not stupid."

"No, but she is scared, Daymir. So very scared of her kingdom falling to ruin, of her people dying. A worthy fear, to be sure. But fear is dangerous, because it makes us desperate and desperation leads to stupidity." She did not move, save for her lips. Her eyes bored into the reflection of his, but even bounced off glass her expression was terrifying. "She believed me when I told her I would raise Athrolan, when I told her I would save her kingdom from falling. She believed I would even restore the Laen to power. So scared was she that she allowed a monster into her city. And you can't even see it."

His eyes were bright when she finally turned back, and cold slipped into her heart. He was afraid, certainly, for fear of her was an instinct, like fear of a storm.

But some men enjoy the sound of thunder, despite the fear. "Ah. Here I am trying to make you understand my power, hoping you'll stop your pursuit, when really, all I'm doing is making you more curious."

"You can think on it, if you wish. Like I said, after the war."

"Lord Daymir, I appreciate the sentiment, and the kindness with which it is offered. You would make a fine companion. I think, though, your offer shows a misunderstanding." She stepped over to where he sat and leaned forward, placing her hand on his. "I am not lost in this dangerous world. Perhaps I was, when I first arrived, but no longer. You forget I am not a human, and will not sit on a human throne. I cannot bear you heirs. I neither need nor seek political power. After this, all I seek is peace."

Daymir's lips tightened. "Do you seek it in the heart of Arrowlash?" The words were not cruel, but his tone was tense.

She winced. "Arrowlash is my ally and guard. Our relationship is no more than that. It is also none of your concern."

Daymir rose abruptly. "Forgive me for imposing on you, Dhoah' Lyne'alea. Good day." He bowed to her and showed himself out. The click of the door closing broke the tentative surface of Alea's emotions and she dropped her face into her hands. *That very well could have been the last proposal I ever receive. The last chance at the life of a woman.* She curled onto the couch, wrapping her arms around her shoulders and wept. *What chance did I ever really have of marrying and growing old beside a kind man? What wife would Creation and Destruction make?* She mourned that life, but a deeper part mourned the girl she once was.

A gentle knock interrupted her thoughts and when she ignored it a second, more persistent one sounded. "Sistermine, it's me. I saw Lord Daymir leave. His face...did you two argue?"

She collected herself then padded to her door. Bren was turning to leave when she opened it. His gaze ran over her tear-stained cheeks and swept her into a tight embrace. He stepped inside, arms still around her, and nudged the door closed with his foot.

"Toar, what happened?" His arms tightened around her and she felt her tears wet his shirt breast. "Did he hurt you?"

She shook her head quickly, pulling away and drying her eyes. "He asked me to marry him."

Bren's brows shot up and he pulled her onto the couch beside him. "Judging by his face, you declined." He ran a hand through his hair. "Is that tea still hot? I think we could both use a cup."

A tiny, real smile bloomed on her face while he poured her a cup. The world was at war and former Lieutenant Barrackborn's greatest concern was his sister's tears. "He was kind and thoughtful and gave me every reason to agree."

"I wondered if he'd propose and if you'd actually agree. I thought he'd ask after the battle, though." He shook his head.

"He offered to let me think about it until then. I can't imagine that life. Am I wrong? What other offers will I have, Bren? I know I'll never be a mother, but I had hoped to be loved. Am I selfish for wanting it all?"

Bren put down his tea and wrapped an arm around her again. "Alea, where are these thoughts coming from? I didn't know you wanted any of this. You could still have children."

"No, my body is not meant for it. I thought it was a curse, but now I think it is the combination of human and Laen blood."

"What do you mean?" The confusion on his open, angular face was almost comical.

"I don't bleed. Other women bleed with the cycles of the moon, twice a month. I never have." She shrugged. "I made my peace with it a while ago, but I still pictured my old age beside another."

"Oh." Bren sat back. "Why are you suddenly afraid of never?"

She sniffed, steadying her breath. "Perhaps, as a soldier, you made peace with mortality years ago. When my home was attacked I saw death—truly saw it—for the first time. Death surrounded me at Fort Shadow in the infirmary tents. With Arman I reversed it even. Somehow, I never realized that even if the world has an after, some people may not. For them, their world ended with this war." She sighed. "Am I making any sense?"

His soft laugh rumbled through her shoulder. "A bit. Seeing death is one thing. Understanding that it can happen to anyone is another. Understanding it can happen to you? Some people never realize that." He rested his chin on her head. "When did you start thinking this way?"

"It was gradual. Part of it came from Arman and Shadow. Seeing death so inglorious, without the rush and fear of danger. Part of it came from studying in Le'yne. As frustrating as my time there was, I learned a lot from the texts they had. I read about the splitting of the world. It is no wonder why they fear me."

She sat up and took a few calming sips of her tea. "I'm sorry. It occurred to me that Lynelle sacrificed herself to split the worlds. It's easier to break than to mend." She was quiet for a moment. "What if I have to do the same to bind them?"

Bren pulled away further to look her full in the face. "You're my only sister and I love you, dammit, and you're not going to die."

She smiled again, broader. "Bren, you're babbling. I love you, too. It's not death that bothers me, mostly. I worry I'll leave things undone. Unsaid."

Bren gripped her hand. "I promise you'll get through this. We all will." He pulled her over and rested her head on his shoulder again.

She let him hold her, her tears drying, the sudden emotions retreating back into her chest. There was another, darker fear that she did not share. She was afraid of herself.

Φ

The 43rd Day of Aeme, 1252
The City of Ceir Athrolan

Alea woke late in the morning, blinking at the bright light streaming in the window. She stretched and the day before rushed to the fore of her memory. She groaned and lay back down. *My focus is waning.* She winced and tossed off her covers. It was late and she should plan for the battles ahead. A soft knock interrupted her perusal of her wardrobe.

Giire smiled as she stepped in at Alea's bidding. "Good morning, Dhoah', I knocked earlier, but you seemed still abed. I brought you some tea and a message from Master Rulhan of the smithy as well." She handed Alea an envelope before pouring a cup of tea.

Alea opened the message hurriedly. "Please inform Master Rulhan he can deliver my armor here. Also, I think a bath would do me good." She paused. "Could you have a note delivered to Lord Daymir?"

Giire curtsied. "Of course. I'll draw up your water." She glanced back at Alea for a moment. "Begging pardon, but you had armor ordered?"

Alea began to undress. "For the battle."

Giire looked down. "You're so mild-mannered, I forget you are a warrior." She stepped into the privy to prepare the bath.

Alea frowned. *Is that what I am?* She wrote a quick note to Daymir then hurried into the bathroom with a happy sigh. *Warrior or not, the luxury of a hot bath will never be lost on me.* As she sank into the water, she thought back to Vielrona. The darkness in her heart then had been a different color, perhaps, but she recognized the signs of the same isolation and depression. *What took me out of that mood, then?*

Giire hummed softly as she worked the tangles from Alea's hair.

Alea suddenly grinned. "Giire, do you often go into the city proper?"

"A few nights, yes. There is dancing and music, not to mention handsome faces." Her hands were gentle.

Alea stepped into the towel that the girl held out, enjoying the rough fabric on her skin. Her mind twisted back to the small purse locked in her desk. "Giire, I have a bit of coin. If I wrote you a list, might you get me a few things?" When she nodded, Alea moved to her desk, drying her hair as she went.

Giire read over the short list Alea handed her a moment later, brows knitting. "Dhoah', why do you want a wig?"

Alea sat on her bed. "Giire, you may have noticed I'm unhappy. It's been a very long time since I laughed and danced and listened to music. I'd like to go out into the city, and I'd like to just be a woman for a night."

Giire's eyes lit up. "I know just the place!"

Φ

The 43rd Day of Aeme, 1252

Tinkling rang through the manor, signaling a message and Daymir pushed away his paperwork. His conversation with Alea the day before left him irritable and in no mood to speak with anyone, even through parchment. Currow brought the envelope up a moment later.

"My lord, Her Majesty wishes to see you before you take supper. And a letter is here from Dhoah' Lyne'alea."

Daymir took the envelope with a frown. "Thank you, Master Currow." He opened it as his steward exited.

> *Lord Daymir,*
>
> *I wanted to apologize for the way our conversation ended. Your offer brought up thoughts and fears that have plagued my mind for some time now, and I cannot face them until after the battle. In another time or place I would be happy to consider marriage and I am honored you thought of me. I hope this will not greatly affect our friendship, for I value it, and would be sad to see it fade.*
>
> *When, and if, you are ready to speak again, you know where to find me.*
>
> *Yours,*
> *Dhoah' Lyne'alea.*

He wanted to reply, but his ill humor would help little. He brought Alea's letter to his study and called for his summer cloak. Even as a child, he had met with his aunt in the evenings for private, casual conversations. It was through these, he was certain, that his interest in politics arose. As gentle as she was, his aunt was a smart woman and knew her post well. Daymir waited as he was announced, then stepped into the anteroom. His manor house was larger than the royal suite, but the finery here was unrivaled. The anteroom led into a large receiving room that adjoined a study, beyond which was the queen's sleeping and dressing quarters. They normally took tea in the more intimate study, but this evening, Tzatia waited for him in the receiving room. Here the decorations were the formal colors of Athrolan, as opposed to the queen's favored lavender. She stared out the window. He could not see her face, but her back was stiff.

"Evening, aunt. Shall I order tea, or do you wish to take supper together?"

"Lord Daymir, I am your queen and your should address me as such." Many would have thought the tremble in her voice was anger. Daymir knew better. It was fear.

"What is it?" He ignored her request for formality. "Who has upset you?"

She turned and he saw, regardless of fear, her face was livid. "You, Daymir!" she faltered. He reached to steady her, but she backed away. "You think you can swindle and pinch and I won't notice? You may be Treasurer, but goodness, I am Queen!"

"What are you talking about?" He stepped towards her again.

She slapped him across the face. "A writ to move thirty-six thousand crown to an account accessible only to you? You think I would fall for this again?"

His mouth dropped open, both at her blow and her words. "Fates, Tzatia. You think that was swindling?" His temper rose. "It was for our future! I am not your husband. I inherit this nation and I intend for it not to be bankwasted when I do."

"Not anymore." Her hands shook as she offered an envelope. It was decorated by her royal and personal seal as well as those of several advisors. It was address to him.

Dread filled him. "'Not anymore,' what?" He opened the envelope quickly. It was a formal document stating his attempt to steal from the crown. It stripped him of his titles and power as Treasurer and his right to the throne. "You're jesting." He rubbed a hand across his eyes. "Tzatia, I was thinking of Athrolan. You have seen Mirik fall to the consequences of war. I was trying to aid our kingdom, not better myself! You can stop this now. Revoke it." Alea's words about fear and deseration echoed in his head.

Her mouth set in a determined line. "It's done. I sent it to the scribes. If your actions were only for the kingdom, why did you propose marriage to Dhoah' Lyne'alea? Was that for us as well? You could have destroyed our alliance!"

"She's interesting and intelligent and would make a good ruler. I enjoy her company."

Tzatia turned, running a hand along the back of her settee. "I no longer recognize you as my heir, or Treasurer of the kingdom. You are stripped of your lordship and gallantry, relieved of all estates, excepting those of your father and excused from court and my person."

He realized then that she was serious. "For what little my word is worth, I only ever thought to raise our home." He bowed. "Forgive me for choosing the wrong path by which to do so. Good night, Your Majesty." He showed himself out and moved stiffly down the hall. He contained himself until he once more stood in his manor. As soon as the door shut, he slumped against the wall of the anteroom, a trembling hand over his eyes. Every constant in his world was gone. He drew a breath, then another. This was what he was good at—clearheaded thoughts while the world crumbled. He never thought it would be his world. He swallowed hard, mind racing, and called for Currow.

"How was your visit with Her Majesty, my lord? You did not stay as long as I expected. Would you like me to order your supper?"

Daymir ignored the offer. "Have all my personal effects packed. They are to be shipped home, to the estate. All my accounts and debts are to be paid off—from my personal funds, please. The furniture not owned by the crown will be sold, as will all horses save for my jumper and charger. All but the nuclear household staff is dismissed with compensation though the end of the month."

"My lord?" Currow stared at Daymir, a deep frown on his face.

Daymir looked up. Currow had served the Xain family since Daymir's father had inherited. They knew each other like family.

"Is this about the funds you transferred?"

"I was safeguarding for after the war, so we would not have empty coffers with which to rebuild. She saw it as swindling, like with Parkvenir. She disinherited me and stripped me of all titles."

"Is there anything else I can do for you, my lord?"

"Stop calling me 'lord.' I am no longer one. I am simply Master Daymir."

Currow bowed his head. "I'll set your affairs in order then, Master Daymir."

"Currow?"

"Yes, sir?"

"I would appreciate your utmost discretion and haste."

"Of course, sir."

Daymir watched him go, then hurried up to his study. It was no longer his, truly. He penned a reply to Alea and sent it out. He was halfway through packing the contents of his desk and bookshelves when the second shock wave of the events hit him. He sunk onto the floor beside the trunk of books. He drew off the ring of the royal house and the seal of Treasurer. All that remained was his personal signet ring, alone on his hand. He felt naked.

Φ

The 1st Day of Lumord, 1252
The Feld de Barran

Dense clouds obscured the windswept rocky fields below. The air whipped as Arman passed, curling around him and through him. It tickled. He grinned, though he wondered if it was truly a smile when his body had no more form than smoke. Leaving Athrolan lifted a mass of lead from his gut. He was not sure it if was due to what he left behind or flew toward. Tzatia had asked him to accompany the fleet, but something deeper drove him south. He crossed leagues in minutes, his unsubstantial body wheeling with each gust of clouds and air.

Ahead, the familiar crest of the Orn de Duhtain rose, barely scraping the underbelly of the clouds. He had seen so much, done so much, that even home looked quaint. *Will Vielrona ever be home again? Will any of them know me?* He bent, diving lower as he grew nearer the city. *Besides, if there were ever a place the Rakos hid, it would be in Vielrona.* The arms of the hills below curled about his home. His smile grew as he caught the brilliant glow of firelight. With so many torches, he must be arriving in the midst of a festival.

He banked again, wheeling closer. The smoke smelled of meat and acrid rot. The rubble below still smoldered. Few walls were left standing. *Fates, not this.* His tears and adrenaline sharpened his eyes, and they caught movement on the edge of the destruction. The fields that had once held cows were now a survivors' camp. The bloated carcasses of livestock were piled high. The fact that some bore marks of butchering spoke to the desperation of those left.

Makeshift lean-tos and tattered shelters clumped in vague groups. There were only enough to house eighty, a hundred at most. Grief caused his concentration to stutter and his bones began to reform. He tumbled from the air, muscle and organs writhing back into place as they solidified. He exploded onto the ground, limbs shaking from horror and pain. Rage billowed. "This was my home!" The voice that tore itself from his throat was not one he recognized. The destruction was greater than he ever imagined, greater than anything he saw at Shadow. It was as if the mountains themselves had tried to swallow the city.

He was suddenly aware of the silence behind him. The camp was still, those closest staring at him. They were too exhausted to be curious, and pain had burnt away any awe that might have shone in their eyes. Arman staggered to his feet and turned toward them. They slowly went back about their work, not caring that a man just materialized from the clouds.

A familiar dark figure cleaned ashes from an old well and Arman stepped closer, waving smoke from his eyes. "Kam?"

The man straightened, blinking at him for a moment. Recognition swept the locksmith's features suddenly and he stepped forward. "Arman?"

Arman nodded, not sure what to say, or how to begin. He could scarcely remember what he had looked like when he left Vielrona. They were separated by several paces, a haze of smoke and what seemed like a lifetime. "What happened?"

The darker man sighed wearily. All the characteristic jesting had gone from his face. "Come have a seat and we'll get you what we can for a drink." He brought the Rakos across the campsite to a small tent and gestured to an overturned crate. "Sit."

Arman folded himself onto the crate, clasping his hands to hide his nerves. A woman emerged from the tent, shot a weak smile at Kam and turned to go.

"Cel, look who came back." Kam's voice stopped her. Her hair was lank and her body thin, save for her pregnant stomach.

"Celly?" Arman stood and swept her into his arms. The cold, awkward spell was broken and he embraced Kam, too.

"Arman, I can't believe you're here!" Celly held him at arms' length. "Your last letter was so grim, I wondered if we'd see you again."

"I wondered myself." He gestured at her abdomen with a grin. "I see your marriage has been fruitful."

She smiled and patted herself. "More than halfway there." A shadow flitted across her face. "I expected to raise him on Gratchen Lane, not in a refugee camp."

Arman looked away. He understood unexpected futures, but he had chosen his. Their child never could. "What the fuck happened?"

"The gods." Kam crouched by their meager fire.

"What?"

"The gods struck us down. I don't know how or why, but the very air turned to poison. Great clouds of brown gas covered the streets. It hit the market first, pouring out of the temples. We never stood a chance."

"When? What of the others?"

"Two weeks ago." Kam stared at the fire. "Wes is gone. Veredy, too."

Arman dropped his head in his hands. The panic in his gut returned with a vengeance. "And Ma?"

Kam shuffled over and placed a hand on Arman's shoulder. "I'm so sorry."

Arman moaned. His mother, Veredy, Wes, they were pieces of him. They were the sand that formed the pearl of his soul. He had built his life around their existence. His chest was too tight for him to speak or breathe. He could barely hear Celly's soft words over the roaring in his head.

"We were able to get her out for a proper burial, more than we could do for Wes and Ver. I can bring you to see her, if you wish."

Arman rose with a stiff nod, still too sick to speak. She took his hand gently and led him through the camp. The dead were laid in achingly long lines. Some trenches lay open beside them, but the process was slow and the manpower weak. Celly stopped at one linen-wrapped form. A metal charm hung from the cord binding the shroud. He slid to his knees beside the body, his hand finding the sunburst charm. His fingers traced the metalwork rays, the holes cut in swirls and loops like flames. It was the piece his father made for her. It hung above their door for as long as he could remember. The sharp metal of the edges drew runnels of blood as his hand clenched around it. Part of him, that nasty voice in the back on his mind, had known this would be what he found. The shock still shook him to his bones.

He wrapped his mother's burnt body in his arms, not caring about the smell. His tears finally came, scalding, burning hotter than his skin ever had. He held her long into the night, rocking in the rain. He told her about Alea and Bren. He told her of his conversations with Eras and the journey north. He wept and laughed in turns. His voice hitched as he explained what he was, what he had always been. It was well into the evening when he finally drew back. "I love you. I wish I'd been here. I hope you were proud. I hope you're at peace." He brushed his hand across her covered face. "I'm proud you were my ma." He kissed her brow and stood, making his way shakily back to the tent where Kam waited.

The locksmith crouched by the campfire, glancing up at Arman's approach. "This isn't the homecoming you deserve."

"It's the one part of me expected."

Kam handed him a tin cup of thin soup. "What brought you back?"

"I'm not sure. Her Majesty Tzatia bid me sail north, with the fleet heading off the Berrin, but I had to come here first."

"Tzatia? Fleet?"

It struck Arman then, how different things had become. "The queen of Athrolan."

Kam's expression was closed. "You want to drag what able men survived into war?"

Arman looked down. "No. Your numbers are too small to make a difference against what we face."

"What do you face?" Kam's low voice was disbelieving. "You found a strange woman in the desert. A month later you ride off with her and we barely hear from you. What happened?"

Arman could not find the words. There was too much to explain, too much that he had avoided for so long. "What have you heard from the north?"

"The Dhoah' Laen came. She's fighting the gods and humans joined both sides." Kam shrugged. "It didn't feel like war, until the attack. Everything was so far away."

"Alea's the Dhoah' Laen. We fight those who wish her dead and the world destroyed. Sounds trite when I put it that way."

"I wondered as much, when the news came. You fit with her, you know. Maybe not at first, but the last weeks you were here, we all could see it."

Arman was grateful his friend did not mention who noticed them most of all. He was not yet ready to hear her name again. He watched Kam's gaze inch over the changes before him.

"Dore Jehan said you flew in on the clouds, formed out of the air."

"Fates, you still listen to the Jehans?" The joke seemed to fall flat for a moment, then Kam snorted. His laughter pealed across the campsite, and tears leaked from the new lines around his eyes. Arman joined him, his belly aching with each guffaw. "You know, after all, I think the Jehan's have been right about everything. Just not when we were ready to hear it."

Kam sighed, mirth fading into fatigue again. "So what are you in all of this?"

"You know the Rakos?"

"You're kidding? Fire in the hands and flying?" Kam poked the fire with a stick. "Could have used that."

The accusation was not lost on Arman. "I'm glad you and Celly have each other. What'll you do now that Vielrona..." He could not bring himself to say the words. "Now?"

Kam shrugged. "We were going to move north, settle in a town. We'd need a place for my work and her cooking and for a baby. I'm too scared to think so far ahead."

Arman frowned suddenly. "I know a place you would be welcome, though it's far." The hope in Kam's eyes set a new ache in Arman's chest. "Travel to Ceir Athrolan and take a boat to Mirik. Alea's brother is the Military Commissioner there, acting king right now. He'll give you a good home and work. If you tell him who you are, he'll take care of everything until you get your bearings."

"It's a long way to travel, but I'll tell Celly." He watched Arman glance north. "You're leaving soon?"

Arman's silence was answer enough and Kam raised his hand to stall him. He ducked into the tent, emerging a moment later with a thick envelope. "I was headed to the message hall when the attack came. Fate's would have it that I bore a letter from your mother." He handed it to Arman. "When will we see you again?"

Arman's jaw was tight. "I wish you both the best of luck. You deserve it." He offered his arm, but not an answer. "Take care of each other."

"You, too." Kam gripped his friend's arm too tightly. "You and Lyne'alea."

Arman turned and disappeared into the darkness without another word. He flung himself into the sky, his grief and rage fueling his ascent. He wondered why, when his future was certain, his skin crawled with the pity in Kam's eyes.

CHAPTER FIFTEEN

The 2nd Day of Lumord, 1252
The City of Ceir Athrolan

ALEA STEPPED INTO THE OFFICERS' quarters, suddenly glad for the confidence respect gave her. She wore somber colors, though the seamstresses seemed to sew little else for her. Her knock on the doorframe was purposeful. "Narier, I need to speak with you."

After a moment he emerged, his face tired and his eyes impatient. "Dhoah' Lyne'alea."

"I have a favor to ask of you."

His lips thinned. "Listen—"

"As the Dhoah' Laen I ask a favor of Narier, captain of my ally's military."

His features relaxed and the relief in his eyes hurt more than she expected. "Right. Of course." His words echoed hers from their last meeting and he stepped aside. "Come in."

"I'd still rather it was private."

His laugh was little more than a sharp exhalation. "No one else is here." It was a sparse room, only the trunks and the coverlets showing any homey personalization.

Alea took a seat at the long table before the small hearth. "I'm sorry for bothering you again."

He raised the wick of the lantern and took a seat across from her. "I'm sorry you think that you bother me."

"Narier, please." She looked down at her hands. She wanted to remain as aloof and practical as possible. The conversation was already veering away from her careful plans. "Please be consistent in how you act. I understand sharing the night and I understand distant civility, but I can't waver between the two. I get enough of that from Arman."

"Right." He straightened and rubbed his hands together. "What can I do for you then?"

"I'm leaving Athrolan within the week. I'm headed east. It doesn't matter if I seem male or female, as long as it's not what I actually am."

"How'd you expect to pull that off?"

"I've got the guts. They won't expect it to be me. I need a patrol uniform. An officer's. Do you have a spare?"

"You're too small."

Alea's eyes narrowed. "You're not that much taller than I am, Narier." She faltered. "Why?"

"Why what?"

Her eyes flicked up to his, the layers of darkness and anger and determination peeling back to show the raw confusion and vulnerability. "I wasn't looking for a lifetime, Narier, just company."

"I can't judge what you did in Shadow, Lyne'alea, because I may have done the same were I in your boots. Doesn't mean it feels right. Doesn't mean the dreams I have are good. You ripped the life right out of those people—allies too. You turned the laws of the world upside down for your guard. You might be great and powerful and fucking beautiful. Doesn't mean you're human. Not anymore."

"Thank you for your honesty. I realize you were being kind before, not telling me all the truth. Thank you for that, as well."

He sighed and scrubbed at his face. "Anything else I can do?"

She rose, shaking her head. The black shutters clanged shut over her heart and eyes once more, but she did not trust her voice.

Φ

Alea wondered at Daymir's brisk response requesting her to visit. It made her nervous, but she hoped his bitterness was waning. *Besides he'd be a fool to try to hurt me.* She made her way quickly to the manor and rang the bell at the gate. *Our courtship, if I want to call it that, was barely two months during a tumultuous time. What did he really think my answer would be?* Sunamen courtships lasted years, sometimes even before the betrothal was announced. *Perhaps the Athrolani do things differently.* It was a moment before Currow let her in. His face was lined and looked more tired than before. "You received the message, Dhoah' Lyne'alea?"

She froze in the doorway of the manor, not answering. Portraits and art were gone, and what was left of the furniture had been covered in drapes. Everything personal was gone.

"I believe he left something for you in the study, Dhoah'. I'll be here if you need anything."

Alea ascended the stairs in a rush, thoughts turning, and pushed opened the study door. The empty bookshelves seemed to echo. A single tome and sheet of parchment waited for her on the desk. She unfolded the latter warily.

> *Dhoah' Lyne'alea,*
>
> *I apologize for not receiving you myself, to explain everything, but I have gone home to my father's estate. My forethought for my country was misinterpreted and thus I must leave my titles and power in Ceir Athrolan for another. The events of the past few days have given me much to think on—your decline of my proposal, Her Majesty disinheriting me and my ultimate return to the country.*
>
> *I wish to apologize for my bitterness during our last visit. I expected a refusal due to your feelings for Arrowlash. I could have understood that—what human man truly competes against a Rakos? My pride was wounded when your choice was based on other concerns. The pain of that wound caused my bitterness. I wish I was through with those thoughts but I am just a man and still frustrated that things did not go as I planned.*
>
> *I left you this letter in part to explain myself, but also to tell you my thoughts on your problem with the gods. You mentioned your bond with Arrowlash was a soul bond. If the gods' powers are tied to their souls, perhaps you could make them bleed soulblood. Would their powers lessen? This book contains a section on the gods' various powers—I thought it might help prepare you. It is the only copy in North Athrolan, and my personal one, so I would take it as a kindness if you keep the stains of tea or god-blood from its pages.*
>
> *I am sorry for my poor attempt at humor, and I wish you well. Perhaps we can meet when this is over. I'm sorry, once again, for how I acted and my assumption about our relationship.*
>
> *Best wishes, Dhoah',*
>
> *Daymir*

Alea lowered the letter slowly and ran a hand over the cover of the tome. It was a thin one and the canvas-covered wood was new, as was the parchment. *I forget that being the foster-daughter of an ihal was not nearly as privileged as I thought. Daymir is wealthier than I realized, to pay for a new scribing of a text—one of which there are few copies.* She tucked the tome and letter carefully under her arm before showing herself out. She would respond, but later, when everything was clearer. Instead, she returned to her room, thoughts running amok.

She was so distracted that she tripped over a trunk in the middle of her room. She frowned at it, rubbing her shin. The chest was made of new wood and decorated by the seal of the palace smithy. She paused, taking a breath. *My armor.* The lid rose easily. The breastplate shone muted silver. The metal curved simply, and two tapering lines decorated the front to show her form. It buckled at the shoulders and waist to a backplate. Beside it were matching greaves and rerebraces. The metal was polished, but not to a high sheen, and the soft glow made Alea smile. *He knew what I meant when I said understated.* She laid the pieces on her bed. Underneath the oilcloth in the trunk was a mail hauberk, treated with a wash that made the metal glint blue in the light. The sleeves reached her elbows and the split skirt to just above the knees. It was heavier than she expected, but not too bad.

She drew it out and placed each piece of armor on the stand that in a normal woman's chambers would hold her best dress. Rulhan's work was beautiful. The backplate had simple swirling designs on its surface, ones she recognized from old Sunamen runes. *Sandstorm. Death. Life.* She reached out, eyes spiraling silver and her skin marbled black. Her fingers traced the patterns of the armor, mentally stitching power into each hammer mark. She withdrew after a moment, guilt uncurling at her actions. *This isn't selfish. If I die, the world goes with me.*

Feeling suddenly restless, she rang for Giire. The woman arrived after a moment, a large bag under her arm. She flashed Alea a grin. "Dhoah', I found what you wanted." Her brows rose at the sight of the armor as she entered, but she looked quickly away. She laid her finds on the bed. The wig was dark blond, the curls stitched up around the crown and the lower half left free. Giire had also found a dress more suited to a night in a tavern than Alea's other outfits.

Giire paused as she smoothed the skirts. "Dhoah' Lyne'alea, aren't you worried about going out alone?"

Alea shrugged. "You said yourself that I was a warrior." She turned, already binding her hair up. Her grin was wicked. "Besides, I thought you could come with me."

Giire's eyes widened. "You barely know me."

Alea stammered to a halt. The woman was right. Giire probably knew Alea much better than Alea knew her. She was not even certain whether the other woman liked her at all. "I'm sorry. I forgot what it was like to work behind everything. I don't know you at all." She echoed her thoughts. "I'm not even sure of your opinion of me."

Giire wrinkled her nose. "You're a bit dark-tempered for my tastes, and I have little interest in weapons or war or healing, like yourself."

Alea turned away, taking her hair down. It had been a stupid idea, and her face flushed with embarrassment. "I'm sorry, Giire. I did not mean to offend you." The hand on her hers was firm. She turned about.

Giire's smile was gentle as she held up the wig. "You like dancing, Dhoah' and that is something I can appreciate. Why don't you come with me to my favorite tavern at the end of the week? We can see if there's anything else we have in common."

Φ

The 5th Day of Lumord, 1252

Arman's every muscle was tense. He knew he needed to focus, but his mind spun wildly off topic. *If I'm not careful, I'll slip and fall to my death.* Days had passed since he rested. He had intended stay a night or two in Vielrona, visit his mother, drink with his friends.

He shoved himself deeper into his thoughts, aiming for the narrowed, taunting eyes in the back of his mind. *Eana. I'll find you.* He flung his mind out, spreading his consciousness over the land. Humans were glittering red pinpricks, tiny fireflies scattered on a bleak landscape. He faltered, wondering briefly at the color.

Eana's answer clattered through his musing. *Fear. Find me.*

His response was closer to a snarl than actual speech. *If you stopped the damned riddling maybe I could! It's like you don't even want me to find you.* He threw his power after his mind, pouring himself into the search. A white-gold flame bloomed on the edge of his mind, and another and another. Four brilliant lights dotted the land ahead of him, leagues apart. *No wonder they think we're dead.*

He dove, spinning east toward the Berrin border. The rolling plains of the Felds became hills separated by shallow streams. In the south were the gray waters of Berme's Eye, the lights of Berrinal bobbing with the swells. As a child he had wondered about the floating city, but after living through so many of the legends he read, he was disinterested. Spindly, stilt-rooted trees covered the great mounds punctuating the flooded lowlands. He flew lower, startling a pair of strange birds half his height. They took off, clacking their red beaks in protest.

One hillock burnt in his mind and he wheeled towards it. It was larger than the others, great stones covered with vines and crumbled by prying roots. *This was a temple. One of ours.* He recognized the statues flanking the caved in doorway, the upheld hands. They matched those in Elanal. He skimmed the ground, weaving along the streams until he materialized at the base of the temple. The ground was rocky and marshy in turns and it took a moment to find a suitable place to camp.

He gathered a few pieces of damp wood and flicked fire at them absently. *I'm here. It's your turn to come and get me.* He settled himself onto the ground and pulled his mother's letter from his shirt. The envelope was charred on one corner and stained. The ordered writing on the front was achingly familiar and he swallowed hard before slitting it open.

> *Dearest Arman,*
>
> *Your letters are a joy and your adventures amazing. I can hear in your words that you're changing. We heard rumors about your allies – the Athrolani for one – and your descriptions are beautiful. I wish I could see everything with my own eyes.*
>
> *Your latest letter said you never had the chance to explain certain things. Something about two ancient bloodlines. The latest news from the north includes a man of the Rakos. It said his given name is Aud'narman. I pretended it coincidence, but there were changes in you even before you left, changes even a mother cannot deny.*
>
> *I hope you found happiness. I hope you found love. The more your life changes the more I understand you'll not come home. At least, not as the man who left. Sometimes I wish it was not so, because you are my baby, my son. If you found contentment, then I am glad.*
>
> *The enclosed was the ring with which I married your father. It now belongs to whatever wife you may find on your journey. Live your life, ride your adventures, love your woman, but never forget us here, who love you and who will always keep a lantern lit for your return, whenever it may come.*
>
> *I will love you, always,*
> *Ma*

Arman upended the envelope over his palm. The ring fell into his hand, heavy and glinting in the firelight. Simple twisted gold held an unpolished sapphire. He slid it onto his smallest finger before returning the letter to his shirt. It was as if she had known. *I'll see you soon.* His dour thoughts were interrupted by a low keening noise. It was too guttural to be a bird, too metallic to be a dog. His gaze flitted between the scraggly trees. No motion caught his eyes. He turned to look at the collapsed temple. *If I were a fallen titanic monster, where would I hide?* The cry came again. It almost sounded like a word, but so crippled and changed it was unrecognizable.

He scrambled to his feet and began to climb the broken stones. His hardened fingers scraped against the cracks, his scales scoring the stone as he passed. Boulders all but closed the temple's door. Arman rapped on the rocks, letting power fill his skin. "Who's home?"

The call came again, clearer now.

"I've come to find you all. War's not over yet." He squeezed through the opening, blinking rapidly to adjust his eyes to the darkness. "Hello?" The noise came again, a rapid hiss that pierced his ears and echoed off the stone. A figure rocked in the shadows, faint light glimmering off the white scales. The angry yellow eyes glowed orange through the lace of bloodshot vessels.

"Came here before, begging, asking, look what happened. Lookie, lookie, begging, begging. Came here before but nothing to be done, nothing."

"This time we're not alone. What's your name?"

"Aral once and Aral again, but not if you ask, not if you beg. Aral, Aral." Arman saw that the creature's left leg ended in a scaled stump. The lower half was rotting under one of the fallen ceiling blocks.

"Hey Aral. I'm Arman." He unbuckled his cloak and pointed at the handprint scarred across the scales of his chest. "You know what this means? This symbol?"

"Laen."

"That's right. There are a few left, but mine, the one bound to me, she's the Dhoah' Laen. She's real. It's time to come out. Time to fight. It'll be the last time. No one else will call you out of your peace, I promise, but now we need you."

The rocking increased, "Nothing left. Don't beg. Nothing left but fear, fear. No promise, no begging, too much fear, fear."

Dread was a cold lump of lead in Arman's stomach. This was a madman, not a soldier.

Φ

The 7th Day of Lumord, 1252
The City of Ceir Athrolan

Alea twirled around a lantern post at the corner of the street. "Is there a particular tavern you enjoy?"

Giire laughed. "My friend's family owns one." She wore an outfit similar to Alea's, a colorful sarafan over bloused sleeves and frothy petticoats. A broad, stiff band held her hair back from her face. "Her husband is in the army, so she works it to keep her mind busy. It's the Wise Hare, in the slums above the naval yards."

"I've been there." Alea kept pace, her worn boots clacking on the stone. She may not have looked Athrolani, but with the yellow wig, she could pass for Vielronan.

Giire snorted. "I can hardly picture that."

Alea smiled. "I met someone there, I needed the anonymity."

Giire glanced over. "I suppose that's hard to come by. You said you've been dancing before. Not here, surely."

"No. I spent a few months in Vielrona before realizing my power. They have fantastic dances—you don't really need to know the steps, only enjoy yourself and skip a lot. What are they like here?" She followed Giire around a corner and down the narrow walk that edged the top of the tier's wall. The view was striking. The city dropped away on one side, a glittering train of embers.

"Perhaps a bit more organized. Lots of stamping and clapping. Some skipping." She shot Alea a grin. "Tonight they will have bards from other places playing, so there will be some new tunes." She turned right and headed down the narrow, overhung alley that Alea recognized. The Wise Hare squatted at the far end. The bright lanterns were cheery, but showed the filth of the street. The sound of music and singing rattled through the cheap, old glass panes. Giire paused on the steps. "Ready?"

Alea grinned and dashed up the stairs behind her. Warmth and light spilled out as they pressed their way in. The room was low and crowded, music pouring from one corner. Tables were stacked haphazardly along one wall to make room for the dancers. Alea wound back to find free stools for the two of them while Giire made for the bar. The heat and music made Alea's head spin and she grinned. *Everyone needs some chaos from time to time.* Alea watched the feet of the dancers carefully. The steps were repetitive and simple, but fast. Her boots tapped in time, mimicking the moves from her chair.

After a minute Giire returned with Alea's purse. "If you're going to do this, you'll do it proper. I ordered fire ale." She pointed to one of the men who seemed the fastest dancer. "He's one of the scribes from the Scribing Guild. Twice a week he performs dances on one of the stages in the warehouse district. He's quite the mover."

Alea glanced at her sidelong. "You fancy him?"

Giire snorted. "Along with half the slums. The other half fancies Bessel's husband's friend, Sousa. He's a proper Athrolani."

A heavily pregnant woman edged through the crowd, two foaming mugs in hand. She grinned down at Giire as she placed them on their table. "Hey there. Juss said you were here. Who's your friend?"

When Giire stumbled over the question Alea held out her hand. "I'm Veredy. Came up north with family and Giire promised to show me about. My ma knows her da."

Bessel shook the hand with a smile. "Good to have ye then. Let me know if Giire gets too rowdy. I've promised her sister to look after her."

Alea grinned. "Promise." When Bessel had gone Alea took a deep sip of the red liquid, wiping froth from her lip with the back of her hand. "I didn't want you to lie to your friend."

Giire glanced over. "You did that rather well."

"Court antics are all just a series of well-coated lies and vague truths. I did come north with family."

"It must be freeing, to be the Dhoah' Laen and thus no longer an object of court."

"It is a title, just as king or gallant or lady. Titles are no less constraining, regardless of their rank. It simply denotes a new set of rules by which to judge and objectify someone." She finished a good portion of her drink before standing. "Now, show me how to make a fool of myself."

The dancing was fast, as Giire promised, and Alea's muscles ached wonderfully halfway through the tune. *This is what freedom feels like. For tonight, one brief moment, I'm just a person, a woman like every other in this bar.* The dancing circle widened and slowed as the best stepped into the circle to showcase their skills. Alea caught Giire's eye and made her way back to the table. After a minute singers took turns standing and singing a verse of the song, the entire crowd joining in for the chorus. Even Giire took a turn, her voice clear and lilting. It was impressive and Alea found herself humming quietly along. The city was large enough to have a hundred such communities. Everyone seemed to know one another, or know someone who did. It was warming and lonely at once. Alea sat back, running a finger along her mug's rim.

"You don't sing?" Giire slid into her seat, breathless and flushed.

"Never!" Alea waved a hand, as if to dispel the thought from the air between them. Her stomach burnt with the alcohol and her head felt pleasantly padded.

"I suppose the Sunamen don't sing. It seems a terribly expressive recreation for so closeted a people."

Alea raised her brows, surprised at the woman's knowledge. "You know the Sunamen well?"

Giire giggled. "I knew one of their ambassador's guards quite well."

Alea snorted. "Well, the Sunamen sung often. It was one of the few times they were free to express." She shrugged. "Unfortunately I have less than little talent. I can't hear notes well enough to sing. They sound nice when played, but I couldn't tell if someone was off key, or if the tune was unpleasant for others."

"You're note-blind." Giire looked delighted. "I'm sorry, I don't mean to make fun, but it's always encouraging to find great people have weaknesses just like us common folk."

"You do realize nobles are no different than you, except in title?"

Giire made a face. "Rather I think we've got the better deal. Bed whom we wish, work for our coin, and have the freedom to spend it."

Alea nodded. "I think I agree." She caught sight of a cloaked man in a far corner. He could have been watching the singers, but the tingling on her arms told her his eyes rested on her instead. "Giire, where's the privy?"

"Out back. There's a two-person shed."

Alea nodded and ducked out the rear door. She stepped into the shadow behind the rubbish pile and waited. Within a moment the man emerged. To anyone else he would have looked intimidating, or at least dangerous. He was partway to the privy when Alea cleared her throat.

"What are you doing, An'thor?"

He froze and glanced over. "I could ask the same. I think I've more a habit for drinking than you."

"I'm fast catching up." The air was cool, but the burn of drink made it a caress on her warm skin. "Did you follow me?"

"Not on anyone's orders, just my own curiosity."

"You're not here to haul me back to Bren for a scolding?"

An'thor snorted. "Hardly. Besides, I think even he would understand this." He leaned against the rear wall of the Hare. "You're trying to burn back the shadow in your mind with alcohol. Trust me, it won't work. Right now, you think it does, but in an hour, a day, it'll be back and angry at your attempt."

She sighed and slumped onto the stoop. "I know. I've tried it before. It wasn't so much the drinking I wanted, but the dancing, the people." She tried to push back her hair, only to realize she still wore the wig. "How'd you recognize me?"

He snorted. "I'm old enough to trust my instincts. If my skin crawls at the sight of a blond girl in a bar I'm willing to bet there's more than meets the eye. Besides, your brows don't match that color, not even a bit."

She sighed. "You think everyone else noticed?"

"Doubtful. They need the visual to recognize a noble. It's all about symbols with humans. They like tidy boxes with clear labels."

"And you don't?"

"Neither of us fit into any box I've yet encountered." His smile was faint but genuine. "Did you want me to walk you home?"

"I think the Destroyer can protect herself on Ceir Athrolan's streets. I think I'd like to wait a while."

"Maybe I'm the one who wants protecting." He glanced over. "You'll be headed north soon. Do you want me to send word to my people on the border?"

"I'll leave next week, the night after the address. I still hope the Crown is in Claimiirn, but if not, I'd be grateful for their help." She fiddled with one of the wig's curls. "I won't be going as the Dhoah' Laen. It's far too dangerous for people to think I'm on the road, and certainly Azirik has spies enough."

An'thor made a show of examining her. "You'll be going as Miss Sell-Love then?"

Alea glared at him. "I do not look like a whore." Her mock anger melted into a smile. "I'll go as a soldier."

"I'm sure Her Majesty will lend you a uniform or two."

"I'm not telling Her Majesty." She stared at the cobbles. "I said I didn't want many to know. You and one other. Not even Bren, until I'm gone at least."

"Who else? Surely not Arman."

Her expression darkened. "I doubt I'll see him before battle. I had a lover in the army. I'll ask him for the uniforms. He's a captain and not too much taller than I."

"I didn't take you for the lover type. Then again, lovers are like drinking, and lessen the loneliness for a while."

Alea nodded. The warmth of alcohol was curling back, pulling away from her mind. A fragile carapace protected her sanity from the jumble of angry, dark thoughts. Someday, soon, it would crack.

An'thor must have seen something of her thoughts on her face. "Whenever I'm close to breaking, it's because something is coming to an end." He jerked his head at the tavern. "You're about to break, Lyne'alea. Care to tell me why?"

"I've learned about all I need to destroy the gods. It's not like I can practice. The only thing left is finding my Crown."

"Don't forget Her Majesty's address—you get to wear a pretty dress and a serious face once more before you go."

She laughed. "I suppose. Such things seem so unimportant."

"And drinking in a slum tavern doesn't?"

Her eyes flicked to his black ones. "You know these little things matter most of all."

He sank onto the stoop with her and drew a flask from his cloak. "I've drunk too much Athrolani liquor to enjoy it anymore." He tipped it back swiftly before handing it over. "So what's your plan, with the gods? I assume you've told no one, protecting them from seeing what you're capable of."

She sipped slowly, enjoying the flavor of wood oil and nutmeg. "It's a bit eerie how well you know me."

"Nonsense. I only know myself." His grin bloomed slowly. "So how are you going to save us all and raise the Laen to power?"

Her eyes narrowed. "I'm going to rip the gods' souls from their bodies." An'thor was silent for several moments and she glanced over, handing back the flask. "Should I have protected you, too?"

He swirled the alcohol in his mouth thoughtfully. "No. Not really. I've seen terrible things—not as horrifying as that, perhaps, but to far better people." He rested his head on the wall of the tavern. "The worst part of what you said is knowing what that will do to you."

"That's why I'm here. I'm drinking on the stoop of a tavern in the slums because in a month's time I might be something too twisted and monstrous to do so. I knew becoming the Dhoah' Laen would change me. I knew I wouldn't be exactly human any more. I knew I'd do terrible things, to myself, to Arman. I never bargained for losing my sanity."

"None of us do." His hand was dry and warm on hers.

She laced her fingers with his, tilting her head back to look at the autumn stars. "I'm scared, An'thor."

He followed her gaze, hand tightening around hers. "Me, too."

CHAPTER SIXTEEN

The 11th Day of Lumord, 1252
The City of Ceir Athrolan

BREN STOOD IN THE CENTER of the throne room. It was swept and polished down to the last corner and the walls were hung with great flags of the capital and cities. The wooden panels were slid back so it adjoined the ballroom. It was an hour before the address would begin and he stared at the throne. *How will I help lead Mirik if I can't even face a foreign nation without nerves?* He was already dressed in his finery, a mass of quilted vermilion. *This is a war address and I look like a peacock.* Slippers on stone interrupted his bitter thoughts. Expecting Alea, he turned with a smile. Tzatia regarded him with empathy. "Thinking on your own responsibilities?"

He looked away sheepishly. "Yes, your majesty. I usually need space to think, and with the streets so crowded this seemed the better place."

"Should I leave you to your thoughts?"

"That might be dangerous." He laughed and offered her his arm. "Care to take a circuit with me?"

"Indeed." She took his arm graciously.

"How are you today?" He set off along the pillared wall. It was a poor substitute for pacing, but it would have to do.

"I look forward to today. It feels as if we have been standing still. Perhaps that stillness will break now." She glanced over. "Soldiers are not the only ones to become stir-crazy, Lord Commissioner."

Curiosity nagged at Bren's tongue. "May I be bold?"

Her eyes crinkled. "You're learning court ways well. What makes you wish to be bold?"

"Daymir, your majesty. Alea told me. I'm sorry something so troubling occurred before battle."

Her face clouded and her chin went up. "He made poor choices and I protected us. I know what he said, but I could not take the risk, not when we are at war."

"Hard choices were not named on a whim. Have our other allies arrived?"

"The Banis emperor's offered troops will arrive soon, and your own men will as well I heard."

"Within the week, though I can only bring just under a hundred and thirty. It's something. And General Aneral returned I saw." He paused. "Have you heard from Arman?"

Her mouth thinned again. "Arrowlash ran out on his promise to accompany our fleet to the north. They waited for him for hours at the docks, but he never arrived. I fear the worst from him."

"With due respect, your majesty, I know him well and he is no deserter. If he left there was a fair reason for it."

"I don't speak of desertion, but of madness, Lord Commissioner." She sighed. "You were raised on war, but I was not. As a young woman I thought the most terrifying choice would be whom I married. I chose wrong, in the end, but I was also wrong in thinking that was the worst choice to make."

"And you've learned the most terrifying?"

"Sending our people to war. I love each of them and I send them to their doom."

"Some, yet, will live." They rounded the chamber, close to where they had begun their walk. "If you forget that, war will drive us all mad. A cause keeps us sane."

"I hope you are right. I cannot fathom fighting the gods, but I do not doubt your sister. I need to trust that we can win, and my faith is sorely tattered." She stepped away. "Forgive my dark musings, but thank you for listening." She smiled. "If you ever have concerns of your own, I will return the favor."

He bowed and watched her walk away, his frown reappearing. *I'll have lines deep enough to swallow someone if I'm not careful.* He laughed at himself. *And now I sound like an old maid.* Thinking on the queen's words, he strode to his room, unlacing his tunic as he went.

Φ

The thunder of conversation seeped from the throne room. Behind the lines of nobles were the officers and higher born commoners that could squeeze into the back of the hall with the scribes and clerks. Their retelling would flood the city streets minutes after the queen dismissed the gathering. Bren peered through the door as they waited to be announced. Advisers ringed the throne's dais and the general and commander flanked the throne itself. Instead of state attire, they wore armor and weapons.

Bren grinned, turning to Alea. "I think we made the right choice." After his conversation with the queen, he donned his new armor. He still wore the vermilion shirt and brown breeches, but his bronze-washed mail and breastplate glinted in the torchlight of the anteroom. A vermilion-trimmed forest green cloak was clipped to the backplate and boiled leather pauldrons.

Like him, Alea wore her armor over her dress, the silver and blue skirts the only softness in her out fit. The loose ends of her hair curled in a breeze Bren could not feel. Kemmer and Aldac stood along one wall, fidgeting.

Alea glanced back at them. "Think of it as a battle. It helps, I promise."

Their laughter died as Tzatia rounded the corner with her two chiefs of staff. Her gray and white dress matched the steel of her eyes as she nodded to them. The herald's piercing call stilled the conversation in the hall beyond and Tzatia breezed through the doors on the tail of her titles.

Alea grabbed Bren's hand, squeezing it tightly for a moment. She had her brother, his men, and a room full of allies. She had never felt more alone.

"I'm with you, sistermine."

"Dhoah' Lyne'alea of Le'yne!"

Her power rose, marbling her skin slightly and shadowing her eyes. The chill of the ocean rolled from her shoulders as she moved down the aisle through the crowd. She was distantly aware of Bren and the other Miriken Commissioners entering behind her. The walk seemed to take no time and forever at once.

"My allies, both legendary and human, I thank you for standing beside Athrolan today as we face the growing clouds of war." Tzatia took Alea's hand, and the commissioners' in turn, then turned to face the crowd, hands clasped before her. "My people, I have called you to this assembly to speak of a threat against us all. It is known that Dhoah' Lyne'alea and her guard, Rakos Arrowlash face genocide. The gods and their human army, led by Azirik of Mirik, are their enemies. As allies to the Dhoah' Laen, they are our enemies as well. Mirik's ally, Berr, attacks our borders daily, and this strengthens our resolve against them. In less than a month's time we march to war. I called you here today to listen to your thoughts, your concerns and to answer them." She sat gracefully in the throne, Alea and the others taking seats beside her. "Those who wish may come forward."

Most of the nobles had family in the military and their questions had been answered weeks ago. Those that stepped forward now were city folk, those who were concerned their crops and goods would be siphoned to feed the soldiers of the campaign or if the city would be without protection.

Tzatia heard each concern with patience Alea could only dream about. Finally the queen raised her hands. "Your concerns are valid. Yes, much of your harvests will feed the army, but you will be compensated, as will those of you who have skills of tanning, smithing and the like. Athrolan is my child, my love, and my greatest priority. I will never leave her unguarded. Our army is marching, as are the men of one of our naval flotilla, led by Commander Dorcal. Much of the navy will remain here. They may be unused to land, but they were born on it, and I trust they will do fine." A smattering of laughter broke out and Tzatia smiled briefly. "A battalion will remain as well."

"Your majesty." An older duchess rose and dropped into a curtsey. "What if our troops cannot defeat Lord Azirik?" She stumbled over the title. With Bren usurping Mirik from under his father's reign, titles were unwieldy things. "What if they come for us?"

Alea raised her hand. "Your Majesty, may I answer?" Alea leaned forward when the queen nodded. "This battle is not to defeat Azirik and his men. Not solely. Azirik has something I need to defeat the gods. I will not allow him to win, which is why we have mustered so many allies."

Now a young man stepped forward, the son of a lending house owner, by the expensive outfit he wore. He knelt on the flagging before them. "Your majesty, Dhoah' Lyne'alea, I have a question about those very allies. The Stonefaced and Ageless, they are strong fighters and an obvious choice, but a new government with few soldiers? Is Azirik still not king?"

A stony silence swept the room while Alea searched for a response.

Bren saved her the trouble. "Azirik was king. As his son, I took the responsibility of my small nation from his incompetent hands. There is a law of Mirik, as in some other lands, that a when a monarch puts another person or persons before his nation, then he might be made crownless. I have followed this law."

"What of our other supposed allies, your majesty?" The man continued, acknowledging Bren's answer with a respectful, but dismissive wave. "You bound us to Dhoah' Lyne'alea. She may stand before us, but she stands alone. She claims power, but what of the strength behind her. Where is her Rakos guard? Has he abandoned her and chosen a better side?"

"You'd best speak with respect when addressing milady, boy." The low voice rumbled through the crowd, cutting the man's tirade short. Mutters sprang up as people turned to peer behind them. The doors to the throne room were open, a frightened page holding his hands out, as if to say he could not prevent the intruder. A few paces into the room stood a bright figure. It was not armor that made him gold, for he wore none, but the curls of the flame in his hair and the coal-bed glow between the scales covering his bare arms.

The inside of Alea's cheek bled from her effort to remain silent.

Arman's grace as he approached the throne was nothing less than predatory. "You ask where your allies are? General Aneral returned from the Hartland with two dozen warriors. Lord Commissioner Barrackborn brings a few hundred men. An'thoriend's people number in the hundreds as well. And now, your other concern about milady's guard is put to rest, for here I am. And I did not come alone." He stopped before the young man, his head cocked like a raptor regarding a rat. The moisture in the air from Alea's power evaporated with a hiss in the heat radiating from his Rakos scales. "So unless you have anything else to add: as you were."

The man backed away into the silent crowd. Arman turned back to the dais, nodding to Tzatia and Bren before his gaze flicked to Alea. He took a knee, one fist touching his brow, lips and chest. "Milady, I bring you more Rakos. I hoped to bring men from Vielrona, but the gods saw to it that nothing was left for me to take." His words were quietly sincere, but his voice tight.

Alea's heard plummeted at the mention of Vielrona. "I thank you, Arrowlash."

He rose and moved to stand behind her. He was close enough that she could have taken his hand. The tension was a physical wall between them, connecting and dividing them at once.

Tzatia rose, the crowd following suit with the rumble of feet upon stone. "This assembly is closed. We thank you for your thoughts and trust that we have soothed any concerns. May fates bring us victory and peace." With the closing "So it is said," still echoing from the dome, Tzatia swept from the room, the others following after her.

Bren's breath burst from him in a cascade of nervous laughter. He turned, sobering at the sight of his sister's face. Alea stopped in the open hall that branched to the various wings. "Please, can we talk?"

Arman was already halfway to the stables. He stopped, but did not turn. "I came long enough to say and do what the damned people needed to see. That's all. I will see you at war."

Φ

Narier arrived just after midnight. The room was dark when he shut the door and the hearth was cold. "No one saw me come, promise. I went through the gardens just in case." He edged in, peering from Alea's made bed to the privy door. "You here, Dhoah'?"

She rose from her silent vigil by the curtained window. "Thank you."

Narier tossed her the pack. "Should be everything you need."

The uniform and armor were just the proper amount of worn. She stripped her gown off, the motions devoid of any seduction, and pulled on the captain's clothes. "I'll be out of the gate within the hour."

"I'll stay here until then, in case anyone saw. They'll think you're me."

"You could always don one of my gowns and stay in the library."

"I fear black is as garish on me as vermilion."

She was grateful for the joking reference to their first conversation, even if it was a poor attempt at humor. She fussed with her hair for a moment. "How do captains wear it? I've seen the general wrap her braid around her head."

"Either that or cropped."

She twisted her braid up and about. The second time her shaking hands dropped her hair pins, he took pity on her. His fingers were gentle at the nape of her neck as he pinned the hair into place. "Alea—"

"Don't, Narier. Please." She jerked away as soon as he finished and grabbed the pack.

"I wasn't going to talk you out of it, or be cruel."

"I know." The door clicked softly shut behind her and her boots echoed along the hall. She was not ready for good-byes.

Φ

The 11th Day of Lumord, 1252

The knock was pointedly quiet on Bren's door. He jerked it open, mouth already thin. "Arman. Should have known."

Arman rolled his eyes. "You have time for a drink?"

"Yes, and so does Alea, I'd warrant." He closed the door and pulled a flask from his desk. "Your boorish behavior does not make me like you much, Rakos."

"You don't need to like me."

"Sure would make things nicer, though, wouldn't it?" He poured them both a few finger-widths and screwed the top back on. "What brings you back here?"

"A long story." He looked down at the alcohol, face shadowed.

Bren frowned. In the weeks that had passed, it looked as if he had lived years. "Vielrona?"

"Fell. The gods destroyed it."

"Gods? I thought they only acted through Azirik."

"Their best power is through him, I think. He created that storm on the Iron Sea. I imagine he did the same. This time it was acid clouds and poisonous gas."

"Your family?"

"My Ma's dead, and my friend Wes and the girl I thought I'd marry."

"I'm sorry, Arman." Bren looked away. "I wish there was something I could do."

Arman glanced up. "There is one thing. Nothing large." When Bren nodded, Arman continued. "I've a friend, only one left, really. He's a locksmith and his name is Kam-Rit Eltena. His wife is Celly. By the time you see them they'll have a babe. They need a home and work. I told them to come north and find you. I told them Mirik would be home now."

"I'll do what I can. We'll need craftsmen surely." Bren sat back. "The woman you wanted to marry—how did you leave things?"

"I ran off with a mysterious woman barely a week after proposing marriage. How do you think we left things?"

"Terrible proposals seem to collect around Alea." Bren laughed and poured another drink.

"You botch one recently?"

"No, but Daymir did, before he was disinherited. Asked Alea to be his queen."

Arman choked on his drink. "You're joking."

"I wish I were. He was fuming when he left, which wasn't a bad sight."

"He wanted her power, I assume?"

"I think he enjoyed her company. The power didn't hurt, though. Part of me is surprised she doesn't have more suitors. Perhaps they're too scared of the rumors." Bren hid a smile. "Even Narier no longer visits her."

"Narier, what does he have to do with the price of Banis silk?"

"He told her she was too powerful, too inhuman for him now. He said it gently, but it was still a pointed reminder about how she is viewed."

"He's a coward."

"You're just unhappy he's bedded her."

Arman's eyes widened and he looked up. "He what?"

Bren's expression sobered quickly. "I thought you knew."

"Knew Narier took advantage of her? What kind of brother are you that would allow that?" Arman grimaced. "What kind of guard am I that I didn't notice? The man beheads people for fate's sake!"

Bren rolled his eyes. "Arman, this is war, soldiers kill people. It was during the siege. He was kind and funny and saw her as a woman."

"You should bed him if you like him that much."

"He's not really my preference, I'm more for the darker men." Bren's deadpan grew serious. "Arman, if she doesn't love you, that's the end of it, but you certainly don't make it easy. She doesn't want a guard, she wants a friend. She wants a lover."

"I do see her as a woman."

"You don't treat her as such."

He hung his head. "I know. I'm too damned scared. I'm too much of a coward." He inhaled sharply. "I found more Rakos. Two, at least. Hopefully they'll find more."

Bren leaned forward. The Rakos were something that even most legends did not dare to touch. "What are they like?"

Arman snorted. "I've only met the one and he's mad. He was trapped in a temple in Berr. Chewed off his own leg years ago. Half the words he says are 'fear.'"

Bren's brows rose. "Sounds like quite the army you've got there."

"I know. I'm hoping they'll prove useful."

"What can they do? Besides put anyone off their meal for a day."

Arman laughed, the sound low and rattling. "The Rakos that changed, like they did, like I am, they weren't called Earth Shakers for nothing." He stood abruptly. "Please don't tell Alea I was here."

Bren stood, raking a hand through his hair. "I don't have to. She knew, last time. Asked me flat out if you'd been here while staring at the window where you jumped. Don't bother pretending."

Arman winced. "Was she angry?"

"More at you than me. You've barely seen her long enough, Arman, but she's changed. That mild girl you had bumping along behind you on the road is gone. She's brilliant and terrifying."

Arman paused in the doorway with a smile. "She always was. You just couldn't see it before. I'm headed south again, I've got more Rakos to find."

"You ought to find that fleet before Tzatia beheads you."

"Let her try. I'm sure the navy can manage on their own. I'll be back for battle."

Bren watched him disappear down the hall. When the hall was deserted, he stepped up to Alea's door, knocking. "Alea? It's me." No answer came and he finally turned away. It was fitting, he supposed, after the unity displayed at the address, that their nights were spent in solitude.

CHAPTER SEVENTEEN

The 12th Day of Lumord, 1252
The City of Ceir Athrolan

BREN HALF EXPECTED ALEA to accompany him to the docks, but his knocking was met with silence. He met Kemmer at the palace gates however, and grinned. The woman's new armor gleamed in the sunlight.

"You look like a general, Kemmer."

She flushed and saluted him, but her grin was wry. "Are you suggesting a promotion?"

Bren snorted and headed towards the docks where Aldac already waited. "I'm barely adjusted to my own new position. We'll talk after the war, eh?"

She fell into step beside him, one hand resting on the head of her axe. "General A'hane does have a fantastic ring to it, Lord Commissioner."

"Insubordinate A'hane has a better one." He flashed the woman a grin. They had made bounds in the weeks working together. Though he joked with her, she was bright and however teasing her suggested promotion was, it warranted some thought. The letters from Mirik were swift and short, as were his responses, but nothing replaced seeing the fruit of his efforts arrive at Athrolan's harbor. He was more than a bit nervous. Aldac stood by the largest naval dock, dressed like Kemmer, though his armor was his own. He saluted Bren, his expression far more serious. "Lord Commissioner. The signal went up half an hour ago. They'll dock within a few minutes."

Chains blocked the naval docks from the others, but a small crowd gathered against them, peering at Bren and his officers. The Miriken would arrive on three of the Athrolani ships, and it had been a long time since Athrolan played host to another army. Another signal flag unfurled from the Naval watch tower in the center of the harbor's entrance. The ships rounded the cliffs and coasted into the shallower blue waters. Bren clenched his jaw against its gaping. They were not Athrolani ships.

The two galleys were long, outfitted with green sails and new hulls. The third ship was larger, almost the size of the Athrolani battle ship. It's prow was narrower, and the men lining the rails were dressed in a familiar bronze and leather armor. Their cloaks and tunics matched the brilliant vermilion of the sails furled along the new wood of the repaired triple masts.

"Kemer, did you know about this?" He tore his eyes away to glance at his first officer.

She shook her head, but her smile was bright. "No, sir. My brother promised a surprise, however. I think he outdid himself."

"I think you have competition for your promotion."

Her laughter drowned in the shouts of the sailors and dock hands as they guided the ships to berth.

Two men stood at the helm of the battleship. The iron hair and weathered face labeled one as Oland, but the other Bren did not know. Arik waved an order to the soldiers as he and his companion disembarking first and striding over to where Bren waited. The soldiers filed out after them, the rumble of armor warming Bren's stomach. Arik paused a few paces away and saluted Bren. His eyes smiled, but his face was serious. "Lord Commissioner Barrackborn."

Bren offered his arm in greeting. "You've done wonders, Arik."

Arik grasped the arm, but raised his chin. "It's Commissioner of the Commons, now." He stepped back and jerked his head at the man standing a pace behind him. "And this is Kole Gallik, Commissioner of Diplomacy and Negotiation."

Something uncurled in Bren's chest at the words. A year ago Mirik was in shambles. A month ago he was acting king of a starved, abandoned city. Now he had a government and army behind him. *Pride.* He took Gallik's arm with a nod. "I look forward to working with you. You've done wonders."

Gallik's grip was firm and his plain face open. "I'm proud to see how far we've come since you arrived."

The final lines of the soldiers disembarked, turning to salute him with a clatter. Bren waved at them, not bothering to contain his impish grin. "Oh, just wait until you see where we're going."

Φ

The 13th Day of Lumord, 1252
The Ruins of Claimiirn

Loneliness was sharpest in the enveloping noise and bustle of Ceir Athrolan. The rolling expanse of hills and forest edging the road was different. There were no meetings or calls for lunch. The noises were hooves on stone and animals preparing for winter. The leaves chattered in the wind. Alea realized she had forgotten how to be alone. There was no need for defenses or verbal sparring. She smiled and it did not feel strange.

The road east had been maintained until it met the small canyon through which they had sailed upon their arrival to Ceir Athrolan. Now, almost at the border, it was barely a worn line of earth. More often she guided herself based on the sun, instead of what may have once been road.

The autumn days were bright and crisp, just cool enough to urge her faster. With nothing to answer to save her own thoughts and those of her persnickety horse, her days were long and easy, her nights dark and often wakeful. It was only after a week that she noticed the first reminder of war.

The trees crowding the narrow road bore marks from passing wagons and the underbrush was battered by boot heels. She slowed, muttering an absent reassurance to her horse. The threads on low hanging branches were green, but that could mean anything. *The average raider would benefit from the camouflage of green wagon canvas.* She spent the next hour on foot, picking out details of the road's previous travelers. The gravel crunching under her boots was a rosy brown. She was no tracker, but an army did little to hide their passing and by the time she emerged on the cliff tops overlooking Claimiirn, she knew enough to hide. The granite cliffs ringed the plains in a U that opened to the treeless hill in the northeast.

Athrolan's penchant for cliff-top capitals did not begin with Ceir Athrolan, it seemed. The walls carved from the opposite cliff face were weathered, but the beauty still echoed. The low-slung sun painted the ruins of the former palace pink. The cliff where Alea crouched once sported a fort, only a few walls still standing. She crept to the edge, relying on the setting sun to blind anyone who happened to glance up. Azirik's army camped below. The mass of tents and picket lines impressed her. *And I thought the outguard was an army.* She stopped counting tents at seventy and began estimating by how many fit under her upheld thumb. She was lucky that Azirik was not using the palace ruins for anything other than storage and officers' tents. After a quick noting of guards' locations, she edged back into the protection of the crumbling fort to wait until nightfall. Perhaps it was the approaching winter, but for the first time during her journey, she wished she could light a fire.

Φ

Midnight guard change was marked by a low trumpet and the muttering of picketed horses. Alea rose and stretched her stiff muscles. They no longer ached from the long days of riding, but lying on cold earth did no one any good. After the burning faded, she tied cloth scraps around her horse's hooves and harness metal. It was a tedious process that did nothing to make friends with the intolerant animal, but when she finished they could have walked into the camp itself unheard.

Satisfied that she had done everything she could, Alea headed off along the cliff top, keeping to the tree line where possible. A trumpet marked the death-hour as she came upon the edge of the palace. The trees had dropped away, but she found a wall that still stood tall enough to hide her mount. After a few fumbling minutes she remembered how to tie the reins in a break-away knot and managed to tether the horse to an overgrown bush. The rough map An'thor had drawn was still folded in her pocket, but she had spent enough evenings pouring over it. The layout burnt on the backs of her eyelids. Her boots scuffed on the rough stone, but save for the two guards flanking the old rear gate, she saw no one.

Claimiirn was built at the beginning of Athrolan's might, and her architects were humble. The halls were narrow and the windows small, protecting against attacks. There was none of the hubris shouted from Ceir Athrolan's gleaming dome and arching aqueducts. *Fourth hall on the right. Eight flights of stairs. Second door on the left.* The treasury was an unlikely home for the Crown, but An'thor promised it would be the best to go there first.

No torches lit the stone, but the moon was bright and high in the sky still. At each window, Alea marked its location. *Four hours until dawn.* It would not do to find the Crown, only to be caught as the sun rose. Her impatience almost won out at the fifth stair, but she forced her boot falls into silence and continued down. She realized belatedly that she was tunneling into the depths of the cliff, and the treasury would be beneath even the level of the plains. The air seemed thicker and she felt the weight of the earth above her.

It was not until she paused outside the treasury door that she heard the footsteps. They were quiet, but steady, and approaching from above. She opened her mouth to breathe silently and crept along the wall. Her fingers found the door latch, cords of tendons standing out as she worked to open it soundlessly. The latch clanked as it opened and the footsteps above stilled. She heard a man's cautious sniff. She hoped he suffered autumn allergies, but there were a dozen more sinister thoughts tumbling through her brain. She stepped backward through the door, feeling her way with a groping hand. The darkness within the treasury was absolute, so thick she could taste the black on her tongue. She swung the door almost closed, holding the latch up with a shaking hand. The stone was cold and damp against her ear as she pressed it to the crack between the wall and door. She focused on counting her breaths. She had slowed them to every twelve seconds when the man finally turned and retreated up the stairs.

She turned, latch forgotten as she fumbled with the flint and hand-torch on her belt. The oil-soaked fluff she packed into the tin box shed only a small circle of light, but it was enough to get her bearings. All gold and finery were stripped. The only remaining hangings were torn or faded. The furniture and chests left were either broken or too heavy to easily remove. All were empty. *I'm in the treasury of one of the wealthiest kingdoms ever to rise, and it looks like a tavern's barren pantry.* She checked every corner, each closed drawer, but there was nothing. She briefly dared to raise her power enough to sense the room around her, but the room was as still as before. She snuffed the tinder box and tucked it back into her pocket after a moment. Her fingertips stung from the heated metal, but she missed the comfort of its light and warmth. She crouched by the cracked door for another minute until her eyes were accustomed to the darkness again before slipping out of the treasury and back up the stairs.

Three flights above the level I entered are the royal chambers. If it's in Claimiirn at all, An'thor said it might be kept there. Blood hissed in her ears as her adrenaline surged again. She was happy to be out from under the tangible press of earth. The palace could have been ruined by neglect. The scars of weapons on stone were eroded by wind and rain. The doors that hung crooked had fallen from their hinges. The sharp edges of windows broken by arrows were long since ground flat. The royal chambers were different. The lock was broken on the doors, like the others, but it seemed even time had not ransacked the rooms. Some things were sacred regardless of race or culture. An empty nursery, with all its broken promises was one such sanctity.

The massive wooden beams caved into the center of the room, the catapulted stone that crushed them shattered across the flagging. The bed was broken beneath and a cradle splintered beside it. Alea's heart ached at the sight. Arman had told her the story of this room. Even with the distance of legend, it was heartbreaking. *An'thor lost his son in this room. In that cradle. Beneath that beam.* She shook away the tugging sorrow and turned to the smaller room that served as a study. The bookshelves were mostly empty, their contents stacked on the desk ready for packing. She opened each drawer quietly, fumbling for the latch of any hidden compartments or false bottoms. Next, she pawed through the chests and the wardrobe. Like the treasury, it was empty. *If the Crown's not here then the Ageless brought it back home. Seems I'm headed to Neneviir.* She turned to the door and stopped.

The moon was still up, the cool light spilling across the dusty, scratched flagging. The doorway and the hall beyond were dark, barely distinguishable from one another. A shadow blocked the door. *Was it there when I came in?* Her eyes burnt as she willed them to see better. It could have been the stone moulding of the door. A cloud could have moved across the moon's face. It could have been a thousand things, but her instinct screamed at her to hide. The doorway was only a few paces away and she sunk back against the wall by the study, biting into her knuckles to keep herself silent. She wanted to run, but she had to be certain the Crown was nowhere in the room. *I'm not touching my power without knowing if someone's there. Last thing I need is for them to know I'm not a captain.*

The night was still warm, but the breeze bore winter's teeth. It whistled curiously through the broken windows, nosed around the crushed beams and eddied out to the hall. As it passed through the doorway, it lifted the vermilion edged cloak of the man standing just outside the moonlight.

Her hand tightened into a fist. He was blocking the only door to the stairway. She would kill if she had to, with her bare hands if necessary.

"I know you're in here. Not sure who you are, but I heard you poking about."

She heard the leather of his boot squeak as he made to move. Without another thought she burst from her cover, pelting across the room and to the broad eastern windows. The stone of the sill was cold against her hands. She glanced down long enough to be sure the ground below was deserted before swinging herself over the sill. Her fingers burnt as she hung for a moment. She heard the man rush across the room. With a last look down, she clenched her teeth and dropped.

Φ

The City of Cair Athrolan

Bren pounded on Alea's door. He expected silence for a day, perhaps a night. This was something else entirely. He knocked for what seemed the thousandth time. "Alea, please!"

"Commissioner Barrackborn?"

Bren turned to see Narier jogging down the hall towards him. The soldier seemed to have just come from drills. "I'm busy right now, Narier."

"Trying to find you sister?" He drew up beside Bren and handed him a letter. "She left this for you. When the servants started gossiping that she'd abandoned us, I figured the game was up."

Concern writhed in Bren's chest like a nest of snakes. "Where, by Toar, is she?"

"She's where she needs to be, sir." Narier bowed a good bye and backed down the hall.

Bren did not watch him go. His gaze fell to the thin letter in his hand. He shouldered open his door, hands shaking as he broke the seal and unfolded the parchment.

Bren,

I'm sorry I'll miss the arrival of your men. I hope you're pleased. I can't wait to hear about it when I see you again.

I'm to the east. If I find Le'yne's Crown in Claimiirn there's a chance I'll return before you get this. If not, however, then I've gone to Neneviir. It's the last piece before the battle, and I can't fight Azirik or bind the world without it.

I hope you understand.

I love you,

Alea

Bren brushed her farewell with a gentle finger before folding the letter into his shirt pocket. Every step farther she took from him, the darker the skies seemed to grow.

Φ

The Ruins of Claimiirn

Blood flooded Alea's mouth as her teeth ground into her lower lip. It was better than screaming at the searing pain in her ankle. She remembered to crouch as she landed to absorb her momentum, but no amount of proper landing made up for uneven ground. She was tempted to make a mad, bumbling run for her horse, but knew the pain clouded her thinking dangerously. The sound of the man descending the stairs drifted through the broken windows of the stairwell. The footfalls paused. She shifted herself as quietly as possible. If he realized she was still there, she would have to run. She gathered her good leg under her carefully and readied herself to spring.

"Don't."

The voice startled her with its nearness. He must have been just paces away. She did not dare to move or respond, but the tone gave her pause.

"I can't see you right now. Keep it that way. If I see you, so will they and I'll have to act." The voice was low and steady, but hummed with energy. "Wait. The moon will set in just under two hours. You'll have enough time to get away before dawn, if no one else finds your horse."

She shifted her weight again, letting her injured leg rest. She felt along her shin and ankle. The bone was straight and unbroken. It was sprained, but she could walk. She breathed a silent sigh and leaned back against the stone. Later she would wonder what he was doing. Later she might question why he let her go. Now there was no time. She had not heard him call for guards, nor had he brought any with him when he followed her upstairs.

"Did you find what you were looking for?"

She could run, she supposed. Even with an injured ankle, she might get to her horse. *If I see you, so will they.* Cold trotted up her back. The ground was damp and the stone behind her hard. The wind that had swirled through the room a minute ago howled through the ruins now. The air smelled sickly, as if something dead had been uncovered when the snow melted. Bren had been like this man, once. She drew a steadying breath. He sat above her, offering her a hand in peace and she was ready to spit in it. *I'm not Arman.* She was tired of paranoia. She was tired of running. "All right."

The silence tightened at her words. "I'll stay with you, if you like, until the moon sets. I can't be sure no one will come, but I'll send them off if they do." There was the sound of fabric against stone and a low sigh. "You must think this a trick or a trap. Let's just say I'm tired, too."

"I didn't say I was tired."

"I hear it in your voice. I recognize that fatigue. You've been fighting a while now, and hard. I'm not saying you're right, but just for tonight, I'd rather talk than kill."

His words were like a journal she had forgotten she wrote. She may never know his name, but in that moment, she knew him better than anyone. "Me, too." She eased herself onto the ground. "Just for tonight." The moon was fat and still golden from summer. The naked hills beyond beckoned it down to bed, not yet lit by the sun. The silence stretched on, broken only by the pounding of her blood and the occasional sigh from above. "What did Azirik say to convince you to fight?"

"My father upheld the gods for as long as I can remember. Fighting for them did not seem like a choice. What about you?"

"What about me?"

"What did they tell you—the queen, the Laen, whoever. Are you Athrolani?"

"No. I'm not really much of anything by birth or raising. Lots of children are like that during war I think. They told me nothing really, nothing I didn't already know. It did not seem like a choice for me either." The ground under her was hard and cold. She had no feeling in her lower legs save for the lancing pain in her ankle whenever she shifted. The sky was a deep blue-green, only a few wispy clouds drifting across. Her breath puffed silently from between her chapped lips. The moon hung low, as if tired from the effort of climbing the dome of the sky. "Why are you doing this?"

"Doing what?"

"Keeping me company while the moon sets." Saying that he was letting her go seemed too dangerous an accusation.

"Perhaps because I finally realized I had a choice all along. I want to make up for all the pain I've caused."

Alea heard her own words from months ago echoing through the broken window. "It is the fault of Mirik, the fault of fate, even the fault of the gods, but it is not yours. No one person is so powerful as that."

The moon slipped happily between the trees, silhouetting their branches. An owl perched on one, feathers ruffled against the cold. It occurred to her suddenly, she had not watched the sky in months.

Finally the plains fell into darkness. The voice above her cracked into use again. "There. The guards should be hard pressed to see you now."

Alea paused, then rose, sensation rushing back into her limbs with agony. She winced and stumbled a few steps before finding her footing. She jogged through the ruins to her horse, heart pounding. She did not dare turn around, but it felt strange to not thank the man.

Φ

The 19th Day of Lumord, 1252

Rocks dotted the bare hills surrounding Claimiirn. Alea's horse picked its way through the mess of stones and scrub grass. Though not mountains in their own right, it was a hard climb. Beyond them, somewhere, was the tundra of the Northlands. Its short summer already passed. The hills all looked alike to Alea, and even with An'thor's carefully penned map, she became turned around twice. They were like the great undulating waves the wind drew in desert sand. *Perhaps long ago some great beast breathed life across this world and these hills are the marks its breath left.*

The clack of hooves on stone was monotonous and wearing on her nerves. Two days of riding and she seemed no closer to meeting the Ageless.

A particularly large hill rose ahead, a tall post erected on its crest. Alea's eyes narrowed. She pulled up, peering through her borrowed spyglass. Each of its four sides bore symbols, like a massive mile marker. She had never seen a mile marker made of iron, or reaching several dozen paces into the sky. She grinned and urged her horse faster.

The door set into the hillside was closed. At first it looked like blackened wood, but as she drew closer, she realized it, too, was iron. Though the hills continued to roll gradually higher, the Ageless seemed to have done even more to hide themselves from the world. Alea riffled through her pack for a moment before drawing out the instructions An'thor carefully detailed to her. A broad circle in the center of the door was polished from countless hands. She laid her hands over the marks, pressing steadily. It receded with a grind. The center was still raised, its edge notched with tally marks. Alea twisted it to the left until it clicked twice, then to the right, listening for five clicks. Lastly she turned it left again for seven. Heavy thuds resounded from within the door as tumblers slid back and gears ground the door upward. *Of course, even their doors wouldn't open normally.* She was beginning to understand An'thor better. *He's like a child with a talented and prideful older sibling.* The door finally thumped to a halt.

A long tunnel burrowed into the mountain, dissolving into darkness. A trough jutted from each wall, and a quick inspection with her fingers told her it was filled with animal fat. She lit it quickly and climbed back into the saddle. The light hissed down the trough, but only made the tunnel seem longer. She nudged her mount inside, her murmurs more to reassure herself than the animal. Several paces inside, the horse's hooves clacked over an iron plate and the door ground closed behind them. *Next time An'thor gives me directions they will not have any tunnels, or narrow halls or dungeon treasuries!*

She steadied her breath and forced herself to recite the poems from her childhood. The tunnel did not curve once, the eerie straightness adding to the illusion that she made no progress. She had worked up to the poems she read in Vielrona when the tunnel ended abruptly. It was another door, but this one was three times the height of a mounted man and equally as broad. The air was noticeably cooler. The circle and tumbler mechanism were the same, though the number of clicks for each direction had changed. Bitter wind squealed through the widening doorway. Beyond were iron gates. The building was unlike anything she had seen, but the pennants and guards dotting the walls told her it was a garrison.

When the door clunked to a halt, she rode through, keeping her shoulders back and head up. *I'm Captain Lenna Grayhill.* Though the brown and gray landscape was stark, the fort ahead was far from deserted. Warriors manned the blood-colored walls, shouting orders and jokes back and forth. Each wore horned helms. Whistled alerts bounced from tower to tower as she approached. No weapons rose to greet her. Either they already expected her, or she was deemed harmless. She hoped it was the former.

At the gate she halted and raised a gloved fist in greeting. "I'm Captain Grayhill from Athrolan." Her shout carried over the wall, loud and sharp in the cold air. "I must speak with your commanding officer."

A smaller door in the gate creaked open and a warrior stepped out. "You come from Domariigo?"

"I do. I trust you received his letter?" She had listened to General Aneral enough to know fewer words were best.

The woman nodded and jerked her head at the fort. "Very well."

The gate rose with a lurch and within moments Alea was dismounting in the courtyard. The building was built in a square, the walls only wide enough to allow a walkway at the top. The only obvious living quarters were a row of rooms along one wall. The rest was open to the elements. What looked like a stable ran along the rearmost wall, steam billowing from the narrow windows cut into the rusted iron. The warriors along the walls watched for a moment before turning back to their work. Alea laughed softly. The horns she thought decorated their helms actually grew from their temples. *Seeing An'thor with his head covered so often made me forget.*

"Athrolani. You're the officer An'thoriend sent?" Everything about the man approaching spoke of the tundra. His furs and leather were thick and battered, as was his snowy skin and ivory ram horns. Like An'thor he wore a tattoo, his of a sword's hilt on his throat and collarbones.

"I am." She offered her arm. "Captain Grayhill. You're the officer here?"

"I'm the one sent to fetch you." He took the arm, his wholly black eyes scanning her face and packs. "Tennic Odrene. We'll take you presently, just loading up the carts." He gestured to the stables. "Come."

The brisk treatment required adjustment after Athrolan's hospitality. Alea expected to stay the evening at the fort before heading further north. As frustrating as traveling was, however, she had missed the constant movement of the road. She fell into step beside him, leading her horse. "This fort, what's it called?"

"Garrison Kaliim, Captain." He stepped through another mechanized door and gestured to the line of stalls. "Leave your horse here then meet me out back. We don't have time to waste."

Alea hurriedly unbuckled her horse's tack and checked the grain and water before shouldering her pack and heading through the door Tennic indicated. The structure of the fort was odd, and the doors alien, but nothing prepared Alea for the sight before her.

They were under the vaulted ceiling of what seemed like a hall. The stacked chests and freight boxes, however, made it seem closer to a ware house. Two parallel bars of iron set into the ground ran the length of the hall, disappearing through a massive open door at the rear. A great contraption crouched on them. It was twice the height of a tall man and made entirely of iron and brass. Clouds of steam billowed from the short chimney at its front. The small cabin behind the steaming chamber was closed off with thick glass windows. The mechanism churned to life as she approached.

Steam drifted from beneath as well, glowing in the light of the oil lamps along its length. Three iron-bound wood carts of almost equal size were clipped behind the iron machine. The middle one bore a narrow staircase leading inside.

Alea hung back while Tennic held a quiet conversation with one of the several men hurrying around the thing.

A boy sidled up to her while she watched the chaos. "You're Athrolani?"

She nodded, still staring at the contraption. Giant pistons on the wheels hissed suddenly. The fresh, smoky smell and the dim lights seemed unreal. "What is this?"

"A steam engine. It runs on heated water and can pull our heaviest freight without effort. We'll ride in that middle cart there."

"You're coming with us?" She finally looked over at the boy. He was milk-pale and had long white-blond curls. The tattoo of a circlet around his brow was bright and new. His temples bulged out with new growth of horns.

"I'm training under my father's men."

"Tennic is your father?"

"No, Edrodene is." He offered her his arm. "Mel'iend Domariigo." He pointed his thumb at the cart. "Come on, I'll get you settled."

She followed him onto the middle cart, feeling like one of the horses they had loaded on minutes before. Narrow wooden benches were bolted to the floor along the sides. Mel'iend grabbed a bundle from a box by the entrance. "You'll need these. I'll pop out while you change."

Alea glanced down at the bundle, then undressed quickly in her spare privacy. Silk leggings and shirt went under her borrowed uniform. She found a seat on the bench and donned silk gloves under her leather ones. She felt like a sausage about to split its skin and despite the cool air she started to sweat. Heavy steps heralded Tennic's entrance, followed by half a dozen other warriors and Mel'iend. The boy handed her dried meat and a cup of water. The meat had enough pepper to make her sneeze, but she was hungry.

Alea's head was swimming. There were too many new faces and new objects to catalogue in her mind, and with her fabricated name, she struggled to find her place amidst it all.

"Was she terrifying?"

She glanced over as Mel'iend slid onto the seat next to her and brandished a belt riveted to the bench. "Who?"

"The Dhoah' Laen. You must have seen her in the city."

Alea swallowed hard. She had not thought of this. "Only from a distance. She was away in Le'yne for much of the time I was stationed in the city. I saw a good deal of her guard though."

"Mel'iend, leave our guest alone." Tennic's voice cut through the thick air.

"I don't mind." Alea turned back to the boy. "You hear many of the stories living up here?"

"All of them. An'thor writes me letters, and sends news. I heard about the Rakos—do they really turn into monsters?"

Alea was taken aback. She had not heard that version of the story. "I think they create them or something. The Dhoah' Laen's guard, he's fearsome. Fights too fast to see, full of all kinds of anger."

"You fancy him?"

Alea started. "Admire him. You can't fancy the sun." A rumbling growl rose from the engine, and steam rolled past the windows of the cart. Wheels ground on rails and the train lurched into motion. They cleared the hall and emerged onto the tundra. The brown scrub grass was already dotted with frost in the valleys. Her white knuckles relaxed their grip on the bench after a few moments.

"Rest while you can. It's a long trip to the capital." Tennic leaned back against the wall. His eyes closed, but Alea would have bet her last coin that he was wide awake.

Her face pressed to the window as she stared out, listening to their metallic heartbeat thundering across the bleak landscape.

CHAPTER EIGHTEEN

The 20th Day of Lumord, 1252
The Tundra of the Northlands

ALEA JOLTED AWAKE. The Ageless stood and stretched around her. The train still hurtled across the landscape, but now it was dark. She wiped the grubby window with her sleeve and peered out. It was night, though she could not have slept for more than an hour. The moon had yet to rise and the stars spilled across the sky. The undulating landscape could have been Sunam, but the dunes and valleys were snow not sand.

Mel'iend glanced over at her as he rose. "We'll just be a minute. Feel free to stretch your legs, just hold on to something if you're going to walk around." He grinned and followed the others into the cart at the front.

Alea rose, rolling stiffness from her cramped shoulders. The rhythmic motion of the carts on the rails was akin to a ship at sea. *Albeit a very stormy sea.* After a moment of peering out the windows along both sides, Alea sat back down. The Northlands were decidedly plain. The snow was only a few handbreadths deep from what she could see. Despite the thick clothes she was no longer sweating, so the temperature seemed to steadily drop. After a moment Mel'iend appeared from the door to the rear cart. Frost rimmed the fur collar of his jacket and made spires from his eyebrows.

"You went outside?" Alea's heart bounced in excitement.

He nodded. "For a bit at least. You want to come?"

She followed him through the rearmost cart, filled with some of the boxes and chests she had seen in the warehouse. "You use this thing to travel because of the cold?"

"Because of impatience. Cold bothers us little." He held the door open for her at the end. "We've got a few, depending on where we're going and the weather. During the deep snow we can't go very far unless the engine has an icebreak on its bow."

A narrow causeway connected the carts, protected from the worst of the wind and cold by a flexible leather sheath. Alea crossed nervously, staring at the white ground flashing between the slats of the walkway. The other railcarts held canvas-covered boxes and barrels. In the rearmost, Mel'iend showed her how to lace up the face of her hood to cover her nose and mouth.

"Trust me, it hurts when the hairs inside your nose freeze." He grinned at her disgust and shouldered open the door. Instead of a causeway, a narrow balcony hung from the back. Mel'iend gestured her onto the walk. It was achingly cold, but the air was fresh and she took a few deep breaths.

"Thank you for coming out with me. I know you just braved the cold."

His soft, hissing laughter surprised her. "We're born for this weather." His face grew serious. "We should make the capital around dawn. Keep your head down and your eyes open."

A shiver completely unrelated to the cold crawled down her spine. "You're the king's son?"

"Warlord. And yes."

"So you'll inherit?"

"Ah. No. Inheritance works differently with us. The staff does not pass by blood, but to the most worthy warrior. It tends to be a cousin or nephew, but that is circumstance only. Warlord Edrodene's uncle was Warlord before him." He shrugged. "I have no wish to rule, and few skills, so I doubt I'll be chosen."

"You're young yet."

"Seventy-two."

Alea's brows shot up. "You look fifteen."

"That's about the age a human becomes an adult, right?"

"A little bit young, but yes."

"Then the ages are comparable."

"You must at least be a decent fighter for Edrodene to allow you to come with this group."

"He wanted me out of the way." His crooked smile reminded her of Arman's.

"How long until dawn?"

"Five hours. The nights are already growing longer. Less than a month and we'll have no sun at all." He pointed to the frost forming along her hood. "We should get back inside, you'll have ice-burn before long."

When she returned to her seat she leaned back, staring at the snow outside. Mel'iend's suggestion to keep her eyes open threw shadows over her excitement and confidence. The Ageless seemed a rough race, however, and perhaps it was only the difference in culture that the boy warned her against.

She did not remember falling asleep again, but she woke several hours later. The cool blue of the northern sky heralded dawn. Tennic was rousing the others and barking orders in a guttural tongue. Seeing she was awake, he jerked a thumb at the windows opposite her. "If you want a view, it'll be out those windows. My men must ready for arrival."

Alea crossed the cart and perched on the newly vacated bench to watch. The snow here was deeper, and Alea realized that perhaps it never truly melted. She shuddered. She could never stand to live in a world so cold and dark. The tracks curved north, affording Alea an expansive view of the white tundra. She made out the shape of mountains ahead, pale against the lightening sky. With the cool, thin air, sunrise was swift. There was no gradual bloom of light and color. The sun exploded from the icy horizon, light billowing across the glittering snow. Alea blinked stars from her eyes and looked north.

There were no mountains. The buildings of Neneviir gleamed in the sunlight. At first it seemed as if the walls were made of glass blocks, but as they neared, curving further, she saw it was not glass, but ice. The blocks were as long as she was tall and stacked together with only the cold and snow to bind them. The spires and minarets were supported by delicate iron frameworks. The rust from the beams and pillars bled red across the blocks.

The city was large, predominantly a single building with sprawling wings and several storeys. The western half was still shadowed by its own bulk, and where the light had yet to touch, Alea saw the walls were lit from within by great oil lamps. A row of arched doorways greeted the steam engine as it glided to a halt before the great iron doors to the city.

Every piece of the building before her, the machines used to get there, even the face of the warriors that guarded the door, told her what it took to live in this bitter environment. *This is where An'thor's strength was born.* There was no compromising in this snow-covered land. Compromise brought death. She swiped at her cheeks, half expecting tears. There were none, but her heart ached.

Mel'iend poked his head through the door to the stairs. "Come on."

She stood and quickly gathered her pack. Her bow would only suffer from the weather, but she missed the statement a visible weapon made. The half dozen warriors that had accompanied her flanked the cart's exit. *Honored guest or prisoner?* When it came to politics, she realized they were often similar.

Tennic glanced over at her. "Edrodene will see you within the hour. We're to eat and warm before the audience. Afterward you'll be given accommodations."

"Thank you." She shouldered her pack and allowed them to escort her up the ice-block stairs and through the doors. She had thought the ice would be slippery, but the constant cold maintained the ridges carved on the surface. There was no courtyard, save the line of stables and berths for the engines. She supposed they rarely received visitors who did not also live there. The doors opened into a wide hall. Despite the inherent chill of the ice, it was comfortable. Straw dusted the floor and heavy oil lamps hung from the ceiling. It was militant, but not savage.

They brought her to a large anteroom equipped with an iron-lined fire pit and several chairs made with fur stretched over an iron frame. *No trees means no wood.*

"We'll be a moment." Tennic pointed to the food lain out. "Help yourself." The Ageless huddled in a far corner, rapidly discussing something in their tongue. Tennic barked a harsh rebuke when Mel'iend faltered, clearly wanting to ask Alea more about the warmer parts of the world.

Tired of sitting, she paced around the room absently. There was no artwork or decoration, only serviceable tables with food and drink. She chose a handful of dried fruit. After a moment she looked over at her escorts. Mel'iend's eyes flicked between hers and Tennic. His expression was that of seasickness.

She met his gaze with a frown. His eyes bored into hers, as if willing her to understand. She dared not reach her mind out to his, but the horror on his face churned her stomach. After warring with herself for a minute, she reached her thoughts out to brush his for a moment, looking away as she did so.

Beware.

She pulled away quickly, before he realized what she had done. The conversation stopped abruptly and Tennic cleared his throat. "Captain, the warlord will see you now. Keep it short."

She nodded once and followed him through the larger doors. The hall was closer to a training court than a throne room. The floor was once again covered in straw. A massive iron fire pit sat in a depression in the center. The tiers surrounding it were covered in fur for lounging.

A set of iron stairs stood across the hall. These too were covered in fur, and an older man sat on the second highest. If the other Ageless were weathered, this man was battered. His bull's horns were chipped and scratched, the marks blackened from smoke. Each hip bore one of the strange weapons An'thor wielded. The metal beads in his dry, untidy braids rattled as he cocked his head. "Why are you here?"

She bowed deeply. "Warlord Edro'dene, I come from Athrolan with orders from Her Majesty Tzatia and our ally the Dhoah' Laen."

"Orders? I'm the lord here, not some human queen or Laen girl."

Alea's nerves began to sing. This was nothing like An'thor promised. "Of course. We share an ally, however. Lord Commissioner Barrackborn has allied Mirik with An'thoriend Domariigo."

"So my brother said. He's never been the brightest. Optimism is an unfortunate disease of the Hotlands. He seems to have contracted a rather strong strain."

"He said I would be allowed to look through your great treasury for an artifact the Dhoah' Laen needs. It's nothing valuable to you, and not fine in its craftsmanship."

Metal clanged as Edrodene slammed his gauntleted fist on a bare spot of stair. "Fine? You think we care about finery here? Are you blind, Captain?"

Her stomach sank. "Forgive me, Warlord. Your people are a powerful enigma to us humans."

He snorted. "As for your rank—you think I'd believe they would send a single captain here without other guards or better instructions? They either have too much faith in you or you are not what they think." A flick of his fingers caused Tennic and the others to draw the strange weapons from the holsters on their belts. A series of metallic clicks rang against the ice walls as their thumbs pulled levers back.

She did not understand how they worked, but she understood a threat when she saw one. She raised her hands slowly. "I come from An'thoriend. I want nothing more than to finish my business here and be on my way."

Edrodene's expression did not flicker and her heart fell. Her thoughts turned to the desolation she had seen upon her arrival. "You're isolated here. It was fine, for a time, but your people are dying, fleeing, and you have no resources. Your machines are all well and good, but you have no one to work them." The growing smile on the warlord's face was grim. "Fates you can't be serious." She sank to her knees and sat back on her heels, hands still raised, but without fear. "You saw what side would give you slaves. You thought the gods and Azirik would help you enslave the world. Your cryptic letter allowed the lie, but I'm not fooled anymore."

"Throw the captain in a cell until I decide what to do with her." Edrodene flicked his hand again before looking away, as if she was no more interesting than the filth under his long, cracked nails.

Her pack was ripped from her shoulder, the force sending her skittering across the floor. She managed to scramble to her feet before two of the men grabbed her by the arms and muscled her through a different door. The stairs down were narrow and twisting. Even with her boots she stumbled often. By the time they emerged into a low hall her shins were bruised and her cheek skinned from the roughly hewn ice wall.

Here the floors and walls were iron, as were the thick bars across the doors of each of the dozen cells. It smelled faintly of decay, even through the cold, and the sickly-sweetness of blood hung in the air. The room at the end of the hall was open. A single oil lamp hung low, illuminating the chair bolted to the floor. She clenched her hands to hide their shaking. She knew an interrogation room when she saw one.

"I don't know what you think to get from me." Her words guttered out when one of the men slammed the side of his fist into her diaphragm. Her breath flew from her lungs and she stumbled sideways. They shoved her into one of the cells unceremoniously and slid the bars shut.

"Whoever you are, the Warlord will find out."

"I'm a captain in Athrolan's army."

The man shrugged before heading back up the stairs with his companion.

Alea watched him go before leaning against the bars. "I'm Lenna Grayhill." Her voice was soft and wheezed over the "h" as she spoke. "I'm an Athrolani captain. I'm Lenna Grayhill." Her words petered out, lips still moving soundlessly as she repeated her false name and rank over and over. Perhaps if she believed it enough, so would they.

It was two hours before anyone appeared, and her stomach was rumbling. Her adrenaline burnt through any food from the past day. This time there were four guards. One she recognized as Mel'iend.

She snarled at him. She had trusted him. A small part of her grinned when he refused to meet her eyes. "You think you'll gain anything from torturing me? I know nothing—General Aneral isn't stupid enough to send a confidant to a strange country, even one we thought to be an ally."

"We don't care about your strategy. We care about why you're here and who you really are." Tennic gestured to Mel'iend. "Read the letter."

Mel'iend cleared his throat. "An'thor, I arrived at dawn on the 31st. Though not the most friendly, the Nenev have been hospitable. I'll begin my search tomorrow. I trust I'll see you soon. Luck and love, Grayhill"

Alea frowned. "You think he'll believe that?"

"Has he seen your handwriting? We can persuade you to write it yourself." Tennic's grin had more teeth than the wind and Alea looked down. "I thought not. Send it out with the next raven." He waited until Mel'iend retreated up the stairs. "Boy has no stomach for learning. It's a shame he's the Warlord's son." His black eyes flicked to Alea. "Now, let's get to learning about you."

The fact that the Ageless used "learning" as a euphemism for torture made her stomach twist tighter. *Should I just reveal my power? Would that stop them?* She had no doubt she could defeat a few guards, but the hundreds of warriors in the city above would be more difficult. *Besides, I'd be hard pressed to escape on horseback.* She grit her teeth as they unlocked her door and dragged her out. She brought her power up, not enough to color her skin or eyes, but enough to envelope her mind. She would feel the pain, but it would be distant. They shoved her into the bolted chair and buckled her arms and legs down. She gathered everything she ever learned, everything that made her Alea, and tucked it behind the walls of darkness.

I am Lenna Grayhill. I'm a captain in Athrolan's army.

The Ageless were not a stupid race, and despite the evidence, were not cruel for the sake of fun. Their abuse consisted of blows and bright lights and superficial wounds. She knew it was to keep her as whole as possible, not to be kind, but she was grateful nonetheless. She felt her lips move, repeating the litany of her identity, but she no longer heard her words. Her thoughts drifted to Reka, and wondered how the woman had fared before her death. Was Azirik cruel? Somehow the only times she pictured him, he was weeping.

Φ

The 25th Day of Lumord, 1252
The Orn de Galin Mountains

It seemed like centuries since Arman had last stood on the slopes of the Orn de Galin. The rocky slopes were stark, hawks circling on the heat waves rising from the outcroppings. Arman drifted upward on his own thermal. A curious bird flew too close, head cocked, eye turned towards the shimmering patch of air. Arman materialized his throat and mouth enough to rattle a warning call at the creature. He did not need distractions now. Below, Aral stretched on a rock, white belly turned to the warm sunlight. His crippled leg was ugly in the light of day, and Arman wondered how much the creature's battered mind would actually help them. The mountain range was quiet, only the low moan of the wind breaking the stillness. He reached out with his mind, as he had before. *Eana, where are you?*

A hideous shriek echoed from the peaks behind him, startling the hawks into flight. *There's a reason nothing lives in these passes.* Arman drifted lower, scanning the tumble of crags and stone. After finding Aral crippled and mad, Arman worried what awaited him with the others. He worried he was glimpsing his own future. A cave opened on a steeper slope below him. Bones littered the outcropping before the entrance. Most were those of animal's, but not all. Arman coasted lower, finally solidifying on the stone before the cave's mouth. At first he thought the creature crouched in the opening was a statue.

It could have been stone, save for the expanding chest. Puffs of smoke rose from the gap in its teeth. It made a low rattling moan, like pebbles shaken from the hillside. It sounded like a death rattle. With the grinding of stone it slowly tilted its head. A hunk of red sinew hung from the claws of its left hand.

Arman still made no move. He did not draw, but his hand stayed resting on the hilt of his knives. The death rattle call sounded again. "Ehnah. Ehnah."

Arman frowned. "Eana? You think I'm Eana?" He lifted his hand from his knife and tapped his chest carefully. "Arman."

The head tilted the other way. "Ahman."

"Probably sounds that way, with my dialect."

Stone ground and the creature's hand rose from its perch and tapped once, twice, on its own armored breast. "Ehnah."

Shock hit Arman's mind as he recognized the golden eyes, the crooked scar. He stepped back, tripping over the bones. Eana's claw tapped rhythmically as he muttered over and over the death rattle of his own name.

Arman raised his hands defensively. "All right, so you're not what I expected. Are any of you sane?"

Aral scrambled down from his perch with the speed of something that had been hunting birds and lizards. He moved like the apes in menagerie caravans, an arm supporting his body when his legs swung forward.

Arman skittered back a few paces. His heel crunched on a skull too large. "You've been eating people, Eana. Is there anything about the Earth Shakers that isn't disgusting?"

Eana made a wholly worse noise that Arman realized belatedly was a laugh. His jaw worked, steaming breath rolling from between his battered teeth. "Not cannibalism."

Arman's brows rose. "So you can speak."

Scales clattered as the creature shrugged. Eana moved to the edge of the outcropping, sharp eyes finding the prone figure of Aral below. "Pathetic."

"You'd be too, if you'd been trapped in your own temple."

Eana's mocking eyes swiveled to look at him pointedly. "Others?"

Arman mimicked the shuddering shrug. "I can sense them, barely. Most shelter in old Laen cities, or temples, like Aral. I'm not sure how many are left—I've found a few dead. Two by their own hands. Claws. The third was poisoned not long ago—perhaps by the gods, same way my city was destroyed. I saw their power, as if it still echoed after they were gone."

"War?"

"The same war we fought centuries ago. Time to finish it." Arman realized each word was a struggle for Eana, the thick tongue and cracked teeth too much for more human speech. As mocking as Eana's eyes were, there was also desperation.

"Help?"

"In the war?" Arman asked.

"Finding. Others."

"Yeah I could use some." Arman looked down. "Thank you, for driving me here. You're a right ass, but it helped. How long have I been hearing your voice, thinking it was my own thoughts?"

"Since I heard yours. Years." He shuffled down the slope.

Arman followed after him, frowning. "You can hear me like I hear you?"

"Started as whispers. Been shouting for months now." He hissed at Aral, the sound of steam on coals. *Get up you bastard. There are others, even if only a few. Don't tell me a missing limb prevents you from flying. I know better.*

The mental tirade startled Arman. "Don't be cruel, Eana. He flew here with me."

"Cruel, cruel," Aral echoed. The creature rose on his good leg, flexing a hand and steadying himself on a crag. At first it looked as if his body rotted, the skin peeling back to muscle and deeper to bone.

Arman backed away as the two dissolved into whirling smoke, spiraling into the clouds and west. *I'll see you at war. Don't be late.*

Don't think we'll miss this. We've waited long enough for you to get your head from your ass.

Φ

The 24th Day of Lumord, 1252

Bren groaned when someone knocked on his door for the fourth time in an hour. "I give up on getting any semblance of work done."

Kemer laughed. "Just ask them to make appointments." Aldac bent over the queen's missives while she and An'thor poured over a strategic map.

"This is war, I doubt Azirik would be so obliging." He heaved himself to his feet.

Eras waited outside, a slight frown curling her copper brows. "Lord Commissioner Barrackborn, I wanted to discuss some plans with your sister, but as I came to call on her, this letter intercepted me." She waved it in the air. "Care to explain what the Dhoah' Laen is doing in Neneviir two weeks before battle?"

Bren looked away. "It's complicated."

An'thor slid from his chair with a rough cough. "I think I'd better explain. Come in, *fetali*."

"This is my room, An'thor, not your parlor."

"I'm your ally and Her Majesty holds a damn fine grudge, so until I have my own, yours will have to do." An'thor leaned on the mantel. "When we met in Mirik, your sister asked a favor of me. She needed to find the Laen's Crown. It was in Claimiirn before she fell, and Lyne'alea suspected it could still be there. I suggested she try Neneviir as well, given the fact that Edrodene ransacked Claimiirn's treasury."

"And you sent her there unguarded?" Eras scoffed.

An'thor rolled his eyes at the general. "Eras, she sent herself. I merely gave her what she needed. May I see that?" An'thor unfolded the letter curiously, skimming it. "She reached the capital."

Bren slumped in his chair. "I still wish you had told me she was leaving."

"And I still agree with her choice not to."

"I'm not Arman, I wouldn't have stopped her. What did she say?"

"Precious little. Says they aren't friendly, but are cooperating. Her handwriting leaves a bit to be desired."

Bren frowned. "What?" He beckoned for the paper. By the time his gaze reached the bottom, his face had twisted into a grimace. "This isn't her handwriting. This isn't her voice. She'd say more, explain more. Complain about the weather."

An'thor grabbed the letter back. His eyes picked out the sharp points on some of the letters, the hard lines at the ends of the sentences. "You're right. This is Mel'iend."

"Who?"

"My nephew. A kind boy, but useless."

"Why would she have him write a letter for her? It can't be that cold."

"She didn't. Something's gone wrong." He tugged the earlier letter from Edrodene from his pocket and scanned it. "'*As always, I weigh the strength of the sides, and the benefits each offers. The choice is clear.*'" He handed it over. "Where does he explicitly name his allies?"

Bren looked it over. "He doesn't. Not once. He could mean anything."

Eras met Bren's eyes. "He's Azirik's. She's been captured. An'thor, take care of this. I'm going to deal with the army. We need to be ready for battle as soon as she returns."

Bren surged to his feet as soon as the general closed the door. "I'm going to get her."

"Like shite you are." An'thor pointed to the stack of papers on Bren's desk. "I understand your sister transcends all else in your mind, but you will lay it aside. You duty is to Mirik now. I'll handle this." When Bren bated, An'thor pushed him firmly back into his seat. "Ready your soldiers. Ready yourself. I know the Nenev, I know the Northlands."

Bren cast a longing look at the door. "All right. But if you fail, I'll gut you."

"If I fail you won't have to." An'thor jogged down the hall to his rooms. Within a minute his packs were ready and he was saddling Theriim. It had been decades since he had last been home. It seemed fitting it would be to make war with his brother.

Φ

The 25th Day of Lumord, 1252
The City of Neneviir

Pain was like water, patient and persistent, worming its way through chinks in the walls until the pressure built up enough to flood. The layers of shadow between her mind and their actions began to crumble.

Her head rocketed back as Tennic's fist rearranged the bones of her nose. Her mind flooded back into her body, her eyes flying open. Her left eyelid was swollen and a stinging on her cheek told her something had split the skin. The fingers of her left hand were black and bent at wrong angles. Nausea hit her stomach like a stone. She heaved, splatters of vomit freezing on the iron floor.

Tennic stepped back, muttering what sounding like a curse in Nenev. "You going to give us anything else?"

"I thought," her voice hitched every few words, "your boots...needed polishing."

The door opened suddenly. Through her bloodshot, good eye Alea recognized Mel'iend. He looked horrified. "Sir, the Warlord wants to see you. Immediately. Something about His Majesty Azirik."

Tennic growled in disgust and gestured sharply to the others. "Put her back. We'll continue this later."

She landed on her knees, the rough iron floor of her cell scratching her skin.

"I'm sorry." The words were low, almost drowned by the muttering of the wind through her barred window.

Alea pushed herself up. Her eye was completely swollen shut now. Mel'iend crouched just outside her cell. "Come to taunt me? Or warn me?" She spit a thick clot of blood from her mouth. "I think I've caught on to the Ageless not being terribly friendly."

He ignored her words. "I had to make sure they were properly gone. You said you came here looking for something. Said it was for the war. We've got plenty of weapons, sure, but I know a fighter and title or not, you're no captain."

Her pride stung at his words. She was never a good actress, but she thought she knew enough of the military to fool an isolated city. "I don't know what you think I am."

He raised his brows pointedly. "Not once did you ask us *who* we thought you were, only *what*. Why are you so convinced we think you're something other than human? And you've got the walk, the stance, the fighter's glare down wonderfully. I almost believe them. That look though," he gestured to her eyes, "that has far too much power and anger for a captain. Whatever you are, you're the damned general."

Her jaw clenched. "You're mad."

"Maybe." He jerked his head at the stairs. "What are you looking for?"

"Allies, that's all. And if you think this sweet innocence will make me talk, you're more stupid than I thought."

"Mad, stupid, you're probably right." The joking act was gone. His black eyes were exhausted and his features broken. "They don't give a shite about me, ma'am. Take me with you and I'll get you out."

Her brows rose. "Help me find what I need and we'll see."

"I'll make the way clear and be back in an hour. Wait here."

"I was planning on waiting in the hall." Her wry smile softened the bitter words. "Go." She shoved herself against the rear wall. Snow had blown in through the barred window, but sitting in a drift was better than being prodded from the door. The blood from her nose dripped down her face, but she was too dazed to stop it. Her vision unfocused as the hot blood melted red canyons through the snow.

Φ

Half an hour had passed when she heard boots on the stairs. She scrambled up. "Mel'iend?"

Tennic appeared before her cell, eyes narrowed. "It seems the Warlord did not actually request our audience. Mel'iend lied." He shoved her cell door open. "What does that coward have planned? He can't possibly think to outsmart us."

"You're right." She raised her hands, backing away. "He's not the bravest. But neither am I. Thought I could stand the questioning. Turns out I'm just too tired of pain. Call me a coward if you wish."

Tennic stepped in, the other warrior following him, weapon leveled at Alea's head. "I think you'll tell us who you are now."

Alea stepped back again, until her back pressed against the hard iron of the rear wall. "The thing is, you don't have to be brave. You just have to be clever." Her power roared through her body. Blackness filled her skin and lightning crawled from her back, burrowing like roots through the iron.

Tennic opened his mouth to scream, but the electricity wormed up both men's boots. Their muscles jerked, bones heating and flesh cooking in a moment. The smell of burning hair and meat flooded the cell as her power bore down. She pushed harder, watching as they fell, still spasming. The life was gone, but she let the lightning puppeteer them across the floor for another minute. The sound of boots pounding on ice broke her concentration and she slumped back against the wall, power curling back into her skin.

"I told you to wait!"

"They got friendly and I wasn't sure you'd get here in time, or at all!"

"Shite." He glanced down at the bodies. "Well. Are they dead?"

"Yes." Alea shoved herself off the wall. "I need my pack. You take care of these two." She slammed her boot into Tennic's face as she passed. The interrogation room still smelled of blood and vomit, and her stomach clenched anew. The table along the back wall held her things, clearly searched. She fumbled with the ties of the pack, one handed when Mel'iend dragged the second body into the room.

"You need help with that?"

"They broke my damned hand."

"Can I see?" He took her hand in his, peering at the bones. "Some of these are just dislocated. Nothing looks crooked. Is there anyone coming?"

Alea ducked her head to peer up the stairs while he continued to examine her fingers. "Nothing yet."

"Good." He grabbed her fingers and tugged them back into place with a swift motion.

A scream ripped from her dry throat and she whirled to glare at him, clutching her hand her to her chest. "Really?"

"You were distracted and that thing would be useless if I didn't." He shrugged. "I've learned things being around too many warriors."

She tried to flex her fingers again. The last two had only been disjointed, but the others were too stiff and painful to move. "Thank you then." She swung her pack over her shoulder. "What about the nose?"

"Can you breathe through it?"

"A bit."

"Then it'll heal all right." He grabbed the weapons from the two dead warriors and headed to the door. "Come on. I'll take you through the rear gate. We'll pass the treasury on our way."

She followed him up the stairs and down a hall. It wound around the Warlord's hall and to the rear of the city before climbing higher. "You only build upwards it seems."

"The ground is too frozen to dig deeply. Our lesser used rooms are higher instead of lower, that's all." He stopped at a large door and began fumbling with the lock. His knobby fingers coaxed it open with his picks after a moment. He shoved the door open and ushered her inside. "I'll stay here to guard. Are you sure it's here?"

She closed her eyes and reached out. The treasury was cold, and the air still. Far in the back, under a rolled carpet and inside a large chest was a leather bag. It buzzed in her mind, a clouded black smudge in her thoughts. "It's here." She navigated through the stacks of books and wardrobes. The chest was thankfully unlocked, but it took her a moment to shove the rug from its top with only one hand. The moment the leather met her hand she shuddered. The Rakos Crown had felt hot and itchy in her hand, but otherwise inert. This was like grasping lightning by the tail. She shoved it inside her shirt, tying the bag's strings to her breastband before weaving her way back to the door. "Got it. Let's go."

He slid the lock back into place, glancing back at her. "You have any plan as to how we're going to leave?"

Alea grinned. "You know how to drive an engine?"

"I have an idea."

"That's more than I do. How do we get there without them seeing us?"

"Luck? They'll be looking for me too, now." Mel'iend broke into a jog. "Can you run?"

"For now." Her adrenaline was wearing thin, but it would carry her home. It had to. She followed after him, not bothering to be quiet. The ice was surprisingly insulating and the sound of their footfalls carried only a short distance. He led her through another series of halls before they emerged behind the line of engine berths. They edged to the engine furthest from the city and ducked to the far side.

Mel'iend handed her his pack and pointed at the engine door. "Hop up into the cabin, I'll grab a few things."

She hoisted herself up into the machine, eying the levers and two things that looked like compasses attached to the wall. A small iron door hid a mound of black rocks and ash.

She heard Mel'iend climb in behind her. "Light her up, I'll manage the speed."

"My powers are ice and water and lightning, not fire!" She said it without thought and winced.

"That's why I brought the torch, ma'am."

She turned to see he did indeed hold a torch from the wall outside. "Sorry."

Either he was more stupid than she thought or he already suspected her true identity. He did not bat an eyelid. "We're escaping from my home and your captors, tension's natural. I'm surprised we haven't had a screaming match yet. Shove this in the coals."

"Right." She poked the mound with the torch gingerly, delighted when they caught. The flames licked high, the coals growing orange. One of the compasses on the wall began to twitch. Mel'iend pumped a lever that must have worked a set of bellows and the coals roared into life. He nudged the door shut with his knee and flicked the latch shut.

"All right. I've seen this before." His tone sounded like he was reassuring himself more than her. After a few moments of tinkering, the engine rumbled and belched a puff of steam from its chimney. "Well if they didn't know, now they do." He depressed a heavy lever on the side and the wheels ground against the rails, lurching into sporadic motion. He depressed it further and the engine lurched again then glided out from under the arched door and onto the tundra. The noise of the engine drowned out any shouts of alarm, but the ping of metal against the sides told her they were most likely under attack.

"Can we go any faster?" She eyed the glass windows. "Metal will hold, but I doubt those will."

"Right. Yes. One minute. I do this too fast and we'll blow cloud-high." They rounded the easy curve in the tracks that led to the city and he grinned. "All right, hold on." He slammed the lever all the way forward. The fire roared and the engine churned before they catapulted forward. The pulse of the wheels on the rails was closer to a rattle and the air screamed over the hard lines of the engine. Mel'iend glanced at her. His eyes were wide with terrified glee. "This is the best day I've had in a while."

She snorted. "My hand is a mess, my ankle is sprained and my nose is broken. Forgive me if I don't share your excitement." Her stomach was beginning to relax, but with the relief came waves of pain she had suppressed during their escape. "They'll probably follow us."

His delight dimmed. "I suppose. It'll take them a bit though. And they'll need at least a cart to carry enough men. We've only got the engine, so we're a bit faster."

"I'll deal with them when they catch up." She sank to the ground, leaning on the hard iron of the cabin walls. "Where are we going? Kaliim?"

Mel'iend made a face. "Yes, let's escape from one Nenev city only to drive right into their garrison. Not your brightest idea."

"I thought we didn't have a choice. The rails only go so many places, I assume." The rumble of the engine buzzed through her skull.

"Well yes, but we could stop before hand. We'd have to travel on foot."

"At least it's warmer there." She heaved a sigh. "How did the Ageless survive in this cold before you developed all these contraptions?"

"You realize Ageless is a slur?" He waved her sheepish apology away. "Doesn't matter. We developed these things precisely because we had to face the cold. Originally we came to the southern border, near Athrolan and Berr, before they were much beyond city-states. We began our work there, gradually moving north when we knew we could. Many think we just thrive in the cold. We do better than most, but the city is heated with generators and radiant heat. We're not tough as all that." He shot her a smile.

"I'm tired of cold, to be honest. I would have liked it more, perhaps, had I not experienced it in a jail cell."

"You grew up in the desert, didn't you?"

She turned to look at him. "How long have you known?"

"I told you, I knew you weren't a captain. I know about General Aneral from An'thor. There is only one other woman who I imagine has that much power and anger in her eyes."

She looked away, a frown growing on her features. "Do you think they knew, too?"

"I doubt it. It pays to be nobody. I've learned to observe much better, since no one takes the time to talk to me mostly."

"Why did they disregard you so much?"

"I spent a lot of time with my uncle when I was younger, and some of his philosophies influenced me too much. Up until a few years ago we corresponded regularly. He and my father don't exactly see on level."

"Have they always been that way?" An'thor seemed a kind, if wounded man. It was no small leap to assume Edrodene might have been the reason. "Why did he trust him at all?"

"Hope, I think. My father was the younger of the two, and the general of the army before the former Warlord died. An'thor was an ambassador in Claimiirn with his wife. Edrodene wanted to invade, and An'thor tried to prevent it." Mel'iend's expression was tight and his eyes narrowed.

Alea winced. "I've heard the aftermath of that story. Never the cause. His son died in that battle, didn't he?"

Mel'iend nodded. "I think that's why An'thor took such an interest in me. His son and I were born around the same time, though I was too young to remember him properly. His name was Elostrii."

"That's a pretty name."

"It's the word for Mother's Breath—the great blue clouds we see at night." He glanced out the window. "If you'd like, I can manage this for a while. You probably need to sleep. Who knows what'll await us further down the rails."

She nodded, hearing that the topic was clearly over. "Wake me if you need to." She curled into the corner. The iron was hard, but warm, and it felt like days since she last slept. Counting back, she realized her last true night's sleep had been over a week ago while traveling to Claimiirn. She shoved her pack into a more comfortable shape and settled in. "Mel'iend?"

"Yeah?"

"Thank you for helping me."

His soft laugh was almost silent against the churning engines. "No, ma'am, thank you."

Φ

Screaming metal jolted Alea awake. She braced herself against the side of the engine. "Fates, that is one way to wake a woman up."

Mel'iend's expression did not lighten. "Ma'am we're almost at Garrison Kaliim. How are we going to make it out of there?"

She winced. "Honestly, I didn't think that far ahead." She hauled herself up to peer through the fogged windows. The fort crouched darkly against the gray backdrop of the southern tundra. "There must be a hundred warriors there."

"Maybe closer to 50. My father is calling everyone home for war."

"Still too many for just us." She closed her eyes. "Too much heat will cause an explosion?"

"Yeah, why?" He caught sight of the power rising in her hands and blanched. "Ma'am, they won't survive a steam engine exploding, but neither will we."

"Only if we're in it." Her lip curled and she grabbed his hand. "We'll open the door. When I tell you to, jump."

"Ma'am—"

"I didn't bring us this far to burn to death." Alea flung the rear door open. The wheels screamed on the rails and she braced herself on the side. "Maximum speed, Mel'iend."

"Right." He unlocked the thin bar that prevented the engine from exceeding safe speeds and slid the lever all the way up. "Full steam ahead."

The engine growled, the fire roaring behind the thick metal of the furnace door. *I may not have fire, but I have water.* She drew the ice, the cold, from the fire. The acrid smell of creosote and fire filled the tiny compartment. The fort jolted closer in the tiny window. Tiny figures waved a welcome, then a more frantic gesture to slow, to stop. "Almost." The massive double doors reared before them. "Now!" Alea launched herself at Mel'iend, her arms locking behind his back as she propelled them through the steam engine's door. They hit the frozen ground, ribs cracking. Alea's shoulder ground into its socket, but her left arm still gripped the boy.

Air rushed past them, sucked into the fort by the fire's hunger. Blackness erupted in Alea's mind and she surrounded them with her power. She could barely focus through the pain. Instead of cool air, icy water enveloped them. She blinked against the sting of salt to find Mel'iend had been stunned by the fall. Her broken hand fumbled over his face and she pinched his nose shut, covering his mouth with her palm. She held her power in place, barely, as the explosion spread over them. The water began to boil at the edges as a second explosion rocked them. Her lungs burnt for air. Finally, the fire retreated to what was left of the fort.

She pulled her power back and the water splashed to the ground. What had been frozen earth was now charred, churned mud. Her skin stung from salt and the heat roiling from the burning fort. She dropped Mel'iend and began slapping his face. "Wake up, you silly boy." Her voice croaked over her aching throat.

It was another moment before he opened his eyes, gasping. "What happened?"

"We jumped, you fainted." She stumbled to her feet and started towards the hills behind the flaming fort. "We need to get out of here." When the Nenev boy did not follow her, she turned back.

He stared at the fort. The flames etched the contours of his face in yellow and black, adding lines he had not earned yet. "Where am I supposed to go?"

"Come with us. An'thor will surely help you."

He shrugged. "He's a solitary man. And what if he does? I'm no good at the sword. Or farming. Or mathematics."

"You're young. But you won't survive by standing in the mud waiting for your father's men to arrive."

"Right." He shrugged deeper into his cloak, though he seemed not to need the warmth, and fell into step behind her.

Alea noticed the rider after two silent, cold hours of walking. After another hour they were within shouting distance of one another.

Mel'iend glanced up from glaring at his boots. "He'll be on us in another minute. This is why I wanted us to take the tunnel."

"Along with anyone who might have survived the explosion? I think not. Besides, whoever they are, they come from Athrolan."

"Or Claimiirn."

Her lips thinned. She wanted to avoid that possibility, though it was far more likely than the option she voiced. "One rider does not worry me, Mel'iend."

Her words were cut off as An'thor's gray charger crested the hill before them at a lope. The warrior drew the horse up and raised a hand. "I wondered if I'd make it in time. Seems I worried for nothing."

Alea jogged the last few paces between them. Her laugh was weak. "Not for nothing. There were a few harrowing minutes."

An'thor dismounted, glancing between her and Mel'iend. "And were you successful?"

"I was." She nodded at Mel'iend. "I have your nephew to thank for that."

An'thor's expression hardened. "About that." He drew the revolver at his hip with a flick. "You're not coming back with us."

"An'thor, don't be ridiculous, he helped me."

Mel'iend raised his shaking hands. "Please. I'm with you." His uncle's only response was to pull the hammer back. "I'm not going back to them, An'thor."

"Pick a direction, I don't care which as long as it's not ours—and start walking. Don't stop until nothing looks familiar."

He backed up several paces then turned and began to walk. When he finally disappeared into the whipping wind, his hands were still raised.

"An'thor, he said he wasn't going back."

"He might have if Neneviir was closer." An'thor returned his gun to his belt and turned to adjust his saddle.

"He could freeze to death!"

"He could return to Edrodene and be ripped to pieces. Worse, he could return and become something I no longer recognize. Given my druthers I'd rather he die in the snow."

"That's not really your choice to make, An'thor."

"Today it was." He whirled. "This world, here in this fucking nightmare of snow and gunpowder, isn't yours. It might be mine, and it's certainly his, but it's not yours and you have no place telling me what choices to make." His voice was an angry rumble and his black eyes narrowed. "And like you have a right to judge me. In a few weeks you'll be deciding the future of every person on this damned world!"

"You think they want me to let them die? Fall to chaos?" Her thoughts jumbled under the black wave in her mind. Her body hurt and her nausea returned. Whatever nerve she hit was unexpected and clearly affecting his level head. This was not an argument she had expected, and not one she was willing to have with An'thor.

"That's not what I'm talking about and you know it! You think Arman's happy with you playing martyr while he becomes a monster?" An'thor's face was twisted. In fear or anger or hatred, she was not sure.

She crossed the distance between them in two strides and gripped him by the collar. "Do you know what happens to a person's mind when they break a law of nature? It doesn't snap, that'd be too easy to fix." Lightning chattered over her shoulders and through her hair. "Something crawls in and makes its home in their thoughts. You looked in my eyes months ago and said you knew what I was afraid of. You can't tell a monster just by looking, An'thor, and the only thing that frightens me is the one I've become!"

An'thor's expression broke with her last word and he cautiously raised his hands. "You're right."

Her remaining thoughts howled in the space her words left. Her power drained from her body. " An'thor."

He placed his palms on her shoulders. When she did not spring away he wrapped his arms around her. "I know."

"I didn't mean to yell."

"Me neither."

"That anger wasn't at you."

"Well I pray we live long enough for Arman to hear it all, and everything left you haven't said." He patted her hair. "My anger wasn't at you either."

"I know. I'm sorry about your son."

His arms tightened, but he said nothing. She felt him swallow hard, and knew he probably did not trust his voice just yet. "Can we go home now, please?"

He pulled away, eyes more tired than ever. "I've got something to take care of first, someone I need to see. Take Theriim, I'll find another mount. It's more important that you make it back."

She climbed wearily into Theriim's saddle. "Stay safe."

He tapped his fist against his brow, lips, and chest. "Luck and love go with you."

The smile that flitted across her face was as haggard as the mountains. "I'll see you for battle.

The Shaking in the Earth

CHAPTER NINETEEN

The 37th Day of Lumord, 1252
The Ruins of Claimiirn

AN'THOR FROZE WHEN THE KING'S eye found him. "Ah, hello milord king."

Azirik's brow quirked. "I thought you were the best in the world."

"Depends on who you ask, I suppose. I thought you were all abed."

Azirik's snorted laughter was not soothing. "You should try sleeping with a vice around your head."

An'thor eyes flicked to the Crown. He had heard the king was mad, heard his devotion had turned to insanity. An'thor knew better: Azirik was sane as any war-time king. Bloody times were not meant for sane men. The Crown glimmered from within the embrace of bruised and angry flesh. Now An'thor wondered if the rumors had been true.

"Would you sit?"

An'thor gaze narrowed. The king should be calling the guard. Azirik's expression was not one of vindication, but of loneliness. The Ageless took the chair by the door. He did not want someone to enter behind him, but he needed an escape route. "Why haven't you killed her yet? That should give you power, enough to attempt it." He gestured to the king's brow.

Azirik snorted again. "Why do you use your sword when you could end any fight with a squeeze of your finger?"

An'thor sat back at that. He had always assumed he knew the king far better than the king knew him. He had forgotten that over forty-five years he'd allowed a lot of little facts to penetrate their conversations. After all, lies were best taken with a dusting of truth. "What do you mean?"

"You have a revolver, a mighty weapon, and yet you have fired it how many times? Four?"

"Six." An'thor rubbed his hand down his scimitar's scabbard. "My blade is the best sword I could have found in Neneviir."

"It's pig iron folded over a dozen times to keep it from shattering. The best your people bothered to make, but still shite."

"And I'd still prefer it. I detest what my people did. I detest what they stand for. The revolver exemplifies both."

Azirik met his gaze. "And likewise, I prefer my own mind. It may be outclassed, it may be weak and twisted to prevent it breaking, but it is my own. This thing is my revolver."

"You aren't afraid they'll strike you down for that admittance?"

"They would lose the power I have over my men, and the connection to my allies. Besides, for a great cause, you would use your revolver. For a great cause, I would use the Crown."

An'thor stared at the man. Something in the king's gaze seared with its intensity. There was nothing he had left to lose, and that made him powerful. There were moves left on the gameboard, still, and An'thor was suddenly certain Azirik still had enough autonomy to sweep his enemy clear.

Φ

The 1st Day of Valemord, 1252
The City of Ceir Athrolan

Bren's mug shattered on the flagging. "Toar, Alea, what happened to you?"

Alea grinned weakly. The benefit of sneaking out of the palace was she had no fanfare to contend with on her return. "The Nenev have an odd way of saying hello."

He shook his head. "You should have brought guards."

"So they could be interrogated? I think not. Could you call your maid in? I'd love a healer. And perhaps something to drink. And food that isn't dried beyond all recognition."

Bren laughed and raised the flask still in his hand. "I'll have to call for new mugs, but you can have some of my wraith." He handed it over, peering at her face. "Did they break your nose?"

"Yes, but Mel'iend said as long as I could still breath through it, it would heal straight. I could barely see out my left eye for half the journey back though." She heaved a sigh. It was a relief to see his face after the ordeal of the last weeks. After a hard sip from the flask she glanced up. "I'm sorry I didn't tell you."

"I'm sorry, too. You were right not to. I might not be as bad as Arman, but I still wouldn't have understood. Did An'thor come with you?"

"He had to take care of something first. He'll be here before long though." She absently picked at the scabs on her left knuckles. "What did he say?"

"The same as before. I told him it was useless lying to you about his visits."

"What happened at Vielrona?"

"Azirik. Well, Azirik wielding the gods' power. I think it was something like the storm on the Iron Sea."

"His friends, his mother?"

"He said Kam was all right. Asked me to give him and his wife and child a home in Mirik. His mother's dead, same with his friend Wes and a woman called Veredy."

Alea groaned. It felt wrong that Veredy had already been dead when Alea had borrowed her name for a night of drinking. "I can't even imagine what he must be thinking."

"I imagine he must feel much like you did a year ago." Bren eyes were sad and gentle. "I'm sorry he hasn't seen you."

"It's funny, he saw me as the Dhoah' Laen when I was as far from that role as could be. Now, when that is all I am, he sees me as a woman. But part of me wonders if we'll ever see on level. Will we always be in this dance? Me leaving when he's arriving?" She shook her head.

He frowned. "What happened in the Northlands? You left angry and cold and lost. You come back almost as changed as when you returned from Le'yne."

She looked down. "I thought I learned to control my power by learning there was no difference between it and myself. Trouble was I didn't know who I was anymore. When you understand something, you can control it. I had to learn who I was, but even more I had to accept it. I can't spend whatever is left of my life terrified of what I am."

He slid from his seat and wrapped his arms around her unceremoniously. "I love you. Whatever you are, whether you accept it or not, I love you." He pulled away and met her eyes. "When do we leave?"

"As soon as General Aneral says the army is ready."

"It's been ready for the past two days. Waiting on you."

"I thought no one knew I was gone."

"They didn't. I told them you were meditating on battle. You haven't been the most sociable the past months, so it wasn't odd that no one had seen you."

Alea glared at him. "I suppose you're right."

Bren rose at Valadai's knock and relayed Alea's requests. "And if you could inform General Aneral that we'd like to speak with her at her earliest convenience."

Alea laughed. "I'm glad I had the forethought to bathe before coming to see you."

Eras arrived before both the food and the healer. Her brows shot up at Alea's appearance. "I learned you went to Neneviir. What happened to your face? Did you slip on the ice?"

"Yes, and they caught me with their fists." Alea grinned. "I had something I needed to get, and An'thoriend's brother was kind enough to relinquish it to me."

Eras's eyes darkened. "I wondered if An'thor was wrong in assuming they would be our allies."

"Edrodene explained that his brother seems to have caught the terrible human disease of optimism."

"He was always an ass." Eras pointed to the chair across from Alea. "Brentemir, may I?" When he nodded, she sat, leaning her elbows on her knees. "What is your plan, Dhoah'?"

"Battle. Within the week. How quickly can you mobilize the men?"

"They can be ready at dawn the day after tomorrow." She glanced at Bren. "And your men, are they ready to march?"

"They arrived a few days after Alea left." He glanced at his sister. "You should have seen it—I've never been more proud. And the Asai arrived shortly afterward." His grin faded and he drew a long breath. "It's been a while since I went into battle, and this one feels different."

Eras glanced up. "You, too?"

Alea glanced between the two. She did not know what they felt, but she agreed everything about this battle tasted differently. *There is certainty in me. Acceptance.* The shadow had not lifted from her spirit, but its blanketing darkness had changed.

Eras looked at her hands, clasped before her. "Dhoah' we're putting a lot of faith in you. This is just the beginning of your battle, but it is the greatest of Athrolan. You made a promise to Her Majesty, and to our people, that Athrolan will not fall. Are you still holding to that promise?"

Alea wondered briefly what Daymir might have said. *I am not so mighty as to keep a city from falling.* She did not look away from the general's gray eyes. "Athrolan will always stand."

Φ

The 3rd Day of Valemord, 1252
The Eastern Forest of Athrolan

Alea noticed the men on the second day of the march. There were five. She began the journey among Indred's men, but after the first day another group of soldiers formed around her. Narier was among them, but she recognized two others. One was a former guard at Daymir's manor and the other she had tended during the siege. None ever spoke to her, but they were clearly a silent rotating guard. She discovered why on their third night after making camp.

The nightmares from Cehn were now speckled with her days trapped in Neneviir. Between them, she woke, bedroll tangled and drenched in sweat. She tumbled off her cot, the images fading slowly from the backs of her eyelids. "Damn."

"Dhoah', you all right?"

Alea turned at the soft voice outside her tent. She rose and peered through the flap. A man stood just outside. She recognized him as one of the men she tended during the siege. "I'm fine, what are you doing?"

"Just keeping an eye out, Dhoah', nothing more."

"You don't have to do that, there are plenty of eyes out tonight."

"Just the same, I'm here." His smile was wary, but genuine.

Her head still pounded and her limbs buzzed. "You were out here before?"

"No, Dhoah', Kal had last night and Narier the one before."

She frowned. She was tired and sorely needed sleep. The thought that these men had taken up her guard without question was uncomfortable. *The fact that I can defend myself aside, this is ridiculous.* She was about to tell the man so, when she caught sight of his face. "You guarded Daymir's house."

"Yes. It's Gord, Dhoah'."

"Thank you, then. Good night." She ducked back into the tent and crawled into her bedroll. Her body ached, but her mind was whirling.

Φ

The 5th Day of Valemord, 1252

Alea shrugged deeper into her cloak and wound her way through the tents until she found the campfire. Narier was alone at the fire, peering into the crackling heat with a vague frown.

"Care for some tea?" Alea held up a tin from her pack and her tin mug.

Narier shrugged. "Might as well." He settled the kettle in the coals and pointed at the fading bruise lingering around her eye. "I see your journey was eventful."

"Rather. I got what I needed, though. Thank you for your help. Then and now."

He grinned. "Gord told me you caught him. Said he thought you were angry at first."

"At first I was. I'm capable of defending myself."

"We all know it, Alea. But you're tired and worn and everyone can see it. You deserve to rest safely."

Her thanks were interrupted by the arrival of a younger man with thick curls. He froze, staring at the woman by his fire. "Fates."

She grinned and patted the ground beside her. "Come on. I won't hurt you. If you insist on guarding me, the least I can do is share my tea."

The man edged over and carefully sat. "Right. Thank you, Dhoah'."

"I don't recognize you." She held out her arm. "What should I call you?"

"I'm Kal Smytheson. I was friends with your guard for a time. Sousa, too."

Alea's response was interrupted by the arrival of the other three.

"And I told her, that's exactly what your sister thought!"

The men crowed with laughter and Kal glanced uneasily at Alea. "Sousa, knock it! We've got company." He looked over apologetically. "Forgive them, Dhoah' they didn't know. They just returned from getting a bottle from the trail army."

Gord flushed, seeing Alea and stammered to a halt. "I'm sorry, Dhoah', I didn't see you."

She waved his apology away. Her time in Vielrona had not been ill spent, and she remembered most of Wes's and Kam's wicked humor. "Nonsense. I'll tell you the one about the Berrin scout and the crow if you share a thumb of that wraith."

Narier snorted into his tea at the expressions on their faces. "I doubt you're what they expected, Alea."

Alea shrugged and smiled at the three still standing. "Come and sit. You with the dark hair must be Sousa, and Gord I know." She held her arm out to the third man. She recognized his face, but could not place where from. "How do I know you?"

"I'm Henack, Dhoah', and you healed me during the siege."

"You were the first man I cared for there. You had an arrow in your thigh."

He smiled. "Yes. You promised it would not rot." He patted the healed limb. "Now I believe it works better than the other."

She laughed and sidled over. "Sit down so I don't have to hurt my neck talking to you. Would you like some tea before it chills?"

Φ

The 7th Day of Valemord, 1252
The City of Ceir Athrolan

Tzatia's mind was as restless as her body was tense. Her forefathers faced onslaughts, not the least of which brought Claimiirn to her knees. They handled them with might and grace and no small amount of retaliation. *And I have proven myself weak and fearful these past months.* Even at her busiest, her thoughts would turn abruptly to Daymir. With distance, she realized that disinheriting the man might have been brash. The queen was nothing, if not stubborn, however.

She scarcely could sit through her corset lacing without pacing. Now she sat in her parlor listening to the details of the army that would crush her city. The corporal across from her looked as grim as she imagined herself. "Tell me when."

"A couple of hours, maybe."

"And you are from the siege at Ceir Felden?"

"I am. It broke several days ago. They left in the dark, and the weather was such we saw nothing but their campfires. They left them burning, to fool us. We didn't know they'd gone until morning."

"And you're certain they are coming here?"

"I got here scarcely before them."

"Thank you for your dedication, Corporal. Go to your barracks, eat and rest."

She was silent for a full minute before she turned to the steward. "Valadai, sound the alarm. Athrolan is under attack." The guards flanking the door snapped to attention as she swept through the door of the throne room. "Leave me!"

She approached the throne when the guards had left. She knelt before it, lacing her shaking hands on her skirts. She knew it was impossible, but she thought she could already hear the enemy hooves. She had not prayed in years, not since the war on the gods began. She missed the comfort it had given her. Now she just thought on her father. "Though I've fallen many a time, I rose on my own. I tried to carry the land as you and grandfather, but I'm faltering now. She promised to keep our crown from shattering, and I pray she succeeds, for I no longer can."

The door behind her creaked and she whirled, ready to reprimand the guards for interrupting her. The words stalled in her mouth at the sight of the figures in the doorway.

At first, Tzatia thought they were some noble women coming to shelter from the battle to come, but a tingle threaded its way up her spine. She rose, head tilting curiously. They wore gray dresses and their hair ranged from black to cloudy gray. The woman at their fore stepped closer. Her eyes, like the others', were dull silver. "Lady queen, we come to offer our protecting."

Tzatia frowned. "Who are you?"

"Your people fight for my daughter, we'll fight for you."

Tzatia's legs gave way, but the woman caught her elbows. "You're the Laen."

The woman nodded. "I'm Elle. These are my sisters, those that would come."

Tzatia collected herself and straightened. "What do you need?"

Elle grinned, and the wolfish gleam in her eyes was suddenly Alea's. "Show us to your ramparts."

Φ

The 6th Day of Valemord, 1252
The Athrolani Camp at Claimiirn

Alea stood on the cliff tops, watching the Miriken below. Anxious thoughts urged the soldier's boots faster. A journey that should have taken over a week had taken only six days. She was among the first to arrive and for the next two hours the army trickled into camp. The sound of hammering tent poles and barked orders faded from her mind as she stared at their enemy. Their arrival had not gone unnoticed and she took dark pleasure in watching the hurried squires and knights sending word. *You'd better be afraid, Azirik. I'll be the death of you.*

"Alea, the general is calling us together." Bren's voice arched over the tents. After a last look at the camp below, she turned and followed him to the officers' camp.

The officers crowded into Eras's tent. The press of armor and road sweat was cloying but familiar. A captain unrolled a map of the plains and cliffs. "We've got an idea of the terrain and their locations. Azirik appears to have most if not all of his troops—roughly two thousand two hundred. Most are cavalry."

"And the Berrin are down there as well, but they're camped behind the ruins." Alea pointed to the place where she had seen the Berrin forces."

"Are there caves in these rocks?" Bren pointed to their path down to what would be a battle field within a day.

Eras shook her head. "That rock is hard. If there are any they are infrequent and small."

"It's difficult to say what Azirik will do," Alea said. "It's safe to assume he will not engage in direct combat, but he will use the gods' power to attack. I cannot say whether he will attack me or the men."

Vinden glanced at her and another man shifted angrily. "Dhoah', is there danger the soldiers should be warned of?"

Alea barely kept the impatience from her face. She was ready to face Azirik now, and the plans were only muddling her thoughts. "I thought soldiers knew battle was dangerous."

"Dhoah'," The general's warning was low but pointed.

"The men will be protected." She only partially listened to the rest of the plans. They would undoubtedly change as Azirik and the Berrin responded. The army was divided into three, Bren leading the various allied troops of Banis, Asai and Miriken, Eras and Raven leading the others. As orders were given the men filed out until only Bren and Alea remained with the colonels, commander and Eras.

The general turned to Alea. "Where will you be?"

"I need a clear view, above the fray."

"The old Claimiirni battlements should do nicely. I'll dispatch a detail of guards for you as well."

"With respect, general, I already seem to have acquired some guards. Perhaps you might consider them."

"I'll look into it. Is there anything else we need to know?"

"Tomorrow, before the charge, I need to see the men. All of them." She glanced up at Eras. "I'll lay protections over them, shielding them from what I'll do. Once my power rises they'll need to be still." She looked over at Bren. "You remember the training court?"

Her brother shuddered. "I wish I didn't. It gave me nightmares, you know."

Eras's stoic expression tightened. "Perhaps you could enlighten us, Lord Commissioner?"

"I need you to pass this through to every man under your command. When you give the signal everyone is to drop to the ground. If you are mounted, get off. You will want to run, to scream, but stay down, no matter what you see."

One of the colonels frowned. "That's it, drop our weapon and take a knee?"

"Only an idiot would drop their weapon," Raven interjected.

Eras ignored them. "Drop and hold and pray to whatever still listens that we live?"

Alea cleared her throat. "I'm still listening, general. Your men will be fine."

"And the signal?" Raven's frown was deep enough to swallow his eyes. "Will we hear it?"

Bren grinned and looked at his sister. "It's her name, and I promise you'll hear it."

Φ

Bren joined Alea and her guards that night. His reception was better than Alea's had been while on the road, but perhaps it was due to the mound of smoked meat and wraith he brought to share. The meat sizzled over the fire as Bren warmed it. He glanced over at Narier. "The Miriken have a tradition before battle—singing and dancing and drinking. I brought my flute. Would you mind a few songs?"

Narier grinned. "It's not like they don't know we're here. Let's make them think we don't give a damn about tomorrow."

Sousa let out his characteristic crowing.

They took turns eating and suggesting songs. After a few, Narier joined Bren's playing with his low, scratching voice. There were drinking songs and war ballads. "Alea, you know any Sunamen war songs?"

"I know many, though they're not Sunamen. I refuse to sing them—I'll send you running to Azirik for protection if I raise my voice." Finally Bren's insistence won out and she began clapping against her leg. "It's Athrolani, so if you know other verses I beg you join in." She hummed a few lines for Bren to copy the notes, though her lack of tune made for a rocky start.

"Well, this is war and I'll probably die
Yes this is the end it seems
But, eh, won't you tell me if I'm wrong
Please tell me what we'll be?"

Narier laughed. "It's an echo song. One of my favorites. We sing back and forth.

"Hey, it's Spring in the thick dark wood
But no wife you'll find for thee
Oh, it's Summer on the cobbled streets
But no babe she'll carry for thee."

Alea whooped, and Sousa joined her next verse,

"Death's a bastard by three and a right boor at that
And we'll never be his, you'll see,
But this is war and we'll probably die
So let's drink to our bitter end."

The lines came faster, the singer alternating with each one. Henack rose and pulled Alea to her feet, spinning around the fire as they shouted the words back and forth.

"You'll have a limp and a scar down your face."
"Well, you'll be fat if battle don't take you!"
"I'll stand tall with my men and sing with the horn."
I'll be grizzled and old before Toar takes me!"
"I'll become king or maybe a duke,

I'll be rich and more handsome you'll see!"

Alea fell back laughing breathlessly. "Dancing is better than singing by far. What other steps might you know?" Across the camp came the sound of others singing, a fiddle and horn joining the raised voices.

"Reka taught me one of the Border dances for victory in battle." When Alea urged Bren, he handed his flute to Kal and began to stomp gracelessly around the flames. After a moment the pattern emerged and Alea joined him. They whirled, the others rising as well, Kal abusing Bren's flute to their steps.

Φ

The music pierced through Arman's mind as he and the other Rakos edged along the outskirts of the camp. The myriad songs and dances combined oddly, but the desperation and joy were not lost on him. He had almost reached the cliff tops when he caught sight of Alea. She was spinning around with Bren, a strange series of steps that looked more like combat than actual dancing. He crept closer before realizing what he had done.

The woman before him was not the Alea he remembered. Eras's hard words about his expectations echoed through his mind. *No, she's not what I expected, but she's everything I could want.* His steps brought him closer still, until he stood in the trees just outside the ring of firelight. Her power pulsed over him, her off-tune singing drawing a smile onto his face. He warred with himself, watching her dancing and feeling the firelight between them. It was likely the last night he would live through and he knew exactly where he wanted to be.

There were three lights that burnt in the heart. The first was the bright, violent flash of passion. The second was a slow steady burn—the approach of spring, knocking ice from the streams and frost from the grass. It was freedom.

The third was brighter than the sun. It boiled through his body, burning everything else away until a single thought remained. *Surrender.* He swallowed hard and stepped into the firelight.

Φ

Alea's breath came in gasps of laughter. The campfire roared higher, shedding light onto the man standing a few paces away. Alea's steps slowed and her breath faltered. Kal's music stopped. The man across the campsite was different. His blonde hair was longer and his tanned skin dusted with strange metallic scales. She would recognize him anywhere, not from the color of his hair or the set of his wiry shoulders, but by the crackling heat of power crashing against her mind. *Of course he'd be here. At the end of all of this.* She felt Bren's eyes fixed on them, but he did not speak.

Arman took a step closer, more like a wary animal than a man. He cautiously extended his hand, the low hum of a tune drifting from his throat. Bren pulled his flute from Kal's loose grip and echoed the notes softly. He played again, faster, the notes dissolving into the liquid of music. Arman's hand still reached between them.

It fit that they would meet at the end of this journey, in the firelight before the glare of battle. She thrust every thought from her mind, every bitter word, and grabbed his hand. The stillness broke and they whirled, the steps coming faster now, more assured as Bren's tune wailed through the night. She danced for victory without hearing the music, pouring her heart into the steps with her Rakos guard. The tears on her cheeks were salty and warm and she was not sure if the sobs racking her body were of laughter or weeping. Her boots and his beat into the still soft ground, and she hoped their steps would shake the very earth under the gods' feet.

CHAPTER TWENTY

The 8th Day of Valemord, 1252
The Athrolani Camp at Claimiirn

THE FIRES WERE BANKED and the remaining music quiet. Alea nestled the kettle further into the fire. She glanced up to see Arman disappearing into the forest. "Arman?" He froze at the sound of her voice and she could see his jaw working. "I understand if you're angry, but could we talk?"

"Resolution before death?"

"As grim minded as you are, you were never a fatalist."

He drew a breath then followed her inside her tent. When she sat on the edge of her cot he took a seat on the chest across from her. His body was that of a man, not the boy who followed her to war a year earlier.

"I can't understand your anger."

He looked down. "A lot of things have changed since we last spoke. Civilly, I mean."

"We both deserve honesty. I haven't always given you that, or known what to say."

"Then I will be honest as well," he offered.

"After this battle the true war starts for me. I fight the gods. I will do terrible things, things that I've damned the gods for. I'd rather not go alone."

"I've learned what this war will do to me, and it's changed my face and my body and my thoughts. What has it done to you?" His eyes were narrowed and glowing in the darkness. "I've asked a dozen people, and none of them, not even Bren, know what you'll do. They have assumptions and the echoes of promises you've made, but you haven't told a single one."

"They won't understand, Arman. I don't blame them, really. Battle has to be a dichotomy. Wars can't be muddled or they'd never be won. I'm letting them believe I'm good, that I'm some benevolent creature come to save the world. And I will save it, but not the way they want me to."

"What are you doing, then? Raising the Laen to power? Creating new gods for them to worship?"

"I'm not making anyone worship the Laen. I'd never make anyone worship them—I barely tolerate them." The vehemence in her voice surprised them both. "No, I think humans have had enough of worshiping. It's time to turn our eyes outward."

His eyes widened. "You can't."

"Arman, it's the only thing left. All the power bound up in the Laen and the gods and even the Rakos, it needs to go back. We're strangling the world just with our existence. I'm not raising the Laen to power. I'm destroying them, too." The confession ripped itself from her heart, leaving her gasping for air to fill its place.

"Then whatever you need from me, I'll give it." His eyes shone with the bravery it took to care for her and the strength needed to leave his world behind.

"You said this has changed you. I'm sorry for that."

"It's all right. Truly." He looked at his hands. "My place has always been here and this creature has always been me. I realized something, too." His pause was not for effect or out of pain. He finally met her eyes. In that moment everything they had feared was bared between them. "Alea, this battle will kill me."

She reached across the distance between them. "Your power lies in sacrifice."

He shook his head. "No. It lies in surrender."

"Then can you trust me? Tomorrow I need there to be no barriers left between our power. Whatever anger you feel, whatever resentment, needs to be set aside. You've begged me to let you into my thoughts. Now it's my turn to ask you to do the same."

"Of course."

"No, Arman. I tried to talk to you while I was in Le'yne. My thoughts just slid right off yours. I could see everything, hear everything in your world. I even screamed for you to hear me, but I was like a ghost."

"You saw everything? Shite. I thought you were angry with me. I thought if I found someone else it would stop hurting. In the end kissing her moved me about as much as a dry history book. She was angry and frightened—she should have been. She thought I chose her because she had dark hair and pale eyes. Truthfully, you're so far above anything I could not really see the resemblance."

"You can't fancy the sun." She laughed softly and waved away his questioning gaze. "I thought I asked you to take me off that pedestal."

"Did I mention I'd been drinking?"

"From my experience that had little to do with it." Her laughter joined his, low and warm in the confines of the tent. "I'm sorry I was distant."

"I'm sorry I was an ass."

"I'm sorry I never let you in."

"I'm sorry I never gave you a reason to." He glanced outside. "It's late and we'll have a damned early morning. I'll let you rest."

She touched his wrist as he went to rise. "Please. When we were on the road you were always there. Just for tonight." He faltered and she edged over on the cot, patting the vacated space.

Finally he toed off his boots, nudging them to sit beside hers. He slid under the coverlet with her, one arm propped behind his head. "I missed you."

She rested their clasped hands on his chest. "And I you." Her eyes slid closed, the lines of worry relaxing for the first time in months. "Good night, Arman."

"Good night, Alea."

Φ

The 9th Day of Valemord, 1252

Alea woke once, shortly before dawn. The body beside her was incredibly warm. She blinked as the face before her came into focus. Arman's features were drastically different. Scales spiraled over his brow and cheeks, larger in the center of his forehead and the bridge of his nose. They were white-gold. The unaffected skin was tanned as always, but with a metallic undertone.

This war is making monsters of us both. Difference is, yours is beautiful. She closed her eyes and nestled closer. There were only a few hours of peace left.

When she woke again it was dawn. Arman was gone and the bed cold. The camp began to bustle outside, the clatter of metal pans and armor sounding through the campsites. She rose quickly and dressed before turning to the chest of armor. A dirty, battered envelope sat atop it.

She did not need the plain script to tell her it was from Arman.

> *Alea,*
>
> *There are so many things I wanted to tell you, to share with you, but never had the words. Now, when I have them, I realize that you probably already know.*
>
> *I know what I said in the gardens in Athrolan, but our bond is the closest to vows, our friendship the closest to marriage as I suspect I'll ever*

come, or ever want to. This ring was the one my father gave to my mother. It doesn't belong to anyone, if not to you.

With everything I have and am,

-A

Alea tipped the envelope over her hand. The gold gleamed dully in the early minutes before sunrise. She tucked the letter away and slid the ring onto her middle finger. Each motion seemed a ritual as she donned her armor. Each added weight was a manifestation of what rested on her shoulders. She was braiding the top half of her hair back when someone rapped on her tent pole.

"Yes?" She turned about, wrapping a leather tie around the end of her plait.

Bren stepped in. He watched her silently for a moment before gesturing to the breast and back plate she had yet to put on. "Would you like help?"

She nodded and allowed him to buckle the metal at each shoulder and about her ribs.

"I saw Arman this morning." Bren's words were soft. "I'm glad he came to see you."

"I am too." She reached for the box that held the two Crowns when Bren grabbed her hand. He examined the ring, his gaze thoughtful. "It's what Arman's father gave his mother," she explained.

"You know what this means to him? What you wearing it means?"

"I know." She shifted. "Bren, I—"

He drew her into a sudden, hard embrace. Their armor clunked as his arms tightened around her. "You can say it later." He drew away. "We should be going, the men are gathering for you to see them."

"I'll be along." She watched him go before sliding the Crown onto her head. It was cold, and sent slivers of tingling pain through her skull as if she had drunk something incredibly cold too quickly. She ducked from the tent and wound through the tents to the cliff tops. The assembled army was quiet, and she could hear the shouts and commotion of their enemy below. The sunlight moved slowly across the fields, inching down the cliffs. Alea moved down the line of men, her steps quick and sure. She reached the first row. She grinned at Narier. Her hand brushed his and she moved down the line, touching hands, faces, shoulders, bleeding cold into their armor and skin. It took the better part of an hour before she was through. Finished, she returned to their front.

"What I gave you allows me to find you and protect you when I must. It will not save your lives against every sword blow, but it will help in the end." She tried not to think of all the faces that would not smile the next day. "You have my deepest gratitude for standing with me today." She fumbled with what to say. There were no words that did not sound trite, or like a battle ballad.

Finally she raised her fist to her brow, her lips, her breast, then threw it into the air. "Luck and love go with you."

Her salute broke the stillness and the men mounted up or drew weapons. The forces moved forth, where the slope down to the fields was more gradual.

Narier appeared, followed by Kal and her other appointed guards. "We'll go scout the battlements. We'll be ready when you are, Dhoah'"

"Thank you Narier." She was moving to follow when she caught sight of the approaching figures. Arman's stride was purposeful, the four creatures loping beside him something out of stories. He stopped a pace away from her. "You have something of mine."

She tugged the Rakos Crown free and placed it gently on his brow, brushing his cheek with her thumb as she drew away. Scales exploded across his skin at the contact. His pupils were blown and flames erupted through his hair. She grinned at him. "You look brilliant, Arman."

His teeth bared in an answering smile. "And you're magnificent."

She squeezed his hand and stepped away. "On my signal, Earth Shaker." She jogged up to the fort. The sound of horses and armor and orders faded as she entered the ruins. She saw the place she had camped weeks before, and found the winding stairs up to what was left of a watch tower. She passed Sousa and Henack on her way, returning their wan smiles. The battlements were broad and high, the granite warming to pink in the sun. She looked down at where Arman waited on the cliffs with the other Rakos. Catching his eye, she grinned wolfishly. *Is it bad that I wish I could see their faces when we let our powers loose?*

His laugh rumbled through her mind. *Ready when you are, milady.*

She watched the army move into place, horses wheeling and weapons gleaming. Below, Arman shrieked and leapt into the air. Power rose into her body, faster than before, pouring through the conduit of her Crown. Black fog erupted from her palms and the battle began.

The connections to her power were multiplied, as if what was once a river now roared as a delta. Every nerve seared with cold. The fields below were vast, covered in waving gold grasses. *It will be a pity to stain it red.* Her thoughts were absent and drifting. Everything was both muffled and magnified through the lens of her power. *Azirik, come on.* The sound of rending metal cut through the air and a mass of bloody-red power bloomed from the ruins of the palace. It expanded, blotting out the rising sun and the scant white clouds high above. The air stained crimson and grew thick and cloying. *Vielrona was destroyed by burning clouds.* The clouds pulsed, with each contraction they spit out sheets of glistening, oily rain.

The crawling wrongness centered around a brilliant spark of copper in her mind's eye. Her fingers twisted, fumbling due to her injured left hand. With a snarl she ripped the bandages and splints away and began again. Her black fog writhed, weaving itself into ropes and bindings of a net. With a flick of her wrists, she flung it over the spark. Azirik's attention swiveled toward her as she tightened her hold. The familiar reek of rot and sickness wafted towards her. *Where have I smelled that?* In her mind she saw the bright blue of Azirik's eyes, bloodshot and stained with jaundice.

Φ

The general drew up, ignoring the stinging in her ribs. This was not the time for distractions. Her piercing whistle rang against armor. Those with halberds rushed to the fore, planting the butts of their weapons as another charge approached. The pain hit her, driving breath from her lungs. She cursed and pulled back, shouting for the colonel of the North Regiment. "Hamacad!"

The man finally crashed through the tangle of weapons and horses, wiping blood from his sword. "General?" His gaze fell to the blood drenching her side. "Shite!" He grabbed her reins and pulled her horse away.

"Enough!" Eras spat blood with her words. "You're acting general now. Leave me!" She slapped his horse's rump with the back of her gauntleted hand. He glanced at her before rushing away to regroup her men. Her dismount was closer to a stumble. Her vision blurred and she ripped her helm off. The Asai rarely thought about their own deaths. It was a given, not something to be fought, and the Asai part of her knew it well. The human part of her mind raged against the relief in her limbs, and the sticky gore covering her tabard. Each breath sputtered through the blood in her throat. She dropped her bow and drew her knife before throwing herself into a knot of Miriken.

Φ

Bren whirled his horse about, twisting his blade in a circle above his head. "Regroup!" The rain splattered thickly against his new armor, the vapor rancid. He drove his men against the wall of Berrin again. He thanked the general silently for sending his charges against men he had never known. The enemy outmatched them by easily a thousand. He signaled for the men to press out, driving the wave of Berrin towards the general's men. It took Bren several sword-swings to realize they were not the only ones protected by power. From the corners of his eyes he caught sight of the glittering coat of red deflecting all but the most direct blows. "Toar!" He blinked sweat from his eyes and whirled into the fray.

Berrin archers found purchase on the cliffs and rained bolts from above. Though distracting at first, the steaming rain did its work, the noxious smell choking air from faltering lungs and burning through exposed skin. Bren caught Hamacad's eye and they signaled to fall back. The sight before them was bitter.

More than half their number littered the fields. The Berrin and Miriken did not pursue them, retreating for the moment to gather their own forces.

Bren grinned. Whatever the cost, they had dented their enemy's number. He trotted over to the commander and colonels. "We took a third perhaps," he noted, drawing up beside them.

"We're being crushed," Colonel Currow spat.

Raven glanced around. "The general?"

Hamacad shook his head. "Fallen. I'm acting now."

Raven snarled and fixed Bren with a glare. "Where's your damned sister? She made a promise to us!"

Bren grabbed the man's tabard. "She promised we would win, she did not promise there wouldn't be a cost!" He thrust the man away and spun his horse. "Those shields Azirik laid are powerful. We'd be drinking to victory already if not for them. Blame that if you must." The thunder of hooves behind them interrupted his next words. "Toar!"

Raven wheeled, blinking against the burning red clouds. "To me!" The men rallied, preparing for whatever new attack approached. A rider dashed past them, then another and a third. Dozens of gray chargers bearing pale, horned warriors.

A crack rang through the battle and gun smoke joined the acrid gas. An'thor broke from the group, slowing as he passed Bren. His teeth were bared in a vicious grin. "You just going to stand there or join in the fun?"

Bren whooped and kicked his mount after them. Raven led his men about the flank again, mirroring Hamacad's infantry in a second charge. Bren's riders streamed after the Ageless warriors. The chaos and smell and noise filled Bren's head, strangling any thought beyond staying alive. His new armor already bore marks, earning the dings and dents he would value and love like those that had marred his own armor. His broadsword looped with the momentum of his charging horse. The mount came to a shuddering halt, pole arm embedded in the muscles of its chest. The squealing animal thudded to the ground, thrashing. Bren's left thigh was pinned under its heavy girth. Bren checked for imminent descending blades, then kicked his right foot from the stirrup, planting it on the seat of the saddle for leverage. He groaned, his leg already beginning to tingle as the weight pinched his nerves. "Dammit!" He shoved again, harder, flexing his trapped limb in an effort to free it. Suddenly two hard arms gripped his chest.

"Help, you damned oaf!" Arman hissed. Bren pushed a third time, wriggling free. He lurched to his feet. Arman backed into the fog. Scales covered his entire body, white and gold and green. Bren staggered, his leg still regaining its feeling. His view of the Rakos was blocked by the bulk of An'thor's borrowed horse.

An'thor grabbed Bren's arm. "Up you get, Barrackborn."

Bren swung himself into the saddle behind An'thor. When he looked for Arman again there was only swirling white smoke.

"You can swing that sword if you want, but if you take my arm with it I'm kicking you from the saddle faster than my blood will cover you."

Bren laughed and held up his sword, shouting to form a phalanx of riders. They punched through the Berrin forces, scattering them to the sides then wheeling to pursue. The Ageless had helped in number, certainly, but what men still stood were marred with blood and Bren could see Miriken scaling the cliff face beneath Alea.

Seeing a rider-less horse, Bren pounded his fist on An'thor shoulder and pointed. He slipped off the gray charger and jogged towards the lighter Athrolani mount whose reins were tangled in a mess of weapons and bodies. He was up in moments, tugging the animal about. All order had gone from the battlefield. Pockets of fighting made it seem as if the ground between the cliffs seethed. Bren rounded as many of his men as he could before leading them towards a dense group of Azirik's men. *Please let there be no familiar faces here.*

Φ

Alea felt Azirik's hold falter. *Azirik, stop!*

You think this is me? You think I have the strength to wield this anymore? You want to destroy the gods? Then come and get me.

She felt the ferocity in his snarl. *Careful what you ask. You should be terrified. The past year cauterized any mercy I could have felt.* Cold bloomed in her abdomen, spinning up her spine and down her limbs. Her focus turned to the sparks of white flames dotting the clouds. *Arman, are they ready?* She felt the brush of power on her mind as he opened his thoughts to her.

We lost Erek, but the rest of us hold strong. What do you need from me?

I need you to mirror what I do, with your fire.

How?

You are connected to the earth and the sun as I am to the ocean and the air. Her voice was gentle.

Alea tested the threads to each of her allies and held them fast with one mental hand. With the other, she drew power from the aquifers deep in the earth. She pulled from the ocean to the north. The power exploded through the Crown. Cold from every ocean in the world answered her gentle beckon. She wove her power into each wave. *This might hurt.*

I've died before, Alea. It can't be much worse. Now!

At Arman's shout, Alea gripped her power. The ground trembled beneath her boots. Her thoughts coalesced into a single word, bursting into Bren's mind, the commanders', the colonels'. *Now.* With a last great tug, she ripped herself open. There was no difference between Alea and Destruction.

Φ

Arman whirled through the clouds, a white spiral of smoke worming through the poisonous brown. He sank through the conduit ringing his brow and into the power beneath. He felt the billowing chill of Alea's breathing, but now he could not distinguish between her breath and his, between the thunder of her heartbeat and his own pulse. He had been wrong. The pain ignited every nerve. He curled in on himself, hands clenched in fists, arms wrapped around his head.

The pain exploded every thought from his mind and his body solidified. He plummeted towards the ground. A grating moan began deep inside his chest, turning into a keening cry that dragged itself from his lips as his power snapped open. His skin burst into flames, a burning ray of light piercing upwards through the clouds from the body of each Rakos. *Sun. Earth.*

His clothes turned to ash, metal dripping from the heat of his body. The flesh between his scales glowed brilliant yellow, like magma in the heart of the earth. He glanced down as he fell. He had seen this before, seen the ground rushing to meet him, seen the body of an Earth Shaker replace his own.

Arman, the fire!

His power punched through the clouds again, light igniting the poisonous air as he channeled the power of the sun. Below, the earth growled. He closed his eyes. *Surrender.*

CHAPTER TWENTY-ONE

The 9th Day of Valemord, 1252
The City of Ceir Athrolan

ELLE CROUCHED BEHIND WHAT was left of the palace's southeast tower. It had been decades since the Laen used their powers in battle. Even then, most who fought, died. But she, who had run for months to find a place to hide her daughter, knew more about deception and bloodshed. Her hands shook and she brought them to her brow. Hooves tore the fields to pieces and the shining white walls of the city were cracked and blackened from Berrin war machines.

Tzatia had taken up a post in the kitchens with the household staff and noble women who would not fight. The eastern wing of the palace was crushed under catapult ballast and the walls threatened to fall. If the walls gave, it would be over.

A young boy dashed from cover to cover, finally sliding down beside her. He offered a water skin in the hand he still had. "Milady Laen, here." His voice cracked from puberty and smoke.

"Thank you." She smiled and took a few sips before handing it back. It was the third time he had brought her water and food. "What are you called?"

"Bren, milady."

She winced at the snap and whistle of another missile being loosed. The air screamed before its passage moments before it crashed into the wall beside her. The stone shuddered. "Excuse me?"

"Vanabren Westing, milady. They call me Bren." His eyes somehow still sparked through fatigue and wariness.

"It's a good name," she offered. "My son's short-name is Bren." She watched the wall with the men below, wondering if it would hold. "That cannot take another hit."

The boy glanced at her. "Athrolan cannot fall, you know. The Dhoah' Laen promised us."

Her heart chafed at the innocence in the words. "I hope not, Bren." She stepped from behind the tower, arrows slicing the air around her. Her body trembled from fear and exhaustion. Power flowed from her hands, holding the stones. Deep moaning filled the air. The sound went on and she realized it came from the north. Wind whipped the ocean's surface, whirling the water into the air. The water continued to rise. The sound deafened her and stinging droplets shot across the waves, collected more and more and racing over the cliffs and hills as if drawn by a great storm. The scent of ocean and salt and time drifted in its wake. *Lyne'alea.* Elle straightened and raised her hands. "Bren, give the others a message!" Her voice arched against the buffeting wind. "We're balance and all things end. Age them. Fray the ropes. Rust their weapons."

The message was passed along the chain of Laen on the ramparts. Pale hands rose, gray hair whipping back. The Berrin did not notice until their catapults no longer shot. The swords rusted from the hilts. Horse leathers dried and cracked.

The battle did not end with the Berrin driven into the hills amidst Athrolani war cries, though the legends would tell it so. The attackers eased back, staring at the sky that still swirled with rain. Their ruined weapons littered the hills and the machines crumbled where they stood. Those who still could disappeared back into the trees. Elle turned as Vanabren emerged from behind the remnants of the tower. His hand shielded his eyes from the smoke and dust in the wet air.

"Your queen shelters in the palace, in the kitchens. Tell her Athrolan is saved."

"Shall I tell her you'll see her when you've rested?"

Elle shook her head and relayed the rest of her message for the queen. She straightened and closed her eyes. They had saved their power for so long, waiting for battle. Now, it was finally over.

Vanabren scrambled down the shattered tower and into the palace. Walls were toppled, rooms destroyed and the royal suites were nothing more than memory. He found his way to the barred doors of the kitchen after three tries. The guards let him through and he slowed, peering through the dark to find the queen. She perched on a barrel of smoked meat, holding quiet conversation with one of the other women.

Her gaze turned to him as he knelt. "What is it?"

"I bring a message from the Laen, your majesty."

"Has the city fallen?"

He dared to look up at her. "Athrolan stands."

Tzatia stared, almost in disbelief. Finally she rose and smoothed her skirts. "Thank you." She turned and issued orders, sending guards and nobles and servants rushing through the palace. Seeing that he had not moved, she glanced back at Vanabren. "Was there something else?"

"Yes, your majesty. Lady Elle, with the black in her hair, told me something else. She said Lyne'alea will win."

Φ

The Ruins of Claimiirn

The blow of Alea's mind against Bren's sent him reeling. Pebbles dislodged and skittered down the cliff faces, larger rocks tumbled after. "Alea!" His voice was joined by that of the commander and the colonels. Officers took it up, her names bounding across the battlefield. The ground heaved, cracking as geysers burst through the stone.

Bren urged his horse alongside An'thor's. "Get out of here! She protected us, not you!" His warning came too late as black water exploding from the screaming earth. He grabbed An'thor's cloak and dragged the man from his horse. The scent of salt filled the air. The fields flooded in minutes and still the water came. Moaning rose in the south and the clouds above burst into flames. The ground shuddered again and gouts of thick magma roared through the dirt. The screams of opposing elements meeting each other drowned out those of the men caught between. Bren shielded his eyes against the battering forces, looking up as water solidified the lava coating his shield of power.

The destruction seemed to last forever, the roaring outside the shell of rock fading slowly. The silence replacing it was far worse. After a moment Bren glanced over at An'thor. Bren had pulled the warrior under the protection just in time. An'thor shook, his eyes wide. His face paled further and he retched.

Bren looked away. What his sister had done was terrible, but he had killed Laen, and nothing twisted the gut worse. He pushed himself to his feet and tested the shell. It was like black glass, shot through with flecks of red and green and blue. After a few solid blows it cracked then shattered.

Bren stumbled free and stopped. He stared at the battlefield before him, heedless of the blood drawn by the razor edges of the glass shell. "An'thor."

"I know."

Corpses were strewn everywhere, those in the lowlands charred to ash and skeletons. Piles of blackened bones marked fallen horses. Water dripped from the higher plain, salty runnels of seawater waving their way back into the earth. The bodies it left were pale and bloated. Flies already gathered. Dotting the fields were other shells along what had been the boundary of the two elements. Others rose from crouches, their armor and uniforms dry and unburnt. There was nothing left of the Berrin or the enemy Miriken that he could see, save a few hundred troops what managed to escape the carnage by climbing into the ruins.

Azirik. Alea's mind-voice howled through Bren's thoughts, devoid of emotion or haste.

"Right." He looked around for a mount, only to wish he had not. The only horses near enough were swollen bodies or blackened grizzle. He staggered across the field to the stairway winding up to the palace. Adrenaline raged in his limbs, but it faded quickly. Hard, cold hands caught him the third time his boots slipped on the granite stairs.

The creature that crouched on the landing before him was not his sister. Her features echoed in the face, but the resemblance ended there. Her hair writhed like black snakes, rivulets of water trickling from her solid black eyes. Shadows filled her skin. "Almost there."

He pulled himself up and followed her silent steps. The journey ended at Claimiirn's great hall. A pair of guards flanked the door, blades drawn. Bren's laugh was closer to a hoarse bark. "Everyone's dead. Forget it."

"Lieutenant Barrackborn, sir?" The younger guard stepped forward, peering closer.

Bren wiped blood and sweat from his eyes. "Captain Sorier?"

"Don't you remember? You made me lieutenant before you left." He frowned, glancing from Bren to the figure beside him. "Is this where you were going?"

"It appears both our roads led here, eh?" Bren swallowed hard, hands tightening on the hilt of his broadsword. He had recognized enough faces under his blows for a dozen lifetimes. "I've about had it with killing for today. Please don't try to stop us."

Sorier glanced at the other guard, a man Bren did not know. "We're not here to stop you, Barrackborn. We're here to escort you."

Bren glanced between them, then over at Alea's sparking eyes. Her hand was ice freezing around his own. "What?"

"Come in and he'll explain. Hurry, though, he's got little time left." Sorier led them into the hall. Unlit torches lined the walls. Trees grew through the cracked flagging and vines draped the pillars. Several tents stood along the rear wall. Azirik slumped in the center of the hall, body still wreathed in bubbling red-brown light. Bren stopped a few paces away, distantly aware of Alea beside him. Azirik's eyes were narrowed in pain and disbelief and a hundred other things that stampeded through Bren's own mind. His hands shook. "Do I have to fight you?"

Azirik jerked his head. The bruised, rotting flesh around the Crown pulsed and blood-laced fluid seeped over the copper. "No. Not anymore." His eyes flicked to Alea. "Hello, again."

Φ

Power thundered through Alea's head, almost drowning the words. *Again?* She took in the mess of Crown and skin and bone on his brow and heard the rattling cough of his voice. The smell of decay met her nose. "It was you. You talked to me while I waited for the moon to set."

Bren turned to look at her, by his expression clearly wondering whether she had lost her wits.

Azirik's body racked with a strangled gasp. After a moment she realized it was a laugh. "Yes. You didn't know?"

"How could I have?"

"I recognized you immediately. If I saw you, so would the gods, and neither of us were ready for that." He hauled himself up until he sat on the flagging. "You think I could see you now?"

Alea shuddered and her power rolled back into her skin, writhing into the Crown on her head and disappearing. She would never look entirely human, but she was recognizable. She tilted her head at him. "You let me go."

"I spent these last months putting everything in place. An'thor was the last piece. I had close to a hundred Ageless just waiting for my word." He swallowed hard. "Tell me what you'll do. Will you raise the Laen to their rightful place?"

She shook her head. Her cheeks were damp and salty. "Is that why you did this? You thought you could reverse everything that ever harmed the Laen? Oh, fates, no." She stepped forward cautiously, ignoring Bren's murmured warning. "No. The gods weren't wrong. Everything has an end. Every reign will fall. Some in fire and some in death and some simply ease away like an old dog in the night. They weren't right, either, though. They are not what comes next." She was a pace away.

"Is it your people? You and your Rakos?"

She knelt beside him and reached out tentatively. She had never felt more vulnerable. This madman gave his last months for her victory. He tore his people, his allies, his masters apart from within and all for her. "No, something new. I don't know exactly, but I know it's coming. It is mighty and different, and beautiful."

"Can't be more beautiful than you." He took her hand. "Take it. Please."

"You won't live though it."

"I know. The world you're saving has no place for people like you and me. We're killers. We are not meant for peace. We might walk in it a while, but never will we fit." He squeezed her hand. "Go on. I'll hold them back for the second it takes, but I can't do it forever."

Alea did not look away, but raised her voice. "Bren. If you wanted to say goodbye, now's the time."

Bren crouched beside her. "I don't know what to say."

"All of my apologies seem too small. You took over Mirik?"

"I'm her Military Commissioner now."

Azirik's sobbing laugh shook his body again. "You were never cut out for being a king."

"Neither were you." Bren's grin was awkward and faint, but Azirik returned it after a moment.

"Are you ready?" Alea met his eyes. She watched him frown as he recognized their color, and the set of her face. He nodded. She rested her hands on either side of his face. "Thank you." Before he could respond, her fingers dug into the twisted, burnt flesh and wrapped around the Crown. Her skin bubbled against the surface of the metal. She clenched her teeth and pulled. The metal popped free with a sickening crack, and she fell back, pieces of skull and blood still clinging to the metal. Azirik slumped onto the stone, blood and power pooling from his head.

Bren staggered back, heaving up everything he had eaten that morning. "Is he gone?"

"Yes." She glanced over at him. "Are you all right?"

His body shook. "That was my king. My commander. Everything I ever knew for almost thirty years."

"I'm sorry."

He glanced up. "It wasn't your fault. It was never your fault." He edged back to Azirik's body, closing the bloodshot eyes.

Alea reached out and gripped his hand. "It wasn't his, either, in the end."

Φ

Bren blinked against the bright rays of sunset as he emerged from the hall. Smoke still drifted low over the burnt and bloody fields. Long graves carved the earth. Infirmary tents lined the base of the cliffs below the Athrolani camp.

Alea glanced over at him. "I've got to get this to my pack. You'll be all right?"

He nodded and sank down onto the stairs. "In a minute."

Sorier crouched beside him, watching Alea go. "She's terrifying."

"She's my sister."

The lieutenant frowned. "What?"

"Azirik's second child." Bren heaved a sigh. "Thank you for seeing sense when he did."

"I saw sense when you did, you know. War turns your guts, for sure, but killing the Laen? That was something else entirely." He paused a moment. "We're prisoners of war, now, I assume."

Bren shook his head. "No. I'm tired of violence and war, Sorier. Take your men, take all the men, and leave. Give it a few months then come home. I'll have Mirik ready for you then."

"We heard there was new ruling there. You took her crown?"

"No. She's an oligarchy now. I'm Lord Commissioner of the Military, acting king until the war is done." He laughed humorlessly. "I guess that's now."

"Sir, there are prisoners, down in the Berrin camp. A patrol taken several months ago. They'll need tending." He stood. "I guess I'll see you in Mirik."

Bren's eyes were too tired to make his smile look sincere. "See you at home." He listened as the man's bootfalls faded into the low din of battle's aftermath. Finally he pulled himself to his feet and tottered down the cliffs and across the field.

A gallant paused as he jogged past him. "Lord Commissioner, good to see you. Thought you fell."

Bren glanced over at the Berrin camp. "There are prisoners in their camp."

"We found them, sir, already bringing them in."

Bren nodded and went to the infirmary tents. They were surrounded by cots and blankets for the hundred of wounded who did not fit in the tents themselves. Healers walked down the rows, checking breaths and wounds. More than once they murmured a few words and closed unseeing eyes. Bren had seen enough battles to be familiar with the screams and moans, but this was different. He led some of these men. He caught sight of a familiar figure as he turned towards the cliffs. Reka lay under a blanket, her skin pale and her braids dirty.

Bren hurried over and crouched beside her. "Reka."

She turned towards his voice. Her eyes were a bloody mess of angry sockets, thin slashes running through them and across her cheeks. A cut sliced through the wing of the butterfly tattoo on her nose. "Bren?"

"How are you doing?"

"I've been better, sir. I fared better than many of the men, if my ears serve me."

Something in his chest twisted. She would live by her ears and hands now. "I've got to see to my men, but I'll be back." He squeezed her hand briefly then headed back up to the officers' tents. He paused at the general's and rapped on the tent pole. "It's Brentemir."

"Come in." The commander's voice was quiet. Bren ducked in. Raven sat at the camp table, head in his hands. Several officers and Asai ranged about him, all equally stoic.

"Commander, sir, I—"

"We'll work till dusk, bringing the wounded and bodies in. We have wagons for the dead. The honored ones at least, to bring them home. The rest we bury here. Fates willing someday we can erect a monument." Raven turned to Vinden. "Keep the men moving until we've finished this."

Bren swallowed. "I'll help." He glanced at Narier. "Where is Alea?"

"Resting, I think."

A soldier burst through the tent flap. "Colonel Hamacad, sir, we found the general."

Raven's face paled and he stood, interrupting Hamacad's order. "Bring her here. Lay her in state." After a moment he cleared his throat. "We've little daylight left. Let's use it while we can."

Bren helped the soldiers in their morbid duty, hauling the bodies of soldiers he never knew. Each was laid to rest beside its companions. The pallor of death fell the same over each, whether human or Asai or Nenev. The evening wound on, gray and cold. Bren staggered to their campsite late. Alea's tent was deserted, the three Crowns perched in their box on her desk. He hung his cloak on his tent pole and ducked inside.

The lit lantern hung from the ridgepole and Kemmer sat on his trunk in the corner. "Lord Commissioner, I just came from the infirmary." She looked down. "Aldac died. He was doing all right for a while, but I think years in the city weakened us. I was with him, when it happened. He said he was honored to have served you, even for such a short time, made me promise to do well by you. He didn't need to, I already would have." It was the most Bren had ever heard the woman say at once. She jerked her head to the east. "You kill him?"

Bren shrugged. "The Crown was part of him. He couldn't survive the removal of it." He sat on his cot. "You're promoted now."

"General?" Her laugh was a hoarse cough.

"Captain of the Guard." He grinned wearily. "But drop the Lord Commissioner bit when we're alone. I need friends now, more than anything else."

"I'll try, sir." She raked a hand through her tangled hair. "What now?"

"Home. It's time to rebuild."

Φ

Alea left the general's tent. It was close to midnight and her body was exhausted. Her mind refused to rest. The battle was only half done for her. What remained would be infinitely harder. The air around her hummed. She repacked her armor in its chest before changing into clean clothes. Her hand froze at the box on her desk. The Rakos Crown glimmered with the others. "Arman?"

She reached out, feeling for the brilliant white-gold spark of his life. There was only darkness. She snapped the box shut and tucked it into her pack.

By the time Bren stopped to check on her, the tent was deserted and she had disappeared into the forest.

Φ

The 11th Day of Valemord, 1252
The City of Ceir Athrolan

Winter sunlight pierced the naked, white branches of the trees. A journey that took the army almost a week, Alea made in just two days. Now she drew up at the tree line. The formerly pristine slope down to the city was churned and scarred. War machines crouched between the tree trunks. Alea's eyes narrowed. The ropes were frayed, the wood rotted. Rust enveloped what metal remained. But for the raw wounds in the stone walls of the city, she could have looked on a battle centuries old.

A hole punched through the false sun of the palace's dome. The walls were breached in three places that she could see. The city was quiet, smoke rising from both cook fires and smashed lanterns. Alea's heart twisted at the sight. *Athrolan was pillaged while her warriors protected me.* Something more tugged at her mind. There was an undertone to the smell of the sea, to the chill of the winter morning. *Laen.* She nudged her horse into a trot and towards the battered gates.

They had yet to open for the morning, though she would be surprised if they did not remain closed for days.

"Halt!"

She shielded her eyes and peered up at the ramparts. "I'm Dhoah' Lyne'alea." A low conversation ensued atop the wall before the gate finally opened. Alea dismounted and tugged her horse into the city.

A woman stood in the center of the rubble-strewn city street. Her clothes were covered with burn holes and stone dust settled on her shoulders and graying hair. "Lyne'alea."

Alea stopped to survey her mother. "Elle." She nodded to the city. "What happened?"

"Athrolan fought your battle, so we fought hers."

"We won."

"Yes. I know. So did we." Elle shifted her weight. "You should rest. We can leave for Mirik in the morning."

Alea shook her head. "I can rest on the ship. The world has waited long enough. I have waited long enough."

"What will you do?" Elle tilted her head.

Alea reached out a tentative hand. "Something terrible. Something necessary." When her mother took her hand, Alea squeezed it. She did not care that her grip twisted bones and ground Arman's ring into her knuckle. With the brief moment of contact, Alea saw the gravity of what she was about to do. "I'm so sorry."

Elle frowned, her face paling. "I don't understand."

"You don't need to. Just be with me. For now." Alea suddenly wished they had the time to be mother and daughter.

Elle looked down. "If you will not wait, then we can at least get this over with." She sent a whistle arcing over the city and palace walls. The other Laen appeared, as tattered as she. Some bore bruises and wounds of more direct battle.

"Together, we can bring you home." She laced her fingers with her daughter's, others coming to take Alea's hand or brush her shoulder.

"Don't waste your power," Alea protested, but her voice was soft. Silver fog writhed around their bodies, threaded between feet and curling across shoulders.

Elle smiled. "Really, Lyne'alea. What do we have to save it for? It may be terrible, I might not understand, but you will not be alone."

Φ

The Isle of Le'yne

Le'yne had changed little. The sky still crackled with its ceaseless energy, and the grasses still waved in the distracted breeze. Alea blinked and turned. She stood on the steps of the great hall. The Laen ranged about her, more exhausted than ever. The rumble of their arrival rippled through the village below and she saw lantern light bloom in the windows of those who had not made the journey to Athrolan.

Alea pushed open the door to the hall. Her feet would not cross the threshold. *How can I turn my back on them with a promise of a victory when they will never see it?* "Elle?"

"I'm here."

"Tell Mera to pack her books. The most important, the best, the rarest. Where I'm going, you can't follow."

"I'll tell her. And I'll see you when you've won."

Alea met her mother's eyes. There was defiance behind the older woman's lie, a strength Alea recognized. She drew a steadying breath and stepped into the hall. The door at the end was still propped open and the stairs unchanged.

She did not stumble in the darkness, her feet forgotten as she descended into the bowels of the earth. She refused to think beyond her next action, refused to listen to the screaming in her mind.

She emerged into the cavern, her boots whispering on the stone as she approached the swollen globe of wounded souls. She knelt, opening the box and laying the Crowns on the ground before her. She stripped her clothes off, raking her fingers through the snarls of her hair until it hung loosely around her. She gripped the Crowns against her naked stomach, relishing the sting of metal against her cool flesh.

First I fight the gods. Then I bind the world. The actions seemed so simple when put into words. She wondered what would be left of her. The Laen would not be there to return whatever it was to Athrolan. Bren would never know what happened to her, down in the darkness of Le'yne and the blackness of her soul.

She clenched her teeth and stepped into the souls. The screaming grew louder and the darkness closer. She gripped the gods' Crown, sinking through the connect to their world. It was akin to the dizziness when she left her body to resurrect Arman. Whistling filled her ears. A beach appeared quite suddenly around her. The air was almost balmy and the rough sand beneath her feet ground as she stepped back. Most of the island was overrun with jungle. Behind her the ocean was flat calm, not a single wave lapped at the strand, even when an eddy of wind caught Alea's hair. She had the distinct feeling that the entire landmass had turned to look at her. She shook it away and moved up the overgrown path before her.

Her journey was quiet and uninterrupted. Her thoughts turned inward. *What steps have I taken to bring me to these? What path did I choose to bring me to this?* Though her hands were unadorned and her body bare, she felt the warm squeeze of the ring on the middle finger of her physical hand. *What friends have I lost to save the world?* At any moment the gods might rain fury upon her, her blood might be drained to stitch the world together.

The trees fell away and a castle rose before her. It was built from the same brown stone that made up the island itself. The wooden gate was barely taller than she, and the double doors carved only with the stylized mountain sprouting a twisting column of smoke that was the gods' symbol. She pushed the doors open carefully and her heartbeat rose to a thunder. Torches lined the brown stone, guttering in the stillness. The hall she followed ended in an arched doorway to a spiral staircase that led up into the dark heights of the castle. The similarity to the stairs she had just descended in Le'yne was not lost on her. She lifted her chin and began the ascent.

The castle's rooftop was large and open. The plants had taken over, tangling across the stone. Some vines and leaves were held back, a path carved through the vegetation to the open, sunken hall in the center of the rooftop.

Chipped, worn pillars held the dome protecting it from whatever weather no longer battered the island. The floor of the hall stepped down into the center, where the gods' symbol rested. Scorch marks marred the copper inlay of their symbol. The pieces of what once had been fine chairs were scattered across the stairs. Only one stood, whole, at the bottom, facing the marred symbol. A man sat, waiting for her. There were others, standing in the shadows, seated on the stairs across from her. She caught herself counting the bloody sparks in her mind. *A dozen, two hundred, it does not matter.* Everything that had brought her there thundered to life in her mind. The months of running, the lives that were lost and changed and the rage that fueled her every step.

"Desmondu!" The ground trembled and plaster rattled from the ceiling at her voice.

The gods turned to stare at her. Desmondu rose. His hair was pale copper and hung in loose curls to his shoulders. A brown robe covered his crimson tunic. His piercing amber eyes narrowed. "You are alone."

Alea smiled. "You've been without us for far too long if you think that matters." She stepped carefully down into the hall, her bare feet hissing on the warm stone. "You know why I'm here. It can't have escaped your notice that the world is unraveling. It's my duty to sew it together. The power that makes your world, your magic, will change."

"It will end."

She laughed, but it was not the sound of mirth. "Nothing ends."

"You will destroy us."

"If you fight me, yes. I just thought you might like a warning."

"You will fall, torn apart, burnt until nothing is left but a mark on the ground. We will fight you until there is nothing left of you to bleed dry." His words rattled like husks on the ground. The other gods rose, converging on his throne. Their eyes were wary, afraid, exhausted.

Alea picked out her brother's oft-invoked god of death, Toar, and his consort, the goddess of the desert mirage Ikate. There were others that she recognized from the temples of her childhood, or from stories. "Very well." She beckoned. The gesture was gentle, almost tender.

Desmondu's laughter faded as copper mist emerged from the floor. It rose slowly, picking up speed as Alea's body filled with blackness. Her irises bled silver until her face shone in the light emanating from orbs brighter than any sun. The mist thickened as she pulled the energy of the gods' realm from the world.

Bolts of bubbling bloody brown exploded against her skin. She ignored the burning. Desmondu shrieked in fury and rushed her. His fist, encased in power, descended on her skull. Something uncurled in the depths of Alea's soulblood, where her heart lay in her physical body. It was gold and scorching in its anger, and familiar as her own power, but it was not her. It raced to the surface, bursting from her skin in an explosion of white fire. She heard nothing through the ringing aftermath in her ears, but the message was unmistakable. *I'll protect you. Do what you must.*

She dragged power from the earth, swallowing it with her own, forcing it into the Crown waiting, clutched with the others in Le'yne. All that was left was their souls. The only thing binding their power to the world were tentative tendrils curled around everything that kept them alive. Tears, held captive in the corners of her eyes, froze. Her fingers sprouted lightning. It writhed, branching myriad times and rooting itself in the chest of each god in turn. Electricity burrowed into their pulsing copper centers and she pulled. Their souls tasted of blood.

Φ

The blast leveled most of the castle. Alea was cocooned in a ball of writhing souls. She was beyond consciousness, beyond enlightenment, beyond death. She was an unborn child, fragile and infinite in its possibilities. Her hands were claws as she ripped the souls apart. Her fingers dripped soulblood as she tore into the barriers between the pieces of the world. She flung the humans' souls into the void, followed by the gods, the Rakos, the Laen. Silver soulblood splattered her face with each violent gesture.

There were three darknesses that grew in the mind. The first was brief and flashing in its anger. But it was small. It was sand in the face of the wind, dust in the face of the rain, noticed only in its absence. The second was slow. It loomed on the edge, muttering and glaring. It was not acknowledged. It could be ignored. Still, it swirled around thoughts, biting them with bitter, savage teeth.

The third was a great law that could not be broken. It was a shadow that fell on a mountain side. It simply waited. It was the night at the edge of the firelight, patient and calm. It was peace. *There are no monsters.*

Only three Crowns hovered in her mind's eye, burning white-gold, stinging bloody-copper and sparking silver-black. She grew or they shrunk, spinning into her palm. She clenched her hand around them absently, as if they were insects. There was stillness. Then the world trembled, shuddering within the fist of Alea's power.

The void around her changed. Images flashed before her, thousands of people, thousands of lives, each imprinted on her mind. Her heartbeat raced, faltered, paused. Her mind was blank consciousness without feeling or judgment. Silence reigned for a second, for an eternity. Waves lapped at Alea's skin, nudging her against a rocky shore.

CHAPTER TWENTY-TWO

The 14th Day of Glasmord, 1252
The City of Mirik

BREN GROANED AS HE LIFTED the heavy lintel into place above the doorway. He shrugged deeper into the wool of his cloak. The air off the ocean was bitterly cold. It took days to lay the honored dead to rest in Athrolan. He arrived in Mirik a week before and began work as soon as his boots hit the cobbles. He pounded a fist against the heavy wood. In a few weeks it would overlook the entrance to someone's home. *Now it's just a pain in my arse.* In the glorious absence of war, Mirik's new military traded swords for hammers. Bren had forgotten how much blisters burnt. It was close to evening now and the lintel was all that was left of his day's work.

He hammered the last of the wooden pegs home, face knotted in concentration. The tool fell from his hands when the scream started. It was not a human scream, he realized, even as he rushed into the street. It was as if the air itself cried out. Lights flickered across the city below and the watchtowers blazed into life. The sea was choppy, like a cup of water, shaken. Great waves surged over the new stone breakwater. Thunderheads thickened from horizon to horizon.

The scream faded to a guttering sound, like pebbles bouncing down a slope. The ocean parted in the east, as if an invisible bowl pressed to its surface. The water roiled and black fog burst from the air above the depression. The sound of rending flesh was followed by a concussive wave of air that knocked him to the ground.

He wondered, briefly if this was the end. As abruptly as it began, everything stopped. Bren pulled himself to his feet. A soft breeze eddied about him, tugging as his cloak. Two islands stood where the ocean had been disturbed, within a long-boat's journey from the cliffs. Faint outlines of buildings dotted the new islands. He found that he was shaking. He took off at a run. He finally stopped in the open air of the harbor, peering up at the sky. He almost expected the stars to have changed.

Others had followed him, the entire city spilling into the streets. "Sir, what is it?" Arik paused, panting, beside Bren. "The air."

He lifted his nose. It was as if he had never smelled fresh air before, and now the soft, crisp breeze came from off the sea. "I know." He thrust his fist into the air, letting out a wild shout. Around him, windows were thrown open, sailors climbed into rigging and guards tossed their helms into the air. They shouted with him, screaming joy across the ocean. Bren fell to his knees. "It's over. She did it."

Kemer wove through the crowd, her frown a stark contrast against the exaltation around her. "Sir!" She slid to a halt beside him. Her eyes glittered with tears that matched his, the ones they were trained to never shed. "Sir, my cousin found your sister." She took his hand. "They just pulled her body from the water."

Φ

The 17th Day of Vurgmord, 1252

Bren leaned his brow against the cool, un-hewn stone of the temple. It was the only such building left standing. The past three mornings he found himself within its enveloping darkness. What he felt could not be called grief. He could not pray, for there were no gods, and he could not talk to Alea. She lay in the palace, barely breathing. After a month of watching her lifeless form, he stopped visiting. Now, instead, he sat in a forgotten temple and talked to her. The black stone seemed to listen.

He turned at the rapping on the stone. "Yes?"

"We were told to ask you about work and housing." The man was roughly Bren's age, though his skin and hair were far darker. A woman stood a pace behind him, smiling tiredly as she murmured to the baby in her arms. "I was told Mirik welcomed refugees. Might you know where to find Brentemir Barrackborn?"

"You already have." Bren held out his hand. "I'm Commissioner Barrackborn. Where was your home?"

"Vielrona."

Sorrow settled around Bren again. "Ah. You're Arman's friend. You're welcome here. Find the stone building on the corner. Talk to Commissioner Oland. He'll set you with a proper house." Bren called through the door as the man turned away. "Did you hear of him?"

"I heard he gave himself for his lady. Good day, sir." The dark man's words were tense and pained.

Bren felt suddenly guilty he did not mourn Arman as deeply. He turned back to the altar. His previous offerings of flowers wilted in the cold. Midwinter was only a week away. His eyes pinched closed at the soft cough behind him. This was his only privacy in the day, and it was precious.

"Am I interrupting?"

Bren's eyes widened. The slight woman was silhouetted by the faint morning sun. He rose to his feet, unable to turn away, even blink. His words stammered from him. "I thought—"

"So did I," Alea answered. Her smile was faint, almost shy. She glanced at the temple. "I heard you, you know."

His own smile eased across his features. He caught her up in his arms, lifting her off the ground. Her arms were hard around his neck and her body thin. "I missed you. I love you."

"And I, you. The city looks wonderful." Her voice faltered. "Bren, the islands, were those my doing?"

"Yes." He pulled away. "It was weeks after the battle and I had begun to wonder."

"Weeks?" She shook her head. "I fought the gods for a long time, then."

Bren squeezed her hand. "It was terrifying here, during the joining. I thought the world had ended."

"It did. At least, the world we knew." She seemed to stare at the flowers, but her focus was far distant. "I was in a dark, strange place, beyond time and sense. I remember it like a dreamer remembers the true world during sleep." She glanced up at the words Bren had carved above the altar during his first visit. "Why did you dedicate a temple to me?"

"When you joined the world, after the terror, there was joy. I can't explain the relief and happiness. It's my experience that people need something to believe in. The hole you left by killing the gods needed to be filled. I felt it fitting you be the one to fill it."

Alea pulled a bag from her belt. She handed it to him. "Did you look in this while I was sleeping?"

"No. I don't think anyone did. Most were too scared." The bag was heavier than it should have been. He untied the strings and peered inside. The crown was a hard, dark metal. He recognized the black glass embedded around the edge. "You made this?"

"That's the Crown for this world. Whole. It is not for me, just as this temple is not mine. It is for whomever comes afterward." The expression flitting about the corners of her eyes was both grieving and relieved.

"Afterward. The battles are over Alea. Life can start."

"I can't stay here, Bren." She looked down. "I'm leaving today. I'll go to the mainland, maybe south. I'm not sure, but I need to see this world a bit. I need the earth under my toes and the sun on my hair for a while."

He wanted to yell at her to stay, beg her to stand with him when he made Kemmer his wife. He wanted to weep until she promised to never leave again. Instead, he sighed. "I'll walk you to the harbor." He took her hand and allowed her to lead him into the sunlight.

Φ

The 21st Day of Vurgmord, 1252
The City of Ceir Athrolan

Alea rode higher into the hills. Her horse's hooves scrabbled on the frozen earth. The clearing opened before her, barren and black. The trees were scarred by fire. She dismounted, and as soon as her boots thudded onto the baked earth, she knew this was where Arman discovered his power. She ran her fingers along a tree trunk, scraping ash from the wood. She pitched her tent facing south, overlooking the Felds beyond. She laid her bedroll carefully, every movement collected, as if a sudden motion would shake the tears from her clenched heart.

The fire she lit was small, and she did not bother to set any soup to boil. She crouched beside the flames, exhausted. She would not rest, though. She had rested enough for a lifetime. The clatter of dry leaves across the hard ground seemed almost like foot falls, almost like speech.

She found herself replying. "I wish we'd said more, that night. I wish I could have been there for you. I'm here now." She lay against the ground, frozen dirt scraping her cheek.

The nervous snorting of her horse woke her. She pushed herself up, blinking to clear her vision. It was dark, the fire nothing more than burning coals. The woods were silent. The horse paced around its picket, eyes rolling. A familiar sensation tickled the back of her mind, but she could not place it. She rose to a crouch, stirring the coals into flame. It was then that she saw the eyes.

They were low, like those of a wolf, and burning yellow. She reached for her bow behind her and nocked an arrow without taking her eyes from the predator. She raised it, breathing like Arman taught her all those months ago. She would never be able to say whether it was the color of the eyes or the heat in them as they met hers that gave her pause, but she relaxed her hold, tilting her head as she peered back. The campfire burst to life between them, casting the trees into bright contract with the dark woods.

Gold scales plated wiry shoulders, and a great bony crest parted the yellow hair down the crown of his head. A clawed hand worked in the dirt, clenching over and over. The scales over his heart fluttered with each beat, flashing the silver of a handprint scar. "Sun."

"No." Her knees gave out and she sat back on her bedroll. "Not this. You thought you'd die. You thought you would fall to your death." She reached out a shaking hand. This was worse than death.

"Sun." The word crackled from his chest again and again.

Even if she had pressed her hands to her ears it would not have blocked the sound. His eyes held none of the familiarity that made him Arman. She moved to touch him but he skittered back. "It's Alea." She inched closer, her words low and careful. "And you're Arman. We met in Vielrona, where the moss turned the rooftops green."

He did not move, but let her creep closer.

"You taught me to shoot and fight and drink there. We stood together in Athrolan's throne room and allied ourselves with her queen, your voice and mine." Her hand stopped beside his and she spread her fingers on the cold ground. The longest one brushed his. The scales there dimmed, retreating to the first knuckle. The skin left behind was pale under its tan, but unmistakably his. The darkness faded as dawn approached.

"We rode north together, just you and me and the white sky in winter," she murmured to him. Her fingers slid over his hand, the scales rough and warm against her cool skin. The scales rolled back up to his forearm.

"I'm Alea and you are Arman. I broke the laws of the world to bring you back when you died. It wasn't so you could protect me. I just couldn't imagine saving a world without you in it." Her arms slid up his and over his shoulders until their noses were just inches apart. Her words were barely more than breath. "I am Alea and you are Arman. We danced on the cliff tops at Claimiirn and all of our enemies trembled at the sound."

His skin was sickly-pale and his hair and beard were overgrown. Angry scars peppered his back. His eyes burnt into hers. The eerie glow faded from his body then, and he was suddenly human. He shoved himself away from her. He scrabbled in the dead leaves, vomiting up stone dust and dried blood. He collapsed on the ground and shuddered. "I need sun."

"The sun will be up soon." He shied from her touch when she reached to help him up. She followed his unsteady gait out onto the outcropping overlooking the dark fields. The sky was gray. He pressed himself to the cold stone, face tilted toward the dawn.

Alea sat a few paces away, watching his chest rise with each breath. His color returned with the day. The faint warmth of the winter sun eased over muscles and skin, chasing madness and darkness from his face. It was afternoon when he finally opened his eyes. They blinked once, twice then swiveled to look at her. "Alea."

She jerked her head in a nod. "I'll make us something to eat." She rose with a soft groan. Her muscles were cramped from sitting still for so long. She scraped snow into a pot absently, every thought on the man sunning himself on the rock behind her. The water had been boiling for several minutes, Alea staring unseeing, when Arman finally approached. He crouched by the fire, heedless of his naked body.

Alea's gaze flicked to him. "Your things are there." She pointed at the tattered pack beside hers.

"I think I want to wash. There's a stream down the hill." He gathered the packet of noodles and meat and pressed it into her hand. "Water's boiled."

She took it and set about preparing the soup. When the soup was set she gathered more wood and unrolled the second bedroll. He recognized her, but more than that she did not know. The world that created them was gone and she was not sure where to turn. The tent was broader and the soup bubbling eagerly by the time he returned. He settled himself by the fire, near enough to touch without crowding her. They ate in silence, sniffing in the cold weather and shivering when a breeze was too insistent.

"That's some faith you had to bring my things."

She laughed softly. "You know far more about faith than I." She poked at the coals to avoid looking at him. "The little piece of you that's in me, it protected me. I knew if it was alive so were you."

He frowned at the flames as if they had given him some great insult. "I thought I was going to die."

"Madness is a kind of death." Her gaze inched from the fire to his boots and up his body to his face. His eyes held understanding.

"I'm sorry we didn't talk of little things that night before the battle."

She drew her glove off and slid her hand to rest on her knee where he could see it. "You think this is such a little thing?" He stared at it, expression unreadable. *Soul bared. Completely.* She swallowed hard and barreled on. "When we were running, every night we slept in different places. We changed horses, changed plans. We even changed our names when we had to. Even my own idea of self changed. And you were there. I was broken and lost with no family in a world I did not know, and when I closed my eyes to sleep, you were there." She slid her hand across the leaves, closer, like she had done the night before. "You are my one permanence."

"And you have been mine, Alea. It's not about finding someone who changes your world, or who molds you into a better person. It's about finding someone that fits with the shape in which you built yourself. You fit. Each step of the way, even when it hurt to see you because what you were told me what I was becoming. We've changed, incredibly, but we've only grown together. You fit." He took her hand and a smile bloomed.

Φ

It took Arman several heart-pounding moments to remember where he was when he awoke. Alea's hand was tangled in his and he extracted it carefully before climbing from his bed roll. Their bodies were too exhausted and their minds too raw for anything more intimate than conversation. He tidied the camp and set water on to boil before slipping out into the forest to hunt. He was dressing the second squirrel when he saw the riders. There were less than a dozen and they rode easily up the hill. He marked the Athrolani uniform and wondered if they were searching for Alea.

His boots were silent as he returned, mind whirling. He did not want to go back to Athrolan. He did not want to see Tzatia and hear the story of war retold myriad times. He glanced at Alea while he packed. *Does she want that life?*

"Is that tea?" Alea sat up, rubbing sleep from her face. Her hair was a tangled mess and one lock sported a twisted dead stick.

He handed her a mug, debating how to ask. Giving her a ring was easy when he thought he would die. Asking her to run into the wilderness was something else entirely. "An Athrolani patrol is on its way up. They'll be here in about twenty minutes." He schooled any emotion from his features. He wanted an honest answer.

"We could live in Athrolan or Mirik. Bren wanted me to stay."

"And live like a noble? Is that what you want?"

"Is there another option? We're war heroes."

Arman kept his eyes fixed on the fire. "If you could go anywhere in the world, where would you choose?"

Her silence was agony to his ears. Somewhere, below, a horse's hoof rang off stone.

"There was that clearing in the Hartland where we stayed our second night after leaving Vielrona. I'd go there. I'd live away from people and memories of what I've been and done. I fear that I owe Bren, owe Athrolan to settle with them."

"When those riders crest this hill your choice will be made for you. I'd miss the open air, but if I had to, I'd live the rest of my life without ever seeing the sky again."

Alea stared at her hands. "What would you do?"

"I can build and we both can hunt. A cabin and a garden would take just a year to build. Winter in the Hartland would be mild." He glanced up and their eyes met. Somewhere, deep inside her chest he felt a gate open in the battered wall erected around her heart. With a smile, he stepped inside.

Φ

An'thor shrugged deeper into his cloak and called for a dismount. The day was steely and cold. The clearing was empty, frozen grasses crunching underfoot. He eyed the tracks. The remains of a fire smoked through the hasty coating of frozen earth. There were marks of a tent and the smell of meat and tea. The tracks of Alea's single horse were evident. There were faint scuff marks from her boots and deeper ones from a larger set. He turned slowly, looking at the marks of two people crouching by a fire. His frown deepened.

"Should we go after them, sir? Her Majesty wanted her back in the city."

An'thor went to stand beside Metters on the outcropping. A horse was just visible on the road, bearing two riders south. He watched them a moment. Finally, he heaved a sigh and pulled himself into the saddle. "There's hot food and good stories back home. Let them have their peace."

END OF REFORGED

ACKNOWLEDGEMENTS

Books are much like humans – there are many places and people that together make them everything they are. If I could thank just a fraction of those people, it would take as many pages as the story that follows.

Of course, there are a few that I cannot help but mention.

My father and my mother instilled a love of storytelling and writing, and the drive to search for the things that filled my mind with awe. It is because of them that I travel, and dig, and wonder. It is because of them that this story began.

I am so grateful to those who read the early and terrible versions of Alea's tale – before she was Alea. Thank you to Lalita and Hilary for being my first readers to "fan-girl" and creating effectively Teams "Arman" and "Bren." Thank you, Emily for driving me mad in sixth grade and allowing me to have the conversation wherein I said "Yes, a book, is a book, is a book, if you love it and try enough."

Thank you to Angie Frazier, who first suggested splitting the first half of Reforged into two books. If I hadn't, I would never have explored the world more fully and found the path to which this story was leading. Your continued support and guidance – as well as your success – was a wonderful inspiration.

Thank you, also, to Ben Donahue, whose incredible talent lent this series its beautiful covers. Your vision and collaboration has helped bring my characters to life.

Thank you to Dr. Greggory Knouff for teaching the fantastic course "Modern U.S. Military History." Your enthusiasm and wealth of political and military knowledge was invaluable

Thank you, also, to the wonderful people who put together National Novel Writing Month and the programers who developed Scrivener and Krita.

Thank you, as well, to all the people and places that have inspired my work and my characters – even, and perhaps especially, the bad ones. Thank you to those who inspire me to be the best I can, and to always "Hold fast to dreams."

Thank you to my wonderful partner for giving me all the room and time to be creative and allowing me to be angry and frustrated and mercurial when writing is not going to plan. It is because of you that this story was finished.

We did not realize the extent of this journey when we began.

SNEAK PEEK AT THE NEXT INSTALLMENT OF BLOOD OF TITANS

CHAPTER ONE

The 27th Day of the Month of Rainfall, 1272
The Forest of the Hartland

Arman stood in the doorway. The bed was made as usual and the desk tidy. The clothes chest was shut and a pair of breeches hung on a hook. *It's all wrong.* The same way his gut had known what Alea was, he knew his son's room was more than empty. *Deserted.*

They had kept the truth of their identities, their bloodlines, from him. They hoped he would be live the life they never could. One of peace. Of anonymity. *Perhaps it was a mistake.* Arman was surprised at his reaction to his son's leaving. He would have thought Alea would panic and he would comfort her. Keplan may not have told them what happened, but Arman would see it was something horrifying.

He stepped into the room hesitantly, as if unwilling to have the last person to cross the threshold be someone other than his son. It was only upon entering that he saw the folded parchment on the pillow. He touched the ragged edge before tucking it into his pocket. He retreated to the main room and set water to boil. Soft footfalls sounded behind him as he took the kettle from the fire and poured two mugs of tea.

"Has he come back?" The circles under Alea's eyes spoke to how well she had slept.

He jerked his chin at the tea cup waiting on the table before her. "I don't think he will for a long time."

"How can you think that?" Her voice rasped from tears and fatigue.

Arman heaved a sigh and sat. "Alea, when I left home I packed my bag, made my bed, swept my floors. Trust me when I say I know what running looks like." Saying it broke his fear, replacing it with a strange mixture of confusion and understanding. "I found a note."

Neither spoke or looked at the letter until the tea leaves had slowed their spinning around the bottoms of the two mugs. Arman opened it carefully, smoothing the tidy crease down the center before drawing a breath.

> *"'Ma, Da,*
>
> *'I cannot imagine what my leaving might do to you, but I hope you understand. Something happened to me. Not an injury or illness, but something deeper than that. I saw things that no one knows, that I shouldn't know, that I've never seen. I do not know why or how, but I know I cannot stay here. Perhaps I am mad, in which case I am saving you from seeing me succumb.*
>
> *'I will be more scared if I am sane.*
>
> *'I hope you do not mind that I took one of Da's drawings, the one of Ma holding me from years ago. I hope you understand I need answers, ones I cannot find here. I love you both.'"*

"Mad? How can he think that?"

"Alea, we denied him the truth. You did to him exactly what your mother did to you."

"I was trying to protect my child!"

"So was she!" Arman's hand shook again, but now it was not panic.

Alea pointed at the backside of the paper. "He wrote more."

Arman turned the letter over. 'Da, I found the letter from the man called An'thor. I cannot fathom why he would need to see me, but I know why you kept it secret. I know you and Ma hid things, things greater than just a letter. I do not understand, but I forgive you.'"

"Letter? What letter?" Alea shifted nervously, refusing to look Arman in the eye.

He was tired of secrets, tired of protecting. *Look where it brought us.* "Tzatia is ill. Dying, probably. She's named whatever child you have. You promised Athrolan's crown would be safe, and I guess she interpreted it differently. An'thor did not say it in so many words, but the meaning was obvious. Keplan may not know what we were, but he damned well knows they want him in the capital." Arman rose, dropping the letter to the table, driving home their son's leaving.

Alea trembled, eyes frantic. "Arman, what have we done?"

Her words paused him as he tugged on his cloak. "I protected you both. You blinded him." The words he threw over his shoulder were more biting that the draft that blew past him. "You better thank fates he forgives you." He slammed out the door. "I'm not sure I could."

Look for the rest of Reforged from Amphibian Press, wherever fine books are sold.

ABOUT THE AUTHOR

V. S. Holmes is an international bestselling author. They created the BLOOD OF TITANS series and the NEL BENTLY BOOKS. *Smoke and Rain*, the award-winning first book in their fantasy quartet, became an international bestseller in 2018. *Travelers* is also included in the Peregrine Moon Lander mission as part of the Writers on the Moon Time Capsule. In addition, they write game content for Stone Blade Entertainment.

As a disabled and non-binary human, they work as an advocate and educator for representation in SFF worlds. When not writing, they work as a contract archaeologist throughout the northeastern U.S. They live with their spouse, a fellow archaeologist, their dog Rory, and own too many books.

www.vsholmes.com

www.ingramcontent.com/pod-product-compliance
Lightning Source LLC
Chambersburg PA
CBHW020353310726
48979CB00015B/2575/J

9781949693355